This book is a work of fiction. All characters, names, locations, and events portrayed in this book are fictional or used in an imaginary manner to entertain, and any resemblance to any real people, situations, or incidents is purely coincidental.

COMPETE
(The Atlantis Grail, Book Two)

Vera Nazarian

Copyright © 2015 by Vera Nazarian
All Rights Reserved.
No portions of this work may be used without permission.

Cover Design Copyright © 2015 by James, GoOnWrite.com

Additional Cover Layout Copyright © 2015 by Vera Nazarian

ISBN-13: 978-1-60762-139-3
ISBN-10: 1-60762-139-8

Trade Paperback Edition

August 15, 2015

A Publication of
Norilana Books
P. O. Box 209
Highgate Center, VT 05459-0209
www.norilana.com

Printed in the United States of America

Compete

The Atlantis Grail: Book Two

Norilana Books
Science Fiction

www.norilana.com

Other Books by Vera Nazarian

Lords of Rainbow
Dreams of the Compass Rose
Salt of the Air
The Perpetual Calendar of Inspiration
The Clock King and the Queen of the Hourglass
Mayhem at Grant-Williams High (YA)
The Duke in His Castle
After the Sundial
Mansfield Park and Mummies
Northanger Abbey and Angels and Dragons
Pride and Platypus: Mr. Darcy's Dreadful Secret
Vampires are from Venus, Werewolves are from Mars:
A Comprehensive Guide to Attracting Supernatural Love

Cobweb Bride Trilogy:
Cobweb Bride
Cobweb Empire
Cobweb Forest

The Atlantis Grail:
Qualify (Book One)
Compete (Book Two)

(Forthcoming)

The Atlantis Grail:
Win (Book Three)
Survive (Book Four)

Pagan Persuasion: All Olympus Descends on Regency

Dedication

To Zinaida Nazarian, my Mother
With all my Love

In Memoriam
1932-2015

And to Tanith Lee
With all my Wonder

In Memoriam
1947-2015

COMPETE

THE ATLANTIS GRAIL
Book Two

VERA NAZARIAN

Chapter 1

June, 2047.

Today is a day unlike any other, in a whole sequence of unbelievable days.

Today we pass the solar orbit of Mars.

And today, five days after Qualifying for rescue and being admitted onboard the giant interplanetary Atlantean starships, we—all ten million of us, teenagers from the doomed planet Earth—have to make a decision that will determine the rest of our lives.

Fleet Cadet or Civilian.

The choice looms before us, inevitable and irrevocable. We've been given five days to think, to consider carefully, to mull it over, while for the first two days the great ships of Atlantis prepare for the immense journey back to the Constellation of Pegasus—loading supplies and resources, cultural and natural treasures of Earth, and taking the measures necessary for transporting all of us safely to the colony planet Atlantis that will now be our new, permanent home.

On the evening of Qualification, and the day immediately after, the Fleet of Atlantis stayed in Earth orbit. For me that time remains a strange, dead blur. . . .

While the transport shuttles ferried supplies and our belongings, we had the chance to contact our families for the last time and say goodbye to our parents and loved ones—to all those who must now remain on Earth, and die from the impact of the extinction-level asteroid . . . while we, the lucky ones, fly onward to the stars.

The asteroid is going to hit Earth seventeen months from now, on November 18, 2048, and there is nothing anyone can do to prevent the destruction of all life on Earth.

I admit, I have a very poor recollection of these past five days. I am still in a stupor, even as I struggle to hide it for the sake of my younger siblings, Gracie and Gordie. It's an awful, mind-numbing combination of despair and grief that started from the moment my older brother George did not Qualify and was denied admittance onto the Atlantean transport shuttle with the rest of us. By now, George is back at home in Highgate Waters, Vermont, with Mom and Dad. I know, because I talked to them, on that same night after passing the Qualification Finals....

I talked to them.

It's a numb blur. Events mixing, memories out of order. I remember being packed into a small, closet-sized cubicle with the softly rounded walls of pale off-white, everything etched with hair-fine intricate designs in lines of gold that all the Atlantean interiors have, bathed in soothing light.... Yes, I was still somewhere onboard that same transport shuttle that had taken us up through the miles of atmosphere and docked with a great ship in Earth orbit.

For whatever reason, they didn't let us off the shuttles immediately. Instead we had to wait, and meanwhile take turns in the communication cubicle chamber. At some point I remember being in line ... glimpses of stressed serious faces of other Qualified Candidates ... hushed teen voices speaking in foreign languages ... and Logan Sangre standing at my side, his serious hazel eyes never leaving me, his strong arms coming around from the back as abruptly he pushes me forward, ahead of his own turn. And suddenly there I am, sitting next to Gracie and Gordie and an Atlantean technician who, I vaguely recall, touches a strange, asymmetrical and lumpy silvery surface, "dials" Earth, and connects us via a video console. The display screen loads and suddenly there's our living room....

I remember thinking how crazy it was to see our old sofa *from outer space* ... Mom's familiar brown-and-beige plaid throw blanket draping the back of it ... and Mom and Dad themselves perched nervously and awkwardly on the edge of that same sofa, staring back at all of us—actually at the smart wall in our living room that now acted like a trans-orbital video conference device.

How weird and horrible we must have looked to *them*—my pinched, pale, exhausted face, Gracie's tear-streaked, red-nosed mess, Gordie's non-typically serious stare from behind smudged glasses—all of us still covered in mud and filth from the Finals, our heads three feet tall, and taking up the whole living room wall, looking out at our parents from the outdated smart-surface, badly in need of an upgrade, and dotted with bad pixels on the bottom....

I don't know why I keep thinking of that dratted old smart wall even now. Maybe it's just another example of unfinished business back on Earth, calling me. I am so *not* done with Earth....

Because there's Mom and Dad and George.

All three of them are waiting to die, together with the rest of the population of Earth who did not Qualify or simply were not eligible for Qualification.

I do not accept it.

It has been my mantra, running through the back of my mind every waking moment, like an earworm song stuck in my brain. Except, unlike an earworm, this is never going to go away.

But—back to that initial time in the shuttle.... After Gracie had wept her heart out and cried some incomprehensible stuff, after Gordie mumbled, I remember saying, "Mom... Dad," in a blank voice that did not—still does *not* seem to belong to me. It isn't me speaking but another seventeen-year-old girl whose arms are no longer skinny and weak sticks, but have some muscle definition, whose face is leaner, older somehow, with sunken cheeks and dead eyes, framed by dark, stringy, dirt-covered hair that hasn't been washed since before the 34-hour insane Qualification Finals ride through the subterranean tunnels underneath the Atlantic Ocean....

I remember seeing Mom's lips quivering as she tried so hard to maintain that artificial empowering smile for our sake, while tears pooled in her eyes, then started sliding down her cheeks in long glistening trails, while she smiled, smiled, smiled at us....

"Gwen, honey," Mom had said at some point in a voice hardly above a whisper, and then put her hand over her mouth at last, to stop the quivering.

I can see it now, branded into my memory. Dad putting his arm around Mom's shoulder in that moment, fingers squeezing her gently, while he speaks to me—is speaking now, and will be always.

"We love you, Gwen, sweetheart, and we are absolutely *proud* of you and Gracie and Gordon, and . . ." Here is where Dad's voice also cracks, as he is about to say, "George," and he can't.

"Take care of each other, sweethearts. Gwen, take care of your sister and brother, you just keep doing what you can, being strong and wonderful, and the best sister to them, as you have always been, as you are! Gordie, you stay strong and take care of your sisters! Gracie, you keep growing and don't let Gwen do everything, okay, sweetie?"

"Stay smart! So, smart, my boy, my girls!" Dad adds, finding his voice again. "And Gwen—we watched you during the—what did they call them, 'Semi-Finals' in Los Angeles, and you were amazing! My goodness—Shoelace Girl!" And Dad laughs, shaking his head in wonder.

"Oh, God . . . you saw that . . ." I mumble. And in that moment my frozen mask of a face breaks down and I am a gusher, as I too begin to shudder with deep sobs like Gracie, wiping my face with the back of my hands . . . sharp motions, angry shaking hands.

The Atlantean sitting silently next to us uses the moment to say very gently and quietly, "Five more minutes."

I nod at him—because I know our fifteen minutes are almost up, and the next teenager needs to call their loved ones on Earth. Everyone in the transport shuttle gets five minutes per call, and we lucked out—since we're all calling the same place, and there's three of us, we get fifteen.

I think of these stupid incidental things. . . . And then I return to the video display. My hungry gaze tries to absorb everything, every tiny beloved detail, my parents, my living room in my home, the sofa, the wooden bookshelf I can barely see behind Dad, the big potted plant in the corner. . . .

"How are you feeling, Mom? How is the weather?" I say stupidly, with a forced smile that's even more fake looking than the one Mom tried to maintain for our sakes.

"Weather's warm, and getting hot, lots of green coming up, soon your Dad will be riding the lawnmower every weekend—"

Gracie makes a little noise, desperately stifled. I smile and sniffle. "Mom, how are you feeling?"

"Oh, I'm fine!" Mom says, eyes blinking wide, making another huge effort. "The pain is much less these few days, and I think the new meds are working, keeping things under control—"

She speaks and I listen, and my mind just whirls like a dumb thing, not registering her words.

"Mom!" I blurt suddenly. "The Atlanteans have this amazing medical technology—it can fix whatever is wrong with you, with anyone—"

And then I go silent and close up. Gordie and Gracie are both staring at me. I cannot raise false hopes, even now, it would not be fair. And yet—

"Is—is George—is he going to be home soon?" I say instead.

Dad's face darkens. "Last we heard when he called, he'll be home in less than six hours. The rioting and civil unrest is quite serious in the larger populated areas, not exactly safe to travel, so he is taking the long and careful roundabout route. He is either taking a connecting flight to New York, or—"

"Time is up," the Atlantean interrupts softly.

"Mom! Dad! Oh God! *Oh God!* I love you! Gracie and Gordie and I, we'll be okay! Both of you, and George, you must *stay alive!*" I chatter uselessly, making every second count, while Gracie does the same thing, and Gordie whispers sullenly, "Bye, Dad, bye Mom . . ." so that we end up speaking in a muddled Lark family chorus.

"Love you always! Love you!" Mom and Dad say almost in unison, and I see the way Mom collapses with weeping against Dad's chest, just as the screen goes dark and the video connection with our home in Vermont is severed.

That was five days ago.
I know that later that same night my brother and sister and I, Logan, and a whole bunch of Qualified Candidates were

finally allowed to exit our shuttle and emerge into a great, brightly lit space within the starship hull interior that had to be the docking bay—an endlessly long round tunnel expanse split in the center by a concave channel tube running along the floor and ceiling, like a subway track between two platforms, through which I assume we had flown in. The oval cutaway shape of the channel tube easily accommodates the largest of the freight shuttles.

Neutral lukewarm air hits us with a blast. . . . No smell, all is clean, sterile. And yet, somehow I know beyond doubt I am breathing *alien* air onboard a spaceship—in its nothingness there's a hint of otherness, a *scent of the stars*.

There is however nothing unusual about the gravity, and it feels just as though we are back on Earth, inside a vast depot.

Except, this place is all pristine cream and off-white, the gleaming hull lined with occasional panels of grey material with gold flecks that must be orichalcum.

It is then that, for the first time since setting foot on the Atlantean mothership, I suddenly think of Command Pilot Aeson Kass.

No—I need to think of *him* from now on as Aeson Kassiopei, son of the Imperator.

An Imperial Crown Prince of Atlantis.

. . . *You matter to him, Lark* . . .

Great ovoid shapes of transport shuttles fill the bay, parked at even intervals along the channel tube on both sides, as far as the eye can see, and crowds of Qualified Candidates and Atlanteans among them, take up most of the area on the floor. . . .

I guess I also need to stop using the designation "Candidates" at this point. We've all Qualified, so officially we're no longer mere Candidates.

So then, what are we? What other word should be used to describe us? Immigrants? Intergalactic refugees? *Homeless?*

Urgent speech and desperate stressed chatter comes from all directions, in all the languages and dialects of Earth—strange foreign vocal inflections, rising and falling tones, harsh gutturals and soft sibilants. . . . Momentarily I am reminded of the Tower of Babel.

There are so many of us! Young people are everywhere, moving or idling, some exiting into smaller tunnels and doorways leading out into the deeper portion of the immense starship around us. Robot vehicles move silently past us, hovering a few feet above the floor, carrying loads of cargo.

Occasionally a great gust of turbulent air comes tearing through the long channel tube section, as from the distance we see another freight shuttle approach at great speed, moving silently and only preceded by the wind tunnel that it generates, cutting the air ahead of itself. The shuttle comes to a smooth hover stop, then rises from the channel and parks itself on either platform side. This happens again and again periodically as more shuttles continue to arrive, while others depart, rising suddenly from their parked spot along the platform, entering the recessed channel and shooting off into the boundless receding distance where I assume somewhere in the end is the exit.

It seems well orchestrated, yet it occurs to me, it's a wonder they don't collide with each other. But I suppose there must be some serious air traffic controlling involved in all this. My head reels. . . .

After a while, none of it matters or makes any sense; all of it is chaos. . . . We mill around, watch the shuttles, watch the crowds, watch each other. We wait, follow directions from bland and expressionless Atlantean officers who scan us, check our token ID data against their hand-held devices. Then we are told to line up and wait some more, are scanned again. . . . All directions are repeated in English, Mandarin Chinese, Hindi, French, Spanish, German, Arabic, Russian. . . .

It occurs to me, where are my friends? Where's Laronda, Dawn, Hasmik, Blayne, and the others? Are they also emerging out of one or more of the great transport shuttles along this same huge shuttle bay, equally dazed and lost, overwhelmed with tragedy and exhaustion? Or are they onboard some other great starship? For that matter, did they even make it?

All throughout, I remember sickly chills riding up and down my limbs, along my clammy dirty skin that is still prickling at the feel of the soggy fabric of my uniform, my hands feeling cold as ice after the subterranean ordeal of the Finals. I see Gracie's equally dirty tear-smudged cheeks smeared with eyeliner, her terrified eyes looking at me constantly—looking for support and strength that in that moment I don't have to give—and Gordie standing awkwardly next to us, filthy and tousled.

Logan Sangre is also nearby, his usually gorgeous dark hair and face a mud-stained mess. For the first time he looks uncertain himself, no longer a confident hotshot high school senior, but very young, a teenage boy lost. And then as though reading my thoughts, Logan gathers himself and closes up emotionally, then casts grim looks around us, while we all scan the crowds for familiar faces and find none.

Get a grip, Gwen Lark, I tell myself silently, over and over. *They need you, you can't afford to fall apart now.*

Just . . . Get. A. Grip.

At some point we finally leave the shuttle bay and are taken through mind-blowingly endless hallways opening into decks and then into more convoluted passages with pale walls etched with ancient looking linear designs of hair-thin gold, beautiful and austere. The ship appears to be immense, so I lose track of any direction very quickly. We are herded in groups of about twenty at a time, regardless of our color Quadrant designations, into long narrow chambers filled with nothing but rows of narrow bunk beds along two walls, four levels high, all the way up to the ceiling, and simply told to take a bed and go to sleep.

"These are not your permanent bed assignments," an Atlantean of indeterminate youthful age with the typical long metallic-gold hair tells us. "This is simply for tonight and the next few days until you are sorted and assigned to your Quadrants and decks, and in some cases, other ships. So, don't worry and don't get too comfortable. Your personal belongings will be located and distributed starting tomorrow. You will also be informed how to have your uniforms cleaned."

"What about getting *ourselves* cleaned? And what about bathrooms?" several Candidates say.

The Atlantean nods and points to the back of the long chamber. "Lavatories with toilets and sinks are at the end of the room, self-explanatory. Showers are somewhat more complicated, but there are pictorial instructions. They resemble your own Earth-style cabin enclosures, but use recycled high-pressure water mist. . . ."

At the same time, another Atlantean crewman walks the rows of our bunks distributing what looks like food energy protein bars and drinking bottles. "These are high-calorie meal rations to give you strength. Eat them now, and then tomorrow for breakfast. Fill these bottles with water from the lavatory sinks—it is sterile and perfectly clean for drinking purposes as well as any other—and keep them with you always—"

"Wait! What is this?" a girl says plaintively. "Aren't we getting real food at some point?"

The Atlantean looks at her sympathetically, but also with a no-nonsense expression. "Yes, you are. And yes, I realize you just went through a tremendous ordeal and require solid sustenance. But for now, this is what you eat and drink. Tomorrow, you will learn more about your ship, and you will learn where we eat real food, what the rules of conduct are, and how we live and perform our duties."

The meal bars are passed out, and the Atlanteans leave two huge containers with more, near the doors, for tomorrow's breakfast.

Great. . . .

I receive my meal bar absentmindedly, chew it while we all stand in a messy line of exhausted teens all pushing and shoving and trying to get water, use the facilities in the back, wash up the best we can.

"How does this work? Where's the toilet paper?" are some of the complaints heard immediately, mostly from the Americans.

"Haven't you heard of a bidet?" a British guy says. "You use the water sprayer thing to wash your bum. Same idea here. Makes sense—in space you recycle your resources."

Finally we get out of there. I collapse into the first available ground-level bunk, right on top of a thin blanket and single pillow. I vaguely remember Gracie taking the bunk directly overhead, and Gordie hunched over in a fetal position in the next one over, on the same first level as mine.

Logan pauses and stands before me momentarily as I lie there. Already I am lost in a silent stupor, but somehow I can tell he's there, hovering over me. . . . Unexpectedly he leans down and brushes his hand gently over my cheek, moving my hair out of my face with a single soothing touch. "Good night, Gwen..." he whispers. "We made it."

I turn my head slightly to watch as he then climbs up to take the next bunk above Gracie on the third level.

Because the ceiling overhead has no direct illumination, I still have no clear sense how big the cabin chamber itself is, or how many other teens there are in this room with us, even after I get up again to use the alien lavatory in the back with all its oddball water sprayers, moving past endless rows of bunks. The lights, strange soft Atlantean illumination, fade into sleeping darkness at some point. They must be set on a day-night timer cycle....

As I fall asleep, I hear, from everywhere around me, soft complex sounds of grief and relieved gratitude—muffled sobs, whispers that sound like prayers in languages I don't recognize, and weeping.

Everywhere, teenagers are crying in the dark.

In the morning of the day right after Qualification—or what must be day according to the flux of the lights—I wake up still mentally numb, and with all my muscles aching, into a bright morning-level "daylight" which fills our sleeping cabin.

What time is it? Earth time? Ship time?

Like an arrow a thought pierces me: *I am in space, on a great starship....*

And then the wonder of it recedes, superseded by grim reality.

George! George is not *here. And neither are Mom and Dad....*

Most of what follows on that first full day onboard is again filled with a daze of unreliable memories—strange sights and sounds, peculiar food, hours of horrible dull waiting and loud noise of young people talking all around us. Beyond using the lavatory or walking up and down the long room past the bunks filled with strangers, there is nothing to do, not even a chance to go through our belongings that are apparently still elsewhere. And none of us even has a clean change of clothing, so no one I know bothers with a shower.

"This is h-e-l-l, hell," Gracie whispers, periodically tugging at my uniform shirt in neurotic boredom. She huddles against me on my lower bunk, as we sit together. Not sure why she is bothering to whisper in this noisy chamber in which the Atlanteans apparently abandoned us. We're basically refugees in an alien shelter.

"Hang in there, Gee Four," I whisper back with what little enthusiasm I can muster for her sake. And I brush my fingers lightly through her grimy hair—at which she surprisingly does not protest in her usual way. "I'm sure they'll come to get us soon and take us someplace better." And then I make meaningful eye contact with Logan who sits next to us.

He gets it that I am just saying whatever blah stuff to keep Gracie calm. He in turn frequently watches the two United Industani guys on the bunk to the right, who give us possibly hostile or maybe just sad looks while they sit and twiddle their thumbs or toss dice on top of a blanket.

Meanwhile a young Spanish kid, directly across from us, mutters some annoying pop song lyrics over and over, as he drums his fingers against his legs, until another girl tells him, *"Basta, por favor, cállate,"* which I know is the equivalent of "Enough already, please, shut up."

My brother Gordie frequently gets up and stomps his feet in place, watching us in silence, then takes a bite of the meal bar that he holds in one hand. I have no idea how Gordie can keep eating even now, after the two bars he's had first thing this morning. They are not bad at all—taste a bit grainy and sweet like carob and honey, and definitely satisfy hunger. However, one is more than enough for me—but not for Gee Three, apparently.

Hours go by as we sit on our bunks, chewing meal bars, talking quietly or loudly, waiting some more, many of us growing restless and bored, and noise levels rising.

"What the hell is going on?" people say over and over. "We Qualified, so what next? When do we get our stuff? Where do we go from here? Are we even *moving* anywhere in these ships?"

Then around noon, or what we are told is ship-board noon-time, we are taken in groups of about thirty to several larger assembly chambers that are classroom-sized, and have large smart wall display screens. We stand and look and listen, as the video displays come alive.

The familiar face of Atlantean Fleet Commander Manakteon Resoi appears before us. He is wearing the usual grey uniform, and we all know him well at this point from so many months of global TV newscasts and interviews back on Earth.

"Good afternoon, young people of Earth," he says, speaking English with just a hint of that lilting accent that we've come to associate with Atlantean pronunciation. English has long been established as the Atlantis-Earth primary and default communication language via agreement with the United Nations. However we notice that now he is also being dubbed into other languages—the walls have small panels along the perimeter that serve as low-volume "speakers" that carry his speech in Mandarin Chinese, Hindi, French, Spanish, German, Arabic and Russian.

"Welcome aboard our starships headed for Atlantis. You are the best of the best, since you have passed all the stages of Qualification and proved yourselves to be capable of integrating into our society—my profound congratulations to you. I realize you have many questions and they will be answered. First, you need to know this. The Fleet is at present stationed in orbit around Earth, while we are still preparing for our long journey. I realize you have said your painful goodbyes to your families. My sympathies are with you and with everyone who must remain. But now you must embrace the fact that you have been granted the privilege of carrying on the future of Earth, and the entire human race. You leave behind the past, and embark on a journey into tomorrow—"

"Wow, is this mate still talking that pretty bullshit again?" a dark-haired teen mutters with an Aussie accent. "Why don't he just cut the crap and tell us what is really happening with us?"

"S-s-s-sh." A girl nudges him.

The Atlantean continues speaking. "In the coming days you will learn much about your role here, and you will develop your potential. But first, you must make a very important personal decision—a choice that will determine your new place in our society. You must choose *what* and *who* you will become."

The Fleet Commander pauses. The steady gaze of his dark, kohl-rimmed eyes holds us immobilized, as he seems to look at us and *through us*, from the display screen. "You have two options. You can either join the Atlantean Fleet as Cadets, pledging your lives and loyalty to Atlantis, or you may remain Civilians and join the general population of Atlantis when we arrive there, twelve of your Earth months from now. . . ."

"Twelve months? Screw that!" some kid behind us mutters and begins to cuss. Gracie and I turn around involuntarily to stare.

"Or what, *dummkopf*? Are you going to get off this boat early? Then go back and stay on Earth. Millions of people will be happy to take your place here," an older German boy tells him with a frown.

"What does this mean for you?" Commander Manakteon Resoi continues. "It means, you have to decide *now* how you will spend the rest of your lives. The military Fleet offers many more privileges and advantages, including higher rank, higher education, and higher pay even after retirement, but it also demands so much more from you, up to and including your life. It is not for everyone. In fact, it is not for the great majority of you. Meanwhile, if you choose a Civilian life—which most of you will—you will have access to education and various trades, and to solid basics. More details will be provided, to assist you with making your final selection. You have five days including today to make this life decision, after which, there will be no going back. You will be assigned to your permanent place on our ships for the rest of this journey, according to your Quadrant and final rank designation, and you will begin your duties and your in-depth education."

Commander Manakteon Resoi grows silent. He allows the information to sink in.

In the new silence, the chamber around me fills with rising mutterings and waves of voices.

"Wow," someone says in American English. "This is wild. What if we can't decide what we want to be?"

"*Pas du tout*, I do not think that is one of our two choices," a French girl replies.

Gracie looks up at me with worried eyes. I turn around, and

Gordie is also watching me. "What—what are we gonna do?"

"Okay, look," I say, blinking in stress. "We don't have to decide just yet. We have several days to think about it. Civilian sounds nice and safe. We'll be okay, right? We—both of you and—" I stop because I almost say "George"—and then I clam up.

In that moment, the Atlantean Commander speaks again.

"The journey to Atlantis itself will take approximately one Earth year—enough time to learn skills and integrate, so that when we arrive on Atlantis, you will feel at home, and you will know exactly what needs to be done. We start this journey and leave Earth's orbit tomorrow, at exactly 8:00 AM, Earth Universal Time Coordinated, accelerating gradually. In about a week we will be outside your solar system. And then we will continue accelerating for six months, reaching incredible speeds within a special *physical flux-state* called a Quantum Stream, at which point we will Jump, crossing an immense light years distance in a blink, and emerge far in the Constellation of Pegasus. There we will decelerate for another six months, then emerge out of the Quantum Stream and arrive in our new solar system on Atlantis."

Commander Manakteon Resoi pauses. "And now, you will begin considering your choice, and you will begin your life with us. There are two thousand ark-ships in the Fleet, including four Imperial Command Ships. Each one of you is currently onboard one such great ark-ship, under the command of an Atlantean captain and crew. Today, you will learn who your captains are, and you will receive further instructions directly from them at the end of my transmission to you. With that, I leave you, and once again, I welcome you to your new life. As of now, you are all Atlanteans."

The display grows dark, replaced by a great square rainbow logo of Atlantis. We all continue staring, and in moments the large screen is refreshed and another face looks back at us. This one is a youthful woman, seeming ageless or merely an older teen, with shoulder-length golden hair and a serious expression.

"Greetings to all of you," she says in a loud no-nonsense voice. "I am Captain Bequa Larei, and you are onboard Ark-Ship 1109. After you make your choice of Fleet Cadet or

Civilian, five days from now, it is likely most of you will remain here and be assigned to this same ship as your permanent living quarters for the rest of our trip. However, a number of you will be reassigned. For now, I want you to get to know the Atlantean Officers in charge of your Barracks and your Residential Section Deck. You will also familiarize yourself with the ship layout. A directory map can be called up at any display screen anywhere on the ship. Get to know this useful schematic because each of the ark-ships is identical, and you will need to know it regardless of what ship you end up being assigned to—"

Captain Larei talks for about ten minutes, telling us important stuff about the ship, the various decks and their functions, the living quarters, the meal halls, the medical sections, the exercise and recreation decks, the classrooms and training centers, the hydroponics and greenhouses and resonance chamber hubs and various ship systems, on and on, blah, blah, blah. . . . My mind glazes over, I admit, which is very much unlike me, who usually soaks up learning and new facts like a sponge. But all I can think of is my brother George, as he was yesterday, riding his hoverboard, as he flies away, receding in the distance, and turns into a tiny speck against the sunset. . . .

I will hear plenty more about this ship in the days ahead, but I will likely never see George again or have as clear a memory of his *face* as I do now.

And so, I tune out mentally and submerge in precious flickering memories. . . . Eventually the Captain's talk is over, and we are led back, and this time taken to a huge shuttle bay similar to the one in which we arrived last night. Since I haven't studied the ship schematic yet, I don't have any idea if it's the same one or not, or if there's even more than one, but it doesn't matter.

Here we are once again scanned by crew officials, and our token ID data is matched to our luggage. So we spend about three more stupendously dull hours waiting in this shuttle bay as robot vehicles ferry our stuff from newly docked freight shuttles. Everything is bundled in pallets, which then get unpacked before our eyes, sorted out, and distributed.

Apparently, while we were all sleeping last night and then hanging out in our barracks half the day, our things were being located and delivered across ships to the proper places.

At some point in the first hour of waiting, I recognize my familiar duffel bag and backpack unloaded by a hovering robot, and I feel a surge of ridiculous tears at the sight. I eagerly take my things—the last familiar things of Earth—and I rummage through them, touching precious books, trinkets, while Gracie and Gordie wait nervously for their own stuff to be delivered.

Eventually we all have our possessions. Which means we have a fresh change of clothing and clean underwear.

Which means we can get properly cleaned up at last.

For the remainder of day one, we and the rest of the Qualified, take showers, eat in Atlantean meal halls, which unsurprisingly resemble Earth cafeterias except for the weird food (about which I will comment later), receive medical attention for injuries acquired during the Finals, and then keel over and sleep in our temporary bunks.

We are awakened the next day at 7:00 AM, UTC, by daylight illumination and Atlantean officers coming to the barracks chambers to give us an hour's notice warning—our departure from Earth orbit will begin shortly.

"There are large observation decks all along the perimeter of this ship, and you may stand and watch out of the windows as the Earth recedes," an Atlantean tells us gently. And then he explains how to get there.

Immediately there is general tumult. Naturally everyone is interested in seeing Earth for the last time, and there is a stampede of sorts. But another Atlantean blows a harsh whistle and we are told to line up in orderly fashion and be ready to go in half an hour, at which point there is a bathroom rush instead.

I vaguely remember holding Gracie's clammy hand as thirty minutes later we race in a big crowd of strangers through the great ship.

"Okay, where are we going?" international voices sound all around us as we jostle.

"Pao, pao! Kuai! Zai na?"

"Where exactly is this observation deck? What time is it?"

"Ta bu zhi dao! Ni zhi dao ma? Shuo shen ma?"

"¿Qué dice? ¡No importa, ahorita, muévete!"

"How much longer? This place is a maze!"

We move in a fast jog for at least fifteen minutes, going through endless deck levels and corridors past sections of the ship for which we still have no words, until we arrive at the outermost perimeter. The narrow corridor opens suddenly into a vast panorama.

Here we grow silent and stop.

The outer hull of the ship is bathed in shadowy twilight on the interior, dimly lit with strips of violet plasma glow near the floor, while the ceiling is cast in darkness. The hull walls are fitted with large, floor-to-ceiling rectangular sections of unbreakable transparent material that looks like glass, spaced regularly every few feet. Through it we see a grand vista of black space sprinkled with crystal clear dots of stars . . . all around, hundreds of silver disks of the Atlantean fleet hover like blossoms in the sea of vacuum . . . and directly below, lies the hemispheric shape of a large bluish planet. . . .

Earth.

Gordie sucks in his breath. And Gracie clutches my fingers tighter, as we all stare.

Logan stands directly behind me, looking grimly at the sight. Everywhere teenagers crowd near the display panels, looking out and beyond. There is mostly hushed silence and occasional reverent whispers.

Minutes later, an androgynous machine *voice* sounds from the hull walls all around us. It is speaking Atlantean, then English, then repeating in other major languages of Earth in a delayed echo of seconds, like a strange linguistic chord.

"Commencing Departure Countdown in ten seconds."

The Atlantean officers and crew standing with us at the observation deck give us silent sympathetic looks.

"Ten . . . nine . . . eight . . ."

Is it really happening? I glance around me suddenly, desperately, at the other young people all around the darkly lit deck.

". . . Seven . . . six . . ."

The Earth—it is heartrendingly beautiful. Great swirls of white clouds float softly, and the continents pass directly below us.

". . . Five . . . four . . ."

There's the Atlantic Ocean, a deep inky blue. And to the left, the shoreline of North America, still cast in night's shadow at 4:00 AM Eastern Time, and sprinkled with golden lights of populated areas . . . the United States. Just there, the northeastern tip, near the Great Lakes and slightly over, but just below Canada, is the tiny triangle that's Vermont . . . Mom and Dad and George are right there, contained within that tiny dot of space, my home.

". . . Three . . . two . . ."

I stare at the spot hungrily, wishing with all my soul to rush toward it, like a speeding bird, a morning lark. My lips part as I whisper silently, gripping my little sister's cold fingers, tight.

". . . One . . ."

"Commence Departure."

And suddenly, there is a deep rumble. It builds somewhere all around the hull of the ship, like an immense chord of plural notes, a grand C Major chord.

And as it builds, the ark-ship starts to tremble. . . . Soon we can feel the vibration all the way to our bones, the buildup of immense unspeakable forces through the floor underneath our feet, the hull walls, the ceiling.

As we look out through the windows, the other ark-ship disks scattered all around us in orbit start to *glow*. Their silver outsides emit a faint violet plasma radiance, so that the metallic orichalcum surfaces begin to "dissolve" visually. In seconds all they seem to be are molten discs of lavender light.

And then it happens.

Gracie makes a stifled sound and squeezes my hand painfully. Because the hemisphere shape of the Earth outside the windows begins to *float away*.

It is so gradual, that at first you experience it as a brief lurch of vertigo, a sudden disorientation in regard to what exactly is moving, you or the world. But in seconds it becomes clear—the movement is external to the self and very *real*.

You perceive that subtle motion in the way the entirety of the Earth begins to fill the view as it slowly *rises* in the window. Soon the partial view transforms into the full shape of the entire planet, as it simultaneously shrinks softly and retreats from us like a balloon lifting skyward, and eventually stabilizes and keeps its relative position in the window.

With each passing minute the planet grows smaller, gently, softly.

There is no urgency in this departure, the visual changes microscopic. And yet, it is an optical illusion, because the speed must be incredible.

In a few more minutes we see the much smaller ball that is the Moon as it emerges from the other side of the Earth, and we pass its orbit, the perspective of distance finally allowing us to see it at that wider angle.

"Oh God . . ." someone whispers behind us in the dark.

"Mom! Daddy!" Gracie says. "I want Mom! *Mommy, Daddy! No!*"

And then she is bawling silently, shoving her face against me, no longer holding back.

She is not the only one. I tremble, holding Gracie against my chest, as the lump inside my own throat pushes at me, but somehow I keep it at bay.

Next to me, Gordie's eyes are a blur. I can see the wet glimmer past his smudged glasses. He sniffles with his nose, shifts from foot to foot, bumping my shoulder with his own.

"Good-bye . . ." teen voices sound in awe and mourning and helpless wonder. Minutes tick away. Half an hour passes, then an hour, and few of us notice.

I continue to watch the retreating sphere of Earth. It is now the size of a penny, so that you can just barely see the white dot that is the Moon—the Earth's satellite's albedo is beginning to match in size just any other star sprinkled in the cosmic background.

The other major reference point is now the Sun, a ball of yellow fire the size of a coin. At some point in the last half hour it has entered the scope of our view and taken up permanent residence in the spacescape. We are told not to look at it directly for more than a few minutes at a time, even though the observation windows are equipped with protective anti-glare shields.

I blink and stare at all of it—the Sun, the Earth, the stars, the black vacuum—allowing myself to consume the grand picture, imprinting it upon my mind's eye. . . .

It is then that I notice that the ship disks of the rest of the Atlantean Fleet outside the window are *lining up* in regular fixed intervals all around us—or maybe they have lined up a while ago, for many long minutes now, and I simply haven't noticed, haven't been paying attention—and we are flying in some kind of formation.

In fact, does it seem that the *motion* itself is leaving a *physical trail?*

And then I am absolutely sure of it, *yes.*

The ark-ships stretch out in a long illusion of a comet-tail behind us and off to the side all around us ... and, I am guessing, just as many are far ahead of us. And it seems that all beyond our formation the stars too acquire an optical illusion of tails, as everything, the entire universe, is being pulled and elongated slightly, from the velocity of our movement.

What did Commander Manakteon Resoi call it?

We are entering a physical state called the Quantum Stream.

Chapter 2

That was three days ago. For three days all we did was watch the Earth and Sun recede outside the observation deck windows. Whenever I went there, the observation decks were always packed with teens staring out at the cosmos—mesmerized, dazed, drunk with the view, blinking at the tiny little blue marble of Earth as it was at some point silhouetted against, and then reflecting the light of the bright spot of pale yellow fire that was our Sun. As for the Sun, wow . . . it was still holding out its relative size and position for the most part, though I know it was microscopically shrinking every time I returned for a gazing session, which was at least every few hours.

And when we got tired of the panorama of space, we would return to our temporary barracks. Since even now we're discouraged from simply wandering the ship aimlessly until we know our duties and place in it, there was nothing else to do. There in the barracks we would sit around and think, often out loud, about the tough choice ahead of us. I remember it in vague snatches—people talking, reminiscing about life on Earth, their families, the current events, the pending destruction.

My sister and brother and Logan, the only people I know who made it here with me on this particular ark-ship—I see their stressed intense faces etched in the unreliable memory of those days, as we go over, point by point, the advantages and disadvantages of each choice.

Meanwhile, how is Earth dealing with our departure? Are there new wars now, more horrible chaos? Does the despair overwhelm our loved ones, now that we are gone?

"Oh God . . . are they okay?" Gracie asks me constantly.

"Yeah, they are," I say. "You know how Dad said, the worst of the unrest is mostly in large urban centers, you know, big cities? So, I am sure they are perfectly fine."

Gracie's expression is unconvinced. Yet again she sits with her feet up on my bunk, fiddling with a cheap bangle bracelet that she took out from her jewelry pouch. It gives her comfort, I guess, like handling the beads of a rosary.

"So, Civilian, right?" I ask, changing the subject.

Gracie scrunches her face. "I guess. Okay, maybe . . . I don't know!" she whines. I knew it would take her mind off the sad thoughts of home. For these past three days Gracie has been changing her mind back and forth on the Cadet or Civilian choice.

"Gracie, seriously. Do you really want to train to be a soldier? To put your life on the line for Atlantis? To potentially kill other people?" I tell her.

Gordie on the other hand is solidly decided, but for some reason won't tell us his choice. My little brother can be so annoyingly stubborn sometimes, so withdrawn into the artistic echo chamber of his own head that I want to shake him and slap him around. I am terrified he is going to make a dangerous wrong choice, but then, who am I to judge what choice is best? And so again, for maybe the millionth time, I wish that George was here to give his smart perspective, his big brother advice.

Because, honestly, even after all the information and reference materials we've been given, we only have a very general idea of what it means to be a Cadet or a Civilian. The former involves joining their military, and rigid discipline and training. The latter, well, basically it's the default position in society.

Unlike my siblings, Logan has made his inevitable decision immediately.

"Gwen, I have to join the Fleet Cadets," he tells me on the night before the fateful Decision Day, as we have come to call it, as we talk quietly away from the others, standing in the semi-anonymous twilight of the observation deck, watching the constant visual anchor that is the Sun disk. The Earth, it is like a small bead, now . . . a pearl on the black velvet of space.

"You understand why, don't you?" he says. "It's part of

what my *orders* are."

By orders, he means the fact that he is part of secret United States government special ops, an organization called Earth Union. And he has been tasked to infiltrate the Atlantean deep layers of society, for reasons that supposedly involve ultimately *doing more* on behalf of Earth than just saving the ten million Qualified at this time of the impending asteroid apocalypse.

How is that even possible? What more is there to be done? How can anyone else on Earth be saved?

I have no idea, and I have serious doubts. But I trust Logan's motives and integrity even if I don't think there's anything he or anyone else in Earth Union can actually accomplish. I believe that Logan *wants* to do the right thing, according to what he believes in. I also know in my heart that Logan Sangre—this remarkable boy I've had a crush on for years, and whom I might actually dare to call *my boyfriend* at this point in our acquaintance—is smart, capable, and not a terrorist.

"As a Cadet, I will be close to the action, close to their military high command," Logan tells me. "I will be listening and watching, and looking for sensitive information that may help us—help Earth."

"Supposing you do find something, how do you expect to relay any of that useful information back to Earth, when we've already left orbit and are more than halfway to Mars by now?"

He looks at me, and smiles very lightly. "That's not something you need to worry about."

Okay, again I have no idea what that means, but I can make an educated guess—Logan either has some kind of fancy special technology to communicate with Earth, or knows someone on the inside, someone Atlantean, and *they* have the means to relay the information back.

As for me? When I start to consider the pros and cons of being a Cadet or a Civilian, I feel a rush of rising panic. And yet, I too have made a very early and firm decision.

Today is the fifth day onboard the ark-ship—Decision Day. Our life decisions will be formally announced today. And yes, incidentally, today is the day we reach and pass the orbit of the proverbial Red Planet. Unfortunately, Mars is somewhere on the other side of the Sun right now, so we won't be able to actually see it as we fly past its orbital boundary, sometime later today, around 2:13 PM, UTC.

Starting at 9:00 AM, we are to be called in groups of about ten people before a panel of Atlantean commanding officers on our ship. All of this is scheduled to happen in the large meeting chamber located near the central hub of the Command Deck. There we will be interviewed individually, our ID tokens scanned and our choices witnessed and recorded. Yes, this is a formal ceremony, and afterward, there will be no going back.

We wake up at 7:00 AM UTC—the ship is functioning on Earth time for our sake. In addition, this is reminiscent of our Qualification training schedule.

Over these past five days I've gotten accustomed to not hearing claxon alarms, but instead seeing a growing *brightness* as it somehow seeps past my closed eyelids. The light itself is sufficient to wake you. I am not sure how it works exactly, even if you have a blanket drawn over your face—but it does. And I admit, as a wake-up method it is far less jarring, so I prefer it.

And so, I open my eyes, squint and stretch tiredly, and then the clarity of stress hits me, as I realize what day it is.

Everywhere around me I hear noises of waking teens and rising conversation. This temporary barracks is co-ed, so boys and girls make their way to the same lavatory facilities in the back of the long chamber, separated only once you're inside, into the men's and women's portions. Apparently now that we're all Qualified, Atlanteans don't seem to care if we fraternize—or maybe we've been simply given a temporary break until we "move in" properly.

In the bunk above me, Gracie is still asleep, curled with her blanket over her head, so I stand up and touch her gently. My younger sister has her usual problem getting up in the morning, regardless of when she went to bed the night before, so I take my time with her. In addition, over the last few days, ever since the trauma of Qualification and losing George, Gracie seems to have reverted to her childish, younger, whiny self. Just like that, she's let go of her tough exterior and semblance of maturity she'd gained from the two months of training with the Red Quadrant. I am guessing it might be a form of post-traumatic stress disorder, and I hope it's temporary.

"Gracie!" I whisper near her ear and tap her shoulder. "Gracie, you need to wake up now, today's the big day. Come on, Gee Four, up, up!"

"No-o-o-o-o!" Gracie moans, clinging to her blanket, and does not move.

Meanwhile I can hear Gordie on the first level bunk closest to mine, waking up and yawning loudly.

In that moment Logan looks down at me from the third level bunk directly above. His dark hair is tousled, and his face is softened with sleep. "Hey, you," he says, in an intimate voice that cracks, and there is something boyishly vulnerable in the way he just stares and blinks at me, and then smiles.

As usual, my heart melts at the sight of his smile. I don't care if Logan is a sleepy mess—he is *Logan*. And in moments he gets down from his bunk with easy athletic movements. Minutes later, I finally manage to drag Gracie down and off we all go to use the facilities, after getting Gordie up also.

We make our way to the closest meal hall, a large cafeteria-like chamber with many long bench tables and a self-serve bar along one wall. Here we eat in haste, what looks to be some kind of breakfast dish of mixed fruits and vegetables that taste vaguely like an egg scramble. The veggies are all grown onboard the ark-ships, inside their hydroponics and greenhouse facilities, and are mostly unknown varieties native to Atlantis, with a few Earth plants thrown in to make our dietary transition less weird. I see tomatoes, mushrooms, and zucchini on my plate in addition to unknown alien stuff. But it all tastes okay, and besides, I am too nervous to care today what it is I'm eating.

"This is yucky," Gracie says, poking at her plate with a fork.

"No, it's not," I respond wearily. "Come on, you need to eat, Gee Four. Please, for once, cut the crap."

"It's okay," Gordie says, shoveling the food in his mouth, as usual.

"It tastes like eggs. I hate eggs," Gracie moans.

"Okay, jeez," I say. And then I point to my tall glass filled with alien fruit juice called *nikkari*—a thick algae-greenish liquid resembling one of those fancy wheat-grass health drinks from a trendy juice-bar bistro back on Earth. "See this? It looks weird but tastes really good. Heavenly, actually, light and fresh like watermelon ambrosia or something. I bet you can just drink it like a protein shake. Try it!"

Gracie stares at the green juice and makes a face.

Gordie reaches over and picks up my glass and takes a swig. "Hey!" he says. "Yummy!"

"See?" I tell Gracie.

But she continues to grimace. "You do realize that Gee Three liking something is empirically meaningless? He's a pig."

At that, Logan, who sits next to me, starts to laugh.

Eventually we get out of the meal hall and hike toward the central hub of the ship in order to line up for the decision ceremony thing. Good thing we're relatively early, because the line is already significant, snaking through several corridors of the command deck.

Teens whisper nervously all around us as we stand, milling about.

Eventually the line starts moving. Atlantean crew members direct us into a large, brightly lit, sterile chamber where we see a slightly elevated dais near the back wall, over which hangs a grand square logo of Atlantis. On the dais is a long table with a panel of seated Atlanteans who look important.

I recognize Captain Bequa Larei in the middle, and on both sides of her are two officers, a total of five people.

Meanwhile, we are lined up before the dais in rows, and we start filling the room.

"Each row will approach the panel of commanding officers," an Atlantean officer tells us. "You will then come up to the Captain, one at a time, give your name, be scanned, and announce your choice, Cadet or Civilian. Your choice will be recorded and you will be given your formal orders and assignment. Now, proceed!"

My heart begins to beat faster. We are in the middle of the room, with about five rows ahead of us. Next to me on the right, Gracie looks very pale and Gordie is not much better. Logan stands on my left and looks composed, his face unreadable. But I sense by his excessive stillness that he is far more affected than he chooses to admit.

The first row of the Qualified approaches the command panel. The first person, a short bulky girl, takes a single step to climb up to the dais and stands before Captain Larei.

"Your name?" Captain Larei says, while the Atlantean officer to her right scans the girl's red ID token.

"Adriana Regalo."

"State your choice. Cadet or Civilian?"

There is a brief pause. And then the girl says, "Civilian."

The captain nods. The Atlantean officer this time to the left of her scans Adriana Regalo's ID token again. "Noted and recorded. You are assigned to this ship, Red Quadrant, Residential Deck One. Proceed there to receive your permanent orders."

The girl nods and then quickly moves out of the way to allow the next person their turn.

This goes on for about ten minutes. Most people choose "Civilian," and are assigned to this ship, though there are a few "Cadet" choices thrown in. The first teen who chooses "Cadet" is told to proceed to "Blue Quadrant, Network Systems, Cadet Deck Two." Everyone stares at the boy as he nods stiffly and gets scanned.

At last it's our row's turn. We step forward.

I exchange glances with my siblings and Logan, and take Gracie's hand briefly. My heart is pounding now, and I feel cold with an approaching sense of doom.

Four people in our row are ahead of us. And then, Gordie.... My younger brother glances at me, scratches his cheek and pushes up his glasses nervously. He then goes up the dais and stops before the captain.

"Gordon Lark," he says gruffly, as an Atlantean officer passes a gadget over his blue token.

"State your choice," says the captain in an emotionless voice.

I clench my fingers into bloodless white-knuckled fists.

"Civilian," Gordie says, after the slightest pause.

I exhale in impossible relief. I think Gordie does too,

because his previously glum expression suddenly lightens up. Indeed, there's almost a smile there, as I see him turn his head back at us slightly.

"You are assigned to this ship, Blue Quadrant, Residential Deck Two. Proceed there to receive your permanent orders," Captain Larei says.

Gordie nods, and steps away.

Gracie is up next.

Again I catch my breath.

Gracie looks at me and her eyes are momentarily terrified. She then steps forward and stands before the captain.

I watch the back of her head, her long dirty-blond hair, and notice how stiffly she stands.

"Grace Lark," she says in a clean steady voice, so that momentarily I am proud of her control after all these days of her being an emotional mess.

And then comes the big question.

Gracie pauses.

I hold my breath and pray.

"Cadet," she says suddenly.

Even the captain must not have seen this coming, because the Atlantean gives Gracie a closer look. And then, apparently liking what she sees, Captain Larei nods.

My heart, oh God, it has gone into overdrive. . . .

Gracie! What have you done? I think, as I forget to breathe.

"Noted and recorded," the captain says, while another officer scans Gracie's token. "You are assigned to this ship, Red Quadrant, Drive and Propulsion, Cadet Deck One. Proceed there to receive your permanent orders."

Oh, Gracie. . . .

And then, it's my turn.

I am still reeling from what has just happened. But I take a deep breath, forcing myself to be clearheaded for what I am about to do.

And then I step forward.

"Your name?"

I stare directly into Captain Larei's kohl-outlined eyes, watch her handsome face and the stern lines of her golden metallic hair.

"Gwenevere Lark," I say in a hard, cold voice that's not my own.

While an Atlantean officer passes his hand-held device over my ID token, I breathe shallow and feel the pulse racing in my temples.

"State your choice. Cadet or Civilian?"

I meet the captain's gaze without blinking.

"Neither," I say. "I choose to be a Citizen."

Chapter 3

There is a strange pause as everyone looks at me.

"You *what?*" Captain Larei says with the beginning of a frown, and widens her eyes, as though coming awake. "What did you say?"

"I choose to be a Citizen of Atlantis," I say clearly, standing as still and straight as possible.

The captain parts her lips, about to speak. In that moment the officer to her right leans in closer and speaks something in Atlantean, pointing to his scanning gadget.

The captain turns to him, glances over at the device, shakes her head in seeming puzzlement.

Moments tick.

Finally Captain Larei returns her attention to me, and her expression reverts to a semblance of composure.

"So," she says in a bland voice, but her eyes follow me with an intense scrutiny. "It looks like your ID has been specially flagged in the system—which is convenient, because now I don't have to deal with your case. Apparently you are being transferred to Imperial Command Ship Two. According to these orders, and regardless of your choice, you have been assigned to Yellow Quadrant, Navigation and Guidance, Command Deck Four. Your commanding officer is Command Pilot Aeson Kassiopei himself, and you report to him directly."

It is now my turn to be stunned. My lips part, and I stare at her.

But Captain Larei nods at me curtly, and the Atlantean officer to her left passes his device over my ID token. "Noted and recorded. Proceed to Shuttle Bay Three to complete your permanent transfer."

I press my lips tight and swallow. And then I step off the dais to allow Logan his turn.

The next few minutes are a mess. Gracie and Gordie and I stand huddled outside in the corridor, looking at each other. It's as if we all gave each other blows to the head and are recovering from the multiple weird, self-inflicted concussions.

Gracie is still defiant from making her gutsy choice of Cadet, but some of her bravado has been diminished by the fact that I am now going to be separated from the two of them. Gordie appears upset again. His frown is back, and his hands are stuck in the pockets of his uniform, which for Gordie is a sign of stress and depression.

"Listen to me," I say. "It's going to be okay! Gracie, I can't believe what you did there, choosing Cadet, of all things—"

"*You* can't believe?" Gracie flares at me. "What about what *you* just did, Gee Two? What the hell did you choose? *Citizen?* What *is* that? And because of that now they transferred you to some other ship—"

"No, they said my transfer was going to happen anyway, regardless of my choice—"

"And not just *any* ship," Gordie cuts in. "She's on Imperial Command Ship Two! That's supposed to be Phoebos's ship! You know, your Command Pilot Kass guy—"

"Not my 'Kass' guy," I interrupt with rising anger. "And he's not Kass, but *Kassiopei!*"

"Whatever!" Gordie shrugs. "What difference does it make?"

Gracie stares at me, as suddenly it sinks in. "Wait! Kassiopei? He's—Isn't that supposed to be their Royal or Imperial or whatever Family?"

"Exactly!" I say, turning to her.

"So he's, what—" Gracie's face pales.

"He's an effing *prince* of Atlantis!" I exclaim. At my raised voice other people in the corridor turn to stare at us.

"Oh, crap . . ." Gracie mutters.

"What? *Damn!*" This time Gordie's jaw drops. "Da-a-a-amn!"

But I am motioning with my hands for them to tone it

down. "Okay, now, listen," I say urgently, continuing what I was originally trying to tell them. "It doesn't matter, okay? Nothing matters except we are going to *survive* this thing, one way or another, all of us. Gracie, you will be careful, and you will stay safe. Yes, I am worried as hell that you picked Cadet as your choice. But somehow I have faith in your abilities—as long as you keep it together and *don't let yourself fall apart*—okay? Gordie—you're *way* smart, and as a Civilian I'm sure you will not get in any trouble if you just do what you're supposed to. Right? *Right?*"

My brother nods reluctantly.

But Gracie continues to look at me fiercely. "How could you do this *Citizen* thing? How *could* you? You abandoned us, knowingly—"

"No! That is *not* what I'm doing!"

"Then what?"

I take a big breath and pause, as my siblings stare at me. So I take Gracie's hand and put my other hand on Gordie's shoulder.

"I had to choose Citizen," I whisper. "Because it's the *only* way I can do something to save Mom and Dad and George. I am going to enter the Games of the Atlantis Grail as soon as we arrive on Atlantis. It's the only way to become a Citizen, and therefore the only way to get our family rescued. The winners of the Atlantis Grail get all their craziest wishes granted! You understand?"

"But—aren't the Games of the Atlantis Grail supposed to be impossible?" Gordie mutters. "No one can win those things! You'll get killed!"

"I know. But I have to *try*," I say. "Besides, I have that Logos voice, remember? It's a huge advantage! I can totally win this thing!"

What I don't say out loud to my brother and sister is that I could not live with myself if I didn't try, and that I am absolutely, hopelessly insane to be attempting something like this.

And that probably, yeah, I *will* get killed in the process. . . .

So maybe Gracie is right. I am about to abandon my only remaining family to selfishly go after an impossibility.

While we continue to talk in agitation, Logan Sangre catches up to us. "Gwen, that was not a smart thing to do, what you did back there," he says immediately, taking my arm. "Citizen? Really? Do you have any idea how much unnecessary attention and trouble this could cause? I mean, I get it, I know what you're trying to do, but there's a better way. You simply choose Cadet, take all these months to train, build yourself up. . . . Then, if you still think you can do it, you enter those goddamn Games when we arrive on Atlantis."

I look at him with a frown. "I thought you, of all people, would understand."

"I do! But I also want you to be safe and careful. And now look, you've been reassigned."

I continue to frown until he sighs, lets go of my arm, and steps back. But then all my anger and hurt deflates as soon as I hear what he says next.

"I've been transferred too," he informs me with an equally serious expression. "I am going to be on Imperial Command Ship One, Red Quadrant, Drive and Propulsion, Cadet Deck One. That's Commander Manakteon Resoi's flagship."

"Oh, man, that's wild!" Gordie exclaims. "You're on the first ship in the Fleet!"

I just look at Logan and bite my lip.

Apparently we're all getting separated.

Well, what did I think was going to happen?

"At least Gee Three and I get to be on the same ship together," Gracie says.

"But not in the same sections," Gordie adds.

But Logan watches me intensely. "So, you're on Command Ship Two," he says. "I don't like it. That's *his* ship. Phoebos, Aeson Kass—or should I say, Kassiopei."

"Yeah," I mutter. "I guess."

"So, did you know who he really was? I mean, about his family—"

"Sort of. . . ." I look up at Logan, feeling a strange heat rising in my cheeks.

"Wait—you *knew?* Did he tell you himself?" Now Logan is starting to frown, and he draws closer to me.

"No!" I hurry to reply, with rising agitation. "Of course he didn't tell me anything like that. It's not like we ever talked about personal stuff, it was all voice training related. I just heard about it from one of the Atlantean Instructors. . . . I mean, I don't think he's hiding it like it's a huge secret or anything, just not advertising the fact that he's some kind of royal. At least not while we were still on Earth. I suppose now that we're here on the ships, we'll learn all kinds of other interesting things about him and the others—"

"The fact that he had you transferred to his ship means he's got special plans for you." Logan is still watching me with a strange expression that I have trouble reading.

"Well, yeah." I blink. "He expects me to use my Logos voice for whatever Atlantean purposes. I bet he will continue to train me."

"I still don't like it. Be careful of him, stay alert. Don't let him—*get* to you."

"Get to me? How?"

Logan takes a deep breath. He begins to say something, but decides against it and stays silent. A long weird pause happens during which he looks at me with somehow vulnerable eyes and I stare back at him, my temples pounding.

When he finally speaks, it's in a more aloof tone. "Whatever it is, we still don't know anything about their long-term plans or real motives, Gwen. It's all just the tip of an iceberg."

I nod. "Yes, it's complicated, I get it."

Logan cranes his head to the side. "Do you?"

I frown then punch him on the arm. "Okay, stop that! Enough, seriously."

But my mind, my pulse continues to race with an inexplicable emotion.

We walk back to our temporary barracks which happens to be somewhere on Residential Deck Four, within the Yellow Quadrant of this ark-ship. Here we collect our duffel bags with our belongings from the small storage units behind wall panels corresponding to our bunks, and proceed outside. Gordie's been assigned to Residential Deck Two, which is in

Blue, so off he goes after giving me an elusive hug—or rather, I hug him and he slips out of my grasp like an eel and pats my shoulder awkwardly.

"I'll see you around, Gee Two and Four," he mumbles.

"Larks stick together!" Gracie and I speak in unison, in a feeble attempt at cheer. I feel an immediate pang of guilt. *Yes, I am abandoning them.*

"Well, I'm heading to Cadet Deck One," Gracie says.

"Okay, I'm sure there's a way to call or communicate from ship to ship," I say. "As soon as we figure it out, we call! And you call too, Gee Three! Promise!"

"Yeah, I promise."

And then I squeeze the life out of Gracie, as we both hug each other, dropping our bags down to the floor.

"You're going to be an awesome Fleet Cadet, Gracie!" I whisper in her ear, as I smooth down her hair around her ears. "You are strong and brave and tough—"

"Shut up!" she says fiercely, because she is still mad at me, but I can see her eyes are glistening wet.

I stand and watch as Gordie and Gracie walk down a corridor together, carrying their bags, and disappear from view, swallowed by the great ark-ship around us—*their* ship, officially.

Logan and I look at each other.

"I am supposed to go to Shuttle Bay Three," I say.

"Shuttle Bay Four, here." He stands gazing at me, not moving, stilled with intensity.

I look up into his hazel eyes. They are warm once again, receptive. "You call me as soon as you figure things out, okay?"

He does not reply. Instead he leans in, and then takes me into a deep embrace, while his lips come down on mine, hard and sweet.

There are no surveillance cameras here, or at least none that matter.

I kiss him back, melting and drowning in those hazel eyes, while my heart hammers inside my chest, and warm honey courses throughout my body at the powerful safe feel of him against me.

But for some reason in that moment I think of another pair

of eyes—the blue eyes finely outlined with darkness that belong to the prince of Atlantis.

Logan and I separate at a junction of corridors leading in different directions on this immense ark-ship. He goes one way, carrying his bags, and I go another. I turn and watch his back momentarily, his confident walk, the toned shape of his tall runner's body, wide shoulders, the fall of his super-dark hair, a rare shade of near black, tinged with a hint of red. As though sensing my gaze, he too pauses, turns his head and nods to me with a smile, and a touch of one hand to his lips in an air kiss.

And then I continue on my way alone.

I walk in the general direction of Shuttle Bay Three, after stopping to consult the ship schematic on the nearest display screen in the corridor. The ship is amazing but we haven't been really allowed to see it properly—to explore or wander about enough to learn our way—and so the schematic is the only means of getting around. After several turns along unfamiliar corridors, I emerge into the huge overwhelming tunnel space that is at least remotely familiar.

At this point I know that all the shuttle bays look perfectly alike. No distinguishing features except a small rainbow square logo and number on the walls at the entrance—which I note, now that I know what to look for. Atlantean numerals resemble ancient Egyptian or even Sumerian etchings, and they are basically comprised of short adjacent lines—one line for "number one," two lines for "two," and so on, until you get to "five" which is four lines bisected by a fifth. This shuttle bay is designated with three short lines.

The shuttles are parked in perfect rows on both sides of the platform tube, with sections of larger freight transport shuttles interspersed with smaller personal flyers—the kind that I first saw explode in the skies over Pennsylvania, in that awful sabotage incident two months ago.

There are not many people about, compared to that first day when we arrived in the ships among the crowds of the Qualified. Except for the endless rows of stationary shuttles, the platforms and bays are mostly empty. I see a handful of Atlantean officers and other workers, and right near the entrance a small cubicle desk area where an official of some kind sits. Next to him a small group of about twenty teens with luggage stand around waiting. I bet they are all transfers to other ships too.

The desk officer looks up at me, and it occurs to me he must be a shuttle traffic controller.

"Hi, I am supposed to report here," I say awkwardly. "I am being transferred to Imperial Command Ship Two."

"Name?"

"Gwen Lark."

The officer scans my token ID to confirm. "Wait here with the others," he says. Then he picks up a communication device and talks in Atlantean to someone.

I nod and switch my heavy bags from one hand to the other.

Half an hour passes. Then, from the distance comes a sudden fierce churning gust of air generated by an approaching wind tunnel, followed by a shuttle. It is one of the smaller personal flyers, moving so fast it appears to be a shooting projectile. But it hovers to an immediate and impossible stop, then shifts sideways onto the platform closest to our side to occupy the first empty slot about fifty feet away.

A few minutes later, a familiar tall Atlantean with super-black skin and short golden hair approaches from the direction of the shuttle. It's Keruvat Ruo, one of my Combat Instructors from Pennsylvania.

Wow, am I glad to see him!

"Instructor Ruo!" I exclaim with surprise and an easy smile.

"Look who's here.... Gwen Lark, glad to see you Qualified." Keruvat's deep booming voice sounds rich and welcome. He smiles at me briefly—and for the first time his smile is without restraint—then he nods to the desk dispatch officer.

Seeing him, the officer stands up from his seat immediately and salutes Keruvat in the Atlantean mode—head inclined slightly, left hand raised, with fingers and thumb forming an angle, palm touching forehead, and thumb touching lips. "My apologies, Pilot Ruo, I did not realize you would be flying this shuttle yourself—"

"CP's orders," Keruvat tells the officer in English, the default language the Atlanteans have been using with us, then glances around at the waiting teens. "So, everyone ready to go? Who else have we got here for ICS-2? The CP—that is, the Command Pilot—sent me to get all of you who are transferring to our ship. I think we've got only three people, am I right? Or is it four?"

"That's correct, four transferring from AS-1109 to ICS-2," the dispatch officer says to Keruvat with crisp efficiency, checking a screen display. And then he turns to the other teens who are waiting. "In addition to Gwen Lark—Jennica Tulls, Lars Hansen, and Alla Vetrova—your Pilot is here. Follow him."

I watch as three figures detach from the group of teens.

The boy, Lars Hansen, is a tall pale Scandinavian, close to six foot-four (and about the same height as Keruvat Ruo), with faded shoulder-length flax-blond hair that looks almost Atlantean, tied in a ponytail. He's got a green token ID and armband, a haughty, tight-lipped expression, and he seems to be older, probably very close to the upper cutoff age for Qualification.

The two girls are very different from each other. I am assuming Alla Vetrova is Russian, or at least Slavic, and if so, she is likely the slim redhead with a blue armband, very short pixie-cut hair, and a reserved, chilly expression. She is slightly shorter than me, but more muscular and toned—which, all things considered, is not that difficult to be, since pretty much everyone who's Qualified is in better physical shape than I am.

The other girl who must be Jennica Tulls is very tall, very dark skinned, African American or possibly from one of the African nations, though with her name I am not entirely sure. She has a red armband and token.

So, looks like I am the only yellow.

We start walking after Pilot Ruo and approach the shuttle. Up-close, the vehicle is not actually parked on the floor as I assumed, but is still hovering a few feet above. I end up being last in line to the retractable stairs, as the other three teens arrogantly get ahead of me—or at least it feels that way, as they all give me blank or hostile glances and probably decide I am inconsequential, even though I seem to know our Pilot.

So many sharp, disturbing memories come as I climb this

staircase into the hatch opening ... images of that burning shuttle at the RQC-3 in Pennsylvania, as I climbed this exact same kind of stairs to rescue the injured Command Pilot Aeson Kass—no, *Kassiopei*. . . .

I blink the memories away and enter the shuttle.

It looks just as I expected it to be, a rounded single chamber, the same central arrangement of six chairs in a rotating suspension harness and a seventh command chair with a hovering control panel, which Keruvat Ruo takes.

"Everyone here understands Earth English? Yes? No? There is a dubbing translator if you need it," he tells us as soon as he sits down, and sings a brief keying sequence in his deep voice, beginning to engage the bumpy touch-surface of the control panel, which in turn activates the hair-fine lines along the hull walls to come awake with golden light. "Move quickly, everyone. First, put away your bags in the wall storage over there. Then, sit down and buckle in. We take off on my count in about a minute."

We hurry to do as we're told, and grab seats, soft and resilient. The harnesses come snaking around us from every direction at the push of a single button in the center, as soon as we connect the two main harness belt sections in our lap. In seconds I am "trapped" in a harness spider web.

"All right, now give me your names and designations. Let's see how well you remember your assignments. Let's start with you—" And Keruvat points at the redhead girl in the seat next to him.

She seems to grow even more stiff than she already is and sits up straight. Her voice is precise and loud, with a strong accent. "Cadet Alla Vetrova, assigned to Blue Quadrant, Network Systems, Cadet Deck Two."

"And you report to?"

The girl pauses. She then says, "I report to you, Pilot Keruvat Ruo."

"Good." Keruvat nods at her, and engages something else in the control panel, so that the walls of the shuttle begin to hum with a strange fine vibration that is different in pitch from the larger transport shuttles I've actually flown on.

"And what about you?" Keruvat glances to his other side at

the boy.

"I am Cadet Lars Hansen, assigned to Green Quadrant, Brake and Shields, Cadet Deck Three. My commanding officer is Pilot Erita Qwas." The older boy's voice is deep and soft, and definitely arrogant.

Hey, it occurs to me, *Erita Qwas happens to be another Instructor from my Pennsylvania RQC, and she's also on this ship to which I am being assigned. Coincidence?*

"And you?" Keruvat nods to the other girl who sits next to Lars Hansen. And then he does something else to the controls, so that suddenly a large portion of the rounded hull wall directly facing us seems to slide apart. A large circular window of some kind of transparent, slightly tinted material is revealed in a semi-circle before us. Through it we can see the brightly lit shuttle bay outside and a portion of the platform beyond which the flying channel tube stretches off into the distance.

We all gasp, because none of us have been inside an Atlantean shuttle that has actual observation widows. Well, looks like these smaller shuttles have a real outside view!

I think back to when I was inside the burning shuttle with Aeson Kassiopei, but I don't recall seeing any windows then—possibly some kind of safety protocol engaged during the crash landing, and caused the hull panels over the viewport to close up?

The girl whom Keruvat addresses, is momentarily distracted enough by the unexpected appearance of the window to stutter at first. Then she gathers herself and says with a light unidentifiable accent, "I am Jennica Tulls, Civilian. I am assigned to Red Quadrant, Residential Deck One. And—I don't think I report to anyone."

"That's correct," Keruvat says to her. "As a Civilian you are not going to have a direct commanding officer. But you will have officers on your deck who will explain things to you when you get there."

And then he turns to me, as I sit on the other side, next to Alla Vetrova. "And finally, Gwen Lark, what is your assignment?"

"Instructor Ruo—I mean, Pilot Ruo," I begin. "It's a little complicated."

"Oh, really?" Keruvat makes a noise that resembles a snort, and turns back to his controls. "What else is new? Is there anything ever *not* complicated when it comes to you, Lark? So, then—is it Civilian or Cadet Lark?"

I blush and mutter, "Neither. I told the captain of this ship that I choose to be a Citizen of Atlantis."

Keruvat is not looking at me, as he is occupied with the controls. But immediately his brows rise and he stops doing whatever he's doing and turns to me. "What? No—don't tell me. You continue to be a troublemaker. The captain must have been relieved to transfer you. Well then, let the CP handle you from now on. What is your assignment?"

"Yellow Quadrant, Navigation and Guidance, Command Deck Four. And my commanding officer is Command Pilot Aeson Kassiopei himself."

Keruvat makes another short sound. If I didn't see the twinkle in his eyes, I might start getting worried. "Deck Four? Hah! Does Oalla know you're coming?"

"You mean—Instructor Oalla Keigeri? She's on this ship too?"

"Yes, Pilot Oalla Keigeri, she's in charge of Cadet Deck Four," Keruvat corrects me, preoccupied with the console before him. He then places his large hand on the controls and sings a short sequence of notes in a deep resonant voice, which makes the control panel light up with strange rainbow color lights underneath the oddly shapeless orichalcum surface. At the same time a series of holographic color light "grids" start popping up, floating in the air above the console, which he quickly manipulates. Immediately the humming sound in the hull rises to a higher octave, responding to Keruvat's actions.

And then Pilot Ruo pauses suddenly and again glances at me. "Wait—did you say *Command* Deck Four or Cadet Deck Four?"

"Command Deck. . . ."

Keruvat continues staring. "No. That can't be right. Are you sure, Lark?"

I blink. "I—I think so, yes."

"That's very unusual." He shakes his head at me. "Command Deck means you will be living in Officers Quarters."

My lips part.

The other three teens in the shuttle who have been listening to us talk, are all staring hard at me.

In that moment our shuttle lurches slightly, then levitates sideways off the platform to enter the flying channel tube.

Pilot Ruo sings another brief sequence then swipes his fingers against the console.

The shuttle shoots forward like an arrow. At the same time we are gripped by g-forces and pressed deep into our seats.

The launch tunnel blurs around us from the incredible speed at which we fly.

Chapter 4

In less than five seconds we burst out of the shuttle bay tunnel, past some kind of shimmering curtain of plasma energy, into the black vacuum of space.

The g-forces dissipate, and suddenly we are floating, smooth and deceptively motionless. Outside the observation window we see the universe and distant specks of stars . . . and all around us, an incredible perfect array of grand ark-ships lined up in a long pattern that resembles a star trail.

The Atlantean ships appear to be fixed in perfect stillness relative to each other. But as we look closer we realize that they are all *moving*—*we* are moving—at such incredible speeds, that the rest of the space around us is gently blurring. Again, that strange optical illusion of tails or extended oval distortions can be seen in all the dots of brightness that are distant stars, galaxies, and other cosmic objects emitting light.

"Ah! Gospodi pomilui. . . ." A gasp comes from one of the teens in the shuttle, Alla Vetrova—an exhalation of pure wonder, followed by something in Russian. The others are just staring. My own jaw falls slack in amazement at the sight.

Our shuttle "hangs" in the same strange suspended illusion of no-motion. And then it turns, rotating so that we see the great disk shape of the ark-ship we just exited begin to fill the left half of the window.

From this vantage point of being outside looking in, the shuttle bay gate directly behind us is a maw of shimmering plasma—an oval spot along the outermost narrow "brim" edge of the saucer shape. All around it the silvery orichalcum surface of the ship disk extends into a gradual sloping rise above and below—defining the shallow saucer "bowl" portion—while the saucer "brim" stretches seemingly for miles horizontally.... And the entirety of it is bathed in the same violet plasma glow, radiating a few feet outward from the hull. I am guessing it's some kind of energy field or shield.

My God, the ship is *huge*, a true metallic colossus.... So immense that nothing comes even close to it on Earth, not the biggest cruise ship or military aircraft carrier. And as we only begin to comprehend the monster thing we just exited, the shuttle makes another small lurch to the right. It moves smoothly and fast, like an orbiting satellite following the curvature of the ship, so that the ark-ship now fills only the distant left edge of the view in the window.

And now we can see another colossal ark-ship about five miles away, and then another one beyond it, receding in size and distance, until it becomes apparent there's a long line of ark-ships stretching out into seeming infinity. And to the right of us, there's a second similar line of ships, stretching parallel to the first. Basically our shuttle is in the five-mile narrow corridor between these two immense streaming lines.

"What kind of flight formation is this?" Lars Hansen asks suddenly.

"You may think of it as a diamond—three parallel lines of ships, flying with a one-ship offset. We happen to be in the channel between two of the three lines. Those of you who are Cadets will learn it very soon, in your Pilot Training classes," Keruvat replies. "For now, simply observe how we fly within the Quantum Stream."

And then he does something, and the shuttle shoots forward along the corridor between the two lines of ships. The shuttle is going so impossibly fast, relative to the rest of the Fleet locked in formation, that the ships appear to be stationary road markers, standing still, while we hurtle forward, passing a ship on alternate sides of us, every two seconds.

This goes on for about five minutes, maybe less. The shuttle slows down just as suddenly as it had accelerated before. Now it begins to fall in line and float alongside another huge ark-ship, visually indistinguishable from the rest.

"There it is," Keruvat says. "That's ICS-2, or Imperial Command Ship Two. Your home for the next twelve Earth months."

Pilot Ruo continues to direct the shuttle smoothly to circle around the ship. At one point as the shuttle turns, giving us a wider view of the cosmos, we see the remote golden ball of fire that is the Sun. We are receding from it, judging by the direction of our movement. And the Earth too is somewhere out there, hidden from view by the line of ships stretching behind us, at this point reduced to a tiny bead of blue light.

"This is amazing," Jennica Tulls whispers.

But in that instant the shuttle lurches again, and for one crazy instant we seem to be flying directly at the ship, about to crash into the hull.... Which turns out to be the shuttle bay opening veiled by plasma.

We arrive inside the shuttle bay of Imperial Command Ship Two, decelerate, and come to a hover stop at a platform deep inside the tunnel. From the shuttle window, I note that everything here is the same as the other ark-ship—a brightly lit open space, with neutral off-white walls and fine gold etchings. Shuttles line the platform on both sides and occasional Atlantean officers and crew move through the bay.

"Unbuckle, and get your belongings," Pilot Ruo tells us, rising from his seat. "Cadet Vetrova, you follow me to Cadet Deck Two. Lark, Hansen, and Tulls—you report to the information and dispatch desk here and they will give you instructions. Welcome, and now, dismissed!"

In moments, we are outside the shuttle. I carry my two bags and stop before the dispatch area. Pilot Ruo and Alla Vetrova head to the nearest exit and disappear.

Lars Hansen and Jennica Tulls remain with me. We are scanned and then we wait.

About ten minutes later three young Atlantean guides approach, consult with the desk, and are assigned to each of us.

"Gwen Lark?" A metallic-haired teenage boy barely older than Gordie approaches me. His expression is serious, somewhat superior, and perfectly controlled. He's wearing a yellow armband. "Follow me."

"Okay," I say, shifting my heavy bags from one hand to the other. "Where are we going?"

"Yellow Quadrant, Command Deck Four," the Atlantean tells me curtly without even looking at me, as we start to walk from the shuttle bay and into a long hallway. "I will show you your living quarters. You will leave your things there and then report immediately to your commanding officer."

I nod and follow him. We move past occasional Atlantean crew members through a maze of sudden contrasts—long corridors illuminated with soothing light then wide brightly lit decks that make me blink from the unexpected radiance—though at this point I am beginning to get some kind of basic grasp of the ark-ship standard layout.

In a nutshell—each great saucer ark-ship is a flattened sphere. The circle is split into four sections from the center, a cross-cut forming four large "pie slices," and each "pie slice" or wedge is allocated to a Quadrant. Yes, that's where that whole "Four Quadrant" notion comes from—four major divisions of function and labor on each of their ships! And, apparently this tradition has been in place for thousands of years, stemming from the time of their original colonization.

There are four shuttle bays in each ship, and they run lengthwise, almost the entire radius length of the ship, effectively making those four cross-cut "lines" that separate each Quadrant wedge.

In the circular heart of the ship, in the very center, is a great spherical chamber called the Resonance Chamber, which is very important for various systems functionality including actual propulsion and flight—but more on this later.

Each Quadrant wedge is cut across horizontally into three sections. The first and innermost smallest section of the wedge, adjacent to the central Resonance Chamber, is the Command Deck, the section where the Atlantean Officers Quarters are located, and where much of the ship control takes place.

The second, middle portion of the wedge, larger and closer to the outside, is the Cadet Deck. This is where the Cadets living quarters and training area is located.

Finally, the outermost largest section, number three, is the Residential Deck. This is where all the Civilians are housed, and it is adjacent to the storage, hydroponics, and other large-scale general life support systems areas closest to the outside hull.

That's the basic breakdown. There are many sub-levels and many corridors connecting the whole thing, but for now, all I need to know is that I am heading toward the heart of the ship—the control and central operations center called the Command Deck.

That's where the Officers Quarters are located, and where supposedly I will be staying.

It is also where *he* is supposed to be—my commanding officer.

Command Pilot Aeson Kassiopei.

My pulse begins to race and my breathing comes fast, as we approach the center of the ship, long before we even arrive at my destination. I don't know why, but I am close to hyperventilating as we emerge past the middle section that's the Cadet Deck and cross the wide dividing corridor gap into the elite "upper" cross-section of the Yellow Quadrant wedge.

The Atlantean walking ahead of me announces nonchalantly, "Command Deck Four." And then he turns into the first corridor.

The hallways here are filled with many frequently spaced doors, unlike the residential decks of the other ship I am familiar with, where the hallways had only occasional doors and each door opened into a huge barracks dorm chamber. Obviously these are smaller cabins meant for individuals.

My guide stops before one of these doors, only three doors away from another cross-corridor. "This one is yours," he says, pointing to a small square logo on the wall next to the door. "Number 28. Remember its location well."

I peer closer and see the same Atlantean numerical etchings marking the surface of the small square. I count five hatch-mark "fives" and a single three-dash character, which together makes number 28.

I also notice there is no door handle or lock. Back on the other ship, the barracks door always slid open automatically when you approached it and was never locked, but apparently not this one.

The Atlantean notices my confusion. "Pass your ID token over this square, and the door will key itself to you. From there on you simply touch it with your fingers to open or close, and no one else but you can come in."

I drop my heavy, book-laden bags down and key my door with my token. It slides open into darkness. The moment I step inside, illumination blooms forth, reaching standard daylight levels. Now I can see the room is very small, a cubicle really. There's a long narrow bunk bed along one wall, and directly above it a bulkhead storage area in place of an upper bunk. Only a couple of feet across is the opposite wall with a small one-person table and bench chair, both retractable and built into the wall, and then a small closet-like enclosure that I can see is a combination retractable toilet stall, sink, and shower, the kind I've become familiar with at the other ship in the common barracks lavatory.

The Atlantean stands quietly at the door watching me.

"Close the door and take five minutes, but no more," he says. "And then we proceed to see your commanding officer. It is bad form to keep an officer waiting."

I frown for a moment, then nod, and touch a similar square on the interior wall, which causes the door to slide shut.

I am now alone in my tiny cabin. Claustrophobia descends on me momentarily and I stand, breathing deeply to calm myself, because my heart is hammering in my chest. I leave my bags on my bed then go to the lavatory enclosure, call up a sink, and splash concentrated water spray on my face, seeing my pale reflection with its newly hollowed cheeks staring back at me in the small narrow mirror that is revealed above the retractable sink.

Then, when my heartbeat slows down sufficiently—or at least enough that it does not threaten to rupture my chest—I open the door.

"I am ready," I say. "Take me to see him."

"Him?" The Atlantean raises one brow. "Pilot Oalla Keigeri will not appreciate your ignorance regarding her."

"What?" I say tiredly. And then it occurs to me—this Atlantean crewman *does not know* who my commanding officer is.

Apparently my ship-board assignment is particularly rare, possibly unique.

"I don't report to Pilot Keigeri," I tell him. "Take me to your Command Pilot—what do you call him—CP. He's my commanding officer, and the one I need to see."

The look on the boy's face is a combination of confusion, amazement, and then an immediate reassessment of me.

A few minutes later we walk through the Command Deck of the Yellow Quadrant, pass the neighboring Red Quadrant Command Deck and cross over into Blue. The Quadrant sections are marked by appropriately colored square logos on the walls of each corridor, which indicates the end of one Quadrant and beginning of another.

"The Command Pilot Quarters and Central Command Office are in the Blue Quadrant," my guide tells me, giving me periodic glances of curiosity. "So why did he assign you to live in Yellow?"

"I've been training with the Yellow Quadrant all this time," I say. "I don't see why that should change."

"But you are a Cadet? How is it that you report directly to the CP?"

"I am not a Cadet," I say.

I think I've managed to confuse the boy enough to render him silent for the moment.

The Atlantean does not speak again until we arrive at a large wide corridor that bears a grand square rainbow logo on the wall. On one side of this hallway is the inner rounded wall that encircles the Resonance Chamber—that central hub that marks the very heart of the ship. And on the other side I see a row of doors, each marked with special ornate insignias, one of which is particularly grand and impressive. There are also two security guards posted at the door.

Here we stop.

"This is the Central Command Office, or CCO," the Atlantean guide tells me in a loud voice, and I realize that he is a little overwhelmed himself. The boy then turns to the guards, and gives a brief salute and then tells them something in Atlantean.

One of the guards glances at me with a blank scrutiny, then raises his wrist, activates some kind of comm device and speaks into it.

A moment later, the door slides open and the guards on both sides step aside.

"Command Pilot Kassiopei will see you now," the guard tells me. "Proceed inside."

I walk past the guards at the door, as my heart begins once again hammering wildly. I take shallow breaths—because it's all I can manage—and enter the chamber.

The Central Command Office is not particularly large, but it is impressive. A wide desk and high-backed chair takes up half the space, and there are four comfortable visitor chairs across from it. About a dozen computer display screens take up the back wall, and directly above is what appears to be a grand digital photograph—a landscape image of impossible beauty, with tall green mountains framing a deep lake, with a castle-like structure of fragile antiquity perched at the cliff-edge of a plateau above the lake, all of it illuminated by a white sun.

Aeson Kassiopei sits working at his desk, and something strange happens to me at the sight of him.

Aeson is the same as I remember him—a composed intelligent face of refined lines and striking lean angles, with serious dark-rimmed eyes of a deep lapis lazuli blue, underneath black brows with a similar faint lapis tint, and lightly bronzed skin, all vaguely reminiscent of Ancient Egypt. Those fine dark lines of contrast around his eyelids—now that I know the truth of his heritage—are beautiful natural markings, not some kind of kohl-based eyeliner or permanent tattoo. And his long hair, a mane of pale metallic gold, is also a true color with which he was born, not a gilded dye that most other Atlanteans wear to honor his Imperial Family Kassiopei.

He is wearing the grey Fleet uniform, and I notice there is an additional gold emblem on his chest, with an insignia similar to what was on the doors of this office. I am guessing it indicates his high rank. And on his left bicep, over his sleeve, I see the black armband—a hero's honor that almost no Atlantean has earned while still living—a mystery about which I still know nothing.

As soon as I approach, he looks up at me.

I feel a painful jolt in my chest and a burning sensation in my cheeks. In fact, I think my entire face explodes in a flaming red blush, and also some kind of crazy choking thing rises up in my throat. . . . So okay, I am just going to pass out now—*No! Get a goddamn grip, Gwen, you idiot!*

"Lark—you made it. Congratulations on Qualifying," he says, after the briefest pause during which his eyes meet mine with lively intensity, and his lips—just for a moment—seem to curve into a shadow of a smile. But he hides it instantly, and resumes displaying a very controlled expression as he continues watching me.

But it is the sound of his voice—clean, deep, familiar—that pierces me on such a visceral level, sending electricity down my skin.

I stand at the doors, like an idiot, unsure of what to do or say. And then I open my big mouth and out comes all this stupid stuff. . . .

"Command Pilot Kass—Oh! I'm sorry—*Kassiopei*—I mean, that is—I don't—I am not sure how to address you properly," I mutter. "For that matter, I don't even know if I am supposed to bow or curtsey or something—I mean—"

"Stop," he says. "Nothing has changed. You may call me Command Pilot Kass or Kassiopei—it is the same thing. 'Kass' used to be my nickname in Fleet Cadet School, a few years ago, back on Poseidon in *Atlantida*. I chose to use it while we were on Earth, simply to minimize exposure. With all the instability and global crises happening on Earth, there was no need to draw unnecessary additional attention to my identity."

"Oh," I say, biting my lip painfully, in order to dissipate the crazy blush, and vaguely try to look away. I finally settle my gaze in the general area of his chin, his throat, even his collar, so as not to meet his gaze. "So then, I don't need to bow or salute or anything?"

"Not at the moment. Though, there may come a time when you will be required to learn and perform the proper salute or other signs of courtesy—during formal occasions." He watches me with a very calm, very composed, almost weary expression. And yet it does not manage to sufficiently disguise his underlying *amusement*.

Oh lord, yes, he *is* amused by me! I am not sure if I should be relieved or insulted.

"Okay," I say softly. And then I dare to look up and face his gaze directly.

There is a pause, during which we look at each other. And then unexpectedly he blinks first.

"Come closer," he says, resting his hands on the surface of his desk. "Take a seat."

I do as I'm told and sit on one of the four chairs, perching somewhat on the edge of the seat. My palms are clammy and I clutch the ends of my uniform shirt.

"Now, tell me, what did you choose before the transfer? I have here some incomprehensible note from Captain Bequa Larei about you not giving her a proper answer? So—what kind of trouble did you start on AS-1109?"

"I merely told her that I choose neither Cadet nor Civilian, but to be a Citizen of Atlantis."

His eyes narrow slightly and he grows very still. "What in the world for? What kind of nonsense is this?"

I take a deep breath and stare back at him. "I want to become a Citizen," I repeat. "Why is that nonsense? Don't I have a free choice in the matter? So, I choose neither Civilian nor your Fleet."

He leans forward over his desk, drawing closer to me. "You have no idea what you are saying. How do you even know about Citizenship? This is advanced material, not something that was supposed to be covered in your Culture Class."

"I know enough to know about the Games of the Atlantis Grail."

"You *what?*" Now he is stunned, and his lips part as he stares at me.

"I know that you hold the Games every year, and Ten lucky winners, called Champions, are crowned, and they get Citizenship, plus all their wishes granted—"

As I speak, I see him shaking his head negatively, and his frown deepens in intensity. "No," he interrupts me. "This is insanity. If you know anything about the Games you also know that all of the other entrants *die*. No one wins, but a handful, and the whole thing is tragic—ancient brutal savagery, an archaic event that should be rightfully abolished, if not for the old laws and traditions—"

"Is there any other way to become a Citizen and get all your wishes granted?"

Aeson exhales loudly, in visible frustration. "You," he says, "are truly *impossible*. Why would you want to be a Citizen anyway? You can live a perfectly comfortable life as a Civilian, or even choose Cadet and become a successful Fleet Officer—"

"I don't want a comfortable life. I want to live an extraordinary one," I say stubbornly. "And I want all my wishes granted."

"What wishes?" He stares at me, craning his neck slightly.

"I wish to have all my family rescued from Earth before the asteroid hits. I wish to have my mother brought to Atlantis and put into that high-tech medical machine to have her cancer removed. I wish my father and my brother George to be here too. That's about it."

"Oh, is that all?" His tone is rich with sarcasm.

But I ignore it. "Well, a decent home to live in would be nice too. And of course higher education, so that I can learn everything I can about this new world I am about to enter—"

He appears to be once more rendered speechless, as he watches me with eyes that bore right through me, it seems, digging deeper and deeper, searching for something, I don't know what. . . .

"And these wishes of yours," he says softly, "do they also include a family at some point?"

"Well of course they do! As I just said, I want Mom and Dad and George—"

"No," he interrupts. "I mean, do you want a family of your own, a marriage union with a loving mate, maybe children. . . ."

As he says this, I feel heat once again rising in my face. "I—haven't thought about it," I reply haltingly. "Probably at some point, yes—but that kind of stuff is not part of my core wishes *right now*. And besides, it does not matter, none of it does. What needs to happen now is the urgent rescue of my parents and George—"

"It's not going to happen," he speaks ruthlessly.

"What?" I open my mouth.

"Let me be blunt. None of what you want is possible. There is no way to rescue your parents, and you cannot become a Citizen. I am sorry that you have been deluded to think that you can do something—"

"No!" I exclaim, standing up suddenly, while dizzying vertigo rises in my head. And then I sense I am about to say the same thing I told him before, back at the National Qualification Center in Colorado, when I accidentally used a compelling power voice on him: *"I do not accept this."*

But I don't. Not this time.

I rein the surge of power back in, as I feel my own prickle of gathering energy along my skin, and I allow my *voice* to dissipate and echo only in my own mind. And then I slowly return to my seat.

I have no idea if Aeson Kassiopei realizes the kind of inner struggle I just had to put down.

Instead I say very softly, "I am sorry, I disagree with your assessment when it comes to my own life and my own choices. I am going to enter the Games of the Atlantis Grail as soon as we arrive on Atlantis. Please tell me the truth. As a free individual, am I forbidden to do so?"

There is a peculiar dark pause. He watches me tragically.

"No," he says. "It is true. You may not be denied this outright."

"Then it is settled."

"No, it is *not*," he says loudly, commandingly, with rising anger. "Although you do have a certain individual right to enter the Games of the Atlantis Grail, according to our laws, you are also on my ship, under my orders. As such, I can forbid you to act in any way that will potentially harm or damage you—and therefore your *voice*—as it relates to matters of Atlantis. Your Logos power voice is an asset and you are hereby ordered to comply with my decision."

"And what if I refuse to comply? Will you incarcerate me?"

In that instant Aeson Kassiopei gets up from his desk. He takes three steps and suddenly towers above me.

In the next instant, he picks me up by the shoulders, raising me up from my seat effortlessly, as though I'm weightless . . . and he holds me briefly, his strong fingers cutting into my arms painfully, his face inches from mine—so close that I can see the dark fringe of his lashes and the sharp line of wonderfully exotic natural pigment around his eyelids . . . And I am also suddenly very aware of his elevated breathing through his slightly parted, chiseled lips.

He then just as suddenly lets me go, so that I fall back in my chair, slack-jawed from the shock of him, his *touch*, his overwhelming *presence*. Even now, the places on my arms where he touched me seem to *ring*, as though branded. . . .

"Gwen Lark," he says very carefully, looking down at me, speaking like a serpent, his voice gone low and dangerous. "Do not *ever* presume to challenge me, or to speak to me in this way again. I have tolerated your outbursts due to your ignorance of proper conduct, and your difficult circumstances. But it all stops now. You will listen and obey orders. Or you will be disciplined."

I feel a surge of crazy emotion rising, as I look up at him, shaking with the overload, and my hands clutch the armrests of the chair. Some really awful, possibly insane blather is about to pour out of me and I cannot stop it, as usual, and frankly, *I don't care*.

"Is this the Command Pilot speaking, or the *Imperial Prince?*" I say with boiling anger. "Should I address you as *Your Highness?* Because it seems to me you're ordering me about, and I am sorry, but technically I have *not* made my so-called 'life choice' or decision yet, and therefore I have not sworn, or promised loyalty, or obedience, or fealty, or *any other junk*—to you or to Atlantis! In fact, I'm not sure I want to, if this is how things are going to be! When Instructor Oalla Keigeri told me that *I mattered to you,* I thought that meant that you actually cared, as a human being, not some kind of tyrant—"

"What?" Aeson's expression grows perfectly still and cold, like stone. He appears to be stunned once more by what I just said. "She did *what?* What did Oalla Keigeri say to you?"

I stare at him, freezing also, my eyes wide open. And then I begin turning red again, red as a beet, or maybe a damn tomato. Oh, crap! What did I just do? What did I just tell him? "Nothing. . . . She said nothing, I mean, not much. . . . She just made it sound like you care—about my well-being, I think?

Or—I am not sure—"

A terrible pause.

He exhales a long held breath. "Well," he says, composing himself suddenly so that he looks perfectly casual, almost relaxed, which I know cannot be right. "Looks like Pilot Keigeri and I need to have a little talk—about overstepping bounds. You can be certain it will not happen again. In the future she will not speak nonsense about things she knows very little about."

I can tell he is very angry, but also, for some reason, he does not look directly at me. Instead, Aeson Kassiopei steps away and goes back to sit down at his desk. He sweeps back his metallic gold hair, puts his hands behind his head and leans back in his chair, still without looking at me. If I didn't know better, I would think he *cannot* face me. Or maybe it's something else?

Whatever it is, I sit in my chair and feel incredibly awkward—for about five very long seconds.

"So," he says.

And then he starts to *laugh*.

It is a clean arrogant sound, perfectly devoid of any emotion, completely in control, and for that reason it is *terrifying*. And as he laughs, he at last looks directly, confidently at me.

"Gwenevere Lark," he says my full name in a sarcastic, terrible, condescending voice, and the unwavering gaze of his eyes is upon me. "Whatever it is you *think* I hold in regards to you—whatever *sentiment* or *weakness* that Oalla Keigeri has so absurdly and mistakenly informed you about—it does not exist."

He pauses, observing the impact of his words. As he does, I feel a wave of cold rising inside me.

And then he continues, softening his words. "*You matter to me* about as much as any other refugee from Earth on this ship. Which is to say, you matter greatly—all of you. But that is all. And I regret that this conversation has turned out to be so inappropriately personal."

"I—I am sorry," I say brokenly, forgetting my own rebellion, while a strange inexplicable feeling of regret floods me, makes me numb. "I did not mean to imply—"

"No, you did not. Very well," he says, sitting forward again. "Then let's not speak of this any longer. As far as the

Games of the Atlantis Grail—the matter is settled also. But—let me make it fair for you. You have *my permission* to enter the Games, *if*, after all these months on my ship, you can demonstrate to me that you have what it takes."

I open my lips and sit up, with a sudden surge of hope.

"But," he continues. "Face it, Lark, you barely made it through Qualification. If you were to enter the Games in the same pathetic condition as you are today, at the same minimal level of physical training, you would not last past the first round. The competition would eat you alive. So, for all practical purposes, we will not dwell on this idiocy ever again."

"But—" I say.

"You will spend the bulk of your time working for me as my aide, reporting to this Central Command Office. After your daily duties, you may use your own time as you wish—to train or not. Also, I will not force you to make a life decision of Fleet Cadet or Civilian until this journey is over—not until I make my final evaluation of you. It is the only exception I will make for you, compared to anyone else—and only because of your unique value to Atlantis. For the duration of our trip to Atlantis, you may choose any classes and train with *both* the Cadets and the Civilians. I will also continue to train you personally in the use of your Logos voice."

"Thank you!" I exclaim. "It is all very reasonable and fair, I agree, *thank you!*"

"Don't thank me yet," he tells me with a faint smirk. "Let's see how you feel in a year from now."

"So, if you find my training adequate by then, you will allow me to enter the Games?"

"Yes."

I smile at him, a big blooming smile of hope and joy—so much so, that he actually seems to be caught up by the sight of me. He cranes his neck slightly, never taking his eyes off my face.

And then reality washes over me.

"Wait," I mutter. "You don't believe I can be ready in a year, do you? And that's why you are saying this . . . only to humor me?"

"Very perceptive as usual, Lark. That's correct. I do not."

"So then you are not really letting me do anything, are you? I am not going to be entering the Games?"

"Not a chance."

I bite my lip and nod at him. A strange new tumult of emotion is rising inside me, churning deep, and oh, it is comprised of so many things . . . there's outrage, hurt, the same deep, bitter regret at the revelation of how he really feels about me—or should I say, how little he feels *for* me—and a fierce burning sense of thwarted rightness.

Well then, Kassiopei, I will show you, I think.

But I keep it all bottled up. "Okay," I say softly. "What is expected of me, as far as daily work here for you?"

"I am glad you show some sense at last." Aeson raises one brow, almost surprised at my composure. "Now then, let's discuss your duties."

And for the next twenty minutes, we do.

Chapter 5

Aeson Kassiopei outlines for me what it is I will be doing as an aide to the Command Pilot's Central Command Office.

"Your primary duties," he says, "will be as records keeper to the CCO. You will observe and record the journey that the Earth refugees make, and you will compile the chronicle into a historical record from an Earth native's perspective. When we arrive on Atlantis, it will be added to our library records and become a part of our common historical record."

"Oh, wow!" I exclaim, unable to hold back. "That's actually amazing, I would love to do this!"

"Yes, I know," he says, looking seriously at me. "You are very bright and observant, extremely detail-oriented, and that's part of the reason I chose you for this task, after having looked over your school records and other details in your personal file."

"I have a file?" I say.

"Everyone does. The information from your Earth schools—in fact your entire education and life history—has been compiled and tallied, together with your Qualification record. Your ID token now holds your complete Earth identity and history. Same goes for every other Qualified teenager from Earth on this ship and in the whole Fleet."

I allow that to sink in.

"A secondary part of your duties," he continues, "will be to assist me in day-to-day regular office tasks, together with my two other regular aides—whom you will meet soon. For that purpose you will learn as much as you can about all functions of the ship. I give you permission to interview the crew and to take notes. You may also come and go freely on all decks, including all four Command Decks, and this office—I've granted your token ID access to enter here, and to use the computer systems at this desk with a basic entry-level clearance. The guards have been notified to allow you to enter freely. If asked, you are always to say you are an Aide to the CCO."

He pauses, and then pulls down one hinged mech arm from the equipment wall behind him, and lowers a display screen with a floating keypad. He swings it around to show me the screen.

I see a login screen and a tablet-style virtual touch-pad English keyboard directly on the screen. Meanwhile the physical keypad below has what looks like alien hieroglyphics, which I realize is the Atlantean character set.

Aeson swings the Atlantean keyboard aside and snaps it closed underneath the display, then rotates the screen even more, so that it lies flat like a tablet before me. "This way you can do data entry in English," he says. "For now. Because your third task is to begin to learn Atlantean. I expect you to have a basic understanding of our core language by the time we arrive on Atlantis."

"Okay," I say. "I can do that. This is all great. I am really excited to be doing this!"

"Good. Your duties will begin tomorrow, eight AM, sharp. First thing when you get here, we will work out your training schedule so that it does not interfere with your duties."

He pauses for a moment, watching me. It seems he is considering what he is about to say next. "As far as your special voice training—it will be incorporated into your regular schedule. But we will have it *off the record*."

"Oh?" I say. "What do you mean? In what sense?"

He continues looking at me with a complex expression, and the long pause extends, becoming unusual.

"Your voice training will literally not be recorded on your schedule. We're going to keep your Logos voice as much as possible a *secret*," he says at last. "Yes, it's true that a number of people in the Fleet currently know about it, including several of my officers, and quite a few of your fellow Qualified Candidates, especially those who were with you at the Pennsylvania RQC-3, and witnessed you levitate that shuttle. . . . Regrettably, there's nothing that can be done in that regard. However, we can minimize any new dissemination of this. From this point onward, you will not mention it to anyone new, including any of your new Instructors here in the Fleet. If asked, you deny it, or change the subject. And then later you report it to me. Any questions, any inquiries about your Logos voice—you tell me immediately."

"Okay. But—why?" I ask.

His gaze upon me is hard and intense. "Because your voice can be used as a political weapon. It can be used as leverage. And so can *you*. As of now, you are under my protection, until we get home to Atlantis, at which point—but we will discuss it when the time comes. For now, all you need to know is that we will work on your voice, but *discreetly*."

"All right." At this point, I'm frowning. He must read all kinds of turmoil on my newly troubled face.

"That's about it," he says with a sudden change of tone, almost flippant. "For the rest of today you may settle in and take it easy." He looks away then again glances into my eyes momentarily. There's a steady intimate expression that I see lurking in his blue eyes which is almost *warm*—but the next moment it is gone, and I am no longer certain it was ever there in the first place.

He sits back, moves the computer out of the way and taps the surface of his desk lightly with one hand. "And now, I believe, it's lunchtime. I'm hungry, so I am heading to the Officers Meal Hall. Come along and I'll show you where it is, since you'll be eating there often from now on."

"Oh . . ." I say. "Am I actually allowed in the Officers Meal Hall?"

Aeson's lips curve into the faintest smile. "As my CCO Aide, you are allowed everywhere."

He gets up.

I quickly follow.

Outside the office doors, the two stationed guards step aside and salute the Command Pilot. He acknowledges them with a brief nod as he walks past them, with me trailing. The guards pay no attention to me whatsoever.

Aeson walks in his typical long stride, so I have to rush to keep up. We arrive at the Officers Meal Hall after taking a few turns along various corridors on Command Deck Two, Blue Quadrant.

The meal hall is a chamber similar to the ones I've eaten in, back on the residential decks of the other ark-ship, except it is considerably smaller in size, with fewer tables, and comfortable dim lighting. The food bar lines one of the walls, and there is an identical selection of food items. No privilege here, nothing to show that officers eat better than the rest of the crew or the Earth refugees.

Somehow it pleases me to see this.

The room is half-full. A tantalizing aroma of warm spices and unfamiliar but appetizing food fills the air. I note that here too all the long bench tables are anchored to the floor, which makes sense onboard a starship. Atlantean officers and other upper-rank personnel sit at the tables, eating from dishes set on trays, and there is the ringing of utensils, and the easy sound of subdued but friendly conversation in the lilting tones of Atlantean, and sometimes English speech, interspersed with occasional laughter.

The moment Aeson Kassiopei enters, the entire meal hall falls silent. All the officers and crew stop eating, rise from their seats and salute the CP.

Aeson acknowledges the room in general with an informal command: "Carry on."

Immediately everyone resumes their meal and conversation. A few people continue looking in his direction, and now I feel eyes on me.

"Grab a tray, get your food," Aeson tells me casually, and proceeds to the lunch bar. I follow him somewhat awkwardly, and watch his tall powerful back and the fall of his golden hair as he interacts with the server who produces a covered tray and what looks like a ready packed bag from around the counter. "Savory *lidairi* and *ero* grains stir fry. Your favorite, Command Pilot," he says.

"Smells great as always. Thank you." Aeson takes the tray and bag, with a nod and a faint smile to the crewman server, and then turns around.

"What are you waiting for?" he tells me, as he finds me staring, holding on to an empty tray.

"I—I was not sure," I say.

Aeson glances around the room, which I now realize is for my sake. "Feel free to approach anyone you might know here. Or take a seat anywhere you like."

"Oh . . ." I mutter. "You're not going to eat here?"

He raises one brow. "No. I usually prefer to eat at my desk. But don't let it stop you."

I nod, but feel a moment of uncertainty. Seriously, what did I think was going to happen? That we were going to have lunch together, just the two of us, the Command Pilot and I? *Yeah, Gwen, you idiot.*

"Enjoy your meal, Lark," he tells me, with a confident glance. "Now, dismissed."

And with those words, Command Pilot Aeson Kassiopei turns away from me and exits the Officers Meal Hall, carrying his take-out lunch.

The moment he's out of the room, I feel a barely perceptible relaxation in the atmosphere, and conversations get louder. Obviously the officers are somewhat constrained by their commanding officer's presence, even when told to be at ease, and he is smart enough to know it.

I realize suddenly the true generous reason Aeson Kassiopei eats at his desk—he does not want to make his crew uncomfortable by his high-ranking presence.

Now that he's gone, I find myself feeling strangely vulnerable. I am all alone in a room full of Atlantean strangers. I take a deep breath, mostly for courage, and go up to the self-serve section of the food bar and pick out some unknown looking dishes that smell promising, and pile stuff on my tray. Then I take a glass and fill it with that same green *nikkari* juice, which I've gotten rather fond of in the last few days.

I stand, looking around the meal hall with a very awkward feeling of being completely out of place.

There is absolutely no one here but Atlanteans, and none of them look familiar. I squint, scanning the tables, and feel overwhelmed. However toward the back I see one dark-haired Atlantean in a sea of metallic gold, and he stands out.

His long raven-black mane makes a stark contrast against the gold. At some point he turns his face slightly, talking with others, and, no way—I know him! It's Xelio Vekahat.

Wow, I think with excitement. *Yet another one of my Instructors is on this ship!*

At this point it cannot be mere coincidence that all these Pennsylvania RQC-3 Instructors are stationed here on Imperial Command Ship Two. They must be Kassiopei's select officers, the best Pilots in the fleet.

They're *astra daimon*.

And this ship is naturally their home base.

Thinking along those lines, I quietly find an empty table out of the way, set down my tray, and eat a lonely alien lunch.

"Are you Gwen Lark?"

I am almost done eating and I look up. It's been at least half an hour, and the Officers Meal Hall is nearly empty. I've tarried here over my food, basically people-watching and not exactly sure what to do with myself for the rest of the day.

A thickset Atlantean teen stands before me. He's possibly older than me, or maybe not, with dark skin, somewhere between deep river clay and brown. His pleasant features are rounded, a flattened nose and blunt chin, with the usual kohl-enhanced eyelids around friendly dark brown eyes, and thick dark brows. His metallic gold hair is short and curling tightly against his scalp. He's wearing a blue armband.

"Yes," I say.

"I am Gennio Rukkat," he says in a slightly nervous tenor and a very light Atlantean accent in his English. "I am an Aide to the CCO just like you. Command Pilot Kassiopei instructed me to find you. You must have many questions, and other things I can help you with, before tomorrow."

"Oh, hi." I smile at him, starting to get up. "Yes, of course, nice to meet you! Thank you so much, I have tons of questions! Let me just get this tray emptied—"

He nods and follows me, while I pick up my empty dishes and take the tray to the recycling receptacle.

"Why don't we take a walk while I show you things and answer your questions?" he says. "And, I hope you forgive me but I really want to make it to the Observation Deck before the scheduled Mars orbit pass."

"Oh, yeah, sure," I say, remembering about the Mars orbit crossing this afternoon. "Is it time already?"

"Almost two o'clock Earth UTC time," Gennio says with excitement, as we exit the Officers Meal Hall and begin walking. "We enter the perihelion region of Mars orbital space at 2:13 PM, and I need to record the image of the Earth Sol as it is in that exact moment."

"Is that for your work?" I glance at him with curiosity. "Is that what you do also, chronicle and record events for the CCO?"

"Oh, no," he tells me with a shy smile. "This is merely personal. I am taking images of the journey for my own astronomy interest. I've photographed your Sun and other stars and cosmic entities at various stages of our approach, and now I am doing the same as we return to Atlantis."

"Sounds kind of awesome," I say, as we quickly turn along the network of corridors heading toward the distant outer hull of the ship. "So, what exactly do you do for the CCO?"

"I oversee the tech—central communication systems and other office computers—basically the CCO machines and their connectivity." He shrugs with a small nervous gesture. "What is it you call it on Earth? Technical support nerd or geek?"

"Oh, yes!" I can't hold back a chuckle. "Okay, I think you and I are going to be new besties."

"Beasties?" The Atlantean glances at me in linguistic confusion. "Wild animals?"

I laugh. "No, *besties*, as in 'best friends,' in old-school underage girl slang—apologies for being silly. It's been a very long day, and it's still only afternoon."

"I understand," he says kindly. Already I am beginning to like this guy very much.

"So," I continue, with excitement of my own. "Now you can show me how to login at the CCO terminal tomorrow. . . . Also, I need to know how to call my sister and brother who are on another ship, how to check the ship location of other Qualified Earth refugees, how to store files, look up data . . . I'm assuming you have search engines and an Atlantean version of the internet, or ship-board intranet—"

    Gennio listens to me rattle away with an easy expression.

    Yes, I think, he and I will be getting along just fine.

Chapter 6

The ICS-2 space Observation Deck is grand and dimly lit, exactly like the one back on Ark-Ship 1109.

Gennio Rukkat and I stop before the floor-to-ceiling tinted windows and look at the immensity of the cosmos outside. Quite a few other people are gathered here too, to watch the momentous non-event that is about to take place. Too bad Mars itself is hidden far out of sight somewhere beyond the Sun, near the opposite point of its elliptical orbit relative to us, and almost in solar conjunction with Earth. It would have been mind-blowing to see it up-close, instead of merely marking the moment we cross some theoretical trajectory path in space. . . .

I glance around and see other Qualified teens with various color armbands and tokens, but no one I know—at least as far as I can tell. Soft conversations in Earth foreign languages sound from all directions. At one point, I am certain, someone recites poetry in classical Latin. And from somewhere else, comes a prayer in Arabic.

"The ship computer is supposed to say when we actually do it. You know, cross the Mars orbit," an older boy says in a confident voice, right next to us.

"You mean a countdown?" a girl responds.

"Yeah."

I turn around.

The boy who speaks is tall and muscular, with an arrogant expression, wavy brown hair and a green armband. I am guessing he is North American, but can't be sure of his accent. The girl is medium-height, with a toned body and waist-long straight dark hair with purple streak highlights. She wears a red armband.

Next to me, Gennio Rukkat looks in their direction and says helpfully, "Actually not a countdown but an extended two-part observance for the duration of the orbit pass. The computer will announce when the vanguard ships of the Fleet enter the perihelion, or closest point of Martian orbit relative to the Sun. And then it will announce when we depart beyond the farthest point of its solar orbital range, or aphelion. The whole event will last about three-point-two minutes, give or take thirty seconds, though I believe it will be closer to exactly three-point-two minutes, based on our current timer calibration, the length of the Fleet formation, and our rate of acceleration. . . ."

"Is that right?" the Earth boy says. "Thanks." And then he and the girl look at each other, raise brows, and compress their mouths, repressing laughter. I recognize thinly veiled mockery, and oh yeah, these two really give off the unpleasant alpha vibes.

But I don't think Gennio notices. "Oh yes, you are welcome," he says. "It really is exciting to experience, even though Mars is not in our viewing range."

"Look!" I distract him, pointing with my hand to a bright point of blue light, like a very bright star. "Is that Earth?" I am pretty sure it is, but I just want to get Gennio to confirm, and to kind of stop talking to the boy and girl next to us.

"It is Earth, that is correct, yes," he says, immediately switching his attention. And then he reaches into the pocket of his uniform and takes out a small Atlantean gadget that looks like a mini-cube made of orichalcum. He presses something and it unfolds into the Atlantean equivalent of a flat rectangle viewfinder with a video display and a micro camera. "Since you mention it, let me just capture Earth in this moment too," he mutters, then lifts up the device and stares through it at the grand spacescape, until the gadget blinks.

In that moment, a bright violet plasma shooting star passes horizontally outside the ship's observation windows. It is followed a second later by two others, and then a third, moving at incredible speed.

"Whoa! Did you see that?" the muscular boy with the green armband says.

"What was that?" the girl echoes him, and so do a few other people.

"Just our shuttles," Gennio says, not taking his eyes off his video gadget. "Likely, these are the advance transports that were supposed to meet up with the Fleet after picking up your Mars Station personnel and shutting down the station, on our way out of the solar system. Makes sense we would rendezvous at the orbital pass."

"Wow! Really?" Now I am genuinely curious. "I never heard anything about that!"

Furthermore, now everyone in hearing range is staring at Gennio and me.

"Oh yes," he says, suddenly a little flustered. "Unlike your older personnel on the Moon, the current Mars Station crew is all seventeen to nineteen and their age makes them eligible for rescue. This was decided a few months ago, in joint agreement with your Earth United Nations. They were supposed to dismantle much of the Mars Station, gut the servers and useful scientific data. . . ."

"Okay, big wow," I say.

"This is completely news to me," the boy from Green says in a hard voice. "Why weren't we told any of this? What the hell? These Mars Station personnel, did they even have to pass Qualification like the rest of us? How come they get special treatment?"

Gennio Rukkat appears to be uncertain how to reply. I have a feeling that what he just told us wasn't exactly supposed to be common knowledge.

"I would think that being on a Mars mission and surviving the seven-month-long trip either via Hohmann transfer orbit or ballistic capture is Qualification enough," I blurt. Okay, maybe I should've just kept my mouth shut, because now the boy turns to me with a withering angry stare.

"Huh?" he says. "What did you say?"

In that moment comes a timely interruption.

"Now entering Mars orbital perihelion." The machine voice sounds at last, echoing throughout the Observation Deck.

Conversations rise and fall in waves as everyone on deck pauses to listen to the voice of the computer and stare at the "nothing" outside, as though they could somehow magically see the Mars-path in space, etched in stardust or something.

"Oh! Oh! There it is!" Gennio says, forgetting everything, turning his camera gadget away from Earth and focusing it on the golden disk of the Sun. "This is the moment I need to capture the Sun. Isn't it exciting!"

The girl and boy next to us make snorting sounds. The boy still looks aggravated but the girl pulls his sleeve and rolls her eyes and then they move away—for which I am glad.

For the next three-point-two minutes, I stand looking at the universe, while Gennio takes endless pictures of the Sun and mutters in excitement, occasionally switching over to Atlantean. "There!" he says at last, holding his index finger in the ready-to-stop-recording position. "I should have enough image data to render a composite video and see if I can observe the micro-evolution in the Sun corona during the whole three-point-two minute passage, and compare it to my identical video taken on Earth approach!"

"Now leaving Mars orbital aphelion," the computer announces in that same instant.

"Wow," I say, impressed. "You really timed that perfectly. Can I look at it when you have it ready?"

"Of course. I can have it ready in an hour—but not now, of course, not this hour but another hour...." Gennio nods with satisfaction, folds his gadget back into a cube, and puts it back in his pocket. There's a look of pure enlightened joy on his face that I've mostly seen on people in physics labs. I know that look, since I've worn it myself on many occasions.

Oh lord, I think. *He is just like me. And we really are nerds.*

For the rest of the afternoon, I wander the ship with Gennio Rukkat, along endless corridors and decks, past Atlantean crewmembers and Earth Qualified refugees going every which way. For once I am letting him talk and point, and I don't pay much attention or ask too many questions—my mind is back in a kind of dark, deep, inner place.

My thoughts flip from sluggish to racing, and I think intermittently and feverishly of everyone I know.... Where are they *right this moment?* Gracie and Gordie, what are they doing on that other ark-ship, and oh, I need to call them somehow.... I think of Mom and Dad and George back home—on Earth, oh

God, they are *so far away* now!

Even now my mind cannot conceive the real cosmic distances, how far away everyone is. . . . Mars! *Mars!* We're past Mars! And supposedly because we are continuing to accelerate like crazy, we might begin to enter the debris field of the Asteroid Belt by midnight tonight! That's almost like the distance from Earth to Mars all over again, but in *one night* instead of the four days it took us to get to Mars! The rate of our acceleration is mind-blowing!

Strange "space vertigo" strikes and overwhelms me all at once, and now I'm dizzy and reeling in my mind. Ever since the Qualification Finals I no longer suffer from a fear of heights. But now, I think, this fear of grand cosmic space has weirdly come to replace it. . . .

And what about Logan? He's on the imperial flagship, settling in as a Cadet to begin his new life and training tomorrow, just like all of us will be doing tomorrow, myself included.

What about Laronda? And my other friends?

Oh, I really need to try to find them!

But first, I need to call my siblings.

And so I interrupt Gennio as he's telling me something remarkable about Atlantean systems networking, and ask him to take me back to the Command Deck and show me how to make ship-to-ship calls.

"Of course," the Atlantean tells me amiably. "Better yet, I can show how you can easily call anyone from the privacy of your own cabin."

"Oh, you can do that?" I say, coming alive. "Oh, that's great!"

We get to my tiny cabin #28 on Command Deck Four, Yellow Quadrant, and Gennio sits down at my single chair-and-table combo, while I sit across from him on the narrow bed, barely managing not to knock my head against the low overhanging storage bulkhead.

Gennio presses a small recessed switch on the table surface and it activates a wall screen I haven't noticed before. "I need your token ID, please. This will key the ship communication line to you."

I hand over my token and watch him as he passes it over the table and calls up a now familiar login screen with a virtual English keyboard.

In minutes I know how to login and how to make shipboard calls, and how to run people searches. I am also set up for text and email.

"There you go," he tells me, somewhat impressed in turn. "You learn fast, that's good. I don't need to explain things over and over to you. Now I'll go while you call your family or friends. I'll see you tomorrow, okay? Maybe see you for the dinner meal? I usually eat at the Blue Quadrant Cadet Deck Meal Hall, or the other Cadet Meal Halls."

"Not at the Officers Meal Hall?"

Gennio shakes his head. "Not as relaxing there. We can eat anywhere we like."

"Oh," I say. "Okay, maybe I'll see you there too!"

He just nods, and exits the cabin.

The moment Gennio leaves, I call Gracie. Apparently wherever she is back on the other ship, her own bunk has a similar video screen built into the wall, and if she is there I can video-call her, or leave a message for later.

"Gracie!" I say, the moment I see my little sister's face up-close in the display. She appears to be in a barracks situation, identical to what we had on the Residential Deck of her ship. The background is noisy with teenage voices, rowdy laughter, and stuff being thrown. So, this is what newbie Red Quadrant Cadets are doing on their first night, I think and smile.

"Gee Two!" Gracie sticks her face so close into the screen that it appears distorted and her nose is big, as in a poorly taken selfie. I notice my sister has a couple of new zits on her chin that she forgot to cover up with her usual concealer makeup. "OMG, Gee Two, where are you? Are you in a little room all alone?"

"Yeah," I tell her, "I got my own cabin. Everything's okay. So, how are you?"

"It's kind of crazy here—" Gracie squeals suddenly as I see someone's hand yank her long hair from the side and a boy's horsey laugh, then another girl's voice speaking in what could possibly be Italian. "Oh man, everything, is okay here too, we got our schedule, classes starting tomorrow, I have Pilot class first thing, which is awesome—oh, stop it, you idiot!" Gracie turns to slap away someone's hand again. Then she laughs. "Okay, Gee Two, I gotta go, call you later!"

And the call goes dark.

"Love you . . ." I mouth the words silently to myself, staring at the disconnected silent display and the main login screen.

Then I try calling my brother Gordie.

Gordie is not there, or at least not anywhere near his bunk to activate the personal line and receive my call. And neither is Logan. I leave messages for both.

I consider if I should call Laronda—and momentarily get a sickening pang of fear that Laronda might not be in the Fleet— what if she didn't make it?

So I decide against it. I feel exhausted, and lie down for a moment. Maybe I can just shut my eyes and that way *not have to think.* . . .

Mom and Dad and George . . . they are so far away now. Farther than humanly imaginable. Back on Earth, which is a tiny blue bead.

So dizzy—the world, the universe, everything is so upside down.

I close my eyes and drown in sleep.

When I wake up, the lights in the cabin have gone down to night level darkness. They are probably motion activated, and since I passed out, there was no motion. However with my movement, they rise to soft evening twilight levels. Reminder to self: next time, ask Gennio if there's a better way to control these lights short of waving my hands about.

I check the small built-in clock in the wall, and it looks like I've not only slept past dinner, but it's close to midnight. Good thing I'm not really hungry, or I'd be screwed.

The cabin is perfectly quiet, and there are no sounds in the hallway outside. It occurs to me, the soundproofing in the ship is very high-end, so maybe I simply cannot hear anything.

I vaguely consider what to do. Going back to sleep makes

sense.

But something makes me get up instead. I use the wash and lavatory facilities, unpack and rummage through my duffel bags and put them away into the overhead storage. I suppose I will also need to ask Gennio tomorrow where the Atlanteans do their laundry. . . .

And then I sit down at the little desk and pull up the screen again, this time using it as a word processor, not a phone line.

I start a new file and title it *"A Chronicle of Earth's Journey to Atlantis, by Gwenevere Lark, Aide to the CCO."*

And then I begin to type.

Chapter 7

I am awoken by the bright shipboard daylight alarm, and it's five minutes after 7:00 AM. That's how long it took my unconscious sleeping mind to surface out of a jumbled nightmare dream filled with dead bodies and subterranean water-filled tunnels into the present reality.

Today is the first day of the rest of my new life.

And yes, incidentally, I am flying through effing outer space, somewhere far beyond Mars, among the rushing debris of the Asteroid Belt, and on approach toward Jupiter. . . .

Of course the debris are not really rushing anywhere. They range in size from microscopic dust to planetoids, and there are huge distances between them, so it's not like we're in danger of hitting anything, but still . . . *Jupiter!*

Last night I got back to sleep really late, after having written approximately five pages of lousy and haphazard notes and narrative that needs to be reworked later, but for now, it's raw and freshly spewed from my mind. And it's something.

If I remember correctly, I didn't stop writing until close to 2:15 AM, when the ship's computer voice intruded into my feverish flow of thoughts, breaking my concentration.

"Now entering the Main Asteroid Belt region," the machine voice announced. Which meant, we're officially out of the rocky inner planets region of the solar system, and on our way toward the gas giants.

Talk about a strange way to fall asleep. . . .

Now, I force myself to get up, shower in the pressurized water-mist stall cubicle, get dressed and step outside the door into the ship corridor, with half an hour to spare before my 8:00 AM morning duties begin at the CCO.

The Officers Meal Hall is the only one I know. So I go there by default, grab breakfast, and eat very quietly in the corner, recognizing no Atlanteans. The officers also eat in a hurry, unlike yesterday's easygoing lunch. This morning they all appear strictly business, with little conversation. I suppose today the routine begins for real, and they all have a boatload of tasks, including our various training classes. . . .

I arrive at the wide Command Deck corridor, just before 8:00 AM, and stop at the guarded doors of the Central Command Office. Already, my heart is pounding like a drum in anticipation of seeing *him*—Command Pilot Kassiopei.

"I am Gwen Lark, Aide to the CCO," I say awkwardly.

The guards let me by without a word.

I enter the office, and there is no one there. There's no sign of Aeson Kassiopei, and Gennio Rukkat is not here either, even though I'd assumed he might be here this morning.

As I stand there, at a loss, I hear a strange scraping sound coming from the floor behind the large desk. Then there's a cough and a grunt, and something that sounds like hard cussing in Atlantean.

I take a step forward. "Hello?"

Someone emerges from underneath the Command Pilot's desk. It's another older teen, medium-height, wiry and slim, with Caucasian-pale skin and freckles. I am willing to bet anything that his long hair, gathered in a segmented ponytail, is bright red underneath that gilded dye. His face is long and lean, and his expression is supremely annoyed. His armband is red, to match his temper.

"What?" he says is a deep voice, speaking decent unaccented English. "Who let you in here? Are you a Cadet? Who are you? Wait, no—are you the new Earth Aide?"

"Yes, I'm Gwen Lark. And you are?"

The Atlantean makes a grimace. "Oh, for crap's sake, I have no time for this." And then he climbs back down underneath the desk.

I stand in the middle of the office, somewhat stunned.

And then I hear, coming from under the desk: "Anu Vei . . ." followed by a grunt and more Atlantean cussing. "I am . . . the other . . . Aide. Come around and help me, girl! Right *now!*"

"Excuse me?" I say, frowning at his tone.

"I said, *move!* Or go get Gennio Rukkat, because you are obviously incompetent—"

"Wait a minute," I say, and my voice is rising to match his. "What is going on here? What do you want me to do, exactly? Look, it's my first day, and I am supposed to get my schedule from Command Pilot Kassiopei, and then discuss with him—"

"As you can see, the CP is not here!" Anu Vei says, still from underneath the desk. "Look—See? Not here! He's in a meeting. As for your damn schedule, did you check your email this morning?"

"What? No. . . ."

"Well, there's your confirmation. You *are* incompetent. Now, get out of here and check your email! You have your Pilot Training, first thing, as in, *right now*—and why is it that *I* know this and you don't?"

"Wait a minute, *what?*" I say, as my temples start to pound with stress and anger. "No one told me to look for any email, in fact I was supposed to see the Command Pilot himself—"

"You are wasting time! Either help me with this desk here, or leave!"

"Okay," I say. "But—"

In that moment the door opens behind us, and I turn around nervously, only to see Gennio Rukkat. Oh, what a relief. . . .

"Gennio!" I exclaim. "Oh, so glad to see you! I am not sure what is going on, or what to do—this person tells me my schedule is in my email? And Command Pilot Kassiopei is in some meeting? I was not told about any—"

"Gennio, at last! Get over here now!" Anu Vei interrupts me ruthlessly and peeks over the desk with a frown.

"Just a moment, Gwen." Gennio smiles briefly then immediately walks past me to the desk. "Anu, what happened?"

The other Atlantean grunts, then motions with his hand, pointing downward.

Seconds later, Gennio goes around and gets under the desk also.

I stand like an idiot for about a minute, listening to them burrow about and knock things, clunk heavy objects, and breathe loudly.

"I am not sure what is happening. Should I go?" I say at last. "Anu, since you know about my Pilot Training, can you at least tell me where it is? It would take me too long to return to my cabin to check the email—"

Gennio peeks over the desk and gives me a mild look. "Oh, don't worry, Gwen. You have plenty of time."

"What?" I say. "But *he* just told me I'm late to my Pilot Training!"

"Who said this?"

"He did! The guy under the desk!"

Gennio makes a soft sound like a chuckle. "Oh," he says. "No, no—Anu just likes to joke with people. It's your first day, right? So, on my first day Anu told me I was on the wrong ship! He told me I had to run back to the shuttle bay and report to ICS-3 instead, which is halfway down the Fleet formation."

"Yeah, and he almost fell for it too." A low sarcastic snort comes from underneath the desk. "If the CP himself hadn't come in at that point, my friend here would've been trying to report to Command Pilot Tahirah Zulei instead, after taking a shuttle flight to ICS-3."

"Oh, that's truly awful!" I say. "How could you do that? You nearly gave me a heart attack."

"Hah!" Anu says in a rough tone. "Deal with it. If you can't deal, you're in the wrong place. How did you even pass Qualification?"

Okay . . . I think. *This Anu guy is a real piece of work. . . .*

I take a deep breath. And then I decide to ignore the jerk.

"Gennio," I say instead. "What is up with my schedule? Do you know anything about it?"

"Oh, sure," Gennio says. "I'm the one who put it together for you, when the CP told me some of the classes you'll need. It is not completely finalized, naturally, since the CP needs to approve it after discussing it with you, but that should happen after he gets back here from his meeting in about an hour."

"So, what classes will I have?"

Gennio pauses to think. "Hmm, there's Pilot Training, definitely—that's priority one. Then there's Culture, Atlantean Language, maybe Combat—or maybe that's optional? Anyway,

I don't recall exactly, except that your first class will be Pilot Training at 1:00 PM today. Why don't we take a look at it in the system? Let me just finish here with Anu, and then we can login and check." And he dives back underneath the table.

"Okay—what exactly are you guys doing?" I take a few steps and finally peer over the desk. I see the tops of two metallic-haired heads as the two guys are leaning over a portion of a lower desk drawer that appears to be broken or detached, and there is a whole lot of alien wiring coming out of there.

"What's that?" I say.

"Nothing," Anu mutters with a frown, glancing up at me very briefly. "Nothing that concerns you, really. At this point, you won't understand it."

"Maybe if you explained it, I would? And maybe I could help?"

"I highly doubt it. You should've helped earlier when I *asked* you—when I needed help moving this drawer panel—at least that would've been at your level of competence."

I feel a twinge of anger returning. This guy is really—and I mean, *really*—getting on my nerves now.

Fortunately Gennio speaks up in his usual mild tone. "It's the networking cables. Something's causing intermittent connectivity failure along the different consoles. They've been having problems, and we replaced some a few days ago, but now the problem is back. The CP told us to check it out, first thing this morning."

I stare at the mess of cables below. "Okay," I say. "I may not know your Atlantean systems but I can probably help with the troubleshooting. The *process* is always the same—a process of elimination. So just tell me what to try and we can test connections maybe?"

"We've already done that, *many* times," Anu says.

"And we've replaced parts," Gennio adds with a sigh. "*Many* parts. Pretty much everything, to be honest."

"Well," I say. "Let's begin from scratch. Take *everything* apart. And this time I will watch and maybe write each step down, so you will know for sure every combination and configuration you already went through."

"We already went through everything!" Anu's voice rises in

new aggravation.

But I ignore him completely. I step around the desk and crawl in between the two of them.

About forty minutes later the CP's desk is lying in pieces all around the room, and so are half the computer consoles. We're all sitting on the floor, tangled in wiring and covered in alien circuit boards. I am passing around Atlantean micro-wrench and screwdriver tools from one guy to the other, jotting down their troubleshooting combinations, and plugging in one cable after another as they tell me.

"Aha!" Gennio exclaims at last, after some successful line connection is made. "I think it's this one! Keep both of those plugged in, Gwen! Don't move! Don't move!"

"Okay, not moving! Just a sec," I mutter, passing the back of my free hand against my forehead, while I hold a loose connection with the other, and a second in my teeth.

"You got it?" Anu wipes the sheen of sweat off his own pale forehead.

"Yeah!"

In that moment the door opens, and Command Pilot Aeson Kassiopei enters his office.

There is a long pause as we all fall motionless.

Aeson takes one step, sees the condition of the room, then freezes in what is possibly stunned silence.

"What?" he says, and his lips part. "What is going *on* here?"

Both Gennio and Anu drop whatever items they're holding, scramble up to their feet, and salute the CP. I remain seated on the floor, cross-legged, my eyes opened wide. A long piece of networking cable is still clutched between my teeth.

Oh my lord, it occurs to me belatedly. *This is so wrong.... Could I possibly look even more like a dog?*

"Command Pilot Kassiopei, with greatest apologies, we are working on the connectivity problem," Gennio mutters. "Fortunately we've just isolated the bad connection—"

"It was her idea to disassemble everything." Anu says in a cool voice, pointing in my direction.

Command Pilot Kassiopei takes that moment to ignore the

two standing aides, and instead focuses his wrath on me. "Gwen Lark," he says very softly, taking a step toward me over a piece of disassembled furniture and a circuit board. "How is it that you've only been here *one day* and you've already managed to take apart my ship?"

I allow the cable to fall from my mouth, and look up at him. "I—I just thought it would make sense to repeat the basic troubleshooting, since they were not having much success—"

Aeson looks at me with a complex expression that is hard to describe. "Is that so? And how well familiar are you with our ship systems that you think you can make repairs?"

"Not at all," I retort. "But then I don't have to be. I am familiar with the *method* of problem solving. It applies to any situation."

Anu makes a choked sound.

"With your permission, Command Pilot," Gennio says in a hurried voice, as though sensing that an explosion is about to occur, "I am certain we are now done and can have everything reassembled and functional in half an hour—"

"You have fifteen minutes," Aeson Kassiopei says, glancing at him and Anu. "I expect everything to be back the way it should be by the time I return."

"Yes, Command Pilot!" The two aides salute again and start picking up parts and connecting lines in a hurry.

Meanwhile the Command Pilot returns his attention to me. "You," he says in an unreadable voice that is low and dark. "Come with me, we are going to discuss your schedule—out in the hall. *Move!*" And he turns from me coldly and again steps past pieces of his desk and exits.

I scramble to get up, nearly tripping on cables, and follow him outside.

As soon as we're in the corridor past the guards, Aeson says without looking in my direction, "Walk with me."

We begin walking along the corridor, and for a few seconds there is only silence. I glance up at him nervously a few times, but mostly keep my eyes on the way ahead. Eventually I can't keep quiet any longer. "I am really sorry," I begin. "It was my fault they took everything apart—"

"No, actually it was not. My aides are qualified technicians. As crewmen, they are solely responsible for their own actions—*and* methodology. What they did was unwisely take the advice of an inexperienced but very *insistent*, know-it-all young girl—"

"Advice, which proved correct!" I exclaim, staring at him, or better to say, at his stern profile, since he still does not look at me.

"That is beside the point."

I struggle to keep my mouth shut. We continue walking.

"And you," he says. "You were out of line. On your first day, you do *not* make recommendations to anyone. You look and listen and *learn*."

"Okay. . . . Understood." I bite my lip, and this time turn away from him and look directly ahead. "It will not happen again."

He finally looks at me. "See that it doesn't."

I nod, silently.

We walk past a few corridors and sections, generally moving in a circle along the wide corridor, as it surrounds, like a donut, the spherical Resonance Chamber at the heart of the ship.

"So, may I ask about my schedule?" I say.

"Yes." He pauses and takes out a small flat gadget that resembles a key card out of his uniform shirt pocket. I stand looking at him curiously, and feel my pulse once more beginning a slow rhythmic pounding in my temples.

Aeson places the card over my yellow token ID, and it flashes briefly. "Your schedule is now programmed into your record. You may consult it any time by reading your token data against any ship console."

"But I thought we were going to discuss my specific classes first, before finalizing?"

"Not much to discuss," he says with another cool, brief look at me. "You are taking Pilot Training, Culture, Language, and Combat. These are the core Cadet classes. Any problem with these selections?"

"No . . . but I am not a Cadet."

"Not yet. But if you are to have this choice available to you at the end of the year, you will need to be ready."

"I see," I mutter. "Okay."

"Furthermore, you also have Navigation, which is part of your continued Yellow Quadrant training, Technology and Systems, which is Civilian general education, and voice training with me, every night at eight PM."

"Okay."

"Finally, you will have Court Protocol taught by a special personal tutor. It is a class that is normally taught to Citizens—"

"Oh!" I exclaim.

But he shakes his head with a cold glance. "Don't get your hopes up. In your case you simply need to become well versed in the standards of interaction with upper ranking members of society, because you are an Aide to the CCO. All my Aides are fluent in matters of protocol since they have to attend a member of the Imperial Family."

"In other words, *you*. . . ."

"Yes." His answer comes very softly.

I nod, feeling my cheeks burn for some reason, as I watch his beautiful profile and the fall of his golden hair.

"Wow, that's a lot of classes," I say. "What about my work hours?"

"I allocated only two classes each day for you. A few days will have three, but no more. Check your schedule and fear not."

"Oh, I am not afraid of an academic overload!" I exclaim.

At my response his lips quiver momentarily, so that I almost think he holds back a smile. "Good," he tells me.

And we head back to the CCO.

Chapter 8

I help Gennio and Anu with the post-assembly cleanup of the office, while Aeson Kassiopei gets his desk back in one piece, calls up his various consoles, and gets to work, promptly ignoring all three of us.

I spend the hours before lunch working at a small console in the corner of the office, next to Anu and Gennio, entering data and occasionally glancing in Aeson's direction, out of simple curiosity. Gennio runs various software diagnostics while Anu looks over email and personnel data and makes catty remarks about random individuals, muttering under his breath. The three of us aides then head out to eat, while the Command Pilot remains working alone in his office, his face serious and absentminded, as he consults what appears to be intricate star charts, and makes occasional face-to-face calls with Atlantean officers.

And then, it's 1:00 PM, and time for my first class onboard the Atlantean starship.

Pilot Training.

"Good luck, Gwen, you'll do fine. This is a very important class!" Gennio waves at me at the end of our meal, while Anu merely nods, as I empty my tray at the Cadet Deck Two Meal Hall. The room is noisy and filled with savory food smells and with Qualified Earth teens, mostly from the Blue Quadrant, since this is their meal hall. Everyone is chattering about the upcoming Pilot Training, which means most of us will be going to the same class in a few minutes.

It's interesting that now the Cadets are all wearing small four-point-star gold buttons next to their ID tokens. I'd noticed it earlier this morning as I passed some of them in the ship corridors—must be a new thing.

I follow the Cadets out of the meal hall, and down a network of corridors to an open deck instruction area, the size of a large classroom. It has about twenty rows of desk-like double-seater cubicles, six per row, each with strange attached circular terminals before them—not precisely computer screens but more like gaming consoles.

"Flight simulators!" a boy exclaims, grabbing one of the places near me.

I think he's right.

I take a seat in the second row, at one of the weird double desks, and watch the room fill up around me. I think I'm the only Yellow in a sea of Blues, with a small sprinkling of Reds and Greens. I'm also the only person without a four-point star button on my uniform.

"Hey, Yellow. You're in the wrong section. Are you supposed to be here?" a serious dark-haired boy with a blue armband says in accented English, glancing at my shirt with its obvious lack of a star button. He looks possibly Latin American.

"Yes," I say curtly. "I am." And I stay silent while he shrugs, then takes the other seat next to me.

I watch as more people arrive, and hear conversations in different languages. To my surprise I see two athletic Asian teens with short blue-black spiked hair, and recognize Erin and Roy Tai, sister and brother, the #1 and #2 top Standing Score contenders from my own Pennsylvania RQC-3. Furthermore, there's also Kadeem Cantrell, African American parkour free runner god and #3 contender. Not surprising at all that they made it through Qualification, or that they were chosen to be on this particular ship ICS-2 under the command of the best Pilot in the Fleet. But it's kind of amazing that I'm going to be in the same class with them. Okay, I'm so out of my league!

At one point I also notice the entrance of two other teens—a muscular arrogant boy with wavy brown hair and a green armband, and a girl with long dark hair with purple highlights and a red armband. They are the same sarcastic pair of alphas from the observation deck the night before, who made smirking fun of Gennio. They don't recognize or notice me, and I am glad.

Another minute, and the room is packed. Every seat is taken, and there are many teens standing in the back, with no place to sit. Noisy waves of conversation move around the deck.

Our Instructor arrives and everyone falls silent.

He is rather unusual—visibly *older* than all the other Atlanteans I have seen to date. If he was an Earth man, I would call him middle-aged, somewhere in his late forties, but of course with Atlanteans you never know, he might as well be ninety. He is average-height, lean and wiry, with deeply tanned skin that has a dry and weathered look, short hair that is not dyed metallic gold but instead is naturally dark, with silver at the temples. He wears a very minimal line of dark kohl highlight around his brown eyes, almost like an afterthought. His expression is so grim and stony that he appears angry even without opening his mouth. The armband on his left uniform sleeve is blue.

The Instructor walks to the front of the classroom and stands coldly, feet apart, before the rows of console desks.

"Attention!" he suddenly barks. "Cadets, stand and salute!"

The room is thrown into momentary chaos. I jump out of my seat together with everyone else, except I have no idea what I'm doing.

Fortunately, neither does most of the class. A few of the Cadets clumsily perform the same salute I've seen the Atlanteans do—head inclined, left hand raised, fingers touching forehead, thumb touching lips.

The Atlantean Instructor watches us in disgust.

"At ease! You are all unfit, and next time you will salute properly. Now, sit down and listen."

Again, the room shakes with the noise of people taking seats.

"I am Mithrat Okoi," says the older Atlantean. "And I will be teaching you Pilot Training. By the time we are done, each one of you will be able to drive and navigate a basic shuttle, and some of you will advance to pilot a variety of more sophisticated spacecrafts."

The Atlantean pauses to glare at us, and the whole classroom stares back in rapt attention.

He points to the flight consoles. "If you require translation from English to another Earth language, use the dubbing earpiece on the side of the console. Language selection is made verbally. From this moment on you will make no excuse for lack of understanding."

As I glance around, a few in the room immediately reach for the translator earpieces.

"Before we begin—" His oppressive gaze again sweeps the room. "Every one of you in this room should be wearing the star insignia of the Fleet Cadet Corps. If there is anyone here without a star, I want you to get up and get out. Do it now!"

I freeze. My heart starts pounding, and I don't dare breathe, or move. Instead I watch from the corner of my eye as at least three people rise from their seats, look around with embarrassment, and quietly leave the classroom.

The kid in the chair next to me gives me a dirty look.

I remain in my seat.

Instructor Okoi starts to pace among the rows of our desks, looking closely at each one of us, as he speaks. "Pilot Training is the core fundamental training you will receive as members of the Fleet. Every refugee from Earth is required to pass basic Pilot Training, but this is a higher-level introductory class, intended for Cadets who will one day attain the rank of Pilots. What does that mean?"

He pauses and stops to point to one of the teens. "You! Tell me what you think it means."

The boy blinks at being singled out. "It means it's a hard class?"

The Atlantean frowns and turns to another student, this one an older girl. He barks out at her: "What else?"

"It—it means we will be expected to excel?" she mutters.

"What else?" And Instructor Okoi moves down the rows and points at Erin Tsai.

"It means that we will cover more material at a faster rate," she says in a cold hard voice, sitting straight-backed at attention, so that the Atlantean nods at her, almost pleased.

"What this means for all of you," he says after a small pause, "is that unless you pass Pilot Training *to my satisfaction*, you will not become a Cadet of the Imperial Fleet of *Atlantida*—

no matter how well you do in any of your other classes. Is that clear?"

We mutter and nod, "Yes."

"Is that clear, *yes sir!*" Instructor Okoi roars at us.

"Yes, sir!" we yell back in unison, raising our voices to parallel his.

"Good!" He approaches the area behind him that has to be a large smart wall, or a projection screen. He taps the surface with his hand, and we see a simulation window view-screen with nothing but stars and space—the same kind I recall seeing on my arriving flight here in the small shuttle.

In that same instant, the display in front of me—and on every one of the student desk consoles—suddenly comes to life with the same view projection. I stare at what looks to be a window into immense interstellar space before me. The illusion is so real, so incredible, that I feel an instant pang of vertigo.

"Whoa! Awesome!" someone exclaims softly.

Other similar voiced reactions sound around the room.

"For the next four months, you will train on these flight simulator consoles," the Atlantean says. "Then, on the fifth month, you will fly real shuttles, *outside*, in the Quantum Stream. At the end of that fifth month, you will take part in the Quantum Stream Race—a grueling Test that will determine your Cadet Preliminary Standing in the Fleet. After the Test, comes the sixth month, during which you will again train indoors, back here on the flight simulators—since it will be Jump Month."

The Atlantean pauses to give emphasis to his words. "That close to the Jump, the Quantum Stream instability will be at its highest, and off limits for beginners. It will be unsafe for anyone but the most experienced Pilots to be flying outside in the Quantum Stream and deviating from standard Fleet formation velocities—unsafe and *deadly*, considering the rate of acceleration we will be experiencing at that point, and up to the very moment of the Jump itself—but more on that later."

At the mention of the Test and the Jump, everyone in the room listens very quietly.

Instructor Okoi watches us like a hawk as he continues talking.

"After we Jump and emerge in our home sector of space

which you know as the Constellation of Pegasus, the seventh month immediately following the Jump will also be unstable and unsafe, as the Fleet begins the deceleration process. Which means, you will again train indoors. However, after that—months eight through twelve—all the way up to our arrival on *Atlantida*, you will be allowed to once again train on real shuttles in the Quantum Stream. You will become proficient by that point. Furthermore, there will be a Final Test during month eleven, at which point you will Compete in a *second* Quantum Stream Race . . . this time for Final Placement in the Fleet. The winners of the second QS Race will receive Pilot Honors, and have their choice of Fleet assignment, in addition to other privileges. The rest of you will be assigned based on your performance, in less desirable positions. Any questions?"

Mithrat Okoi ends and looks around at us.

There is mostly awkward silence. And then from the back, comes a boy's voice, oddly familiar.

"What does it take for a Pilot to become *astra daimon?*"

I turn around to look, and other heads turn, all around me.

The speaker is Blayne Dubois.

My mouth opens in a smile of happy excitement. *Blayne! Blayne made it, and he's on our ship!*

Blayne is in the very back of the room, and I notice that he is not seated at a flight simulator console, or in a wheelchair. . . . Instead he is upright and on a hoverboard, using his lower body strength to keep the board at a near vertical angle and maintain the special Limited Mobility position he has practiced for so long, with me and Aeson Kassiopei. This way he appears to be almost "standing upright" on his own. Wow, he looks almost effortless as he does it! And, furthermore, no more wheelchair—he's got his own hoverboard at last!

The teens notice that he's on a hoverboard, and obviously they have no idea about his normal use of a wheelchair, so they stare in curiosity.

Instructor Okoi meanwhile, gives Blayne an appraising look, noting his very competent LM position on the hoverboard. "You ask a fair question, Cadet. Your name?"

"Blayne Dubois."

I crane my neck, and yes, there's definitely a Cadet star on

Blayne's uniform chest.

"Cadet Blayne Dubois," Instructor Okoi says. "You ask about becoming *astra daimon*, the best in the Fleet, and your question itself gives you credit. Unfortunately, I must disappoint you upfront—you and everyone else in this room."

The Atlantean turns from Blayne to span all of us with his steel gaze, and there is faint derision written there. "Not one of you here will ever be *astra daimon*. Most of you will be competent Pilots, some of you will even be excellent, and some will be lucky just to fly a shuttle without crashing. *Astra daimon* are the elite—a brotherhood of the best, after years of working together intimately in life-and-death situations, and absolute camaraderie. It is not an honor to which you can aspire, but a recognition of such flawless excellence that can only be earned from the other highest ranking Pilots. From my rather vast experience, none of you here are the material from which such Pilots are made. As for your brave question, Cadet Dubois—ask me again at the end of the year, and we'll see how I answer you."

Mithrat Okoi then ignores Blayne, and addresses the rest of us again. "And now, Cadets—turn to the person sitting next to you at the same console. Take note, this is your flight partner for the rest of the year until further notice—your Co-Pilot, who will be flying with you on all your shuttle runs. Don't like your choice? Too bad, you are stuck with each other. The only way you can be separated now is if you crash and die—"

Immediately there are waves of unhappy whispers in the room.

"And those of you standing in the back who have no flight console seat—turn to the person standing to your right and introduce yourself to your new partner. Next time you will arrive early enough to have a seat and a console."

In that moment, the dark-haired Latino boy sitting next to me raises his hand. "Excuse me," he says sullenly. "This girl next to me—she's not a Cadet. She has no star. Can I get another partner?"

I feel a sudden blast of cold in my gut.

Instructor Okoi turns his grim face to us, and then starts walking toward our flight simulator console. He stops in front of me, and glances at my uniform, and the lonesome Yellow token on my chest.

"*You*—did you somehow *miss* hearing my instruction at the beginning of this class?" he says, leaning down over me. "Where is your Cadet Insignia?"

I look up at him. "I am not a Cadet," I say softly. "But I *am* supposed to be in this class."

"Is that so?" The Atlantean's tone sends another wave of cold fear through me.

"I am an Aide to the CCO . . ." I mutter, so quietly that even I barely hear me speak.

Mithrat Okoi gives me another closer look. "Your name?" he says, and this time his tone is neutral.

"Gwen Lark."

There is an unpleasant pause.

"Gwen Lark, you may stay in my class." And then the Instructor looks over to the Latino boy who snitched on me. "And *your* name, Cadet?"

The boy appears somewhat puzzled, and frowns, glancing from me to the Instructor. "Hugo Moreno," he says. "So, what about her? Does that mean she—"

"It means, Cadet Hugo Moreno, she is your partner," Instructor Okoi says, turning away from the two of us, and returning to the front of the room.

"You better not screw me over," Hugo Moreno whispers to me in the moment the Instructor's back is turned.

I part my lips in outrage.

Great, I think. *This is possibly the most important class, and I'm stuck for a whole year with a jerk for a partner.*

About forty minutes later we have learned the names, positions, and functions of various instruments on the flight consoles, and our homework is to memorize them. We've also received a very brief rundown of the Four Primary Systems involved in Piloting, the principles being the same whether it's a great starship or a small shuttle.

"Memorize these concepts and terms," Instructor Okoi tells us loudly. "Red Quadrant controls Drive and Propulsion. Blue Quadrant controls Network Systems and Central Command.

Green Quadrant controls Brake and Shields. Yellow Quadrant controls Navigation and Guidance."

"In other words," a boy mutters behind me, "Red is 'Go' and Green is 'Stop'—that's all kinds of backwards and messed up, the total opposite of traffic lights on Earth. Wonder, how come?"

A few snickers are heard.

"And hey, Blue is the CPU or brains and central nervous system, while Yellow is supposed to be some kind of GPS?" another boy says.

Instructor Okoi glances in the direction of the speakers. "Use whatever comparisons you like, if it helps you remember," he says in a hard voice. "But the next time you open your mouth and speak in class without permission, you will be disciplined. Now, *silence!*"

There are no more flippant comments after that.

Mithrat Okoi stands watching us coldly, and then he continues. "In addition to the Four Primary Systems, there are other types of secondary systems involved. What is missing, that we have not discussed? Who can tell me?"

A girl with a blue armband and red pixie-cut hair raises her hand. I recognize Alla Vetrova, the Russian girl from the shuttle ride during our transfer to ICS-2. "Weapons!" she says in a confident voice. "How can a military Fleet not have weapons?"

"You are correct." Instructor Okoi nods at her. "Weapons is indeed one of the important sub-systems on each ship. However, its implementation is managed by all the Four Quadrants—which makes it something we call a *broad sub-system*. No ship can fire a weapon without the coordinated effort of all the Four Primary Systems, as a security measure. We will learn more about this in the days ahead. What else?"

"Life support!" another girl says.

"Good, yes. Life Support is also a broad sub-system common to all the Four Quadrants. Anything else?"

"What about sewers and water filtration and food production? That's part of Hydroponics?"

Mithrat Okoi nods yet again. "In part, yes. There is a more accurate breakdown, but again, you will learn the specifics later. For now, this is sufficient."

The Instructor speaks for a few more minutes. Eventually we are dismissed.

"See you tomorrow," I tell Hugo Moreno as we get up from our seats.

He glances at me like I'm a nobody. "Yeah, whatever."

I sigh and start to leave. It's after 2:00 PM, and I am supposed to be back at work at the CCO at 2:15.

However, there's Blayne Dubois talking to some people in the back of the instruction deck, as he skillfully turns his hoverboard around, levitating upright. It looks like they're asking him about his board, or basically just checking out whatever his deal is. It won't really make me late if I stop just for a minute to say "hi."

I hurry toward him. "Blayne! Hey, Dubois!"

He looks around at the sound of my excited voice, and there's the familiar toss of his messy longish dark hair out of his face, partly covering his blue eyes. As soon as he sees me, his one eyebrow rises and he gives me the faintest smile.

"Hey, Lark. Here you are. Upbeat as usual."

"Yeah!" I make a half-smile, half-grimace. "Good to see you made it! And, you're here on this ship!"

"Yeah, well, the CP had me transferred here. I guess he has some kind of plans for my bright future." Blayne smirks, as he orients the board partly in my direction, so he is looking straight at me.

"Same here," I say. "I am an Aide to the CCO. Which means I basically work in his office part time, and take classes part time."

Blayne raises one brow again. "Hmm, that explains your freaky presence in this Cadet-only class. So, a Civilian?"

"*Undecided*, actually." I speak carefully. It occurs to me that it's best not to get into too much detail of what my real plans are, at least not here in public.

"They let you do that?"

"Only until the end of the year, then the CP supposedly evaluates me."

In that moment I glance to the side and see the two arrogant alphas—green armband muscular guy and purple streaked hair girl, from the observation deck the night before—and they are standing right there, listening to Blayne and me talk. I realize they are among those who stayed behind to ask him stuff and check out his hover ride.

"So who are you exactly?" the purple hair girl says to me. "You two know each other?"

"Just taking this class, I guess," I say. "And yeah, Blayne and I were in the same RQC."

"Nice. . . . So, both of you get special treatment," the Green guy says, narrowing his eyes. "He gets the sweet ride, and you get to take your sweet old time and hold off on choosing your future, unlike us dirty peasant rabble. Tell me, who do I need to kiss or kill to get me one of these?" And he points to the board.

"You just need to be in a wheelchair," Blayne tells him in a voice gone quiet.

The Green guy blinks, taken aback momentarily.

In that moment the purple haired girl's smart jewelry pendant starts making a beeping "ding" noise, which must be her clock app. "Hey, we've got the next class in ten," she says to him. "Let's go, Trey. Just drop it."

I glance at Blayne. "Sorry, I have to go too," I tell him, biting my lip. "Hey, want to grab dinner later?"

"Yeah, hey, go . . ." he tells me with a kind of dark abstraction that I've seen in him often previously, when he is reminded of his disability. He turns his back on Trey and the girl, ignoring them. At which point the rest of the gawking Cadets disperse.

"See you in the Yellow Quadrant, Cadet Deck Four Meal Hall? Around five-thirty?"

"Sure."

And then Blayne sings a brief note sequence, which makes his hoverboard flatten and rise three feet above the floor. He nods at me and flies away, lying on his stomach like an Olympic Skeleton rider. In just two seconds he disappears down the long corridor, out of sight.

I hurry in the other direction.

Chapter 9

When I get back to the Central Command Office, I am definitely late. I tiptoe in past the guards, the door opens, and I hear voices inside.

Aeson Kassiopei is speaking in soft Atlantean with someone via video at his desk. The back of his chair is half-turned so that he appears in profile, and the mech arm of the video display monitor is angled so that you can barely see the screen or the person on the other end.

I glance briefly in his direction, and my face flames with heat for a moment, just from hearing the deep pleasant sound of his voice.... So I take even breaths to calm my nerves.

Meanwhile Gennio and Anu are working on their usual consoles near the walls.

"You're late!" Anu mouths the words at me as soon as I am near.

"Sorry!" I whisper, and pull out my own console, and roll up a chair.

"Hush! Quiet!" Gennio gestures with his finger to mouth, and then points to Aeson.

I nod, and settle in.

And then I again glance with curiosity, because the person on the other end of the conversation is female and speaks in a somehow familiar, somewhat superior voice.

Oh, wow . . . it occurs to me. This is the same girl I heard Kassiopei video-talking with once before, back on Earth, when I was in his office at the Pennsylvania RQC-3.

Back then, it had first crossed my mind that he was communicating directly with Atlantis, *in real time*, without any kind of temporal delay . . . and it blew me away. The amazing idea and the impossible mechanics and physics involved distracted me so much that I didn't have time to wonder about the identity of the female.

But now . . . That girl—my God, I did not see her face *then*, only the fall of her very pale, metallic-gold hair, but she sounded fancy and upper-class, and she appeared to be someplace very beautiful, with greenery and waterfalls in the background. And now as I glance over, seeing only a portion of the screen, I manage to *see* her face.

The Atlantean girl is striking. If Oalla Keigeri can be called merely beautiful, then this one is *perfect*, so beautiful she is *unreal*, like a porcelain doll.

Great eyes, of an unusual green-gold tint, somewhere between hazel and honey. They are outlined finely by kohl and luxurious blue-black lashes, underneath delicate arching brows. Her lips are full and sensual, colored with a pearly rose tint, so that a gloss reflection falls upon them, emphasizing the sexy rounded shape against the translucent pallor of her skin.

Her flowing golden hair cascades down, far beyond the video screen, and some strands are intricately braided, threaded with jeweled metallic rope that hangs in garlands. Similar fine strands of metal garland encircle her forehead, and a single pendant jewel descends between her brows. She's an impossible cross between a delicate elvish goddess and Nefertiti.

Okay, I need to stop ogling, because—well, because it's none of my business. I have work to do, the continuing chronicle of our journey to write.

I force myself to look away, call up the English keyboard, open my word processor file . . . and then I fall into a daze again and simply listen to the tones of their voices—*his* and *hers*. Aeson's confident cool voice has acquired an additional soft inflection, almost gentle. And she, okay, wow . . . The last time I heard her talk she sounded bored, petulant and arrogant. But now she is still somewhat superior, but much more sweet, and she is speaking in an almost caressing tone.

Something strange starts to rise deep inside me, an inexplicable turbulent sense of unrest.

I look up again, because I feel stupidly unable to concentrate. And I don't even know why. . . .

I reach over and gently nudge Gennio. "Who is that?" I whisper.

Gennio glances at me. "It's Lady Tiri—Tirinea Fuorai."

"Who is she?"

"Hush!" Anu interrupts, hissing at both of us.

Gennio nods then continues, whispering even more quietly. "Very important . . . high ranking lady! Tell you later."

"Okay. . . ."

But I can't get my mind to focus on anything. Eventually the video call ends, and Aeson disconnects their line, after saying something extremely pleasant, so that the girl fades out on soft laughter.

He then turns his chair and momentarily glances at us. I catch his fleeting gaze and it's as if I am seared by a force of bright daylight. . . . And then he looks away, and calls up another display screen.

For the next hour I try to focus on my writing, but it's close to impossible. Eventually Aeson gets up, briskly stretches his arms behind him, then heads out to oversee something in another part of the ship. He merely nods at us briefly, and we are once again left alone in his office.

"Okay, where's he going now?" I ask.

"Shields Resonance Room, Lower Deck," Anu says with a tone of chronic annoyance. "They've been having problems with field calibration. Then he'll probably do his gym workout before dinner, then back here again until nine. Sometimes he wanders the ship doing random deck checks. Then more work here in the CCO, calls and meetings. Eventually he might get to his private quarters and bed by midnight, unless he decides to do a midnight jog around the ship via the observation deck, as some of the officers like to do. Let's see, I can probably give you his entire schedule for the next five days. Want me to keep going?"

"Enough, Anu," Gennio says, with a sigh. "She will learn the CP's schedule soon enough. This is only her first day. You will make her crazy."

"Too late," I say with a tired smile. "I think I'm already there."

Anu makes a snort sound.

I decide to use the moment to ask Gennio about that girl.

"So who was she exactly, that very dressed up caller who was talking to him just now?" I say in a casual voice.

"You mean, Lady Tiri?" Gennio takes a deep breath. "How to put it? She is—well, it's complicated."

"What do you mean?"

"He means, she may be the next Imperial Consort," Anu interrupts. "You really need to learn the intricacy of our court politics, Earth girl. Your Court Protocol training cannot come soon enough."

"No, no. . . . Well, nothing is certain yet," Gennio says. "So we cannot assume anything until it is formally announced—I mean, until the Command Pilot, that is, the Imperial Prince Aeson Kassiopei announces his choice for Imperial Consort."

"But it's pretty much a given," Anu says. "*She*'s a given. Everyone in the capital expects it to be her, Lady Tirinea, of the noble family Fuorai. She is the frontrunner in the media circus— to borrow your wonderful Earth slang—the media circus that surrounds the choosing of the Bride of the next Imperator."

The cold feeling that has been burrowing in my gut makes itself known full force, washes over me. What is wrong with me, all of a sudden?

"So," I mutter in confusion. "The Imperial Prince Aeson Kassiopei is getting married?"

Gennio nods. "Yes, by law he has to choose a Consort within three years after reaching the age of sixteen. Otherwise— there are repercussions."

"And may I ask how old he is now?" I say softly.

"Eighteen Atlantean years, as of—let me think—the equivalent of last Earth October," Anu says. "Which is close to twenty of your Earth years."

"I see."

"As soon as we arrive on *Atlantida*," Gennio adds, "he is supposed to make his announcement. The Imperator expects it, the Court expects it, the public expects it. He's been putting it off long enough. There are several possible contenders, all from noble prominent families—"

I bite my lip. "Putting it off? Is he in love with this Lady Tiri or not?"

Anu snorts again, rudely. "In love? What kind of stupid

Earth crap do you think? This is the Imperator and the Kassiopei Family we're talking about. They don't 'love.' They make alliances. They exchange DNA to produce the next generation of their ancient bloodline of gods—"

"Anu! Cut it out!" Gennio says in a loud voice the like of which I've never heard him use. "You are crossing the line, speaking in such a crass manner about the Imperial Family."

"Oh, please. She's going to hear all kinds of things about Kassiopei soon enough. Might as well start her off early." Anu raises one eyebrow and gives me a sarcastic look.

But Gennio shakes his head. "Don't listen to him, Gwen," he says. "Because whatever things you might hear about the Kassiopei, they don't apply to our CP. There's a reason he wears the black armband of honor. And when he chooses his Imperial Consort, it would only be for the right reasons."

"What right reasons?" Anu snorts. "Even the most honorable man cannot escape his obligations when he's a Kassiopei."

I remain silent, processing all this, and finding that somehow I am very disturbed.

In that moment, a disembodied machine voice sounds from the walls of the CCO.

"Thirty minute warning. Approaching Jupiter orbital perihelion," the ship computer says.

A very timely interruption.

"Oh! We have to see this!" Gennio exclaims, forgetting his upset, and in fact forgetting everything else. His pleasant face lights up with intellectual energy. "To the Observation Deck! Must run! *Now!*"

I sit up. "Are we allowed to leave our work?"

"For something like that, oh yes!" Gennio closes out his work files and swings the console back into the wall, getting up in a hurry. "Especially since Jupiter will be visible! But only for a minute—or a few seconds! Let's go!"

He has me at "Jupiter" and "visible." I fly out of my chair.

But Anu glances up at us with a show of boredom, and just shrugs. "Naturally Gennio can never resist the pull of a fellow gas giant. And apparently neither can the Earth girl. Go on, you two, I think I'll stay right here."

We hurry to the observation deck at a true run, while Gennio chatters all the way, telling me various facts of this particular orbital passage. Apparently we are not the only ones. Other teens and quite a few Atlantean crewmembers move quickly throughout the various corridors and decks, and everyone's converging on one side of the ship—the side which will have a real view of Jupiter.

"It will only be a brief flyby," Gennio tells me, panting for air, as we reach the crowded observation deck. "It is true that Jupiter has a much wider orbital range than Mars, not to mention, it is huge and easiest to see even from a greater distance. But at the rate of our acceleration, we are already traveling multiple times faster than we were when we crossed the Mars orbital region."

"So, what does it mean, as far as our actual glimpse of Jupiter?" I say, pushing past Cadets and Civilians and Atlanteans through the tight corridor that opens on the observation deck, after Gennio who leads the way.

"All right, quick numbers here," Gennio blurts. "Distance from Earth to Sol, your sun, is approximately 150 million kilometers. Distance from Earth to Mars is about 55 million kilometers. Distance from Mars to Jupiter is about 533 million kilometers. But the acceleration rate of our Fleet is sharply exponential. So we might see Jupiter in a very strange visual trajectory. Maybe—to give you an example from Earth—you drive your car on the road, and a sign post flies by. . . . Poof!"

"Are you saying Jupiter will be like that?"

Gennio smiles. "Sort of—but, just watch!"

And so we stand, bumping shoulders with everyone in the twilight of the observation deck, and stare at the great empty universe and the distant elongated dots of stars. The Sun is not visible from this particular side of the observation deck that spans in a perfect circle the entire outer hull of the ark-ship, so it's even more difficult to have a frame of reference. And the micro-bead of the Earth too is somewhere out of sight.

"Now entering Jupiter orbital perihelion," says the ship's computer.

"There! Oh! Look!" People all around the deck exclaim.

A pale orange ball the size of a large marble makes its presence on the farthest right of the visible windows. Even as we stare, it hurtles past us, so that boys and girls rush to move from window to window, "following" its horizontal trajectory across our visual field.

"Okay, that thing is giant in reality, but looks so tiny!" a girl exclaims.

"*Mon Dieu!* I thought we would be closer! *Merde!*" another girl says. "We must be so far away from it!"

"Yeah, and moving so incredibly fast!" a boy says.

Only about forty-five seconds elapse, and Jupiter disappears on the far left of the visual field.

"Now leaving Jupiter orbital aphelion," the machine voice sounds immediately after, telling us what we just witnessed.

"Wow. . . ." I exhale. Apparently I've held my breath for most of the flyby.

"Beautiful, wasn't it?" Gennio says, smiling blissfully at me.

Wordlessly I nod.

We return to the CCO and Anu greets us with a mumble-grunt. Aeson Kassiopei has not been back to his office yet, so we resume our tasks until 4:00 PM when according to my schedule I have my second class for today.

"You should run, or you'll miss Culture Class," Gennio says as I fumble with my console, unsuccessfully trying to snap it back into the wall. "Leave it, I'll take care of it for you—go."

"Thanks!" I say, and head out.

By now, the guards outside the CCO doors are used to seeing me enter and exit, so I rush by them, on the way to the Yellow Quadrant Residential Deck Four, where the class is held.

I move at a run through a few long corridors, exit the Blue Quadrant, cross through Green, and arrive in Yellow, all in under three minutes. Then for five minutes more I make my way down through Yellow, moving from the center of the ship outward. I pass the halfway point—a wide dividing corridor separating the Cadet Deck from the Residential Deck—and find the classroom area in another large open space.

The room has ordinary desks and chairs of a streamlined

shape, simple writing surfaces, with no unusual consoles or machinery. The desks are long table benches seating at least six people, and they curve in elegant semi-circle rows facing the front of the classroom where the Instructor stands, speaking already.

I am definitely late, because the room is full, so I barely squeeze in at a bench in the back row next to an Asian girl with a Yellow ID token. She is also visibly missing a Cadet star. A few other late arrivals end up standing in the back, with no more bench seats remaining.

Our Culture Instructor is another older teen, who could be my age. She has the usual metallic gold hair, but it's gathered behind her in an updo knot of some sort, and pinned tightly, so that her oval face has a slightly severe look, with not a hair out of place. However her kohl-highlighted eyes are friendly brown, and her expression is generally benevolent. She is a little on the curvy side, but her uniform sits well on her, emphasizing her pleasing figure. The armband she wears is yellow.

"For those of you who are still coming in, please try not to be late in the future, because our time on this ship is precious. The year will fly by, and you still have so much to learn in this one short class," the Instructor tells us in a soothing-balm voice that I recognize immediately as a *power voice*, namely that of the Storyteller. I am immediately reminded of my first Atlantis Culture Instructor Nefir Mekei back in Pennsylvania.

"I am Nilara Gradat," says the Instructor. "And I will be conveying to you not only cold facts—the kind you already learned in your brief classes during Qualification on Earth—but the true *spirit* of life on Atlantis. This way, when you first arrive, you will smell the scent of the land and it will be instantly familiar to you. When you hear the language, it will sound like home. And when you see the people, you will find them welcome and comfortable, like family."

"Not if they are *como mi familia!*" A boy chuckles. Then he grows quiet, suddenly remembering his family, and the reality of what's coming to Earth.

Nilara Gradat ignores the outburst and continues, looking over us with a serene gaze. "The things you will learn in this class will help you understand *Atlantida*, and us. Notice, this is a mixed class, and some of you are Cadets, while others are Civilians. This is because the concepts you will learn here apply to everyone in our society. There are no tests in this class, only common sense and wisdom that will help you personally. I want you to feel free to speak to me any time after class, if you need help with any aspect of Atlantean life. My office is #34 here on Residential Deck Four."

A few whispers sound around the room.

A boy raises his hand. "If no tests, how do you know we learn anything?"

Instructor Gradat smiles at him. "I will know by the way you respond a year from today. And, speaking of years—do you know that a year on Atlantis lasts longer and has different seasons and months than Earth?"

I look up with interest.

"We have long seasons that last four months, not three. And instead of Spring, Summer, Autumn, and Winter, we have Green, Red, Yellow, and Blue. For example, right now it is Blue season on *Atlantida's* upper hemisphere, cold and bleak."

"So, Blue is Winter?" a girl asks.

"Approximately, yes," Nilara Gradat replies. "We will therefore keep to the Atlantean Seasonal Calendar here on the ships, for the duration of our journey, so that you get used to it, even though the duration will still be short and based on your Earth seasons."

The Instructor pauses and begins to gently pace the room before us. "The first two seasons you will experience on our ships are Blue and Green, for three Earth months each. Then there will be the Jump. That is the first half of our journey. Immediately after, we will enter the seasons of Red and Yellow. At the end of Yellow we will arrive on Atlantis, and from there on you will experience the true longer seasons on the surface of the planet."

There are a few whispers, and then another boy raises his hand. "Okay, is an actual *year* really necessary to get to Atlantis from Earth? I mean, a whole frigging year, that's kind of a super exact number. Kind of a weird, unnatural coincidence—"

Nilara Gradat nods. "I see what you're saying. And, no, you are correct, an exact year is not precisely necessary. There are many variations in interstellar travel, based on the type of space vessel being used, the number of ships in the Fleet, the rate of acceleration, and some other factors. Together they generally amount to a time period relatively close to an Earth Year. A single light ship traveling at ultimate speed can probably make the trip in four to five Earth months, but certainly not the entire Fleet. This journey calendar was carefully planned and set, in order to transport the whole Fleet safely, and also to give you time to acclimate. We could have flown a bit faster, but it would have been unsafe for the number of ark-ships involved. The stability of the Quantum Stream *state* depends on so many variables, and these were deemed to be the best-case scenario. You might ask your Pilot Training Instructor for a more detailed explanation. Any other questions?"

"What kind of holidays do you have?" someone asks.

"Excellent question." Instructor Gradat takes out a gadget and suddenly all our ID tokens flash brightly. "I just sent out a Holiday and Months Calendar to all of you. Next time you check your schedules you will see the Atlantean seasons and holidays for each day."

She pauses again, as we peek at our tokens momentarily. "Some of our major seasonal holidays are similar to what you have on Earth. We have Light Feast celebrated in the coldest heart of Blue, when families gather around feast tables and light cozy bright fires to keep the cold away. There is the Burning Night in the hottest middle of Red when a different kind of fire is lit, bonfires in the dark night, filled with dancing and wild fun. There is Gold Harvest in Yellow, a day when we eat and remember the past, the good things and the people we love. And Flower Day in Green when we are dressed up in garlands and everyone must wear fresh flowers or get teased.... And of course there is Landing Day, to commemorate the ancient Original Colony of Old *Atlantida*, at the site of Poseidon, where stands the colossal Atlantis Grail monument of orichalcum and gold...."

I raise my hand, because as usual it happens to me in class—my big mouth opens and out comes stuff. "Are these religious holidays? Do you have religion on Atlantis?" I say. "Faith? Belief in a God or gods?"

Instructor Gradat turns to me with a curious glance. "An interesting and important question. What is your name?"

"Gwen Lark."

"Thank you for asking, Civilian Lark—"

I don't bother to correct her calling me a Civilian.

"Yes, there are many faiths and religions on Atlantis, old gods and new ones," Nilara Gradat says. "We will learn more about this vital aspect of our life in future classes. But in short—our world is both secular and faith-based. We have advanced science and theology, and we have learned how to reconcile both. Therefore some traditions are steeped in ancient beliefs and others are steeped in common sense. Same thing with the holidays, they have secular and religious aspects. And not everyone believes everything, or even the same thing."

"So," I blurt suddenly, risking all kinds of things. "Forgive me if this is inappropriate, but . . . do you actually worship the Imperial Family Kassiopei as gods? Sort of like Ancient Egyptians did their pharaohs?"

There is a long pause of weird silence.

Nilara Gradat stands looking at me, as though I really did confound her.

And then she speaks very softly, very quietly.

"Yes. . . . Some of us do."

She then looks away from me, and changes the subject.

Okay, I am still sort of reeling from that answer, while Instructor Gradat is already covering other material.

If they worship Kassiopei, for real, then what must it mean in practical terms? I think. *How, exactly? And even more importantly, why?*

". . . it is something that you will truly enjoy. Can you imagine, dancing in low gravity and then zero gravity?" Nilara Gradat is saying, and there are some excited whispers going around the classroom.

What did I miss? I try to focus my mind and pay attention to the class.

Quite a few people raise their hands. "So what are these dances like?" a girl asks.

Nilara claps her hands together and smiles. "First, you'll be happy to know that Fleet Commander Manakteon Resoi has agreed to let us have four Zero-G Dances during this journey, so that there will be one dance held each season! And each Quadrant will host. For example, Blue will host this first season's Zero-G Dance. The dance itself will happen inside the great spherical chamber in the heart of each ship—you know it as the Resonance Chamber."

"Wait," a stern boy with a Cadet star on his chest says. "Isn't the Resonance Chamber used to drive the ship? I thought it's filled with your computers and tech, like a monster propulsion engine room or something?"

For the first time, Instructor Gradat laughs, in her sonorous voice. "Oh, goodness, not exactly—the Resonance Chamber is simply an empty room, shaped like a great hollow ball the size of your concert hall or a lesser sports stadium on Earth. It is used for all kinds of things, including ship systems, crew assemblies, competitions, and dances."

"Whoa!" the boy says. "That's kind of crazy. You dance inside the same room where you make the ship fly?"

"The inner surface of the Resonance Chamber consists of various layers of orichalcum and other special materials that are exposed or covered as needed, to engage various functions. Think of your Earth vegetable, the onion, and the many layers that can be pulled back. Each layer is sensitive to sound in a different way, and is connected to an entirely different ship system and acoustically *isolated* from the others. You will learn more in your Technology and Systems class. But for now, just be aware that yes, when the Resonance Chamber is set a certain way, it is perfectly safe to go inside it and do all kinds of things, including physical training—and dancing!"

"Okay, mind-blown!" a girl exclaims.

"Wait till you go inside and see it!" Instructor Gradat says, looking around at us with energy. "Each Quadrant decorates the interior based on the theme of the Dance. Just as you do on Earth, people get dressed up in formal wear, and invite dates—friends, significant others. You will be able to invite anyone you like when it's your Quadrant's turn to host the dance."

"Can we invite people from other ships?" a boy asks.

Instructor Gradat nods. "Yes, you may . . . as long as you

conduct yourselves appropriately."

"What does that mean?" someone says. "So, are we allowed to mess around? You know, hooking up, dating other people, or is that still forbidden, like during Qualification?"

Nilara Gradat takes a deep breath and looks around at us. "This is a complicated question, and I am not the best person to answer it. Furthermore, you are supposed to get a formal sex-and-relationships talk from your Dorms and Barracks officers, either tonight or tomorrow morning. But since you bring it up now—*please* see a medical tech or doctor after class and ask them about what *options* you have, and all their repercussions."

The Instructor pauses.

"Let me be blunt. If any of you get pregnant and give birth to a child during this year we are in interstellar space, you will *deeply* regret it. First, your child *will* be born with serious defects—you will learn more about this and the dangers of the Jump to human physiology in future classes. Second—you will have the responsibility of caring for an infant, and one with special requirements, before we even arrive. Third—if you are a Cadet, you will be denied various Fleet privileges if you have the burden of a child and no family unit. So, don't even think about it. Just—don't."

"What about birth control? Don't you have that kind of thing on Atlantis?"

Instructor Gradat homes in on the speaker and shakes her head. "*Don't even think about it.* Honestly, I am not being a prude. I am being realistic. The risks to your bodies during pregnancy and to your potential children's bodies are *critical* while we are on this journey. And no birth control is completely reliable. . . . Besides, most of you really *are* too young, and few of you are ready for sex—even if you think you are, and even if you think your hardships give you a special excuse and some kind of 'break.' For goodness sake, give yourselves a year at least, to come to terms, to understand your new life, to arrive in Atlantis, before you start breeding like your proverbial Earth rabbits!"

Snickers and giggles fill the room, but the Instructor is not smiling.

"How did this discussion ever deteriorate from simple

dance dates to sex?" she says sternly. "Think of it this way—you Qualified. You are strong enough to get a grip on your hormones. So don't screw up now! For your own sake, don't ruin your future! But—you are more than welcome to ask a date out to dance. *Just* to dance. Maybe, a kiss. Anything more—talk to a doctor! Is that clear?"

"Yes!" the class answers almost in unison. Some people still give each other meaningful looks, roll their eyes, and hold back giggles. Eventually they settle down.

"Good!" Nilara Gradat exhales in some relief. "Now, let me continue telling you about the Zero-G Dance. Where was I? Yes—the decorated Resonance Chamber. When it's time to go inside, portions of the floor are hover-raised so that there is a flat surface upon which to begin the dancing. Then, as different types of dance music play, gravity is manipulated! Some dances are in low gravity, so you can jump up really high, while others are in mixed gravity so you adapt your movements to the music. And yet others require no gravity at all, so the floor falls away and you float around the great expanse, holding your partner or spinning all by yourself—oh, it's absolutely amazing! I love zero-g dancing so much, have loved it since I was a little girl back on *Atlantida!*"

Many hands fly up this time, as everyone has questions. We've been loosened up by the "sex talk" enough to at least participate.

Yes, it's silly to dream of dancing at a time such as this, but it's understandable, I think, sinking into an unexpected mental quagmire. After so much stress and tragedy, everyone wants to let off steam, especially considering that everything else is still so uncertain. And yet. . . .

Somewhere out there, the Earth . . . a tiny pixel dust mote, millions of miles away . . . waiting, even now, to be struck by the asteroid . . . just a tiny point in space, with everything and everyone you know and love, all life destroyed—

No, do not think.

I force myself back from the dark place and focus on the here and now.

"You probably wonder how the zero-g dancing came about," Instructor Gradat says. "And the answer might surprise you. It's one of our most ancient cultural traditions on *Atlantida* and it stems from thousands of years ago, and our original colonization. When the Ancient Atlantean refugees from Earth arrived on this new planet, they had few means of entertainment, and zero-g dancing happened to be something they did on their ships along their way. When they landed and established that first colony, the tradition remained. Since then, all Atlantean dance halls and entertainment centers have gravity manipulation—one of the few traditions that were never outlived."

"Okay, this really does sound like fun," the Asian girl next to me whispers, nudging me lightly.

I nod, but my attention is once again wandering.

Culture Class is over at 5:00 PM, and now I get to meet Blayne Dubois for dinner. After an hour of all that surprisingly lightweight class material—you might call it a relaxing oasis of emotional popcorn and bubblegum, with a touch of unplanned sex ed thrown in—sorry about the awful pun—I hurry to see him. I should be feeling some degree of carefree excitement, but for some reason the idea of dancing has left me depressed.

I get to Cadet Meal Hall Four early, and it's a crowded mess. All the day's classes have been let out, and our first day is officially over. Yellow Quadrant Cadets and a smattering of others are clamoring loudly at the food lines, and all the tables are packed with people, noise, and chatter in strange languages.

I stand at the doors and peek inside, but don't see Blayne or his hoverboard anywhere.

"Hey, move it! Going in or out?" someone says to me, and I get shoved slightly, as a tall older boy with a yellow armband displaces me from the doors roughly and goes inside. I get slammed back and end up pressed against the wall as a crowded stream of mostly Green Cadets continues past me, heading inside. A whole contingent of them—and they are speaking Chinese very loudly.

Finally I see Blayne down the corridor. He hovers near-upright once again, keeping his board in an LM position, moving slowly toward me in a stream of people. I suppose he cannot keep his hoverboard flat in this crowd, so he's being courteous. Those nearest him stare in curiosity, but apparently Blayne must be used to it by now, because his expression is bland, like he doesn't care. Which is probably not too far from the truth.

I raise my hand and wave at him.

He nods, and finally makes it close enough so we can speak.

"Lark, is there any other less hellish place we can eat?" he says loudly near my ear, over the din. His long hair sweeps into his eyes as he leans in to hear my answer.

"How about the Residential Deck Meal Hall?" I shout.

"Probably just as bad, if not worse. There are more Civilians than Cadets."

"We could wait a little?"

"I'm starving," he tells me.

I get a daring idea. "We could try the Officers Meal Hall in Blue," I say. "As an Aide to the CCO I have access. And you can be my guest!"

Blayne raises one brow. "Sure, why not. At worst, they kick me out and mildly spank you for your gall in bringing me."

I smile and roll my eyes. "Then let's go!"

Minutes later we're in the Blue Quadrant, approaching the Command Deck. Blayne is levitating next to me, keeping the nose of his board up at a 30-degree angle, so that he's not lying completely flat but resting on an incline, high enough so that he can speak to me face to face.

Now that we're out of the densely populated areas and on the Atlantean-officers-and-crew section of the ship, the corridors are manageable, and we get to our destination in no time.

"So how has life as an Aide been so far?" Blayne asks, glancing at me sideways.

"About as exciting as I imagined," I say, as we arrive at the doors of the Officers Meal Hall. "It's only been one day, but feels like a whole week of insanity crammed in." And I start telling him about the other two Aides and the office.

The Officers Meal Hall is thankfully not over-crowded. I blink at the soothing dim lighting and see some empty tables, and hear plenty of lilting Atlantean conversation and occasional laughter. There are no Atlanteans I know present. Again I feel a little self-conscious coming in here, but it dissipates as soon as I take a step inside, with Blayne following me via hoverboard.

As Blayne and I move to get our trays and step up to the food bar—that is, I step up while Blayne floats several feet above the floor—I do note a few curious glances in our direction, and several long appraising looks at Blayne and his excellent command of the hoverboard in LM style. That's because he skillfully controls the board with his lower body while managing to balance himself upright and hold his food tray with both hands as if he has no disability. But no one says anything, and so I take a deep breath and forcibly ignore everyone else.

Blayne on the other hand becomes a little stiff. "You're sure this is okay, me being here?" he says at one point. "Just let me know if not. . . ."

"Yeah, it's fine," I tell him confidently, pouring myself a tall glass of *nikkari* juice.

We fill our plates with something alien but pleasantly aromatic, and grab seats at an empty table. Blayne maneuvers the board so that he can transfer himself over to the bench seat. Once seated, he manually adjusts his lower extremities, and softly hums a sequence so that the board remains hovering upright next to his seat. I glance over at his motionless "dead" feet, the pristine sneakers that never walked the floor, and the clean tube socks. . . .

"I'm really glad you got that hoverboard at last," I say a few minutes after we've been chewing in silence. "How did you convince them to let you have it?"

Blayne looks up, after forking a big chunk of some kind of swirly noodle-like dish with pungent greens. "Believe it or not, it's the same board I had from the Finals. When they Qualified me and let me inside the shuttle, I told them I needed a wheelchair, so they just let me keep it."

"Wow. . . . Just like that?"

"Just like that."

I make a small snort sound and chew my food.

Then, after a few moments I take a deep breath and tell him about George.

Blayne looks at me seriously as I am talking, and his blue eyes are intense and unblinking. "I'm really sorry," he says when I'm done. "I know how much your brother means to you—and your sister. And—" He grows silent and stares at his food.

It occurs to me that he is thinking about his own siblings back on Earth, who never Qualified at all. I suddenly feel guilty bringing up George when Gracie and Gordie are here with us and okay, while Blayne has no one at all.

So I quickly change the subject and mutter something about the CCO and classes and the recent orbital pass of Jupiter. Blayne listens to me, eating quietly, nodding occasionally.

"Gwen Lark."

With a start I hear a low and cool voice coming from behind. I turn around and look up, and see a tall Atlantean with raven-black hair standing over me. A mane of glorious long hair, so dark it's bluish black.... A stone-cold handsome face, lean and hard, looking down at me impassively.... Intense dark brown eyes highlighted in kohl.

It's Xelio Vekahat.

"Oh, Instructor Vekahat!" I say, almost choking on my food. "Hi!"

For a moment he says nothing, and his expression is stony, while his eyes seem to bore into mine. Is he here to admonish me for being here? Or maybe for bringing Blayne into the Officers Meal Hall?

But the next moment his face changes and his lips curve up into a remarkable smile. "Congratulations, Gwen," he says. "It is very good that you Qualified. I was certain you would—Shoelace Girl."

"Oh!" I say, and my lips part in surprise, while I smile back at him. "Thank you, Instructor Vek—"

"The proper address now would be Pilot Vekahat," he corrects me, continuing to look at me with amusement. "But you may call me Xelio—or Xel. I think the formalities are mostly behind us, and since you're not one of my Cadets, you've earned the right."

"Okay . . ." I mumble. "Thank you."

"So, Gwen," he says, stepping over the bench and sitting down next to me at our table, and completely ignoring Blayne.

"How do you like being on board an Imperial Command Ship? Is Kass treating you well? Hope there are no beatings. What exactly are you now, *his personal* Aide?"

Even beyond the sarcasm, there is something odd in the way he says it, putting emphasis on the words "his" and "personal." Furthermore, I feel oddly uncomfortable at his overwhelming masculine proximity, the musky faint scent coming from him. . . . In that moment I recall the amazing, bronzed, muscular torso underneath the uniform that sits so well on him, recall his perfect warrior moves from Combat Training.

"Everything is great so far," I say, glancing briefly in his eyes. "And yes, I am an Aide to the CCO. The work is very interesting. . . ."

"I'll bet." Xelio continues looking at me closely, as though he is just now seeing me in a new light, examining me under a microscope, and that smile is now a faint permanent fixture on his face.

I blink, then look away at Blayne who is watching us interact with a kind of semi-bored bland look that he often has. Meanwhile he continues eating.

"This—this is Blayne Dubois," I say awkwardly. "He is a Cadet and—"

"I know who he is." Xelio turns to look at Blayne and gives him a brief nod of acknowledgement.

I grow silent and there is a very awkward pause while Xelio once more watches me, which is now making me silently crazy. Why doesn't he say anything? What is this?

Fortunately in a few more seconds, the Atlantean takes a deep breath and sits back somewhat. "I think your *baidao* stew is getting cold," he says comfortably. "So I'll let you eat in peace."

"Oh, no, it's okay," I mumble, trying to be polite.

"It's fine." All of a sudden Xelio leans toward me and places his large hand over mine—a very light, brief touch. "If you have questions, if you need help with anything, at any time, let me know."

His palm is strong, warm, and there is a brief electric sensation at the point where our skin makes contact. . . . And then he lets go, and gets up, stepping over the bench. "Have a tasty meal, Gwen—and you too, Cadet."

As I glance up at him, open-mouthed, he pauses again and says, "I mean it—any time."

And then he walks away and exits the meal hall.

I am still staring in the wake of his tall back and that mane of black hair, when Blayne says with a typical smirk, "Well, that was interesting, Lark. If I didn't know better, I'd say that guy has the hots for you."

"What?" My mouth falls open even wider. "That's ridiculous!"

Blayne snorts and takes another forkful. "You're right," he says. "Obviously he must be into *me*, and just using you to get closer to my own desirable self."

Chapter 10

We finish eating eventually, Blayne gets back on his board, and we escape the Officers Meal Hall without seeing anyone else familiar. Blayne tells me he is beat, and then flies off to his Cadet Deck for a supposed nap. Knowing Blayne, I bet he'll just go to read his ebooks until lights out, hiding somewhere in a corner of his barracks, maybe lying on his bunk. He'd told me at one point, when we were still back on Earth during Qualification, that he prefers the really old-school text-and-image ebooks, not the Holo-Stories or 3Dbooks, and he's downloaded enough ebooks reading material onto his tablet to last him ten lifetimes. Lucky guy!

I head back to my own cabin. Suddenly I am exhausted too. It's as if the weight of the strange day has come crashing down on me. It is not even 7:00 PM, and I definitely need to get some rest before my 8:00 PM secret voice training class with Command Pilot Aeson Kassiopei.

I turn down into the corridor on Command Deck Four and walk the length of it, staring at the Atlantean numerals on each door until I get to cabin #28.

As soon as I enter my room, the sensor lights go on. Then a small beep comes from the wall over the table with the built-in computer display console area.

I turn toward it, and the screen lights up. The system tells me there's a video phone message from Laronda Aimes. The time stamp says she called about twenty minutes ago.

Laronda! OMG! She made it! Yes! Laronda made it!

I plop on the chair with excitement and call up the vid-phone message.

There's loud noise in the background, and then Laronda's

familiar grin and short relaxed bob-hair with its blond streak highlights falling over her forehead fills up the screen, and she practically yells into the camera. "Gwen! Gwen Lark! Hey, *girlfriend!* It's me! Me, *moi!* Where are you, Shoelace Girl? Hanging out with your fancy-pants Command Pilot? Call me! I'm in my Barracks, baby! Ark-Ship 809, Cadet Deck Four!" And she points to the Cadet star button on her chest with her nails, freshly painted dark red and sleek-looking against her dark brown skin, and sticks her tongue out at me. Then the picture fades out.

Oh my lord, I think, *Laronda is a Cadet!* How in the world did that happen?

I immediately activate the callback function, and then wait as the ship-to-ship system tries to access her direct line.

Five seconds later, the screen comes back on again, and there's Laronda, this time live. At once, both she and I scream and squeal and make kissy-faces at each other.

"Oh wow, you are a Cadet, you crazy, cray cray craaazy!" I exclaim.

"I know!" Laronda again points to her Cadet star insignia. "I figured, what have I got to lose? And as a Cadet I'll get better opportunities and probably more dough eventually—or whatever they use for currency."

And then she opens her eyes wide at me, and points at my own chest with only an ID token. "And you! What is this? What are you? Civilian? No way! I was so sure you went military too, what with the Imperial Command Ship assignment—"

"I'm neither, actually." And then I tell her the whole story.

"An Aide to the CCO? Holy crap! What is that?" Laronda shakes her head. "And your Phoebos guy, the CP—oh my gawd!" she suddenly screams. "He's a *prince!* A goddamn Imperial Crown Prince! What the Eff, Girl? How did that happen? Did you know? That he's a prince? Kass is Kassiopei? Oh. My. Gawd!"

"I know!" I chuckle and snort.

"So—how is he? Any different? All 'princey' and full of himself?"

I smile. "Yeah, he is. . . . Same as before, actually." And I describe some of what took place, leaving out most of the really weird tense conversation between him and me. Because, to be honest, I'm not even sure of how to speak about it to anyone, not even a friend like Laronda. However, I do mention my plans for entering the Games of the Atlantis Grail, and his negative reaction.

"Well, for once, he's right!" Laronda exclaims. "This is crazy stupid! How can you even think about entering their Death Olympics? I mean, imagine you had to enter ordinary Earth Olympics. Let's be real for a moment—would you qualify for the Olympic Trials in, let's say, figure skating? Pole vaulting? Gymnastics? Weightlifting? No? Then hell no, you wouldn't qualify for any crazy Atlantean events either! Come on, girl! Give it up!"

I take a deep breath. "I can't...." And I tell her about George. Then about Mom and her cancer, and Dad, and—

I trail off.... It occurs to me yet again, *I have no right indeed*. Everyone else, Laronda included, is suffering the same loss of family as I am. What gives me the right to think I can do anything about mine?

But at the same time, the crazy mantra resumes in the back of my mind, drilling into my consciousness. It's the same words I've heard for many days now, over and over....

I do not accept it.

Meanwhile, Laronda's serious face watches me from the video screen. "Oh, no, not *George*," she whispers. "I am so sorry, girl. So sorry!" And Laronda's eyes fill up with tears.

At which point my own eyes start getting fuzzy too, and the screen blurs.

I take a deep shuddering breath, and then I tell her, "Okay, I need to stop, I know. I'm sorry, this is selfish crap on my part. You have your own little brother Jamil back at home, and your Auntie Janice... *I know*."

"Hush..." Laronda tells me, wiping her eyes and her runny nose with her sleeve.

Home. Where is 'home' anyway? Even now, we are hurtling through space, millions of miles away....

We stare at each other for a few long moments in silence.

Then Laronda perks up, and changes the subject and tells me the good stuff. For example, it turns out, Dawn Williams and

Hasmik Tigranian are both on her ship.

"Oh, yeah?" I smile, wiping away the moisture in my own eyes.

"At the end of the Finals, Dawn kind of saved my butt!" Laronda says. "When that cavern explosion happened, and then we were all flying up through that long terrifying chute up to the surface of the Atlantic Ocean, Dawn kept me and Hasmik both from bumping into the walls. She made sure we flew straight, and then we all sort of held each other and our hoverboards close together, and we all got out! Next thing we know, we're in an Atlantean shuttle, all of us Qualified, and rising up into Earth orbit!"

I laugh with joy. "So where are they now?"

Laronda rolls her eyes. "Both chicas went Civilian on me! Can you believe it? They're together on Residential Deck Four!"

I shake my head and grin.

"I mean, Dawn, *Dawn!*" Laronda continues. "She's all tough and has the best scores, and then she goes and becomes a Civilian! She told me she has no interest in fighting or butt-kicking and just wants to make it to Atlantis and settle down in peace, study biology and agriculture, and maybe raise the Atlantean equivalent of chickens!"

I giggle and Laronda snorts. We continue talking for a few more minutes until I realize what time it is.

"Oh, crud!" I exclaim. "I have to go! I have to see Command Pilot Kassiopei!"

"Huh? This late?" Laronda raises one brow.

"Yes, it's my voice training." I figure, since Laronda already knows all about my special Logos voice, it makes no difference if I tell her I am still getting voice lessons. But just in case, I warn her: "By the way, please don't mention it to anyone else, okay? About my freaky power voice, I mean. The CP wants me to keep it discreet."

"So, one-on-one private lessons with a yummy-hot commanding officer who's also a prince, eh?" Laronda again raises one very meaningful brow and then wiggles it. "Don't worry, my lips are sealed."

I bite my lip, and she bursts out laughing.

It's almost 8:00 PM when I come rushing up to the CCO. It's the evening shift for the crew, and the guards at the doors have been changed. These two new ones don't know me, so I have to explain myself and then one of the guards calls the CP via his wrist device, then waits for verification.

At last I am allowed inside.

As I walk in, I see Aeson Kassiopei standing up behind his desk, and he is in the process of turning off several screens and retracting the swinging mech arms back away from his work surface. I manage to catch a glimpse of one before the display goes blank, and it appears to be a news feed of Earth, a scene of urban chaos and orange flames and burning buildings. On the bottom of the screen the marquee strip in English has the words "nuclear reactor sabotage" and below it, something like "orange alert terror threat."

I stop in my tracks and stare. Aeson turns in that moment, seeing me, and immediately my pulse awakens and begins to pound in my temples at the sight of his cool clear gaze, his dark lapis-blue eyes trained on me impassively.

"Take a seat," he tells me without any other preliminaries.

"Was that Earth?" I ask nervously, feeling a wave of cold enter my gut. "What is happening there?"

"Nothing . . . it does not concern you." His answer is soft, and he does not look at me, while he continues to turn off the equipment.

"But—I just saw everything burning!" I exclaim.

He pauses to glance at me. "Don't. . . . Don't look, don't *think*. It is not something that can be helped, and it does not help you to dwell on it."

"How can you say that?" My lips part and I take a step closer. "It's Earth! My family is out there! My *home*, everything!"

"I know." He stands motionless, watching me. "But your home is now here, and on Atlantis. You have to let go."

"Easy for you to say!"

"No, actually, it is not." He points to one of the four visitor chairs before his desk. "Now, please sit. We have work to do."

I frown, and step across and sit down in the closest chair.

He takes a deep breath and sits at his desk also. I watch his profile, the tired hollows of his lean cheeks, the fall of his golden metallic hair. It has been a long day for him too.

He then reaches for a small box, which I recognize to be the familiar sound damper box containing orichalcum pieces—it's the same box we've been using to train with, back in Colorado.

I stare at it as though it's my last connection with Earth. Which is nonsense, but it's how my mind is working now, attaching significance to little things.

"How was your first day?" he asks me suddenly, as he opens the box to take out several charcoal-grey pieces with fine gold flecks. Orichalcum is like fool's gold—or better to say, magician's gold—sparkling with hidden yellow under bright lights, and dull grey the rest of the time.

"Okay . . ." I mumble, still frowning, angry at his refusal to speak about Earth. "The classes were fine. I think I'm going to enjoy Pilot Training, and Culture."

"Good. And what do you think of your two fellow Aides? Not counting this morning's incident, any work issues?"

"Gennio is great. He's been helping me with many things. Anu is—"

At my hesitation, I notice Aeson Kassiopei glances at me briefly, and the corners of his mouth almost imperceptibly turn up. "Anu is Anu," the Command Pilot says. "He's a bitter pill to swallow at first, but you will get used to him."

I make a small sound of sarcasm.

But now he's all business. Ignoring my reaction he points to the orichalcum that's sitting on the desk surface before us. "Today's voice lesson will involve temperature. You will learn to change the quantum state of orichalcum to heat it up and cool it down."

I sit up straight with interest. "You can do that?"

He notes my heightened attention and continues. "In your Earth physics terms, it involves *quantum harmonic oscillation*—but not exactly. There are many additional parameters involved in eliciting this particular thermal reaction via acoustics. For now, all you need to know is that you are influencing the vibration frequency of orichalcum."

"Wait! Is this similar to those awful burning batons during the Semi-Finals?" I recall with a shudder.

Command Pilot Kassiopei watches my growing dismay at the memory of the hellish Qualification ordeal I went through . . . those last moments of Semi-Finals, with me holding on to the burning baton with one hand and to my sister Gracie with the other (that other hand was attached to my wounded arm, with a bullet lodged inside), as we rose up in the air toward the shuttle over Los Angeles. That baton—it had burned my hand right through to the bone. . . . If not for the high-end Atlantean medical technology that restored my limb after Semi-Finals, I would have no hand right now. In fact, I might not have *both* hands.

"Yes, it's a similar process," he says. "The batons were keyed on a more complex level, to remain cool and inert when submerged in water, but to heat up when in contact with air. Today, you will attempt a much simpler variant."

He looks down at the small lumps of orichalcum and points to one. "This one," he says. "Watch."

And then he sings a complex note sequence in his rich deep voice, the sound of which sends electricity through me and makes the surface of my skin pucker up and my fine hairs stand on end.

The piece of orichalcum rises, floating a few inches over the top of the desk. And then it starts to glow. The change is imperceptible at first, but with each passing second the metal glows brighter, from deep red to white-hot.

"Put your finger close to it but don't touch," Aeson tells me. "Can you feel the heat?"

I move my hand toward the levitating piece. Just as he described, I feel radiating warmth, then significant heat coming from the flaming orichalcum.

"Yes . . . wow. . . ."

I keep my hand raised, my fingers trembling, as I stare in wonder.

"Careful," he says. "And now, this—to stop the thermal reaction."

And he sings again.

When the sequence is done, I note the way the burning piece starts immediately to fade in brightness. This cooling process seems to happen much faster.

"Can I touch it now?"

"In a minute. Still too hot." And he continues looking at the floating lump of metal.

I look up suddenly, because a strange other memory comes to me. And I just have to ask. . . .

"Command Pilot Kassiopei," I say softly, watching his averted eyes, the amazing thick fringe of his lashes. "Back then, during the Semi-Finals, when you were in that shuttle in the very end. . . . You put your bare hand directly on the burning baton and pulled us inside—what command did you use to make the baton cool down instantly, so you could hold it?"

Aeson does not respond at once. Instead, I note he grows somewhat still. "I didn't use any command. There was no time," he says at last, in a tone that might be almost careless.

For a moment I don't process the meaning. And then I *get it*, and I am stunned.

"Oh my God . . ." I whisper. "You mean you *held* it while it was still *burning* and you pulled us in? What about your hand? What must have happened to your own hand? You burned your hand, didn't you?"

He looks up in that moment, looks into my eyes. His gaze is clear and profound and filled with intensity that cuts through me like a shaft of light.

"Hands can be repaired," he says. "You know it for yourself."

My lips part as I stare at him in wonder. "How badly was it hurt?"

"It was repaired. It doesn't matter."

But I don't relent. "Oh, wow! Thank you! I had no idea at what cost you saved our lives!"

But he simply nods at the piece of cooling orichalcum floating in the air between us. "Lark," he says. "Your turn to make it burn."

About fifteen minutes of singing later, I am still unable to elicit the quantum thermal reaction necessary to create the heat. While I practice, Aeson opens up a console and starts working on something. Periodically I glance up to watch his face in quarter-turn, the composed fine angles of his lean jaw, the way he presses his lips into a controlled line as he focuses on the work before him.

At some point I must have paused way too long, and spaced out while looking at him. Because without taking his eyes away from his task he says, "Stop staring and continue. There is nothing here of any concern to you."

I feel an instant flush of heat in my cheeks. "Sorry . . ." I mumble. He must think I'm trying to see what's up on his display screen. Better he thinks so than realizes I am staring at *him*.

So I fake a yawn and put a palm over my mouth. "Long day . . . I'm a little tired."

He finally looks at me. "All right. It's your first day, and it's close to eight-thirty. You may go. Also—there's supposed to be a mandatory group lecture given to all Earth refugees, Cadets and Civilians, in their residential quarters, in about fifteen minutes. It's about—matters of personal health and—" He pauses, and blinks momentarily, which I've discovered, is his only "tell," the only crack in his control. "—and sexual conduct. You need to attend."

"Okay," I say, while my brows rise. "Oh, but I don't have a dorm or barracks. I'm in my own cabin on Command Deck Four. . . . So where do I go?"

"Feel free to choose any nearest Civilian residential dorm or Cadet barracks. It doesn't matter," he tells me curtly, once again turning his face away.

"All right. But are you sure I need this?" I say, just before I rise from my chair. "My Culture Instructor gave us an abbreviated version today, basically preaching abstinence for the duration of our trip. So, I get it—space flight is developmentally bad for my body and bad for pregnancies. It's not like I plan to have kids—"

"You have a boyfriend," he says suddenly. "If you plan to—be *intimate*, you will need to know this. So, yes, you need to attend. Now, dismissed!"

I get up in a hurry—not only because his tone has become menacingly cold, hard, and unyielding but because my cheeks are now flaming in embarrassment—and then I flee his office.

Since I don't have a Cadet star and don't want to be conspicuous, I drop by Residential Deck Four, Yellow Quadrant, and go find a Civilian dorm. It looks exactly like that shipboard dorm we were first placed into on our first day, with ceiling-high rows of bunk beds, and a narrow corridor between them, with washrooms in the back—I'm assuming it's the standard personal quarters layout for all the dorms and barracks on each ship. I perch against the wall next to complete strangers and listen to an Atlantean officer give a ten-minute sex conduct talk to a room full of annoyed teens.

For the most part, it's not anything I haven't already heard. Except for one thing, which is suddenly made clear to us, with all its striking implications. . . .

"All of you chosen for rescue, ages twelve through nineteen," the Atlantean officer is saying, "are best suited to travel through interstellar space and survive the effects of the Quantum Stream, and especially the Jump. Your hormone levels are sufficiently high that the inevitable cell damage that occurs can be self-repaired by your strong young bodies. Children younger than you and adults older than you *cannot* handle the effects without significant irreparable harm to their bodies and *minds*. Yes, even our advanced medical technology cannot fix this level of damage. And pregnancies at this time will result in tragedies."

A dark-brown skinned girl with long African locks raises her hand. "So are you saying that the only reason we are being *rescued* is that we can survive this journey? Oh sweet Jesus! Is that why you wouldn't take adults or babies? All those other people left behind on Earth?"

"Yes," says the Atlantean, keeping his face impassive. "That is mostly correct."

The dorm quarters are suddenly filled with noisy tumult. Everyone's talking all at once.

The Atlantean raises his hands for silence.

"How come none of this was said back on Earth?" a boy cries out. "Those people had the right to know!"

"Yeah, not to mention, so did we!" another boy yells. "We should've been told that this is an unsafe option!"

"Be quiet, all of you!" The Atlantean officer raises his

voice and it rolls through the room like a peal of thunder. He's using a *power voice*, it occurs to me—because as soon as he speaks, the dorm goes silent, as though everyone's been mildly stunned. So, this is a form of crowd control. My mind is racing as I stand and listen.

"Knowing this—would it really have made a difference as far as your ultimate choices?" the Atlantean officer continues. "You were given the opportunity to be rescued. All of you gladly and wisely took it. And as for your loved ones on Earth who did not Qualify due to age—would it have been kinder for them to know they were doomed outright? That they could not even *hope* to step aboard our ark-ships? In my opinion—and the opinion of the Atlantis Central Agency—the less painful information was disseminated, the better for everyone, your loved ones included."

As the Atlantean speaks, my mind races with another horrible realization. My parents! Oh, God! If this is true then Mom and Dad would not be able to survive the trip to Atlantis anyway, even if I could somehow smuggle them on board!

No! *No!*

I do not accept this.

I stand shaking, clenching white-knuckled fingers against my uniform shirt, while wave after cold wave washes over me, filling my insides....

But then, in the middle of all this numbness, a bright thought comes.

What about my Pilot Training Instructor Mithrat Okoi? Compared to the other Atlantean officers and crew who are all teens our age, he's ancient! He has to be way over the safe age for interstellar flight, and yet he's on this ship!

And, for that matter, what about the only other "old" Atlantean I know, the Fleet Commander himself? Yes, he seems younger than Instructor Okoi. But still, Manakteon Resoi has to be at least twice as old as any of the other Atlanteans in the Fleet!

So, how is it that *they* are allowed to be here?

I frown, thinking.... And I resolve to grab and "interrogate" the one friendly and reliable source of knowledge, as soon as I can find him—Gennio Rukkat.

The sex-and-health talk goes on for about five more minutes. The Atlantean officer concludes by telling us about the location of the nearest medical facilities on this deck, and that we all have to see a doctor as soon as possible for a physical exam and hormonal evaluation.

It will be used to determine our personal physical condition—not only in regards to birth control for family planning, but to regulate hormone levels for those of us who might require hormonal treatments for other medical conditions, and for overall balancing.

Apparently our physiology must be checked, and then some of us might have to be variously medicated and tweaked just to keep our bodies safe from the stress of interstellar space and the dreaded Jump six months from now. In short—hormonal balance is something they are going to keep track of very carefully, for all of us, male and female, for as long as we are on this trip.

"Don't worry, for the majority of you there will be no treatment necessary," the Atlantean adds. "But for some of you, yes, minor adjustments will be needed to survive the trip in good health."

Suddenly the androgynous, now familiar machine voice comes from the walls of the ship around us.

"Thirty minute warning. Approaching Saturn orbital perihelion," the ship computer announces, cutting off the Atlantean officer's final words.

"All right, we are pretty much done here, so you are all free to go," he says. "According to our flight trajectory calculations, Saturn is going to be visible, so you might want to attend this final planetary fly-by. Also—this is probably the last opportunity you will have to see Earth with the naked eye. Once we are beyond Saturn, Earth is much too small to observe without magnification unless you have extraordinary eyesight. Go, take that final look."

At his words, the room gets noisy again.

My chest feels a painful twinge. So I race, together with most of the dorm, to the observation deck.

Everyone wants to say that final goodbye to Earth.

Chapter 11

Saturn's a big draw, but I'm guessing it's mostly the notion of a final glimpse of Earth that brings everyone to the outside windows.

There are so many people on the ICS-2 Observation Deck this time that it's elbow-room only. Once again, the fly-by pass will only be seen from one side of the ship, so everyone has converged here.

I push my way inward, jostled by other teens, hearing the din of many languages all around me, smelling sweaty humanity.

In this messy crowd, there's no one I know, and I wonder momentarily if Blayne has made it here with his hoverboard. I scan the vicinity, but if Blayne's here, there's no sign of him. Seriously, there's got to be thousands of people on this ship, and it feels like they all crammed onto this one deck.

I think of my siblings, Gracie and Gordie, probably also crammed in a similar observation deck on their own ark-ship, and elsewhere in the Fleet, Laronda, Dawn, Hasmik, Logan. . . .

I wish Gennio was here.

"How close will we be when we pass Saturn? Anyone know?" a skinny dark boy asks behind me.

"No idea," the girl immediately next to me says. "I hope we at least get to see the Rings. I mean Jupiter was a big 'ole let down. Or should I say a teeny tiny one."

"At least we got to see Jupiter at all," I say, as I crane my neck to look over the crowd at the large windows and the blackness of space beyond. There are hardly any stars visible, only rich darkness.

"Okay, that bright thing on the left, what is it?" a boy says. And now that everyone notices, voices rise in amazement.

"*Nyet, ne mozhet bitz—neuzheli eto sontse?*"
"*¡Sí, creo que esto es el Sol!*"
"Is that the Sun? No way! That's tiny!"

And as we point and stare at the far left of the panorama, there's only one solitary star-sized object, but extraordinarily bright, and it has to be the Sun.

Wow....

The Sun. It has grown so unbelievably remote.... All that's left of the familiar orange fire disk is now smaller than the head of a pin.... But it's still powerful enough to cause retinal damage, even at this distance, if we stare at it directly without the shielding filter on the windows.

"What about Earth? Can anyone see it?"

"*Now entering Saturn orbital perihelion,*" the ship's computer says.

Instantly the crowd goes silent.

And then we see it.

It starts as a tiny point of light in the general center of the window panorama, and it grows in split seconds to immense proportions, filling up all the observation windows with faded yellow pallor, like a balloon being blown up—and oh, the Rings! They are huge! Great oval fixtures spanning the whole cosmic vista outside unfurl like great wings, all in a *split second*....

Saturn is hurtling directly at us! Or we are crashing into it!

There's not even time to blink!

People on the observation deck scream, because suddenly we are being swallowed by Saturn's immense albedo. There is no more black space outside, *only Saturn*, casting the grand illusion of a universe of soft pallor and light, and the Rings are overwhelming ... and oh lord, did I just see one of its many moons briefly silhouetted against the Rings? Atlas? Titan?

There is no time for the mind to acknowledge or correctly process anything that's suddenly visible out there, because it's all happening too crazy-fast....

We fall, we crash ... we plummet into mist pallor.

And we emerge on the other side, having seen none of it really, none of the faint field of ice particles born of moon geyser plumes that comprise the Ring *through* which we just passed—probably the most visually prominent outer A Ring or the Cassini Division between Rings A and B, or maybe it's the B Ring?

And just like that, it's all gone.

"Now leaving Saturn orbital aphelion," the computer says.

And once again, there is only blackness, the dark void. And there's the Sun again, a pin of angry blinding light.

"Oh, f— me . . ." comes someone's voice in the general silence. "That was—just wild! How fast *are* we going?"

"¡Madre de Dios, sálvanos!"

"I don't know, but I just crapped my pants!"

People start giggling and cussing and chattering, in various languages, which seems to be the normal human reaction to stress and to anything kind of mind-blowing. And then someone points to an area of space slightly below the Sun and off to the right.

"Look! That tiny bluish thing—is that *Earth?*"

Once again we grow silent as we strain our eyes and stare at something that's not quite a star.

"Wow . . ." a boy says behind me. "It's the Pale Blue Dot. It's almost that size now, isn't it? That's our home! Damn. . . ."

And as he says it, I remember the world-famous old photograph taken fifty-seven years ago by the Voyager One space probe leaving Earth. It turned around and took a final picture of Earth, and our planet was the size of a pixel captured in a fractured ray of sunlight, to paraphrase the classic astronomer Carl Sagan.

This is what it looked like.

But wait, no! I recall. *No, it did not—not quite.*

The original "Pale Blue Dot" was photographed somewhere about six billion kilometers away from Earth, beyond the orbit of Pluto.

This, our present location, is similar the other Pale Blue Dot photo—actually the third-ever selfie taken of our planet—and this one's the Cassini spacecraft version, taken twenty-three years later by NASA scientist Carolyn Porco who wanted to improve on the original. That famous stunning mosaic of images taken from the shadow of Saturn, with the grand panorama of the Rings and the tiny dot of Earth, is called "The Day the Earth Smiled."

And that's what Earth looks like, right effing now—from just over a billion kilometers away.

Except, today no one is smiling there.

It's close to 10:00 PM, and the crowds on the observation deck have thinned out. All barracks and dorms adhere to the 10:00 PM lights out, so most people want to get back in time for bed after a very long first official day as Civilians and Cadets.

A few, such as myself, linger, gazing into the dark cosmic panorama outside the ship's array of floor-to-ceiling windows.

I stand and breathe and look. Moments float away in silence.

As an Aide to the CCO, unassigned to any standard shipboard group, I don't really have to be anywhere. I have no lights-out in my small private cabin—the lights go on and off based on my activity level.

It occurs to me, how strange my personal situation is, compared to the others on board this ship. In some ways I am even more *isolated* and lonely than I imagined I would be. At least during Qualification I was a Candidate like the others. But now, I'm somewhere in the surreal halfway position between being an Earth refugee and an Atlantean crewmember.

Neither here nor there. An aimless nobody, out of place.

I don't belong.

The strange depressive thoughts haunt me. At the same time my mind is numb with the new awareness of the nil chances that my parents have for rescue.

I don't know how much time passes, as I stand, staring out at the black cosmos outside. Fifteen minutes at least, maybe half an hour. In some ways it's calming to stare at the void. . . . Stare and think.

The illumination of the observation deck is soft and low, a kind of permanent twilight. The floor plasma lights supply just enough light to move around safely. I suppose it's intentional, to allow those who choose to be here to meditate upon the view of the universe.

At some point, I am pretty much alone for real. No one else is here on this portion of the deck; everyone has gone to bed. An occasional Atlantean crewmember on duty passes the corridor, but that's it.

There's just the Earth and me.

Hungrily I stare at it—the faint *dot* of blue—tiny, infinitesimal, precious, vulnerable, even now receding beyond my eyes' ability to see. It is my last anchor, my one and only point of connection, of familiarity, of *sanity*. Even so, a few more minutes, seconds, incalculable moments, and I begin to doubt if I'm looking at anything at all.

And after what might be another quarter of an hour . . .

"Good-bye, little Pale Blue Dot," I whisper. But silently, stubbornly, I tell myself, *This is not good-bye. No, I do not accept it. Somehow, I will come back.*

And then, I see it no more.

The Earth has dissolved into the darkness, has been swallowed by the cosmic grandeur all around. Only Sol is outside the window, our Sun—and now it alone remains an anchor point of visual reference.

A sudden "space vertigo" strikes me, a recent replacement for my one-time fear of heights. My head is swimming, and I can barely stand upright.

I stagger, taking a few steps to right myself, put my hand out toward the nearest corridor wall behind me, the inner wall of the deck opposite the windows. I am shaking. . . . And without knowing how it happened, I realize my face is now wet, is streaming with tears. . . .

In that moment, I get the strange sensation that I am being *watched*.

Someone, in the shadows of the observation deck, is staring at me.

With a burst of inexplicable panic I look around, and then my breath hitches.

There *is* someone. A man is standing in the narrow dark place between two window panels, just off to the side. How did I not see him?

In the faint light all I can distinguish is the pallor of his long hair, and the faint glimmer of unblinking intense eyes, trained upon me. He is motionless and silent. Has he been there all this time?

How long?

I take in a deep shuddering breath, while a sudden burst of anger strikes me. How dare this stranger intrude upon my moment of privacy?

I take a step toward the windows, toward him, acknowledging his presence.

In the same moment he separates from the shadows and comes forward toward me.

It is Aeson Kassiopei.

"Oh!" I exclaim, feeling an immediate embarrassment. "Command Pilot, I'm sorry I didn't see you." And I hastily wipe my eyes. But of course he's seen me bawl for the last ten minutes, so it's not like it makes any difference.

But he says nothing in reply, only continues to look at me. What is he doing here?

"It's really late, I know, I should be getting back . . ." I mutter.

"Go . . . get some rest," he says quietly, speaking at last.

Now that I can see his face, his features in the twilight illumination of the deck are rendered softer, sharp lean lines turned to shadows, so the focus is all on his eyes. . . . In that strange moment, they are the eyes of an angel.

"Okay . . ." I whisper, while a swell of mindless feeling surges through me.

But he only nods, turns away from me, and walks quickly in the direction of the interior of the ship.

I get back to my own cabin, and there's a message from Logan. It's time-stamped with 9:53 PM.

My pulse pounds and I play it immediately, feeling weird guilt for not being there when he called.

Logan's handsome serious face comes on the screen, with the background of noisy barracks of ICS-1, the Fleet flagship. The ambience is no different than Gracie's or Laronda's barracks. But Logan's demeanor is hard and businesslike.

"Gwen," he says. "I really need to talk to you. Wherever you are, please give me a call as soon as you return, regardless of time. We have lights-out at ten, which is in a few minutes, but it doesn't matter. No one around here will sleep immediately, and we can whisper in the dark."

And the screen goes blank.

I frown, wondering what could be so important that Logan needs to talk to me after lights-out.

So I call him.

This time the screen goes live with darkness and the hum of near-silence in the background, and Logan's face is lit only by the glare of the video screen in the wall of his bunk.

"Gwen!" he says in a whisper, and a smile warms his face.

"Logan! What's going on?" I whisper to match him.

"How was your day?" he begins, throwing a brief glance behind him in the dark.

"Crazy, but survived!" I smile back tiredly. "And you?"

"Same here. Cadet training is as brutal as Qualification. And here on ICS-1 they don't mess around. Everything is competition-based. Everyone wants to be the best, to stand out, to please the Commander, to get noticed—"

"Hey," I whisper. "I don't think you called me so urgently just to talk about your training? What's really up?"

Logan's lips curl up into a flirty smile. "Can't a guy just call up his girl in the middle of the night to tell her he misses her?"

At the sight of his smile, his expression, I can't help feeling a warm wave flow over me, so I grin. "I miss you too. But seriously, what's up?"

But Logan continues to smile. And then he whispers, "I *need* to see you."

My cheeks flame briefly. "Okay, didn't you guys just get that same sex talk we did? You know, the one about *not doing anything* beyond kissing?"

His smile deepens into a wicked grin showing his healthy white teeth. "Why, what did you have in mind?"

"*Logan!* Jeez!" In my smiling outrage I exclaim his name loudly, so that he points his finger to his lips in a hush gesture.

And then I sober up. "Bad news," I say suddenly. "They told us about the hormones and the ages for rescue and how older people cannot survive the Jump. So that means my parents—"

As I am talking I see his expression grow serious.

"Gwen," he interrupts me gently. "It's partly why I need to

see you. We need to talk—*in person*. So you need to find a way to get me on your ship—as soon as possible. Tomorrow."

"What do you mean?" I say. "Okay, now you're scaring me. What? What is it, what did you learn?"

Logan takes a deep breath. "There are things I need to say in private. To you—and to your CP."

"What?" My jaw drops. "You want to talk to Aeson Kassiopei? Why?"

"Not now," he says. "Not on a call like this. Just—promise me you will get me on board your ship first thing tomorrow, under any pretense. It is urgent. I'm certain your commanding officer will appreciate what I have to say."

"I don't know—I don't know if I can manage it—"

"I know you can. Just do it."

I frown. But he looks at me so earnestly that I cannot help nodding. "Okay. . . ."

"Good," he says, exhaling in some relief, as though he'd been waiting for me to make this decision. And then he adds, "Because your parents' lives, and the lives of everyone on Earth, depend on this."

Chapter 12

It's pretty much impossible to sleep after that. I spend an hour lying in bed, with the cabin lights dimmed due to my inactivity, agonizing about what Logan said, what I need to do in the morning. What in the world is going on? What can be so important that would require him to show up here on this ship and talk to Command Pilot Aeson Kassiopei in person?

I have no memory of falling asleep. But when the 7:00 AM daylight alarm engages, I am pulled out of a stress-dream in which I see Gracie and Gordie and myself running through some kind of dark dripping tunnel, with George somewhere far ahead of us, calling us after him. . . .

About twenty minutes later, I head out to the Officers Meal Hall, where I eat Atlantean breakfast food without tasting anything. I watch the officers eat in a hurry, and at some point I see Pilots Keruvat Ruo and Oalla Keigeri walk in, and head to the food bar.

Oalla Keigeri is a beautiful Atlantean girl about my height, with a perfect hourglass figure, slim and powerful. Her golden hair falls to her shoulders framing a gorgeous face of stunning beauty—the kind of face that made Earth guys drop their jaws and salivate, when we first had her as our Yellow Quadrant Combat Instructor back at the Pennsylvania RQC-3.

Now I am more used to her stunning looks, used to seeing Oalla as a real person—not just a merciless taskmistress, but as a tough and fair instructor, and a loyal friend to Kassiopei.

According to my schedule, I have a class with her today, in fact, later in the day.

I consider getting up and walking over to their table. . . . Only—what will I have to say? I am still not entirely comfortable being in the Officers Meal Hall, and even though I know both Keruvat and Oalla, I would never presume to impose on them, because they are high-ranking officers, Pilots in charge of two of the Quadrants on this ship, Blue and Yellow.

But a crazy thought comes to me. What if I just flat-out asked them for a shuttle ride to go pick up Logan? There's got to be someone on this huge ship who's getting on a shuttle to get to ICS-1 today. Maybe I can hitch a ride? After all, Keruvat did bring me here in the first place.

As my brain churns through these partially crazy ideas, I look up from my barely eaten food and see Gennio Rukkat and Anu Vei, my two fellow Aides, heading toward my table.

"Good morning, Gwen," Gennio says, putting down his tray comfortably next to mine and sitting down. "We thought we'd eat here today. Anu says they have better *rigavi* rolls here than in the Cadets Meal Hall."

"Well, they *do*," Anu says in a grumpy, sleepy voice, without even nodding at me. He places his tray on the opposite side, so that he is facing both me and Gennio, across the long bench table. And then he goes back to the food bar to get drinks and some kind of crispy waffle thing that's colored orange with streaks of green.

"Hi," I say, smiling lightly at Gennio. The Atlantean radiates such pleasant calm that suddenly I am glad for the company.

And then, before Anu comes back, I take the opportunity to ask a blunt question. "Gennio," I speak quickly. "I just remembered something from yesterday. Can you tell me how is it that older Atlanteans such as Instructor Mithrat Okoi, or Commander Manakteon Resoi are able to withstand interstellar travel? Unless I'm missing something, they're not teenagers and don't fall within the 'safe' age range. So how will they survive the Jump?"

Gennio is busy chewing, entirely preoccupied with the contents on his plate, but my question seems to affect him. He pauses and swallows, and looks up at me with his big brown eyes.

"Oh!" he says. "Interesting observation. Let me see if I can explain the circumstances briefly. You see, for people who are of an unsafe age for the Quantum Stream and the Jump, there are cold storage capsules. When the time comes, they will be placed in the capsule chamber and put in stasis, so their micro-cellular activity is minimal, basically stalled, and they sleep through the dangerous portions of the trip—"

"Who? What?" Anu returns to the table, interrupting Gennio rudely. He's carrying two glasses, one piping-hot, and giving off a sweet aroma reminiscent of pastries and a bakery.

"Oh, I was just explaining to Gwen about cold storage chambers for those who require it for Jump safety."

"You were?" Anu sits down and puts a stirring utensil inside the hot drink. The Atlantean utensil looks like a cross between a stirring stick and an Earth spork, slim and narrow with a two-pronged end. If you turn it right side up, you get a two-pronged trident, the kind that belongs to the Ancient Greek God Hades.

"What's that?" I say, pointing to the utensil. Not sure why, but I want to distract Anu from our present conversation. I'd prefer to talk to Gennio on this subject that's so important to me, without Anu's latent hostility and oddball interruptions.

"What—this?" Anu raises one brow and glances at the drink. "This is *lvikao*. You drink it, like your Earth coffee or tea. But much better."

"No, I mean that stirring stick thing."

"Stirring stick thing is a *kipt*."

"Okay." I nod.

Meanwhile Gennio takes another huge bite from his plate and chews with satisfaction, forgetting what he was saying. In some way, Gennio endearingly reminds me of my brother Gordie and his absolute blissful abandon when chowing down.

But Anu is not giving up so easily. He pokes Gennio's hand with the hot dripping end of his *kipt* that he just took out of the glass. "You were saying?"

"Oh!" Gennio resumes. "The cold storage capsule, yes. They have them on all the ships for those who are underage or over the age of safety."

I resign myself to the fact that we're having this conversation with Anu present. "So, is this a common thing? Why can't they just put all the Earth adults and small children in those capsules and rescue them too?"

"I am sorry to say, but there are not that many of these capsules, not even on Atlantis," Gennio says. "I think, there's only ten on each ship. They are very expensive and very high-tech. We don't have that many available. Only for VIP use and emergency use. They are a kind of quantum state life boats."

"I see." I pause and exhale, as all kinds of enthusiastic ideas circulate through my head. Suddenly I feel *so much better* about things in general, including my original plan for saving my parents.

No matter how much of a long-shot it is, *there's hope!* They can survive the Jump!

As I mull over this new information, Anu says to Gennio, "So are you coming with me to pick up You-Know-Who from ICS-1? I need a co-pilot and Baritei is stuck on a shift at Hydroponics."

I freeze, with my fork halfway to my mouth.

What? No. Way.

This kind of coincidence cannot be real.

"Are you going to fly a shuttle to the flagship?" I say, staring at Anu.

"No, I am going to walk on my knuckles," he says, rolling his eyes. "*Of course* I'm taking a shuttle. It's for your own damn Court Protocol Class at 3:00 PM tonight. What's His Name hates to pilot in the Quantum Stream, so he needs to be ferried across like the Imperator Himself."

"Who?"

"Consul Suval Denu! Who else? Your exalted Court Protocol Instructor!"

"Oh," Gennio says with a minor shudder. *"Him."*

I look from one to the other, not liking the sound of this. "Who is he?" I say. "What's wrong with him?"

Anu makes a snort.

"Oh, nothing's wrong," Gennio hurries to say in a placating way. "He is just a little—"

"Oh, you'll see him soon enough." Anu makes another even more rude snort and takes a deep swig from the steaming glass of *lvikao*. The delicious pastry aroma from the glass wafts at me.

"So when are you going there?" I ask. "Can I come with

you, please?"

Both the aides give me a curious look.

"You want to come on the shuttle?" Gennio says. "I don't know if that's a good idea.... The CP may not expect you to leave this ship—"

"Oh, for crap's sake, let her come," Anu says. "It's not like she has anything important to do besides scribbling. Her Pilot Training Class is at 1:00 and this is going to take no more than half an hour. It's educational!"

"Are we going now? When are we going?" I straighten in my seat, while my thoughts race.... *I need to call Logan immediately and tell him I'm coming.*

"As soon as we're done here. No need to check in at the CCO, I already sent an email to the CP that we're all coming in an hour late."

"You did not!" Gennio exclaims, horrified.

"No, of course I didn't, fat-brain." Anu puts down his glass. "You are going to go over there and tell him yourself. Make something up, if necessary. Then meet me and Earth girl over at Shuttle Bay Two."

Apparently, in addition to the usual non-intrusive general weapons scan everyone gets upon arrival in any shuttle bay, there's also a mandatory high-security scan before boarding a shuttle for the Imperial flagship. Fifteen minutes later, after being scanned by guards for unauthorized weapons, Anu and I stand on a drafty shuttle bay platform next to a small saucer shuttle, feeling the wind corridor motion of the air in the long concave tube down below the platform, a few steps away.

The shuttle is the exact same personal flyer model I am now used to. It is inert, hovering in a parked position about three feet off the floor of the bay.

Anu stands idly, with crossed hands, as we wait for Gennio to show up. He says nothing and doesn't even look at me.

Earlier, I managed to excuse myself on account of needing to use the bathroom, and dropped by my cabin where I left a hasty video message for Logan that I'm on my way. And now I'm here, shifting from foot to foot nervously, and hoping that Gennio convinces Command Pilot Aeson Kassiopei that there's a good reason for this shuttle trip.

A few minutes later, Gennio comes running.

"So?" Anu asks.

"All is fine. We can all go." Gennio glances at both of us with an expression of relief. "The CP did not even say anything, just told us to be back within the hour."

"Great!" Anu slaps one hand against his thigh, then immediately turns to the shuttle hatch. He sings a brief sequence in a low baritone and the hatch opens.

We climb up the short ladder and go inside.

I follow them from behind, and pause momentarily as the familiar ivory-cream interior of the rounded hull greets me. Wall panels of slate-grey orichalcum alternating with pale cream with embossed spiral designs circle the chamber. In the center there are six seats in a suspension harness, and a seventh command chair with a hovering control panel before it.

Gennio makes a move toward the command chair, but Anu is there first. Overtaking him, Anu slides into the main pilot chair and says, "No, you co-pilot today. Pull up the secondary console."

Gennio nods and takes the closest of the six seats next to the command chair.

And then they both look at me.

"Well, don't just stand there," Anu points me to the other adjacent chair on the other side of him. "Sit down and watch how it's done!"

I take the seat and glance over at the main control panel that's hovering before Anu.

"Gwen, engage your safety harness, please," Gennio says to me from his chair on the other side of Anu.

And then we all buckle in. I pull the belt-level harness together, and as it joins at the buckle, the vertical harnesses descend from all directions, whipping like snakes, which never ceases to startle me.

Gennio hums a soft tenor sequence and one of the panels separates from the walls and levitates toward him, turning its nether side up to reveal a console.

"Wow, neat!" I say.

Anu stares at me. "Now, you do it. Might as well grab a

console and help pilot, since you're here."

"What?" I panic, and my brows rise. "Are you crazy? I don't know how to do anything yet! I mean, I just had *one class* yesterday—my first ever, where they barely taught us the names of buttons and function keys. We never got to do any flight simulator stuff yet! I don't even know how to turn this console thing on—"

"Yeah, yeah, whatever." Anu gives me a brief disgusted look. "Just do what we do, there's nothing to it. Takes about five minutes to figure out—"

"No, Anu," Gennio interrupts. "She is just learning, you can't expect her to—"

"Sure I can." Anu glares at Gennio. "Are you forgetting our own pilot school?"

And then he turns to me. "Listen, Earth girl, when they teach us to pilot back on Atlantis, they just stick us in a shuttle and make us do it—*all in one day*. The Instructor Pilot sits down and shows you, and you try it until you get it right, or you crash and die. None of that fancy flight simulator nonsense. You're in a damn shuttle, aren't you? So you've got everything you need to learn. Now, *learn*—unless you are an idiot with half a brain or less! Which I'm guessing you are!"

As I listen to Anu's tirade, I feel my face grow hot with anger. Me, an idiot? What about *him?* What the hell is he thinking?

As I stare in outrage, he makes another sarcastic snort. "Just as I thought. You *are* too stupid to learn like an Atlantean. I have no idea why the CP made you an Aide, unless he just wants a female around the CCO, so he can look at you when you bend over—"

"Anu!" Gennio exclaims in a serious voice. "That's quite enough! You are really out of line! You need to apologize—"

Me? I'm so angry, I am white-knuckled as I clench my fists, and my head is beyond hot. I imagine mashing my fist into Anu's pasty long face. *I am going to break his face and crack his nose and.* . . .

Instead I take a deep breath. And then I say, fiercely, through my teeth, "Anu Vei, apparently you aren't afraid to die. Because *I am about to kill us all.* I am going to pilot this shuttle right now. Show me what to do."

"No, Gwen, please, don't—" Gennio begins.

But I shake my head. My face is locked in an implacable expression. *"Show me!"* I exclaim, thinking back on what sequence Gennio sang a few moments ago. "How do I call up the console?"

"It's somewhat advanced," Gennio mutters nervously. "You need to *auto-key* the panel to yourself first, then call it to you. See those walls, the panels that are grey are all potential consoles—"

I guess Gennio has no idea how much voice training I've had.

"Like this?" I say. And then I focus on the nearest orichalcum wall panel and sing the sequence that's quite familiar by now, keying and calling it to me like a hoverboard.

Anu and Gennio start at the rich sound of my mezzo-soprano, and then stare as the panel obediently hovers in my direction.

I easily command it to turn over, and the console is revealed.

"Now what?" I say in a hard voice.

Gennio's mouth has parted. "Wait! You really are serious?" he says.

"Deadly serious." I glare at him and Anu.

Anu makes a grunt noise. It's a sound of satisfaction.

Moments later, all three of us have the controls "on," with the ready lights enabled—dim pulsing colors moving in response to the faintest sound under the bumpy touch surface— as long as you keep your fingers on it. Meanwhile, the window shields on the hull walls directly opposite us have come down, revealing flight windows with the outside view of the shuttle bay.

I glance back and forth from the keys of my console to the observation windows before us. I'm shaking slightly, with a combination of anger, terror, and stubborn resolve.

Just for a moment I remember the stress of having to take driver's education back at school in Vermont. I flash back to my poor Dad attempting to teach me to drive, in one of our older cars.... Oh lord, I was so bad! Even on my last attempt four months ago, I flunked the written test out of sheer terror, despite knowing all the answers, and barely missed getting a learner's permit.

This—this is so much worse. Infinitely worse. It's so *not* like driving a car on Earth.

I am going to die.

And I am going to take two other people with me.

"Okay, Gwen," Gennio repeats, for like the tenth time. "Remember, there are four basic functions. Red and Green control the Propulsion, also known as Thrust, and Brake—in other words, Go and Stop. Yellow and Blue control the direction and course correction. Yellow sets the initial course, Blue refines and balances it according to environmental factors, adjusting and controlling the overall flight."

"Got it," I say breathlessly.

"One very advanced Pilot can perform all four functions and fly alone. But for best results and best safety, you need at least two Pilots per vehicle," Gennio continues.

"And in a large spacecraft like an ark-ship, you need four Pilots," Anu interrupts.

"Right. Fortunately we are in a small shuttle," Gennio continues. "Now, the main Pilot—in our case, Anu—will handle the primary Thrust and Brake functions. I, the Co-Pilot will handle the Navigation and course correction Adjustments."

"No, you won't," Anu says. "*She* will Navigate. She's Yellow, so might as well let her perform her proper function. You just handle your own Blue crap."

Then Anu glances at me disdainfully. "You have the easy part—setting course. We're simply going to a nearby ship, so plotting the mini-course is a no-brainer."

"But if you were Navigating the whole Fleet across vast interstellar space, that would be a different matter," Gennio says. "Very difficult, probably the most difficult task of all. Imagine—if you set the wrong course across stars, we get lost and we die."

"Exactly. But for now, Earth girl, you just Navigate us across a tiny ship-to-ship length of the Fleet—easy! While fat-brain here—he has to course-correct and control the initial path and trajectory you set, all while compensating for our own variable speed and the Quantum Stream general velocity—all of which is the Blue control function."

"Slow down! Too much! Too much information—this is probably very confusing to her," Gennio says with a worried frown. "Are you sure, Gwen, can you handle this?"

"Yeah," I say, while my gut fills with cold terror. "Now tell me how to Navigate."

Chapter 13

"First," Gennio says, "we start the shuttle. The main Pilot sings a Major keying sequence while holding down this four-color ignition key." And he points to a kind of raised bump in the bottom center of the console where four different-color lights race in a circle around each other. I recognize it from having memorized it the night before for my Pilot Training class.

"Go ahead, put your finger on it, Earth girl," Anu says. "If you don't, you won't be recognized by the shuttle as a Pilot for this flight. All Pilots must make contact and be keyed to the shuttle console."

I place my index finger on the ignition key and watch the two Aides do the same.

Anu, followed by Gennio, both sing a simple three-note sequence, and I follow their lead.

In that moment the hull walls of the shuttle come alive, and a low harmonic hum rises. Hair-line threads of golden light race around the etchings in the hull. . . . Somehow I can feel an echo of that fine vibration where my finger touches the panel.

I realize it is my literal *connection* to the ship.

Next, Gennio shows me how to call up the Navigation Grid. "Each of the Pilots has access to four virtual coordinate grids, depending on need. They are hologram projections that pop up above the console and you can do things like plot coordinates, for example to go from point A to point B."

He points with his finger to each of the four corners of the console. "These buttons call up grids. Red, top right corner button is Propulsion Grid. Green, bottom right, is Brake Grid. Blue, top left, is Adjustment Grid. Yellow, bottom left, is Navigation Grid."

"Okay," I say, while the shuttle is vibrating all around us.

"You can tap any of the four corners to switch between grids any given moment." And Gennio demonstrates by tapping the yellow corner.

Immediately a rectangle grid of yellow light shines brightly over his console, like a ghostly laptop display screen. I see fine lines marking grid squares stand up in the air, appearing out of nowhere.

Next Gennio switches to blue, and a blue grid pops up, then a green one, then a red one. "You can make it 3D if you tap it twice." And the moment he does, the red rectangle suddenly morphs and extends, taking up a strange three-dimensional space, as though a translucent box of light is hovering over the console.

"Wow!" I say. And then I tap the yellow corner key on my own console. Up pops my Navigation Grid, golden-yellow. I tap it again, and it elongates into 3D space.

"Enough playing," Anu says. "Time to get going."

Gennio bites his lip nervously, then tells me, "All right, this is how you set up the Navigation itinerary. First, you choose Destination." And he presses a spot on the console smart surface that's right next to the yellow corner grid button—basically swipes his finger off to the side.

Immediately a small secondary grid appears in the air over Gennio's console, right next to the main Yellow grid. I replicate his movement by sliding my own finger across in a swipe. A similar yellow square pops up before me. It is populated by rows of weird Atlantean symbols that blaze yellow, like an array of angry alien emoji drones.

"What's that?" I say, while my mind goes, *"oh, crap."*

"Okay." Gennio points to the very first one on top left. "See that *circle* character? That represents you, in other words, this ship. That's like the Home button, okay?"

"Okay...."

"See the four-point star character right next to it? That's the Fleet Menu. In other words, you can use it to call up a list of all the ships in the Fleet."

"Got it. What about the other weird characters?"

Gennio shakes his head. "Don't worry about them. They're

other menus. Ignore them for now. All you need is the Fleet Menu."

"All right."

"Now, tap the Fleet Menu."

I do as he says, raising my finger up in the air to touch the projected holo-character star made of yellow light.

At once the character expands into a long scrolling menu of Atlantean numbers, in three columns.

"Holy crap!" I exclaim.

"Just a visual representation of our actual Fleet formation—three adjacent columns of ships, each one a number, lined up the exact same way we're flying in space right now," Gennio says. "Now, to scroll up and down, just touch the edge of this menu grid on either side."

I make a scared sound and *very* gently move my trembling finger to engage the scroll function. The numbers start moving down through the air. I slide my finger in the other direction, and they scroll up.

"Good," Gennio says. "Now comes the easy part—find the ICS-1 flagship and tap it. That will choose it as our flight Destination."

"But I don't really know how to read these numbers." I bite my lip. "I only know how to count to maybe twenty in Atlantean?"

"Hah! Congratulations, you've achieved the reading level of an Atlantean three-year-old," Anu says with a snort.

"You know what?" I turn in a burst of fury, and glare at Anu. "One more word from your filthy mouth and I will stuff my fist in it!"

"Whoa!" Anu makes a hoarse laugh and sits back from me. "Earth girl's got a bite!"

"You just shut your Atlantean trap!"

Gennio shakes his head at both of us. "Please, Gwen. Okay, let's just continue, please." And he points to the moving columns of numbers. "Fortunately all you need is to count to four in Atlantean. There are four Imperial Command ships in the Fleet. They are all in the middle row. And they are spread out evenly, the entire length of the Fleet. Unlike the other ark-ships, each Imperial Command Ship is designated by a large circle, with a number inside. ICS-1 is at the very beginning of the formation, so just scroll up all the way until you see a circle with a #1 in it. By the way, there we are, ICS-2, see it?"

As he points, I see a big bright circle with two dashes in it, among the sea of numbers—our own current ark-ship. It inches downward slowly, eventually disappearing off screen. I scroll with my finger to speed up the movement, passing hundreds of numbers, and finally reach the top of the menu. Just as Gennio said, there's the other big circle with one dash, up on the very top.

"Now, tap it to select our Destination."

I do as I'm told.

In that instant something weird happens. The Fleet Menu grid disappears and instead two circles suddenly pop up on the main Navigation grid. They float in the air—the circle with #1, our Destination, is on top, and a blank circle designating us, the shuttle, on the bottom.

"That's it, Navigation set!" Gennio says. "You did it, Gwen, good job!"

I exhale in relief. "Okay, now what?"

"Now, I take over, and fly!" Anu says harshly.

And he puts his fingers on the red corner, calling up the Propulsion Grid, then sings a brief major key sequence.

The vibration in the hull of the shuttle around us increases. I watch the window and see the view outside shifting. We start to move, drifting off the platform to the side and into the concave drive tunnel.

At the same time I see that Gennio puts his fingers on the blue corner and calls up the Adjustment Grid. He sings a minor key sequence, and starts manipulating the blue circle that represents our shuttle, to keep it centered along a perforated line that must be a vertical guide.

Anu taps twice to take his Propulsion Grid 3D. And then he sings again.

The shuttle suddenly blasts forward along the launch tunnel.

I grit my teeth and hold back a scream.

We burst outside past the violet plasma shield and into empty space. Black vacuum fills the flight windows. The shuttle makes a turnabout—while Gennio is busy manipulating the Blue grid. Once again, as that first time with Pilot Keruvat Ruo, we end up in an "alley" between two formations, two vast rows of ships stretching in both directions to the invisible horizon.

Now thinking back, I remember all of it—all the things that Keruvat Ruo was doing on that flight—the swift flashes of color grids popping up above his console, the sequences he was singing. Neither I, nor the other three Earth refugees on that shuttle were paying any attention to what the Pilot was doing back then, completely occupied by the view of the black cosmos.

But now—oh, it all comes rushing back. Now that I have an actual perspective, a basic *understanding* of sorts, now I remember and care. Pilot Keruvat Ruo was brilliant! But no, it suddenly sinks in—not just brilliant, he was a *virtuoso*. That's how good he was, how amazingly coordinated and fast on the controls. He needed no co-pilot. . . .

"Ready, Gennio?" Anu says, throwing me a sideways glance. "I am about to fly us out of here, fast!"

Gennio merely nods. I realize they are talking mostly for my own benefit.

"Watch, Earth girl, this is how you increase speed and go forward."

Anu continues holding down the red corner. In addition he now places his other hand on the center of the console touch surface, right above the ignition button. He slowly swipes his finger *outward*—away from himself and out to the console upper edge.

As he does so, I hear the shuttle hull vibrate at a higher pitch. At the same time the view outside starts to blur with motion—we are speeding up, as we coast through the corridor between formations. Faster and faster we fly. . . . Soon, ships on both sides flash past us, appearing as stationary road markers while we seem to be the only thing in motion.

I have no idea how all of it works. But it must be the nature of the Quantum Stream—apparently it creates some kind of space-time bubble around the Fleet. The term I've heard used is a different "phase-space." We're basically contained within our own unique mini-universe of velocity and relativity. I expect they'll be teaching us more about it in classes at some point.

"We will fly all the way to the front of the Fleet," Gennio says without taking his eyes off his Blue grid, which he is watching like a hawk, making sure the blue circle ship marker remains lined up against the guide.

"How long do we fly like this?" I say a few minutes later, trying to keep my breath even.

"One third of the length of the Fleet. The Imperial Command Ships are spaced out evenly, dividing the formation into three segments," Anu says. "We're now probably about halfway between ICS-2 and ICS-1, so, almost there."

"How do you know? How do you know when to stop?"

Anu snorts. "I don't. That's *your* job to tell me. Watch your own Yellow Nav grid and tell me if we are close."

"What?" My mouth falls open.

"Oh and if we *don't* stop in time, we will overshoot, and pass the flagship," Anu adds almost gleefully. "Which will kick us out of the Quantum Stream and into standard interstellar space—in the middle of nowhere, uncharted, with no way of getting back. There we will coast for days until our life support runs out—or, if we're lucky, we run into something potentially incendiary, like the gravity well of a nearby star, which will instantly take us out of our misery. In either case we die a horrible death while cursing you."

"What?" A wave of panic engulfs me. I feel my hands trembling while my temples pound. I stare helplessly at the Yellow grid before me. "What do I do? What? *What?* What am I looking at here? Quickly! Please, Gennio, *help me!*"

"It's okay, Gwen," Gennio glances at me calmly. "Technically, Anu, we're still within the solar system confines so we're not interstellar, but it is still deadly. If we fell out of the Quantum Stream we would be lost, completely on our own, and yes, eventually die. But anyway, Gwen, there is plenty of time. See the two yellow circles, how the bottom one—our shuttle—is slowly nearing the top one?"

"Yes!"

"Okay, now see those little notches on the vertical guide?

When there's only *one* notch gap left between the two circles, that's the optimal Braking distance."

I stare like crazy at the Yellow grid projection, and count the notches silently. "Okay, I think there are two?"

Gennio quickly releases the blue corner of his console and taps yellow, making different color holo grids replace each other in the blink of an eye. He glances at Yellow and tells me, "Yes, you are correct." Then he instantaneously flips back to Blue and continues his own task.

"So what do I do?" I mutter, while we continue rushing onward and the windows show endless formation ships flashing by. "Hello! *Gennio!*"

"Oh," he says. "Sorry. Just tap the shuttle circle twice. That will signal the Brake system. At that point Anu will initiate the Braking process."

"Okay, got it!" I forget everything else in the world around me and stare at the two yellow circles of light as they slowly converge in the air grid before me.

Seconds tick away. . . . At last the shuttle circle touches the last notch closest to the circle representing ICS-1. "Now!" I say and double-tap the shuttle circle.

In that moment the circle on my Yellow grid starts blinking. At the same time Anu's Red grid flashes once, then his circle flares really bright and stays that way.

"Engaging Brake!" Anu releases the Red grid and pulls up Green. Holding the green corner with one hand, he slowly swipes the center of the touch surface, this time down, toward himself and closer to the rainbow ignition key on the very bottom.

The nature of the hum in the walls immediately changes. The motion outside the windows slows down, and we coast softer and finally come to a smooth floating stop before an arkship at the tip of the formation, beyond which there is *nothing*—no more ships, only black space and distant on-rushing stars.

It is Imperial Command Ship One.

I remember to breathe, as Anu switches back over to Red, and sings a turnabout sequence while swiping his fingers in a circular motion along the middle of the console. At the same time Gennio on his Blue grid continues to fine-tune our position relative to the linear vertical guide.

As the shuttle approaches ICS-1, the great hull of the ship grows to fill the entirety of the view. Next, we plummet toward a violet plasma-cloaked opening, pass the shield energy barrier and enter the long tube of the shuttle bay.

A few seconds of violent motion while the tunnel blurs with speed around us—and this time I note how Anu switches rapid-fire from Red to Green in order to engage Thrust then Brake—and then we coast over to a platform.

We have arrived.

I release a long-held breath and sit back in the chair. No, really I collapse. I think there's a sheen of sweat on my forehead. . . .

"Hey, not done yet!" Anu glances at me and points to the console, which remains lit.

"Now," Gennio says, "we need to disengage the shuttle drive and park it, turn the power off, then un-key ourselves individually from the console. Like this—"

He presses the ignition key with the four-color circling lights, and sings the same three-note major sequence that originally turned the shuttle on. Immediately the living sound of the ship ceases around us. The hull goes silent and the golden lights stop racing along the hair-fine etchings. At the same time, the shuttle makes a small lurch, like an elevator pausing, and stops in place, motionless.

"And now the power off." Gennio sweeps his fingers along the *underside* of the panel. His console goes dark.

Finally, Gennio sings a sequence to levitate the panel back over to the wall and un-key it.

Anu performs similar steps with his own console, except that, being primary, it remains hovering before his seat. And then he looks at me.

I do what Gennio did, and watch my console return to the wall.

"*Now* we're done."

As soon as we emerge from the shuttle and into the ICS-1 shuttle bay, we are met by guards wearing prominent

Imperial insignias on their uniforms, and holstered weapons at their belts. Similar insignias decorate the walls.

Before we take any more steps inside the ship, they scan us *again*. I realize it's likely normal routine, and security is probably extra-tight on the Commander's own ship.

While Gennio and Anu talk to the guards in Atlantean, I just stand there, looking around.

Okay, now that my unexpected Piloting ordeal is over, time to get my brain back in gear—*Logan*. I wonder how to find him, and start making plans to slip away from the guys temporarily.

But they're done talking. Gennio turns back to me. "We are clear to proceed. Come along, Gwen, we need to find Consul Denu's chambers, on Command Deck Three. The guards called ahead to let him know we're coming, so he will be waiting for us."

"Just follow the scent of too much perfume, essential oils, slaughtered flowers, musk . . ." Anu says. "Directly to his door."

"Okay . . ." I say, not knowing what to think.

Gennio winces, then wrinkles his forehead. "Yeah. The Consul is a little . . . extravagant."

Anu makes a tremendous snort of sarcasm. "A little."

We start walking.

Ten minutes later, after moving through the usual network of corridors, from deck to deck, we reach the Green Quadrant Command Deck in the interior hub.

The hallways here seem to be filled with more people, more Atlantean guards, more protocol in general. Apparently it's not too far from the Commander's own private chambers, since he embraces the Green Quadrant as his base of command.

The greater corridor that runs between the flagship Central Command Office and the Resonance Chamber is decorated with Imperial insignias every few feet. At the doors of the CCO itself, not two but four guards stand on duty.

We pass this VIP area carefully, staring at the impassive guards with a variety of holstered guns and blade weapons at their belts, who pay no attention to us. And then we turn into a lesser corridor and into the Command Deck hallway filled with officers' cabins, a section similar to my own cabin hallway.

"What's his number again?" Anu asks.

In reply Gennio pauses before a door. "Here, I think. Number eleven."

"Okay.... Ready?" Anu slaps his hands against his sides, which I am beginning to recognize as his nervous tic. And then he steps up to the door and passes his hand over the square button on the wall. It must also function as a kind of doorbell, or maybe an intercom.

"Consul Suval Denu, may we come in?" he says loudly.

After a moment the door opens.

When Anu mentioned perfume and flowers, he was not too far off.... I've long since stopped noticing the clean but slightly sterile nature of the air inside the Atlantean ships, but now a blast of aromatic perfume greets us, like walking into a cosmetics store in a mall back on Earth—but much *worse*.

The cabin quarters are large, similar to the CCO office space back on our own ship, but the décor is frilly splendor, in delicate shades of lavender, mauve, rich plum and burgundy, interspersed with underlying earth tones of cinnamon brown, coral, and carnelian. Everywhere I see fabrics cascading from the walls, gold embellishments, and vanity mirrors on side tables. In the center of the room is a large bed covered in pillows of all shapes and strewn with layers of sheets and embroidered coverlets.

A slim, slight, middle-aged Atlantean man in a grand gold wig and a long sage-yellow robe stands haughtily near the doors, next to a packed trunk, also covered with gold embellishments and upholstered with rich deep red fabric.

I admit my jaw must have dropped, and I am staring at him, unblinking. Good lord, the *wig!* It is a strange Ancient Egyptian-looking or Mesopotamian hybrid—something that maybe King Hammurabi wore, or an Egyptian pharaoh—but made of pure golden hair, tightly braided and coiled and woven in rows of micro-pleats.

His skin is warm suntan, similar to Aeson Kassiopei's coloration. His face is oval, lean, elegant, and his dark brown eyes are outlined in kohl, while his brows bear the sheen of lapis lazuli, all artfully precise, perfect. He is even wearing some kind of softly glittering dark henna gloss on his austere lips.

Around his neck is a wide Egyptian-style collar, lying

heavy like an aegis over his chest, and made of gold and precious inlay. The rich sage robe is delicately embroidered, with a golden hem that falls to his ankles, where I can see sandal-like woven boots, also trimmed with gold and precious stones.

It's as if a being of ancient royalty has come to life and stepped forth from a pyramid or temple wall painting. *He is unreal!*

I continue to stare, while both Anu and Gennio quickly incline their heads and do the formal salute with their left hand touching lips and forehead.

And then comes his voice—a musical delicate tenor, cultured and refined and absolutely regal.

"Anu Vei and Gennio Rukkat. You are late," Consul Suval Denu says in perfect English, enunciating every word. "Come and take my travel wardrobe and we will proceed." And then he motions with one manicured hand to the large trunk.

"Our apologies for the delay." Anu and Gennio both step inside and take the trunk, picking it up by the handle on each side. Apparently it's heavy, because both boys make an effort to lift.

Consul Denu barely glances behind him. "Kem will carry my Scents and Personal Art boxes, so you will not touch them."

Only now do I see, in the corner of the room, a young dark-haired boy, barely older than Gracie, quietly perched on a low footstool. He too wears a tunic robe, but much shorter and simpler, rich brown, over dark blue pants. Immediately the boy scrambles up and goes to the side table to pick up four large ornate boxes that he carefully stacks on top of each other until his face is no longer visible. I have no idea how the boy can see past them and still walk. The contents of the boxes make clanking and clinking noises.

It occurs to me that these are the first true *civilian* Atlanteans I've seen who are not wearing the Fleet uniforms. Furthermore, the Consul himself has to be a *citizen*.

In that moment Consul Denu notices me. His gaze stops upon me, cool and serpentine.

"Who is this?" he inquires.

"Hi, I am Gwen Lark," I say as politely as possible. "I am

also an Aide to the CCO."

For a moment the Atlantean says nothing, only examines me, looking me up and down with critical disapproval.

And then he says, "Ah, yes. You must be the new student. Very well, girl, you may approach and carry one of my boxes. Kem, give her something to carry. Something least consequential."

Before I can say anything, the boy Kem—apparently some kind of assistant of the Consul—comes up to me and gently hands me off the topmost box, so that at least now the pile of boxes precariously balanced in his arms only goes up to his chin. I receive the box with a kind of minor dread.

"Do be careful, all of you," Consul Denu remarks in a bland voice. "Now, let us go, we must not keep the Imperial Lord waiting. Lead me to your transport ship."

And Consul Suval Denu motions for us to go before him.

Minutes later, walking as quickly as we can with our various clanking burdens, we make it back to the same shuttle bay.

Consul Denu moves gracefully behind us, his posture upright, and his light pace that of a swan—a very annoying pompous swan in a golden wig. Periodically he makes snide yet perfectly dignified observations about the ship, the tedious corridors, the sad lack of decorum in the members of the crew passing around us. And, oh yes, he constantly reminds us to be careful with his things.

"Kem, keep the Scents upright. Always upright! Gwen Lark, both hands must be in firm contact with the lid and the box for proper closure and balance. And as for balance, Anu Vei, do not walk ahead of Gennio Rukkat, or the delicate handles of the wardrobe will be warped. Walk side by side—the corridor is rather narrow but still sufficient to accommodate you both. . . ."

Another minute of this and I have a feeling either Anu or Gennio will turn around and strangle this man. Their faces are drawn, lips held tight, and they are both huffing with the exertion of carrying the heavy trunk. Meanwhile Kem is patiently walking next to me, as we carry the boxes filled with unknown bottles, cosmetics or other trinkets. What in heaven's name is Personal Art?

As we enter the shuttle bay, the two Aides increase speed, so that they are almost running with the trunk. We stride quickly after them, past Atlantean crew and guards and their tedious scanners.

Just as we reach our shuttle, I hear a familiar voice call out my name.

"Gwen! Gwen Lark!"

I turn around, and it's Logan.

Chapter 14

Logan Sangre strides quickly in our direction from the end of the platform where apparently he's been waiting for us.

At the sight of Logan's striking tall figure, and his familiar handsome features, my pulse starts to race with excitement, while pleasant warmth floods my cheeks. Logan looks so damn good in the Fleet uniform!

"Thanks for coming, Gwen," he says, with a casual light smile, but a very intense look in his eyes. And then he bends close to plant a kiss on the side of my mouth, grazing my cheek and trailing up, and simultaneously whispers in my ear, "*Perfect timing.*"

"Hey, of course," I say, somewhat flustered, and then I glance back at the others in my party, expecting all kinds of things.

But no one is looking at me. Anu and Gennio have set the trunk down temporarily, and now they stand at the staircase leading to the open hatch of the shuttle, ceremoniously allowing Consul Denu to climb up the stairs ahead of them, followed by Kem.

Without looking around, the Consul disappears into the shuttle, followed by his attendant.

That's when I open my mouth and say, "Guys, this is Logan, he is coming with us."

The two Aides turn around. Anu blinks, glances from me to Logan and frowns. "What?" he says. "He's what?"

Gennio just looks on with a slightly nervous expression.

I take a step forward assertively, and pull Logan by the hand after me.

"Hey," Logan says to them with an easy smile. "I am Cadet

Logan Sangre. I will be coming with you to ICS-2."

"You what?" Anu frowns and turns his head sideways, examining Logan.

"Who exactly is this, Gwen?" Gennio says.

And then Anu looks down and notices my hand holding Logan's. "Oh," he says while his brows rise. "Oh, hell no! This is your boyfriend, Earth girl! So *that's* why you wanted to come along with us to the flagship? So you could see him? No way are we taking your boyfriend for a ride! And you, get lost, Cadet! Don't you have some classes you should be in right now? I am reporting you to your commanding officer—"

"Whoa! Hold it," Logan says, putting up his hand with a very businesslike change of expression, going from easygoing to stone-hard in the span of a second. "I am going on an errand, and this has nothing to do with Gwen. You need to let me come with you, this is Fleet business."

"Oh yeah?" Anu continues looking sideways. "What kind of Fleet business? I was not informed of any kind of—"

"Anu Vei." To disguise my uncertainty and my nerves, I make my voice as firm as possible. "Enough. He is coming with us." And then I turn to Gennio. "Look, I will vouch for Logan, he is an excellent and exemplary Candidate and now a Cadet, and he needs to see our CP. . . . Okay? This is important, no joke."

Gennio purses his lips. "Okay, Gwen, we were not told about this. I am sorry, but this is really not appropriate, I'm afraid. Unless we are ordered by the CP directly, we cannot just pick random people up on the shuttle."

I take a deep breath. "Understood," I say. "But this is an exception. Please, just this once. At worst, you can blame it all on *me*. But you'll see, the CP will approve this, I know. Trust me, okay?"

"This is crazy," Anu says. "I say, no."

"Hello?" In that moment Kem is back, peering at us from the doorway of the shuttle. "The Consul says to hurry up!"

The Aides glance at him. "Tell the Consul we are coming!" Anu exclaims.

"I don't know." Gennio looks at me then at Logan. "If maybe you can tell me what this is regarding? You say Fleet business, but what is it?"

Logan trains his compelling hazel-eyed gaze upon the Atlantean boy. "It is, but I am not at liberty to speak to you about it. It is high-level and concerns your Command Pilot only."

Gennio bites his lip. "Can anyone verify this? Your commanding officer?"

"Come on, let's just go," I say. "Consul Denu is waiting. And Logan's just another passenger. *I take full responsibility!*"

"All right," Gennio says thoughtfully. "But I really don't like it."

"You don't have to like it." Holding on to the Consul's box with one hand, I push Logan forward with the other, and we climb the staircase leading into the shuttle.

Once on board, Logan eases up on the intensity and becomes his usual charming self. He also takes a seat strategically as far away from me as possible, on the other side of Gennio, while I end up seated in an end seat next to Kem.

Consul Denu sits pompously in the seat right next to Anu's main Pilot chair. The shuttle seats are all taken, except for one, and that last one becomes the repository for the Consul's grand trunk.

"Strap it in." The Consul points one elegant claw-like finger with its long painted nail to the trunk in the end chair, and Gennio rises sadly from his co-pilot seat and pulls the trunk's seat belt together and engages the harness around it. As he does this, Anu sits, rolling his eyes.

"And who is this?" Now Consul Denu has noticed Logan, and is examining him with some suspicion.

Logan gives him a confident smile, followed by a perfectly executed Atlantean salute, ending with his head in a slightly inclined position. "I am Cadet Logan Sangre. It is a privilege to share this shuttle with you."

"Very pretty posture, hmmm." The Consul raises his chin at him, then brings it down in a faintest nod. "It is refreshing to see at least some Imperial Fleet Cadets who follow proper protocol on their second day."

And then Logan is ignored.

Anu and Gennio start up the shuttle, and this time there is no pretense to engage me in the piloting process—they are too tired and stressed to bother.

The hull sings the now familiar melody, we coast off the platform and enter the shuttle bay tunnel. This time, as we blast off, I don't bother watching the view outside the window. Instead all my focused attention is on the two pilot consoles, the constant rapid flipping around of the four holo-grids, key functions, and the process of flying.

We arrive back on ICS-2, and once more everyone gets to carry Consul Denu's belongings. Even Logan volunteers, and gets handed a medium-sized ornate box.

"Let the pretty Cadet take the Face Colors box. It is the least fragile," the Consul says graciously.

We walk from the shuttle, and past the usual guard station where we are stopped only briefly for scanning. Seeing the splendid figure of Consul Suval Denu, the Atlantean guards come to order, and rain salutes upon him as he sails by.

A minor mishap happens, just as we are about to enter the closest shuttle bay exit corridor leading inside the ship. Kem and Logan walk behind us, bringing up the rear. It is unclear who runs into whom, and who drops what first, but I hear a minor crash behind us. I turn around, and there's Logan's box on the floor, lid off, and what seems to be a hundred small chalks or cosmetics sticks of various delicate colors rolling about all over the floor and under the feet of the guards.

Logan cusses softly and squats down, starting to pick them up one at a time, while Kem is barely holding on to his two boxes of Scents, which are teetering in his grasp.

"Oh, no!" I exclaim, and turn to help Kem get a better grip on his burden.

Meanwhile we hear a horrified tenor exclamation behind us.

Consul Suval Denu stops and raises both trembling hands before him. "Oh Gods! My Personal Art! What clumsy idiocy!"

"Apologies, my lord!" Kem mutters, speaking for the first time in a faint high voice, "Oh, my greatest apologies!" As I help him hold on to his things, I doubt he is in any way at fault, but he seems to be used to taking the blame regardless.

"It is all entirely my fault, Consul!" Logan says, looking up from the floor, his hands full of the crazy color-stick things. And they just keep falling through his fingers and rolling off, going under the feet of the nearby guards, rolling away in all directions.

"No! Stop!" Consul Denu's voice has risen in pitch so that he is screeching at the guards. "You, do not move your feet, you clumsy oafs! And you! Either stand still or carefully pick up! Move it! You three, pick up, now! Carefully! Gently!"

And now four Atlantean guards join Logan on the floor chasing the paint sticks, bending over, colliding with each other, in absolute subservient chaos.

The rest of us, Anu, Gennio, Kem and myself watch in horror. Logan looks up at us periodically, giving us pointed glances, and at some point stumbles backwards and crashes lightly into a guard, nearly bumping heads.

It is so ridiculous, that any other time I would laugh—and I'm sure so would Logan. But we have to keep our faces straight for the benefit of Consul Denu.

When it is all done, and all the lost pieces are accounted for and back in their precious box, Logan picks it up and makes a show of hanging his head with guilt, then shakes his head sadly. "Once again, I am extremely sorry, but I believe everything is back safely. My sincere apologies."

The Consul gives him an incinerating glare. "I retract my good opinion of you, Cadet. You are far too clumsy and not worthy of Imperial service. Kem, take his box away immediately. Good thing it was not the Scents he dropped."

And with these words Consul Suval Denu turns his back and exits the shuttle bay.

By the time we get back to Command Deck Two, the inner hub of the Blue Quadrant, Consul Denu announces that he is in no condition to be seen by the Imperial Lord—apparently that's the proper Court designation for the Crown Prince, in other words, Aeson Kassiopei—instead, the Consul must rest and freshen up.

And so we take the Consul to his temporary guest quarters

here on our ship, which are in the VIP officers section, near the CP's own quarters, in the corridor right around the corner from the main hallway and the CCO.

While Anu and Gennio carry the Consul's trunk and settle him in, I tell them that Logan and I must go directly to see the CP.

And with that, we turn the corner and take a deep breath. Logan looks at me and I look at Logan, and we hold our lips in a tight line. Then both of us burst out laughing. But it's only for a moment.

"Wow!" I say. "That was stunning!"

"Intense!" Logan says, wiggling one brow and grinning at me. He reaches out with his hand to sweep a stray lock of hair that's gotten loose from my ponytail and got stuck to my slightly sticky forehead. His touch sends a pleasant tingle along my skin. As he does that, his fingers linger, and his expression grows serious.

He starts to lean in closer to my lips, but I put my hand up against his hard chest and hiss at him with a half-smile, "Logan! Not here! Come on, let's do this thing. Take care of your business."

He purses his lips regretfully, then nods, smiling at me again. "Okay, I'll take a rain-check on that very yummy mouth of yours. Fine, are you ready? Let's go see your CP."

"Right around the corner." And as I say it, my pulse starts racing double time, in a combination of inexplicable uncertainty and stress.

Did I do the right thing, bringing Logan here? I suddenly wonder.

"You sure this is going to be okay?" I ask him, as these new doubts assail me, and we start walking.

"Oh, yes," he replies, and his face is composed.

"You never told me how serious it is, what it's really about?"

"In a minute, you'll see."

And we are at the doors of the CCO.

The two guards are the same from last morning, so they know me. They give Logan only a brief look, while one guard calls the CP on his wrist comm. Apparently Command Pilot Kassiopei is in his office, otherwise they'd have just let us in without checking first.

The doors open and I go inside, followed by Logan.

Aeson Kassiopei is at his desk, and he barely glances up. However, as soon as he notices Logan enter right after me, his gaze focuses and suddenly he looks at us with his full attention.

"Command Pilot Kassiopei," I say, feeling my head pound. "I'm sorry for this somewhat unexpected thing, but—this is my friend Logan Sangre—Cadet Logan Sangre. And he has something very important to discuss with you. He came all the way from the flagship, and—"

"What's going on?" Aeson Kassiopei interrupts me, resting his hands on the surface of his desk. His voice is cool as he observes Logan and me.

In that moment Logan steps forward past me, moving me off to the side with one gentle but firm hand. He then performs the formal salute in a crisp, businesslike manner, for the CP's benefit.

"With your permission, Command Pilot Kassiopei," Logan says. "I have something very important for you."

And in the next moment Logan flicks his wrist and points a small but lethal Atlantean gun at Aeson Kassiopei.

I cry out, while an instant wave of cold, horrible panic hits me in the gut. *"Logan!"*

Meanwhile, Aeson has gone very still, and merely watches Logan with an unblinking serpent stare. His hands remain motionless, resting calmly on the surface of his desk.

"Logan!" I scream again. "What are you *doing?*"

But the two young men ignore me. Their deadly gazes remain locked on each other.

"I can take you out with a single shot, right now," Logan says quietly, calmly, like a demon.

Aeson does not blink.

There is a moment of impossible frozen time.

And then Logan lowers the gun and flicks his wrist to put the weapon away, back into his sleeve, in a remarkable sleight-of-hand move. "Fortunately," he says, "it is not why I am here at all."

"Fortunately for you," Aeson Kassiopei tells him. And then he slowly lifts the palm of his own elegant hand from the surface of his desk, and I see a similarly discreet but lethal gun pointing at Logan. The micro-weapon is nearly flat, easy to conceal, and can be operated with one finger. I recall it's called a needle-gun because it fires a series of tiny needle-like lasers close together in a line, forming a slicing "blade" of light.

"I am pleased to not have to kill you today, Cadet Sangre," he says casually, and then makes a similar subtle wrist-flip to put away his gun. He then sits back in his seat, a picture of infuriating and impossible composure. "Now. Tell me why you're really here."

Logan seems to be impressed. He raises one brow and nods to acknowledge the unexpected stalemate. "Command Pilot, this was a necessary demonstration—"

That's when I exhale loudly in impossible relief. And now a wave of anger at Logan has flooded me. "Are you insane?" I exclaim. "What the hell did you just do? How *dare you* raise a weapon at him like that? And how do you even have a gun? My God! I brought you here on my good honest word—"

But in that moment Aeson raises the palm of his hand to me, to signal silence.

I shut up.

"A demonstration," Logan continues. "I needed to show you how relatively easy it is to pass through all your layers of security, procure a weapon and be in a position to threaten or assassinate even the highest officer on your ships."

Aeson Kassiopei watches him impassively. "And your point?"

"My point," Logan says seriously, "is that I have been given real information that there is going to be a high-level hostage situation involving all the Imperial Command Ships. And it's going to happen within the next few days and possibly as early as in the next few hours."

"Go on." Aeson's expression is unreadable.

Logan takes a step forward and points to a chair before the desk. "May I?"

"Sit."

He sits down slowly across from the Command Pilot, acting as a well-trained soldier who knows when not to make any drastic movements. "I am going to tell you something that puts me at cross-purposes with my own original orders. First, you need to know that I am a member of an Earth organization called Earth Union. We are *not* terrorists. Earth Union is sanctioned by the United States Government and the United Nations as a special operations task force to protect the interests of the planet Earth, in light of the present crisis." He pauses to observe Kassiopei's reaction. There is none.

"We are mostly observers," Logan continues. "However, we have also been trained to mobilize and act upon specific orders if we receive them. Let me be honest—our interests lie first and foremost with Earth. And the joint governments have tasked us with ensuring that certain *arrangements* between Earth and Atlantis authorities are carried out as agreed."

"Arrangements?" Aeson speaks for the first time. "Elaborate."

Logan puts his fingers on the surface of the desk and taps them lightly against the smooth polish. "I am aware that the Imperator has made specific promises to Earth governments—promises in regards to rescue, use of Earth resources, and the asteroid itself."

"And what are these promises?"

Logan makes a small sound. "I would think *you* are familiar with it. Because, with my low clearance level, I'm not. I have not been briefed on the fine details, only that the clandestine arrangement exists. In short, I know that there is a standing promise to rescue a much greater portion of the population than just the Qualified teenagers. Also, that in exchange for a percentage of Earth's natural resources and mining rights, the asteroid impact will be lessened significantly, so that there will not be an Extinction Level Event, but a survivable situation."

Aeson Kassiopei sits up in his chair and moves forward, closer to Logan, as they face each other across the desk.

"This so-called intelligence," he says. "How do you have it? Who on the Atlantean side has supplied you with it?"

"I may not reveal this information—yet."

Aeson's lips move into the faintest shadow of a smile.

"How convenient. You have told me nothing specific, but enough to have you incarcerated for plotting and treason against Atlantis."

"I am not done," Logan replies. "Please allow me to continue."

Aeson's expression, as he remains leaning forward, is terrifying. "I am waiting."

Logan nods and his fingers continue to lightly sweep the desk. "I realize, Command Pilot, that you may not want to reveal to me your own level of involvement, and I do not expect any less from you. However, this is what must be shared. My fellow Earth Union operatives and I have been planted in the Fleet, and all subtle measures have been taken to place us in the most key positions possible. We are on each of the four Imperial Command Ships. And we have been ordered to prepare to make our move before the Fleet leaves the solar system."

Aeson Kassiopei watches him, unblinking. "A few hours after midnight tonight the Fleet will pass the orbital region of Uranus," he says thoughtfully. "Then, sometime after midnight the next day, we pass Neptune, and enter the Kuiper Belt region. By late afternoon, two days from now, we will be beyond Pluto, and approaching the end of your Sun's heliosphere and entering true interstellar space. By the end of the third or fourth day, we will be moving through the final outer regions of the Oort Cloud, the absolute last marker defining the outer edges of your system's reach."

Logan nods. "This means we have only four days to carry out our orders—to take hostage the Commander and all three Command Pilots, including yourself. We are to hold all of you to assure the agreement terms are carried out."

"And if they're not?"

Logan's expression is grave. "Then we are authorized to use extreme persuasive measures, up to and including execution of hostages."

"Assuming all of this is true, why are you telling me this?" Aeson observes Logan's face, every tiny muscle motion. "Why should I believe the words of a traitor to his own command?"

As they speak, I find that I am frozen motionless, with such an impossible mixture of emotion, confusion, and cold realization of new facts that I have forgotten to breathe.

"I have betrayed my orders, because I remain loyal to Earth, not some bureaucrats," Logan says with a new level of forcefulness. "And because I have reason to believe that the organization I serve has been corrupted from the inside. Indeed, the corruption lies at the very top with the government leaders, including the United States President herself."

Aeson moves his head slightly, shifting in his seat. "Tell me more," he says. "You must tell me so much more before I can understand or might be willing to believe you. Begin with explaining this corruption."

Logan sighs. A sense of weariness comes over him. "I've learned a few things overnight. And I put the facts together. First, I now know the reasons for your very peculiar age restrictions for Qualification. If they are indeed true, then *there can be no mass rescue* of the Earth population, not even with the availability of the cold storage capsules—they are enough only for a handful of VIPs. That's point one, and a guarantee of at least one broken promise. Second, we've been promised that several of your Fleet ships will remain in orbit around Earth, ready to perform the terms, including various rescue functions and modification of the asteroid's trajectory or whatever means you were going to use. But according to our satellite, radar, and other imaging tech, we find no ships remaining in orbit—"

"So . . . someone from Atlantis actually *promised* you that the asteroid can be moved from its impact trajectory?" Aeson Kassiopei says. "Name some names for me."

"My source tells me the promise was made by the Imperator himself directly to an assembly session of Earth Union at the United Nations, via videoconference, four months ago."

"I see. And what was my Father getting in exchange for this transaction?"

"That, I don't know."

"You are not making this very easy for yourself."

Logan nods. "I am giving you as much information as I have. But allow me to finish—the one most troublesome thing I've learned yesterday, relates to the President and other high command. It turns out, upon receiving the urgent news from us about the age-based limitations for rescue of the general population, President Donahue and other Earth Union leaders did not show any *surprise* or *concern*—no concern at all that billions of people on Earth were going to perish after all. Instead, as soon as we relayed the information, our final orders were given to us—to stand by for the hostage taking operation."

"You say 'we relayed.' Who else is working with you directly, on your ship?"

"There is one other operative that I know personally," Logan says. "It's the truth—he is the only one I know. Earth Union policy is, we are only given one other individual's contact information at a time, so that if we are individually compromised the rest of the operatives remain viable. I can reveal his name to you because he and I both agree that Earth Union has been corrupted—has taken the wrong course of action, and gone too far. My operations partner is Cadet Daniel Tover. Both of us are assigned to ICS-1. However, we are not alone. Each Imperial Command Ship has *three pairs* of EU operatives. There are four more people who are still on that ship, ready to carry out EU orders and take Commander Manakteon Resoi hostage. Meanwhile, there are six people on *your* ship who are ready to enact the same orders with you. And same thing for ICS-3 and ICS-4."

Command Pilot Aeson Kassiopei takes a deep breath and exhales, sitting back deeper in his chair, and momentarily turns away from Logan. "All right," he says. "There is sufficient troubling information here that I am going to take your words under advisement. I know you haven't told me the full story. But for now this is enough."

Logan continues watching him.

"You do realize that you're taking a different kind of risk in speaking with me about this?" Aeson says, again turning to face the other. "And I don't mean incarceration for treason against Atlantis. Cadet Sangre—you think you know me? How easily you assume that I'm not in fact already working with Earth Union directly. I could be working on behalf of my Father with Earth Union, and you've just stupidly revealed your fundamental Earth Union doubts and disloyalty to me. You are at my mercy, Cadet. Well?"

Logan shakes his head slowly and does not look away.

"No," he says. "I think not. I believe you are not involved, Command Pilot, because I have a certain idea of your integrity."

Aeson Kassiopei raises one brow in the closest semblance of sarcasm yet. "How so?"

"That." And Logan points to the black armband on Aeson's left bicep. "I know that you wear the mark of a hero. And I respect that. I do not see how you would be involved in such reprehensible dealings."

There is another pause of silence.

"It appears, Cadet Sangre, that we have something in common," Command Pilot Kassiopei says. He then leans forward again, placing his hands on his desk. "You will therefore tell me everything you know—*again*. Start from the beginning. How you were recruited, who is your handler, and who is your Atlantean contact, here in the Fleet. If you hold back, it will do neither of us any good. Prove to me that you are genuinely motivated to save lives."

Logan thinks for a moment, then nods. And he begins to speak.

Chapter 15

Kassiopei and Logan talk for the next twenty minutes, while I breathe shallow and stand perfectly still, my body approaching muscle atrophy, while my senses take everything in. At some point, Gennio and Anu arrive in the office, but seeing the intensity in the room, they pause at the doors.

I silently motion for them to come in and sit down. And then all three of us perch on our usual seats near the walls.

"What's going on?" Gennio whispers to me, motioning with his head to the CP and Logan talking at the desk in moderately quiet voices. Now that I've stepped farther away, I can no longer hear them—at least not well enough to clearly tell what they're saying, so I begin to fidget in agony. Gennio must see my extraordinary level of agitation, and the unrest in my posture.

But I only shake my head negatively, continuing to stare at the two speakers, Cadet and Command Pilot, trying to catch snatches of words. It's like a bomb has exploded in my head. I no longer know what to think or feel or. . . .

Anu looks at them then back at me. "Must be really serious," he finally mumbles.

"Yes!" I whisper fiercely. "It *is*."

Finally another ten minutes later, it appears the conversation or interview is done.

"I am officially transferring you to my ship, Cadet Sangre," Aeson Kassiopei says loudly. "As of now, you report to me directly. Any problem with that?"

Logan nods. "No, I am honored."

"We will speak more on this later. For now, I'll make the arrangements for transfer." Aeson pulls up a mech arm with a monitor and console, then starts keying in something.

Logan watches the CP's movements.

"Your new assignment is ICS-2, Red Quadrant Cadet Deck One. The official commanding officer in charge is Pilot Xelio Vekahat, but he will be informed of the actual arrangement. If anyone asks, you report to him. This must be kept discreet."

"Understood."

Aeson observes him. "One more thing—how did you get that gun past the ship security, both here and on the flagship?"

Logan smiles. "I didn't. The gun was never unauthorized. I simply took it off one of your guards at the shuttle bay, *after* we were scanned. You might ask Gwen about the little incident near the exit doors with the dropped box of cosmetics—"

"Oh, no, you don't mean—" I exclaim, putting one hand to my mouth. "That box you carried for Consul Denu? That was on purpose?"

Logan glances at me briefly and grins. "Oh, yeah. Did you think it was an accident? All those rolling paints underfoot, four guards crawling around on the floor, bumping into me, their weapons holsters unattended. I could have stripped them of multiple weapons and probably their underpants too. My thanks to Consul Denu and his luggage for providing such an easy scenario."

Anu makes a snort and bites his lip, but there's a blissful stifled smile on his face. I think he's just been seriously impressed by Logan. Either that, or he just really, really has it in for Consul Denu, and Logan has made his day.

But Command Pilot Aeson Kassiopei is not smiling. "All right. I am sure I'll be hearing about it from the Consul himself at some point." He merely nods. "In that case, we're done here for now. Cadet Sangre, dismissed."

Logan stands up, and makes another salute. Aeson watches him with an unreadable expression. For a moment they look at each other.

Aeson Kassiopei finally glances in our direction.

And when his serious gaze rests on me, I feel the pressure equivalent of the weight of a mountain. "Lark," he tells me. "You may walk outside with Cadet Sangre. But return here shortly."

I nod, and then I follow Logan outside the CCO.

As soon as Logan and I are in the hallway and around the corner, beyond the hearing of the guards, I turn around and glare at him.

"How could you do that to me? How?" I say, and my voice, my whole body, everything is trembling with an overflow of emotion. "You made me look like an idiot! And you put my reliability in question! How could you not *warn me* about what you were going to do?"

Logan watches me with a serious, gentle look in his hazel eyes, and turns his face sideways with an apologetic soft expression, as he continues to observe me. "Gwen, I couldn't," he says at last. His voice is mild and remorseful. "I couldn't risk you saying no to me, and not letting me get here, get on that shuttle. It was too important that I make contact ASAP. Now that you know the gravity of the situation, you must see why it had to be done."

"Okay, yes, I understand it's bad. But you could have told me, *warned* me you were going to pull that awful gun trick. I thought you were going to *kill* him!"

"You need to trust me. You know me better than that."

But I am not letting up. "Or—or, he was going to kill *you!* Don't you get it? You were *both* this close to killing each other! All for a stupid, crappy demonstration! You could've simply showed him the gun in your pocket and explained how you got it, via a breach in security, or—or whatever! There was no need for a ridiculous Wild West showdown! I couldn't bear it if *either* of you got hurt!"

In that moment Logan grows still and an odd frown appears on his face. "So you *do* care about him after all," he says in a cool voice.

"Huh?" I stare at him, beginning to frown myself. "I what?"

"You care about him."

My mouth drops. "What are you talking about? Hell yeah, I care about him getting hurt, just as I care about you getting hurt! He's an honorable guy and a great commanding officer! What's not to care?"

In that moment Logan shakes his head and smiles again, his

intense expression evaporating—I am guessing, forcibly. "Never mind. Okay, let's not worry about it. All right—I need to find my way around this ship, find my new Barracks. I am guessing the Cadet class schedule is the same?"

I blink at the lightning-fast change of topic. "So we're done talking about what just happened in there?"

"Yeah, for now. The CP will call me if he has any more questions. But for the moment, he's been warned about what's coming, and he will handle it. Ball's in his court." Logan speaks almost casually, as we start to walk down the corridor, and then he cranes his neck at me and gives me his devastating smile. "So, babe, see you for lunch?"

"Don't you babe me, you a-hole jerk!" But I am beginning to crack under the thousand-watt beauty of that smile.

Logan reaches out and brushes one finger against my cheek. "Later," he says. And he starts walking away from me down the corridor.

"Jerk!" I say to his back.

And I return to the CCO.

When I approach the CCO doors, there's Anu and Gennio, standing outside, looking serious. "What?" I say. "What's going on?"

Anu shrugs, with a cool expression. "Nothing. The CP kicked us out. We have to wait out here."

"He's talking to the Imperator, his Father," Gennio adds. "Whenever he does that, we are not allowed to be inside for the duration of the call."

"Oh." I stand, looking at them, at the impassive guards. It occurs to me to wonder—*is Aeson Kassiopei discussing with the Imperator the news he's just learned from Logan?* I wouldn't be surprised.

"So what are we supposed to do now?"

Gennio examines his fingernails then scratches the back of his head. "We wait."

"It's almost eleven," Anu says with a world-weary roll of his eyes. "We could have early lunch."

Gennio glances at him in reproach. "We can't just leave like that, we have work to do."

"I know, fat-brain. I am only dreaming."

So we stand like that for a few more minutes, milling about the hall, and probably getting on the guards' nerves. The guys tell me about how Consul Denu made them set up his stuff all over his guest quarters and install three wall mirrors.

"Oh—the Consul said to tell you, Gwen, that he will see you for your first Court Protocol class at 3:00 PM today, in his quarters—it's the same cabin, number eleven, just as it was on the flagship," Gennio recalls.

"Okay." I purse my lips.

"Lucky you," Anu says.

Eventually we are allowed back inside the CCO. There we see Command Pilot Kassiopei in a grim mood, pacing the room. He must have just ended his video call with the Imperator, because the screen still displays the Imperial logo at his desk.

Seeing me, Aeson gives me a quick piercing glance, then looks away. With one swift motion he passes one hand through his long metallic hair, sweeps it out of the way, almost with irritation, and moves a few strands from his forehead. Then he returns to his desk, barely acknowledging us, and starts making a series of calls.

For minutes he talks in a cold commanding tone, in Atlantean, to various ranking officers. Gennio and Anu listen discreetly, frequently glancing up from their consoles.

I tap Gennio with my hand. "What's he saying?"

"Security. He's talking to different ships security officers. Setting extra procedures in place."

"Yeah," Anu says. "Whatever news your boyfriend had about that hostage threat, the CP's taking it seriously."

"Good," I say.

But my mood remains stressed, volatile, impossible to put into words. On the one hand, I am relieved that everything turned out okay with Logan coming here, that his intel was *real*. But I am still very disturbed with *how* it was all handled by Logan, the way he used our relationship, my trust in him, to do a risky thing that could have backfired terribly. And then there's the nature of the situation itself, the whole thing with Earth Union, with what our President was planning. I am far from clear on the details, but it's enough to know that shady dealings were being planned behind the scenes, things the general public was never aware of. Promises made by the Imperator of Atlantis to a handful of Earth bigwigs. *False* promises. And they in turn had made false promises and explanations to the rest of us.

And so I try to concentrate on my work, and instead end up distracted.

Eventually I give up trying. I think and brood.

After a hasty lunch, eaten with the aides in the Blue Cadet Meal Hall, I have Pilot Training at 1:00 PM. It's the only class on my schedule that I have every day, in addition to my secret voice training.

I get to the learning deck section allocated to our class, with the flight simulator consoles, in a big hurry—trying to be as early as possible, so as to have a seat. I manage to snag one in the second row. Once again, the room is packed and fills up fast, with more students than available double console desks. I see Blayne Dubois and wave to him, as he finds a console seat not too far away from me and skillfully moves his body and limbs over from the hoverboard into the chair.

"So, Lark. We meet again. Another day, another Pilot Training class, imagine that," Blayne says with a faint smile, and stows the hoverboard away under the desk.

"Yeah, crazy, I know." I smile back. "There's more than one class! Who knew?"

My partner, Hugo Moreno, arrives and plops into the seat next to me, giving me a dull mumble for a greeting.

"Hey," I say. "I grabbed us a decent console near the front."

"Uh-huh," he mumbles, then looks away from me as though I don't exist and signals to a few Cadets he knows. One of those guys is Trey—that same alpha aggressive jerk who's friends with the purple-streaked long-haired girl whose name I still don't know, and who both made fun of Gennio that first day on the ICS-2 Observation Deck during the Mars orbital pass. Just lucky for me, they both settle down at the double console right next to Hugo and start blabbing loudly.

I look around for more familiar faces, and see the hotshot Tsai siblings arrive. Erin sits down right in front of me in the first row, so I have a view of her ramrod-straight back, and her spiked blue-black hair. Her brother Roy sits in the spot in front of Hugo.

There's Kadeem Cantrell, sauntering easily, and his partner, some French girl I don't know. Apparently Kadeem speaks French fluently, because they are talking together and laughing softly as they settle in.

And then I see Logan. My gut does a somersault, and my pulse starts racing. And then I tell myself, *Okay, so what?* Of course Logan would be in this class, this is the most advanced Cadet Pilot Training section. Where else would he be?

Logan sees me, smiles and waves to me. He then starts moving in my direction.

I'm not sure I'm ready to see him. So I keep my expression stern.

"Gwen. . . ." He stops next to our console desk and leans forward to rest his hand over mine. "Where were you? I thought we were going to have lunch?"

I raise my brows. "We were? Oh, I wasn't sure if you made hard plans. Or if you were going to *spring it on me*."

Logan's mouth tightens. "Come on, that's not fair."

"Sure it is." I look up at him. "I am still ticked off at you, Sangre. Really, I am."

"Okay, I deserve it. But let's talk about it later, okay?"

"Right," I mutter.

Logan squeezes my hand, and then retreats to find a seat. As he does, I notice how Hugo and Trey and the purple-hair girl all look him over curiously.

Especially the girl.

Yeah, I bet, I think. Logan's so easy on the eyes, and he's new in class and on this ship. It won't be long before all the girls take notice and ogle him like hormonal vultures. Ugh. . . . I really should be used to it by now. That's what I get for being with a hot guy.

Am I with this guy? I think suddenly, out of left field. So far we've kissed a lot, and made out pretty heavily a few times, barely making it to second base, but nothing beyond that. Logan's been a perfect gentleman, never insisting on anything more than what I'm ready for. . . . Which is good, because I don't think I am ready for anything else, not now, not with the world being what it is, my parents, siblings, my family, Earth, Atlantis, *uncertainty*. . . . Damn.

Yeah, he's the perfect boyfriend. And I have to admit it, he's a true friend, not to mention, brilliant company. I know he really cares about me. And, my God, I've been in love, or "in obsession" with him for years—pretty much since I've started high school in Vermont. But this whole weird incident, the way he sometimes puts his so-called orders, duty, convictions, before everything else? On the one hand I admire him for it, but on the other hand, I feel a little *lost*. Trust is such a strange thing.

Okay, why am I even thinking about this now?

Again, the sickening onslaught of doubt—indeed, a real fancy cocktail of doubts and insecurities and stress—starts digging at me.

In a few moments, our Pilot Training Instructor arrives. Mithrat Okoi enters the room and immediately we all spring up and salute.

"You may sit," he tells us curtly. His manner is the same as yesterday—hard, implacable, serious.

And then he gets right into it.

"Yesterday's homework was to memorize the flight console layout," Instructor Okoi says. "Today, we run the first simulation flight."

He flicks the remote device he is holding and suddenly all our display screens come to life. Each smart screen shows the same identical view of a shuttle bay from a platform, the kind you would get from a parked shuttle.

"Today you will learn how to take a basic shuttle from the stop position into the launch tunnel and then outside. You will fly a short distance, return to the shuttle bay, and power off."

The Instructor slowly paces before us, speaking. "You will also learn the four basic function grids and the roles they play during flight. . . ."

As he speaks, I realize suddenly that everything he's saying so far, *I already know how to do*.

"First, you and your partner will decide who is the Pilot and who is the Co-Pilot on this simulation."

The class erupts into whispers.

Hugo nudges me at once. "I'm the Pilot. Got it?"

"All right." I nod.

"And now," Instructor Okoi continues, "Here is how we begin the power-on. The Pilot and the Co-Pilot both—place one hand on the underside of the console before you. The light indicators on the surface of the console indicate the power is on and ready."

I do as I'm told, and see my console light up in a familiar way. Hugo does the same to his own side.

"Now, step one—you auto-key yourself to the ship. Both the Pilot and the Co-Pilot must do this procedure before they can operate the vehicle—"

The Instructor continues speaking, giving us step-by-step basic console instructions, and again, I *know everything* he's about to say.

I am kind of mind-blown. This is wild! Everything from this morning's crazy shuttle flight comes rushing back to me, and I sit there, listening, and going through the motions along with the rest of the class.

It occurs to me that it might be best that I just play along and not draw any unnecessary attention to myself. However it becomes really tough watching Hugo fumble with his Red and Green grids, as he constantly calls up the wrong menus or swipes the touch-surface in the wrong direction. Our poor simulation shuttle lurches along, bumping against the launch tunnel walls, sending up wicked sparks flying from the tunnel surface we grind past—silly realistic display shows them too—and I groan and hold my breath in frustration as we finally blast out, and then almost collide with the outer hull of the simulation ark-ship we just exited.

"Watch it! Keep it straight!" I exclaim yet again, as I try in futility to adjust our ship's motion against the Blue gridline.

"You shut up," Hugo tells me, and I see he's wiping sweat from his forehead.

But we're not alone. Everywhere around the room I hear Cadets swearing, exclaiming, yelling at their partners, while now and then a few horrible explosions sound from some of the consoles, indicating a catastrophic crash and end to the simulation.

Hugo and I manage to not crash our sim-shuttle until the very end when we are on our return lap. Hugo flips to Red, swipes to engage Thrust, but moves his finger widely so that it deviates too far from a straight line. And so we come in from the outside, launch homeward into the tunnel, but wander off to the side and high-speed-slam into the shuttle bay platform. There is a big ear-deafening BOOM, and our simulation goes dark.

"Great!" I exclaim. "Just great!"

Hugo looks ready to kill me, and cusses loudly. "You think you can do better?"

"I'm not even going to bother to respond to that," I say.

"Oh, yeah?" He leans in to me, frowning full-force, and his dark eyes are scary.

"Yeah." I'm so furious I don't even flinch. "A cracked-up monkey can do better!"

In that moment Instructor Okoi claps his hands together to signal the class for general silence. "Attention!" he says. "So far your performance has been deplorable. For the rest of the hour, each one of you will take turns being the Pilot and Co-Pilot. You are going to practice this over and over, and you *will not* leave this classroom until you complete *three* shuttle run scenarios in a row without crashing!"

Groans are heard all over.

My partner Hugo cusses hard.

I shake my head in disgust.

In that moment Erin Tsai raises her hand.

"Yes?" Instructor Okoi nods to her.

"Why are there audible explosions in this simulation?" she asks. "I thought sound waves needed particles of matter to travel through, and in a space vacuum there would be no sound?"

Mithrat Okoi nods. "You are correct. There is insufficient density of matter in space to allow sound to travel. However this simulation is not real space—it is designed for your benefit. The *sound* should remind you, every time you hear a violent explosion, that it is what happens to you if you make one tiny mistake—you die violently, and may be additionally responsible for the death of others. Does that answer your question?"

"Yes, sir."

"Good. Now, continue practicing your exercise."

For the next half hour we take many turns piloting the shuttle in the scenario.

Okay, I admit it—on my first actual attempt as main Pilot, handling Thrust and Brake is harder than it seems. Although I have a solid grasp of the process, I find some of my swipes are shaky. As a result, I also crash us into the launch tunnel on re-entry, just as Hugo did when he was Pilot. But at least I do it fewer times than Hugo, who manages to mess up the Blue-Yellow grids entirely, as he Co-Pilots me in grim hostility, making our shuttle wobble and deviate from its course like a drunken sailor.

The classroom around us is full of exploding noise and frustrated Cadets. Even Erin and Roy in front of us crash periodically.

Instructor Okoi paces between our rows of console desks, observing our pathetic attempts with an expression of doom on his face.

"This is just messed-up stupid crap!" Hugo mutters fiercely for the umpteenth time as we go Boom, and punches the side of the console with his fist.

"Okay, we need to get out of here," I say with frustration. "So, can we get at least one clean run?"

"Maybe we would if I had another partner!" Hugo frowns at me.

"Okay, you know what? This is bull," I say. "You're the one messing up two out of three times. Why don't you stop blaming me and do your part! Focus, already!"

"I don't need to listen to you, bitch! You're not even a Cadet!"

I snort in fury. "Oh yeah? Well, you're just stuck with me. Deal with it!"

Hugo cusses again.

I groan.

And then we begin yet another frustrating shuttle run.

Chapter 16

I've no idea how late it is, but most of the class has stayed past the hour, trying to complete the assignment of three clean runs in a row. The console desk in the front row just before us is now empty—Erin and Roy got through their exercise cleanly and left ten minutes ago. To my right, on the other side of Hugo, Trey and the purple-hair girl are still at it. And so is Blayne and his partner, a few desks down.

I glance around to see if Logan is still here also, but I don't see him. Not sure where he sat down, so he might still be somewhere in the back rows.

I am beginning to get worried. It feels like it's already after 2:30, and I have another class at 3:00 PM with Consul Denu. The last thing I want is to be late to *that* one.

We finally complete two clean runs in a row. Hugo is sweating profusely.

"Just one more," I mutter. "One more! We can do it!"

"Okay, yeah, we can do it!" he echoes me.

It's my turn as the Pilot, so I take us out very carefully, engaging the Thrust, staring fiercely at the Red grid. All is well. Then my fingers tremble on the swipe, snagging against the console surface.

There's a familiar BOOM.

I don't know what just happened, but I crashed us in the launch tunnel before we even left the shuttle bay.

Again.

Hugo growls at me.

"Sorry! Crap! So sorry," I mumble, and we start over, with run one.

When we finally manage to get three clean scenarios in a row, we are almost the last people in the room. Only one other console desk is occupied with an unlucky pair of Cadets. One of them is a round-faced Asian girl, big and bulky, barely fitting into her desk. She slouches over in absolute shame as her partner, a wiry Latina with braids, screams at her in Spanish. I feel for her, really, I do.

"You suck!" Hugo tells me as he starts running out of the open classroom deck area into the nearest corridor on his way to his next class.

I ignore his outburst—because okay, he's kind of right, this time. I did screw us up badly on that final run. Instead I hurry to my own class with trepidation. It's definitely after 3:00 PM, and I am so late!

I arrive on Command Deck Two, find the first VIP quarters hallway, and look for Cabin #11. Passing my hand over the square ID pad, I say my name and ask for permission to enter.

I stand, breathing fast, when the door slides open. A whiff of perfume greets me, followed by the regal voice of the Consul. "You may enter."

I take a step inside, and just wow—in only an afternoon this cabin must have been transformed from a sterile military-style functional space into a frilly oasis, almost an exact replica of the Consul's personal quarters back on the flagship.

Kem is moving around the large room in quiet harmony, arranging fabrics and moving pieces of décor. As it's happening, Consul Suval Denu lounges in a large folding chair lined with cushions, eyes closed, hands folded in his lap upon a mini-pillow, his feet, in their intricate, jewel-encrusted footwear propped up on a tiny foot-rest. I'm guessing the fancy folding chair was one of the things inside that grand trunk, because there's just no way an Atlantean ark-ship would simply have that kind of furniture lying around.

"Gwen Lark, it is poor form, you are late," the Consul tells me after a pause of uncomfortable silence. He opens his eyes and immediately glances at a small digital Earth clock sitting on the side table, which reads 3:19 PM.

I stand, holding my hands together awkwardly.

"Nineteen of your Earth minutes after the hour." The

Consul's long-nailed finger points at the clock. I watch the glitter of gold and the play of light from the sparkling stones, coming from the three rings on his hand.

"I'm really sorry," I say. "My Pilot Training class ran overtime. I came here as fast as I could."

"Your first lesson in Court Protocol," Consul Denu says, looking in my eyes with a sharp gaze. "Make no excuses for your behavior. Simply make the appropriate apology. And then volunteer for appropriate punishment."

"Huh? Okay." I raise my brows.

But the Consul stares back at me with unblinking disdain.

"Your second lesson is never to use non-existent words or animalistic sounds worthy of a gurgling infant child in your adult communication. At the Court of the Imperator, the appropriate response is 'yes' or 'no' followed by the honorific 'My Imperial Sovereign' if you address the Imperator Himself, 'My Imperial Lord' if you address the Crown Prince Heir, 'My Lord' if you address a member of the Elite Nobility of *Atlantida*, or 'Sir' if you address a ranking Citizen who is not otherwise of noble blood. There are other fine distinctions, but this is sufficient for now."

"All right," I say. "So how do I address the women?"

Consul Denu narrows his eyes. "You are rather more impertinent than expected. Therefore this lesson time must take into account the additional training in humility. I am also told that you have a tendency to speak out of line and beyond your rank. We will work on that."

My lips part of their own accord. *Oh, is that what you've been told about me?* I feel a fierce stab of irritation at Aeson Kassiopei. But I say nothing and hold my breath then slowly release.

Consul Denu notices my effort and nods. "Speaking your mind at Court can be the equivalent of a death sentence. And if I understand correctly, the Imperial Lord finds you sufficiently useful that you must be kept alive. I will therefore make every effort to improve your chances."

I look at him and still say nothing. Nobody ever said I don't learn fast (admittedly, except when it comes to P.E. and physical activity, or, okay, that crappy shuttle Piloting).

Consul Denu observes my continuing silence with satisfaction, and takes a comfortable deep breath. "Now then. You may approach me and sit down—in that chair. And we will begin our actual lessons."

Nearly forty minutes later I escape from the perfumed prison of Consul Denu's quarters. After our rough start, apparently the Consul decided he must first introduce me to his own elegant pedigree. So, for the rest of our class I get to hear him discuss his family tree with all its prominent ancestors, going back several thousand years to the original colonization of Atlantis. Admittedly there are useful and fascinating snippets of planetary history in all that—global events including two major floods, several world war cycles, and other stuff that gave me an idea of civilizations on Altantis, but good lord! The roster of names and ranks! I hope the next class is more Protocol and less Consul Suval Denu.

Unfortunately my schedule today includes yet another class. It's Combat at 4:00 PM, over at the Yellow Quadrant, with Oalla Keigeri. I am exhausted from all the crazy pressure since this morning—and it's only day two of us having assumed our official roles in the Fleet.

Combat Training is held in the mid-sized gym area on Cadet Deck Four. The room is once again open-space, with freely connecting corridors leading into the rest of the ship Unlike Earth gyms, this one is more like a martial arts dojo, a wide-open studio space with a hard floor and optional mats rolled up along the walls. I also notice the glaring lack of standard gym equipment such as rowing machines, steppers, stationary bikes or treadmills. Instead, there's a designated sparring area in the middle, and off to the side, a wall with a punching-bag-like surface instead of paneling. Next to it are stacked hand weights in various unusual shapes and sizes.

When I get to the gym, the room is already full. Cadets with yellow armbands are predominant, and once again I feel a little weird with no Cadet star on my uniform.

Oalla Keigeri walks in and blows her whistle. Immediately the Cadets come to order, and line up in rows without having to be told. After all, she is their commanding officer, the Pilot in charge of the Yellow Quadrant on this ship.

I get into a row near the back.

"Good afternoon, Cadets!"

In response we salute, with our left hand to lips and forehead.

Oalla shakes her head. "Now, give me the Form Salute of *Atlantida!*"

This time we perform the four-part Form Salute we'd been taught back on Earth before the Qualification Semi-Finals. It consists of a series of full-body movements and is supposed to be the brief form of the ancient Er-Du Salute given during formal Combat. I have no idea what the full extended Form is like, and I suppose at some point they will teach us, but for now, I struggle to remember how to do this short form version.

One. Step with right foot to the side, widen stance. Bring two fists together, knuckles touching, arms bent at chest-level.

Two. Open fists, palms facing out. Touch the tip of the thumb and index finger of one hand to the corresponding other so that the empty space between the two hands forms a triangle.

Three. Bring the two palms together, thumbs still away from other fingers at an angle. Draw the "praying" hands toward you, so the thumbs touch the chest. At the same time bend your head down so that the fingertips touch your forehead. Bend the knees, maintaining the wide stance.

Four. Separate the hands, lifting them outward into a sweeping arc. Return hands, palms down against your sides. Straighten your knees, as you bring the right leg back in, feet together.

I manage to do the Salute the best I can and then stand in the lineup with the others.

Oalla Keigeri observes us coldly. "How quickly you forget," she says, shaking her head. "This is the first Er-Du class since you Qualified, and today we'll see how much else you have forgotten in just a few days without practice. As Cadets, you will no longer have the luxury of forgetting your training. If you continue to perform poorly, you will not only earn demerits—you will earn *punishment.*"

She blows her whistle again and tells us to line up in double rows, facing each other.

We rush to do as we're told.

"Now, give me First Form, Floating Swan!"

An hour later, pouring sweat, and nearly dead, I stagger out of the gym. The rest of the class does not fare much better.

Pilot Keigeri puts us through the entire Primary Twelve Forms cycle, over and over. No sparring, no stretching, no running laps, no hoverboards. We simply perform the Twelve Forms in order, starting with Floating Swan. And when we get to the last one, Shielding Stone, we start again at the beginning.

Without rest.

At some point the exhaustion turns into lightheadedness, and I have no idea how I manage to stay upright. But, it's over at last, and now I wander back to my cabin on Command Deck Four, through corridors busy with other Cadets and Civilians returning from their classes. I really need a shower, because, pouring sweat, ick. . . . Dinner can wait.

As soon as I get showered and cleaned up, it occurs to me I probably should check up on Gracie and Gordie. I haven't talked to my little brother since I got transferred to ICS-2, and although he's a Civilian and is unlikely to get into much trouble, still. . . . What kind of a big sister am I, not to see how he's doing? So I call up the video display screen from my cabin's wall and start to make the call, when a beep sounds outside my door.

It's Logan.

He stands at my door with a grin, and I swear, he could be holding an "I'm sorry" rose between his teeth if he had one at his disposal.

"Hey, jerk," I say, letting him in. "How did you find my room?"

"They have computers, you know. With search engines."

"Crappy Atlantean search engines," I say, continuing the verbal game.

But Logan takes one step inside my tiny room, and suddenly his hands go around me. His mouth closes hungrily over mine, and oh, forget it, brain. . . . *Forget everything.* The sweet honey starts to pour, and I have honey in my veins, not blood but sweet coursing weakness. . . .

I lift my hands automatically and grasp the back of his

strong neck, feeling the soft wavy locks of his oh-so-dark brown hair with its secret reddish highlights, as he takes my breath away from me.

Holy lord, my temples are pounding. . . .

We disengage at last, and Logan looks at me steadily with his impossible hazel eyes. "So, dinner?"

"Huh?" I say. And for some reason I'm instantly reminded of Consul Denu's weird admonishment to not use "animalistic or gurgling infant noises in adult speech."

So I make a light snort, and Logan raises one brow. "Dinner is funny? We could go to your Yellow Quadrant meal hall, or mine. Or any other—"

"Well, I was going to call my brother Gordie, and then check on Gracie too."

He glances around my tiny sterile cabin. "Nice place you got here, by the way. An actual private room of your very own. . . . And as for your bro, he's probably already at dinner. It might be best to try him later."

I make another laugh sound. "Knowing Gee Three and food, you're probably right. Wonder how he's doing, though? A little worried. No, a *lot* worried."

Logan gives me a curious look. "We can talk on the way. And I'm sure he's doing just fine."

And so we head for the nearest meal hall, which happens to be Cadet Deck Four Meal Hall.

It's close to 6:00 PM and the place is still busy as usual at this time, filled with unfamiliar but pleasant edible smells. Whatever's on today's menu is faintly spicy and savory with herbs, reminiscent of Mediterranean food.

There are only a few empty tables. Cadets with Yellow Quadrant armbands fill the hall, with a few other colors in the mix. I see no one without a four-point star pin. I also see no one I know.

I take that back—there's Blayne Dubois, settled quietly with his back against the wall, his hoverboard out of sight, which I am guessing means it's stowed underfoot. He's bent close over his bowl of soup or stew, typical curtain of hair falling to cover half his face. He is eating absentmindedly with a spoon in one hand while reading something on his tablet. No one else is sitting next to him, and he's oblivious to the world.

"There's Blayne!" I say to Logan.

"Uhm, I was hoping it would be just the two of us for dinner, so we can talk."

"We can talk with Blayne there," I say. "He's completely trustworthy and a friend."

"Gwen...." Logan touches my arm lightly. "I want to really talk. One-on-one. About what happened."

"Okay." I bite my lip.... I am not entirely happy. Just because his kiss back in my cabin temporarily lowered my IQ points, doesn't mean I can't think just fine, *now*.

And so we get our trays, get our bowls filled with the aromatic stew stuff, and fill up the drinking glasses.

Logan gets us a table in the middle and we sit down, across from each other.

"Okay," I say, looking up at him seriously. "Talk."

Logan sighs, picks up his glass and takes a deep swig. The glass is steaming hot, so I think it's *lvikao*. I still haven't tasted that stuff and I'm momentarily curious.

"Look," he says, staring into my eyes seriously. "I am really, *really* sorry. About not warning you today. I know it was a shocker, and yeah, it was important that it would all look real enough to make an impact on your CP—"

I put down my spoon, clattering it against the bowl. "So you used my raw, terrified, freak-out reaction as part of the 'look real' scenario? Logan, that's *depressing*—depressing that you don't think I can be counted on to keep my face straight or just stay out of your way if needed. I still insist you should've told me. I'm a big girl, I can handle *subtlety*. I feel used."

"I know. I used you. I *did*. I suck for doing it. But again, there was a life and death crisis." He pauses, glances around the room briefly with a kind of absentminded expression that disguises a razor-sharp perusal. "And it still *is*. Still going on. Do you *understand*? Nothing has broken yet ... no attempt has been made by EU. Which means that, even with my warning, with the new enhanced security and state of readiness, your CP, the other two CPs, and the Commander, are still at risk. And so are all the rest of us."

I frown. "Yes, I get that it's going to hit the fan any

moment. You don't need to remind me. It's part of what's making me soul sick in addition to everything else. We're hurtling through outer space; *nothing*'s any longer real except these damn ark-ships. And some kind of violence is potentially going to erupt, while I can't even get to my baby brother and sister because they're stuck on some other dratted ark-ship that's also hurtling through outer space, while the rest of my family is stuck back on Earth all because that damned asteroid is going to destroy *everything*—"

The burn of tears is starting to coalesce in my eyes. I swallow quickly, then raise the spoon of stew and put it in my mouth. I chew by force.

Logan watches me with intensity, and his expression is sympathetic and vulnerable—completely honest.

A tray clatters loudly to the floor behind us.

I start, and Logan starts. We both turn around.

For a moment it looks like some kid dropped their tray and bowl. And then, I blink, and I see that it's not.

The kid fell. And he's not getting up.

Then I hear a soft *zing* sound. Not a pop, but a zing, the sound of an Atlantean mid-range small-caliber laser handgun. I know that sound because of several target practice sessions during Combat classes—I've fired one. It's also the kind of gun that guards use.

Another Cadet falls—this one's only several tables away, standing with her tray talking to someone, an easy target shot in the back.

Immediately there's screaming mayhem. I see flashes of individuals with black masks covering their faces, rushing inside the dining area, holding weapons, pointing, firing. . . .

"Down!" Logan shouts, grabbing my hand. Moving with lightning reflex, he pulls me automatically down, so we both hit the floor, lying on our stomachs between two tables.

I am not sure what is happening, but I see many feet, people stumbling, running in all directions. . . . Cries of fear and pain. . . . Bodies hitting the floor.

It's impossible to tell who's who, how many shooters are there—in that first vivid moment I remember seeing at least four masks, but I can't be sure.

Logan is holding me tight. After we fall, he sidles near, and now lies covering me with his body. I feel the rigid hard muscles of his arms and chest, crushing me to the floor as he whispers, "Don't move, don't breathe. . . ."

Temples pounding, I lie there, until we hear voices issuing commands in Spanish, Chinese, maybe some other language.

And then someone says in English, loudly, "Attention! This is Terra Patria. You are all going to listen and do as you're told. If you are *alive*, and on the floor, get up, now. If you don't get up, you will be shot. We start shooting bodies on the floor, row by row. Starting now! Get up if you want to *live!*"

Logan cusses under his breath. He locks his intense gaze with mine.

And then he and I both get back on our feet, very slowly.

We stand, looking at the meal hall full of fallen bodies, sounds of fear, soft weeping. About thirty people in addition to ourselves, are still alive, standing quietly all around the room, frozen in place.

The masked assailants are all dressed in the same uniforms as the rest of us, wearing armbands of all four colors, and Cadet stars. There are six of them, three male and three female, and they carry a variety of Atlantean weapons among them, including a few big guns and rifles. Where in heaven's name did they get those?

One of the masked guys, dark-haired, big and muscular, with a green armband, yells out, "All of you, move over to that wall, away from the food bar. Go! And keep your hands up, where we can see you!"

Holy crap, I *recognize* that voice. It's Trey. It has to be. Same big build, same a-hole swagger. And, Terra Patria, really? WTF?

Damn. . . .

We obey the instruction, and move in a careful hurry, stepping over the few bodies in our way, toward the back of the meal hall.

And then I notice, still seated in his chair, right where he's been eating, there's Blayne Dubois. At first, with an ice-cold shock to my gut, I think he's been shot dead. But no—I see a flash of his blue eyes registering mine—he is simply very, very still, staring quietly at us as we all crowd near his table.

I realize in that moment of horror that, without his hoverboard that's still stuck on the floor, Blayne *cannot* get up.

Chapter 17

We stand in a sorry crowd of very scared teens in the back of the meal hall. I glance at Blayne who's still seated and motionless, and move as close to him as I can. Logan moves with me, his fingers touching mine briefly.

The six shooters herd us up against the wall, and four of them remain while two move aside to whisper among themselves. Then I see one of the two, a girl, step away and quietly exit the room though the entrance, still brandishing her gun. I have a feeling she's been told to guard the entryway.

"All right, everyone!" Masked a-hole Trey speaks again, loudly. "This is what's going to happen here. You are all going to stand quietly against the wall and do what we tell you to do, or you get shot. Right now, remain quiet. Got that? *¿Comprende?*"

Some of the people nod, but most of us remain motionless and silent, watching.

While Trey is speaking, two other guys pace slowly, looking at us, while the two girls stand off to the sides, guns pointed.

"You—why are you sitting? Get up! *Now!*" A masked guy notices Blayne seated against the wall and points a gun at him.

Blayne blinks. "I can't, my feet don't work, sorry," he says softly. "I need my hoverboard just to stand. It's under the table."

"What the hell?" The guy steps closer. It looks like he's about to shoot Blayne.

"No, wait!" I exclaim. I'm trembling, and now my stupid big fat mouth goes into overdrive. "He really can't! He's disabled! Please let him be!" I say loudly in a high-pitched squeaky voice.

The guy with the gun whirls toward me. I see his eyes through the slits of his black fabric mask, considering me.

Trey, who seems to be their leader, hears and looks at us, then takes the steps to narrow the distance. He looks closely at me, then Blayne. "Hey, I know you two," he says crudely. "You're the 'special treatment' cases, aren't you? The girl who's not a Cadet and not a Civ, and the boy who's got the fancy hoverboard?"

As Trey speaks, I see Logan's eyes watching me with a very intense burning gaze. Oh, his gaze—it's pleading me to be careful. . . .

"So," Trey says, moving in closer to me. "You're what? An Aide to the CCO? That's just great! With him and you, we've got us a nice pair of bargaining chips. *And* a hoverboard!" And he kicks the table where Blayne is sitting, which is fastened to the floor, and doesn't budge. So he bends under to look for the board.

"What do you want?" I ask, watching his movements. "What do you hope to achieve with this? You just killed a bunch of innocent people!"

In reply I receive a hard blow against the side of my head from the other masked gunman who's right next to me. The impact sends me backwards, reeling, so that for a moment I see *black nothing* and stars. Logan's hands reach out and close around me, keeping me upright while I blank out, keeping me from falling. A few barely repressed gasps sound from the other hostages.

"All of you shut up! And you, *you* especially, just shut your mouth," Trey tells me, straightening, with the hoverboard pulled out from underneath the table and now in his hand. He approaches, dragging the inert length of orichalcum against the floor and leans in, hissing in my face, as I blink from the harsh blow. "But before you do, what's your name?"

"Gwen Lark," I mumble.

Trey smirks. "Okay, Gwen Lark! Now, we're going to make a few calls, and you'll be speaking for us."

He then sets down the hoverboard in the middle of the floor, grabs hold of my arm and pulls me forward.

"Hey!" Logan speaks up, trying to keep his hold on me.

"Let go, or you get shot in the face," Trey tells him, followed by an obscenity.

Logan grows silent and releases me, but his eyes are dark with fury.

The rest of the hostages are barely breathing.

Trey pulls me roughly behind him, and we approach the opposite side of the room with the food bar where a small wall computer console is visible. I step over the body of an Atlantean food server, a kid with metallic hair, no older than Gracie. He's lying on his side, glassy blue eyes wide open, still holding a stew ladle in one dead hand, while the large tray is overturned on the heating pad surface, globs of aromatic stuff dripping down from the counter. Blood is pooling from the wound on his chest and it's mixing with the spilled stew on the floor.

Suddenly I start to gag. I'm about to be sick all over my uniform, but I hold back the reflex, just barely. Glancing behind me, I see the crowd of hostages, Logan and Blayne among them. Many terrified eyes watch me move, while the armed assailants continue to point guns at them.

"All right, here we go!" Trey pushes me to the wall with the console. "Now, Gwen, baby girl, you're going to call up the CCO and ask for your commanding officer."

"And if I don't?" I don't know what kind of crazy crap in my head makes me say that.

"If you don't, I shoot your brains out."

I start to punch in the call. Immediately I get a low beep tone—a null signal indicator, meaning that there's no one in the office at the moment. Crap!

"Okay, it's not answering," I say. "He's not there. He's probably having dinner."

Trey leans in close to my face so I see the black fabric of his mask and his two glittering eyes. I also smell cheap musk body spray for men. "So, where would he be now? You know his schedule, right?"

"Actually I don't." And then I remember. Aeson Kassiopei works out before dinner. "I think he might be in the gym. . . ."

"Then call him there!"

"I don't know what gym—"

"Keep being an idiot and I start shooting your body parts.

Call him now!"

My pulse is thundering now, and honestly I don't know what to do. So I try something that Gennio had taught me about—a ship-wide general VIP intercom for public announcements only, otherwise a big no-no. Its use is reserved solely for Commanders, Command Pilots, Captains and other authorized high-end personnel.

I punch in the classified PA code, and speak into the console. "Command Pilot Kassiopei, this is urgent. . . . Please call Yellow Quadrant Cadet Deck Four Meal Hall—*right now.*" As I say the words, I hear my own unsteady voice amplified and echoing from the very walls of the ship around me.

There is a long moment of silence.

I start counting seconds in my head. *Four . . . Five . . . Six . . .*

"Well? Why doesn't he answer?" Trey pokes my shoulder with the muzzle of his gun. "Call again!"

I gulp. Then I begin punching the PA code again.

Before I'm done, the video display comes alive, and I see the face of Aeson Kassiopei, up-close, staring into the camera. The remarkable close-up reveals the stunning detail of his lapis-lazuli blue eyes highlighted in a shadow fringe of jet-black lashes, that natural "kohl" outline around the lids, dark eyebrows with the faintest hint of lapis gloss, straight nose and hard austere line of lips—altogether the face of a demon. He is grim with intensity, and his forehead is covered with a light sheen of sweat, with strands of pale golden hair sticking to his skin. As far as I can tell, his bronzed upper body is naked. . . . He must've been working out, because behind him I see the sparring area and walls of a gym.

"This is Command Pilot Aeson Kassiopei," he says in a cold hard voice. And he looks straight at me.

But Trey shoves me out of the way and keeps his gun to my chest.

"Command Pilot!" he says. "This is Terra Patria, and as you can see we have your little office Aide, and your favorite hoverboard boy, and a dining room full of other hostages. Sorry to say, we had to shoot about half of them, but still, we've got plenty more, maybe thirty-five people left alive here. So if you want them to stay that way, how about we talk?"

Aeson does not blink. "What do you want?"

"Straight to the point, I like it!" Trey shuffles momentarily, adjusting his grip on the gun, and then he points with the gun at the video screen and starts speaking, sounding like he's memorized a script.

"Terra Patria has several demands for Atlantis. First, you are going to take this ship and turn it around and head directly back to Earth. Second—you're going to take a detour to drop most of us off back on the planet, and then you will take the empty ship and fly toward the asteroid while it's still a good ways away from impact. Third—you will crash this ship right into the asteroid, going at full speed. The resulting multi-megaton explosion should take care of the asteroid, problem solved. Fourth—you will take your entire damn Fleet and get the hell out of our solar system, and never come back!"

A moment of silence.

Kassiopei's face is a frozen mask. "It's not going to happen," he says calmly.

Trey pokes my shoulder with his gun. "Oh, yeah? Well, that's not something we want to hear."

Aeson watches him. Then he glances at the rest of the room. "You know you're not getting out of this alive. Let everyone go, and I promise you a fair trial and your life, together with the lives of others in your group."

Trey cusses. "You're kidding me, right? So I'm going to begin shooting some hostages. Starting with *this* girl." And he strokes the gun across my chest, sweeping it to the left, to position it directly over my heart. "Gonna count to three, Command Pilot, and little Gwen Lark here is going to be one ugly bloody mess—"

Aeson blinks. "Wait," he says. And his voice becomes *hollow*, dark, unrecognizable.

Trey makes a snorting laugh. "What? What did you say? I don't think I heard you, Command Pilot—"

"I said, wait." Aeson looks at Trey with serpent eyes. "I am coming over."

"Oh, you're coming here? When?"

"Ten minutes."

Trey nods, again waving the gun that he's taken from my chest. "Great! Be here and we can talk terms and details. Because I promise you, if you don't, none of these people will be alive by the end of the hour. It's all on your head. Oh, and be sure to come alone. If we see guards with you, we start shooting hostages."

"I am on my way," Aeson says. "I will come alone. Harm no one." And the display screen goes dark.

I stagger back as Trey shoves me roughly and takes me back into the group of hostages, leaving me to stand near the wall next to Logan and some terrified girl Cadet.

"You okay?" Logan whispers.

I reply by widening my eyes. Because two guns are pointed at me and him.

"No talking," a masked girl says harshly.

So for the next ten minutes we stand, breathing and waiting. A few whimpers and sniffles sound around the room, but mostly there's silence. The gun-toting assailants seem high-strung. They talk occasionally in quiet tense voices, while pacing before us, and I can't tell what is being said. Furthermore, not all of it is in English.

At some point, Trey walks closer to the exit corridor and says loudly, "Jenny, can you see anyone coming?"

"Not yet," a girl's voice replies from outside the meal hall near the entrance.

And then, a few minutes later, her voice sounds again. "He's here."

Trey slaps his leg with the side of the gun and stops pacing. Through the mask, his eyes glitter with excitement. "Disarm him. Check carefully and take all the weapons he might have on him. Then let him in here."

"Okay...."

Another minute passes. And then Aeson Kassiopei enters the meal hall. His hands are lowered at his sides and he is once again fully dressed and wearing his uniform shirt.

Without saying a word he walks quickly toward the hostage takers, straight-backed and unyielding.

Trey orients in his direction, with his gun pointing at

Kassiopei. The other four masked Terra Patria members linger momentarily with indecision, some of them eventually deciding to keep their weapons aimed at us.

"Command Pilot!" Trey says. "Welcome! Come closer and let's talk."

But Aeson does not reply and keeps moving toward him. His face is frozen in a cold, expressionless, focused mask. When he gets to the middle of the room his gaze flashes with life. . . .

And suddenly, everything seems to go slow motion.

I watch as his hands move in tandem, wrists fly up and twist, strong elegant fingers flashing with impossible speed. And then he fires, with both hands simultaneously—rapid, multiple lightning-fast micro-volleys of pure laser light from two needle-guns—aiming perfectly five times.

At five different targets.

The first one to fall is Trey. He goes crashing down, and before he even hits the floor, Aeson Kassiopei is firing elsewhere.

Down goes the masked girl nearest me, with an exhaled breath and the hiss of scorching flesh and fabric. Then, a fraction of a second later, the guy nearest her, crumples. There's no time to blink, and the remaining boy and girl collapse in a lifeless heap on top of each other. . . .

Not one of them has had time to fire their various weapons.

Aeson Kassiopei stands in the middle of the room, breathing silently—a demon of destruction. He makes no sound, but I can see his chest rise and fall.

His glance sweeps all of us. Then he walks, stepping over the fallen bodies—both terrorists in masks, and ordinary innocent Cadets who had been shot earlier. At the console wall he pauses, keys in a security code. "All clear," he says coldly into the wall speaker.

As armed Atlantean guards move in from the entrance, the CP finally turns his attention to us.

"Is everyone okay?" he says, approaching our large group of hostages swiftly.

Then it's like a dam busting, as hostages start talking at him all at once. Voices rise, nervous, emotional. A few people hug, others sit down at the nearest tables and put their heads down in aftershock. "Oh, thank God!" some exclaim. Meanwhile others just yell out random expletives.

"F— me, did you see that?" a badly shaken Cadet behind us babbles with emotion, glancing from Blayne to me, to Logan. "He's a *maniac!* He just walked in and took out five people in two seconds! Alone and no backup! Oh, man!"

Blayne snorts in relief. "Yeah. That's why he's the CP."

"Thank you, Command Pilot!" a girl cries, with tears in her eyes. "Oh, thank you so much! I thought I was going to die! I really did! Wow!" She looks like she's about to hug him.

Aeson nods at her, at all the rest of them, as he moves through the crowd. He then raises one hand for silence. "All right, everyone!" he says loudly. "If you are injured, go to the medical deck immediately. If you need help getting there, security will assist you. Everyone else, please clear the room! As you exit, give your names and get processed by security at the doors, so we can keep track of what happened here. Expect to be briefly questioned at a later date, but there is nothing for you to worry about. Now, dismissed!"

He finishes speaking, and heads directly toward Logan and me.

Meanwhile, the Atlantean security guards begin moving all around the room, examining the fallen victims, looking for possible survivors, and dealing with the crime scene.

I must say, I am stunned, shell-shocked and kind of overcome right now. *I don't know what just happened.* When Aeson Kassiopei nears me at last—when he looks down at me in that very first second, with a very strange expression in his eyes, I don't know what it is, what to say, how to react to him.

"Lark, are you okay?" he says, standing directly before me.

"Oh yeah, I'm okay . . ." I mutter. "So sorry I had to use that PA system, I know I am not supposed to do that, I am so sorry—"

He motions with his head negligently. "You did the right thing."

"She got hit, hard, right here," Logan says, pointing to the side of my head.

Honestly, I'd forgotten! It's true that my head is kind of stinging in that spot near the side of my temple, and I bet I'm developing a honking ugly bruise.

Command Pilot Kassiopei examines the side of my head, and his expression becomes veiled, unreadable, somewhat distanced. He nods, coolly. "There's a swelling. You'll need to get to medical deck, as soon as possible, after we're done here."

"Oh, but I'm okay—"

But Aeson Kassiopei is no longer looking at me. His attention is now on Blayne, and he is inquiring if he's hurt.

"Just need my board back, and I'm completely okay, thanks," Blayne says with a light crooked smile. "No bodily harm, only damaged pride."

"Good." Aeson switches to Logan. "You're unhurt, Sangre?"

Logan nods.

"In that case, grab a gun." Aeson points to the closest fallen weapon on the floor near one of the masked Terra Patria. "And come with me. We're under attack."

I stare with confusion, but Logan shows no surprise. He leans down, picking up a mid-range handgun. He checks it proficiently, then retrieves a belt holster from the fallen, and attaches it to his waist. "Where are we going?"

"This was a distraction, an opening act," the Command Pilot says curtly, and begins to walk. At the same time he wordlessly signals a few of the guards, and they use wrist comms to relay low-voiced Atlantean commands to others elsewhere. Then they fall in line behind us.

"Yeah, I got that. Terra Patria idiots used by EU to create multiple attack points." Logan follows him, and I trail after.

"We're going to Command Deck Two. Apparently, guards there are not answering, so the assumption is, they're down. The CCO is currently *taken*." Aeson glances at Logan, then at me briefly, as we all move rapidly to the exit of the meal hall. "Your Earth Union ops did a clever number, agitating the Terra Patria so-called idiots and staging an incident here in the wide open public space, while apparently the CCO was the primary target."

"Too bad for them, you were elsewhere," Logan says.

"Too bad for the CCO, actually." Aeson keeps his face averted from us, looking straight ahead, so I can only see his three-quarters profile. "Yes, I've been varying my schedule, but not enough. I should have been at the CCO twenty minutes earlier. If I'd been there, the present *situation* developing in my office would not have happened."

I catch no glimpse of his eyes, but the proud disdain radiating from him is palpable. If I hadn't witnessed his amazing weapons performance in the meal hall just now, I would think him arrogant, but he is perfectly serious. *Holy crap*, I think, *he is absolutely confident his presence would've prevented the takeover. . . .*

And the truly scary thing is, he's probably right. After all, he just killed five people.

No, I take that back, *he killed six*.

Because, as we exit the Cadet Deck Four Meal Hall, the sixth terrorist—Jenny, the girl who was sent by Trey to guard the entrance—is lying there on the floor, only a few feet into the corridor, in a pool of her own blood. And she's still holding several weapons.

Aeson steps over her, then quickly leans down and picks up a standard handgun from her hand and returns it to his own empty weapon holster.

He then resumes walking quickly.

We follow.

Chapter 18

We walk swiftly through corridors toward the ship's interior where the Command Decks are located, crossing over into the Blue Quadrant.

Aeson Kassiopei periodically talks into his small wrist comm in Atlantean.

When we're just a few corridors away from the hub with the CCO, we pause. The CP touches a small section of paneling on the wall and calls up a display console. We stand and watch as he enters codes and a multi-screen mini-display comes alive. Surveillance images of the hallways around the CCO show two dead guards at the doors and three masked operatives standing with weapons. Another surveillance scene shows the interior of the CCO itself, where two masked individuals occupy the CP's own desk. Mech arms are supporting several monitors as they peer into them. One person is keying something into a console.

"If they've figured out how to use your general surveillance network and broken through even the lowest security levels, they can probably see us now, out here," Logan says in a low voice.

"Assume it is so," Aeson replies coldly. "It is likely they've also seen what happened in the meal hall, so there will not be an element of surprise. For the moment I've disabled the highest security access from the CCO, so at least they won't be able to affect the vulnerable ship systems from there."

"Are these Earth Union?" I whisper, standing next to Logan.

"Most certainly," Logan replies. "Notice their body positions and well-coordinated movements. Terra Patria was a disorganized mess. I'm sorry to say, my fellow EU ops are real military and far better trained."

"Is there a way to talk to them, maybe get them to recognize what's really going on?"

Aeson Kassiopei glances at me suddenly. "Lark," he says. "You need to be somewhere else. I want you to turn around and return to the Yellow Quadrant and go directly to the medical deck. Then get back to your personal quarters, lock your door, and stay there."

"I—I mean, okay." I blink tiredly. He's right, I'm not sure why I'm here exactly. This is kind of crazy. I have a concussion. I've just been in a hostage situation. And now I am surrounded by a bunch of military guys—Logan included—and taking part in a high security operation to retake the Central Command Office? WTF?

"Too late, she can't go back, at least not down that same hallway. They're coming this way." Logan points to a display of another corridor juncture, where half a dozen more masked terrorists are moving in a disorderly fashion but quickly, weapons drawn. Apparently Earth Union got more Terra Patria members involved. Or maybe these are yet another group of foolish teen rebels. At this point, who the hell knows?

My head *hurts*. It really hurts now. I definitely have a concussion.

"Not a problem. This ship's security patrols will soon be after them, cutting them off from behind," Aeson says. "But meanwhile they can do some potential damage here. So we need to keep moving." He then talks through his wrist comm again, and starts to walk, taking a turn at the next corridor junction.

Again, we all follow.

We pause a few minutes later, and I lean against the wall tiredly and watch the guards and the CP talk among themselves. We learn meanwhile, that similar hostage operations have taken place at all the four Imperial Command Ships.

"The flagship is safe. Commander Resoi's forces have isolated and captured the Earth Union operatives there," Aeson Kassiopei remarks to Logan, and glances at me casually. "Less fortunately, the situation at ICS-4 is not so good. Command Pilot Quarar Ritazet is one of the hostages. Now, tell me again, Sangre, what specific initial demands can we expect from your people?"

While Logan is talking quietly, I zone out momentarily, and think about how safe or unsafe it is, theoretically, to fire weapons on board a starship. Won't all these randomly fired lasers cut through the walls and all the layers of the hull, and depressurize us? Or doesn't it work that way? I recall the Atlanteans employ these funky purple plasma shields. . . . Do plasma shields serve as secondary airlocks and prevent pressure loss? How does pressure loss work, exactly?

Pressure loss. . . .

"Gwen?" Logan touches me on the shoulder gently. "Gwen, we really need to get you out of here."

I really must've zoned out. Because even Aeson is staring at me now, with his supremely intense *hull-piercing* gaze, while four of the guards stand checking weapons.

"It's going to get a little hot out here, very soon, so. . . ." Logan points me to the nearest cabin door. Apparently we're in another officers' residential corridor, and this must be someone's empty quarters. "Can we get this door opened for her, someone? Is there a security override to unlock—"

"No time!" Aeson Kassiopei interrupts, motioning to a guard. "Give her a gun, *now*."

And as the guard complies, handing me a standard handgun, there is an explosion of noise around the corner of the next corridor, and it's coming straight at us.

"Move!"

The CP's voice blasts us into action. Suddenly we are all running down the corridor, and everyone's firearms are drawn. I run the best I can, holding my gun in a shaking hand, while Logan pulls me by the hand behind him, faster, faster!

The corridor is long but there's a junction coming up ahead in about fifty feet, where we can make a turn and use the corners for staking out defensive positions.

Unfortunately before we get there, there is new noise directly before us. It's coming from up ahead where that same junction is—running feet and subdued voices speaking a mix of Earth English, Chinese, and Spanish. At least half a dozen masked and armed teens turn the corner.

Kassiopei is in the lead, with two guards, both of them in

the direct line of fire.

"Drop down!" he yells, and moves like lightning in the front position, putting one knee down, anchoring his leg with his boot, aiming two guns from the low stance, and signaling all of us to fall behind him.

Logan pushes me down forcibly before I know what's happening, so I end up crouching on the floor against the corridor wall, panting heavily. The rest of our group falls in line, all six Atlantean security. Four of them drop in similar floor positions next to the CP, while two bring up the rear behind us, so that Logan and I are protectively encircled.

And then in the next few split seconds a crazy thing happens.

Aeson Kassiopei *sings*.

His low voice goes dark and complex, forming a minor keying sequence. And suddenly the orichalcum panels lining the corridor start coming apart from the walls, ripped violently by the force of his command. . . .

They fly through the air and stop suddenly, levitate in place, standing up vertically, forming a protective barrier.

He is ripping the ship apart to do this, to create a barricade!

In principle it's exactly what I'd done during the Qualification Finals, in the flooding tunnels underneath the Atlantic Ocean, using hoverboards to barricade us against flooding waters.

Only here, it's a barricade against firepower.

Command Pilot Kassiopei concludes the sequence with the panels lining up four feet tall and three feet wide on both sides of the corridor, and a similar structure behind us, leaving a narrow opening in the middle. The result is four new barrier walls behind which we can hide from enemy fire. . . . Will it hold?

I stare in stunned wonder at the exposed metal hull interior of the corridor walls stretching all around us, showing wiring in places, and small air vents where the panels used to be.

Aeson goes silent, then signals for the security guards with a nod of his head.

It all happens in a matter of seconds, as the two groups of rebel terrorists converge on us from the two opposite sides of the corridor.

And then comes the firefight.

Aeson Kassiopei takes aim around the barricade walls, and his handgun fires precise calculated zing volleys. There are yells of pain on the other side, and the fire is returned. The guards take turns firing and pulling back around the barricade panels.

Meanwhile, a similar thing is happening behind us. The two guards in the rear start firing at the other group attacking us. With a single intense glance at me, Logan joins them, firing with practiced accuracy.

I cringe against the wall, holding the gun uselessly in my hand, wanting instinctively to put my head down and my hands over my eyes. Instead I freeze in place. My marksmanship is barely functional, beginner level at best. Usually I need both hands held steady on the gun just to hit the easy target at a firing range. Here, with moving real live targets, I'm useless.

Meanwhile, there is only *zing, zing, zing*, coming from all directions. . . .

My pulse pounds and seconds tick.

With my peripheral vision, I watch Command Pilot Kassiopei fire relentlessly. His profile is impassive, and he reloads periodically, hands moving impossibly fast to replace charge cartridges. At one point he glances behind at all of us, including *me*—hard blue eyes meeting mine in a searing gaze. He barks commands in Atlantean to the guards, and then resumes firing.

Moments later, a few of the terrorists attempt to storm the barricades.

A tall bulky teen rushes past the levitating panel barrier behind me, throws himself with a roar at one of the Atlantean guards, grappling with him, even though he's been scorched in the leg by someone on our side.

Logan and the remaining guard turn to deal with him, while two more terrorists come through.

In the crazy seconds while all of this is happening, it occurs to me to wonder if these are Earth Union or Terra Patria. No, they look out of control, disorderly, so must be Terra Patria. . . .

I raise my gun and press the trigger, firing in the general direction of the oncoming enemy. My hand shakes badly, and I only manage to scorch the opposite wall. A big girl with guns in both hands rushes through the opening, sees me, turns directly at me. . . .

I squeeze my eyes shut . . . this is it, *I am about to die.*

But the girl goes down immediately, her face scorched with a blast of lightning. She crumples in a pile at my feet, and I glance to my left, only to see Command Pilot Kassiopei at my side.

With one strong hand Aeson Kassiopei pushes me back against the wall and down. I can feel his hard painful grip against my arm, then the shoulder, as he leans in, covering me with his torso. Strands of his long pale metallic hair sweep against my face, as he immediately turns and fires again, his back to me, so that I am wedged between him and the wall.

I suck in my breath in terror, as the hum and whine and *zing, zing* sounds increase and multiply all around us, accompanied by the scorching hiss of metal, as more terrorists storm the barricade.

Aeson's powerful back is before me, and he is the only living barrier between me and the fire hell. . . .

In those instants I have no idea who else is out there, who's alive—Logan, the other Atlantean guards—no clue. I think I hear their voices, but I can't be sure, because the zing and screech of lasers is overwhelming.

"Lark! Gun!" Aeson cries to me without turning, reaching behind him with one hand. I relinquish my handgun to him, and he takes it to replace one of the two he's been using that must've run out of ammunition. Great, now he's out of cartridges. . . .

I continue to cower behind him, uselessly, as he resumes firing with my gun.

And then it's over.

A sudden silence comes. I can only hear his elevated breathing as Aeson straightens slowly and stands, breathing heavily. Before him is a pile of fallen bodies, and pools of blood. Levitating wall panels bob in the air lightly from the various hard impacts. . . . Two Atlanteans and Logan crouch with weapons bared, in various corners of the barricade.

Everyone else is dead.

Kassiopei puts out one hand with the gun up to signal

"wait," then slowly walks to look around the corridor. He stands in the space between barricades, looking in both directions, then announces, "All clear—for now."

We all rise from our spots. I find that I can barely stand, and my knees feel like putty from squatting tensely in a bad position.

Logan immediately comes up to me. His face is grim, and he has a few scorch marks on his sleeves where the lasers barely missed him. The other Atlanteans are similarly marked.

When Aeson Kassiopei turns again, I can see the front of his uniform. He also has burn marks on him, and his one shoulder has scorched fabric and a small red stain that appears to be his own blood. . . .

"Gwen! Are you okay?" Logan holds me with his both hands on my shoulders, examines my face gently.

"Yeah. . . . What about you?" I mutter, blinking with tension. And I continue glancing at the Command Pilot and the other two Atlanteans.

Aeson Kassiopei goes to examine the bodies of the fallen Atlantean guards. He touches a few of them gently, then straightens back up. . . . For one fleeting instant the look on his face is *different*. Then it goes blank.

Next, he speaks into his wrist comm in Atlantean. When he is done, he glances around and then quickly sings another note sequence.

The hovering orichalcum panels come crashing to the floor, suddenly inert.

We all stare at them for a few seconds.

But Kassiopei ignores them and turns to Logan and me.

His expression is guarded, cold, and yet it manages to affect me in a strange wordless way, so that I feel my throat closing up and an impossible tension building inside me . . . and suddenly I just want to weep.

I don't even know why.

Maybe because of all the *dead*.

Or maybe it's just the way he looks at me, as he stands there, *seemingly* cold as ice.

Because I realize suddenly, *it is only the surface*.

Inside, he is all fire.

"Sangre," he says in the meantime, glancing at Logan. "I want you to take her down this way, turn right and try any of the doors in that hallway. Use security code 58927 to override the locks. Make sure she gets inside and secures the door. . . . Then, return here."

"What—" I start to say.

But Command Pilot Kassiopei returns his gaze to me, and it scalds me with raw force. "Go with him. *Right now*."

I nod wordlessly, and start walking, with Logan holding me by the arm, so as not to trip over bodies . . . and all that slippery blood.

We turn the corner, try several doors, until one reacts to the security code and opens.

I pause, staring stupidly at it.

Logan looks at me gently. "Okay, you just saw how bad it is. . . . So you need to get *inside* and stay down. Don't open the door to anyone until we come back for you, okay? Not until this is over."

"Okay." I breathe faintly. "And yeah, I know. . . . I'm pretty useless, just a stupid burden. I'll get out of your way. And you—all of you—please don't get killed. *Please*."

Dazed, I watch Logan's grave face as the cabin door slides closed, separating me from him—from all of them—and shutting me inside a very small enclosed space, similar to my own cabin.

I tremble and take several deep breaths, like a stunned idiot. And then a sudden overflow of emotion builds up in the back of my throat.

It breaks inside me.

And I start to cry.

I stand crying silently, for I don't know how long, until my sobs turn into dry heaving shudders. At some point I end up seated on the bed bunk of a stranger, some unknown officer whose cabin I've taken over.

The motion activated cabin lights slowly dim, because I've stopped moving. They come back on gently when I raise my hands to wipe my face and rub the back of my nose.

There's no sound outside, only the soft steady hiss of circulating air through the cabin vents. I hear nothing through the door. Once again I wonder if the sealed doors on the ship are truly soundproof or if there's just no action out there. Are all of them—Logan, the CP, the two remaining guards—just being very quiet? Or are they even still in the corridor around the corner? They must have gone. . . .

Minutes tick. . . . I get up slowly and go to the tiny lavatory sink and rinse my face under running water, patting the bruised and concussed side of my head gently. My head feels puffy, swollen.

Suddenly there's a huge *explosion* outside.

Rather, it's the combined hiss and zing and whine of multiple Atlantean weapons being fired simultaneously at *very* close proximity, the pounding of many feet, people running, the shouts of voices, Earth and Atlantean, orders being issued, human cries. . . .

I freeze, my insides grown cold in horror, plunged into an overwhelming despair. Sounds like another gun battle is taking place in the corridor right outside.

Oh, God. . . .

I feel useless. I need to go out there and *do* something.

I need to help them!

But they told me to stay inside and wait. After all, what can I do?

I am not a soldier.

I listen, my breath suspended . . . *slowly exhale, slowly inhale*. My heartbeat is hammering.

A lull in the action and noise level. . . . Then the sounds redouble. More pounding feet, shouts, mixed voices. They move past the door and recede, going further down the corridor. Until it all fades.

Dead silence.

I stand, breathing.

Then I return to sit down on the cot. My fingers touch the fuzzy plain surface of the serviceable beige blanket.

And time blurs.

For the next two hours at least, I sit and listen to periods of silence followed by periods of activity outside. There are no more shots fired in the hallway, at least not like that one big flurry of explosive violence in the very beginning.... I hear groups of people moving past, mostly speaking Atlantean, so I'm assuming they're ship's crew and security forces.

My God, what is happening out there?

And what about my sister and brother? What's happening on Gracie and Gordie's ship? Is it being taken over too? *Are they okay?*

Terrible chaotic thoughts plague me.... I figure out how to call up a clock app on the small wall display, and it shows me 9:43 PM.

Stupidly it occurs to me that now I'm late to my 8:00 PM voice training with Command Pilot Kassiopei.

Holy lord... is Aeson Kassiopei even *alive?* And what about Logan, and the security guards? And for that matter, where's Gennio Rukkat and Anu Vei, the two other CCO Aides, I wonder in a sudden burst of panic. Did they get hurt when the CCO was being occupied?

I sit on the cot, and breathe, and see in my mind's eye the dead bodies lying around the meal hall. All those dead kids.... Even that awful a-hole Trey, dead and highly deserving of what he had coming—but he's only a stupid, evil, messed up boy.

He *was*. He's dead now.

All of them.

The wall clock shows 10:45 PM when the walls come alive with the sound of an amplified male voice on the PA system, steady, confident, wonderfully *familiar*. It startles me—pulls me out of a daze and makes me almost jump out of my skin—so that my heart starts hammering as I listen.

"This is Command Pilot Aeson Kassiopei. The situation on Imperial Command Ship Two has been contained. I am pleased to confirm that the rest of the Fleet is also back under control of Atlantean forces."

There is a pause. And then Kassiopei's voice resumes. "All crew and personnel on this ship, with the exception of special security and other designated sections—your orders are to return to your personal quarters, dormitories and barracks, and stay there until morning when we resume our regular ship schedule at 8:00 AM. At present I am establishing a ship-wide curfew. Stay in your quarters. I repeat, stay in your quarters. If you require emergency medical attention, enter code 117 from the nearest console. Medical personnel will be sent to you. This is all."

And there is silence.

I breathe in deeply, in a kind of quiet joyful relief that comes from hearing the living voice of a person that you thought dead. So, the CP is *alive*, and the situation is under control! But what about Logan? My heart races with a weird cocktail of new worry.

I stand up, and feel an immediate head rush—my head is definitely not doing well.

I consider going outside, but remember Logan mentioning that someone will come for me.

But Command Pilot Kassiopei did say, *return to your quarters*.

Just as I open the cabin door, step outside and take my chances, I see Logan walking along the corridor toward me.

And the corridor itself . . . oh wow, what a horrible ugly scene, just as bad as the other corridor we were in with the barricades. . . . Several fallen bodies, Cadets and Atlanteans . . . floor streaked with red, actual puddles of blood, scorch marks on the wall panels. It occurs to me in a bizarre aside, that apparently these Atlantean laser weapons don't damage the walls enough to pierce the hull. Because the door of my cabin looks terribly scorched on the outside, but none of it got through to the inside.

"Logan!" I exclaim weakly, and move toward him, meeting him halfway, and realizing that I am unsteady on my feet. "Thank God, you're okay!"

Logan looks exhausted and his uniform is more scorched, and splattered with even more red, but none of it's his own—at least I don't think. He's got a minor bruise on his jaw, streaks of grime around his hands, arms and elbows, even his uniform knees, where he must've been down on the floor again. Belatedly I recall that my own uniform is likely stained also after that horrifying meal hall hostage incident, and then the firefight in the corridor.

His face is grim, hair tousled, but he manages a smile for me.

"Gwen . . ." he mutters, taking me in a strong embrace. "It's okay, everything is okay. We got 'em. *All of them.*"

I hold on to him, my fingers grasping the back of his neck, and just breathe. He meanwhile nuzzles my forehead and gently touches the swelling on the side.

"Okay," he mutters after a few seconds of breathing into my hair. "Now let's take you to medical—CP's orders. He sent me to make sure. Not that I wouldn't have come for you on my own. . . ."

"He—he's unhurt? Everyone else okay too? Right?" I say in a daze, as we start walking, stepping carefully over slippery blood-stained floor panels, past bodies, on our way to the Yellow Quadrant. Such empty vacuous questions—I'm not even sure who I'm asking about, who's unhurt. *So many people died needlessly.*

"Oh God!" I come to a halt, my brain waking up. "I need to call Gracie and Gordie!"

But Logan shakes his head and gives me a reassuring squeeze. "Call them later. I'm sure they're just fine. Their ships were unaffected, remember? Only the four Imperial Command Ships were targeted."

I nod, and we continue moving.

Now and then, various Atlantean personnel and Earth Cadets and Civilians hurry past us in the ship corridors.

Logan supports me around the waist and tells me in snatches what happened in the last few hours—how they've re-taken the CCO and the rest of the ship.

I listen and nod, lightheaded, nausea rising in my stomach.

It has to be the concussion, I think. A few moments more of this walking motion, and I am going to be violently sick.

Chapter 19

The medical deck area is located in Residential Deck Four. There's supposed to be one in each Quadrant, but this one's closest to my residence, so Logan gets me there.

There's a line in the front waiting section when we arrive. Teens with minor injuries wait while those who are seriously hurt get seen first—typical triage. I see a few with bloody scratches, and several scorch wounds from the laser guns, but most are simply badly traumatized. There are quite a few Atlantean crew members among the more seriously injured.

A young boy hyperventilates. A girl Cadet is wheezing with an asthma attack. Two young kids babble incoherently about being betrayed by Earth, and how there's more secret terrorists coming for us, and how we're all doomed to die before we even make it to Atlantis. . . . The doctors and med techs move rapidly, taking us through to the back where the examination rooms are, but it's still at least half an hour until I get seen.

"A concussion," the no-nonsense young Atlantean medic says, shining a light in my eye and making me follow his fingers. He's another older teen, and I stare at his neatly trimmed short metallic hair and his angular chin, while he passes some kind of scan gadget over my forehead and then there's a tingling heat sensation along my skin.

"I've taken care of the worst of it. Now, get some rest, and have someone wake you every two hours," he tells me at last, turning off the machine.

"Oh?" I mutter. "I thought if you have a concussion you're not allowed to sleep at all, or you fall into a coma or die, or something?"

The medic shakes his head. "A myth, for the most part.

Your symptoms must be watched, but otherwise rest is good. Set a timer and have someone wake you to make sure your symptoms do not get worse. You are free to go."

I figure, this med tech has a huge line of other more seriously injured people to deal with. So I vacate the room, and Logan's waiting for me outside.

"I'll watch you tonight," he tells me, as we head back to my cabin on Command Deck Four.

I glance up at him, despite the heavy dull ache in my head that's aggravated by every movement. "No, Logan, that's crazy, you need your own rest," I say. "You've been in *battle!*"

But his hazel eyes are warm and he smiles lightly. "You make it sound so awesome. But, no, I'll stay with you tonight. That is, if you are comfortable with me being there, you know, alone with you in your cabin. Just you and me—" And he wiggles his eyebrows meaningfully, following it up with another slightly tired, slightly flirty smile.

"Oh, you—you, *silly.*" I blink weakly, attempting to smile also, and both of us stop at the doors of my cabin.

Inside, Logan turns his back while I threaten to hit him if he peeks, and hurriedly undress, wash up, then pull on my sleeping shirt and pajama bottoms. I lie down and he makes me comfortable on my bunk bed cot, covering me with the sheet and blanket, arranging it around me gently. Then he turns to the wall clock, which shows a little after midnight, and sets the alarm for two-hour intervals. I look at him as he sits there, watching me, soon almost nodding off in the narrow hard chair near the wall, just two feet away. Did I mention the cabin is a tiny closet?

"Logan," I mutter softly, as the cabin lights fade due to our motionless inactivity.

"Huh?" In the twilight I see him barely open his eyes, as his head is lolling to the side.

"Logan, get your butt here. . . . There's plenty of room for you to lie down."

He blinks, the glitter of his eyes more alert than it was a second ago. "Are you sure?"

"Oh, yeah." I scoot back against the wall, making room for him. "If you lie next to me, then you'll be able to tell if I die in my sleep from this concussion thing. Okay? I'm relying on you to *not* let me die, mister."

And I giggle drunkenly, both from tiredness, and from the stupid effects of the concussion, and just possibly from something the medic did to my head.

The cabin lights come on stronger, because Logan is up and moving. Without taking his eyes off me he removes his stained uniform shirt, then his boots and pants, so he's naked to the waist, only wearing his boxers.

Oh. My. God.

Yes, I'm injured and dead-tired. But still, I gulp and forget to breathe. . . .

In the next moment, I feel his solid muscular body next to mine. The bunk mattress makes a small creaking noise. There's only a thin blanket between us.

Logan moves slowly, gently to lie beside me, and puts one hand around me, the other behind his head. He arranges the pillow so that my head does not bump the wall. I rest my cheek in the crook of his arm. If I weren't so stupid-tired, I'd be melting now, melting at the wild, sensual, musky scent of him, all around me. . . . And if he weren't so stupid-tired he might be trying to nuzzle my neck and feel under my shirt.

Instead, he sighs, and closes his eyes. And then he falls asleep before I can count to five.

Apparently I fall asleep very soon after, because the next thing I remember is the voice of the ship's computer, pulling me out of a dreamless void.

"Now entering Uranus orbital perihelion. . . ."

"Oh, no! Uranus! I need to see Uranus! I mean, no, wait—" I mumble thickly, attempting to rise—causing the room motion sensors to increase light levels—and discovering that Logan's face is hidden in my neck, and he is breathing into my hair deeply, like a baby. Immediately he stirs, takes in a deep shuddering breath, grunts lightly, rearranges his warm arms around me, and then his one eye comes open. "What about my anus?" he mumbles with a sleepy mischievous little boy smile.

I groan and poke him in the ribs with my elbow. (Such perfectly-defined, muscular abdomen and ribs!) But he only grabs my hand around the wrist and strokes my palm with his thumb, sending an immediate sensual pang up my arm. He's smiling widely now, still partially muddled with sleep, and his jaw is slack in relaxation. I put my hand on it, and feel prickly new stubble. My, what a beautiful jaw line. . . . And yet again I think: *What in heaven's name is this perfect male specimen doing in my bed?*

"*Now leaving Uranus orbital aphelion,*" the computer says.

"A-a-and, so much for that sphincter. . . . I must say, that was rather fast." Logan raises one brow, watching me softly. "Did you notice how the intervals between those orbital passes are getting closer and closer together, despite the increasing unimaginable distances between planets?"

"Uh-huh. Hey, what happened to the alarm?" I say. "And yes, Sangre, I'm *not* dead, if you care to ask."

He points to the wall. "Look, still six minutes to go. The ship computer woke us early. And yes, Ms. Gwenevere Lark, you appear to be fully alive and fully functional."

But then he becomes serious, and gently turns my head to examine my bruised area. Each point where his strong fingers touch me rings with sensual awareness. "How does your head feel? Any different?"

I wrinkle my nose. "Still a dull ache. Not too bad, though. Better, I guess."

"No nausea?"

"Nope. But I need to pee. . . ."

He smiles, and starts getting up to let me out of the bunk. "Great. I'm going to turn to the wall, while you use the luxury facilities."

He does, and I do. It's a little awkward, but oh well. Then I get back in bed, and he climbs after me. We cuddle, for all of three minutes.

"Now, go back to sleep." And Logan leans in to brush his lips gently over mine.

I close my eyes, feeling the languid honey starting its flow, inundating me with pleasant warmth. I'm completely surrounded by Logan.

And I sleep.

In the morning, I wake up with the 7:00 AM "alarm" lights. I feel much better, no headache, but Logan is gone.

And then I remember. . . .

It goes like this:

At some point about two hours ago, he stirs lightly, barely rousing me with his movement, but not enough to fully regain consciousness—at least not at first. But in those first moments, as he moves restlessly in his sleep, I can feel something against the side of my leg. With only a thin blanket between us, I realize that his lower body is pressing against me, and oh wow, something is *down there.* Just as I come to the realization, he shudders and wakes up fully, saying, "Oh, God . . . sorry! Sorry!" And then he hastily pulls back from me and gets out of bed, turning around so that I cannot see the front of his boxers.

"Damn! My apologies, Gwen!"

I remember Logan's face in those moments, vulnerable and flushed at the same time, as he mutters with sleepy embarrassment, beginning to put his uniform back on. "Okay, it's almost time for your second alarm wake-up. And on that note—time for me to get out of here. . . ."

I remember staring at him, my own face starting to burn with a crazy red flush. And then I recall saying, "I think that *was* the wake-up alarm." *I can't believe that came out of my mouth!*

He laughs suddenly, and I put a hand over my face and laugh too, and the situation is diffused.

Before leaving, he dutifully checks me to make sure I can answer sleepy questions, and my head is not hurting any worse. Then he tucks the blanket around me, and leaves the room to return to his own Cadet barracks—even though it's still curfew.

That was two hours ago.

And now I yawn, sit up, and put my hand over my mouth, stunned to think what almost happened. Well, actually, nothing much happened . . . at least I don't think it did. I giggle to myself.

Poor Logan.

With the new day, the grim realities of last night come rushing in. On my way to breakfast at the Officers Meal Hall on Command Deck Two, I walk through ship corridors past other grave-faced people.

This morning, breakfast is served and eaten hurriedly, and

the meal hall is nearly empty. Few Atlantean officers are present, because I'm guessing the ship-wide cleanup is still going on, and everyone has been deployed to deal with it.

Last night Logan had told me some of the details of what had happened, but I was too sick to pay proper attention. And now I finish up eating and hurry to the CCO, arriving fifteen minutes early for the 8:00 AM shift.

The wide corridor that runs between the VIP offices including the CCO and the inner hub of the Resonance Chamber is filled with Atlantean personnel, mostly officers. Looks like a meeting is going on and it's spilled out into the hallway. There's a new set of guards at the doors, and I realize with a stab of sorrow that those two young guys I'd gotten used to seeing, are now *dead*.

The Command Pilot himself is standing right outside the doors, talking to the group of officers in Atlantean. He looks exhausted and extraordinarily serious. Judging by the bleak expression in his heavy-lidded eyes, the messy unkempt fall of his golden hair, and the shadow of stubble on his lean cheeks and jaw, he hasn't slept, washed, or even been to bed at all this night. At least he has a new uniform shirt on, without the grime and blood splatter. I suspect the main reason he bothered to replace it was to cover up that significant bloodstain from the seeping wound on his shoulder. . . .

I feel a gut-wrenching pang of worry. *I hope he had a doctor look at it!*

I stop and pause a few feet away from the crowd and suddenly notice Gennio's familiar curly head, and Anu right next to him.

Thank goodness, both the boys survived! I mean, Anu is a jerk, but I'm happy he's alive. And Gennio—oh, what a relief!

Gennio sees me and waves. "Gwen! There you are! You're okay, good! We're supposed to wait until the meeting is over then we can go back inside the office. We're going to be checking the systems for harmful sabotage and other possible damage—"

I nod and stop right next to them. "So glad you guys are okay too! What's going on?"

"They're going to be dealing with the Earth Union

prisoners," Anu tells me.

I blink. For some reason the notion that there would be live *prisoners* after this event never occurred to me. *Idiot me!* Of course there's going to be people alive from the EU side. "Oh, really?" I say. "Wow. What's going to happen to them?"

Anu shrugs. "They will probably go on trial and be executed for treason."

The way he says it, sends a cold chill of *reality* through me.

"Well, you don't know that for a fact," Gennio retorts. "They will definitely stand trial, but they were just soldiers following Earth Union orders, so not sure if execution will be warranted. It's a really unfortunate, complicated situation."

My mind is suddenly reeling. *Execution. . . .*

"How exactly did the CP contain the whole awful incident yesterday?" I ask, because suddenly now I need to know everything that happened.

And Gennio and Anu tell me.

"It was really intricate," Anu says, leaning against the hallway wall and folding his arms. "Excellent, smart strategy, exactly the kind that our CP is famous for. First, the four Pilots in charge of the Four Quadrants did a ship-wide sweep with their security teams, starting with the outside perimeter and moving inward, deck-by-deck. Then they surrounded the pockets of hostility. There were several fire exchanges—"

"You mean, firefights?" I say.

"Yeah. But they were all over quickly. Many terrorists got shot, the rest captured and sitting in security cells right now. Pilot Xelio Vekahat's Red team captured two of the Earth Union operatives, while the CP's own teams together with Pilot Keruvat Ruo's Blue teams got three more, plus a bunch of Terra Patria. The last one of the Earth Union ops was taken by Pilot Oalla Keigeri's Yellow team. Oh, and Pilot Erita Qwas's Green team got the remaining Terra Patria cells near Hydroponics and Storage."

"How did they get the CCO back?"

Anu snorts. "They gassed it."

"They *what?* Oh my God!" My mouth falls open.

"Oh, no, it's okay—it was just sleeping gas, sent in directly through the air vents," Gennio says mildly. "Actually that was the least violent part of the recapture. The Earth Union ops inside the office got knocked out, and then the CP's team went in with masks and just took them."

"Also the CP's idea," Anu adds thoughtfully. "Kind of funny, one kind of mask trumps another. Poetic too!" And he makes a whistling sound.

I stand, processing the information.

Meanwhile, I watch the Atlantean meeting in the corridor start to disperse. It occurs to me, all the Four Quadrant commanding officer Pilots are here. As more people leave, I finally notice Oalla and Keruvat, next to Xelio and Erita, talking at the doors of the CCO with Command Pilot Kassiopei and several other ranking officers I don't know. Eventually they too head out, and the CP returns inside the office.

As they pass Gennio, Anu, and me in the corridor, Oalla nods at us.

Meanwhile raven-haired Xelio gives me a lingering glance and a brief smile that goes all the way to his very dark eyes. *"Nefero eos, vati impero pharikone,"* he says to us in passing, but looks at me as he says it.

I stare in his wake in minor confusion, then glance to Gennio. "What was that?"

But Anu interrupts. "Hah! Just in time for your Atlantean language class. You have it today, right?"

I frown, thinking. *Wow, I didn't even check my schedule for today*, that's how thrown off I am by all the awful recent events. "Yeah, I think so. . . ."

Anu raises one eyebrow and says in a superior tone, "You think so? You should know, Earth girl. It's your class schedule, after all. By the way, want to know what Pilot Vekahat just told you? He said, 'good morning, Earth girl, you are like a putrid fish in a poo-poo bucket.'"

"No, he did not!" Gennio shakes his head, frowning. "He merely said, 'good morning, imperial aides,' to all of us."

Anu makes a rude noise. "Yeah, same difference."

"Anu," I say tiredly. "You are disgusting."

And then we get called in to enter the CCO.

Command Pilot Kassiopei stands next to his desk, adjusting the mech arms of various monitors and consoles that have been moved out of place while the CCO was occupied by the terrorists. His movements are tired, and as we enter, he turns around and nods to us to approach.

"Do a primary level deep sweep of the software and hardware in this office," he says to Gennio. "I want you to disassemble *everything* to board and component level and check for anything missing or anything that does not belong. Then run full diagnostics."

"Yes, Command Pilot!" Gennio immediately pushes his way through and starts climbing under the desk.

The CP turns to Anu. "I want you to do a line signal trace for all central net connections. Start with my office and cover all the primary ship systems. Watch for router anomalies, intrusions, and line diversions. Log everything you find."

"At once, Command Pilot!" Anu nods energetically and then moves in next to Gennio, and begins pulling apart wall panels.

Aeson Kassiopei stands watching them for a few seconds. He then turns to me, looks at my forehead and injured side. "How's your head, Lark?" I notice the tone of his voice is unusually bland, and his eyes are barely staying open.

"Oh, I'm fine, Command Pilot," I say. And then I keep going. "But I think you need to get some rest! Look at you—you're going to pass out! Did you get some medical attention for that wound? Please tell me you did! What happened here?" I point to his shoulder.

He watches me speak, and his lips part. He slowly raises one brow. Could it be actual *amusement?* For once I think he's too tired to hide it. "Your attention is noted, Lark, thank you. And now, in fact, I'm going to get some sleep. For the next two hours, I'll be in my quarters. I am not to be disturbed. The only exception is, if the Imperator calls here. . . . Or if there's more trouble. Otherwise, do *not* wake me up before 10:00 AM. Clear on that?"

"Oh, yes!" I say, and press my lips tight to hold back a wide smile of satisfaction. *He's taking my advice!*

Anu and Gennio glance up at him from their work, and voice their agreement.

"Good." Aeson Kassiopei nods. His gaze meanwhile is still glued on me. "Now, get some work done also. I believe you have a historical chronicle to write. Last night's unfortunate events should provide you with much new material."

"Yes, sir!" I say and put my hand up to my forehead in a silly version of an Earth military salute.

But he only shakes his head tiredly and continues to look at me with wide-open, very blue eyes. Yes, he's *definitely* too exhausted to reprimand me for impropriety.

"Just get to work," he repeats softly. Then he blinks.

And he turns away from me and leaves the CCO.

Chapter 20

For the next hour I try to concentrate on writing up the events of last night, while they're still fresh in my mind. As I key in my work, Gennio and Anu move around me in the office. Several times I am forced to save my file and wait while they disconnect me, check various systems and re-initialize the computers.

"Oh, not again, Anu! I just lost a paragraph of work!" I mutter in frustration, as the pasty-faced annoying boy pushes past me and pulls out a connector or a panel that makes my display go blank.

"Only one more connection check," he says. "Besides, your blogging can wait. It's not important anyway."

I turn my head at him and frown. "This is not blogging," I say in a hard voice. "I don't blog."

"Oh, yeah?" Anu glares at me while rolling up a length of network cable. "Then what is it?"

"I am recording events. Unbiased, without embellishment or expressing my own opinion. Blogging is mostly opinion and perspective. This is reporting factual events—*journalism*."

"Yeah, whatever." Anu rolls his eyes.

So I ignore him and continue typing. So far, I've chronicled the entire hostage incident, and then the corridor gun battle. Horrible images of the firefight resurge before my eyes, the *zing* of laser firearms, the falling people, the blood. . . . I visualize the levitating wall panels forming the crazy barricades, as Aeson Kassiopei fires his weapon relentlessly. . . .

And then something occurs to me. "Hey, Gennio?" I look up. "Can I ask you something? Yesterday, the CP was involved in a bunch of serious hostile exchanges. Why didn't he simply use a *compelling voice* to just command the terrorists to stop and surrender? I mean, wouldn't it have saved a bunch of lives—?"

As I speak, Gennio pauses whatever he's doing and looks up at me. And so does Anu.

"He can't do that," Gennio says. "If you mean the kind of *power voice* that *compels* others, that's illegal. Wait—how do you know about that anyway? It's really bad, Gwen. No one on Atlantis is allowed to use it."

"Except the Imperator." Anu corrects him.

"Well, yes," Gennio continues. "But the Imperator is not going to use it either, unless it's under very rare, carefully controlled special circumstances, such as formal ritual at Court, or during an emergency."

"Okay . . . but wasn't it an emergency yesterday?" I say. "I mean, if Imperial Crown Prince Aeson Kassiopei is going to be Imperator one day, don't you think he could make an exception, in the middle of a life-and-death firefight?"

Gennio purses his lips and frowns. "I don't think so," he says. "It doesn't work that way. By law, he may not, not until he is Imperator. There's a good reason it's illegal to *compel*. Throughout history, whenever the *compelling voice* was used, there were many bad reactions, damage to the minds of the recipients, and some awful side effects. That's why they stopped allowing it."

"Yeah, it causes irreversible brain damage in some people, and the effects in general are unpredictable," Anu says.

I watch them intently. "How so?"

Gennio thinks. "Well, for one thing, it doesn't always work the way it's intended. People's minds and brains are wired differently, so when they are compelled, they may do *weird* things. If you compel a person to drop their weapon, for example, one person may hesitate and fire first, *then* drop, so it's not safe."

Anu snorts. "Not to mention it affects *everyone* in hearing range. If the CP used a *compelling voice* during the fight, everyone, including his own security team, would be affected by the command. Can you imagine if the guards dropped their weapons too? Ha-ha-ha!"

"That's not funny." Gennio shakes his head at Anu.

"Wow," I mutter. "Okay. So how does the Imperator use it then?"

"As I said, during ritual, or under emergency circumstances. Such as during times of war. Even so, special earplugs are issued to the Imperial special forces. They put them in, in order to remain unaffected."

"Yeah." Anu nods. "Those earplugs are part of standard combat gear. In the old days they used to issue them to all soldiers because of random unpredictable enemy attacks. Now, just the special forces."

"I see. . . ." I take a deep breath, while various thought gears are turning inside my head. I remember now how badly Kassiopei reacted to my accidental use of the *compelling voice* on him, back at the NQC in Colorado. *Holy crap! I had no idea it could cause brain damage! I almost caused an injury!*

So, that explains many things. I was such a fool. . . . I tried to make him teach me how to use it, and he was justifiably angry.

Wow. Just, wow.

So I continue working on the chronicle, while the guys continue doing repair and diagnostics on the computers around the office.

Command Pilot Aeson Kassiopei returns to the CCO around 10:30 AM. He still looks grim and tired, but at least he's cleaned up, shaved, and wearing a crisp new change of clothing. And his eyes are once again clear and focused.

I've no idea how he's capable of such swift recovery. After only two hours of sleep I'd still be a pitiful mess.

"How is everything?" the CP asks the two Aides, without glancing at me.

Gennio and Anu report on the details. So far, it looks like Earth Union had not attempted any sabotage within the systems, but there was some non-standard comm line usage that was traced back to them.

"Good work, continue looking," Kassiopei tells them.

And then he leaves again, this time to deal with the incarcerated prisoners, various staff meetings, and other pressing business after the terrorist events.

"He won't be back for hours," Anu tells us, sniffling his nose loudly. "Let's redecorate the office. How about pink and orange?"

But Gennio is too engrossed in the diagnostics to even react to the stupidity.

Meanwhile, I check email and see a general in-coming text message with the Fleet logo. Apparently it's from the ICS-1 flagship to the CCO staff on all the four Imperial Command Ships. Commander Manakteon Resoi is going to be addressing the entire Fleet later today, to give an update on the situation. So I tell the guys.

"When is he speaking?" Anu asks.

"At five o'clock."

"Okay, plenty of time to get that inspirational speech ready."

"Well, he will definitely need to say something to raise morale," Gennio says. "Because I'm sure all the Earth refugees are very frightened and feeling uncertain right now."

"Myself included," I add.

It's true. I honestly don't know what to think any more—about *anything*.

And then I take a deep breath and ask. "What the terrorists claim about the asteroid, about how it was promised to the Earth governments that its impact could be diverted or minimized—is any of that true? Can Atlantis do that? Can you nuke it or something? Or move it more out of the way?"

Gennio frowns. Anu widens his eyes.

"I really doubt it," Gennio says. "The asteroid is huge, remember? It's the size of a small planetoid. Even if we blasted it with various weapons, it would not be enough. In fact, I believe they already tried doing some of that. Remember, the various joint expeditions, with Earth oversight? They landed on the surface, Earth and Atlantean teams. They did all kinds of things. That was months ago."

"Okay," I say. But at this point I'm not entirely convinced. And although I believe that Gennio—and yes, even Anu—are telling the truth, I also believe they may not *know* everything.

So that leaves one thing. At some point I will need to ask Command Pilot Kassiopei.

After lunch, I have my 1:00 PM Pilot Training class. When I get to the classroom area, the Cadets are talking loudly in a small crowd, some arguing in nervous high-strung voices, and no one is rushing to claim the flight simulator desk console seats.

I sit down at an empty desk and look around, hoping to catch a glimpse of Blayne Dubois or Logan Sangre. Neither of them is here yet.

There's also the noticeable absence of Trey, the Terra Patria terrorist. And his friend, the alpha girl with the purple-streaked hair is missing also. I bet she was one of the terrorists too, probably got gunned down in the meal hall with Trey. . . .

"Hey, anyone seen Trey Smith?" I hear a familiar boy's grating voice, and it's my partner Hugo Moreno. He's talking to a couple of Blue Cadets.

"He was one of them, got shot by the CP himself," a Cadet says.

"Really?" Hugo whistles. "No way! Too bad."

"Yeah, well . . . Terra Patria. Screw 'em with a yardstick." And the Cadet cusses.

"What about his chick, what was her name, Brie? Gabriella Walton? Purple hair?"

"Yeah, Brie Walton. Not sure. I think she's alive. Supposedly she was with the other group, Earth Union. So, probably a prisoner. Unless they shot her too. . . . Anyway, Trey was just a stupid dick. But she was smart, one of the masterminds. . . ."

"Oh, yeah?"

They continue to talk a few feet from me, and then Hugo looks around carelessly, sees me and gives me the usual semi-hostile look of disgust.

Today I don't bother saying anything, not even "hi" to him.

When the Instructor arrives, we come to order, and resume working on our shuttle flight scenarios. Instructor Mithrat Okoi is grim, impassive, and gets right into the class material, and does not say anything about what happened yesterday, which is probably for the best.

A fter class, I return to the CCO at 2:30 PM, and the two Aides are mostly done with the tech diagnostics, while the CP is still not in the office.

"He hasn't returned yet," Gennio tells me.

"Yeah." Anu looks up from his console. "Meanwhile everyone's been calling him. The Atlantis Central Agency's Presiding Corrector and like his entire ACA office has called directly from Poseidon's Imperial Court, in regards to the Earth Union prisoners. Oh, and of course there's Consul Denu—the Consul 'respectfully demands' to see the Imperial Lord as soon as he is available. And he's been calling every half hour. Oh yeah, the CP's really going to love *that*."

I listen to them talk, then pull up my own console. According to my schedule, my other class today is Atlantis Language, at 4:00 PM, so I have time to do some tasks.

As I sit working, it's as busy as they say. Calls keep coming in, as the main video monitor resonates with various musical tones every few minutes. Gennio takes the incoming calls dutifully and I hear him reply in a formal polite tone in Atlantean, then take messages and disconnect. Several times I recognize the whiny nasal voice of Consul Denu.

Every time the Consul calls, Anu holds his nose, makes a fanning motion with the other hand, and looks at me.

I roll my eyes.

At about 3:30 PM, Command Pilot Kassiopei finally returns. He walks in, and his expression is like a thundercloud. Has he been interrogating prisoners? Dealing with his security teams? Disposing of the dead? Whatever it is, I don't dare to ask, and it's really none of my business.

Gennio relays all the messages, and the CP nods at him, then gets in his own chair and starts calling people back.

In a few minutes, while Kassiopei is on a call with some security personnel, there is an incoming buzz from the guards at the door. Apparently, Consul Suval Denu is here in person, to see the CP.

Command Pilot Kassiopei looks away from the video screen and frowns. "All right, send him in," he says tiredly, then ends his current call.

The door opens and Consul Denu enters, in his great golden

wig, and attired in a white robe trimmed with scarlet and gold. A whiff of flowers, fruit, and musk precedes him.

The moment the Consul steps inside and sees Kassiopei, he immediately bows deeply to the waist and performs an intricate gesture with his hands, which is both ridiculous and elegant at the same time—I can't explain how, it just is.

"What bright pleasure it is for this Humble Servant to see My Imperial Lord Kassiopei on this day," says the Consul, with an ingratiating smile, speaking English. "I hope My Imperial Lord is well and might receive the Compliments of Light—"

In reply, Aeson nods at him and interrupts, while his own voice and intonation becomes more formal than usual. "My dear Consul Denu, please, no need for Court ceremony. As I've told you many times previously, while we are in the Fleet, under military jurisdiction, I expect you to do me the courtesy of treating me as an Imperial officer, not a prince. Now, what can I do for you?"

"Ah, but My Imperial Lord, you present me with such a dire commandment, for it is nigh impossible to forget the bright presence of the Imperial Crown Prince and glorious hero of Ae-Leiterra, and son of the Imperial House Kassiopei of *Atlantida*—"

"Enough, *please*." Aeson puts his hand up to halt the Consul's speech. At the same time he glances briefly at us, and his gaze meets mine in a fleeting moment of intensity before moving on. I notice his face is starting to flush with color.

It's kind of wild, because *I have never seen Aeson Kassiopei blush before. . . .*

And it looks amazing. Aeson's bronzed skin acquires a deeper rich tone, and he looks truly flustered, and kind of, well . . . *charming*.

I stare at him in curiosity, and listen as Consul Denu continues to heap exorbitant praise and superlatives, while at the same time begging excuses for doing so. It occurs to me—the Consul is far more *sly* than he lets on. He is also doing all of it in English, and I wonder if some of it is for my own benefit, because he glances at me and the other Aides as he speaks, as though to check our reaction.

At last he comes to the point, and basically it's nothing

more than a social visit. Apparently the Consul simply *had* to present himself before the Imperial Lord, and reaffirm his desire and pleasure in offering his continued services in the educational capacity.

"Yes, thank you," Kassiopei tells him. "I value and appreciate your time and effort in educating my newest Aide in Court Protocol."

"After only one class, and a minor incident of tardiness, the girl is proving herself to be a promising pupil," Consul Denu says, glancing at me benevolently.

"Good. But now, I do believe she has another class to attend." And the CP looks meaningfully at me. "Lark, you have Language at four?"

"Yes," I say.

Kassiopei nods. "Then you must get going. And be sure to see the Consul out, as unfortunately I have other pressing business having to do with the tragic events of yesterday—"

"Why, yes, yes, of course!" the Consul exclaims. "I must indeed get going myself, for I must never be in the way of My Imperial Lord's duties at this difficult time! Yes, indeed—"

And that's how Consul Denu and I both find ourselves outside the CCO, and the office door shuts behind us.

I make hasty excuses to Consul Suval Denu and flee his perfumed presence.

My first official Atlantis Language class is held in the Yellow Quadrant Residential Deck Four. The classroom is similar to the one where Culture class was held—basic austere desks, no computer consoles.

I arrive early, and watch the classroom area fill to capacity with an even mix of Civilians and Cadets, of all the four Quadrants. There's no one here I know. No, wait, one person who looks slightly familiar—the big and husky Asian girl from my Pilot Training Class, the one who together with her partner were the last ones to finish the flight simulation yesterday. She has a round face and a permanently stressed expression, and barely fits in her seat. Her uniform, with its Cadet star and green armband, also seems to be a tight fit, straining her shoulders and seeming a bit short in the sleeves and legs. In addition to everything, it probably doesn't make things any less awkward for her.

I figure, what the heck, and sit down next to her.

"Hi," I say, with a smile. "I'm Gwen Lark, and we have the same Pilot Training class. The one with all the awful shuttle flight simulations."

The girl is silent and stares back at me with immediate alarm, as though she doesn't expect any good to come from interactions with strangers.

"Sorry," I say. "You speak English?"

"Yes. . . ." Her reply comes after a long pause, in a deep soft voice.

"What's your name?"

Another pause. "Chiyoko Sato."

"Nice to meet you." So, I think, sounds like she's Japanese. And it's still unclear if her English is sufficient to communicate.

Before I can say anything else, our Language Instructor arrives in the room.

She is a petite, exquisitely beautiful teen with delicate features, medium brown skin of a hue somewhere between olive and bronze, shoulder-length metal gold hair with straight bangs cut across her forehead so that they almost cover her kohl-dark brows, and a dreamy expression. Her uniform sleeve sports a yellow armband.

The Instructor stops in the front of the class and turns to us, saying, *"Nefero dea, scolariat!"*

Her speaking voice—oh, it's like song. Pure, resonant, gorgeous. And it's especially amazing to think so, considering that every single person here can sing and is musically inclined, yet she still manages to stand out.

"Good afternoon, class!" she repeats, this time in English. "I am Chior Kla, and I am your Atlantean Language Instructor."

The classroom full of Cadets and Civilians watches her with growing interest.

Instructor Chior Kla smiles at us, and looks widely around the room. "All of you, you are so fortunate," she says. "Your Earth languages are all so beautiful! So intricate, glorious, musical! On my way here, I have spent many months studying the various language families and groupings that Earth has produced since the last time Atlanteans were here with you, sharing the planet of our origin. Most languages have common roots, like great trees and vines, and many of them entwine lovingly, mixing together to form new hybrids. At the time of Old Atlantis, our vibrant language was thriving and giving offshoots, which later became your Ancient Egyptian and Ancient Greek, among others. Thus, when you study the language of *Atlantida*, you will recognize many roots of words that you already know in your modern languages."

Instructor Kla pauses. "How many of you have studied a language other than your native language? Raise your hands!"

I glance around me and see most hands go up, including my own. Next to me, Chiyoko Sato also raises her hand.

"Oh, wonderful!" Instructor Kla exclaims. "Then you already know what it's like to think in a different way about the same thing. Because that's all a new language is—a slightly *different* way of thinking and looking at the same world. It's like putting on multi-colored sunglasses. It enriches your thought processes and blows up your imagination like a balloon. And it gives you the mysterious power to express yourself to others who normally might not be able to understand you."

Chior Kla paces among the rows of our desks, and looks at us. "Now, I will tell you a secret. But first, I ask you this—what do you think is the *purpose* of language?"

A girl behind me raises her hand. "Is it to communicate?"

Chior Kla smiles. "Of course, but that's just the most obvious purpose of language. What else?"

"To share your own life with other people?" a boy says.

"Definitely. What else?"

I raise my hand with excitement. Yes, here I go again, me and my super-uber blab power taking over my mouth. "I think, language gives you the ability to become someone else," I say. "When you speak, you are no longer you, but a vessel for the *thing* that must be expressed, the meaning."

Chior Kla pauses and nods at me. "What is your name, Civilian?"

"Gwen Lark," I reply. Again, not going to correct the misconception that I'm a Civilian.

"Thank you for a wonderful new insight today, Gwen Lark.

Because you have illustrated one part of the secret I am about to share."

And then she looks around at us, and her eyes—which I notice are the color of yellowish-orange amber—are filled with poetry. "The secret purpose of language is to *change everything*. And by everything I mean, your life, the life of others, the planet, the universe itself. Language is action, movement, life itself. It initiates progress, evolution. Language creates. If I recall correctly—in one of your ancient Earth holy books, there's the notion that 'in the beginning was the word.' I think it's a beautiful metaphor. Because if you think about it, the world itself is made up of metaphors—meaningful thought and image constructs."

"Okay, this is too weird. I'm getting a big-ass headache," a boy whispers behind me.

But most of the class is listening with curiosity. Because, yeah, this Instructor is definitely a little weird, but that's what kind of makes her weirdly irresistible.

"Now, you might have studied *metaphors* and *similes* in your own language classes back on Earth," says Instructor Kla. "Who can tell me what they are?"

My hand shoots up, but so does a whole bunch of other people's.

"Yes?" Instructor Kla nods to the girl right next to me—Chiyoko Sato.

"Similes and metaphors are both figures of speech," Chiyoko says, in a clear deep alto voice. "They both let you describe and compare things by means of analogies or abstractions. A simile uses comparison words 'like' and 'as,' while a metaphor uses the word 'is' or any other, to describe. For example, 'my heart is like a flower' is a simile, while "my heart is a flower' is a metaphor."

"Nicely said," Instructor Kla says. "What is your name, Cadet?"

"I am Chiyoko Sato," the girl repeats, this time in a less enthusiastic manner.

"Thank you, Cadet Sato. Metaphors and similes are just some of the many parts of speech, complex constructs made up of words to convey meaning," Instructor Kla continues. "How many of you know what a *synonym* is?"

A dark-skinned boy says, "That's just a word that means the same thing as another."

Chior Kla nods at him, then once more turns to all the rest of us. "What if I told you that the word 'heart'—or *corazón, coeur, sertse, sin, seert, herz, hart, cuore, uummat, cridhe, kardia* or any other of the thousands different language forms of the same thing we all have beating inside our chest cavity—is just a synonym? Because you can think of different languages as merely *vast groups of synonyms* of each other. So the more languages you learn, the more words you know to mean the same thing—which makes each thing you know that much more rich, powerful, wonderful! Suddenly that thing inside your chest—that coeur, sertse, heart—is no longer merely *one*, but *many!*"

I admit, my mind is racing with excitement. I find that now I am listening with all my heart—if such a thing is possible.

"And on that note," Chior Kla says, Let us begin learning the beautiful language of *Atlantida*, a proto-language for so many of your modern ones."

For the next half an hour, Instructor Kla teaches us some basic words. We all learn the Atlantean greeting "good morning," "good afternoon," and "good night," which is *nefero eos, nefero dea,* and *nefero niktos*. And then we learn how to say goodbye, which is *hetep-nete*.

We also learn that Atlantean nouns have genders—male, female, and neuter—and that some words have different meanings if they are *sung* as opposed to merely *spoken*.

Okay, that kind of blows my mind. . . .

"Forget the basics, what I really want to know is some juicy Atlantean cuss words," a boy says to his fellow Cadets and Civs, as they laugh on their way out of the room, as soon as we are dismissed.

I say bye to Chiyoko, the Japanese girl next to me who seems to have such a nice command of verbal knowledge. I'm definitely impressed.

She only nods shyly without even looking me in the eyes, and heads out, walking with a slouch as if to hide her big shape and height.

Next, instead of heading to dinner, I return to the CCO. I remember about the speech that the Fleet Commander is going to give at five. I should be there to hear it with the rest of the CCO staff.

When I get there, Anu and Gennio are working inside, and so is the Command Pilot who, as usual, is talking to someone on the video screen in Atlantean.

Now that I've had some basics, I find that I suddenly appreciate the lilting beauty of the language he uses. . . . And it certainly doesn't hurt that Kassiopei has such a deep, pleasing voice.

"Gwen!" I look up and Anu is poking me with the end of a digital tablet stylus. "So, what did you learn? Can you speak Atlantean now?"

"Oh, yeah," I say. "*Hetep-nete,* Anu."

Anu makes a horse-laugh sound while Gennio chuckles. Command Pilot Kassiopei peers at us with a minor frown then resumes his current video conversation.

We all shut up.

A few minutes later, it's time for the Commander's speech.

The ship's PA system comes alive with the strong measured voice of Commander Manakteon Resoi.

In that moment, I think pretty much everyone hearing this is a little afraid of what he's about to tell us.

Chapter 21

"Good afternoon, young people of Earth and Atlantis," Commander Resoi says. "The regretful situation of last night has been resolved, and the terrorist factions are in custody. In the next months, they will be further investigated and tried for their criminal activity. In the meantime I grieve with all of you for the great loss of lives, especially at a time such as now when every human life means so much to all of us.

"I want you to be secure in the knowledge that none of this will happen again. For as long as you are in my Fleet under my protection, you have my promise, and the promise of the Atlantis Central Agency, and the Imperator Himself, that your lives, and the precious lives of everyone undergoing this journey are safe.

"You, children of Earth, are *safe from harm*. And your continued presence on these Ark-Ships will from now on be a positive time of learning, fruitful effort, and mutual cooperation between the crew and the welcome refugees."

Commander Manakteon Resoi pauses, allowing the meaning to sink in. And then he continues. "Today is the third day of your formal duties in the Fleet. To mark the occasion of your entry into the life and routine of Atlantis, I designate a formal Celebration Day in three days from now—it will approximately mark the time during which we will be leaving the heliosphere of your solar system and entering interstellar space. As the Fleet moves through the Oort Cloud, on this first calendar month of Blue, the Blue Quadrants on each ship will host a Zero Gravity Dance. You will learn more about this joyous event from your commanding officers, and you will at last have the opportunity to experience a true ancient tradition of Atlantis."

The Commander's speech ends.

Gennio and Anu glance curiously at the CP who sits at his desk, to gauge his reaction. But Aeson Kassiopei is silent, grave and thoughtful.

"This is good, isn't it?" I say at last. I remember the excited big deal my Culture Instructor had made about this Zero-G Dance stuff. I'm definitely curious to learn more, even though I likely won't be taking part.

Because yeah, in case it's unclear, *Gwen Lark the Dork does not dance*, doesn't know *how* to dance, and doesn't *want* to know.

Instantly I'm reminded of the essence of living hell that is high school dances, and the horrible lonely wallflower experience I've had during the few that I've regretfully attended at Mapleroad Jackson High, back in Vermont—mostly by force, due to the evil machinations of my best friend Ann Finnbar.

So, yes, normal teen dances are the worst atrocity perpetrated upon klutzy nerds like me. But Gwen the Dork (still speaking of herself in third person) is more than fascinated by the physics and mechanics of this space version of the thing. I mean, *zero gravity dancing*, wow!

As I think all this, Aeson Kassiopei gets up and turns off the nearest monitor. "I am heading to dinner," he says coldly.

"No gym?" Anu asks.

"Not today."

And the CP exits the office.

"Well, *he's* in a bad mood," Anu mutters, glancing at us as the door closes.

"Why?" I ask.

Gennio looks at me. "I think the CP feels this is poor timing. Dancing is frivolous, and we've just had a tragedy. So much still going on. All that recovery work left to do."

"Besides, he's never been a fan of dances, especially since he has to deal with all that crap at the Imperial Court. He really hates dancing," Anu says with a snort. "He has to dance with all those court ladies who throw themselves at him."

"Something we have in common," I mutter, momentarily imagining Aeson Kassiopei in a grand ballroom surrounded by crazed girls in fancy outfits that look a little bit like the fashions worn by Consul Denu. "Not the 'court ladies throwing themselves at me' part, but the 'I hate dancing' part. But I'm really eager to learn how the Zero-G part works."

"Let's go to eat dinner, and I'll tell you all about it," Gennio says.

We eat at the Cadet Deck Two Meal Hall, among crowds of mostly subdued teens, still recovering from the bloody ordeal of yesterday. Gennio and Anu blab non-stop about how the Resonance Chamber will be set up for the Dance, and how they will likely have to do a lot of the preliminary tech setup.

As I listen, only with part of my attention, I keep thinking about where Logan is, and how my sister and brother are doing, and for that matter how Laronda and the rest of my friends are.

"So there are all these layers of sound-sensitive orichalcum panels," Gennio is saying. "And they line the entire Resonance Chamber, floor and ceiling."

"Uh-huh," I reply, taking a bite of my sweet-sour-savory noodle and greens dish called *varoite*.

"And the floor panels are the most fun part. Because they will be levitated up and down during the dance, each section separately from the others, so that people end up on different levels, and then when the gravity drops out, *you fly!*"

"Wow," I say. "I still can't really visualize it, but I guess I'll see it in action."

"Oh yeah, you will," Anu says. "Because it's part of our job to make sure the tech behind the Zero-G works properly, and in time with the music. Blue is hosting this first dance, so the CCO has to get involved, whether the CP likes it or not. I mean, he'll probably farm out the official welcome announcements stuff to Pilot Keruvat Ruo, but still, he'll have to make an appearance—"

"Okay, now I'm a little confused," I say. "Why are we, the CCO, involved, exactly? Isn't Pilot Ruo in charge of the Blue Quadrant? So, how is it the CP's business?"

The Atlantean gives me a look, this time as if I'd said something truly ridiculous. "What else would it be? It's *his* Quadrant."

"Wait, *what?* Oh . . ." I exhale. Suddenly a whole lot of

things snap into place and become clear. "So—does it mean that before Command Pilot Kassiopei got to wear the *black* armband he wore *blue?*"

"Yes, of course." Anu grows silent, almost respectful. And then he ruins it and adds, rolling his eyes at me, "What did you think, stupid Earth girl?"

I raise my brows. "Well, actually I didn't think anything. . . . I mean, I didn't really *know*. How could I?"

"Yes, our CP originally pledged himself to Blue," Gennio tells me. "He is the best marksman in the Fleet—that's a Blue distinction. In Fleet School, he ranked in first place for marksmanship. He was so far ahead of everyone else that he broke the curve. He can shoot multiple targets with his eyes closed. And he can shoot faster than anyone in recent history."

"Okay," I mutter, thinking about what I've witnessed during the meal hall hostage shootout. "I can believe that. . . ."

At that point the guys forget about the Zero-G Dance and start talking about target practice scores, so I zone out, and finish my dinner mostly with my own thoughts.

A little before 8:00 PM I head back to the CCO for my voice training. It's been a long day, rather unexciting compared to yesterday, but with much thinking in retrospect. As I walk the ship's corridors, I see cleanup still happening, as Atlantean crews scrub and sterilize decks, and wash the blood residue from the floor and wall panels.

Where are the bodies? What happened to all those people who died, both Earth and Atlantean? The grim thought plagues me.

The guards at the CCO doors let me pass, and I find Aeson Kassiopei is inside. He sits before a darkened screen, leaning back in his chair, hands resting behind his head, eyes shut.

The moment I walk in, his eyes fly open. "Lark," he says. "Good, you're here."

"Sorry I'm a little early," I say, feeling a familiar elevated pulse beating in my temples, which happens every time we're alone.

"There will be no voice training today."

"Oh?" I pause.

"Instead, you will come with me." He gets up from his desk and I turn after him in confusion.

"Where are we going?" I mutter, trying to match his long stride as we walk outside past the guards, and head down the corridor.

But Aeson Kassiopei does not turn to look at me, and doesn't say anything. We continue walking past several sections of Command Deck Two, then cross over to the Cadet Deck, and continue to the Residential Deck, all the while moving outward, away from the hub center of the ship.

Finally, in a long dimly lit corridor designated as Storage—which I only know from studying the ship's layout map, never having been here before—we pause before a series of doors leading into a closed and isolated sub-corridor section. In other words, we will have to go down to *lower* levels—something that again I've never done before on an ark-ship. Everything I know so far is located on the same main ship level—Command, Cadet, Residential Decks, the central hub with the Resonance Chamber, the space observation deck, et cetera.

What's down there? I believe some of it is designated as Hydroponics decks, and the rest? More storage? Machinery?

As I stand and wonder, Aeson Kassiopei takes out a key access card and swipes it over a security panel. The doors slide open, and we are inside another corridor that stretches for about twenty feet and then ends in a corkscrew metal staircase.

The Command Pilot goes down the stairs first, and I follow, our boots clanging against metal. The echoes here are significant, by their acoustics suggesting the presence of more metal.

We keep going down the dizzying spiral of stairs, passing several levels marked with Atlantean numerals. When we get to Five, we come to a stop. There are more levels below, but Aeson Kassiopei steps off and enters the corridor on Five. It is long and dimly lit also, as though there's a need to conserve lights, or maybe no need for them.

Rows of doors fill both sides of the corridor. Two sets of guards patrol slowly down its length. The CP swipes his key card over one door, and we enter.

The room is small, dimly lit, and there is no one else inside.

However, one whole wall is a one-way observation window into a brightly lit small cell—a questioning room. The cell is bare of furnishings except for a hard table and two chairs. Two people are inside, sitting across the table from each other.

One of them is Logan Sangre. The other is a girl with long dark hair with purple streak highlights and a red armband. She has a dark bruise on her face, while her hair and uniform is a mess. I recognize her as Trey Smith's girlfriend, Brie Walton.

A single untouched glass of water stands on the table before her.

"Oh my God . . ." I whisper. "What's going on?"

What's Logan doing here?

Aeson Kassiopei glances at me. He then touches a console near the wall and suddenly I can hear what's being said in the other room, as if I'm there.

". . . Tell me, when and where was the order given? All I need is the time and location," Logan is saying in a cold measured voice.

The girl says nothing, only continues staring at him from underneath dark straight brows. She is both fierce and strangely calm at the same time.

And then at last I understand. *Logan is interrogating her.*

"Sangre has been working here all day," Kassiopei says suddenly. "He is good. I am impressed with his methods. He succeeded in getting two of the Earth Union to provide solid intelligence."

"Wow," I say. "So that's why I didn't see him in any of the classes or anywhere, not since he left my room this morning—"

As I say it, I realize suddenly how it must sound, and my face flushes with heat. What must Command Pilot Kassiopei think? That Logan and I spent the night together? I mean, we *did*, but it wasn't like *that*, and Logan was just there to make sure my concussed head was okay overnight.

I glance up to gauge his reaction, and I see Aeson Kassiopei is looking at me strangely.

His eyes—in the low illumination of this room, there is a bared, raw glitter in them, liquid and *intimate*. He doesn't say anything. Instead, he blinks and looks away from me, as though unable or unwilling to meet my gaze in that instant, and once again observes the two people in the other room.

"This Earth Union operative, Gabriella Walton, has been particularly difficult," he says in a neutral voice. "However, I expect your boyfriend will convince her to talk—eventually."

"My boyfriend—" I begin to say, then grow silent, because, really, what was I about to say anyway? "I am glad Logan is being useful," I say instead.

"Should I trust him?"

The question comes suddenly. And I am taken aback by it.

"What do you mean?" I glance up at Kassiopei.

"I said—should I trust him?" Aeson Kassiopei repeats, looking at me closely, and his gaze is suddenly piercing and intense.

I frown. And then I say, very softly, after the tiniest pause. "I do."

Aeson Kassiopei nods. "In that case, so will I."

And as I consider the peculiarity of this, and his answer, he nods, then tells me, "That is all, Lark. I wanted to show you this, and to have your confirmation. You may go now, you have seen enough. Sangre will be here, working on her for at least a few more hours."

And then the CP exits the small dark one-way observation room, with me in tow.

We return to the upper levels, walking back along the same dim corridor, and when I ask what else is down here, the CP tells me that some of it is auxiliary storage, and some of it includes places for keeping prisoners—an incarceration deck. Finally, as we enter the corkscrew stairwell, and I smell a whiff of acrid smoke and burning fumes coming from another level below, he tells me there are *incinerators* there.

As we rise up the stairs and emerge on the main level, several Atlantean crew move past us, carrying what appears to be bodies in tarps. They use a special service elevator that's located next to the stairwell, and go down.

"So the dead—they are getting incinerated . . ." I say in a soft voice.

Aeson nods at me sorrowfully. "Yes. The dead must be disposed of cleanly, to prevent the spread of infection in such a tightly enclosed space as a starship. None of this was foreseen, and we are not equipped to carry so many corpses in storage. We have enough cold storage facilities for standard circumstances of death, but nothing like this."

"So they must burn. . . ." I glance at him. "This might be a stupid question, but you don't simply jettison bodies into space?"

Aeson's gaze hardens even more. "We don't. We consider it disrespectful to the dead. It is also not very safe, especially not while we are in the Quantum Stream."

"I see. . . . And are there no funeral services, no prayers said over them?"

Looking straight ahead before him, he says, "Not prayers—but *songs*. On Atlantis we say goodbye to the dead by singing them onward to the great mystery of whatever comes next."

"Do you believe in an afterlife?" I ask. And in that instant as I wonder what God or gods the Atlanteans worship, or *he* worships—or if he personally even worships anything at all—I remember that some people deify the Imperial Family Kassiopei.

Aeson Kassiopei remains silent for a few moments. And then he says, "I prefer not to talk about it. . . . Maybe some other time."

Respecting his wishes, I say nothing.

We walk back the rest of the way toward the inner hub area in general silence.

"You are free to go, Lark," he tells me, as we approach the Command Deck sections. "I will see you tomorrow." His expression is closed off, weary, and unreadable.

I nod, and watch his straight proud back, as he walks away from me.

Something strange prompts me to whisper in his wake.

Nefero niktos. . . .

But he does not hear me.

Chapter 22

Sometime after midnight, I am awakened out of a troubled sleep by the now familiar androgynous voice of the ship's computer.

"Now entering Neptune orbital perihelion. . . ."

About five seconds later, it comes back on with:

"Now leaving Neptune orbital aphelion."

And then, another ten seconds later:

"Now entering the Kuiper Belt region. On approach with heliopause."

I lie awake in the soft darkness, motionless so as not to trigger the light sensors. And I try to think—to imagine the impossible cosmic distance that now separates me from the tiny ball of rock called Earth, upon which I was born.

My Mom and Dad, my brother George, everyone and everything I know, is billions of kilometers away, *literally*.

Billions.

It's not really something any human being can imagine. It's completely off the human scale.

And just trying to visualize, to imagine any of it, brings back that sickening dizziness that I'm beginning to call *space vertigo*. My head, still not completely recovered from the concussion of a day ago, begins to hurt again.

I have no idea how, but eventually I fall back asleep.

The next day is completely uneventful. In the morning, when I get to the CCO, no one else is there except Anu, who informs me that the CP is doing ship-wide general inspection and will likely be out all day, and that Gennio is gone to do some other errands until late afternoon.

"I am going to be in Hydroponics in an hour, so you will need to watch the office until your first class. What and when is your first class, Earth girl?"

"Not until 1:00 PM," I say, turning on my work console. "And it's Pilot Training. It's *always* Pilot Training, remember?"

"Excellent. Then you can answer the calls this morning."

I frown at Anu, while my stomach starts to turn queasy with butterflies. I really don't like where this is going. "Okay, what am I supposed to do if they talk to me in Atlantean?"

"Talk to them in English. They will understand. Everyone studied your English before we got deployed here."

"What if the *Imperator* calls?"

Anu makes a loud snort of laughter. "He knows English too."

"Oh, crap . . ." I mutter. "How would I even begin to talk to him?"

"Ask Consul Denu. He's supposed to be teaching you all the correct Imperial Protocol."

"Oh, lord, no," I say. But Anu is right. If I need help in this area, the Consul is the one person to turn to. But do I really want to open that perfumed can of worms by calling him now?

Oh, no. . . . Just, no.

Seeing my dour expression, Anu laughs and laughs.

I really, really, *really* want to kill the snotty jerk. I swear, one of these days. . . .

Somehow I survive the morning after the little jerk goes to Hydroponics, leaving me completely alone in the office. Lucky for me, no one calls except for one very serious looking, elegantly dressed Atlantean official from Poseidon, who fortunately addresses me in perfect English, and a couple of officers from other ships. I tell them all the CP is unavailable, and ask if they would care to call back or leave a message.

So this is what it feels like to be a receptionist or an administrative assistant or secretary, I wonder with minor irritation. Nothing wrong with it if you actually *know* what you're supposed to be doing!

After a quick lunch in the Officers Meal Hall, I stop by my cabin where I attempt to finally call my brother and sister, to see how they've been faring. Gracie's line doesn't answer, so I leave a message. And Gordie's is also unresponsive, so I leave him one too. In a nutshell it's an "I'm alive, all is well, how are you, call me please," kind of message.

And then it's off to Pilot Training.

Today we are doing a different kind of flight simulation. Instructor Mithrat Okoi assigns us a straight flight path between imaginary obstacles.

"You will launch from the shuttle bay flight tunnel. And this time, as you exit the ship, you will continue going in a straight line, avoiding any obstacle that comes in your way," the Instructor tells us, pacing our rows of console desks. "There will be a variety of obstacles placed before you, both stationary and moving, and it is your responsibility as Pilot and Co-Pilot to deal with them accordingly."

Erin Tsai, in the front seat as usual, raises her hand. "Sir, how exactly do we deal with the obstacles? Can you please elaborate?"

"You have three options," Instructor Okoi says. "First and best choice, you bypass the obstacle by going around it. Second, you destroy the obstacle—blast it out of your way by engaging your ship's weapons system. Third, you crash into the obstacle, and you are destroyed, ending the scenario."

Sitting to my right, Hugo Moreno gives me a dirty look. "I get to shoot, okay? I'm the one firing the weapons!" he hisses in my ear.

"Right, whatever," I reply.

"In order to deploy your ship's weapons," the Instructor says, "the Pilot and the Co-Pilot must *both* be involved—"

I glance at Hugo and raise one brow triumphantly. He only glares at me.

"Both of you must act in tandem, since this is a joint process," Instructor Okoi continues. "Remember, Weapons is a general sub-system, requiring a balanced approach. It's a safeguard against potential abuse of the system, and against hasty decisions."

This time Roy Tsai raises his hand. "So, how do we engage the weapons system?"

"To initialize Weapons, the Pilot simultaneously presses

both the Red and Green Grid buttons on the right, while the Co-Pilot simultaneously presses both the Blue and Yellow on the left. Do it now!"

Hugo and I press two of the corners each on our consoles, with him acting as Pilot and me as Co-Pilot. Immediately all four grids are activated. In seconds, they *blend*, and the color of the hologram transitions to pure white.

Everyone in the classroom stares at this new White Grid floating in the air over each of our consoles.

"This is your Weapons System," Instructor Okoi announces. "The white circle indicates your own ship and its present location. Any other color objects that populate the grid are either other friendly vessels, or enemy targets—ranging from simple training scenario obstacles to actual full-fledged enemy forces. And now, observe!"

He presses his hand-held device and suddenly the grid before each Cadet is filled with different color circles, scattered in random locations in the grid-space all around our own white circle.

"This is your enemy or your colleague," Instructor Okoi tells us. "Your task is to first identify who is who, then avoid the enemy or destroy them."

"How do we fire?" a girl asks.

"You *don't*. First, the Pilot and Co-Pilot need to mark the items on the grid as hostile or friendly. Press the large four-color rainbow button on the bottom of your console. When the Weapons Grid is active, it serves as a Select toggle button. Now, for the sake of our scenario, let's assume that all the orange circles are our allies—other Fleet ships, or friendlies. Toggle the Select button until the rainbow lights are steady, which indicates Friendly. Now use your fingers to touch-select each friendly entity in the grid—"

We do as we're told, touching the hologram orange circles floating in the air before us with our fingers. Each one I touch suddenly gets a white line border around it.

"And now," Instructor Okoi says, "press the Select button again. You've just isolated your allies from potential friendly fire, and marked them as safe. This tells the Weapons System not to fire on these entities under any circumstances."

"Okay," a boy asks. "This is kind of complicated. What if there are more than one type of enemy or more than one type of friend or ally—"

Mithrat Okoi glances at the speaker. "Valid questions. War is complicated. It is precisely why these preliminaries and careful pre-selection is so important before any battle is fought or actual fire exchanged. The answer to your question will be covered in detail at a later date. For now, assume that the rest of the grid entities are hostiles."

He pauses, looking at us grimly. "At this point the Weapons Grid is defined. Next comes the moment some of you have been eagerly waiting for—you will launch weapons."

Instructor Okoi points to the nearest Cadet's console. "Now Pilots, swipe the touch surface in the direction you want to fire. And Co-Pilots, also swipe in any direction you want to fire. The weapons will fire in a 90-degree wide burst, with your swipe serving as the vector aimed at the target. If both the Pilot and Co-Pilot swipes overlap, the common overlap zone will receive additional firepower. Try it!"

I swipe to the right. Next to me, Hugo swipes straight ahead.

Immediately our grid comes alive with a wave of golden light that flares outward from the white circle in two directions to match our motion. All the objects in the way of the flare get obliterated and disappear off the grid. At the same time we hear multiple explosions.

The same thing is happening all around the classroom. "Whoa! Awesome!" Cadets exclaim, clap, and there are hoots and excited laughter.

"Silence!" Instructor Okoi roars at us. "This is *not* a gaming console. This is a *war console*. You've just theoretically obliterated thousands of lives. *Real lives.* You are never to react this way again in this classroom, or you will be disciplined."

It's like he threw a bucket of cold water at the room. Silence reigns, with only a few residual explosions sounding from various consoles all around us.

I watch, holding my breath.

"Now," the Instructor says quietly. "As I was saying in the beginning of this portion of class, you have before you a scenario with obstacles. Your responsibility is to decide how to handle them. Destroy or bypass. You will fly the shuttle forward, until you get a clean run all the way to the end of the formation. Each moment, you will have to make the choice of 'destroy or bypass.' Now you know how to switch to the Weapons Grid. I recommend you use it as little as possible in your simulation flight. No one leaves the room until you have successfully completed one clean run. Now, proceed!"

And the Instructor resets our consoles to the beginning of the scenario.

Hugo groans, and I groan.

And we begin the simulation.

About two hours later I get out of Pilot Training. Hugo hates me, and I hate him, and the whole class seems to hate each other. For now, I think it's sufficient to say that all of us suck badly at Piloting. I mean, given real ships, we would all die and kill each other in horrible flaming crashes. . . .

I drop by the CCO at 3:30 PM and this time I find Gennio there.

"Hey, Gwen!" He looks up from his work. "So have you been to see the heavy-duty 3D printers yet?"

"Huh?" I say. "What?"

"Oh, sorry! I thought you just had your Technology and Systems Class, never mind. That's your next class. It's down on Seven next to Hydroponics."

"Yeah, I have that class at 4:00 PM. What are you talking about exactly?"

Gennio smiles at me with an expression closest to mischief that I've seen in this boy yet. "You are going to love the 3D printers. They make everything, including your new formal outfits for the Zero-G Dance. I know all the girls are super excited, because you get to choose the fabric and the fashion, and all that kind of thing."

Formal fashions? Fabric? Who does Gennio take me for? As a card-carrying *nerd*, I am perfectly satisfied with my appearance-ignorant status. I own functional clothes that fit me comfortably and protect me from the elements. If it hadn't been for my Mom—who never insisted, only made tactful and subtle suggestions whenever she steered me (again, tactfully) to the appropriate clothing section of the mall department stores—I would look worse than frumpy. I would look like wilderness grandma, and also own maybe two outfits and alternate-wear them every other day.

As soon as my natural fashion tendencies (or lack of) were established, we had it all worked out. For years, Mom would simply buy my clothes and I would let her. Seriously, if it hadn't been for Mom's general good taste, bullies in school would've eaten me alive and made even worse fun of my looks and outfits. As is, at least she kept me decently inconspicuous. In our family, Mom, Gracie, and George are the somewhat fashion-conscious ones. While Dad, Gordie, and I—we don't give a crap.

That's why Mom pretty much dresses all three of us—or did. . . .

Because Mom is billions of kilometers away, on a tiny dust mote in space, and she will never dress me again. . . .

With a sudden gut-wrenching pang I think of Mom, and family, and everyone again, as Gennio tells me all this girly stuff, assuming I'm interested.

Maybe I *should* be, it occurs to me momentarily. Now that I'm sort of dating someone. . . . What would Logan think if he ever saw me nicely dressed, and possibly wearing actual makeup and cosmetics?

And then I get a weird fleeting thought—what would Command Pilot Aeson Kassiopei think if *he* saw me all dressed up?

I can count on my hands the number of times in my life I've been really nicely put together. Most of them involved going to the Opera to attend Mom's own infrequent performances. And even in those cases I did as little as possible to my appearance. I wore lipstick, eyeliner and mascara maybe three times, and hated it—the horrid gunk got in my eyes. And it made me look *weird*—like someone else—which kind of scared me.

What would happen, I think suddenly, if I tried again? If I went all out and got dressed up, made up, and did something fancy to my hair?

I mean, I don't even *have* any nice clothes packed in my duffel bags, just practical stuff.

Okay, now I'm really curious about those 3D printers. And once more I feel a lonely strange sense of not belonging anywhere—since I'm not a Cadet or a Civilian, I don't even have the dorms and barracks officers to tell me what's going on with the Zero-G Dance preparation.

All I've got is Gennio. And if he hadn't mentioned the 3D printers, I would have no clue at all, not even enough to ask anyone.

At 4:00 PM I head to the remote outer section of Red Quadrant Residential Deck One, near Storage. Here I get scanned by guards who verify my class schedule before admitting me past secure doors inside the locked dim corridor. It's similar to the one I'd seen last night with Aeson Kassiopei when we visited the interrogation room.

Here I, and a few other Cadets and Civs on their way to the same class, go down another corkscrew stairwell to level Seven. We emerge in unexpected brightness—a glassed hallway that walls off a sudden great open space, brightly lit with daylight illumination.

It is stunning. . . .

On the other side of the glass is a green oasis. Trees and shrubs and climbing vines fill a greenhouse that must span the entire length and width of the ark-ship, because I see no end, no horizon line. . . . Earth plants mingle with what appears to be strange alien Atlantean vegetation. They hang, cleverly suspended from special support beams overhead, into shallow troughs or deep containers of running water, their roots growing directly in the water without any presence of soil.

The water must contain a perfect balance of nutrients and chemicals necessary for growth, I realize. And it flows abundantly everywhere, including sprinklers and mist delivery systems.

So . . . this is Hydroponics. This is the deck that provides the ark-ship with food, oxygen, and other things necessary for life support.

An Atlantean stands at the end of the short hallway. He is tall and somewhat big, with short golden hair and reddish-brown skin, and a blue armband on his uniform sleeve. His features are pleasant, soft and rounded, and he reminds me a little bit of Gennio—he could be Gennio's slightly older brother. "Over here, everyone!" he says in a loud comfortable voice, waving to those of us newcomers who are still coming in from the spiraling stairwell.

At some point, when the hallway is so packed there seems to be no standing room, the Atlantean opens a glass entrance into the Hydroponics section, and motions for us to follow him inside.

A blast of glorious oxygen-rich air hits us, together with fine mist spray. There's also the surprising sound of birdsong and the buzz of living insects.

Wow, I think, *this is not just a greenhouse but a true ecosystem!*

The Atlantean stops at an open area near the entrance, and we gather around him. "I am Klavit Xotoi," he tells us, "and I will be teaching you Technology and Systems. Most of what we'll be doing in the coming months is learning how everything on this ship works. We will observe the various systems, starting with this one. Hydroponics is the largest and most vital of the general systems, and the H-Deck makes up the entirety of the ship on Level Seven. In the coming days we will learn all about it. . . ."

As Instructor Xotoi speaks, I look around in wonder, and so does everyone else.

"My God . . . it's like the Garden of Eden," a Civilian girl whispers in reverence.

As we stare at this incredible place, I notice eight-feet tall, flat stacks of grey material, piled in rows, not too far from the entrance. It has the look of orichalcum, and I realize all at once that it's stacks upon stacks of hoverboards.

"Now, before we continue, I want each one of you to grab a hoverboard from over there," Instructor Xotoi says in the very same moment that I realize it. "The nature of Hydroponics makes it nearly impossible to work here without having the ability to access the growing trees and plants at any height level, all the way up to the ceiling—which, as you can see, stretches about seventy feet to accommodate most common varieties of trees. Some of the crops here are so delicate that the only way to harvest them gently is from above, via hoverboard, without disturbing their ground root systems, and without having to walk through endless expanses of water. Furthermore, since the H-Deck area itself is so vast, the most efficient way to get around here is via hover flight. So—get your boards, key them to yourself, and let's get going!"

In moments, everyone around me starts singing the keying sequence, in some cases ending up in a minor vocal tug-of-war for possession of specific boards. I quickly pick one and key it with practiced notes before anyone else does.

My board comes flying toward me, and I get on top, straddling it by habit. A few people stand up, in snowboarder and skateboarder style, but I notice that many choose to sit, just like me. Momentarily I flash back to the dark horrible subterranean tunnels of Qualification Finals during which we all had to lie on top of our hoverboards for the duration of what seemed to be a hellish eternity. . . .

As soon as the whole class is airborne, Instructor Klavit Xotoi tells us to follow him. And then he commands his hoverboard to rise and starts to move into the heart of the green oasis.

An hour later, after completing a high-speed overview flight tour of H-Deck, with all its green growing wonders, we return to the entrance area that leads back upstairs to main level, and surrender our hoverboards. I feel strangely refreshed and at peace, as though I've been out on the surface of a planet for the last hour, flying in the gentle breeze among fragrant greenery, instead of in the bowels of a huge starship.

Others in the class seem to feel the same way. Hydroponics almost made us forget.

"Next class, we will continue on H-Deck," the Instructor tells us. "But now, we make a short detour to the Manufacturing Deck. It's up on Level Six. Since we have the Zero-G Dance coming up the day after tomorrow, and many of you will require things such as new clothing, I've been asked to demonstrate to you our 3D Printing process."

Many girls and quite a few boys clap in excitement. I suppose their commanding officers had told them all about it, and what to expect.

We turn into the corridor on Six, and another large area presents itself to view. Although much smaller than Hydroponics, it's still an impressive warehouse of machinery and materials. Rows of industrial 3D printers line the walls, and rows of various organic and artificial raw "ink" materials fill storage containers up to the ceiling.

Atlantean crew members move about, working the machines, and levitating robot vehicles transport boxes around from one pallet to another.

The Instructor talks in Atlantean to a few of the crew here, and then takes us to a smaller office enclosure where we are shown how to enter specific printer programs into consoles.

"Once you have your clothing program ready, you simply email it to the 3D printer device driver app which will queue the specific print job for you. The finished product—in this case, your new outfit—will be manufactured, and then delivered for pickup here at the end of the assembly line. You will be notified via email when it's ready, and you can come get it the day after tomorrow, before the Dance."

The Instructor points out the various raw materials containers. "These are the material ink compounds that will be used to create an endless variety of clothing fabrics." He turns to point to another section of the office containing memory storage drive chips. "And here is a huge library of Earth and Atlantean fashion, historical and modern. Most of it already resides in the Fleet Network Cloud for your immediate access, but if anything is missing, it can be requested here, to be manually loaded into flash memory for your use. Just email us with the catalog item number."

A girl raises her hand. "How long do we have to get our programs ready for printing?"

Klavit Xotoi thinks. "I suggest you don't wait any longer than by noon tomorrow to submit your program. The 3D printers will be extremely busy, even running non-stop 24/7, and it takes at least ten minutes to assemble a single outfit, assuming a basic three piece including matching shoes. There are thousands of you on this ship, and only so many printers. So please be considerate of others and don't wait until the last minute."

Another girl raises her hand. "As far as our personal body measurements, how accurate will these outfits be?"

"Perfectly accurate, considering that you begin your program with a body scan." And Klavit Xotoi points to the opposite end of the warehouse. "Incidentally, body scan machines can be found over there in Section M-12. Once you are scanned, your measurements variables will be permanently matched to your ID token and stored for future use, as well as also used to populate the 3D printer template. Then you build your dressy outfit from there on."

I take a deep breath and raise my hand. "This may be a dumb question, but do we *have* to wear these fancy formal outfits in order to attend the Dance?"

Klavit Xotoi raises one brow and looks at me curiously. "Civilian, you are absolutely *not* required to have such an outfit. It is voluntary. In fact, you are free to attend while wearing your everyday uniform and boots, if you so choose. However, most people do prefer to get dressed up for the occasion of the Zero-G Dance."

"Oh, super," I say. "In that case, that's a relief."

It's settled—I am so *not* getting dressed up!

Chapter 23

Most of the teens in the class look at me funny after I make that last remark, but I don't care. Technology and Systems Class is over, and I head back to grab dinner, and think about what to do for the rest of the evening.

Briefly I think of Logan, and then of my sister Gracie, and Gordie, and Laronda. Haven't seen any of them for a while. And come to think of it, Blayne Dubois wasn't in Pilot Training either today or yesterday—at least I don't remember seeing him there.

I eat alone at the Officers Meal Hall in Command Deck Two. It occurs to me that I am actively avoiding returning to that Yellow Quadrant Cadet Deck Meal Hall where the hostage situation took place. Honestly, I don't think I can bear seeing that room again. The dead bodies will always stay in my mind's eye.

Meanwhile this room feels safer somehow. I glance around and see familiar Atlantean officers, including Oalla Keigeri and Keruvat Ruo. A few officers even nod at me in passing.

Incidentally, there's no sign of Command Pilot Kassiopei anywhere. I wonder where he is, and if he ever actually eats like a normal human being, since I've never encountered him in this meal hall or any other—at least not since that very first day when he showed me the way here.

I am so alone. . . .

"Gwen Lark."

I look up and see a petite Atlantean girl standing behind me. She is holding a tray with food and has a slightly shy expression on her face. "May I join you?"

"Oh!" I say. "Oh, sure! Please, sit down!" Okay, I didn't

expect this. I have no idea who this person is, but I think I've seen her in the meal hall before.

The girl puts down her tray very carefully across the narrow table from me, and takes the bench seat facing me. She is very slender, with a curvy hourglass figure and porcelain-rosy skin. Her features are pixie-like, and her heart-shaped face—framed by short metal-gold hair in a blunt cut—has a charming low-key beauty. She wears a green armband around her slim arm.

"If I may introduce myself, I am Vazara Hotat, and my Assignment is in Brake and Shields," she says in a sweet, highly pitched voice with just a trace of an Atlantean accent. "You don't know me, but Gennio Rukkat asked me to make friends with you—that is, if you don't mind?"

My brows rise, but I am smiling at her. "Of course I don't mind. I could use a friend—and thank you. That was very nice of Gennio, considering that I'm somewhat isolated in my present odd position as CCO Aide who's also an Earth refugee—all my siblings and most of my friends are on other ships. And since I don't live in a dorm or barracks with other people, I seem to miss out on a lot of what's happening."

"Well, I am not an expert on what's happening," she says, picking up her glass of *nikkari*. "But I think I can help just a little with the basics. For example, have you decided what you are going to wear to the Zero-G Dance? I can help you with your program and show you some of the common fashion trends in Poseidon, and even what they wear at Court—"

"Wow," I say. "Believe it or not, I'm all set in that department."

Vazara raises one very pixie-ish brow. "Oh, really? And Gennio was all worried that you had completely no idea."

I snort. "Gennio is very sweet, and I appreciate his efforts—and yours. But, yes, I'm all set. It's very simple—I am simply wearing my Fleet uniform."

The Atlantean girl's smile disappears, replaced with immediate concern, and she stops eating. "Oh, no!" she says. "But that's not good! Everyone dresses up for the Dance, it's an old tradition. How else would you enjoy yourself when you are up there in perfect weightlessness? Your outfit should be dreamy and gorgeous when you fly with your partner!"

I pick up a bite of something alien and spicy with my fork after swirling it around on my plate. "Well . . ." I mutter. And then I explain to Vazara that I don't expect to be doing much flying or much dancing. "If anything," I say, "I'll be operating the Zero-G tech together with Gennio, and making sure the levitation and gravity transitions happen properly with the music. Now that to me is the most exciting part of this event. I can't wait to see how it all works!"

But Vazara does not give up. "You know, I can show you how we dance in *Atlantida*—all the latest modern dances. It's really easy and so much fun! You can learn in a few hours!"

Poor girl. . . . She has no clue she is talking to Gwen the Klutz.

"Look, I really appreciate it," I tell her. "But, maybe next time. I'm really not up to dancing right now. And I'm sure you have better things to do than get your feet crushed by an elephant. Besides, wouldn't all the boys be looking up the girls' fancy skirts as they're flying around, up there in Zero-G? I don't really want to deal with any of that silliness. . . ."

"Oh, goodness, no!" Vazara bites her lip with the effort of explaining it to me. "The outfits are made cleverly to hide your underclothing—either in the way they fold and unfold during dancing, or with extra hidden layers that cover you from below as you fly. And in some cases you can always wear additional form-fitting shorts underneath."

But I shake my head. "Sounds way too complicated."

Vazara watches me sadly. "All right, but please let me know if you change your mind. I am very eager to help you!"

I smile. "Yes, I can see."

We chat for a while longer, and I find that Vazara is extremely pleasant, but somewhat too "girly" for my usual kind of pal. She goes on and on about formal dresses, shoes, party decorations, shoes, and dance music—and did I mention, shoes?—until my eyes start to glaze over. I admit I miss my friend Ann Finnbar from back home in Vermont, and I seriously miss Laronda, Dawn, and Hasmik, my Qualification friends.

At last we part, and I promise Vazara that the moment I

need any help whatsoever, I will contact her or drop by her quarters in the Green Quadrant, Command Deck Three.

Yeah, *that's* likely not going to happen, at least not in the near future.

I return to my cabin and plop down on my bunk and think. *Just, think.*

Where is Logan? Is he still doing the interrogations down in the bowels of the ship? Yet again I flash back to the image of Logan—grim, intense, and surprisingly cold and clinical in his levels of patience—facing off that tough Earth Union girl. . . . That's definitely a new side of Logan I've never seen before—hard and calculating. I'm not too sure what to think of it.

And then I recall the look in another person's eyes, when we were down there in that one-way observation chamber adjacent to the interrogation room. Aeson Kassiopei, watching me with raw, inexplicable eyes. . . .

Talking about—where is the CP? Do we have the voice training today or not?

A strange little twinge of concern comes to me. I haven't seen him all day.

At 8:00 PM, I arrive dutifully at the CCO, and the guards let me inside, and there's no one there. I sit around for about ten minutes, waiting. Then it occurs to me to check my email.

There's a message from Command Pilot Kassiopei:

"Lark, my apologies, but we have to cancel your voice training again for tonight. I am going to be unavailable all night. I will see you tomorrow. —A. K."

The message is terse and typical, and for some reason I can easily imagine it being spoken in his deep cool voice.

Okay, why exactly am I thinking about this?

Frustrated at myself, I get back to my cabin, grab a favorite old book from my duffel bag and try to read a little before bedtime.

It doesn't occur to me to check my video messages until it's after 10:00 PM, lights out in all the dorms and barracks.

Because there's a message from Gracie.

"Hey, Gee Two!" my sister Gracie says, peering closely into the camera, with her noisy barracks in the background. Somehow, in just a few days, she looks all grown up and serious, with her hair gathered neatly behind her and her Cadet Insignia star pinned on her uniform. "Sorry I missed your calls, but things are pretty busy here, we don't get much time off. Talking about time off—we all got permission to attend the Zero-G Dance on other ships, but only if someone invites us. So—here's our chance to hang, if you invite me over to your ship! I really wanna see ICS-2, and party with you. Okay, I know you don't party, but you know what I mean—anyway, call me!"

Oh, great, I think with excitement. *A chance to see my little sis! I can invite Gracie here for the Zero-G Dance!*

And so I go to bed, resolving to get Gracie over here, one way or another.

Instead of solid sleep, I get woken several times in the night by the voice of the ship's computer, announcing various trans-Neptunian Kuiper Belt Objects, including Pluto, Eris, Makemake and Haumea.

"Now in orbital range of dwarf planet Pluto...."

And on, and on. Seriously, I get it; it's unbelievably cool. I mean, *Pluto!* So amazing, and it even has a heart-shaped area on its surface! But for once I am too cranky with sleep.

And then, toward morning, I hear:

"Now entering heliopause."

A few seconds later, the next ominous announcement makes my pulse race and wakes me up completely from a shallow sleep:

"Now leaving solar system heliosphere.... Interstellar space begins in ten seconds...."

I bolt upright, almost hitting my head against the low overhang of the storage compartment directly above my bunk.

Dear God, this is it.

We are out—out of the solar system, beyond the safety bubble of the solar winds, having reached the boundary where the solar wind pressure equalizes with the pressure of the interstellar medium of our galaxy.

Cold sweat breaks out on my forehead. My heart palpitates with full-blown panic, with space vertigo.

If it's any consolation, I whisper to myself, *at least we're*

still in the Milky Way.
　　For now.

In the morning, to my amazement, the CCO is filled with people. Not only is Aeson Kassiopei there, but so are Anu, Gennio, and a constant stream of officers and crew who drop by every few minutes to ask the CP for various permissions and specifications, in regard to the Blue Quadrant-hosted Zero Gravity Dance event.

How crazy-big is this thing going to be anyway?

The moment I walk in, Anu hands me a handheld tablet with a checklist of tasks and the event schedule for the big day tomorrow.

"What's this?" I say, meanwhile glancing in the direction of the CP.

This morning Aeson Kassiopei looks even more icy and irritated than usual, a particularly lethal combination that creates a perfect storm of disdain on his handsome lean face. As a result, his responses to the various officers are curt and somewhat dismissive, while he barely glances away from his work and focuses on his screen.

He must really hate this, I think.

"Check your email for more incoming instructions," Anu says. "This is the timeline for every ark-ship. The Dance itself begins at 7:00 PM, and runs until midnight on all ships. But first, see all these other things that must happen tomorrow. And here on ICS-2, we are responsible for them!"

"Great," I mutter. "Resonance Chamber panels diagnostics and sound check at 9:00 AM . . . Decorations start at 11:00 AM . . . Lighting at 1:00 PM . . . Music programming at 2:00 PM. . . ." I look up. "So, no other work or classes scheduled for tomorrow?"

Anu snorts. "Why? Would you like some of my work added to your schedule?"

I roll my eyes at him and return to scanning the list.

And then I fill up with courage and ask about my sister.

"Command Pilot," I say. "What must I do to have my sister Gracie formally invited here to our ship for tomorrow's Dance?"

Aeson Kassiopei looks up at me. "What?"

"My sister," I repeat. "I want to invite Gracie here."

"That is fine," he says. "Talk to Gennio and have him check the personnel balance sheet." And then his attention returns to the display.

"Okay...."

I turn to Gennio and he explains to me that the number of personnel physically present on each ship has to be specially accounted for—literally. It has something to do with the maximum weight limits allocated to each vessel in order to maintain the required flight velocities, and to retain the formation balance necessary to keep us all within the Quantum Stream.

"Wow, I had no idea it's so complicated."

"Oh, yes." Gennio nods thoughtfully. "Each ark-ship has to carefully preserve the weight range throughout our journey. For every person, shuttle, or unit of freight that leaves one ship, approximately that much needs to be brought over from another ship, within a specific tolerance ratio. People and things come and go all the time between ships, but the ship systems keep careful track of all arrivals and departures—"

"So each time one person comes and goes, it can mess things up?" I say, thinking with sudden guilt about how I basically stowed Logan away on a shuttle and brought him over here without asking.

"One person is no big deal," Anu says. "But with all these people getting invited to other ships for the Dance, everyone will be coming and going all over the place, all on the same day. So we have to be extra careful not to upset the weight balance everywhere. That's why we have personnel balance sheets. The system automatically checks it for discrepancies and dangerous weight fluctuations across the Fleet."

Gennio types on his console. "Okay," he says. "I just allocated Grace Lark to ICS-2 for tomorrow, so she is cleared to arrive after 8:00 AM and can stay until midnight."

"Thanks, Gennio!" I smile at him.

And then I glance down at the checklist on the tablet in my hands. "This is crazy . . ." I mutter. "All this effort for some silly dance."

"Agreed." It's the Command Pilot who responds. He looks

at me momentarily and I see the weariness in his gaze hiding underneath the general irritation. "And yet," he adds, "it's necessary and has to happen. It's a morale booster, intended to make people forget the bad, at least for a short while."

"Yeah, I get it." I watch him steadily, but he quickly looks away.

The rest of the day is a hassle-filled mess. The other two CCO Aides and I are sent on errands all over the ship, checking the Manufacturing Deck where the 3D printers are cranking out endless production items, testing points of various networked systems, and otherwise getting ready for tomorrow's precise schedule.

Most of the time I simply tag along and watch and observe, and help occasionally with whatever Gennio and Anu delegate to me—mostly easy tasks such as handling and carrying computer parts. As a result of this, I also don't get to attend any classes. Oh, I think, Hugo is going to be *so very mad* at me for not showing up to Pilot Training....

"Will there be food and drink at the Dance?" I ask at some point as we are testing network lines somewhere on Cadet Deck Two.

"Yes, basic refreshments," Gennio says. "But drinks in closed containers only, because of constantly changing gravity."

I imagine a giant room filled with weightless dancing people and millions of airborne floating droplets of liquid. *Yeah, no.* That's not a bright idea.

"I'm surprised you guys would risk any drinks at all," I say. "Spills happen. Can't expect every single person to be careful with their closed beer containers. Especially if they're already drunk."

Anu glances at me. "No alcohol," he says. "There's no liquor allowed during Zero-G Dances."

Gennio nods. "The combination of changing gravity and alcohol can make people really sick."

"Good to know." I file that away under interesting facts— nothing that would ever affect *me* personally, since I don't drink, but hey, good to know.

After dinner I call Gracie, and let her know she's been approved and is coming over tomorrow. Gracie expresses her joy at me through the screen by reverting to her inner twelve-year-old self and squealing loudly. Then I get to hear about her fancy formal outfit that she'd just emailed to the 3D printer on her ship, and how she's going to dress up in blue, because everyone will be dressed in blue, and how Blue is awesome for hosting the Dance.

She then tells me how even Gordie, our socially-oblivious brother, is into the idea of Zero-G Dancing—and not only because he's in Blue, and his Quadrant is hosting, but just because—and he's going to go to the dance held on their own ship and check things out. "I bet Gee Three will just stand at the wall like a doofus and stare at the special effects till his mouth falls open." Gracie giggles.

"How's Gordie doing?" I ask.

"Dunno, I don't see him all that much, but yeah, he's doing pretty well. He loves being assigned to Networked Systems—or is it Network Systems? Whatever—now he's discovered Hydroponics, so it's all cool. He can hang out with the plants and draw them. Better than people. Better than girls, definitely. Wanna bet, he won't even notice all the hot outfits on the girls tomorrow—"

"Gracie," I say. "Please don't overdo it, okay? Just don't wear anything too outrageous that would make Mom worried."

Gracie sticks her tongue out at me. And then just like that she goes serious. "I miss Mom . . ." she says softly, frowning.

"I know." I give her a virtual finger kiss against the display screen. "So—see you tomorrow morning after eight—"

I want to add *"I love you"* but Gracie nods, frowns even more, and suddenly disconnects the call.

I linger, staring at the blank screen and wonder if my little sister is now crying.

Chapter 24

Today is Zero Gravity Dance Day. Yes, it's only the first of four such Dances scheduled throughout the months of our journey. One for each season, and this one's Blue.

I wake up with the 7:00 AM gradual lights, and feel a strange zing of excitement. My own crisp and clean change of uniform is folded on the chair, ready for me.

Atlantean laundry facilities are spare and there's always a line to use the super high-speed wash-and-dry combo units down at the end of each deck. But last night I managed to run my clothing through, and now I'm all set for today, with a fresh new bra and undies, and that very pretty starched and pressed looking uniform. As far as uniforms, we all have two sets each, so I get to wear my perfectly clean one in honor of Dance Day.

Just for a brief moment I regret not having a special dress to wear to this thing. And then I tell my stupid brain to cut it out.

I don't dress up. I don't dance. Remember, Gwen numbskull Lark?

Besides, after all the upcoming work in the Resonance Chamber today, I hardly expect my clean new uniform to still be fresh and unblemished. Oh, well.

I shower and put on the clean uniform, and consider doing something different with my hair. A stern, pasty-pale, tired girl looks back at me from the mirror, with long hair that's starting to form waves already, even though it's ratty wet. And so I decide to just do the ponytail for now. Maybe, when it's time for the actual dance I can run back to my room and freshen up a bit, and maybe brush my hair and wear it loose. . . .

I rush through breakfast, seeing no one I know in the Officers Meal Hall, and then head directly for the shuttle bay that's supposed to produce my sister. I don't have to be anywhere until 9:00 AM when we begin work at the Resonance Chamber, so I hang out at the bay for at least fifteen minutes past eight, watching the crazy-busy traffic.

It is absolutely a madhouse today. Shuttles arrive and depart every minute, kicking up major wind in the launch tunnel, and the platforms are filled with Earth teens and Atlanteans. People carry bags and formal jacket suits and dresses neatly wrapped in plastic, and a few brave souls are already dressed up—which I think is insane, since they have a whole day to kill before the Dance. Some of the Cadets are wearing white dress uniforms, trimmed with gold braid around the collar and sleeves. I realize these must be parade uniforms of the Atlantean Fleet, and they look *sharp*.

Happy, rowdy teen noises come from everywhere, squealing, yells of greeting in various Earth languages, as people meet their dates arriving from other ships.

I watch a few couples kiss and linger, as they come together, and I think about Logan. I haven't seen him for the last several days, so I wonder how it will be.... At this rate, I'm uncertain if he will even show up for the Dance.

Eventually, Gracie's shuttle arrives. I see her come down the short ladder, and oh, wow—Gracie's wearing the fancy white Cadet dress uniform! And right behind her I see a familiar hoverboard, and on it, Blayne Dubois. He's hovering upright in the LM Form, dressed in his everyday grey uniform. Gracie turns to him to say something, and laughs loudly as she takes the last step off the bottom rung.

They both see me and Gracie waves. "Gwen!"

I move through the platform crowds toward them. "Gracie, there you are! And, wow! *Look at you!*"

Gracie beams at me and straightens up her posture. "You like?" Then she adds, "And no, there's no uber-foofy blue prom dress outfit, I was just messing with you last night...."

I notice her hair is tightly pulled back and pinned smartly up, and her usual raccoon eyeliner has been toned down to resemble the Atlantean fine-line kohl fashion—it actually looks good! And I have to admit, my little sister looks darn good overall. The sharp perfect creases of her uniform pants are flawless, her boots shine, shirt has no wrinkles, red armband is tied impeccably, Cadet Insignia star pinned in proper place, and the whole thing sits so well on her, that I am amazed. Even her pearl stud earrings are in good taste!

I make a move to hug her, and actually pause. "May I touch you?" I whisper with an open mouth.

In reply Gracie reaches out to me and we hug, carefully, but for a nice extended moment.

When we come apart, Gracie turns to glance at Blayne. "It's so cool that Blayne happened to be on the same shuttle with me," she says. "We got to blab!"

"Hey, Lark," Blayne says to me, moving his longish hair slightly out of his eyes. "I guess I should specify *which* Lark, now," he adds with a faint smile, without looking at Gracie.

We laugh.

"So what are you doing on the shuttle?" I ask him, as we start moving from the platform toward the exit and the interior of the ship. Blayne softly sings the note sequences to advance his hoverboard, still in the upright position, while he maintains his lower body hold on it. Wow, but he's gotten good—it's almost unnoticeable that he's not actually standing.

"I don't remember if I told you," he says, "but the CP assigned me to teach LM Forms to a few of the Combat classes. Yeah, I know, pretty wild—I guess he thinks I'm ridiculously decent enough at it. So anyway, I get to go around the Fleet and do the classes on different ships."

"Yeah," Gracie exclaims. "Blayne was coming back from teaching, which I think is super awesome." And then she looks at him and back at me quickly.

We get scanned by the security at the exit, then proceed to the interior.

"That's super impressive, actually," I say to Blayne. "But I'm not too surprised. You're really rocking the LM Forms, Dubois."

"I am, aren't I?" he adds with a sarcastic smile, and barely looks from me to Gracie, who smiles widely at him. "Good thing they found *something* for me to do around here."

"Aww, come on!" Gracie exclaims, and then punches Blayne on the arm, so that he says, "Oww."

We laugh again.

"You guys had breakfast yet?" I ask.

They both nod.

"Have anything major scheduled for today?" I ask Blayne.

"Not in particular." He shifts on the board slightly.

"Do you mind watching Gracie for a bit, while I go deal with the Resonance Chamber for the next hour? All the CCO Aides have to do acoustic tests in the room—"

"*Watching* me?" Gracie interrupts with outrage. "Hey! I'm not five! Blayne and I can just go hang out for a while, but it's not like he's babysitting me, because that's a rotten thing to say, Gee Two!"

"Okay, okay!" I put up my arms. "Blayne, can you please go hang with Gracie for a while?"

"Sure," he says, after the slightest pause. "I was actually going to get a nap and catch up on my reading, since we get the day off—"

"Some of us don't get the day off," I counter. "And besides, the Dance starts at seven, so not much of a day."

"Since I'm not going," he says. "I get the whole day and night all to myself. Pretty nifty."

"What?" both Gracie and I exclaim simultaneously.

"You're not going?" I say. "Don't you want to see the amazing weightlessness and all that low gravity dancing? It's supposed to be spectacular. Just the observable physics alone is worth it!"

"Nah," he says. "Not my scene."

"Not my scene either," I say. "But still, fascinating—"

"Aww, come on, Blayne! Noooo!" Gracie whines. "You absolutely have to come! That's crazy, you can't miss this Dance! Noooo!"

Blayne sticks one hand in his ear. "Oww, oww," he says. "Pitch too high, ruptured my eardrum, lower volume please, Lark Two."

"Lark Two? WTF?" Gracie puts her hands on her hips and glares at Blayne full-on.

"Oh, jeez . . ." He shakes his head. But there's just a tiny trace of a smile in the corners of his mouth.

"Okay, look," I say to Gracie, because suddenly I get it. *Duh, what an idiot I am sometimes.* "He just doesn't want to go, because, well, use your brain. He's not going to be comfortable there, with other people dancing." I don't say it, but I hope Gracie figures out my meaning, *the boy can't exactly dance without the use of his legs.*

But Gracie frowns at me, glances at Blayne and then back to me.

There's a pause.

"In case it's unclear, I'm not exactly fleet-footed," Blayne says suddenly. It's as if he's read my mind.

Gracie continues to look from him to me. "No, no," she says. "Both of *you* need to use *your* brains! It's a *zero-gravity* dance! As in, weightlessness! So it doesn't matter if he can walk or not. When it's low gravity, he can sit it out, but he can definitely *dance* in Zero-G!"

Okay, wow. Gracie's absolutely right.

Blayne and I stare at each other, then Blayne raises one brow. "Lark Two has a point."

"Lark Two?" Gracie ruins the effect of her moment of brilliance and whines again. "Cut that out, that's just way confusing! I'm Gee Four and she's Gee Two, and no one's Lark Anything. Want me to start calling you Bee One?"

"Too bad and too late. As of today, we've officially got a Lark Two," Blayne says, with a sarcastic crooked smile.

"No, we don't!"

"I dub thee Lark Two—"

"Okay, okay," I say, realizing it's almost 9:00 AM. "I'm going to be late to work, so please behave, Gracie—and Blayne, hang out with her please, okay?"

And as Gracie looks away momentarily, I mouth silently to Blayne, *"Watch her, I beg you!"*

He raises one brow then rolls his eyes. "Yeah, okay, got it."

And then he sings a tone sequence and deftly turns the board around in the corridor. "Come along, Lark Two, I've got an Imperial Command Ship to show you."

I leave them be and run to the Command Deck Two central hub, toward the Resonance Chamber. By the time I make it to the CCO corridor, I see the numbers of Atlantean crew hurrying back and forth, and can finally gauge the serious level of work that's about to take place.

I haven't noticed any doors to the Resonance Chamber before, but now I realize that they have been there all along—almost seamless floor-to-ceiling panels facing the junction where the corridor turns, and the corner CCO office stands.

They stand open now, and as I approach I see a softly lit great interior, beckoning me inside.

I walk past several crew members doing something to wall panels in the hallway right next to the entrance, and then I go in—or rather, I take a step. . . .

Holy lord in heaven, wow!

I am inside an immense sphere—a hollow ball the size of a football field.

How is that even possible? This spherical chamber is immense, it goes up hundreds of feet in all directions, and it's at the center of this ship.

How huge must the ark-ship *itself* really be, to fit this sphere? I recall seeing what an ark-ship looks like on approach via shuttle. . . . But even so, the miles of hull going up and down and across don't properly register. My mind cannot grasp the dimensions. I try to think of some kind of analogy, and the closest I imagine is a round fruit, like a peach, with a pit in its center—that would be the proportions of the Resonance Chamber to the rest of the starship. Except, the starship is not a sphere but a flattened saucer. . . . It occurs to me, the Resonance Chamber sphere probably defines the *height* of the ark-ship. Imagine if someone took a peach and flattened it under a press, but enough to leave the pit intact. That's the starship!

As I'm thinking these crazy thoughts, some Atlantean pushes past me into the chamber, carrying things, so I get out of his way, and step inside.

Okay, let me explain what I'm actually stepping on.

The spot at the doors where I'm standing is the exact widest circumference level of the sphere. Half the dome is above my head, and the other half is below—an upside-down dome, or a great bowl, dropping off into a dizzying empty space, lit with a soft milky illumination that seems to have no source and is seeping through the smooth glassy panels themselves.

A ten-foot wide walkway runs in a donut circle all around

the inside of the sphere chamber. Upon it, people are working—currently doing acoustical diagnostics and testing the orichalcum underside portions of the panels that comprise the sphere's walls. . . . In the next few hours, others will be setting up the tables and refreshment stations, putting up decorations, installing special lighting and the musical DJ stations.

I step into the walkway, and look down at the "bowl" area, momentarily getting some of my old fear of heights back—there's no railing at all, and the drop is pretty tremendous. . . .

"Gwen, over here!"

I turn, and it's Gennio, about a hundred feet away on the walkway, doing something to the panel before him.

I approach quickly and see that he's holding a three-by-four-foot, gently concave panel that he's unsnapped from the wall. There's a solid orichalcum layer revealed in the wall underneath, but this outer panel itself is smoothly polished and resembles milky-white frosted glass.

"Hey," I say. "Please don't tell me you have to pop out every single one of these panels in this chamber?"

Gennio laughs. "Oh, no! This device tells me which ones need to be checked, so I simply walk around the room perimeter—and Anu too, and a few other techs—and when a panel is flagged, we pop it out and test it." He then takes the panel and puts it gently back in its spot with a snap. Once in place, the panel fits seamlessly into the wall of the sphere.

"How do you remove it? There's no edge or anything I can see," I mutter.

Gennio hands me a similar small gadget from his pocket. "Here, simply pass it over the panel and it will be electro-magnetically released from its bond.

"What about all the panels all the way up there? The ones on top of the ceiling, and at the bottom of the bowl? Can we go down there?"

"Sure, if anything down there is flagged, or up there, we go up, or we go down." Gennio points to a panel about ten feet down along the curvature of the bowl. "There's one faulty one there."

"How do we get down to it? Do we jump?" I speak only partly in jest.

"Hey, Gwen Lark, Earth girl!"

I turn to see Anu moving toward us from the opposite direction of the walkway. He's actually not *on* the walkway itself but alongside it, suspended in the air, gliding on top of a hoverboard in a loose skateboarder stance.

"Aha," I say. "So *that's* how you get down to the bottom and up to the ceiling."

"Precisely," Gennio says. And then he points to a stack of hoverboards a few feet away on the walkway. "Just grab one whenever you need it."

Now that they mention it, I see in the distance quite a few Atlanteans on hoverboards levitating at various points near the ceiling or down in the bowl below, as they perform diagnostics work.

I look around, and smile slowly. "This place is awesome!" I say.

A few minutes later I am moving around the room on my own, checking the panels as Gennio and Anu taught me.

The device is easy to use, a small intuitive touchpad, and the functions are nearly automated. I pull panels, test them against the device, return them back in their slots. When needed I take a hoverboard and use it to rise up or go down to reach a distant spot. The sensation of floating around this great chamber fills me with odd excitement and anticipation for the Dance tonight.

"I know there will be thousands of people here," I say to the guys at some point. "Where will they all fit? This walkway is going to be way overcrowded."

Anu makes a loud horse-laugh. "Want to start showing her the floor lifts?" he says to Gennio, while giving me sly looks.

"Oh!" Gennio looks up from his panel tile. "It's all movable, Gwen," he says.

"What?"

"The bottom part of the room."

"Huh?" I frown. I still don't quite get it.

"Like this—" Gennio does something on his touch pad. And then as I watch, a section of the bowl below, made up of about ten connected panels, starts to slowly rise toward us, like an elevator. It separates like an onion layer from the floor of the chamber, and a darker layer of orichalcum is revealed underneath.

The section stops moving exactly at the level of the walkway and hovers in place.

"Wow . . ." I say.

"Now, imagine the whole floor below rising up like that," Gennio says. "The Dance will begin with the floor raised to this main level. Each single panel is individually adjustable, so we can raise and lower any part of this chamber at will."

I stare up. "What about the ceiling tiles? Can you bring them down too?"

"Sure." Anu nods. "But why would you want to? Nobody is going to stand upside down on the ceiling. During weightlessness they will just be flying around all over the place anyway."

But Gennio responds to my question thoughtfully. "You know, if needed, gravity can be completely reversed on the ship. . . . So that the ceiling could theoretically function as the floor. In which case, yes, we can manipulate the ceiling panels exactly the same way. Of course I can't imagine *why* we would need to flip gravity upside down—"

"Hmm," I say, as my imagination starts working its way into crazy town. "What if the ship was stuck or crashed somewhere, and it was flipped over, and we were all walking on the ceiling, so then—"

"You are pitifully crazy, Earth girl." Anu shakes his head at me in superior disgust.

"No, wait!" I say. I am on a roll. "What if we're in the gravity well of some kind of star or a black hole that exerts a strong gravitational pull at the ship from the wrong direction, then flipping gravity inside the ship would make sense!"

Gennio and Anu both give me strange looks.

"I think you have work to do," Anu tells me. "Over there, two more panels are calling you personally by name. 'Check me, check me, crazy Earth girl!' they say—"

I sigh and get back to it.

A little over an hour later we're done with the acoustic diagnostics.

"That's it for us," Gennio says, as we walk back inside the corridor. "Decoration begins at 11:00 AM, but that's another Blue Quadrant crew team's responsibility."

"Oh, really?" I say, perking up. "So we don't need to do anything for that, or for Lighting at 1:00 PM, or Music Programming at 2:00 PM?"

"Nope." Anu wipes the back of his sticky forehead tiredly. "That's for the other Blue losers. As Aides for the CCO, we're done here."

"Blue losers?" I raise one brow.

"Just ignore him," Gennio tells me. "He's with the Red Quadrant and thinks his Quadrant will do a better job when it's their turn to host the Zero-G Dance."

"Heh!" Anu wiggles his brows meaningfully. "We always do a better job. That's why we're number one!"

"Not true!" Gennio is getting visibly annoyed, judging by the way he fiddles with his handheld, putting it away in his pocket finally. "The Quadrants are theoretically equal in function and importance. The numbering is just an old tradition—"

"Oh, yeah?" Now Anu glares at him. "Then how come Red is always number one in nearly everything we do? And Blue is number two? Oh, and mustn't forget the losers Green in third place and last place super-losers Yellow!"

"Hey!" I say. "I'm Yellow. Don't knock us."

"I don't have to, you knock yourselves every time just fine!"

"Don't listen to him, Gwen." Gennio rubs his head furiously. "It's only somewhat true—there's a tendency for Red to be more aggressive in achievement, and Blue to be more precise. Green is more steadfast and persistent, and Yellow is creative and original. But that's about it. All other tendencies are artificial—just a bunch of myth."

"Yeah, yeah, tell it to yourselves, losers." Anu starts walking away, head held high. "Wait till the Quantum Stream Races, when Red will win all the top spots and smash you, and leave you Blues and Yellows wailing in the back like fatty blubber fish."

"Whatever, jerk." I say softly in his wake.

And I go to look for Gracie.

The rest of the afternoon goes by quickly. Blayne and Gracie are missing for most of it, and I have no idea where to look. But I'm not too worried—I'll see them for dinner and definitely at the Dance.

At around 6:30 PM we get back from the Cadet Deck Four Meal Hall. Blayne escapes to his barracks for a nap, promising he will make an appearance at the Dance. Gracie and I head to my personal cabin, to freshen up and do the girly stuff before the Dance begins. And by girly stuff I mean mostly watch Gracie wash up, apply last minute makeup, brush hair, and fuss nervously about the stupid little things related to our looks.

"Do you have to be there exactly at seven?" Gracie asks, as she stands before my tiny sink mirror and pulls back her eyelid and looks deeply inside her eyeball.

At least that's what it looks to me like she's doing. . . . But she tells me she's curling her eyelashes with eyelash curlers that look like medieval torture implements, then applying eyeliner, sparkly eye shadow, and mascara, then putting in false strip lashes. She is also using an eyebrow pencil, a blemish cover-up stick, and powder foundation makeup, and finally lip liner and lipstick.

Honestly, I have no idea what she's doing—her makeup bag is laid out on my bunk and frightening cosmetic stuff is everywhere. I get a momentary flashback to Consul Denu—at least there's no perfume. Back home I never had to deal with seeing all this monstrous beauty ritual happening outside the privacy of her own room, but now, here we are. . . . What can I do, I love my sister.

"No," I reply to her question. "As far as I know I don't need to be there right at seven. Gennio, one of the other CCO Aides will be on duty for most of the night—he's one of the guys in charge of the gravity synchronization with the music, together with some other guys from the Blue team."

"Oooh! Sounds so awesome!" Gracie makes a giggle sound, and applies blush while sucking in her cheek then smiling to make the cheek "apple" stand out—apparently that's how you're supposed to apply blush properly.

There is one consolation at least. She's wearing her nice white Cadet uniform, and there is no horrendous dress.

"Almost done!" Gracie says, after unpinning her long dirty-blond hair because she's decided to wear it down after all, at the last minute. "Just going to brush out my hair one more time."

"Okay, I need to do that too, after you're done," I say, tugging my own ponytail by the rubber band to release my mess of long hair.

"Hey!" Gracie stops doing everything and turns around to look at me. "Where's your honeybunch Logan?"

"Oh." I purse my lips. "I think he might be working now, but I'm sure I'll see him at the Dance." I don't tell Gracie how Logan's been reassigned here to ICS-2, or under what circumstances.

"Oh, cool." She gets back to her hair fussing. "He's way yummy-dreamy, and hope everything is going great for you two."

"Yeah," I say, smiling lightly. "I guess...."

"You guess? Aww come on, Gee Two, let me know, details, spill!"

"Oh, hush, silly," I tell her. "It's private."

Gracie stops again and spins around. "OMG! You guys *did* it!"

"Gracie!" My mouth falls open. "How rude! And *no*, we have *not*, and you shouldn't ask that kind of thing."

"Okay . . . sorry." But she makes a silly face and turns back to the mirror.

That's when I start to blush with a delayed reaction. Thank goodness she's no longer looking at me.

Besides, it's almost time to go.

Chapter 25

At last we head to the Dance.

Yes, I got to brush my hair, and my ordinary uniform seems to be okay, with nothing out of place. So now we make our way through crowds of teens—overdressed, stunningly dressed, and wearing every imaginable trendy varieties of look-at-me outfits.

Even before we reach the Command Deck corridor, we can hear the music.

It's a light pounding Earth bass rhythm, and the song's a recent pop-chart hit.

Great, I think, with a pang of rising fear, *it's high school dance hell all over again.*

But Gracie's got a big happy grin on her face and she is buzzing with excitement.

We turn the corner, and we see . . . *blue.*

The light ambience is coming from the hallway, seeping softly to color all things—walls, floor, ceiling, even the moving shadows and human shapes—and it's pulsing in time to the music. People are packed in the corridor, moving past Atlantean guards in crisp parade uniforms.

I see an ocean of girls with slinky black dresses showing cleavage, long legs and bare backs, intricate hairdos, amazing striking makeup, weird pseudo-historical outfits, feathers, sparkling fabrics predominately blue in color, gaudy lipstick on fat puffy kiss-me lips, gloss and black kohl. . . . I see guys with slicked-back hair, spiky hair, weaves and long locks and curls and buzz-cuts, wearing jackets, shirts and formal tuxes, and everywhere white-and-gold dress uniforms of the Fleet.

And we haven't even entered the Resonance Chamber yet!

"I am seriously underdressed," I mutter.

"Yeah, you are!" Gracie says. "Want to head back to your place and maybe find something else to wear?"

"Oh, no. . . ." I shrug. "I don't own anything nice anyway."

So we keep going.

Finally, we're at the doors, going inside.

The milky-white sterile sphere from this morning has been completely *transformed*.

The place is magic. A grand world of shades of *blue*, with a deep velvet sky overhead, so dark blue it's almost black, and the illusion of stars sprinkled all around. Garlands of snowflakes and cobweb-fine glittering tassels cascade from various points along the dome. Suspended upon tassels, tiny micro-lights glimmer, like blue, white, and gold fireflies.

The wall panels closest to the bottom are glowing and pulsing in subtle blue transitions of shadow-to-light, and the floor has been raised up to the main level, so that the immense crowds fill the middle of the humongous chamber.

Groups of people are milling around the perimeter near the drink stations. Many are dancing, but nothing out of the ordinary yet—they haven't started the gravity manipulations.

I push inside, after Gracie, and try to look around in this super dense crowd for a glimpse of anyone at all who might be familiar. . . .

At least I know where to look for Gennio, since he's stationed near the walls close to the entrance, and watching a small computer station.

I look to the rows of seats lining the perimeter and see quite a few girls and boys sitting quietly, or just milling near the walls. Some of them are really dressed up, others not so much. But they all have that awkward look, where they're not quite sure what they're doing here exactly . . . and I recognize myself in them.

These are the awkward geeks, the nerds, the loners and outsiders, the uncool losers who don't belong. None of them will get asked to dance tonight. And none of them will dare to ask anyone else. If not for my current assigned duties in general, I would be one of these wallflowers. . . .

My sympathetic gaze keeps moving along these people,

drawn to them with a sense of camaraderie. At one point I see a vaguely familiar, large, bulky girl, sitting with shoulders slumped forward, staring out into the room with a dull gaze. She is dressed up in a big sparkly navy-blue dress, her hair is up with ribbons, and she has dark makeup on. I recognize Chiyoko Sato, the Japanese girl from my Pilot Training.

Momentarily I consider going up to her and saying "hi."

"This is nuts! How are we ever going to find anyone in this huge place?" Gracie says, tapping my arm.

I return my attention back to my sister.

"Just get these things—couple locators," a girl in bright makeup next to us says. She's holding two small glowing blue pins in her hands. "They're handing them out at that station." And she points, then turns away.

Gracie and I shove our way to the wall and see a line of people. Atlanteans are handing out the blue-light pins in pairs.

"How does it work?" a boy asks.

"Just pin one on, and then give the other to your friend," the Atlantean girl explains. "The pins transmit your location with blinks. Long blink intervals mean you're far away. Faster blinks mean you are getting closer. Solid steady light is when you're standing next to each other."

"Hey, neat!"

I grab a pair and so does Gracie. I pin one on and pin the second on her sleeve. The pins remain steady blue.

"There," I say. "Now we can find each other."

"Great." She looks at the other pair in her hand then looks around us with a searching gaze. "I'll save these until I see Blayne. He'd better come! He promised!"

I smile. "Don't worry, he'll be here. If he promised, you can trust him to show. Boy's reliable."

"Yeah," she says, biting her lip. "I know. He *saved me*, remember?" And she continues to throw quick glances around.

Immediately I think of those last critical minutes during Qualification Finals when Gracie fell off her hoverboard as we were flying out of the subterranean chute tunnel, and Blayne caught her and held her with one hand in a Grip of Friendship, pulling her to safety. Apparently it's really made an impression on Gracie. I don't blame her—Blayne really *did* save her life.

If I didn't know my sister better, I'd think she's somewhat nervous. But Gracie is always high-strung, so this is not really something I can be sure about—normal stressed Gracie versus extra-tense.

"Why don't we go check the seats that line the walls?" I say. "He might already be here and—"

"Attention, Cadets, Civilians and Crew! Blue welcomes you!" A loud booming voice interrupts us, coming through the acoustic system in the walls like the voice of God—namely, echoing as though a deity has spoken from somewhere very far, such as Mount Olympus—while at the same time the dance music fades into silence. I recognize the voice belonging to Pilot Keruvat Ruo.

"Today, in this cold Season of Blue, may you be warmed by the presence of friends who were once strangers!"

Crowds of teens clap and hoot.

I glance around the immense expanse of the spherical chamber, trying to see where it's coming from—where Keruvat Ruo is—but it's impossible. He might be speaking from some other room. . . .

No, wait, I see him. Right in the middle of the great dance floor, a small circular portion of the floor has been raised about five feet. It's floating in the air, and now a spotlight is slowly blooming upon it. Pilot Ruo stands there, illuminated from all sides, dressed in the white uniform of the Fleet, in sharp contrast with his rich velvet-black skin. His metallic gold hair gleams with a nimbus of brightness, tinted blue with the ambient lighting.

"All right," he booms at us. "Are you ready for the Zero Gravity Dance?"

The room screams back at him, *"Yeah!"*

"Great! Just remember, there will be only one warning! The Music Mage will say, 'Gravity changing now!' and the rest will be a surprise! So expect low gravity, no gravity, and everything in between! Are you ready?"

"Yeah!"

"What's the magic warning?"

"Gravity changing now!" the thousands of teens roar in reply.

"That's right! You got it! Now, Dance! *Orahemai!*"

And the spotlight on Pilot Ruo fades, his section of floor descends back to main level, while at the same time a high-energy popular dance song blasts out of the glorious acoustic system, and everyone is once again dancing, jumping, and everyone *screams*. . . .

"Oh, no, I *love* that song!" Gracie shouts in my ear. "I wanna dance!"

"Go ahead!" I shout back with a smile.

Gracie makes big eyes at me. "But I don't want to dance alone! I wanna dance with someone!"

"Okay. . . ." We're still at the periphery, not too far from the closest entrance, so I look around over swaying and jumping people, desperately trying to see anyone I know for Gracie to dance with.

"Let's try over there near those other wall stations," I say, pulling her by the arm.

We squeeze, shimmy and shove our way to the closest wall area where seats line the perimeter and where the main acoustic station is located. I see the small partially walled off glass cube and inside is Gennio with a couple other Atlantean guys I don't know and one girl, whom I recognize as Vazara Hotat. All the boys wear the white parade uniforms, and look sharp. Meanwhile, Vazara is a sparkling azure nymph made of glitter and netting, like a sea creature. Her hair is threaded with pale blue flowers and her eyes are great smoky kohl.

Once again I feel oddly out of place in my dowdy plain uniform.

"Gwen!" Gennio waves with one hand, and with another he manipulates a smooth touch-console with a holo-grid projection in white. The whole workstation is floating in the air before him like a tropical island.

We crowd around the cube and I yell, "My sister Gracie wants to dance—any volunteers?"

"Sure," says one of the Atlantean boys, about Gracie's age. "I'm not up for Mixing until later, so yeah. Let's dance!"

"What's your name?" Gracie yells.

"Baritei Gaido! Just call me Bari!"

And off they go, disappearing into the crowd in the middle

of the dance floor.

"How's it going?" I ask Gennio.

"Pretty good!" He points to his console holo-station.

"You look good!" I say, pointing instead to his uniform.

"Thanks, you too," he replies politely.

I cringe, laughing. "Nah, I know I look like junk, but that's okay. I'm here to see the physics magic! Talking about—who's the Music Mage? Is that you?" I ask.

But Gennio shakes his head and points to Vazara.

And just on cue, she demonstrates. The Atlantean girl winks at me, swaying in perfect rhythm to the music, and then she raises a tiny gadget to her mouth.

"Gravity changing now . . ." she whispers mysteriously, in a sexy siren voice that resounds and echoes all through the room, amplified to sound like a goddess. And as she does so, the beat of the music slows, changing to another song, and at the same time the floor seems to drop out from under me in a sickening falling sensation.

But no! *It's the gravity!*

In seconds I feel lighter and the peculiar sensation of falling is overwhelming, relentless.

Everyone in the great chamber screams. . . . And then, people start jumping! It's crazy, because each jump sends you floating up several feet, effortlessly, like a trampoline, so that in a short while people start doing acrobatic tumbling moves, and it's all in time to the music.

"Whoa!" Teens shout all around me. Even the ones who are not dancing, start moving their bodies, curiously examining their hands, and a few leap in place with woots and screams.

"My hair is floating!" a girl exclaims nearby, twirling in place. I watch her long red hair twirl around, seeming in slow motion, like a movie special effect, and it's absolutely *unreal. . . .*

I admit, even I jump up in place to test the low gravity. "This is so damn cool!" I say to Gennio, who only nods at me.

A minute later the song ends and Music Mage Vazara speaks once more into her tiny mike: *"Gravity changing now!"*

Her thundering goddess voice sounds, and then. . . .

The world is falling.

Complete *weightlessness*, while a classical slow dance plays, switching into the gentle swaying rhythm of an Earth waltz.

I stare in amazement as the *whole dance floor* suddenly begins to move. Slowly it falls away, sinking down gently as a feather, leaving only the ten-foot walkway perimeter around the Resonance Chamber intact . . . while the thousands of people in the middle remain in place, *suspended in the air* over a great hollow bowl.

Oh. My. God.

I am floating inches off the floor. Gennio is floating. The whole world around us is floating. . . .

I watch, mesmerized, as many couples figure things out and take hold of each other, pushing off upward, so that they float up like balloons into the great blue expanse. Couples twirl, embracing, holding hands, holding waists, holding nothing at all but their fingertips touching. . . .

"Careful," Gennio tells me, as I start to float upward. "You might want to anchor yourself, since this is not the dance floor portion, and when gravity comes back you might fall down hard."

"Oh—yeah," I say, enchanted.

The song ends, and Vazara says the magic phrase in a voice that echoes with mischief. *"Gravity changing now!"*

And the dance beat picks up speed again, while gravity starts to bloom, increasing very gently, while at the same time the floor below starts rising, so that all the dancers floating on the ceiling have the chance to come down safely.

I am back on the floor, feeling weight returning.

"This is stunning!" I say to Gennio.

"Thanks," he says matter-of-factly.

In that moment, it occurs to me to ask something else. "By the way, where is the Command Pilot? Is he here?" I glance around in curiosity.

"Oh, yes." Gennio points to a distant spot along the walkway. "The CP is moving around the room, making sure things are okay. Last time I saw him, he was over there. Not on the actual dance floor section, of course, just around in the stations area on the walkway."

"Of course," I say. "Naturally he wouldn't be dancing. Not from what you guys told me about his dislike of dancing."

"Oh, no, not the CP." Gennio almost laughs. "He dislikes this whole event, but he is in charge of things for this first dance, so he must be here. But—no dancing."

"No dancing, I get it." I laugh softly.

And then I glance around again, peering in the distance, and this time I see him. Aeson Kassipei is standing talking to someone near one of the stations.

And wow, he is wearing the white-and-gold dress uniform of the Fleet. He looks commanding, stunning, indescribable, with his long golden hair brushed back neatly, his chiseled profile . . . his almost arrogant posture . . . the piercing glance of his eyes as he turns momentarily in our direction. . . .

Holy lord. . . . My heart starts pounding suddenly.

"Yeah, I see him," I say to Gennio, simply because I kind of have to say something.

"Gwen! There you are!"

I turn at the familiar voice and Logan is standing behind me.

Oh, my lord. . . .

Logan looks amazing. He is wearing the white-and-gold Cadet uniform, and his super-dark-brown hair reflects the faintest hint of red, tinted demonic blue with the room ambience, as it falls beautifully around his forehead in soft waves. His hazel eyes look down at me with a hidden promise, and there's a faint smile on his perfect lips.

"Wow," I say, looking up at him. "You look—you're all dressed up!"

He pulls one brow in a mock frown and shapes his lips in a pout. "And you're *not*. Darn . . . I was really hoping to see you all amazing and extra-special tonight."

"Oh! Well," I say, and my lips part, while I start to blush in embarrassment. "You know me—I'm sorry, I didn't think—I mean, you're aware I'm a klutz. I don't really know how to do the girly stuff—or the dances, or makeup, or dress up or anything—" As I mutter, I'm getting more and more flustered.

"Oh, no, don't worry about it," he adds with a soft smile. "It's okay, really."

"No it's not, I'm sorry—"

"Really, it's *fine*." He takes me by the arm and leans in closer to my face. "I don't really care how you look, you are always beautiful—"

"Oh, phooey!" I slap his arm in continued shame. "Thanks for being nice, but I messed up tonight, didn't I?"

It's true, I think. *I didn't think of how Logan would feel seeing me all dull and boring.* What kind of a rotten girlfriend am I anyway?

"You're perfect," he tells me, still near my ear, and then whispers, "I really missed you these past three days. . . ."

I raise my hand to touch his cheek. "The CP kept you busy, I know." And then I manage a quick glance in the direction of Aeson Kassiopei, who has his back turned as he speaks to someone in the distance.

"You have no idea." Logan notes the direction of my glance, then shakes his head and looks at me closely. "But in any case, it's done for now, and tonight we *party*."

Oh, crap. . . . Again I get a cold sinking sense of dread. And I get a flashback of high school. "Eeep. Party? Okay, you remember those school dances in the MJHS auditorium?" I mutter. "I went to a few and it was kind of seriously awful. All I know is, I stood near the wall, on the gross sticky floor, in puddles of spilled punch."

He snorts. "Oh, yeah, I remember those things. They were pretty lousy. You know, my band played quite a few of them. The only decent thing was the smuggled beer."

Yeah, Logan was in a band, lead guitar, back in high school. Yet another reminder of how much of a loser I am compared to this amazing boy.

"Hey!" Logan recalls suddenly. "Did you get one of those people locator pin pairs?" He is looking at the one that's presently blinking on my chest next to my token ID.

"Oh, yeah," I mutter, looking down at my chest. "That's for locating Gracie. She is out there dancing—"

"Aww," Logan makes the silly pout face again. "You didn't save a pair for us—you and me?"

"Oh, crap!" I say, putting my hand up to my mouth. "Okay, can we get another set? I'm such a classic idiot tonight!"

"No, you're not." He grins at me, while taking out a pair of blue pins from his own pocket. "Fortunately I have mine right here." And Logan pins another pin on the other side of my chest so that I have two, and pins his own matching one to his chest.

"Now, let's go dance, my classic one!"

"Oh, no, Logan, please, no! You know I dance like a hippo! I will step all over your toes and mess up your nice shiny boots—"

But even as I continue to protest, Logan sweeps me into his arms and pulls me with him into the dance crowd.

Chapter 26

"*G*ravity *changing now!*"
The seductive voice of the Music Mage speaks at us out of the airy dome—for whatever countless time this evening—as the music track changes to low gravity.

Logan and I sway-float in a slow amazing embrace, with him holding my lower back and waist, and his face nuzzling my ear, while my hands are wound around his neck as we gently come down from the ceiling after a zero gravity dance—possibly my tenth one this night.

Wow, zero gravity dancing.

Since the first time I've experienced this amazing sensation, it never ceases to amaze. At first, when the dance floor falls away, and you remain floating in the air, the feeling is a mixture of panic-dream and vertigo. . . .

Your brain cannot *understand* what is happening with the sudden lack of gravity, so it tries to compensate, and as a result it feels like you're falling, endlessly.

Falling . . . falling . . . falling. . . .

It's a little like being on an amusement park roller coaster—that moment when the coaster falls down steeply and you scream because you have to—it's what your body does in reflex. Now, take that moment of falling, and just extend it, sickeningly.

At first it's queasy and unpleasant. But then something inside you adapts. And there's a flood of amazing natural *euphoria*. You are swimming through the air, a strange magic aerial fish, and the sense of freedom lets you feel suddenly invincible, able to do anything, *be* anything.

You look down, and there's the floor, far below, and it's *not* rushing toward you sickeningly. Instead, the rules of physics have changed. Suddenly you can fly. You are in control of the universe, existing within the moment—completely *alive.*

You look up toward the ceiling, and you can reach out and touch it, with a single push off. . . . Just let go of someone's hand and aim high!

It helps the illusion of grandeur that tonight the ceiling is a dome of stars, velvet cosmic darkness sprinkled with light. You can touch them now. Just once, just for tonight. . . . And you *do.*

And oh, the music! The lighting! It all works together, as you begin to turn softly, swept away by the common rhythm. You circle each other, you tumble and spin and move with your partner, and each one of you corrects the motion of the other with the lightest touch. You're now a part of an endless circle dance, and your hair floats wildly, and your clothing merely kisses your skin, brushing past you in the air. . . .

Even now, everything I describe is insufficient. You *have* to be there—to soar, to breathe it in completely—in order to understand.

Well, it's now been at least three hours, and I'm in a sweet state of exhaustion and over-stimulated senses. . . .

And I think back on what happened earlier.

After my initial shy protest, Logan dragged me to the dance floor and patiently showed me all kinds of moves, both for the fast dances and the slow intimate ones. Wow, the boy can dance! We were rocking out during the fast bass-rhythm tracks, and the low gravity jumping was pure magic.

"You can dance just fine," he told me. "You have such an amazing singing voice and that indicates you have an underlying sense of rhythm—all you must do is stop holding yourself back. Just let go, and let it take you. Your body knows how to move—"

At some point after the first hour, it happened. I stopped being particularly awkward and just let myself relax. I think I did step on his toes quite a few times at first, but it got better. He laughed at me, and then picked me up and placed my feet on top of his and just carried me around like a doll, stepping for the both of us. And that wasn't even during the low or Zero-G, but normal gravity. Did I mention Logan is way strong too?

There were at least two kisses. Once, at the end of a very

sexy twisting dance, we ended with our bodies pressed tight together and his lips brushing mine, and then lingering deeply. And the second kiss happened as we were floating way up on the top near the dome ceiling, with no one too close to our location. That's when Logan put his hand around my throat possessively, in a strange, intense and raw gesture that did not hurt but somehow made me sensually vulnerable, and sent electric tingles coursing throughout me. And he crushed his mouth against mine, so that for an instant I could not breathe.

"Whoa!" I gasped, as we finally came apart.

"Sorry, too much?" he whispered hoarsely.

But I shook my head and smiled at him, and then glanced around in light embarrassment. I thought I saw Command Pilot Aeson Kassiopei down on the walkway below, and for some reason I really hoped he did *not* see this.

I recall how Logan saw me glance down in that direction, and I think he figured out who I was looking at, because he frowned momentarily, but said nothing.

That was over the course of the last three hours—throughout which I was blissful and yet inexplicably *restless* at the same time, my senses buzzing, constantly glancing around the room, constantly distracted even though I was with Logan.

What was I doing, and why?

And now, in this transition between dances, my hair still floating around us, I stare dreamily over Logan's shoulder. . . . And I *think*.

I see Gracie not too far across the dance floor, dancing with Blayne—or to be more accurate, holding hands as they float down from the ceiling as the low gravity takes hold. Gracie skillfully guides Blayne over to his hoverboard that's levitating upright nearby, and he adjusts his lower body on top of the board, fixing himself in the LM Form. . . . As they turn, I see he is actually smiling widely at her. And oh yeah, there's a blue pin on his sleeve, and Gracie has a matching one, both glowing steady blue to indicate perfect proximity.

"Thirsty?" Logan disengages from me and I nod. We head over to the nearest drink station and grab two covered glasses with special straws, while we wait out this fast dance, the oldie classic "Bad Romance" by the venerable diva of our grandparents' generation, Lady Gaga. We stop by Gennio's gravity sound station and say "hi," while Gennio is taking a break and another Atlantean is working the gravity device.

The crowd in the great sphere chamber has thinned out somewhat, as some of the people have left for the night. Still two more hours to go until midnight, but at least there's now more room to move freely, and it's actually more fun. Those of us who are still here are either on duty, or are consummate dancers. Or, in my case, just fascinated with the whole thing.

I turn and blink and see the rows of seats against the room perimeter where the wallflowers sit. Only a few of them still remain. Most of the chairs are now empty—just a few drink glasses rest on the seats, forgotten. A lonely boy or girl sits here and there, watching the dancing crowd.

I see that Chiyoko Sato has not moved from her spot, not even to get a drink. It's a weird empty feeling to see her frozen like that, slouching. She is sad and large and kind of beautiful.

"Gravity changing now!"

The dance tempo slows down again, and gravity slowly starts to fade.

Suddenly I see *him*.

Aeson Kassiopei walks—slow, graceful, confident—past others in the crowd, and stops before the seated girl, Chiyoko Sato. He speaks to her.

Chiyoko looks up at him, startled, in surprise. There's an almost frightened look on her face, the look of a wild bird.

And then he reaches out to her, offering his hand.

Chiyoko Sato nods slowly, then takes the Command Pilot's hand, and rises.

He continues to hold her hand, as they move gliding toward the dance floor. There he puts his other hand around her waist, remaining straight backed and perfect in his elegant stance, and guides her into an amazing version of a waltz.

They float upward, rising like clouds, joining the other couples in the gentle dreamy weightlessness and the glorious music of reeds and violins and sounds of heaven. . . .

Aeson's pale gold hair floats around in a halo, fanning out gently. As he turns via floating motion at one point, I see a soft genuine smile on his face as he looks down at her . . . while

Chiyoko's face is transfixed with surprise and wonder. . . .

I stare, absolutely stunned, frozen motionless, craning my neck up, my lips parted.

"Wow . . ." I whisper. "That is the most amazing, kindest, honorable thing. . . . That poor girl—he just asked her to dance and swept her away—And he *doesn't* even dance!"

"Gwen. . . ."

I turn around, my eyes wide with emotion, wild electricity buzzing through me.

Logan is looking at me seriously, strangely.

"Did you see that?" I say to him, pointing. "That was the most impressive—"

But Logan interrupts me, speaking in a flat voice devoid of emotion. "I can't do this anymore."

I blink. "What?" Something about Logan's tone sobers me immediately, and the emotional euphoria flees.

"This," he says. "All of *this*." And he motions with his head to me and then looks up in the direction of the weightless dancers, and Aeson Kassiopei.

"Huh?" I say. "What do you mean?"

"You know what I mean."

I frown, as the cool strangeness starts rising inside me. "No, actually I don't."

Logan shakes his head slightly, and continues looking at me, and his expression is now hard and remote. "It's you," he says. "You and *him*."

"What?"

"Wow, amazing. You really don't want to admit it, even now. Not even to *yourself*."

I am suddenly very cold. "Admit what?" I say, and my voice is unsteady.

"Oh, come on!" Logan is frowning and speaks quickly, breathlessly. "Look at you—you've been watching him—your Command Pilot Kassiopei—for the entire duration of the time you and I've been dancing. All these hours, every few minutes you turn around and you look as though you've lost something—you look for *him*. What do you think that is?"

"I—I don't—I am not—" I stutter, beginning to hyperventilate.

But Logan is relentless. "Listen, I care about you. I *need* you. I really do. I—I think I am in love with you. . . . This is *killing* me. But—" He pauses, as though gathering himself for something superhuman, and his eyes are raw, wounded. "But I can't be the one you *settle* for. I need to be the one you choose. The one you *want to be with* above all others—really, truly. Not an afterthought. Not because you can't have *someone else*."

"Oh my God, what? What are you talking about?" My voice is rising in anger, while a lump is forming in the back of my throat. "Are you saying you think I am *interested* in the Command Pilot? Like *that?*"

"Will you for once cut the crap, Gwen?" Logan puts his hands painfully around my shoulders, and speaks fiercely, leaning close in my face, so that I actually have to take a step back from him and almost float upward, because of general weightlessness. "You're not 'interested,' you are damn *obsessed!* Remember, I know how you operate! The same way you used to look at me in school, when you thought I didn't know—"

"Operate? How I *operate?*" I exclaim. "That's just the meanest, most despicable thing to say! You're the one here who's the *operative!*"

"Yes, operate!" He continues as though not hearing me, and gives my shoulders a hard shake. "And now, this thing that you're feeling for him—it's the same damn crush, but times a thousand! You watch him, you look at him—even during Qualification, back on Earth, all that time you spent training with him—tell me, do you really pretend even now that you're not attracted, that you're indifferent, that you're not *in love* with him?"

"I—I am—" I stand or possibly float, mouth open, breath snagging, and feel the tears brimming in my eyes, while the blue-lit dance floor all around us starts to fade and blur in my field of vision. Another moment and my tears will form into tiny droplets of liquid and float away. . . .

What is he saying? What is happening?

"Stop it!" I say to Logan. "Just—*stop it!*" And I push him back so that he releases his hold on me and just stands, semi-floating, breathing fast, staring wildly, desperately into my eyes.

I have never seen Logan like this—*crazed*, for lack of a better word.

And I—I have never felt like this. What is happening to me?

I am crazed too.

"*Gravity changing now!*"

Apparently the zero gravity dance is over, and gravity starts returning, and neither one of us cares or notices.

The things he just said—awful, biting, cruel things.

They are—they are possibly *true*.

"Okay, tell me," he says persistently. "Tell me you are completely *indifferent* toward him and I will apologize and beat myself up and forget this conversation ever took place. Well? Am I totally full of crap? Are you indifferent toward Kassiopei? Can you tell me that much at least? Can you, please—"

"I—" I open my mouth, and my breath catches suddenly. "I—*cannot*."

In that moment as I say it, Logan's eyes become tragic.

He lets out a shuddering breath, and his head hangs down powerlessly. Then he passes his hand roughly against the back of his hair. And he looks up at me, this time radiating cold.

"I knew it," he says in a soft, dead voice.

"I am . . . sorry." I stare at him, breathing fast, while the tears that had been brimming in my eyes now run endlessly down my cheeks.

"It's all right," he says, looking away, past me. "I think we're done here."

And with those words, Logan Sangre turns around and leaves me standing. He walks away in rapid strides, and I see his hand reach for the blue pin on his uniform, rip it off violently, and toss it on the floor behind him.

The pin lands, rolls and stops some distance away from my feet, and starts blinking to indicate the loss of proximity.

So does its mate, the corresponding pin on my chest.

I stand completely alone in the sphere chamber filled with people, blue light, and pulsing music, feeling that someone has slammed me over my head.

With my peripheral vision I see that Chiyoko Sato has

returned to her seat, and she looks different somehow, bright and *alive*. She is even holding a drink in her hand. Her dance partner, Aeson Kassiopei is long gone.

I turn around, pass the back of my hand over my face in haste to rub away the tears, and then see my sister Gracie and Blayne, both headed in my direction.

Crap. . . . Can't let Gracie see me like this.

I sniffle to clear my sinuses, then make a happy face before they get here.

"Great dancing, guys!" I say brightly.

"Oh, yeah, I never thought I'd say this, ever," Blayne says thoughtfully. "But I'm pooped from dancing."

Gracie tugs him on the arm and says she'll be back to get them drinks.

"I can get my own, you know," Blayne protests.

"No, I'll get them! You go over there and *sit!*"

"Oh, jeez. . . . All right."

When Gracie leaves, I nod to Blayne. "Hope she's not driving you too crazy," I say with a struggle at a smile.

"She's fine." He snorts lightly.

"Good." I nod, then point to the nearest empty seats. "Why don't you do what my sis says, and get some rest for your leg muscles. I'll be back too—need to replace my own drink."

While Blayne remains behind, I hurry over to the drinks station, while my mind is roiling in a strange, complicated party-mix of emotional states—unrest, upset, despair, confusion, anger (no—fury), worry, fear (no—terror), euphoria, *insight*.

Gracie is carrying two glasses, and I stop her momentarily. "Gee Four," I say, touching her arm. "What are you doing with Blayne? What do you think this is? He's a wonderful human being and he does not deserve to get hurt. Are you messing with him?"

"Huh?" Gracie pauses and stares at me with a frown. "Why would you say something awful like that? I'm hanging out with Blayne because he is awesome! Why would I ever hurt him?"

"Okay, fine," I say and tap her on the arm again. "But let me just say this once and I won't say it again. If you *hurt* that boy in any way, I will kill you. Got that?"

Gracie's mouth drops. "What is wrong with you?" she says.

"Why are you being such a witch all of a sudden?"

"I'm not," I say in a hard voice. "I'm simply giving a public service announcement or a heads up. Now, go on and party, sis. Make sure Blayne has a good time."

"O-okay. . . ." Gracie gives me another look. "Are you sure you're okay?"

"Oh, yeah," I mutter. "Actually I think I'm going to be heading back to my room. I know it's not midnight yet, but to quote our buddy Blayne, 'I'm pooped,' and I'm sure you can get back to the shuttle bay safely on your own. Just don't stay too late. The ship-to-ship shuttles are all waiting and scheduled to ferry people after the dance, but only for about half an hour."

"Gee Two. . . . Did something happen? Where's Logan?"

Damn this girl, but my baby sister is astute.

I bite my lip and smile.

"He left," I say.

Now Gracie gives me her full attention. "Why? What happened?"

I take a deep shuddering breath. "I think, sis, Logan and I just broke up."

Chapter 27

"What?" Gracie stares at me, and her lips part. She is completely deadly serious. "Gwen, what happened?"

I stand very still, trying to control my breathing, and just shake my head at her. There is only so much control I can maintain, after all this time—all the pent up things over these days and months, culminating in this one *thing*—before it takes me.

I must not fall apart.

Not now, not before Gracie.

"Well," I say, carefully choosing words. "He and I said some things, and for the most part, it was actually—"

"What?"

How do I even begin to explain? How can I tell my sister what I myself have trouble parsing right now?

Logan told me I had *feelings* for Aeson Kassiopei.

He accused me and he judged me. And he put it out there in the open, in hard terms that were cold and undeniable, laying it all out in its white-hot scalding *truth* before my stupid unconscious mind.

Logan was right—*is* right.

I am not indifferent.

I try to reason with myself. Reasoning is good. It provides focus and clarity.

So, what exactly do I think/know/feel, when it comes to Command Pilot Aeson Kassiopei, Phoebos, *astra daimon*, Imperial Crown Prince, son of the Imperator of *Atlantida*, and my commanding officer?

He's the guy who dances with the wallflower.

The guy who eats alone at his desk instead of the meal hall, so as not to make his subordinates feel uncomfortable, and works around the clock.

Who goes in like a madman, guns blazing, and saves lives—including my own life—after I save his.

Who trains me and gives me orders, and looks at me sharply.

He's the guy with intelligent blue eyes, who wears the black armband of a hero because he once gave his life and *died* for Atlantis—a mystery I still don't understand.

He's the guy who's so far out of my league that it can be measured by galaxies, literally.

Who's going to marry a beautiful princess of the Imperial Court as soon as we arrive on Atlantis.

Who's going to be Imperator, and whose family is worshiped like gods.

Who possibly holds the fate of my family and my parents, not to mention Earth, in his hands.

The guy who, I was once told, cares about me in some way.

. . . *You matter to him, Lark.* . . .

And the guy who, when confronted, laughs in my face, and tells me he *does not*.

I take another deep breath to steady myself.

"Gracie," I say. "It's a complicated mess. Some of it is my fault. Mostly, it is not anyone's fault."

But Gracie continues looking at me with concern, still holding the two glasses in her now shaking hands. "What did Logan do? What did the jerk do?"

"Nothing. He told me some hard things about myself that are true. And I have to admit, I've been unfair to him."

Gracie frowns. "How so?"

I make a stupid little laugh noise and point at myself and at my plain uniform. "For one thing, I didn't dress up. There you have it. I'm kind of a crappy girlfriend."

"No! No way! That's just junk! You mean you had a fight over your outfit? What a horrid jerk to make something out of it—"

"Nah. That's just a minor symptom of the problem," I say softly. "The problem is, I care about Logan, but—I also have these stupid feelings for someone else. And—they are—nothing is ever going to come of it."

"Oh . . . wow." Gracie's mouth opens again. "You like—I think I know who it is—"

"Gracie, don't. . . ." I interrupt.

But she bites her lip and whispers. "It's Kassiopei, isn't it?"

"Damn," I say tiredly. And then I add. "Is it that obvious?"

She cranes her neck at me. "Well, not really, at least not too much, don't worry. But I think most of us kind of knew you two had something going on—"

"That's the thing, *nothing* is going on!" I exclaim in a sudden burst of emotion. "Nothing! Yes, okay, I'm attracted to him somewhat, but it's ridiculous. He's my commanding officer, and a damn prince! The whole crazy unrealistic thing is just— Why am I even discussing this with you now, Gracie? You need to get back to Blayne, and we can talk later—"

"Oh! But this is so important!" my sister says. And then she leans in to me and whispers loudly with a smile, "I kind of think he likes you back."

I make a gesture of disgust. "That's enough," I say. "I need to go."

And before Gracie can say or do anything else to rip my heart apart, I get out of there, walking with determination past the remaining dancers, until I'm out of the great blue chamber.

I don't start crying until I reach my cabin and close the door.

The next morning, I wake up and it hits me all over, like an ice-cold bucket of despair.

Logan and I are no longer together.

I have feelings for Kassiopei.

I am so damn screwed.

Moving apathetically, I take my time getting ready, as I shower, dress, then head to breakfast in the Officers Meal Hall where I hardly eat more than a mouthful.

How in the world will I face him? And by *him*, I don't mean Logan, but the CP. The crazy thing is, it's not like anything has changed between the two of us—*I'm* the one who has changed.

Okay, get a grip, I tell myself. *You have no time for this crap. You have to work. You have to learn as much as you can about everything you can. You have to train yourself, and you have to keep going. . . . And at some point, somehow, you have your family to save.*

Remember the Atlantis Grail?

And I go to the CCO.

Thankfully Aeson Kassiopei is not there. However, the post-dance cleanup is going on in the central hub corridor right next to us, and Gennio and Anu are both late. So I end up having to handle a number of Atlantean officers who come by to see the CP. By the time the other two aides arrive, nearly an hour late, I am ready to hide somewhere.

"Great job at the dance last night," I say instead to Gennio, who looks sleepy and tired this morning from his long shift at the Zero-G Dance.

He mumbles something with a smile, then begins his work.

Anu yawns deeply like a crocodile, and works also.

I open my file and start a new chapter in the chronicle of the journey of Earth refugees that I've been writing.

The rest of the day passes like a bad hallucinogenic dream of various office tasks, classes, meal halls.

I don't see Aeson Kassiopei until our 8:00 PM voice training session. As I arrive at the doors of the CCO and pause while the guards admit me inside, my heart is hammering so wildly that I think I am going to die.

The Command Pilot sits at his desk, working on a console. The moment I walk in, he looks up. "Come on in," he says, and swings the console-and-monitor unit mech arm out of the way, clearing the desk surface.

His expression is unreadable and his eyes watch me steadily as I approach—while I maintain an illusion of as much calm as possible—while inside me oceans of emotion are churning.

"Hi," I say, breathing shallow.

His one brow rises slightly at my oddly casual, monosyllabic greeting.

Okay, what did I just say? That was suspicious. Not to mention, stupid. I should've said, "Good evening, Command Pilot." Or maybe not—that would've been too formal, so even worse.

Okay, this is crazy.

As my thoughts go into panic mode, I take a seat across from him at his desk.

Aeson Kassiopei continues watching me silently. I wonder if he noticed something unusual about me? Am I staring too hard at him? Am I meeting his gaze too directly, head on—or not enough?

Am I being sufficiently *normal?*

Okay, what does that even mean, what's being normal for me?

"Remind me what we were doing the last time?" he says, as he takes out the familiar soundproof box with the pieces of orichalcum and sets it on the desk. And then he remembers. "Oh, that's right, it was the heat generating exercise."

"Oh, yes," I say. And because I think of *heat*, and then remember again the Semi-Finals in Los Angeles, when he put his bare hand on the burning baton and saved me and Gracie, my face suddenly erupts in a horrible deep flush.

He is not looking at me as he takes out one lump of orichalcum and begins to sing the complex series of notes to cause the piece to levitate and then undergo the incendiary reaction. His dark, beautifully low voice sends cascading shivers through me. . . . The piece starts glowing angry rose-red as it hangs in the air before us.

"If I recall, the last time you had some trouble," he says, glancing up at me in that instant while I am trying to control my breathing enough to dissipate the blush. "Let's see if you can replicate the sequence this time around."

And he sets a new inert piece before me.

I keep my eyes down, avoiding any direct confrontation with his gaze, as I try to sing the difficult array of notes he just demonstrated.

Once again I am unsuccessful.

"Take your time," he says, and again turns to his console, to do the usual tasks while waiting for me to achieve the new vocal ability in practice.

I glance up at him periodically, fleeting and quick, and his face is composed as he concentrates on the work. As usual, his lips are held in a tight line when he is particularly engrossed.

And, God forgive me, I start examining him blatantly, shamelessly noting every tiny detail about him, in those moments as I continue to look up. This is no longer unconscious and innocent on my part—this is me *checking him out* and being aware of it, *knowing* precisely what I'm doing.

"What is it?" he says, glancing at me eventually. "You're distracted, you're not paying attention."

"Oh, sorry," I mutter. "I was just thinking about how incredible the Zero-G Dance was last night. I had no idea that kind of thing could even exist!" And I smile shyly, then have to look away, because his so-very-blue eyes—oh, he is *looking* at me.

"You seemed to have a good time," he says, after the slightest pause. He does not smile back, but his expression is bland, or maybe controlled. "It's a fine old Atlantis tradition, zero gravity dancing. There will be more chances for you to experience it in the coming months. . . . All right, now try again. This time, focus on holding the sharp notes a little longer." And he nods to the orichalcum piece lying before me.

I get back to my efforts. It's futile; I'm incapable of concentrating tonight—at least not this soon after my new-found awareness of my feelings toward him. Having him so close, and having to do a focused task just now is an impossibility.

Get. A. Grip. Idiot. Gwen.

By the way, the incidental absurdity of it doesn't escape me—I'm supposed to generate *heat* in an inert piece of alien metal, all the while I'm burning inside.

Slow, *slow* burn.

I have no idea how I'm going to survive—this evening, tomorrow, all the coming days, for as long as I have to work alongside him until we arrive in Atlantis.

And then what?

I try not to think too far ahead.

One day, one moment at a time.

This is the point in the recounting of events when things become blurry. Time stretches out into a long daily routine.

There's no reason for me to describe every day, and for that matter every week that follows. I wake up every day, go in to work, take classes, see my fellow CCO aides, my commanding officer, all while I maintain a careful wall of composure that eventually becomes second nature—because it must.

The Fleet has left the solar system, and the vast reaches of the Oort Cloud which is the final, quasi-theoretical marker of the Sun's influence. Whenever I go to the shadowy ICS-2 Observation Deck, to stare at the perfect darkness of interstellar space, there's no more Sun to look for—not even as a bright, remote, blinding pinpoint of light. The Sun has faded into yet another distant, anonymous star and dissolved into the surrounding cosmic expanse. Nothing remains now as a frame of reference except the surrounding ark-ships of the Fleet itself, seeming to be stationary objects of violet plasma, as they stretch out into an endless formation all around us.

I have no idea where we are in space. . . .

The Atlantean Blue season—abbreviated artificially into three Earth-style months—finds me studying and spending much time in the Pilot Training flight simulator classroom, even during after hours.

The Pilot Training itself is arduous and slow progress. Hugo Moreno and I work together very poorly, and our improvement is marked in tiny daily increments. But then, so is it with most every other Cadet in this advanced training classroom taught by ruthless taskmaster Mithrat Okoi.

Every day we practice endless variations of shuttle run scenarios, with and without weapons grids, enemy obstacles, and other complications. As a working pair, I think we're relatively average in our achievement, and that seems to annoy Hugo to the extreme. He greets me with grumbles and frowns, and tends to blame me for every failed run. "Your fault, Gwen Lark, again—so stupid. You slow me down, man! Way down!"

Other people in the class show markedly faster improvement. Erin and Roy Tsai are one of the top three Pilot and Co-Pilot pairs, together with the Russian girl Alla Vetrova and her South African partner Conrad Hart, plus Leopold Deller from Austria and his partner DeeDee Kim from the Philippines.

Logan is in the class of course, but he and I have been avoiding each other for days, now—which is turning into weeks.

We're completely polite if forced to be in the same room, which happens a few times in classrooms, meal halls, and even at the CCO—since Logan still does work for the CP, and those Earth Union criminal procedures are ongoing, in conjunction with the Atlantis Central Agency and the Poseidon courts. But otherwise Logan never looks at me directly or meets my eyes, and all our contact is forced. I have no idea if Aeson Kassiopei has noticed—how could he not, seeing how chilly Logan and I are with each other?—but the Command Pilot does not say anything.

So, did I screw it up big-time, by breaking up with Logan Sangre?

Let me think. . . . Logan was the perfect boyfriend. He's been my dream for so long and he made me happy. Yeah, I still have feelings for him, even *right frigging now*. They are not the same mushy overwhelming, all-consuming feelings, but they are there, and I do *care* about him. I miss his sensual strength, his soulful kisses, the touch of his hands. . . . And yes, I continue to agonize over this decision many late nights as I lie in my tiny solitary cabin, listening to the gentle hum of the air in the vents.

However, I also can't deny the reality. Which is—I can no longer give all my emotional attention and attachment to Logan, and that's unfair in a relationship such as ours was supposed to be. Was I ever in love with Logan? I think so. But I was also so much younger than I am now, and he was my first intense crush.

Besides, stuff like this is a distraction. I have serious work to do, and a mission, a *goal*, to take care of my family. Whatever my feelings might be just now—for anyone—it will have to get on the back burner. . . .

I know—easier said than done.

My other classes are proceeding well. Consul Suval Denu sees me once every few days in his perfumed personal quarters to teach me Imperial Protocol, and now I know a thing or two about life at Court—and how precarious and insanely ritualized it is—and how each member of the Imperial Family is to be treated. For example, I've learned that the proper term to use is *Archaeon Imperator*, and that the present one, Aeson's father, is Romhutat Kassiopei, the Archaeon Imperator of *Atlantida*.

I've also learned that Aeson Kassiopei has a younger sister, the Imperial Princess Manala Kassiopei, and their mother is Devora Kassiopei, the Archaeona Imperatris of *Atlantida*, who is known as the most beautiful woman of her generation.

This probably explains, I think, *the stunning physical appearance of her son. . . .*

Furthermore, under the tutelage of Consul Denu, I've also picked up another unexpected skill. It's the ability to maintain a subtle new level of composure under trying circumstances and to hide my turbulent emotions behind a neutral or pleasant mask. It's proving to be very useful whenever I am in the presence of my commanding officer Aeson Kassiopei.

In Atlantean language class, I've picked up enough basic phrases from our Instructor Chior Kla to at least recognize a few words spoken by the Atlantean officers and crew in the meal halls (and a few cuss words from Anu Vei). But after only a few weeks, I and the rest of my fellow Cadet and Civilian classmates, have a long way to go before we can speak Atlantean well enough to hold a proper conversation.

Meanwhile, I am doing reasonably well in Combat class, taught by Oalla Keigeri. The Twelve Forms of Er-Du are becoming second nature, and I spar well enough to be in the top third of my class.

It's also interesting to note that whenever I practice my Forms at one of the gyms, I often find Pilot Xelio Vekahat is there too, working out with weights and punching bags, naked to the waist, covered in sweat, and beautiful enough to make me turn away and blush. He glances my way and acknowledges me with a confident smile, which makes me recall the times during Qualification on Earth when I first had to work with him on the Forms. After his workout, he sometimes lingers, watching me move, and I find the almost tangible sensation of his gaze upon me a strangely stimulating thing.

There's no question that Xelio Vekahat, with his long midnight hair and sensual eyes, is also completely out of my league. But for an awkward nerd like me it's nice just to be noticed for once. I don't think it's anything more than that, but I enjoy the charge of energy I get during these workouts.

Oalla Keigeri is also the Instructor for my Navigation Class. I haven't mentioned Navigation before, because it's a very specialized short tech course for members of the Yellow Quadrant only, held just once a week. We get to learn the in-depth function of the Yellow Navigation Grid, and also the role of *sharp* notes in various command sequences.

In a nutshell—sharp notes compensate for the natural *degradation of pitch* that happens over an extended duration of time (a weird form of acoustic entropy at the quantum level). They are used to fine-tune the Grid itself and other instruments that require pitch precision.

During Technology and Systems classes, Instructor Klavit Xotoi takes us on frequent tours of the ship and makes us disassemble things down to their basic components. Some people find it tedious, or icky—as in the case of sewage and recycling systems—but personally I love it. My favorite part still remains the Hydroponics greenhouse deck. Instant peace and Zen-state relaxation.

Overall I find Culture classes with Nilara Gradat to be the most casual and relaxing. After all, Instructor Gradat was the one who first taught us about zero gravity dancing. We learn other basic aspects of everyday Atlantean life—the kind of entertainment they have, and their equivalent of films and television, books, and games. Atlanteans love to tell stories through music, so their equivalent of opera is a very big deal on Poseidon.

Of course, the serious stuff is also interesting. One of the aspects of Atlantean society is the early age at which children begin to study and assume adult responsibilities. "You will find that we have very young people doing work that you might find surprising," Nilara Gradat tells us. "If you think this Fleet is full of teens, wait till you see our towns and cities and the kinds of business trades that are handled by your peers."

The bulk of my time outside classes is taken up by work at the CCO. Gennio, Anu, and I have arrived at a basic common routine in our various tasks, and I find I'm comfortable around them. Even Anu is slowly growing on me, even though he's still a real prick. Meanwhile my chronicle of the journey of Earth refugees to Atlantis is turning into a book filled with fascinating events and descriptions.

Back in my cabin I call up Gracie and Laronda on a regular

basis. We gossip, chat, and make things a little easier for each other. "Girl, I still can't believe about you and Logan!" Laronda tells me every time, mourning my breakup. "How'd you let that boy go? You were so perfect together!"

"Apparently not perfect enough," I say, and try to change the subject.

I've even chatted with Dawn and Hasmik a few times, though my brother Gordie seems to be an elusive fish and almost never calls me back, no matter how many messages I leave. Seems like he's always doing a shift at his ark-ship's Hydroponics, and I don't blame him.

Meanwhile, I've discovered that Gracie calls Blayne almost every day, and I don't know, but is something happening there? Not sure, considering Blayne is about two or three years older than my sis, who's going to be turning thirteen very soon—her birthday is August 14, which is in the middle of the third Blue month of the arbitrary Atlantean journey calendar. I trust Blayne way more than I do my own sister, so whatever it is, I'm not too alarmed.

At the end of three months of Blue, Gracie turns thirteen, and we enter Green, the Atlantean equivalent of spring. During the first week of the first Green month—our fourth month in space—there's a second Zero-G Dance, this one hosted by the Green Quadrant.

Since officially the CCO has nothing to do with it, and I'm in no mood to dance or remember what happened the last time, I skip the dance entirely.

I hear it goes quite well, with the Resonance Chamber decorated like a stunning green garden filled with flowers, and Pilot Erita Qwas having her Green Quadrant organize a scavenger hunt in the middle of the event.

What's far more exciting for me is that at the end of that month, *real* Pilot Training begins—we finally get to train on real shuttles outside.

During the second month of Green (our fifth month in space) is our only chance to practice actual live flight runs before our first test—the Semi-Final Quantum Stream Race.

The Race is scheduled for the final week of the second

Green month. That's right before the dangerous third month of Green begins—our sixth month in space, also called Jump month—when the Quantum Stream becomes too deadly and unstable for beginners.

The Race is the day after tomorrow.

It's what we've been training for, our first major Test.

The Quantum Stream Race will determine our Cadet Preliminary Standing in the Fleet.

And for me, it might make a huge difference in *status*.

For the moment, I'm still neither a Cadet nor a Civilian.

But if I succeed in this Cadet event, I might be able to convince Command Pilot Aeson Kassiopei to allow me to proceed with my insane plans regarding the Games of the Atlantis Grail.

The only thing I've got to lose is . . . *everything*.

Chapter 28

I wake up on the day before the Quantum Stream Race with the gloomy knowledge that our Pilot Standing Scores will be posted today, which will determine our entry order for tomorrow.

The problem is, Hugo and I are probably in the bottom third of all our classmates. Our last three shuttle runs outside were precarious, terrifying, and at one point I thought we were going to die.

I'm not kidding.

That's how bad we work together and how poorly both of us seem to perform. . . .

We've had a total of five runs outside. That's how many learning flight opportunities each pair of Cadet Pilots in the Fleet gets—on a tight, carefully coordinated rotation schedule—due to the limited number of actual shuttles and the hundreds of thousands of Cadets. So we had to use our turns carefully.

Our first shuttle run happened two weeks ago. As usual, Hugo was Pilot, handling the Red/Green Grids, and I the Co-Pilot on Blue/Yellow—with Instructor Mithrat Okoi supervising us remotely via audio-link.

We launched, entered the flight lane between ark-ship formations and then flew in a straight line for the entire length of the Fleet in one direction, then returned. It was *terrifying*. Hugo's hands were shaking during both the launch and braking swipes, and I had to compensate like crazy to keep us straight and on course.

Flying in the same direction as the Fleet is called *streaming*. Flying in the opposite direction, against the Quantum Stream is called *ripping*.

We *streamed* okay, then did the necessary turnabout before reaching the terminal anchor ships in formation which are either ICS-1 in the very front or ICS-4 in the very rear. As we were *ripping* back, and it was time to brake, I signaled the timing on the Yellow Grid, but Hugo ignored me for about three long seconds. So we almost overshot our home ship, and heard the loud angry shouts from Instructor Okoi: "Engage Brake now! Cadet Pilot Moreno, wake up! Use the damn Brake!"

We circled back around ICS-2 and barely made it into our designated shuttle bay.

After we parked and exited the shuttle, with the whole class waiting for us to complete our lousy first turn, we got to see Instructor Okoi's thundercloud expression and hear his disdainful assessment of our performance.

"Embarrassing first run. You do *not* hesitate, ever," he told both of us, but was looking mostly at Hugo. "This earns you *one point* out of a possible five. Very poorly done."

And that was that. Most other people in the class got at least a solid 3, and some, like the Tsai siblings, Alla Vetrova and Conrad Hart, and even Logan and his partner Oliver Parker, got 4s and 5s. Logan gave me a cool stare as he watched us get the crappy low points and the tongue lashing from the Instructor.

The next four runs we did in the following days were slight improvements, but we only earned one 3, which was on the third run, and the rest were 2s. Overall, a pitiful 2-Point Average, which is not something you want.

Well, today we get to see the culmination of our shame....

I shower and get dressed, skip breakfast, and head directly to the wide corridor junction between the Yellow Quadrant Cadet and Command Decks. On the walls here are several smart boards that are supposed to display the Pilot Pairs and our Standings, starting at 7:30 AM. The same boards are a posted in all the Four Quadrants, all around this hub corridor.

A crowd of teens is gathering very quickly. Girls and boys stare up at the boards periodically, waiting for their numbers to roll around, and discuss nervously and loudly. Most of the Cadets here are from the Yellow Quadrant, although I see a few Blues, Greens and Reds who happen to be in the area of this deck. Apparently the Atlanteans don't separate our scores by specific classes, and everyone's Standing numbers are simply listed in order, based on the total number of Cadets on *this* particular ship.

I know the same thing is happening today all across the Fleet, as Cadets get their Pilot Standings. I think of Gracie, and I *know* for a fact her scores are going to be better than ours. Gracie and her Pilot partner got 3s and 4s on their five live runs. *Way to go, sis.*

I stand in the crowd, getting elbowed by other teens, looking at the running vertical scroll marquee of alphabetical names followed by the name of their partner, and then the score. Each person's name gets mentioned twice during the marquee, so that everyone gets alphabetized in turn, with the partner name in parentheses.

An alternate marquee, to the right, lists the Pilot Standing Numbers first, followed by names. Here I see that Pair #1 is Alla Vetrova and Conrad Hart, followed by Erin and Roy Tsai at #2. Why am I not surprised? I also notice that Logan Sangre and Oliver Parker come in at #7.

Meanwhile, Hugo is not here, not on this deck. He is probably checking the smart board over at the Blue Quadrant portion of the corridor.

My name comes up first before his, alphabetically. I squint and see:

Lark, Gwenevere (Moreno, Hugo) – 547

Oh yeah, that's bad. . . . Considering there are 624 Cadet Pilot Pairs on ICS-2, we are not rock-bottom, but pretty close to it. And I can safely bet we're among the three lowest scoring pairs in our specific Pilot Training class, which is supposed to be the advanced, higher level class.

I turn around and see Blayne Dubois on his hoverboard, levitating upright a few feet away. His face looks mellow.

"Hey, Dubois!" I say. "What did you and Leon get?"

"Hey, Lark." He shrugs, craning his neck in his usual gesture to move the longish hair away from his blue eyes. "No idea yet. Waiting to see my name or Leon's."

"My score is just awful," I say.

He nods thoughtfully. "Well, don't sweat it too much, it's just a number. Not the End of all Things. That comes tomorrow during the Race."

"Thanks, very encouraging." I make a pitiful snort.

"Any time, it's what I do. Want to grab breakfast?" he says.

"Sure."

He pauses in that moment to stare at the board. "Ah, there we go—*Madongo, Leon (Dubois, Blayne) – 351*. Okay, I suppose."

And then we head to the meal hall, where most of us are too nervous to eat.

I show up at the CCO for work at 8:00 AM, and fidget nervously for the next two hours in anticipation of the next Quantum Stream Race prep-related event on today's schedule. At least Command Pilot Kassiopei is not in the office this morning to see me be all pitiful and stressed out, but Anu and Gennio give me funny looks.

"I think it's okay if you need to leave early," Gennio tells me at last, about fifteen minutes before 10:00 AM. That's when the Quantum Stream Safety Lecture is supposed to take place over at the Pilot Training classroom.

"Please, I beg you, *go* already. Go to your QS Safety Lecture early, Earth girl," Anu moans. "Watching you makes me want to do bad things to myself—but mostly others—such as fat-brain here. If you don't leave now, I will torment Gennio until he soils his uniform pants, and it will be all your fault."

Finally I give in and rush to my Pilot Training class for the special lecture.

The classroom deck with the flight simulators is packed with students already. I manage to grab one of the few remaining empty double console desks, and moments later Hugo shows up and takes the other seat, giving me the usual hard glare.

Instructor Mithrat Okoi stands before us like an old general, waiting to begin. Today the flight simulator screens remain blank and dark. Instead there is a large smart board in the back, which lights up at 10:00 AM on the dot. *"Quantum Stream Safety"* is the bold headline on top.

"Attention, Cadets!" the Instructor begins with the usual bark command.

We rise up quickly in unison, salute, and return to our seats.

Mithrat Okoi nods at us grimly. "This is your last class before the QS Race. Today we will not practice—today we will discuss what awaits you tomorrow. First and foremost we will review Quantum Stream Flight Safety. You think you know the dangers? We are going to go over them one more time, because you really *don't*. Knowing with your mind is not the same as being there, faced with death. Because one wrong move, and you *are* dead."

Instructor Okoi begins to pace in his usual manner among our rows of desks.

"First—we are in the final week of the pre-Jump month. The velocities outside are now phenomenal, and instability is *rising* every *second*. Which means that in one week, the only ones who will even be able to Pilot outside in the QS space will be the Officer Pilots in charge of your Quadrants. No rote Fleet Pilot will be allowed outside, not even a good one. Only the *astra daimon*. Do you understand what that means?"

We stare at him, and there is perfect silence. Most of the Cadets in the room barely dare to breathe.

Because yes, we have all seen it, first hand—those last few times we were outside on practice runs, we could see it—what's out there. . . .

There is no more "normal interstellar space" outside.

The universe is nearing a *blur*.

If you look at it, the *color of space* itself is *different* now, no longer pure black with occasional spots or patches of remote color radiance to indicate stars, galaxies or nebulae. Now, everything is *one* color. It's a strange surreal *off-black*, a lighter "space," almost a deep shade of grey, as though the entirety of the cosmos has been stirred up and put through the blender, resulting in a homogeneous mix of darkness and faint light, with the final product being dark roiling grey, like a field of static.

When Hugo and I flew last, we saw that terrible terrifying grey, no individual stars, no true light or dark, with nothing but Fleet ships lined up in formation, and the universe itself so uniform that it felt claustrophobic, as though it was encroaching upon us from all sides, a great nothing, squeezing us. . . .

Instructor Okoi continues. "Knowing how tough things are out there right now, it is vital that you understand and follow the safety rules properly. These are the rules, and we are going to discuss them one by one." He presses his handheld and a list appears on the smart board:

Quantum Stream Safety

1. Do not under any circumstances breach the Boundary demarcation of the Quantum Stream zone.

2. Maintain your flight course. Adhere to straight lines.

3. Avoid making sudden sharp movements or turns.

4. In case of obstacles, slow down first, then engage in evasive maneuvers.

5. Brake earlier than normal.

6. Surrender right of way to any other ship in your immediate vicinity if they are too close to the QS Boundary, allowing them to stay inside the Stream.

7. If you have the misfortune to breach and fall outside the QS Boundary, follow the QS Breach Emergency Protocol, or QSBEP-1.

"Now, the first and most important item on this list," Instructor Okoi tells us, "is this one. *Do not under any circumstances breach the boundary demarcation of the Quantum Stream zone.* What does it mean?"

He pauses to call up a chart of the three-column Fleet formation on the smart board. "The boundary is defined by the one kilometer corridor of space surrounding the Fleet on all sides. The boundary extends out beyond the exterior formation columns of ships on the right and left of the Stream, which are columns #1 and #3. It also extends out forward, before the flagship ICS-1, and behind the anchor ship ICS-4 in the rear. Stay within the zone! If you pass or fall out of this safe area of Stream space, you will end up *outside*, somewhere in the unknown vastness of interstellar space. That is a death sentence."

Erin Tsai raises her hand. "Instructor Okoi, what about the special instances when vessels coming from the *outside* have to merge with the Fleet within the Quantum Stream? How is that possible?"

Mithrat Okoi looks at her. "Are you referring to rendezvous maneuvers, such as the Mars station personnel pickup? Those are done under very controlled circumstances. First of all, approach and entry maneuvers are only allowed very *early on* in the journey, when the common Fleet velocities are not at their height. We are long past that relatively safe point. Second, only the most skilled *astra daimon* can do a *planned re-entry* into the QS field space from the outside, using QS frequency 'future projections.' This is advanced Piloting that *some* of you will be allowed to study in your second year—and most of you will not study at all. In short—Breaching the QS Boundary right now will get you killed."

"But what about the Emergency Protocol?"

"We will come to it in a moment. But—let me say this now, before you start to grow lax, thinking of it as a fallback. The QS Breach Emergency Protocol is *not* going to save you, unless you are very, very lucky, or very, very good. Most people who breach the QS zone do not come back. So do not plan on using it. Instead, plan to avoid the circumstances altogether."

Erin nods quietly.

"Item two," the Instructor says, once again calling up the list on the smart board. "*Maintain your flight course. Adhere to straight lines.* This might seem self-explanatory, but you need to remember that sometimes there will be circumstances forcing you to change course. If you are faced with such, do it wisely, and plot your new course with care, using the most straightforward route. Simple is always best. Hence, straight lines."

He points to the next item. "Number three. *Avoid making sudden sharp movements or turns.* This is the most common cause of breaching the boundary. Do not do it! Lose control, and you lose everything!

"Item four. *In case of obstacles, slow down first, then engage in evasive maneuvers.* I don't care if it costs you time in the Race. Would your rather lose time and get a lower score or lose your life? Slow down!"

"Okay, now I'm ready to crap my pants . . ." a Cadet nearby whispers.

Someone else giggles.

Mithrat Okoi turns in the direction of the noise and locates both the speaker and the person who laughed. He walks up to them in rapid strides. "You, and you," he says, leaning over them. His handheld device scans the two Cadets' ID tokens. "Demerits to both. Your outburst just cost you five places in you Pilot Standings."

Oh, crap. . . .

The class goes completely silent after that.

"Item five," the Instructor continues as though nothing happened. *"Brake earlier than normal.* This ensures precision, and is your best bet when the Quantum Stream is at the height of instability. All ship approaches should be done with greater care than normal at this time. Entering the shuttle bay upon return is one of your most risky maneuvers during the Race. This is where most accidents happen.

"Item six. *Surrender right of way to any other ship in your immediate vicinity if they are too close to the QS Boundary, allowing them to stay inside the Stream.* This means that if you see another shuttle next to you, and your movement might throw them off and cast them into the boundary, do not do it! Desist, and let them pass, especially if it looks like they are already in trouble. It is the honorable thing to do. If anything, consider this—you will never become *astra daimon* unless you act with honor toward others. If you have the slightest aspiration in that direction, then stay honor-bound."

Instructor Okoi pauses momentarily, glancing around the room.

We stare back at him, full of tension.

"Now," he says, "we come to the last critical item, number seven. *If you have the misfortune to breach and fall outside the QS Boundary, follow the QS Breach Emergency Protocol, or QSBEP-1."*

Mithrat Okoi turns to the smart board and calls up another list. This one has "QSBEP-1" on the top header. "This is the Emergency Protocol. If you find yourself thrown out of the

Stream, do not waste a single second. Make every attempt to follow the protocol, item by item, before you panic or give up and resign yourself to death. Note that this will be posted inside your shuttle next to your console during the Race, so that you can refer to it at a glance. Please, I repeat—if you have to follow this protocol, do it immediately, as soon as you realize you are out of the QS zone. Do not panic, do not hesitate, act!"

We stare at the new terrifying list on the board:

QSBEP-1 Emergency Instructions

1. Listen to the space around you in all directions for any QS signal trace.

2. Sing the exact frequency to match quantum resonance until shuttle acknowledges the match and is keyed. Synch the shuttle to the QS field.

3. Plot the signal coordinates onto the Navigation Grid.

4. Set new course and pursue the QS field immediately.

5. Re-enter the Quantum Stream zone as soon as you are within reach.

"Memorize this list," Mithrat Okoi says. "Let's break it down. Item one. *Listen to the space around you in all directions for any QS signal trace.* When a ship first breaches the QS and is thrown out into normal interstellar space, it immediately loses its *acoustic resonance charge*—the force that keeps it within the Quantum Stream—and becomes inert. The first few seconds are therefore critical. You and your ship are 'dead in the water,' but still within range of the Stream, and quantum traces packed with acoustics can be picked up on shuttle resonance scanners. Use them to grab those final shadow 'echo-remnants' of the Quantum Stream before they dissipate completely!

"How does it work? Sound cannot travel in ordinary space without matter, but a quantum field contains or traps acoustics temporarily, together with everything else. If you can locate the QS field, you might be able to access the sound frequency 'trapped' inside. Therefore, immediately turn on your resonance scanners and set them to *global scan mode*."

Instructor Okoi pauses. "Item two. *Sing the exact frequency to match quantum resonance until shuttle acknowledges the match and is keyed. Synch the shuttle to the QS field.* Assuming you got lucky and found a QS field trace out there, and your resonance scanner has picked up and recognized the sound frequency, now you yourself must replicate it. Basically you are now responsible for keying your inert shuttle back to the original frequency of the QS field. Without being keyed, you are still *out of phase* with the Quantum Stream and everything inside it, and cannot re-enter the QS field from the outside—even if by some miracle you are flying right alongside it. Think of yourself and the shuttle as being stuck in one dimension, while the whole Fleet is inside the QS field bubble in another dimension. You have to be synched up in order to interact."

The class is paying super-intense attention right now, and yeah, this stuff is hard. Normally I love schoolwork, but right now even *my* head hurts. . . .

"Item three. *Plot the signal origin coordinates onto the Navigation Grid.* How do you do it? Basically, once your shuttle is keyed, your Navigation Grid will auto-populate itself with the origin coordinates as your destination. You will see the destination circle pop up once again. However, to finalize course, you must Select and then confirm manually.

"Item four. *Set new course and pursue the QS field immediately.* This means, once you manually acknowledge the Destination, you have to fly your shuttle there, so do it! Engage the Red Propulsion Grid, swipe the forward Thrust, and fly as fast as you can!

"Item five. *Re-enter the Quantum Stream zone as soon as you are within reach.* This is self-explanatory. As you speed up and gain proximity to the QS field signal trace—the progress of which you can see on the Yellow Navigation Grid, as the two dots approach each other—you will have the chance to merge back into the QS field. Do it! This is your only chance!"

The Instructor goes silent for a few moments and observes the impact on our faces.

All I can think is, *Wow. This is terrifying.*

How in the world are we supposed to go out there tomorrow, now that we've had our pants scared off?

"Any questions on the QS Breach Emergency Protocol?"

No one raises any hands.

Instructor Okoi nods. "Fine. Your shuttle inspection begins at 1:00 PM today. All Pilot Pairs assigned to each specific shuttle must perform the vessel inspection together. It will be crowded, but you will manage. Remember, the condition of your shuttles will be added to your final scores tomorrow. Now, dismissed!"

I get out of there and return to the CCO, in a grim mood. Work goes poorly because my mind is not on it, and then I grab a quick solitary lunch at the Officers Meal Hall. I escape here whenever I want to get away from all other Earth teens—such as today. At this point I need time away from the entire crazy Cadet preliminary QS Race frenzy that's buzzing in all the usual Cadet places. Here it's relatively quiet. The Atlantean officers are just having an ordinary lunch. If I can pretend for a moment I'm one of them, maybe my heart will stop racing. . . .

Unfortunately it's not to be. I see Aeson Kassiopei come into the meal hall to pick up his usual bagged lunch. As always, the moment he's seen in the room, everyone stands up and salutes. Aeson has to acknowledge them, and command them to be at ease.

I watch his fleeting strained expression that is revealed just for a moment before his lapis-blue eyes become veiled, as he turns to the food server, takes his food, and walks out, proud and straight-backed.

And for that one moment, as always, with a twinge in my heart I feel sorry for him—for his position, and the distance he must keep.

I'll see him back at the CCO later. But now, the shuttle inspection awaits.

At 1:00 PM I am at Shuttle Bay One, in a crowd of my Pilot Training classmates and a bunch of Cadets from other classes. Our shuttles are parked in rows, on both sides of the platform, and we go looking for our assigned ones.

Hugo and I got shuttle #72, and it's somewhere in the middle of the lineup. By the time we get to it, we see it's open, ladder down, and other Cadet Pairs are crawling all over it, inside and outside, doing underbelly inspection.

There are six Pilot Pairs assigned to each vessel. We are all supposed to follow a standard checklist and redundantly examine each item on the list, even if another Pair has just gone through it.

"Okay, I'll take the first ten items and you take the next," I say to Hugo.

He frowns. "No, I'll take the first ten."

I frown and roll my eyes. "Okay. Fine, you take the next ten and I'll take the first."

"Okay—no, wait!" He really glares at me. "What are you saying?"

"Haven't you ever watched old-fashioned comedy routines?"

"Uhm—what? No! Just cut the crap, okay!"

I snort and let him take the first ten. Which means he climbs inside the shuttle while I deal with the exterior, bumping shoulders and knocking heads with the other Cadet Pairs inspecting the same parts, while we all crawl underneath in the hover space, between the floor and the shuttle underside.

Half an hour later we switch and this time I get to go inside while Hugo crawls underneath.

Eventually we're done and turn in our checklists with our recommended repair instructions and notes to our Instructor. This ship inspection is also part of our final Test Score, so we have to be careful and thorough.

I get back to the CCO, do some more semi-distracted work, listening to Anu complain about some personnel schedules to the CP, and then it's dinner and a small break in my cabin.

I call up Gracie and wish her luck. Gracie gives me a finger kiss against the screen and I know she is nervous as hell. Meanwhile, her whole barracks sounds like a zoo at feeding time. Yeah, she isn't the only one.

"It's going to be okay, Gee Four," I whisper with a gentle tired smile. "Just be careful, stay a little slow, and it's okay, no one says you have to win this stupid Race!"

"I know," she yells back, because she has to, over the din in the background. "I just want to place a little higher than average. Especially considering all the pressure to score high points for our Quadrant. You do know they are keeping track of cumulative points for all Cadets who are with Red, and we're supposed to try to beat the averages of the Blues and Greens and Yellows—"

"Okay, yes, of course!" I hurry to reassure her. "But it just means you can still aim to do well for yourself, but be more on the careful side as you do it."

"Yup!" She pauses with a silly shy smile. "Have you seen Blayne today?" she asks. "How is he? Doing okay?"

"Oh, don't worry about Blayne," I tell her. "His score is a decent one. He'll do fine."

She snorts. "I know! Just wanted to know if he is stressing at all. Hope not!"

"Oh no, the boy is calm and sarcastic as usual. All's well."

"Oh good." She exhales in relief.

I can't hold back a smile of my own.

Later that night I go to my voice training. I get to the CCO at 8:00 PM, and for the first fifteen minutes everything is routine as usual—Aeson Kassiopei has me practice our latest voice exercise while he works on something else. But suddenly, in the middle of things he shuts off his computer with a snap and turns to me with a steady look.

"Lark," he says. "Enough for today. Put that away for now. . . ."

"Oh?" I look up at him with a composed expression, and drop the orichalcum piece that I'm manipulating.

Over these many weeks I've perfected the blank calm look that I've cultivated especially for *him*. It's now become an easy habit, like putting on a Halloween sad mask. Why sad? Because, underneath it, I'm nothing but a trembling, vulnerable, raw *wound* that's refusing to heal. I realize how emotional and pathetic that sounds . . . but now that I've acknowledged my stupid feelings with my conscious rational *higher* mind, there's no use lying to myself any more or putting a pretty spin on it. Might as well face it.

But oh, how well I've disguised it from him.

He has no idea what's happening inside me every time I'm in the same room with him.

"I want to speak to you about tomorrow's Quantum Stream Race," Aeson Kassiopei says, while his intense gaze rests upon me.

"Okay...."

"I want you to be very careful. Do not take unnecessary risks. It doesn't matter how well or poorly you place."

"It does to me." I continue looking at him.

He, in turn, continues watching me. "Why?" His tone has become particularly soft.

"Because I have to do well enough so that when the year is over I can enter the Games of the Atlantis Grail."

His expression darkens. "Oh, no . . . don't. Not that again. Look, I thought we've come to an understanding about it, the futility, the dangers involved."

"Maybe *you* have, Command Pilot Kassiopei," I say coldly, while inside me turbulence is rising. "I am still resolved."

There's a strange pause. His eyes—oh, the pure, serene clarity of his relentless gaze.

"You are *not* resolved. I do not permit you to take unnecessary risks," he says, still speaking softly. But now there is a strange *power* to his charismatic voice, an insidious slithering force that comes up from deep in the ground and rises to permeate my skin with sweet languorous darkness. . . . Every word he utters falls with precision like a stone.

Wait—is he using a compelling *power voice on me?*

I blink and shake my head. And suddenly, like a flash of lightning, I am furious.

Oh my God. . . . Yes, he is!

So *that's* what it's like. I am certain of it!

"I'm sorry, Command Pilot," I say, pretending not to notice, pretending to be agreeable and acquiescent. "I'm tired and I need to go back to my room early. Need to get some rest before the Race. May I be excused, please?"

His gaze continues to overwhelm me, but now his lips hold back a smile.

I know—I can almost *see* it. And I am so mad I could slap him!

"Very well," he says, this time speaking normally. "You may go, Lark. Get well rested and take it easy tomorrow."

"Oh, I will," I say, almost sweetly—that's how furious I am now.

And then I get out of there before I do anything I might regret.

I am so going to win this damned QS Race tomorrow.

Chapter 29

The morning of the Quantum Stream Race finds me in high energy and strangely charged after the previous night. I find I am still angry at Kassiopei for attempting to *compel* me, and for some reason failing to do so—or at least me being well enough aware of it that it doesn't "take."

Hah! So much for all that fine talk from Gennio and Anu about the *compelling power voice* being illegal and immoral, not to mention dangerous enough to cause brain damage. So, does that mean that Kassiopei can get away with using it when others can't?

However, I get it. He *is* concerned, and I, with my Logos voice, am still an asset for Atlantis that must be protected at any cost.

And it's not like he compelled me to do something awful. He merely tried to keep me safe and *sedate*.

But oh, he is so going to regret it. . . .

I smile grimly to myself as I get dressed and head for breakfast. I have exactly fifteen minutes, before I have to report to Shuttle Bay One at 8:00 AM for the QS Race lineup.

I arrive early, but already the crowd of Cadets in Shuttle Bay One is overwhelming. The mind-blowing fact is, in this exact moment, the same thing is happening in Shuttle Bays Two, Three, and Four, and in every other ark-ship shuttle bay in the Fleet.

Everyone is crisply dressed in sharp clean uniforms, polished boots, and Cadet Star Insignias glittering on chests. Faces look nervous, determined—everyone wants to do well on this flight test, since it will determine a great deal of our futures (for some of us even more so than others, I think). Atlantean guards and officers direct us to our places where we line up to wait near our assigned parked shuttles.

Basically the Quantum Stream Race is a complicated relay. Each shuttle gets a series of six Pilot Pairs over the course of the Race, and each Pair goes up against ten others at a time.

It works like this:

The Fleet formation is made up of three long columns or lines of ships stretching to the horizon—columns #1, #2, and #3. The four Imperial Command Ships are all located in the middle column, which is #2. They are spaced along even intervals throughout the length of the Fleet. ICS-1 is in the very front, while ICS-4 is in the very end. The two long empty channels between the three formation columns are the racing lanes.

Shuttles launch from every ark-ship's four shuttle bays, emerge outside (on the right side of the ship if coming from columns #1 and #2, and on the left if column #3) and wait in a vertical "pancake stack" with ten other shuttles, at the designated starting point near the "racing lane."

The starting point is marked by a hologram light projection that beams out from each ark-ship, casting a wide strip of color light across the racing lane. This holo-strip serves both as the Start and Finish Line for each leg of the relay Race.

Each shuttle begins and ends its turn next to its home ship by crossing the Start/Finish strip. But first it must complete a circle around the Fleet, racing against ten others.

Ten shuttles at a time—each coming from a single vertical pancake stack—enter the racing lane and wait for the start signal. When the signal sounds, off they go. Thirty seconds later, the next vertical stack of ten (from one of the other shuttle bays, rotating in order) enters the racing lane, and so on.

The "racetrack" course stretches along the channel between the formations in a super-elongated circle. You fly straight between formations, *streaming* in the same direction as the Quantum Stream, until you reach the ICS-1 flagship up at the very head of the Fleet.

Here, you make a hard left turn into the space between the flagship and the second ark-ship in the middle formation column—taking care not to overshoot the flagship—and cross over to the other flight channel lane, which is the one you use to return, this time *ripping* against the Quantum Stream.

When you reach the anchor ship, ICS-4, which is the last ship in the Fleet, you again make a hard left turn in the space between ICS-4 and the second-to-last ship, and emerge in the original race lane where you started. Now you fly straight again until you reach your home ship and the Finish Line.

Note that if your home ship happens to be in column #1, you begin your race by moving in the "return" lane. You have to first fly *ripping* against the Stream toward ICS-4 in the back, then turn and *stream* toward ICS-1—basically you are still going in the same direction in a circle, but the *order* of which ship you reach first (ICS-1 or ICS-4) is reversed.

Yeah, it sounds complicated, but really it's simple—you fly to one end of the Fleet, turn around, fly to the other end, and come home to your ship, all while circling the middle formation column #2.

The time it takes you to complete the course, by crossing the Start/Finish Line, is marked as your Race Score. After you cross the Finish Line, you return back into the same shuttle bay, park the shuttle, and surrender it to the next Pilot Pair for their turn in the relay.

The six Pilot Pairs who use the same shuttle also share a common Shuttle Team Score that gets added to the individual Pilot Pair Score. This ensures that every effort is made to work well with the Cadet Pairs going before and after you—so that the shuttle is in good shape for each leg of the Race.

And now, about the scores. . . .

We've been told that the *top three* highest scoring Cadet Pairs from each ship will receive distinctions, including Quadrant distinctions. And the top 200 Cadet Pairs overall, will receive First Fleet Honors.

"Attention, Cadets!" the booming voice of Instructor Mithrat Okoi echoes from the walls of the shuttle bay around us. I'm guessing he is being transmitted to all the four shuttle bays of Imperial Command Ship Two.

We grow quiet immediately.

"Welcome to your first Quantum Stream Race. Pilot Pairs,

line up! On my mark—first Pair, you have control of the shuttle. Go!"

Hugo and I are the third Pair in our line. He looks very pale and withdrawn this morning, like he hadn't slept properly, and gives me dark frowning stares. I, on the other hand, probably look too wound up, still feeling cocky after the previous night.

We watch tensely as all around us the first two Cadets in every line run for their shuttles and climb inside. Seconds later, the shuttles come alive, move off the platforms and start entering the launch channel, ten seconds apart.

I realize that traffic controllers give them timing instructions from inside the shuttles, but it still looks very random and terrifying. It's a wonder they don't collide in the busy launch tunnel.

Once again the terrifying reality of what's happening slams me with panic.

Breathe, Gwen, breathe. . . .

I can do this.

Seconds tick, then minutes. We have no idea what is happening outside, out there in the Quantum Stream. . . . All we know is that it takes about 15 minutes to complete the course of this length on the average, and the time to beat is 10 minutes, a record set by some Atlantean Cadet back home.

Fifteen minutes later, the first of the shuttles start returning. The wind churn in the launch tunnel is incredible as the small flyers come bursting in, slow to a stop and park on their platform spots. Pilots emerge in haste, looking dazed and overwhelmed, and signal their replacements to take over the shuttles.

Immediately those in the second batch of Pilot Pairs go running to claim the shuttles.

Another minute, and our shuttle #72 returns.

As soon as the Cadet Pilots immediately ahead of us run to take control of our shuttle, I find myself standing in the very front of our line, with Hugo breathing down my neck.

The Cadets in the first Pilot Pair that has just returned with our shuttle stand looking somewhat bewildered. Then the girl starts yelling at the boy, and he shows a cringe-worthy expression of disgust.

"Hey, so how was it?" Hugo calls out to them.

"It sucked, hard," the girl says, whirling around. "We nearly lost control. That first hard left turn up in front of the Fleet—watch it! This bozo here almost made us overshoot the flagship and Breach! And oh, the lane itself is so crowded, tons of other shuttles, just horrible!" And she continues giving her partner a hard time.

"Great," Hugo mutters. And he glares at me.

"What?" I say.

"Nothing. You just keep it cool, okay? We can't afford to mess up."

"I know. And—you first," I say.

A few minutes later it's our turn.

Shuttle #72 comes in, the Pilot Pair before us climbs out, and hands it over to us.

"Go, go!" Hugo cries to me.

And we race for it.

As soon as we're inside the shuttle, Hugo grabs the Pilot chair and I take the Co-Pilot one next to him. Immediately I buckle in and call up a console panel from the wall, keying it to me, while Hugo is still messing with his harness button, with trembling fingers.

"Move it, Moreno!" I say in a hard voice uncustomary to me. "Or would you like me to take the Pilot chair instead?"

"Shut up!" he growls and gets his harness together, then keys himself to the console.

Both of us swipe the undersides of our respective consoles, making them light up. At the same time the window shields separate automatically, revealing the viewport with the crowded scene of Shuttle Bay One outside.

"Hurry!" I say. "Sing the ignition sequence already!"

Hugo glares at me as he sings the 3-note sequence while holding down the large button with the four-color racing lights—as the Pilot he has to go first—and I as Co-Pilot immediately do the same thing.

The shuttle comes alive with a low harmonic hum. Hair-fine threads of golden light race around the etchings on the hull.

I glance up and see something new—the two panels flanking the viewport on both sides light up in bright red text, in

English, and oh crap... it's the *QSBEP-1 Emergency Instructions* list, posted in duplicate, one on each side of the shuttle, like a grim reminder.

Hugo notices it too, because I see him stare momentarily.

Another thing we notice also is the appearance of a large readout in the center above the viewport. This is our Race Clock. It will be digitally displaying our progress in real time.

In that moment the voice of the Atlantean automated air traffic controller sounds from the walls. *"Ten second warning.... Shuttle #72, prepare to enter the launch channel."*

Hugo and I go crazy, as we pop up our grids, and Hugo coasts us over to the edge of the platform.

"... three ... two ... one ... You may enter the launch channel."

Hugo sings the sequence, and then his Red Grid goes 3D.

We are now off the platform and in the channel.

"Shuttle #72, you may launch now!"

Hugo swipes to engage the Thrust.

We blast off.

The tunnel blurs around us and in seconds we are outside in the muddy grey spacescape. The saucer hull wall of ICS-2 looms behind us.

Meanwhile, the "racing lane" area just ahead is full of speeding shuttles already in the Race. They pass by us like meteors, bullets, or specks of plasma light....

Oh, wow! How are we ever going to *merge* into that hellish speeding traffic?

"Okay, get in the stack! Now!" I yell, wildly entering corrections on the Blue Grid, because I see it—the stack of shuttles that had emerged just before us from the same shuttle bay, lining up in a vertical array next to our ark-ship.

They are our competition.

And directly ahead of them, the Start/Finish hologram projection stretches out like a virtual suspension bridge—a tightrope made of golden light across the racing lane... It continues for five kilometers, ending at the next formation column.

Yeah, did I mention, the racing lane is several kilometers wide?

"I know! I know!" Hugo yells, and positions us into the array, about a hundred feet away from the hologram strip of light.

We come in as the third "pancake" from the bottom. And in seconds another shuttle takes the spot right above us so that we can see its purple plasma underbelly as it moves in . . . then another comes in, until there are seven more shuttles directly overhead.

We wait on the sideline in our stack of ten.

"Pilots, prepare to enter the Race! Ten second warning. . . ."

Hugo and I flip between grids like crazy. While he preps us for the Thrust on the Red Grid, I flip to Yellow and set Destination to be our own starting position—in other words our own ship, ICS-2. That way the shuttle will know what general course to take as we steer it manually.

". . . three . . . two . . . one . . . Start!"

In that same moment our Race Clock readout lights up with an initial 00:00, and the milliseconds start flying.

Our shuttle lurches, and we careen like crazy, merging into the racing lane. The shuttles above and below us do the same. We all time our entries so as to avoid hitting each other and all those other racing objects.

Hugo sings in a nervous voice that's barely on pitch, and then swipes the Thrust.

Holy lord in heaven.

We blast forward like a comet. . . .

The racing lane stretches out before us into infinity. The hologram Start/Finish Lanes projected from every ship in the Fleet form a strange pattern of stripes before us, directly in our way, so that it feels like we are moving through an actual physical tunnel lit intermittently with golden lines. My vision starts to go haywire.

Okay, that was *not* expected.

Hugo bites his lip and swipes right and left constantly to veer us away from the slower shuttles in our way as we catch up with some of them. Meanwhile, other shuttles pass us by, going faster. . . .

I hold my breath and manipulate the Blue Grid wildly,

adjusting for Hugo's wild maneuvers.

Each time we pass an ark-ship, there's a new stack of ten shuttles—either waiting on the sidelines to enter the racing lane, or in the process of merging in. . . . This complicates things to an insane degree, because now we also have to constantly watch for new merging shuttles in addition to what's *already* in the lane with us.

At least there's an equal number of shuttles *exiting* the lane as they cross their own ships' Finish Lines, so that the overall balance of traffic remains the same.

"Over there! Damn!" Hugo exclaims, as we see what looks like a burning crash explosion up ahead, as two shuttles collide . . . and the flames are immediately extinguished by the space vacuum.

"To the right, up, up!" I scream, working the Blue Grid, while Hugo circle-swipes on Red, and we barely miss running into a pile of debris, then keep going. Other shuttles similarly maneuver around the unexpected, tragic obstacle.

Oh my God. . . . Those poor kids just died in that crash.

But I cannot allow my mind to wander. So I take in a shuddering breath and keep working the Blue Grid, keeping us as straight and even as possible.

A quick glance at the Clock, and the readout says 07:34.

At this point we're almost at the front of the Fleet formation and the ICS-1 flagship is coming up.

"Shuttle #72, prepare to turn left ahead. . . . Fleet termination, ten second warning."

Hugo does not respond—he's busy swerving around a group of shuttles.

That's when I realize we're coming in too fast.

"Start to Brake!" I exclaim. "Brake now!"

"I know! Shut the f— up!"

Hugo flips to Green and swipes down, slowing us barely in the nick of time, because the flagship is right there, and so is the turning channel—that last five kilometer gap between ICS-1 and the ship directly behind it. . . . If we don't make this turn, we overshoot the flagship and Breach out of the Quantum Steam.

Hugo flips to Red, circle-swipes, and we turn into the space belonging to the middle column #2, and go sideways then spin about slightly—I go crazy on Blue Grid, trying to compensate the wobble—and then we emerge into the opposite direction racing lane.

"Merge! Go!" I scream.

And we do . . . just barely. A whole bunch of other shuttles are also making this hard turn. It's a zoo!

But at least we're flying in a straight line once more.

I check the Clock readout and it shows 09:47.

Once again, the hologram Start/Finish Line projections from the ark-ships in formation flash by us, in the optical illusion of stripes, as we hurtle through the channel, this time *ripping* against the Stream toward the end of the Fleet.

"How much time?" Hugo mutters without taking his eyes off his Red Grid.

"Ten-seventeen on the Clock," I reply, glancing up fast.

He cusses.

We still have to make one hard turn before we can get to the Finish Line and our own ark-ship. And with less than four minutes left to make the 15-minute Average, our time is not good at all.

"Go faster!" I yell.

Hugo growls and swipes the Thrust to increase speed. The way seems relatively clear up ahead, so at last we have a brief opportunity to make up some time we lost while slowing down and making the turn.

I admit, we're really moving scary-*fast* now, passing a bunch of shuttles. Hugo seems to have found his rhythm. The Clock shows we have just over two minutes to go before the 15-minute Average.

"Shuttle #72, prepare to turn left ahead.... Fleet termination, ten second warning."

Okay, now we're nearing the anchor ship, ICS-4, and the end of the Fleet.

"Doing good, get ready to Brake, Hugo!" I say, watching the Yellow Grid notches.

"Okay, got it!" he shouts back, then engages the Green Brake.

We coast smoothly up to the cross-channel just before the anchor ship ICS-4.

Hugo circle-swipes, as we maneuver the turn, and I circle-swipe to micro-adjust.

Just as we're coming out of the turn, ready to merge into the racing lane and the home stretch, there are three shuttles that come hard on our tail, and two of them spin out.

They hurtle *directly at us*. . . .

Hugo cusses, freezes momentarily.

"Go!" I scream.

And then Hugo flips to Red and starts to maneuver us wildly out of the way of the oncoming disaster.

We spin out also, as we merge crookedly into the racing lane, coming at a super-wide angle.

"*No!* Don't hit that ark-ship!" I scream, as my fingers fly on the Blue Grid.

Hugo reacts by swinging us even more out of alignment, until we are drifting out of the racing lane completely and starting to spin in a circle, completely losing our sense of direction.

"Brake! Brake! Just Brake!" I yell, as the violet plasma-coated hull of a nearby ark-ship starts to loom closer and closer. We've swung out of the racing lane completely and are about to slam into the column #3 formation space on the other side.

"Turn back! Turn! Move right!"

Hugo is circle-swiping uselessly, still on the Red Grid when he should be switching to Green to Brake.

Finally he flips to Green and swipes to slow down.

Our shuttle starts to slow and coast, and the angle of our drift widens even more, as though in slow motion.

We are now *past* the column #3 formation and still moving . . . slipping out of control and spinning farther out into the muddled off-black abyss that stretches only a single kilometer beyond the edge of the formation.

We come to it softly. . . .

As we pass the Quantum Stream Boundary, it feels gentle, a mild prickling, like a static curtain moving all around us. The shuttle lights flicker, as though a charge is being drained.

And then the view outside the window changes. It's no longer homogeneous ugly grey but rich living *black*.

The Fleet is gone.

But oh, the stars! There are stars all around us once again! Billions of them! They are sharp and in focus... and we are drifting alone among the mauve and rose and gold radiance of a glorious, unknown giant nebula.

Stunningly beautiful.

Not a bad place to die.

Chapter 30

Panic hits me with a surge of adrenaline. It blasts through my moment of stark, cold, debilitating, idiot *paralysis*.

"The Emergency Protocol . . ." I whimper, while I stare at the glorious colored stars and giant nebula . . . and at Hugo, turned to stone next to me.

"Oh my God . . ." he whimpers also. He is still in paralysis mode.

It seems, both of us have lost our voices from the terror.

I regain mine quickly. "Hugo! Wake up! Get a goddamn grip!"

I breathe heavily, wildly, panting with frantic panic. My pulse hammers in my temples, as I turn to the *QSBEP-1 Emergency Instructions* list that's lit up in red text on the wall panel before me.

There's not a second to lose, I recall. We have to hurry, because the Quantum Stream field trace dissipates almost instantly.

"Okay, what! What do we do?" Hugo mutters, looking like he's about to weep.

We both stare at the Emergency Protocol.

"Okay," I speak in a crazed hurry. "We listen to the space around us in all directions for any QS signal trace. Which means—turn the resonance scanners on!"

"Okay, yes," Hugo responds. "Right! We use Global Scan Mode!"

We activate the resonance scanners and listen.

The ship's acoustic grid crackles to life all around us, as we start hearing the eerie *silence* of space from the hull itself, with occasional pulsar bursts of unknown radio frequency, interpreted by the ship as dull bursts of faint static.

"How long do we listen?" Hugo exclaims after a while.

"I don't know!" I am starting to hyperventilate at this point, and a lump is rising in the back of my throat.

"So, we keep listening!" Hugo looks at me, then looks out at the glorious space vista outside, fidgets in his seat.

"Yeah . . ." I say. "We kind of have to. This is the first step in the Emergency Protocol and we can't proceed past it."

"Oh, God . . . oh, God. . . ."

About five minutes later, as the shuttle resonance scanners cycle on all frequencies, we're still picking up only faint crackle echoes of distant radio waves from the stars. None of them are even close to being the Quantum Stream field traces.

Our only chances and our luck have come and gone, many, many long minutes ago.

It's time to face it, but neither one of us—Hugo or myself—can.

We're cut off.

We're going to *die here*.

I listen with intense focused attention to the resonance scan going on around us. Empty eerie crackle, punctuated by silence.

My eyes are brimming with moisture now, and the lump in the back of my throat is choking me.

Gracie. . . . I'm never going to see my sister again.

Nor my little brother Gordie. Or George. My entire family back on Earth—I won't be able to help them, or even stupidly die in the Games of the Atlantis Grail while trying to help them.

And I will never see *him* again.

Aeson Kassiopei.

"Hey! What was that?" Hugo reacts desperately at a small blip noise, followed by a hollow reverb echo.

I tense up and listen fiercely.

But it's all nothing.

"Okay, is there anything in these damn instructions we can do? *Anything?*" Hugo says after another few minutes.

I frown, and stare at the red text, my mouth moving over the lines silently, reading the items over and over. Willing them to have a hidden magic solution.

"Instructor Okoi said our shuttle would lose the *acoustic resonance charge* that connects it to the Stream."

Hugo stares. "Yeah? So? What does that mean, what can we do?"

"Nothing," I say. "I don't know, I guess—thinking out loud."

How long does it take to die in space? Will it be oxygen depletion? Dehydration? Starvation? Sickening thoughts start intruding.

The worst part is, I have no real idea of how well Atlantean shuttles handle life support. We never got around to studying it in detail, but from what I vaguely recall, the small personal flyer shuttle's system gives us about a month of resources, if we conserve everything.

Great, I think, *I get to die slowly, over a month, with Hugo Moreno going crazy next to me.*

More minutes pass. Hugo cusses constantly, both in English and Spanish—I think it helps him to relieve tension, and to be honest I don't really blame him.

"Okay," he mutters, partly to himself. "What, what, what? What does this next instruction say? What does it mean, 'Sing the exact frequency to match quantum resonance until shuttle acknowledges the match and is keyed. Synch the shuttle to the QS field.' What the hell is that? Maybe we can start singing some random crap?"

I frown. "I guess we could."

So for the next minute Hugo sets the resonance scanners to "Record" mode and tries keying the shuttle with various note sequences. His voice is shaky and breathless, so mostly the resonance scanners just respond with: "Sequence unrecognized. Repeat sequence."

"Why don't you try it?" he says at last.

And I do. I sing a few sequences in a much better tone and on pitch. However all I get is this from the scanners: "Sequence recorded."

"Now what?" Hugo glances from me to the Emergency Protocol list.

"I have no idea!" I exclaim. "I don't even know what we're *doing* now, this is bull!"

"Yeah, well," he yells back at me. "Why didn't the Goldilocks idiots just keep an audio recording of the Quantum Stream frequency *on file*, here in their goddamn shuttle computers? So that we wouldn't have to go hunting for it on the sonar?"

My mouth drops. "Because, idiot," I say, "it doesn't *exist* in *real time!* Hello! Weren't you listening in class all these weeks? It's not a real frequency, it's a *quantum* one, and it's in constant flux and in a state of probability! The Quantum Stream is a probability field, not a discrete thing you can record, and if we could just bottle it up so easily, there wouldn't be a problem now, would there be?"

Hugo frowns like a thundercloud at me.

"The reason we have to go chasing the field trace out *there* is because the QS frequency is modulating! It *changes* every damn moment! We can only hope to capture it quickly enough in real time and synch to it before it changes again!"

"Yeah, well, that's crazy and impossible!"

"Exactly!" I yell. "That's why the QSBEP-1 Emergency Protocol almost never works! It's more luck than anything!"

"Well, screw this—this—" And again Hugo goes off into curses.

I put my head down and bump it against my console. I rub my temples, pull at my ponytail, yank it hard, and look up again periodically.

There has to be something, I think. *Maybe I can beat it into my stupid brain.*

Something.

Minutes turn into half an hour.

Think, Gwen, think!

Out of nothing else to do, I sit up again, and make the resonance scanners play back the last known recorded QS field frequency before we Breached the Stream and lost the acoustic resonance charge on the shuttle. A series of five tones sound in a chord progression.

Hugo turns to me and watches dully. "What is it? What are you doing?"

"Playing back the last known QS field frequency before we Breached."

"Can we use it?"

"No. It's useless. It's no longer the real time frequency of the Stream."

Hugo slams his fist on his console.

"You know what?" I say. "Let's just go ahead and pretend this is the correct frequency. So I am going to key the shuttle to it. Why not, right?"

"Whatever," he mumbles in despair. "Yeah, do it. . . ."

So I sing the sequence, and the resonance scanners pick it up, and the shuttle hull responds, coming alive with golden lights along the etchings.

"Hey," I say with false bravado. "At least we're not dead in the water. We can pretend we're going somewhere! Yay!"

And then I muse. "Okay, what are the next steps in the Emergency Protocol?"

Hugo reads out loud: "*Plot the signal coordinates onto the Navigation Grid. . . . Set new course and pursue the QS field immediately.*"

Why the hell not? I think. And I call up the Yellow Grid, then the Fleet sub-menu, and scroll down to find ICS-2.

I tap it, and the Destination circle appears on the Navigation Grid next to our shuttle. Since at present it's not to be found anywhere in *real space*, the circle designating the ark-ship just floats there, bumping our shuttle circle—adjacent to us, as though the Grid doesn't know what to do with it or where to plot it.

"There you are, cute little itty-bitty ark-ship," I mutter with black humor. And I poke the hologram with my finger to select the Destination.

And now, all that's left is to sing the major sequence to activate the Destination.

"I wish . . ." I mutter. "I wish I could just call you to me, like a hoverboard. Wouldn't that be lovely?"

Hugo frowns at me and rolls his eyes.

Yeah, right. I should roll my own eyes at myself, right about now.

And then a silly thought from an old physics class comes to me. It's the notion of *quantum entanglement*.

Basically, it's the idea that two particles can be "entangled" or bound together on a quantum level in some creepy, spooky, mysterious way, and made to share common properties. When separated by any distance, they remain weirdly connected. Whatever you do to one of them has a direct effect on the other, even if it's billions of miles away.

Or something like that.

"Little ark ship," I say. "This is creepy and insane. But I am going to call you to me."

I set the resonance scanners to "Broadcast" mode.

And then I take a deep breath, and think about the Fleet and the ark-ships, and all the people on them, flying through space in formation, bound together in the Quantum Stream, somewhere out there, encased in their personal quantum bubble, out of phase with the rest of the universe.

Just a little while ago, I was a part of all that, I was one of you. . . .

Entangled together.

I sing the keying sequence in a clear, clean, *compelling power voice* of perfect focused intensity.

I call the *Quantum Stream itself* to me.

The resonance scanners broadcast my voice into the vast empty recesses of the cosmos.

I sing and sing, over and over again, desperate and strangely serene, while Hugo watches me, mesmerized. . . .

And then, as we stare outside the window at the black velvet of space and the flood of stars in the grand nebula, *something* changes.

Something out there begins to blur.

The universe is dissolving before our very eyes, as if a cosmic whirlwind has passed and stirred up the stars and blended them . . . and everything is suddenly off-black, a static wall of grey.

I'm not entirely sure what's happening.

"Oh God! Look! *Look!*" Hugo points at the viewport.

Out there in the distance of a few hundred kilometers I see light specks of purple plasma, like a hive of speeding fireflies stretched out in a long linear formation. . . .

"Holy crap! It's the Fleet!" Hugo exclaims.

I stop singing. "Go! Go!" I am crying now, while my head

starts to pound.

Hugo comes alive with a wild yell, then flips to the Red Grid and engages the Thrust.

We blast forward like a bullet.

Toward the Fleet.

We fly up to the exterior formation column #3, and merge into the 5-kilometer space between ships. The all-companying grey field that is the Quantum Steam seems to *come with us*—indeed, to be all around us—and at no point does it seem like we entered or passed the Boundary zone back into the QS space.

It's as if we've been inside a mini-bubble of the QS field all along.

That makes no sense.

But right now I don't give a damn. And neither does Hugo.

We fly the shuttle like crazy, merging into the racing lane—it appears to be significantly free of traffic at this point.

I suppose the Race is over by now. After all, we were gone for over half an hour. . . . In fact, our Race Clock readout shows 67:06. Oh, well.

We arrive at ICS-2, enter the shuttle bay launch tunnel past shields of plasma, and then emerge inside and park on the platform that's now filled with other stationary shuttles. The depot is nearly empty of people.

Hugo is making gleeful chuckling noises, and he and I grin widely at one another as we turn off the shuttle. Right now, all we're feeling is crazy relief.

"We did it! We effing *did it*, Gwen!" he exclaims, as we climb out and down the ladder.

Outside, several Atlantean guards wait for us, and there's Instructor Mithrat Okoi, standing at the platform, pale and grim and unyielding.

He turns directly at us.

"Cadets, attention!"

Both Hugo and I salute. Yeah, I know, I'm not a Cadet, but everyone always forgets. What can I do?

"The Quantum Stream Race is over! You are late, and you've just earned yourselves a disgraceful Score that puts you in *last place!* Where have you been, Cadet Moreno, Cadet Lark?" Instructor Okoi roars at us.

We stand, our gleeful euphoria fading.

"We were—not sure, sir!" Hugo says quietly. And he glances at me.

I take a deep breath and speak haltingly. "We were outside the Quantum Stream, sir. Somewhere in interstellar space . . . for the last half hour, sir. We got lucky somehow. And—and we got back inside."

"You *what?*" Now Mithrat Okoi is staring at us hard, and his brow is furrowed in a frown.

Hugo and I stand stiffly, trying not to look directly at him.

"Are you saying you Breached and you managed to *return* somehow?" There is anger and disbelief in the Instructor's tone. "Impossible! How did you get back?"

"We—" I begin. "Okay, there was just interstellar space and no QS field trace, even though we kept listening for it. So we just tried a bunch of different things—"

"And nothing was working," Hugo adds. "Until I told her to sing a frequency—what was it, oh yeah, the last recorded QS field frequency that the resonance scanners had saved."

I ignore the blatant lie that Hugo just told—about him telling me to sing it when it was my idea all along—and continue. "I keyed the shuttle to the last recorded frequency, sir. But—"

"But what?"

"It didn't seem to make any difference. What I tried next however, might have been the real solution—"

Instructor Okoi cuts me off to check his handheld gadget that starts buzzing. "Enough—save your explanations," he says to us, looking up after a moment. "Command Pilot Kassiopei informs me that you are to go directly to his office—both of you—right *now! Go!*"

We salute again, then turn and head at a run for the shuttle bay exit.

We arrive at the CCO, panting for breath, and terrified, yet strangely upbeat. The guards allow us inside, and as we enter the office, there's the CP. . . .

Aeson Kassiopei is pacing near his desk. My heart immediately lurches wildly at the sight of him. What I feel in that moment is indescribable—joy, relief, madness. . . . Oh, how I want to rush at him and *hug* him, because I thought I'd never see him again—

The moment he sees us however, he whirls around and stops.

My God. His expression is terrifying. His gaze—it has the impact of a thunderstorm and it *buries us* with furious intensity.

"Moreno and Lark! *Where have you been?*" The words come down like hammer blows. He is not using a power voice but he might as well be.

I cringe, and Hugo cringes also.

All my crazy happy feelings at the sight of Kassiopei—they have been obliterated and replaced with fear. My breath has been knocked out of me.

But I force myself to look up and meet his gaze. "I am very sorry, Command Pilot," I say. "We were making our final turn in the Race when we Breached out of the Quantum Stream. And then we somehow got back in."

"You certainly did."

Aeson Kassiopei is looking at *me*—only me alone, ignoring Hugo completely—and together with boiling fury there is something haunting and *primal* in his eyes.

My pulse starts pounding again.

A moment of silence.

"Your shuttle," Kassiopei says. "It disappeared completely off the Fleet Grid. Missing for *forty-nine minutes.*"

"Yes, that would be the time we were out there in interstellar space . . ." Hugo says carefully.

I nod.

"And then," the Command Pilot continues, glancing at Hugo briefly but returning all his attention to me, "and then ICS-2 Shuttle #72 miraculously reappeared."

"Yes . . ." I say softly.

Aeson Kassiopei frowns at me. I can tell his breathing is strangely elevated as he holds himself in check . . . just barely.

"Here's the thing," he says. "In the *exact* moment when shuttle #72 reappeared on the Grid, the global QS sensors registered a sharp irregular change in the frequency of the entire Quantum Stream. But that is not all—the new QS field frequency was the same as that of your incoming shuttle."

"So . . . what does that mean?" Hugo mutters.

"It means—" The CP pauses, while his gaze bores into me, again ignoring Hugo. And then he says softly: "What happened was impossible—a fluke. Consider yourselves lucky to be alive."

I stare. Hugo stares.

Aeson Kassiopei looks away from us and begins to pace. "Cadet Moreno," he says. "You are dismissed. Return to your barracks. Your QS Race Score is 23 out of a possible 100, which puts both of you in the dismal #624 last place for this ship. Be glad you are alive."

"Thank you, Command Pilot," Hugo says. "I am. . . ."

And he salutes, gives me a fleeting nervous glance, and exits the office.

I remain alone with Aeson Kassiopei.

Chapter 31

For a few seconds neither one of us says anything. And then Kassiopei goes to his desk and sits down in his chair. He leans back and puts his hands behind his head.

"Sit down, Lark. We need to talk."

I approach his desk stiffly and take one of the visitor chairs. I sit motionless, watching the level of his chin, because right this moment I find it very hard to meet his eyes. Because again, the feelings inside me are churning . . . such an unstable mixture of joy, relief, terror. . . .

"All right, what really happened out there?" he says in a hard voice, watching me. "Tell me everything."

And I do. I speak haltingly, trying to skip the parts where Hugo and I froze up so badly and lost valuable moments at the very beginning. When I'm done, I look up.

Aeson's expression in that moment is raw and terrifying. I see that he is now leaning forward, with his elbows resting on the desk, and one of his hands is clenched in a fist, pressing hard against the polished surface.

"What you did," he says. "It is not something that has ever been done by anyone who is not of Imperial Kassiopei blood."

I blink. "Oh. . . . What did I do exactly?"

"You *keyed* the Quantum Stream to *yourself*." His gaze sears me like fire. "It had nothing to do with the shuttle you were piloting. It was all *you*. You did not merge back into the Quantum Stream by matching its natural frequency. You did something that *forced* the Quantum Stream to match its frequency to *yours!*"

"But—" Suddenly I am feeling breathless and faint. "How does that work? I thought you could only *key* orichalcum objects?"

Command Pilot Kassiopei exhales. "Orichalcum can be keyed because it has unusual quantum-level properties. It happens to be uniquely unstable at the quantum level, permanently. Orichalcum is a transitional metal, always in quantum flux, and for that reason it can be manipulated in unusual ways."

He pauses, runs his fingers slowly along the surface of his desk. "To acoustically levitate an object in regular 3D space, sound waves must bombard the object from three directions, surrounding it. Orichalcum, being in quantum flux, *entangles itself* with sound waves at a molecular level so that at any given moment its particles instead *surround* the sound. It 'wraps' itself against sound, creating the same effect. Instead of being surrounded by sound waves, it surrounds sound waves at the quantum level."

"That's wild," I whisper.

"The reason I tell you this is because you need to understand that quantum level manipulation lies at the heart of everything—all our technology." He never takes his gaze off me. "What I've just told you is something no other Earth scientist, no Earth human being knows. And the reason I tell you this is because your abilities are amazing—even for an Atlantean."

I breathe very slowly. "Wow. Thanks—I guess?"

Aeson Kassiopei continues watching me, and after a time his face darkens. "I—" he says suddenly. "I didn't know what to *think* in that moment when you were *gone*. That moment when your shuttle dropped off the Fleet Grid, was—"

His words trail off.

There's silence.

I meet his eyes.

"In short—I am very glad you made it back," he speaks at last, almost gruffly. *No, that can't be right.... Is he in some kind of discomfort? No!*

"I'm glad too." And I allow myself a tiny little smile.

But he immediately frowns, his expression hardening, as though slamming on a mask. "Now then, what happened today needs to remain a secret. There will be questions raised by the Commander, but we will not be disclosing details of the

Quantum Stream anomaly to anyone else. The public will only know that you and Moreno managed to get back by normal means—you found the right frequency, matched it, keyed the shuttle to it, et cetera. In fact, do whatever it takes to convince your own Pilot partner that's what happened, so that he also doesn't talk in a way to raise suspicions and questions."

"Okay." I nod. "What then should I do if people ask probing questions?"

He raises one brow. "You tell them whatever is in the Emergency Protocol. In the meantime, you and Moreno are officially in last place, and you get no special treatment, no 'extra credit' score for making it back alive out of the Breach."

I purse my lips. "Doesn't bode well for my progress as a Pilot, does it?"

He snorts, sounding oddly pleased. "No, it does not."

But then he looks up at me and says, "However—well done, Lark."

And I am dismissed.

The next few days after the Quantum Stream Race turn into a weird combination of humiliation and celebrity worship.

Word spreads among the Cadets about what happened to us, the infamous last-place Pilot Pair who came in dead last yet managed to get back safely from a QS Breach. Cadets whisper, and then it gets around to the Civilians and other Atlanteans, until pretty much all of ICS-2 knows what we did and what happened to us. And yeah, supposedly word gets around to other ships in the Fleet too.

Yeah, we're semi-famous.

Some people look down at us as losers. They're right, we did get the lowest score possible for a Pilot Pair on our ship, in the QS Race.

And the Cadets who were in line after us to use our shuttle #72 in the Race are pretty ticked off at us. They had to be reassigned to other shuttle lineups and lost some valuable time in the race, because of us. Not to mention, our Team Score really suffered a hit.

However, most Cadets also think it's kind of hotshot awesome what we did. Pretty soon we're referred to as "the

Cadet Pilots who Survived the Breach." In some ways we're getting just as much attention as the top scoring Cadet Pilot Pairs on ICS-2.

In terms of overall achievement, the Blue Quadrant is in the lead, followed by Red, Green and Yellow. The first place winner on our ship is Alla Vetrova and her partner Conrad Hart, with a perfect 100 score, which gives them both ark-ship distinctions and First Fleet Honors. Then Erin and Roy Tsai come in second with a 99 score and distinctions. Neither one of these placements is a shocker—both pairs are Blues, and we've all been expecting them to take the top spots. However, the surprise is the third-place Pair—Logan Sangre and Oliver Parker, moving up from seventh place in their standings, and receiving a 98 score and distinctions.

And then there's us, the notorious losers.

Hugo goes around puffed up, bragging to everyone he can. I think he's honestly forgotten—or made himself conveniently forget—what actually happened, and now tells people that we followed the Emergency Protocol to a letter, reacted quickly and appropriately, and that's what saved our brilliant butts.

Yeah, I let him talk. . . .

Meanwhile Gracie calls me, scared to death, and I have to reassure her I'm okay and all is well. Gracie tells me she did decently on her own QS Race, and got a 78 score. Way to go, Gracie! I'm kind of amazed, in a really good way. And I'm so proud of my sister.

Then, oh wow, out of the blue, Gordie calls me!

"I thought you'd forgotten your big sis, Gee Three," I say, seeing my little brother's usual smudged eyeglasses and loopy grin in the video display. I think I see a lot of greenhouse plants in the background. He must be on his ship's H-deck.

"Oh yeah, no. . . . Hey, that was smoking hot," Gordie tells me. "You guys Breached and then came back! Whoa!"

"When you put it that way, you make us sound like whales," I say with a snort.

"Heh!" Gordie snorts back.

"Love yah, Gee Three!" I smile at him.

He just mumbles something back, totally flustered. Typical Gordie reaction.

I talk to my little bro some more, and then it's like an old-fashioned phone switchboard here in my cabin. The moment we disconnect, in comes Laronda's call.

"Laronda!" I exclaim.

"You're alive!" she screams at me. And then we blab for at least half an hour. I learn that Laronda's Cadet Pilot Pair Score was a healthy 67 for the QS Race.

"Girl, I am entirely happy with it," she says. "Now all we gotta do is keep training and survive the big Final Race, months from now. And you—you have to catch up, okay? Okay?"

"Okay," I say. "Believe me, I know. But right now, as far as I'm concerned, being in last place is better than being dead."

"Oh, yeah." Laronda shakes her head at me.

I don't tell Laronda, or anyone else what actually happened. I think Command Pilot Kassiopei is right. I did something kind of amazing, something I don't even understand, and we have to keep it under wraps for now.

The next days and weeks continue in the same general routine, as we come to the end of the middle month of Green season, and enter the third and last Green month before the Jump.

Yeah, it's Jump Month. . . .

The Quantum Stream instability outside has now reached critical levels, and no one but the *astra daimon* is allowed to fly. So we're all back to training on the flight simulator consoles in the classrooms.

In our Pilot Training classes, Instructor Okoi treats Hugo Moreno and me the same as he does everyone else, but Hugo is now both easier and more difficult to deal with. After our shared ordeal in interstellar space, he's no longer as hard on me as he was before. But his macho posturing has become extremely annoying.

The only good thing is, now when we practice the various flight scenarios, Hugo does not begrudge me being the Pilot whenever we have to swap roles. "Go ahead, Gwen," he says benevolently. "You can Pilot this one."

Often, as we sit in class, there's Logan Sangre and his partner, a few desks away. Sometimes, when I look up, I see

Logan secretly watching me with an intense hard gaze. But the moment our eyes meet, he quickly looks away. Yeah, there are still many complicated, weird, unresolved *feelings* there, between Logan and me. . . . But neither one of us wants to take that first step . . . and so, nothing has changed between us.

Meanwhile, the two other CCO Aides, Gennio and Anu, might be somewhat impressed with me, now that I've Breached the Quantum Stream and come back safely. Gennio tells me I did a great job in that shuttle. Anu of course just says, "You got lucky, Earth girl. There's a saying in my home village, 'the gods take special care of idiots.'"

"Anu," I retort. "As the village idiot, you illustrate this saying perfectly."

I often meet up with Blayne Dubois for lunch or dinner. Blayne got a very nice 83 Pilot Pair Score on the QS Race, and he is doing quite well. He also tells me he still teaches the LM forms several times a week, in Combat classes all over the Fleet.

"What can I say, I've got a nice gig going, Lark," he says with a light smirk. "I can make a career of it and retire with benefits." And then he adds, "So, how's Lark Two? Has the wild child perpetrated any new drama since the last time we talked?"

"What, you mean since last night?" I say with a tiny wicked smile. "Gracie told me you guys were taking up video screen time for over an hour."

"Oh, yeah . . . well, slight exaggeration as usual." Blayne is suddenly very engrossed with moving around the food on his plate. But there's definitely a shadow smile there, hiding underneath all that hair that's falling over his forehead.

My other classes are proceeding reasonably well. Atlantean Language class is fascinating. Although I still can't speak *Atlanteo*, I think I can now pick up at least some of what's being said around me whenever I'm at the Officers Meal Hall. Navigation, Technology and Systems, and Culture classes are all proceeding at a pace.

However, what's most surprising is how much I am getting out of Consul Denu's Court Protocol sessions. The Consul may seem like a perfumed fop, but I realize now it is a deceptive crafty illusion, a front to cover his true powerful aspect.

Consul Suval Denu is a master diplomat and a master of

subtle manipulation, observation, and insight. Very few things escape his notice, and as a result, I am learning to be on my guard around him, more so than with anyone else. . . . Because I sense that with a little more time and subtle examination of my behavior, he will know exactly how I *feel* about the Imperial Prince.

And that simply cannot happen.

My Combat class with Oalla Keigeri is progressing well also. I haven't talked much with Pilot Keigeri, but when I do, she's a combination of friendly and businesslike, and finds my Er-Du progress sufficient.

I also notice that ever since I Qualified, Oalla seems to keep all our conversations to a professional level. Not once has she breached the subject of what she told me back on Earth, about how much "I matter" to Kassiopei. It occurs to me—maybe she got reprimanded by the CP for chatting with me, and is now trying to keep an appropriate distance.

However, it's quite a different matter between me and Xelio Vekahat. We still see each other almost every day at the gym, and he stops by to talk after every workout. On the day after the QS Race, he comes up to congratulate me on getting safely back from Breaching out of the Quantum Stream.

"Your talents never cease to amaze me, Gwen Lark," he says with a steady look and a smile. "I'm definitely impressed."

"Thanks. . . ." I wipe the workout sweat off my forehead with the back of my hand. I'm dripping wet, and feel a little uncomfortable under the steady hot gaze of his so-very-dark eyes.

And then I get a crazy idea. "Pilot Vekahat—Xelio," I say, craning my neck slightly. "You said once that you can help me if I needed help."

He raises one handsome raven brow. "Yes, of course. My offer stands."

"Good!" I say. "Because I think I need your help. I need to train physically—train *hard*. I need to become not merely decent at Er-Du and weapons Combat, but really, really *good*—before the year is over and before we get to Atlantis."

"Is that so? And what's the reason?" Xelio takes a step closer, so that his face is very close to mine, and continues to observe me with intensity.

I take a deep breath. "I plan to enter the Games of the Atlantis Grail."

"What?"

Okay, Xelio did not see that coming. He makes a laughing sound. "Are you insane?"

I shake my head. "No, I mean it. I am resolved to enter and *win* this thing. I need to become a Citizen of Atlantis. And I need you to help me become physically strong. Can you do that?"

His brows rise and he continues chuckling. "Does the CP know about these crazy plans of yours?"

I nod. "Oh yes. And he disapproves entirely. He also told me that unless I can prove I'm capable of it, by the end of the year, he will not allow me to enter the Games. So, I must prove him wrong."

Since I'm not smiling at all, Xelio stops laughing and looks at me seriously.

"Very well," he says unexpectedly, and his eyes cut through me with intense sensual regard. "Proving Kass wrong is a welcome challenge. Yes, I think I'll enjoy this. We'll begin tomorrow."

Chapter 32

It is definitely the heart of Jump Month.
What does it mean? It means that the preparations for the Jump are ongoing, everywhere, and the Fleet is on alert.

A sense of urgency has gripped us, and it's somewhat hard to put into words.

Our velocity continues rising, but it is no longer anything that can be described, not even in mathematical terms—at least not ones I've studied back on Earth. In terms of literary metaphor, *we are going infernally fast.* . . .

When you go to the ICS-2 Observation Deck, it's a terrifying, depressing sight, evoking visceral terror. Outside the windows, the universe is a uniform deep grey blur now. Nothing to see, not even vague shadows of stars, only the closest neighbor ark-ships in formation.

It's as though *nothing* in the world exists, only *us*. And for that reason, most people no longer visit the observation decks of the Fleet ark-ships during these last weeks.

The things we are taught about the Jump process in our various classes are also intimidating.

"During the final week leading up to the Jump," Instructor Mithrat Okoi tells us, "all Fleet Pilots will remain inside. At this time, no one will be allowed to fly ship-to-ship in the Stream—not even the *astra daimon*. Your classwork on flight simulators will proceed as usual, but on the day immediately preceding and following the Jump, there will be no classes held."

"The experience of the Jump is highly complex and individualized," Instructor Nilara Gradat tells us in Culture Class, on the day she has a guest doctor attending the lecture, to answer our medical questions. "As the fabric of the Quantum

Stream around us grows more and more unstable, even the presence of the ship's powerful shields and various life support systems is inadequate to protect living beings from all the effects. Many people suffer what is called *Jump sickness*—both before and after the Jump itself."

Immediately hands go up, as concerned students want to know more.

"Jump sickness symptoms include disorientation, dizziness, loss of consciousness, and various forms of agitation, temporary loss of motor function," the Atlantean doctor picks up at this point and speaks to us. "Some of you might experience nausea, difficulty breathing, elevated pulse rates and panic, others a full body flush and circulation issues. There is also the danger of panic attacks causing you to harm yourself accidentally."

Nilara Gradat nods. "For that reason, everyone on the ship—passengers and crew—will be confined to their sleeping bunks, where you will engage the safety harness system. You will lie down and stay flat in bed at least fifteen minutes before the Jump and fifteen minutes after. Fortunately the effects dissipate quickly, and most of you should be sufficiently recovered within the hour."

A girl raises her hand and asks tremulously. "How does the actual moment of the Jump feel? Does it—*hurt?*"

The doctor shakes his head. "No, it is painless, but it can feel like a momentary loss of consciousness for most people, which is not particularly pleasant. That's why we strongly recommend you lie in your bed and try not to move too much. The ship's automated system will issue a thirty-minute warning countdown, to give you plenty of time to prepare."

And then we are told: "You will undergo physical examinations to once again test your hormone levels. If the hormonal balance in your body does not match the safe range, you will be given treatments the day before the Jump."

In the meantime, our Technology and Systems Instructor, Klavit Xitoi, informs us of another aspect of the process. "To protect against the effects of the Jump, we employ a Stasis System. For that purpose, there's a cold storage chamber on Deck Level 5. It contains ten emergency storage capsules for those on this ship who are most vulnerable. That includes anyone over and under the safe age."

He adds: "Some of your older instructors will be using the capsules, and some of you on this ship who test most poorly on the hormone level exams will be chosen to go into the capsules—all for your own safety. Unfortunately the selection is limited to a handful of individuals, and they will be chosen on the recommendation of the medical team."

Instructor Xitoi then takes us on a tour of the Stasis Deck. We go down the spiral stairwells to Level 5, and then into a large brightly lit chamber with two rows of five capsules, surrounded by computer consoles. They look like large glass coffins, and we are given an explanation on how to operate them.

"One thing you don't need to worry about," Instructor Xitoi says in conclusion, "is the fact that all the ark-ships employ an automated Jump Protocol, so that once the Jump System is engaged, no personnel on duty are necessary. The ship takes care of the whole Jump process. So there is absolutely nothing to be afraid of."

Yeah, right. . . .

Overall, I would say most of us are now sufficiently terrified that we can't wait for this Jump nightmare to be over already.

At last, Jump Day is here.
The day before, I go in to the medical deck for my hormone level exam, and fortunately I'm within normal range, so I don't get any hormone boosters. Some of the other teens are less fortunate, and they end up with a variety of shots and have to drink some kind of clear liquid that supposedly tastes foul.

I check up on my siblings, and apparently both test as safely within normal range, so no boosters for them, thank goodness.

Today, everyone's duties on board the ship are very light. I wake up at 7:00 AM, feeling nervous butterflies in my stomach as though it's a day of competition of some sort. I force myself to eat breakfast, then head to the CCO.

The Command Pilot is away doing ship inspections, so it's basically Gennio, Anu and myself for the next couple of hours. They are running major Jump System diagnostics, and I help as much as I am able, which is not too much at all. This system is so critical that I am not allowed to touch anything, only respond by reading off status code numbers on the screen when asked.

The Jump itself is scheduled for 2:35 PM this afternoon. That's when the Fleet will finally reach the necessary optimal velocity to achieve the Jump.

"Don't eat a big lunch," Anu mumbles to us as we work on multiple consoles. "Unless you want to be tossing up the contents of your stomach from Jump sickness."

"Is that from personal experience?" I ask.

"Yeah," Anu tells me. "During the first Jump on our way to Earth, I got to watch fat-brain here throw up after the Jump. He puked all over the place. Everything he ate for lunch was on the floor—"

"No, I did not," Gennio says with a frown without looking up from his own consoles. "Enough, Anu."

"Okay, but it would've been funny if you did!" And Anu makes a rude laugh.

"Seriously, Anu," I mutter. "Are you a five-year-old? What's with all the stupid?"

"Hey, you just watch your lunch, Earth girl, this is no joke!"

Gennio and I both roll our eyes tiredly.

However when lunchtime rolls around, I have no appetite, so I eat and drink almost nothing, Anu's warning ringing in my mind. Besides, there is hardly time to linger since the Pre-Jump Protocol is about to be implemented all across the ark-ships of the Fleet.

And as Aides to the CCO, we assist the CP in part with some of it.

Our schedule is as follows:

At 1:00 PM, Pre-Jump Protocol begins—which means that everyone is officially placed in "ready" mode. That's when Atlantean crew members and Earth refugees are ordered to begin winding up their regular duties, to finish up whatever they are doing and report to their personal quarters by 2:00 PM.

At 1:30 PM, the ten individuals who are to occupy the cold storage capsules are to report to the Cold Storage Deck on Level

5. On our ship that includes the two older adults Instructor Mithrat Okoi, and Consul Suval Denu, plus eight at-risk Cadets and Civilians chosen by doctors.

At 2:05 PM, Command Pilot Kassiopei initiates the automated Jump Protocol. That's when the Jump System takes over, and begins the thirty-minute warning Jump Countdown.

At 2:20 PM, fifteen minutes before the Jump, everyone has to be lying down in their beds, with harnesses engaged.

"Be sure to remove any constricting clothing, shoes, jewelry, sharp objects—anything that might potentially cause you accidental harm if you are incapacitated," we are told by the medical techs. "Also, keep your water bottles readily available and within reach."

At 2:34 PM, one minute before the Jump, we are to lie as still as possible, take deep breaths, and wait.

At 2:35 PM, the Jump happens. The Fleet will leave the galactic neighborhood of Earth and *jump* instantaneously to the galactic neighborhood of Atlantis, somewhere in the Constellation of Pegasus, the Great Square.

At 2:50 PM, depending on our physical condition post-Jump, we may get up and out of bed, and are allowed to resume our regular day.

"If you are still experiencing heavy symptoms of Jump sickness by 3:00 PM, be sure to report to the nearest medical deck," we are told.

And so it begins.

The CCO Aides are scheduled to briefly assist in the cold storage chamber at 1:30 PM. Gennio, Anu, and I head down to Deck 5, through ship corridors filled with stressed out rushing people. When we get there, we see at least five doctors or med techs on duty, and the cold storage capsules are open.

Instructor Mithrat Okoi arrives punctually, the first person there. We watch him being prepped by the medics. He confidently climbs into the capsule and lies down. Gennio and Anu supervise the system functionality while the medical techs get to work attaching instruments and sensors to Mithrat Okoi's body.

"Are you ready, sir?" an Atlantean tech asks politely.

"Proceed," Mithrat Okoi says calmly and closes his eyes.

The capsule glass lid comes down and is closed over him, and then the controls engaged, flooding the chamber with a milk-pale ice mist.

Gennio steps up to verify that all is running smoothly.

The eight teens who are to be stored in the capsules are next. I watch with sympathy the three very young girls and the one much older girl—both at the extreme ends of the safe age range—and the two very young boys and two older boys. All of them have a frightened, haunted look, and I don't blame them.

The teens are processed one at a time, and each time a capsule closes over one of them the others watch with growing terror.

"There's nothing to be afraid of," an Atlantean female doctor says gently to the youngest little girls and boys. "You'll wake up very soon and you won't feel a thing!"

"Yeah, you're lucky," Anu mutters to one older teen already lying down with a resigned look, as he checks his capsule's controls for the last time. "You get to bypass Jump sickness, while we don't. I'll be happy to trade places with you, man."

The reassurance seems to work, because the teen exhales in visible relief and closes his eyes.

Wow, I think. *Anu actually said something useful*.

In minutes the last of the high-risk teens are now safely stored in their capsules, and it's almost 2:00 PM when Consul Denu arrives, running very late, with his assistant Kem running behind him with a bag, and the aura of perfume wafting after.

"Here, my boy, begin by taking my robe and the accessories," Consul Denu says, starting to disrobe ceremoniously. Even now, he is still wearing his golden wig.

The techs stand waiting patiently for the layers of Consul Denu's outfit to be cast aside, while he stands, mostly letting Kem do the removal. Lastly, comes the grand gold wig, and I think all of us—Anu, Gennio, myself, all the doctors and techs—stare in mesmerized suspense to see what's underneath.

Underneath the wig, Consul Denu is bald as an egg.

I think I'm as stunned as everyone, but we all hold in our reaction politely.

Amazingly enough, the Consul observes us comfortably in that moment, with the tiniest fleeting smile on his face. "So now you come to the mystery of mysteries, the heart and crux of things," he tells us in a poetic tone mixing sarcasm and aplomb. "The humble servant of the Imperator is revealed, and he is a bird without feathers." His glance travels around us, lingering on us Aides especially. And he winks at me.

"Come, don't be shy," he says at last to the medic techs. "Put me up in this extremely expensive machine, and let it perform its job."

And Consul Denu climbs inside the remaining empty capsule, with the assistance of at least three people. As he lies there getting prepped, he waves his manicured hand elegantly in our direction, and at Kem in particular. "Now, run along, Kem, and hurry to your own cabin. You may hold on to my things until after the Event. For now, you must get in bed, stay there safely, and try not to move too much, for it can be a highly unpleasant experience—"

Consul Denu is still talking when the capsule lid comes down over him. Immediately the air of the chamber is freed of much of its perfume, though some of it remains on the clothing and things that Kem is holding.

"Yes, my Lord," Kem mutters, at this point to no one in particular. But he still remains standing, as though at attention.

Anu and I take a peek at the console instruments next to Consul Denu, and we see the mist fill the capsule, and momentarily glimpse the Consul inside, resting like an alien mummified doll creature in courtly makeup.

"All right, we're done here," Gennio says, just as the thirty-minute warning Jump Countdown begins over the ship's public announcement system.

"Attention all personnel. . . . Thirty minute warning. . . . Jump sequence initializing now. . . ."

"Okay, let's get out of here, we're running late," Anu mutters.

I turn to Kem and touch him on the arm. "Hey! The Consul will be fine, go on to your cabin," I say to him gently. "Hurry now! He wants you to be safe! Go!"

He looks at me with a very stressed, lost little boy look,

then nods.

And we all vacate the chamber, running through the corridors, up the spiral stairs to main level, then on to our Command Decks and our respective quarters.

I get to my cabin in ten minutes, with the ship countdown loudly accompanying me every minute. The corridors are mostly empty now as the last of the stragglers arrive at their quarters.

Once inside, I close the door, splash my face with cold water. I feel strangely lightheaded, and it seems like I'm seeing dots swimming before my eyes.

It occurs to me, these might be the first symptoms of Jump sickness.

I am not too worried however. They are minor and all I need to do is get in bed. I pull off my boots, and my socks. Then I take off my uniform shirt, leaving my tank top and bra underneath. My uniform pants are generally loose on me, so I leave them on. I'm not wearing any jewelry, so nothing to worry about there. I remove the rubber band holding my ponytail and loosen my hair, so that I can lie down with my head resting comfortably.

"Twenty minutes to Jump . . ." the ship computer says.

I fill up my water bottle at the sink and place it on the small table. Then reconsider and stick it on the floor directly next to the bed so that I can reach for it if I'm too sick to move. . . .

Finally I lie down, fluff the pillow underneath my head and take a few nervous breaths. Then I find the emergency harness button and depress it. I've never had to use the bunk harness before, so it's kind of weird to see the many harness belts immediately snake down and enclose the outside, so that it looks like the bunk bed is held inside a net, or maybe I'm behind the bars of a silly bed jail.

"Nineteen minutes to Jump . . ."

I lie, trying to control my breathing and the sudden pounding of my pulse. *No, Gwen you are not having a panic attack*, I tell myself. *Breathe, breathe.*

I listen to my pulse and the hum of the air coming from the vents.

And then I hear a sharp sound of someone *retching* outside in the hallway.

A few seconds later it is followed by moans of pain.

Oh crap. Who's out there?

I consider ignoring it, but then it comes again.

"Seventeen minutes to Jump . . ."

With a sudden burst of adrenaline, I push the harness button, releasing myself from the safety cocoon, then get up and move to the door.

I open it and peer outside into the corridor.

Apparently I'm not the only one. A few other cabin doors slide open nearby as various Atlantean officers and crew look out.

And then I see Kem.

Kem is semi-collapsed on the floor, with his back resting against the wall panels. He is moaning and he looks red and sweaty.

"Oh no! Kem!" I exclaim, as I move toward him and squat down at his side, feeling his forehead. "Are you okay? What are you doing here?"

The boy looks up at me, and I see he's flushed a deep red. "Can't . . ." he mutters. Need to get to my cabin . . . can't. My eyes are fuzzy, can't read walls, section numbers. . . ."

"Need some help?" One of the other Atlanteans says.

"No, thanks, I got it," I say.

"You're sure?"

"Yeah, I know where he lives."

"Fifteen minutes to Jump. . . ."

"Okay," I say to Kem, taking hold of him around the shoulders and waist and helping him get up. "Let's take you to Command Deck Two—you're on Four now."

"Oh," he mumbles, staggering, as we begin walking as quickly as possible, while cabin doors start closing around us as other Atlanteans return to their quarters.

We get to Command Deck Two at a slow run, moving through empty corridors.

"Twelve minutes to Jump . . ." says the computer as I turn into the second VIP corridor and get Kem up to his own cabin, which is only a few doors down from Consul Denu's elegant

large quarters.

"Hurry! Lie down and stay down!" I say in a commanding big sister voice, plunking him down on the bed, where he collapses, moaning. I grab a water bottle and fill it partway in seconds flat, then place it on the floor nearby. I also press his bunk harness button.

"Okay, sorry but I have to get back!" I exclaim, panting.

"Seven minutes to Jump. . . ."

"Thanks so much," he mutters.

"Just try not to throw up on yourself," I say. "Keep your head turned sideways!"

"Okay. . . ."

And then I get out of his cabin and begin to run.

I turn a few corners and run through the CCO central hub corridor, right before the main offices.

"Five minutes to Jump. . . ."

I notice, for once there are no guards stationed on duty at the CCO doors. They must be in their own bunks by now. In that moment, the doors open, and out comes Aeson Kassiopei. He looks grim and tense, and just as he turns his head, he sees me.

"Lark! What the hell are you doing here?" He frowns and takes a few steps in my direction.

"Oh!" I pause, panting hard from running, while many dots are now swimming before my eyes, like weird static. "I was just helping Kem to get back to his room, he has Jump sickness, and he got lost—"

"You are disobeying direct orders! Get back to your quarters immediately!" he says in a hard voice, catching up to me.

"Okay, but I was just—"

"Go! *Run!*"

"Four minutes to Jump. . . ."

I turn and start hurrying, and hear his rapid footsteps behind me.

"No, wait! Too late, you won't make it back in time!"

I hear his voice at the same time as I feel his powerful grip on my arm, as he starts pulling me with him.

"What?" I mutter, as we hurry around the corner, and into

the first VIP corridor.

"No time," he repeats, as we stop before the first door. He opens it, and pushes me inside with both hands, his fingers pressing into my arms painfully.

The cabin is small, almost the same size as mine, and only the table is longer. The pristinely made bunk with a blanket and single pillow, and a storage hull overhead is possibly a bit larger.... But I can't be sure now, because my head is beginning to go around, and I stagger in place until he has to catch me by the elbows.

"Where are we?" I mutter. Meanwhile my mind starts to race with strange excitement, because he is standing right next to me, and there's nowhere to go, and I can smell the musky scent of him *up-close*, and feel the strands of his golden hair as he moves around, clearing things off the table surface....

"My quarters," he says curtly.

Okay, I did *not* see that coming. "But—but this is such a tiny room, it's just like mine!" I say in surprise.

In reply he merely pushes me down on the bed. "Sit. And now, lie down, carefully. Watch your head."

I obey and lie back, resting my head against *his* pillow, while this insane overflow of emotion starts bubbling inside me.

I am lying on *his* bed.

"Two minutes to Jump...."

I lie and watch in a strange surreal daze as he starts pulling off his own boots and then loosens the collar of his uniform shirt, unbuttoning the top three buttons, then proceeds to remove various small firearms and key cards from his pockets, dumping them on the surface of the table.

When he's done, he turns to me. His face is blank, emotionless. "Scoot over, closer to the wall," he tells me.

My lips part. But I do as he says, pushing myself as far against the wall as I can, while my temples are pounding so fast I feel like I'm about to explode....

In the next instant the bed creaks slightly as he sits down, then stretches carefully on the bed, *right next to me.*

Okay, I think I am going to die....

The bunk is only slightly larger than my own tiny cot, but it's barely enough for two people. I briefly recall how Logan had to embrace me tight in order for both of us to fit on my bed.

Oh my God.

Aeson Kassiopei rests his head against the pillow next to me, and his long metallic hair falls soft against my neck, his strong shoulder touching mine. He then rises up again, and moves in closer to me, and momentarily looks at my face. "Lift your head," he says near my ear. I feel his warm breath wash over my cheek.

I raise my head, and he moves the pillow closer to me so that most of it is under my head, cradling it against the hard wall panel.

And then he puts his arm up and around and behind my head against the wall, because there's basically nowhere else to rest it, short of embracing me full-body.

"One minute to Jump. . . ."

There's a pause while we both listen, lying next to each other, stiff and motionless.

And then suddenly, it's as if he makes a difficult decision. He moves again, and his arm comes down and wraps around me, and keeps going. . . . And I find myself lifted from underneath by the shoulders, and pulled up against his chest, so that now I am lying in the crook of his arm, while his body is pressing against mine, the entire length of him.

"Fifty seconds to Jump. . . ."

He reaches over with his other hand and pushes the harness button. The restraints come down snaking around us, enclosing us into a safety cocoon.

My head is against his chest and I am surrounded. . . . I can hear his strong beating heart and feel the hard muscular planes of his body underneath me. He is so warm, so large, and I am drowning in the warmth and strength. . . .

"Twenty seconds to Jump. . . ."

"Lark," he says in his deep voice, speaking calmly, and I feel the vibration of his voice inside his chest, powerful, rich, against my cheek. "Keep your head down and try to relax."

"Okay . . ." I whisper, while my pulse races erratically, at the same time as my head is swimming in a strange warm crazy stream.

"Ten seconds to Jump. . . ."

His breathing is so calm, so even ... hypnotic.... I lie against his chest and watch him through the fringe of my eyelashes, his stunning profile, the angles of his chiseled jaw, as he lies staring directly up at the bulkhead over our heads, and never at me.

"Nine ... eight ... seven ..."

"Close your eyes," he says softly. And then his face turns at last, and his lapis blue eyes are upon me, profound, solemn, filled with intensity.

"Six ... five ... four ..."

"Breathe ... Gwen."

My heart stumbles wildly, skips a beat at the strange intimate sound of his voice, as he says my name—not "Lark" but *"Gwen."* And I feel his chest rising and falling, as he breathes with a regular rhythm, setting an example for my own body, so I breathe also, in tandem with him.

"Three ... two...."

"Just breathe."

"One...."

Jump.

The world goes out.

We Jump.

Chapter 33

I surface out of an abyss, rising up like a drowning swimmer, fighting to regain consciousness through a thick indescribable fog. . . .

It's as if I've been splintered into a *billion trillion* particles and reformed on the quantum level.

Which I *have* been.

My head feels heavy like an anvil, and at the same time it's on fire.

I am on fire.

For a moment I am disoriented and I don't know or understand anything—I don't know *what* or *where* I am.

And then consciousness returns, and with it, the idea of drawing breath.

Breathe, Gwen, breathe.

I find that I cannot breathe.

I struggle for air, and then I suck in a deep breath sharply, and my eyes fly open as I lurch upward, heaving deeply, gasping.

In that moment I remember everything. I recall my surroundings and where I am.

I turn my head, my body squirming, gasping for air, and I see *him*.

He is lying next to me and partly *under* me, still unconscious, head slightly turned, breathing deeply, thick long eyelashes resting against his cheek. His skin is flushed slightly, and I see the bronzed lines of his neck where his shirt has been unbuttoned.

I shudder again, trying to catch my breath while panic hits me with a wild surge, a tidal wave of emotion, and once again I am drowning in it.

In that moment his chest expands, rises, takes a deep breath and he shifts under me. His eyelids flutter and he comes awake—he opens his eyes and his lips part on an exhalation.

In that moment I push against his chest with both my arms and elbows, while my pulse goes into overdrive, and I moan and gasp for air.

"It's okay . . ." he says in a thick voice, letting me struggle. "Lie still. Try to lie still. Breathe slowly now—"

In response I struggle again, my hands pushing wildly against him, and I try to get up, bumping my head painfully against the bulkhead overheard. The pain only serves to agitate me further.

My hands grasp at his shoulders, pull his golden hair—oh how soft it is, how long I've wanted to touch his hair like this, feel the delicate texture of this natural gold—and at my touch his eyelids flutter suddenly and he stiffens.

I sit up and pant, and my fingers grasp at his hair, digging deeply into his scalp, and he *lets* me.

It's strange, but as I regain my breath, and part of my mind, it occurs to me—*I am pulling his hair and somehow it's okay?*

"It's okay, Gwen," he says again, as though he's reading my mind. He is breathing evenly, but his lips have now come together in a tight line—a sign of his exerted control.

And then panic hits me again, and I am flailing and fighting for breath, and now I try to climb out of the bunk. My hands rip at him, at his hair, at the harness restraints all around us. And he only holds me lightly, letting me strike at him, and repeats in a soft suddenly breathless voice, "It's okay, just breathe."

I moan in frustration, while my face, my neck, every inch of the surface of my skin is now burning up.

Heat rises throughout my flesh and I don't know what to do with it, I need to *rip it out* of me. I tear at it, at my own skin, my own hair, pull at the harness, the blanket underneath us, my fingers digging into his shirt.

"Hold on just a few minutes longer," he whispers. "It's okay."

I rip at his shirt, grasp at my own tank top, pulling at it, as I begin to climb over him, and I hit my head against the bulkhead again, moan in pain, but don't even care—I have to get out, get away from my own burning skin. . . .

My tank top snags against something, and then I feel the clasp of my bra snap in the back and loosen suddenly.

I pause momentarily, while reality washes over me in strange slow motion.

And then the impossible happens. *I pop out from underneath my bra.*

Immediately I sag a little. Okay—I'm not huge in the chest but I *am* on the large side, and the last time my Mom took me to get fitted for a bra they told me I was growing out of a C cup and will have to go to a D soon. So yeah, it's normal to sag a bit when you're pushing past C, without wearing some kind of support. However what's really bad is to be wearing a short tank top that pulls up really easily.

And it happens. . . . The tank top rolls up from the bottom, and oh my God, *I fall out completely.*

I am topless naked in front of my commanding officer, Command Pilot Aeson Kassiopei.

I freeze.

And he freezes also.

The moment elongates—it's another Jump, another universe is being created around us—and I watch his face as he looks at me . . . at my naked chest hanging in his face.

His expression—I don't think I have words for it. His eyes, they go *dark* and they are all pupils, no blue. . . .

I am burning up with embarrassment. Waves of shame travel through me, while warm heat is rising.

And then, just as suddenly, I no longer care. Embarrassment fades back and in its place fierce energy floods me. Something wordless, powerful, rises up, giving me a surge of strength. . . . I *know* I really should pull down that top. Instead I feel *wanton* and shameless, almost *gleeful* that he sees me like this, is looking at me, at my *body*.

Seeing me. . . .

I make a small sound, a whimper.

And he continues watching me, petrified. There is no sound, only his breathing . . . it is elevated and loud, but he never parts his lips, keeping a straight line.

Perfect control.

And then slowly he moves his hands up, strong fingers splayed wide open, sliding against the curve of my waist, my sides, and he holds me, suspended over him. Where he touches my bare skin, I am scalded with fire. . . .

Just as I think the moment cannot end, he moves again. His one hand reaches up and unexpectedly he cups my breast, lingering. And then he squeezes, *hard*.

My lips part at his touch, and an electric shock surges through me. . . . I moan and move against him involuntarily, because this is insane, *this is not happening*.

In response, his other hand takes my other breast, and he presses them together, and his thumbs brush against the tips.

My God, I move again at the strange stab of pleasure . . . I am above him, and my one hand again digs into his hair, while my other hand slides down, trembling, along his warm throat, his shoulder, then sweeps against the hard lines of his muscular torso. All the while as I *touch him*, he remains silent, breathing forcefully, and he continues to scoop my breasts up with his warm long fingers, then flattens them back down hard against my ribs. . . .

"That's enough now," he says suddenly, in a rough voice, letting go of me, just like that.

I pant, breathlessly, feeling shock at the sudden loss of his touch. And as I glance down at his uniform pants, I notice the *condition* of his crotch. All this time I've been moving against him unconsciously, and now—now I am mesmerized. . . .

Something wild, primal prompts me to move my hand down. And then I do the unthinkable. I cup my hand against *him*. It's only fair, since *he* held me first.

"No . . ." he says immediately, sucking his breath in sharply. "Don't do that. . . ."

I linger only for a moment and let go.

"No, don't . . ." he says again, so that now I'm unsure of his meaning. Only his eyes are in agony.

But it's too late. His breath hitches sharply. . . . His lips part. . . . And the next instant I see the beginnings of a dark stain on his uniform fabric.

His face flames wildly, and he pulls away from me, putting

his hands over his crotch, cussing in Atlantean. "No, damn it, this *cannot* be happening!" he exclaims roughly, and then starts to laugh. Which makes it terrifying.

And as I pause, completely stunned, he exclaims suddenly, "Out! Get *out!*"

I am shaking now. *My God, what is happening?*

"Go! Just—just get out of here, Lark!" he continues saying ruthlessly, chuckling bitterly at himself as he turns his face from me. Next he fumbles with one hand to find the harness button and releases the restraint, while I start climbing over him to get out of his bed.

"Please, cover yourself . . ." he says, averting his eyes, with dark sarcasm, as soon as I'm off him and on the outside of the bed. "And put your damn bra back on. . . ."

But then he shakes his head as though clearing his head of a fog.

"No, wait!" he says suddenly, raises one hand to point at the nearby chair and table. "Don't go! You cannot leave yet. No. . . . Over there—go sit—sit down and put your head down on the table. . . . Just ten more minutes, and it will be safe."

I finally find my voice. "I'm sorry . . ." I say with emotion, while a tidal wave rises, choking me. "I am so sorry!"

"Not your fault," he says. "It's all mine." But he continues looking away and is now turned to the wall entirely.

I stagger upright, dizzy with a head rush, and then barely take a step before I land in the seat. Hastily I pull down my dratted tank top over my chest and try to fit myself back inside the bra cups—the bra is useless, I think there's something wrong with the clasp. And then, resting my elbows on the tabletop next to his needle-guns and gadgets, I put my head down, and tremble, and just breathe. . . .

Breathe, Gwen, breathe. . . .

A few minutes later, I look up, while my mind is now very *clear*, at the same time as I am absolutely embarrassed, humiliated, and mortified with pure unadulterated *horror*.

Or maybe *he* is.

I don't know. I can no longer tell.

"You may go now," he says suddenly, still lying down and facing the wall.

"Are you—are you okay?" I mutter.

"It's only Jump sickness, Lark," he says in a hard voice without looking at me.

"That was Jump sickness?" I open my mouth.

"Yes . . ." he says after only the slightest pause. "Now, go! I am going to get *cleaned up* now, and you—you are going to *go*."

"Okay," I whisper.

And I flee his quarters.

I don't really know how I manage to make it back to my own cabin, as I rush through the corridors of the ship, holding my hands crossed over my chest to keep the awful little tank top in place—after all, it's just underwear—and in addition I am also stupidly barefoot.

Since it's been twenty minutes after the Jump, there are people in the hallways now, some of them looking dazed, others recovered completely as if nothing happened.

Once in my own room, I close the door and collapse on my own bed, folding myself up in a fetal position. I lie on my side, trembling, rocking, and shuddering in delayed reaction shock.

And then the tears come. . . .

They are tears of humiliation, pain, confusion—just an absolute emotional overload.

Maybe it's still Jump sickness?

To hell with Jump sickness! *No,* I think, *this is something far more complicated.*

What had just happened between me and Kassiopei? What was it?

How am I ever going to *face him* again, after today?

And then it occurs to me, *how is he ever going to face me?*

Because, yeah, he definitely underwent an experience that affected him just as much if not more, and I think it meant something. I think there is *something* there—something between us.

But what is it?

I lie in bed for over an hour, examining everything with as much clinical detachment as possible, coming to grips with my own emotions. And then I change clothing, put my full uniform back on, and venture outside my cabin.

I don't bother to go looking for Gennio and Anu, or returning to assist at the cold storage chamber on Deck 5. In fact, I don't even pretend I'm capable of doing anything useful right now. If anyone asks, I can blame it all on Jump sickness. Let them handle the revival of the people in stasis. I am taking the rest of this damn day off.

Time to get a solid meal—possibly in a very remote meal hall where I am not likely to meet anyone I know. And once I get back, I will call Gracie and Gordie to make sure they're okay after the Jump.

As I head to dinner, something else occurs to me suddenly: *right now, the Fleet, all of us, we're in a very different part of the universe.*

Wow.... We've made it halfway across the uncharted cosmic divide. We are now in the galactic neighborhood of Atlantis.

And my home, Earth? The solar system? The Milky Way Galaxy?

They are all now so infinitely far away.

Chapter 34

Now that we've Jumped, we've officially entered the first month of Red season, the Atlantean equivalent of summer.

The next morning after the Jump, the first official day of summer on the Atlantean calendar, I go in to the CCO, having steeled myself emotionally. I decide that the best course of action is to simply face Command Pilot Aeson Kassiopei directly and not flinch, and be polite and businesslike.

Act as if nothing happened, Gwen, I tell myself.

But when I get there, he's not in.

Gennio and Anu tell me the CP is off at some kind of series of meetings, and he is going to be gone for most of the day.

"So, how did you enjoy your first Jump?" Anu asks with a raised brow. "Barf much?"

"No problem," I tell him, thinking, *lord, if they only knew*.

"Did you get sick?" Gennio looks up at me mildly. "I did not see you back here afterwards, so not sure if you were okay, or too sick."

"No, not too badly." I shrug, putting on a calm face. "Got a little dizzy, stayed in bed longer. Everything's fine. Sorry I didn't think to let you know I'd be out. How did everything go with the cold storage revival?"

"Fine as usual," Anu says. "You didn't miss much. The two old guys survived, so did five of the eight Earth kids. Three of them—not so lucky. Frozen dead like your Earth ice cream pops."

"What?" I part my mouth in horror.

"Oh, stop it, Anu!" Gennio shakes his head. "Never mind him, Gwen, no one died, he is just joking as usual."

"Okay, then," I say. "Anu, one of these days. . . ."

But he just snorts and turns back to his console.

The rest of the day is uneventful, except that while I'm at the office, I keep expecting the Command Pilot to walk in at any moment, and he does *not*.

"More systems inspections," Gennio says. "All the post-Jump protocol stuff that the CP has to supervise. He'll be out all day."

And then I check my email and I see a message from Kassiopei.

Immediately my heart jolts painfully, and I open the email with trepidation. It's short and to the point: *"Voice training will be cancelled for tonight. —A. K."*

Yeah, why am I not surprised?

As far as classes, I attend Pilot Training, where Instructor Mithrat Okoi seems to be fine and perfectly healthy after his cold storage capsule experience yesterday. He lectures us in the usual hard voice, pacing before the classroom.

"Flight simulator training will continue indoors for one more month," he says. "The first month after the Jump is considered equally unstable as the previous one, and none of you are allowed to fly outside. Yes, we are now *decelerating*, but the process is gradual, and it will take us another six months to reach velocities that will allow us to slow down and stop, just as we arrive on Atlantis."

And then Instructor Okoi reminds us: "Your Final Pilot Test will be the second Quantum Stream Race, and your skills and abilities will reveal the kind of Pilots you are to become, including your roles in the Fleet. There will be one major notable change for the Second QS Race—you will no longer be constrained to your current flight partners and will be able to choose anyone as your Pilot Pair."

That gets everyone in the room excited, myself included. *I no longer have to fly with Hugo!* I think gleefully.

Meanwhile I see Hugo give me an evaluating stare, then come to some kind of conclusion and start looking around the room. Oh yeah, the boy is going to switch partners! So long, Hugo!

"Enough! Make your Pilot Pair arrangements *after* class!"

the Instructor raises his voice, and the Cadets immediately settle down. However, everyone continues glancing around the room discreetly, for the rest of the class period.

I look around also, and see Logan, as usual not too far away. He does not look at me and appears absorbed with his flight console—but I know he's been watching me.

Then I notice Blayne a few seats away also. He looks occupied with his partner too.

There's plenty of time to find a new flight partner, I decide. Anyone's got to be better than Hugo.

The following day at the CCO, the Command Pilot is still noticeably absent.

I am almost frustrated by the fact, because, to be honest, I'd like to get it over with. Just see him, face him, deal with that hard initial moment. . . .

And then for a brief time I wonder, *is he actively avoiding me?*

No, that cannot be.

And indeed, my theory is discredited, because Aeson Kassiopei comes in around 2:00 PM in the afternoon, just as all three of us Aides are working.

We all get up and salute as usual. My heart starts pounding with stress. I take short shallow breaths and try not to let my rising flush overwhelm my face completely.

Breathe, Gwen, breathe. . . .

Aeson's expression is cold and determined, and he looks particularly sharp today, well put together. He nods at all of us curtly, and does not even make eye contact with me. . . . He gets behind his desk and calls up multiple workstation consoles. I count mech arm monitors, and there are at least five today, obscuring his desk.

Wow. . . . Is he literally hiding behind them from me? I cast the idiotic thought aside, and try to concentrate on my work file.

The next few hours crawl at an excruciating pace, and finally it's almost dinnertime. I have no idea what kind of work I've been doing, but all I know is, I survived being in the same office space with him without combusting. Of course, the worst is still to come—tonight's voice training session, one-on-one.

At some point the CP turns off his tech equipment, gets up swiftly and walks out past us without looking, on his way to the gym before dinner. I glance up just barely in time to see his proud, stiffly-held back and the fall of his long gold hair as the door shuts on him.

I exhale a long-held breath. . . .

Okay, this is not going to be easy.

The other Aides and I head out also, to grab dinner.

And then I get back to my cabin where I kill some time, waiting for 8:00 PM.

At 8:00 PM sharp, I arrive back at the CCO. The guards allow me inside after a brief consult with the CP over their wrist devices—which usually means the Command Pilot is busy or on an important call.

Which proves to be the case.

I enter, pulse racing wildly, breathing evenly to compose myself. And I see a single display console turned around, its back facing me, and Aeson Kassiopei talking in soft Atlantean tones to someone. Immediately I recognize the feminine lilting voice of the speaker on the other end.

Oh, crap. . . . It's that girl.

Lady Tiri whatshername. Tirinea Fuorai.

A blast of elemental anger strikes me in the gut. It is so sudden, so unexpected, that I am stunned enough to pause, before I advance any further inside the room. What am I feeling? *What is it?* I don't think I understand the feeling.

It's jealousy.

I'm absolutely freaking jealous of this Lady Tiri, and I am so damn angry—at her, at him, at *myself.* . . .

I stop to listen, while Aeson ignores me completely and continues speaking, and I see a faint smile on his lips, a smile that makes me melt, because I have never seen it before . . . I have never seen him smile, *sensuously,* like that . . . not for anyone.

Everything inside me is twisting—heart, lungs, my gut—they are seized with a cold unfamiliar emotion that's made up of darkness.

And then, the worst part is, I listen to them speak *Atlanteo,* and because I've been studying the language, I am picking up a few words here and there. Not the real gist, but the individual terms and phrases. . . . Terms, such as "sweet" and "I can't wait to see you."

At least I haven't heard the word "love" being used.

In *Atlanteo*, love is *"amrevet."* And the word for "lover" is *"amreve"* while "beloved" is *"amrevu."* Again, none of these forms are being used.

I listen, barely breathing, still standing near the door.

Then I decide to advance forward.

In that same moment, their conversation ends, and he disconnects the call.

As I approach him, his soft expression evaporates, and he is a blank mask of no emotion.

"Good evening," he says, looking at me like an unblinking serpent. "Take a seat."

Damn him. . . .

I sit down in my usual spot and rest my hands in my lap.

He looks at me, and I look at him. *Steady, steady now. Don't let him see you blink first.*

"How are you?" I say.

I don't think he expected that. So his one brow rises and he moves his head slightly. "Fine, thanks," he says. "And you?"

Well, that was brilliant.

But then I take a deep breath and decide to go direct.

"Command Pilot Kassiopei, I hope what happened at the time of the Jump is not an issue between us. I am sorry—about whatever it was."

His gaze upon me is intense suddenly, so intense that I find I'm drowning in it, in *him*. "It was nothing," he says coldly. "Nothing happened. The Jump affects everyone in different unexpected ways. Unusual physical reactions and responses happen, but they are temporary and *meaningless*. It's over. Think nothing of it and move on."

"Oh," I say. "Okay."

"Now, if you yourself still find any lingering symptoms, it's a good idea to see a doctor." He watches me as he says this. "In your case, I hope you recovered quickly afterwards, and are not still upset about the uncomfortable circumstances."

"I'm fine," I say, keeping my voice steady, while a lump is starting to rise at the back of my throat. *No, I'm not going to cry in front of him.*

Never again.

Well, then, I think bitterly. *He considers it meaningless.*

Meanwhile he calmly looks away from me, reaches for the orichalcum sound damper box, to begin tonight's voice lesson.

I guess *that* conversation is over.

The next day is mostly a repeat of the previous one. I work, attend classes, have voice training that evening, and things are cool and businesslike between us.

In fact, things have gotten chillier than ever. It seems that whatever brief *connection* I thought we had, has not only been lost, but has been stamped out and put down mercilessly.

Aeson Kassiopei has either decided to keep his distance from me for whatever reason, or he really does not care at all about me—at least not in that intimate way about which I still dare to dream.

I do not accept that.

What I don't accept is the *not knowing*. I realize our situation is hopeless. There are worlds of rank, upbringing, cultural and ethnic difference and separation between us. He is a top-ranking Fleet officer and Imperial Prince of a semi-divine ancient dynasty, destined to marry into the highest aristocracy of Atlantis. As far as I know, according to their laws and traditions, I'm not even fit to wipe dust off his shoes—a nobody refugee from Earth, entirely at his mercy, and a fool to think otherwise. There can never be anything between us.

But if I could only *know* for one true moment that he cares or has *feelings* for me, I could live with that. Even if I never saw him again after I got to Atlantis—at which point he would deliver me into whatever branch of public service that my Logos voice condemns me to.

In one way or another, before our journey ends, before our regular personal contact is over, I resolve to find out.

And then, later that night, just before bed and Fleet barracks curfew, I talk to Laronda.

I call her up, because I'm soul sick. And I tell her everything.

And I mean, *everything* that happened during the Jump.

Laronda listens as I go into details, and her mouth falls open.

"What? Girl, *no!* No way! He did *what?*"

I blush furiously as I describe it.

Laronda puts her hand up to cover her mouth and starts to giggle. "Oh, wow! You mean he—in his *pants?*"

"Yeah."

Laronda is holding her mouth with both hands now and her eyes are so round. She rocks back and forth and nearly hyperventilates. Finally she catches a breath and fans her face with her hands and shakes her head in disbelief.

"Okay, I'm sorry," she mutters. "Seriously, I hope you know I mean no disrespect—the guy is totally amazing and imposing and yeah, he terrifies me. I'm just freaking out here, on your behalf. This is not me laughing—this is me going *nuts!*"

"I know. . . ."

Laronda continues fanning her face and saying, "Sweet lord almighty!"

"You—you won't mention any of this to anyone, right?" I whisper.

"Oh, hell no! Are you kidding me? My lips are zipped and sealed and stored away in the back of a freezer!"

I nod, silently, shaking slightly.

"Okay, listen, girl . . ." she says at last, taking a deep breath. "You better watch out. At this rate he's going to put a baby inside you, and then what are you gonna do?"

"But nothing happened!" I exclaim, my face flaming red.

"Not *yet!*"

"At this rate, nothing ever will. . . ." I bite my lips painfully and wrap my arms around me.

"Wait—" Laronda peers at me sideways, her face moving in to take up much of the video screen. "Do you *want* something to happen? Do you—want to be with him, with your prince? Well? Spill it!"

"I—he's not my prince," I mutter. "And, I don't know. I—"

"You really like him, don't you?" Laronda is no longer

fidgeting around or haranguing me, but looking at me wisely.

I pause for a moment.

"Yeah," I say. "I think I do."

"More than Logan?"

"I don't know . . . maybe . . . *yes*."

"Wow." Laronda sits back now, drawing away from the screen close-up. "In that case, girlfriend, you're pretty much screwed. Unless the Atlantean prince plans to take you as his mistress or concubine, or whatever ho-slut hookup girl thing they call it over there—"

"Oh, stop it," I say. "The word for lover is *'amreve.'*"

And I begin to cry.

Chapter 35

This very same week in the first month of Red, they announce the third Zero-G Dance—this one hosted by the Red Quadrant.

Since the instability of the Quantum Stream outside is still high, and the velocities are unsafe for ship-to-ship travel, with the usual exception of *astra daimon* hotshot Pilots, we are mostly confined to our own ships for this particular Dance.

Which means, I can't invite Gracie. Or Laronda. Or anyone else located elsewhere in the Fleet.

At first I consider skipping it—like I skipped the Green Dance. After all, I'm a fragile emotional wreck right now, barely functional, even though I don't show it and put on a brave front.

But then something happens that makes me change my mind in a big way.

That night after my workout at the gym, after our hard sparring practice together, Xelio Vekahat asks me to go as his Date.

Let me repeat that, and explain the capital letter "D" in Date. This is Pilot Xelio Vekahat, the commanding officer in charge of the whole Red Quadrant on ICS-2. And he asks *me* to accompany *him* to the Zero-G Dance hosted by his Quadrant, in the official capacity as his one and only formal guest and significant other.

So yeah, date is probably an understatement.

"So, Gwen what are your plans for the Red Dance?" he says, standing very near me as he holds up my arm to correct my Er-Du stance.

"I'm not sure," I say. "I don't know if I'm going."

One of Xelio's brows goes up and he peers at me closely as

though stunned. I find his proximity and his facial expression both sarcastic and incredibly hot. "Of course you are. I want you to come as my official date."

"Oh . . ." I say, my body stilling in the stance, as my poor mind tries to register this unexpected and frankly mind-blowing notion.

"Well?" he says, the gaze of his black eyes caressing me. "Is it really that hard? Say yes."

"I—okay," I mutter. "I mean, yes. Wow, thank you. . . . Are you sure?"

"Why would I not be?" Now he's smiling at me.

"But—" My lips part and I suppose I'm having a deer-in-the-headlights moment. "Don't you have any other real girls to ask?"

"Real?" His other brow goes up and now he's definitely amused. "Are you saying, you're not *real*, Gwen? Or is there something about you I need to know? Not a girl? Not human, maybe? I know—maybe you're that wooden boy puppet from the old Earth children's story?"

I snort and start feeling warm all over. A flush is rising, and my cheeks, my face, all of me is lit up. That was a dumb thing to say.

"I mean," I start to backtrack, "maybe you have someone better to ask out."

"Better how?"

Oh God, please don't make me say it. . . . I think he's intentionally torturing me.

I take a big breath. "Someone less ridiculous and more good looking."

"I like ridiculous," he says, examining me closely, while the smile is still on his lips. "And I like what I see—Shoelace Girl."

"Oh, lord, no!" I purse my lips and shake my head. But I'm smiling too. "You're never going to let me off for that incident, are you?"

"Never." He leans in and suddenly kisses my cheek.

I feel an immediate conflagration of flames rising.

Yeah, I'm going to the Red Dance.

Talking about flames—*fire* is the theme of the Red Zero-G Dance. In three days, the Resonance Chamber will be decorated in every shade of burning, incendiary, combustible, infernal shade of crimson, scarlet, ruby, *red* there is.

When I ask Xelio awkwardly what I need to do for the Dance, he simply tells me, "Be there, wear red."

Okay, I think, *I suppose I can do that*. And then I think—*Help! Someone! Anyone!* I have no idea how to really dress up, and as Xelio's formal date I will need to look stunning.

And then a really intense new fire lights up under me—here's my opportunity to do something that will make Command Pilot Kassiopei take a second look at me.

What do I need? Definitely an outfit, hair, and makeup. And then something else, for the wow factor. But—what?

I spend most of the next morning at work semi-daydreaming. I space out so often that Anu and Gennio notice my absentminded idiocy.

"Hey, Earth girl! Wake up!" Anu tosses a small computer component at me, hitting me on the back of the head, as I stare at the same screen for the last five minutes without moving. Obviously Aeson Kassiopei is not in the office this morning, else Anu would at least pretend to be businesslike and curb the rowdy.

"Anything wrong, Gwen?" Gennio asks with a glance from his work console.

"No, sorry, I was just thinking about what to wear for the Zero-G Dance," I admit honestly.

"Oh, you could ask Vazara Hotat for help with that," Gennio says with a smile.

The Music Mage! I recall Vazara's classy stylish looks and her definite talent in the area of fashion and makeup. Plus, didn't she offer to help me, back during the Blue Dance?

"Great idea! Thanks Gennio!" I exclaim. "I'll go talk to her after this."

"No, you won't." Anu snorts. "Vaz is stuck on another Ark-Ship today, and she won't get a ride back to ICS-2 until the day after tomorrow, right before the Dance."

"Oh, drat." I purse my lips.

"Why, what do you need exactly? Is it just the 3D printer

pattern for your outfit?" Gennio tries helpfully. "Because I think I have a bunch of those things on file. Maybe you can scroll through them and find something you like."

"Okay, thanks." But I am still pretty much lost at sea, here.

What I need is my little sis Gracie. Okay, I'll call her tonight. But what I also need is for Gracie to magically materialize in my cabin with her big pouch of makeup. And that's not going to happen.

I freeze for another long helpless moment, trying to think where I can get my hands on that girly stuff. I don't really know any girls on this ship, at least not well enough to ask them to borrow their personal cosmetics. Because, yeah, that would be a class act—not.

"Can the 3D printer print cosmetics?" I ask the guys pitifully after a few more useless moments.

"Sure, probably," Gennio says. "If you like, I can lend you my own eyeliner Paint stick, but it's the only item I have, and I don't think that's adequate for your needs."

"Hey, if you need that stuff, you can always ask Consul Denu!" Anu makes another loud laughing sound.

I pause momentarily. "Hmm, that's not a bad idea. Do you think he has the right kind of makeup that's okay to wear at the Zero-G Dance?"

"Hah!" Anu exchanges a superior glance with Gennio. "The Consul has everything. He has the most expensive stuff you wear at Court."

"Oh, good." I nod. "Because I need to look really nice."

"Oh, yeah? How come?" Anu giggles. "Have a big date or something? Is it your boyfriend Sangre?"

I sigh. "Logan is not my boyfriend—not anymore," I say quietly. "And yes, actually I do have a big date. I'm going with the person in charge of the Red Dance—Pilot Xelio Vekahat."

"Whoa!" Anu's mouth falls open. I think, for the first time ever, I've managed to impress him. "No way, you have a date with *Xelio?*"

"Who has a date with Xelio?"

We all turn around and it's Command Pilot Kassiopei. Apparently he's entered the room quietly, and now stands behind us, listening.

Immediately my face betrays me as I start to feel the heat explode in my cheeks. Idiot Anu simply *had* to raise his voice in that second and yell out on top of his lungs, didn't he? Ugh. . . .

"*She* does!" Anu says, pointing at me. And then we all remember our place and scramble up to salute.

"What's going on here?" Aeson ignores the salute and his cool eyes turn to me, focusing.

"Oh, nothing, Command Pilot," I respond, looking at the level of his chin.

"She has a date with Pilot Vekahat!" Anu continues gaping at me.

"Is that so?" Aeson resumes walking toward his desk as though nothing is amiss.

"Yes, for the Zero-G Dance," I mutter.

"You're not going with Sangre?" Aeson sits down in his chair and once more looks directly at me.

"No," I say. "I'm not."

"He's not her boyfriend anymore!" Anu says loudly.

"Enough, Anu." Now the Command Pilot is looking at me very closely. There's a very strange expression on his face.

I blink.

There's a somewhat long pause.

And then Aeson Kassiopei says comfortably, "You're in luck. Xel is a very skilled dancer. You'll enjoy the Dance." And with infuriating calm he nods to all of us, and starts up his consoles.

For the rest of the shift I hide my face in my own work.

After lunch I am more than happy to escape to Pilot Training Class. Anything to avoid Kassiopei and the CCO.

When I get to the classroom deck, I see Cadets wandering all over the room, talking loudly, and I remember that this is pretty much the time when we're supposed to make arrangements for our new Pilot Partners. Everyone's mingling, talking. . . .

I see Hugo Moreno laughing loudly and confidently with some guy, one of his buddies, and I'm guessing that's his new Co-Pilot.

But the interesting thing is, quite a few people choose to

remain with their original partners. I see Logan and Oliver sharing a double console desk as usual. So is Blayne and his partner Leon Madongo, a wiry, soft-spoken Kenyan teen.

I stand kind of awkwardly, looking around. And for a moment I get a painful flashback to high school and being picked last for P.E. team sports. . . . Seems like not much has changed in that department.

And then my gaze connects with Chiyoko Sato. The big girl is standing at the back of the classroom, looking lost, just like me. . . . I remember the day of our very first shuttle run flight simulator assignment, when Hugo and I were nearly the last people in the room, and so was Chiyoko and her partner, a Latina girl with braids, who was yelling at her and giving her a hard time. That same girl is now far across the room, having found another partner.

Okay, I think, why not?

So I walk up to Chiyoko, who looks at me, her round face wearing the usual slightly startled expression.

"Hey," I say. "Want to be my Pilot Partner?"

There is a pause.

"Okay . . ." Chiyoko says quietly.

"My name is Gwen Lark," I remind her.

"I know."

Yeah, I suppose she does. Hugo and I are the notorious losers of the previous Race. Now I'm kind of surprised she just agreed to work with me. I even feel a little guilty that she's stuck with me.

Chiyoko and I find a console desk and take our seats. "Do you want to be the Pilot or the Co-Pilot?" I ask her carefully.

Her quiet answer again comes after the slightest pause. "I don't care."

I smile. "I don't care either." And then I glance at her. "We can figure that out after we practice together and see how it goes."

"Okay."

Chiyoko is apparently a girl of few words. Which is just fine with me.

All in all, this is definitely better than dealing with Hugo.

And then Instructor Okoi comes in and begins the class.

Afterwards I get a brief shift back at the CCO, and then have my Court Protocol class with Consul Denu. I arrive at the Consul's quarters precisely on time, as the Consul demands of me, and knock politely.

Kem opens the door with a tiny friendly nod, and I go inside where Consul Suval Denu reposes in his comfortable chair, reading one of his elegant Atlantean literary journals on an Atlantean equivalent of a tablet. One thing I've learned over the course of my studies with him is that literature is considered to be a very high art in Atlantis, with a long, rich tradition, together with opera, chamber music, and other cultural forms of human expression. Consul Denu is a great connoisseur of the arts, and is incredibly well-read—something that I find most impressive about him.

Really, the more I know Consul Denu, the more I realize the complexity of this man. Underneath the extravagant foppish attire and manners—which I realize now is a kind of disguise, a ritualized costume—he combines the delicate subtlety of a poet and the steely mind of a diplomat.

I make a formal Atlantean high-ranking woman's greeting, which is a form of a curtsey and salute combined—something he again expects of me. And then, before we begin today's class, I politely tell him about my sudden needs in the cosmetics department.

"I hope I'm not overstepping, Consul Denu," I say, "But this isn't just a date. I have an obligation to look appropriately *good* for the Red Dance, since Pilot Xelio Vekahat himself has invited me. So I'm wondering if I might ask your help with my makeup?"

The Consul raises one arched brow at me, and looks me over. "My dear, yes, I see. Your obligation in this case is undeniable. And since I have all this at my disposal, I am happy to assist. But tell me, what will you wear?"

I sigh. "I'm still not sure," I mutter. "I only know it must be red."

"Ah, well you need to be sure by tomorrow, considering the Dance is the day after."

"Okay, I am going to look at a whole bunch of dress

patterns tonight."

"You do that. And once you find the right one, send the file here so I can take a look at it. Remember, skin art must always match the outfit."

I thank him genuinely, and we proceed with the class.

That night, my voice training with Aeson Kassiopei is an exercise in emotional torture—at least it feels that way for me.

He never brings up anything about the Red Dance or my upcoming date with Xelio, or even that now he knows for a fact that Logan and I are no longer together.

It's as if he cares about *none* of it.

Soon, I feel overwhelming despair gathering inside me.

And when the half hour is over, I flee back to my own cabin while the despair rings loudly in my head, and then transforms into blazing *anger*.

I pull up my console and call up the search engine to find an appropriate beautiful dress. But all I can think of is not beautiful or elegant or stunning, but angry, crazy, wild.

It's how I feel. And I need to channel this feeling into whatever it is I am going to wear.

I try to consult again the huge database of historical costumes from the previous dances. I think about the theme—red, heat, fire. And then I submerge deep inside myself and think—what do I have inside me that can express that *red* in a powerful way?

Because I need that wow factor.

Looking to get inspired, I open up the information page for the Red Dance itself, to see what's on the program. And then I see it—interspersed with the actual zero gravity dancing there will be short vocal performances, open to the public, a kind of Atlantean version of karaoke. There's even a footnote about how much Atlanteans love and value singing and music.

And then my wild idea hits me.

I think of Mom, singing opera to me when I was a kid. And me, singing along with her. *Wow*, I think. *I still remember so many of the gorgeous arias she did, that I can probably easily repeat them.* When I was little, I sang along with her—in a child's voice, but still, I memorized the music and words. . . . All I would need to do now is call up the score and music and brush up on it overnight and I will be ready for the Red Dance.

And in that instant, everything—my look, my outfit, my song—comes to me in tongues of blazing red fire.

I open up the costume database and start looking for the template so I can build upon it the perfect costume for the Red Zero-G Dance. An hour later I'm done, and I send it off to the 3D printer, along with my body measurements template. And then I send a copy to Consul Denu, to let him figure out my matching cosmetics.

Finally, I look up the old operatic score and start remembering how it goes. . . .

My *red* song.

Then I send it to the Red Dance scheduling, to reserve my place in the vocalist lineup.

Chapter 36

The next day—the day before the Red Zero-G Dance—is a madhouse, filled with the usual ship-wide aura of excitement.

Everywhere across the Fleet, teens are getting their outfits manufactured, keeping the 3D printers running non-stop. For many people it started even earlier, the night before, but I only know that my own costume is scheduled for pickup after 4:30 PM.

Anu is gone for most of the morning, since he's aligned with the Red Quadrant and therefore has to help out with various Red Dance preparations. In his case, it's acoustic tech stuff similar to Gennio's role during the Blue Dance. And tomorrow, when the main setup and prep schedule begins, he'll be gone again.

Gennio and I work in comfortable silence, and the CP is in and out of the office, making brief appearances, and then going to take care of ship business elsewhere.

It's almost relaxing.

When Kassiopei returns just before lunch and gets behind his desk, I throw frequent glances at him, feeling hyper and upbeat. *I can't wait for him to see me tomorrow.*

Only, there's one fear that hits me suddenly. . . .

Will he be there?

Aeson Kassiopei *hates* dancing. He has no particular Quadrant obligations to be at the Red Dance. What if he decides not to attend at all?

I am so unsettled by the thought that all my crazed preparation will go to waste, that I actually gather the courage to broach the subject.

"Command Pilot," I say carefully. "Are there any particular duties the CCO has tomorrow at the Zero-G Dance?"

Aeson looks up from his work, frowning at being interrupted. "What?"

I repeat the question.

"No, we have nothing scheduled," he says, looking at me with an unreadable expression.

"Will you be attending to supervise, or anything?" There, I said it. I asked him point-blank.

"I will not be supervising," he says, after the slightest pause. "As the ICS-2 commanding officer however, I do need to make an appearance. It will likely be brief."

Disappointment strikes me hard.

"I hope you stay long enough to hear me sing," I say suddenly.

His one brow rises as he looks at me. "Oh," he says. "You signed up to be a vocalist?"

"Yup." I allow myself a tiny brave smile.

He pauses, then nods. "It should be interesting to evaluate how your voice handles a musical piece. I'll try to stay long enough to hear your performance."

Later that afternoon I run to Manufacturing Deck on Level Six to pick up my completed outfit. It is pristinely wrapped in discreet plastic, and comes with matching shoes and all the accessories. All I'm missing is jewelry, but I tell myself sparkly bling is entirely unnecessary—I'll look just fine without it.

I call up Gracie. This is the time for last minute advice, and I carefully open up the plastic to show her the costume.

"Oh!" Gracie parts her mouth and says, "Wooooooow! Gee Two, I can't believe you're wearing that! That's just—"

"Awesome?" I finish for her.

"Well, yeah!" She continues gaping. "But I was gonna say, that doesn't even seem like you! That's just *intense!* And the fact that you're going with Pilot Xelio Vekahat? *Wow!*"

I smile at my sister. "I know," I say.

My smile—it is almost *wicked*.

I wake up in the morning of Red Dance day, super energized. All regular classes and work is cancelled, since each Dance day is basically a Fleet holiday.

I take my time lingering at breakfast. And then, since I don't have to be at the CCO today at all, I consider either taking a long walk around the ship, or doing a short gym workout. But I decide against both, since I want to conserve every ounce of my strength—emotional and physical—for my upcoming performance tonight.

So instead I spend several hours holed up in my cabin, intermittently reading, laying out my costume for tonight, going over the music score of the aria I will be singing, actually singing it softly a few times, and then finally napping.

I break for lunch, then get back to it again, until dinner.

As the time grows closer to the Dance, I find that I am too nervous to eat.

Instead, I take a long shower, and then start fussing and putting on the *dress*.

At 6:30 PM, as I am not even close to being done with my hair—which I'm attempting to pin up into a tight updo, either a bun or chignon—I hear a soft tone sound at the door. I open it to find Kem standing there, holding a big box and a bag.

"Hello, Gwen, Consul Denu sent me to help you dress," he says timidly with a smile.

"Oh!" I exclaim, holding my hair with one hand, and trying not to do any damage to my *dress*. "Thank you *so much!* I didn't realize it was so late already, I was going to come by his quarters to pick up the makeup—"

"No need." Kem points to the things he is holding, "I have everything here. May I come in?"

"Oh yeah, of course!"

Kem steps into the tiny cabin and starts setting up on the table surface.

"Your dress is very beautiful," he says. "Consul Denu wanted me to say he approves your choice and color, and he has the recommended matching color Paints selected for you. I am going to apply the Paints in Imperial Court fashion, which will give you the most high couture look."

"Oh my goodness," I mutter, "I didn't realize you would be

doing my makeup! I'm sorry to put you to all this trouble! Are you sure? Maybe I can just do it myself?"

Kem shakes his head. "Oh no, it's no trouble at all—it is what I do. And it's the least I can do, after your very kind help during the Jump when I was so sick. For which I remain very thankful."

"Oh," I say, smiling. "Okay then."

He nods shyly. And then he becomes businesslike.

"Gwen, please let go of your hair and stand up straight."

I drop my partially pinned-up hair and do as he tells me.

"Now turn, please."

Kem looks at me critically, his gaze sweeping up and down. This is what he sees. . . .

The *dress.*

It is the color of blood. Deep dark blood, a profound midnight red that's the closest to black I could make it when I chose the hue—Spanish flamenco at midnight.

The shape of the dress begins as a tight sleeveless sheath on top, with a plunging round neckline, clinging to my chest, waist, and hips like a second skin. . . . And then, as the delicate soft fabric flows down past my thighs and below, it starts to flare out gently around the legs all the way to my ankles—not in stiff flamenco fashion, but loose-hanging, fine as cobwebs, so that only if I spin or float in Zero-G, the skirt becomes a gradual great bell of translucent gauze around my feet. . . .

The fabric itself, delicate yet durable, has a mother-of-pearl sheen to it, so that it reflects the light, with a gradation from pure black to shimmering red.

The matching pair of deep red shoes with sharp pointy toes has slim two-inch heels—not too high, because I am just too much of a klutz to risk a dangerous mishap. They are basically pumps with abbreviated stilettos. I've tried them on, and I think I can manage to walk in them without tripping over myself.

Right now I'm barefoot, and the shoes are sitting on the floor, while I turn around in front of Kem to show him the fit of the dress.

"Very lovely," he says. "Now let's begin with your hair, and then I will apply Paints last."

"What? You're doing my hair too?" I glance at him with

utmost relief. "Oh, thank God! Thank you so much! As you can see, I'm not doing too well here on my own!" And I point to my mess of an updo that appears to be done by a monkey.

"Of course," he says. "Now, sit. And I will re-do your hair."

Half an hour later, my hair is pulled tight against my scalp, with a gorgeous, compactly wound bun near the top of my head—everything is skin-tight, clean, austere lines, with not a wisp out of place. Because my hair is long and thick, Kem has to make a crown of braids to frame and circle the bun around its base. This hairstyle, with the bun raised high above the nape, does wonders—it reveals that my neck is far more elegant than I thought.

"On Atlantis, the current hair trends do not allow messy asymmetry. So, no hanging single curls or locks on any sides. You will instead look stern and perfect."

"Sounds good to me," I say with a smile, glancing at the small mirror and the sophisticated girl looking back at me.

"And now, the makeup." And Kem begins working on my face.

First he uses a special foundation matte powder that is applied so lightly that it appears invisible, but adds a hint of both color and porcelain pallor to the skin of my face, neck, and upper chest. In a moment of quantum paradox, suddenly my skin appears ethereal. . . . Next, he uses a variety of color sticks to blend amazing dramatic shadows over my eyes, with the subtlety of a true artist. Then he applies gentle blush that finds and emphasizes my high cheekbones. Finally comes the razor-intense kohl eyeliner and mascara that transform my eyes into deep stunning things.

"My eyebrows are kind of thick—do you need to pluck anything?" I ask in trepidation.

"No," he replies. "Plucking eyebrows is actually a common misconception—most women and men already have the natural brow shape that perfectly defines and emphasizes their eye socket. When they pluck, to make the ridiculous up-sweeping arches, they in fact detract from the true expressiveness of their face. Unless the brows are already naturally thin, plucked eyebrows take away the potential *force* and *fierceness* hidden in you, and change your face—not in a good way."

"Wow," I mutter. "Sounds like a whole philosophy there."

"Yes, it is. It is also an art, and you study it," he says with some pride. "It's true, in some cases, some adjustment is necessary to the features. But in your case, Gwen, you make it easy. Your eyebrows are neither too thick nor too thin, but perfectly shaped. They frame your eyes with power and distinction. And—no need for false eyelashes. Your natural eyelashes are precisely enough. I simply darkened the colors all around to emphasize the beauty of your wonderful blue irises."

The very last is the lip color. He outlines my lips, then fills them with a rich blood-red cosmetic that has the juicy gloss of crushed cherries and black ink.

"Your lips have a truly fine harmonious shape. A full lower lip such as yours makes it easy to sculpt colors. Open your mouth. . . ."

I do as I'm told, and he continues fine-tuning the gradation of lip color at the corners with a fine-tipped brush.

When he is done, I look *amazing*.

Seriously, I can't even begin to describe how good he made me look.

This is not me. . . .

I am someone else—a beautiful, shadowy, mysterious female.

I look fierce. Seductive. Dangerous.

I look like her, the one who will sing the *Habanera* tonight, with the intention to *devastate*.

Carmen.

I try to stand up, but Kem tells me firmly he is not done yet. "And now, the finishing touches," he says with a little pleased smile.

He reaches into his magic bag and opens another small box. Inside is a beautiful jewel pendant—a great blood-red ruby, fixed in a delicate black metal filigree setting. The ruby is not faceted, but a smooth rounded cabochon. It is surrounded by tiny, sharply faceted black crystals that dance with black fire. Next to it in the box are two matching earrings, consisting of similar smaller ruby studs with sparkling garlands of black jewels, shaped like eyes of a peacock.

"This is on loan from Consul Denu's personal collection," Kem says, putting the chain around my neck and attaching the clasp from the back. "Wear it tonight with Consul Denu's compliments and his thanks."

The chain slips with a cool pressure around my neck and the pendant dips down to rest provocatively in my cleavage, where it sparkles with an infernal light. I am so unused to this kind of thing that its placement actually makes me blush.

"Oh wow, this is gorgeous and looks expensive!" I say with worry.

"It is both," Kem replies with a smile. "But Consul Denu wants to thank you on my behalf—again, for helping me."

"I should be thanking both of you so much!"

"Your ears are pierced?"

"Yes."

Kem nods. "Good. These are for pierced ears, though I have an alternate set of clip-ons, which are a part of the collection. Some Atlantean high-ranking families do not pierce or in any way mar their flesh, so there must always be alternatives."

Kem puts the earrings on me, and they are surprisingly light and comfortable, with the deep red studs adding almost no weight, and the exquisite peacock fringes dangling almost down to my shoulders.... They brush feather-softly against my cheeks and throat like ghostly kisses....

"One more thing," Kem says. He opens the bag again, and takes out two long evening gloves that match my dress in deep red-black color.

"Oh, wow . . ." I say. "Where did you get this made? How?"

"3D printer," he says with a little smile.

But then I notice they are not actually gloves—they're a strange cross between fingerless gloves and just sleeves that go up just past the elbows. I pull the sleeves on and see there is a ring on each that attaches to the middle finger, connecting the sleeve fabric to the hand, forming an elegant "V." I slide the rings on.

"*Now* we're done," Kem says, looking at me with satisfaction. "But wait—no, one more last thing. . . ."

He reaches into his bag one more time, and this time takes out a single large flower, fresh from the Hydroponics deck, its closely cropped stem enclosed in a small special hydrating tip. It's a deep crimson carnation. "This is from me," he says. "For your hair, to complete your themed costume."

"My God, you are amazing!" I exclaim, while Kem carefully pins the gorgeous hothouse blossom to the side of my head.

"There," he says. "It is specially coated so the freshness should last the entire evening."

I stand up, slip on my high-heeled shoes. . . . Take a few steps and glimpse myself sideways in the small mirror.

A creature from another dimension—a dimension of shadows and black ruddy flames—passes by me in the mirror.

"Go on," Kem says. "The Dance has started. I will see you there."

It's just after 7:00 PM when I move through the large people-packed corridor in the central hub near the CCO, toward the entrance to the Resonance Chamber.

Red light fills the hallway, and stains all of us with passionate crimson highlights.

Inside, the music comes like thunder, a heavy dance beat.

I walk carefully, unused to my high-heeled shoes, not to mention the entire rest of me, alien, exotic, dramatic. Right now I'm feeling like a combination of Cinderella and a military commando on a mission. After all, I *am* wearing all that war paint—oops, I mean, face paint.

I'm supposed to meet Xelio somewhere near the music tech sound station, not far from the inside entrance.

Surrounded by a crowd of other gorgeously overdressed teens, I take a deep breath and enter the Resonance Chamber.

Oh, wow. . . .

It's as if I've entered the heart of a deep red jewel—a blood drop—or possibly the innards of a great red giant star. . . .

The grand spherical expanse is lit up in strange sinuous red light. It's all furious pale crimson radiance up near the ceiling . . . and then it starts fading in a smooth gradation to a deep, almost-black crimson at the level of the currently flat, upraised floor. The floor itself looks like a bed of simmering coals, or maybe a lava flow that's ready to break through a thin black crust. . . .

The walls of the chamber, I notice, are decorated at regular intervals with long slim objects that appear to be blazing columns of white light. I try to make out what they are, and suddenly I get it—they are *swords*—translucent swords, with blades made of an unknown glass-like material and filled on the inside with hard white radiance.

Absolutely stunning. . . .

Thousands of teens fill the center of the dance floor, moving to the hard beat. I see girls wearing every shade of red, and Cadets in white uniforms trimmed with gold. Soon I realize, as I look around, that my own dress is possibly the deepest darkest shade of red that I can see. . . . In this universe of red, I am darkness personified, a dramatic dark goddess silhouetted against hell flames. . . .

All around the perimeter, where the donut walkway runs around the width of the sphere, the usual stations are set up. I start scanning the room for familiar faces, while I gradually make my way through the crowd to the nearest station where they're giving out couple locator pins.

An Atlantean girl hands me a pair of red pins, and I take them, clutch them in my slightly trembling fingers. I recall suddenly the last time I had to deal with these pins—except they were blue and Logan tore his off angrily and left me standing. . . .

Stop, just stop, do not think. . . .

Where is Xelio?

Just as I start to wonder, I see him, only a few steps away, near the sound tech station, talking to several Atlantean crew members. I think I see Anu among them.

My lord, but Xelio is *hot*. . . . He is wearing the white Fleet uniform, trimmed with gold around the collar and sleeves, and his long black hair is brushed back neatly and gathered behind him in a segmented tail, each segment held by a slim angry-red silk band. His uniform sits on him with sleek precision, emphasizing his beautiful wide shoulders and the elegant line of his back. My gaze trails lower—yes, I'm brazen tonight!—and he is tight and muscular in all the right places.

I see his half-turned profile, and the cocky grin as he laughs with his officers and crew. Damn, the guy is charming and a little scary, all at the same time.

I am almost afraid of approaching him. A pang of doubt plagues me suddenly. *Seriously, what am I doing here?* I think. *I am Gwen the Awkward Dork. And he is sleek, confident, hotshot, stunning....*

In that moment, Xelio turns around and sees me.

And as he does, he grows absolutely still. The smile leaves his face. And he just stares.

There is a long scary moment, a deadly pause.

And then Pilot Xelio Vekahat walks toward me, and stops just an arm's length away.

"Hi, Xelio," I say in a slightly breathless voice.

His black eyes are infinitely focused on me.

"Gwen..." he says, after a smallest pause. "I—I had no idea...."

A stab of nerves hits me. "What?" I say, and my voice is so quiet now, that I suspect he can barely hear me over the din of the crowds and the music.

"You are—" he pauses again, and in that one moment the expression of his face is so serious it is almost vulnerable, startled—as though he's *lost* in me.

"Is something wrong?" I whisper.

But then he shakes his head, and his normal confident expression returns. "Nothing is wrong.... To the contrary—you are *stunning*, Gwen Lark. You made me forget my thoughts and took my breath away. I had no idea you could be like this."

I gulp. "Is that a good thing?"

In answer he takes a step, closing the distance between us, and his arm wraps around mine, pressing it to his side almost possessively. Then his hand slips down, his warm large fingers sensuously clasping my own.

"Come," he says, looking intently at me from up-close, devouring every inch of my face, then allowing his gaze to wander downward, along the skin of my neck, and lower, where a blood ruby reposes in the cleft between my breasts. "You are a goddess. And tonight, you are *mine*."

And in that moment all my doubts, all my nagging fears recede.

Because, really, from the very first moment, I *could* see it in his eyes tonight, an appraisal of me, and I could *see* that he was genuinely overwhelmed. But I simply did not believe myself, as usual.

But—not any more.

A surge of confident power fills me and I smile up at him as we begin to walk through the crowd.

Just for a moment, Xel pauses. He opens his other hand and brings it up so that I might observe two glowing red pins sitting on his palm. Wordlessly he attaches one to the side of my dress, then changes his mind, and puts it on my unattached right sleeve, where it winks on my upper arm below my elbow. "Forgive me, I don't want to mar the perfection that is you . . ." he whispers, as he sticks the other pin carelessly on the front of his own uniform.

"Thank you," I whisper back. And then I open my hand and show him my own pair of pins. "What shall I do with these?"

"Obviously you may not part with them either, and no one else may have it." He smiles, then takes one from me and pins it right next to the first pin on his uniform. And he takes the remaining one in my palm and pins it on my other sleeve, in perfect symmetry, so that now I have one on each arm.

"Two eyes, to watch you with," he says, pointing to the two pins on his uniform. "Both mated to yours."

I laugh. "Very silly, Xelio. But at least now we can be *twice* as certain we will not lose each other in this crazy crowd."

As I am talking, I notice he is watching me relentlessly, consuming me with his eyes. He observes me from head to toe, and then begins again.

"All right, stop that!" I say with a smile, and slap his arm lightly.

"What?"

"Stop looking at me like that!"

"Like what?"

"I don't know. Like I'm some kind of weirdo. Like you haven't seen me before."

His expression deepens. "But I *haven't* seen you before.

You are beyond words."

"You're not so bad yourself, Pilot Vekahat," I say, because honestly, I'm getting a little uncomfortable here, unused to this kind of thing—this kind of attention.

Flashbacks of Logan. . . .

Xel blinks, surfacing into awareness, as though again he cannot help himself.

Am I really having this amazing effect on him, or is he simply being the super polite date?

But before I think too far in that direction, he takes my hand again, and squeezes it warmly. "Want to open the Dance with me? Let's go, *im nefira!*"

Momentarily I am stumped by that Atlantean term. But then, as he pulls me forward into the thicket of the dance floor, I remember that it means "my beauty."

We arrive in the center of the dance floor and stop. Xelio nods lightly to someone—I am guessing to someone in one of the distant tech stations on the walkway—and suddenly the music fades and a small gap opens around us as people step away . . . because a section of floor panels directly underneath us detaches from the rest of the floor. . . . Suddenly we are *rising*, just the two of us, until we hover about ten feet above everyone.

A spotlight falls upon us. Xelio and I are bathed in a radiant crimson beam of light.

Immediately the dance crowd screams.

Xel turns his head to look around and smiles his wicked confident smile. Still holding my hand he taps some kind of tiny button at his collar. And then he exclaims in a deep, ringing voice radiating masculine power that echoes godlike from all sides of the spherical chamber around us:

"Attention, Cadets, Civilians and Crew! Red welcomes you!"

The crowd screams again.

What a surreal moment. . . .

My pulse races wildly. Okay, I should be cowering with terror . . . to be in such a spotlight, with thousands of people looking at us—both at him and at me.

Instead I am exultant. He squeezes my hand, and I squeeze

back, brazenly.

And I think he realizes it—he senses that in that wild instant, he and I, we are a perfect power match.

"Today, in this fiery Season of Red, may you burn with the joy of celebration among true friends who stand at your side! Turn to the one next to you! Look in their eyes and find the fire!"

His soaring voice thunders, only to be answered by the thunder of the crowd.

"And now," Xel says, with a mischievous look at me. "You all know what happens when the Music Mage says the magic warning?"

He nods at me, leans in so that his microphone button is inches away from my lips.

And I get it. . . . I exclaim in reply, "Gravity changing now!"

Even as I speak, I hear my voice transform, amplify, and echo from the walls around us. A wild, *insane* euphoria overtakes me.

Thousands of teens respond, this time to me, with another roar.

Xel winks at me and then speaks to them again.

"So, what's the magic warning?"

"Gravity changing now!" the crowd screams in reply.

"Perfect! Now, Dance! *Orahemai!*"

Immediately the music explodes, and the crowd goes wild with dancing, while we smoothly descend back to the floor level.

"That was fun!" I exclaim, as he pulls me to him, and we get out of the thicket, on our way to the periphery.

"Let me take care of a few things quickly," Xelio tells me with a meaningful look. "And then we dance!"

"Okay!" I grin at him, as we push through the dancing crowd.

We come up to the glassed-off sound tech station. I see Anu in there with three other boys, none of whom I recognize.

Anu looks up momentarily from the hovering sound console, sees Xelio and nods, and then his gaze falls on me as I wait outside.

I smile brightly at him, and watch as he does a double-take, and his jaw drops as he sees me. He mouths something to me but I cannot hear him from outside the cube, and I don't bother going in.

Let Anu have his little moment of shock, I think with grim satisfaction.

Yeah, I look good tonight. Tomorrow it might be back to dowdy, plain, dorky Gwen, but tonight. . . .

While Xel consults with the guys in the booth, I look around the crowd. I am searching for a certain someone, and *he* is not here yet.

Command Pilot Kassiopei.

At least I don't see him in this crowd.

However, somewhere on the dance floor I see Logan. He is in his impressive white Cadet uniform, dancing with a blonde with long gorgeous hair and a tight body encased in a slinky little red dress. I have no idea who she is, but knowing Logan, I'm sure he had his pick of the hottest girls around the ship.

My heart does a funny little jump, but I take a deep breath and turn away.

No, nothing is going to spoil this night for me. . . .

Let Logan dance with whomever he pleases.

Chapter 37

Xelio finally gets away from the sound station and comes up to me with a slow sensual smile.

"Sorry," he says. "Now that's over, you and I can enjoy ourselves. How are you feeling so far?"

"Pretty good." I smile at him.

"Damn, you're stunning . . ." he says, as his black eyes take in my glowing expression and once again he seems startled by me. I can tell he really means it.

"Thank you," I reply, once again not knowing how best to respond.

"No, thank *you*—for being so beautiful." He pauses. "No, what's that word you used?—real. You are so damn *real* that you take my breath away."

"You know," I say, "I'm going to be singing later tonight?"

"Oh, yeah?" He leans in to me. "You signed up for a vocalist spot? I'm impressed! And knowing your voice, I expect it will be incredible."

I allow a tiny smile, as I think, *Oh, wait till you hear me, Xel*.

"Yup," I say. "I am on at 8:15 PM."

"Gravity changing now. . . ." A velvet-smooth male voice comes like magic from the walls around us.

I briefly think of Vazara Hotat, but it's definitely another person in the Music Mage role tonight. And whoever he is, he sounds very good.

The beat slows down, and suddenly the sensation of falling is here, as the low gravity takes hold.

As usual people scream, and everyone starts jumping to take advantage of the acrobatics.

I let out a small squeal of excitement and Xelio laughs with me as he takes me by the hands, and sweeps me onto the dance floor. With every motion we start floating up like dandelions, and oh, my dress! The ethereal bell skirt unfurls and swirls around me like the spiral arms of a galaxy....

I throw back my head and exclaim in pure delight, and then feel Xelio's hands close around my slender waist as he lifts me up, and spins me, and he is grinning in exultation.

Time ceases to exist as we spin and twirl to the beat. The dance is short however, and soon the Music Mage speaks again.

"Gravity changing now...."

This time the music beat slows down completely, and a gentle sweet song takes over, vocal heavenly harmonies interspersed with flute and reeds and strings.

There is no gravity now, and the floor below—a bed of red coals and lava—starts to fall away, revealing the spherical bowl abyss of the Resonance Chamber underneath us.

And we remain in place, floating, as though suspended over the heart of a volcano.

The illusion is so powerful that there's a volcano below us that people scream, and point, with crazy emotion.

"Whoa!" I exclaim, looking down past my floating skirt and my elegant shoes, while we begin to float away upward, propelled by our own bodily motion. "That's simply amazing!"

Xel only looks at me, smiling, as he holds me by the waist. And then—because of the magical sense of the world slowing down in the suspended state of the zero gravity dance—the longer he looks in my eyes, the more his smile fades, and his expression again grows serious, startled, *vulnerable*. It's as if he's forgotten how to maintain the confident exterior, and now the *real* underlying person is coming through—a guy who is so deeply affected, that he can no longer pretend otherwise.

In fact, I think he's so taken by me, that he doesn't even attempt to kiss me or in any way make a move.

Wow, I realize suddenly. *He is afraid*. Not of me, but of damaging some fragile airy thing that he suddenly sees in me. Because, yes, I can see it in his eyes, the awe and wonder... and with it, the *distance*.

And in that moment of understanding, it makes me sad.

"Xel!" I say, caught up by the intensity of the moment. "Hey! It's *me*—still me, you know, don't you? Gwen the doofus nerd! Remember? Shoelace Girl!"

He blinks and then he smiles again. "I know," he says. But the way he says it, strangely, I don't think he even understands the change in his perception that has taken root.

The song ends.

"Gravity changing now!" the Music Mage exclaims with mischief, and suddenly a fast energetic track comes on, while gravity blooms forth, returning.

All of us, airborne couples gliding near the ceiling, start to float down softly, and then land on our feet just in time to touch down on the floor that once again rises to meet us, flattening at the main level of the walkways.

"Want something to drink?" he says, still holding me around the waist almost gingerly, but his confident smile returns.

"Sure!" I nod.

We move off the dance floor toward the walkway, while my thoughts flitter about wildly, wondering again where Aeson Kassiopei is, and if he even made it to the Dance.

Xelio and I make our way to the nearest drink station, where Xel gets in line for us, telling me to wait by the glassed-off area of the tech cube, out of the push-and-shove traffic zone. Grateful to him for dealing with the drink crowd, I move away and stand, watching the dancers.

And then I turn, and see *them*.

Command Pilot Kassiopei, wearing his Fleet dress uniform, white and gold, walks slowly with Oalla Keigeri and Keruvat Ruo, from the direction of the entrance.

They must've just arrived, I realize.

Keruvat is also dressed in the full parade uniform, tall and gorgeous. Oalla on the other hand, wears a long red dress, sleek and bright like a flame. Her golden hair falls loosely around her shoulders, and it is threaded with many ruby-red jewels that catch fire in the bright pulsing lights. Her heels are at least three inches tall, and she steps effortlessly with perfect grace. And her face, when she turns, is made up in elegant high-fashion, with dramatic colors.

Immediately my heart lurches in my chest and I feel my

pulse picking up, racing. . . .

I watch Kassiopei approach, and he is splendid, regal, spectacular—I run out of crazy words for him in my mind, as I stare, wildly.

When they are just a few feet away, talking and laughing among themselves, I turn my back to them—to *him*—because suddenly I am the same nervous awkward girl, who cannot even walk easily in two-inch heels, much less face *him*.

They pause, almost next to me, still not seeing me. In that moment Xelio emerges from the drink station, carrying two tall covered glasses with straws.

He sees Kassiopei and the other Pilots and waves to them with one glass.

"There you are, Kass," Xelio says, flashing a wicked smile. "Glad you bothered to show. Though, I'm amazed you're here this early."

"Sorry we've missed your opening, Xel," Oalla says, coming up to him and bumping his arm in an easy, relaxed manner of longtime friends.

Aeson, standing almost next to me, and literally not seeing me, folds his arms casually—his favorite stance—and simply stares at Xelio with a faint hint of a smile.

"Nice job, so far, Pilot."

"Why, thank you, Command Pilot." And Xelio grins, at the same time as he attempts an insolent salute while still holding the ice-clinking glasses in both hands.

"Love your color scheme," Keruvat says in his deep voice. "Remind me what this color is called—is it by any chance—*red?*"

Xel snorts. There is general chuckling.

"So, Xel, where's your date?" Oalla asks suddenly. "Hope you didn't frighten her too badly with your delightful charming personality?"

Xel raises one brow, and then takes a step in my direction.

"There she is!" he says with a softening smile.

I turn my head around, and then the rest of me, turning to face them all.

Everyone glances, and in that moment I see Aeson Kassiopei, as his gaze alights upon me. . . .

He is *transformed*.

Aeson sees me, and I swear, he jolts in place slightly. Then he frowns, grows perfectly still, and his lips part.

He stares at me in disbelief, and I look back at him.

A warm flush starts rising from a deep place inside me . . . rising, rising. Good thing I'm wearing so much makeup that my blush is probably invisible. What a wonderful disguise.

"Lark?" Aeson Kassiopei asks.

"Yes?" I say, looking up at him. Even though I feel breathless and I'm blushing like crazy, a tiny little smile of triumph wants to break through and settle on my blood-cherry-red gloss-covered lips.

"I—I didn't recognize you, sorry," he says coldly. And he continues staring with great big wide-open eyes.

"Gwen Lark?" Oalla exclaims. "Is that you? *No!* But, you look amazing! I didn't recognize you either, wow! What a gorgeous dress! And I love your makeup! You could be at the Imperial Court, looking like that!"

"Thank you," I say softy.

Keruvat nods appreciatively, and they all look at me now, examining me as if I'm an exotic zoo specimen.

"Here you go." Xelio interrupts the moment by handing me my drink.

"Thanks," I say, glancing at him with a smile. And then I add, "Hey, do you know what time it is? My vocal performance is at 8:15."

I momentarily glance back at the others, and my God, they are all still staring at me.

Furthermore, *he* is staring at me—Kassiopei.

He is so still, so perfectly unbelievably *motionless*, that I actually wonder if something is wrong with me.

"Don't worry," Xel tells me, checking a small gadget he pulls out of his pocket. "The performances begin at 8:00 PM, which is in ten minutes from now, and looks like you are the second person in the lineup."

"Great!" I smile brightly, and turn to all of them. "All right, you must hear me sing!"

"I wouldn't miss it for the world," Oalla says, smiling back at me. And then she sees Aeson Kassiopei, still frozen motionless, still *looking at me*, and she nudges him on the arm. "Kass? Hey!"

"Yes?" He blinks as though coming awake and gives his attention to her at last, tearing himself away from me.

"We're going to stick around long enough to hear Lark perform, all right?"

He nods. "That's fine." And now, he is no longer looking at me at all.

They go to get drinks, and then the Command Pilot walks around the perimeter, his arrogant back turned to me, as he checks out the room.

I watch the back of his head, the sleeked-back golden hair, as he moves off into the crowd, retreating from me.

And then I sip my drink through the straw, careful not to damage my perfect lip makeup.

Xelio stands at my side and glances in the direction of the CP. "So, your commanding officer is his usual uptight self tonight, which is to say—" He never quite finishes the sentence, but there's a wicked smile on his lips.

"Oh, yes," I reply with a little wicked smile of my own.

Soon, it will be time for my song.

There is still time for a couple of dance sets before they have the intermission for the vocal performances.

"Gravity changing now!"

The moment the beat slows down to the low gravity style of dance, we feel the sensation of falling again.

"Let's go!" I exclaim to Xelio, and pull him by the arm toward the dance floor. Suddenly I am feeling confident and energetic, and *I want to dance*.

We find the beat and start moving together, and Xelio spins me, while I dip and turn, and my skirt flies like butterfly wings.

Whenever I can manage it during the turns, I glance around quickly to see if Aeson Kassiopei is anywhere nearby.

And eventually, yes, I feel someone's eyes on me . . . I feel *him* looking.

Sure enough, the Command Pilot stands far off at the edge of the walkway, turned in our direction, as though observing the dancing crowd.

But he is looking directly at *me*.

How do I know this?

I've felt the impact of that gaze before. Its weight is familiar. I would never mistake it for anything else. It has the force of a storm and the pressure of a mountain. Even from this distance, I can see his unblinking eyes trained relentlessly upon me, *watching*, piercing me.

Oh yes, now *he sees me*, I think. *Good, let him look. . . . He sees what I can be like, at last.* What did Xelio call me? A goddess—even if only for tonight.

And yet, in that moment, curious, I start to compare certain things. I compare how Xelio looks at me and how Aeson looks at me—and it is *not* the same thing at all.

Tonight, Xelio has shown a kind of *reverence* toward me. I can see the distance of growing worship reflected in his black eyes whenever his gaze makes contact with mine. That's because Xel is now seeing me as something fragile and unattainable—a goddess, a queen.

But there is *no worship* in the intense gaze of Kassiopei.

The way he looks at me—his strange intimate *knowledge* of me is instead a troubling burden. It's as if he's taken me apart a million times and put me back together again. And now he's *branding* me with his gaze, marking the surreal goddess as an impostor, in order to reveal me once again as an ordinary plain old "Gwen."

I don't even know what that means. I have no words for it.

I just know that the way he is looking at me now is making *me* vulnerable and open to him.

There is only one thing to do now, to save myself.

I need to sing my song.

Chapter 38

It's close to 8:10 PM, and five minutes before my performance. The dance floor has been reformed into a stage, with most of the center panel tiles hover-raised ten feet to create a wide floating circle, upon which multiple spotlights shine.

The person up first is finishing their song—a soulful classic folk ballad accompanied by acoustic guitars. I think it's a piece by Peter, Paul, and Mary, called "500 Miles" about being far from one's home, and it brings everyone's mood down significantly.

The singer's face is projected on the walls of the sphere in a mosaic of giant stadium screens, so that everyone can see her performance up-close. The crowd sways gently, listening to the lovely voice, amplified to stadium-level. The singer, a tall girl with red hair, ends with a deep sorrowful bow. As she straightens back up, and the audience claps loudly, I see her face is glistening with tears.

I stand waiting my turn, just a few feet away at the base of the stage, near the lowest of the ascending panels that form a hovering staircase for the performers.

"By all that's sacred, I hope your song is more upbeat." Xelio is standing right next to me and now whispers in my ear, while attaching my touch-microphone button just before I go up. "I'd hate to have it said that the entire ark-ship wept at a Red Dance. What will it do for my Quadrant's reputation?"

I turn to him with a confident smile. "Don't worry, Xel." And as I start to go up the stairs, I smile again—saucy, flirty, powerful. Throwing him a bright parting glance I add, "I promise, you won't be weeping. Instead, I suggest you hold on to something!"

I step onto the stage, and walk to the middle of the circle, which is about 20 feet in diameter. My heels make clicking noises that echo around the grand acoustics of the spherical chamber.

I stand, and glance around me at the huge crowd of teens, bathed in red glow. All attention is upon me.

Again the fleeting thought comes to me—I should be terrified.

Instead, my gaze searches hungrily for a glimpse of Aeson Kassiopei.

And—there he is. Once again he's on the walkway perimeter, which is far in the distance from the vantage point of my spot on the stage. I just barely see him, standing casually, arms folded, next to Oalla Keigeri.

Good thing there are stadium screens, I think, *or he would never see me from where he is.*

And now—now everyone is going to see me.

I take a deep breath, smile, and tap my microphone button.

Immediately my face in all its dramatic, fiercely painted glory fills the giant screens along the perimeter. And the first rhythmic power-notes of the *Habanera* fill the chamber.

I begin to sing.

The *Habanera*, or *"L'amour est un oiseau rebelle,"* is an aria from Bizet's opera *Carmen*, sung by the titular character. It is a song of seduction and freedom, a strange thing of paradox. "Love is a bird in rebellion," sings the seductress, sultry, powerful, playful, while she's teasing and provoking a soldier who pretends to ignore her while he secretly desires her.

My rich mezzo soprano voice begins deep and low, rising from the depths of my chest. And then it pours forth like honey. . . .

The song is a duel of power. Love, or the bird, comes and goes however it pleases. You set it free and it may or may not come back. You chase it, and it never does. But the moment you stop going after it, there it is, chasing you.

Wow, not sure how much of a metaphor this is of me and Aeson and our weird relationship, but it feels real and it feels like it applies to us.

And so I sing. . . .

During the first stanza I stand motionless, finding my sound, controlling the perfect output of my voice. And then I loosen up and begin to stalk the stage, allowing my voice to control me.

My voice soars, and the recorded orchestral accompaniment frames its rich timbre, while I turn in all directions and express the passion of Carmen.

No—it is my *own* passion.

I am passion, I am Gwen, and Carmen does not live here anymore.

As I move fiercely about the stage, I glance down into the audience, to see their attentive faces, as teens from Earth and Atlantis watch me in fascination.

And then I see *him*.

Aeson Kassiopei stands directly before me, in the front row. He must have changed his mind and decided to watch me from up-close. As I glance next to him, I see Keruvat and Oalla with Xelio—all the Pilots watching me with rapt attention.

But the only one that matters now is Kassiopei. . . .

My daring gaze flashes in his direction once more, and possibly he catches me looking at him, and he blinks, then his lips part. . . . He is gazing at me in wonder.

I don't think I've *ever* seen him look at me this way. There is innocence . . . raw, vulnerable *need* . . . a fragile opening up of inner layers. Through his gaze, in all its clear focus, a long-submerged mystery finally comes to light.

I smile and tease and seduce . . . and even when I turn away, I still sing to him.

With every new glance in his direction, I see the progression of changes in him taking shape.

He trembles, his face deepens in color. He is under so much strain that for a moment he appears to be ill. . . . With all his being, he now strives toward me.

And then the music escalates, the music is on fire. . . . I sing fiercely and my voice strikes the air like a whip, then modulates and purrs in the low register, alternating the moments of passion. I glance in his direction again. . . .

He still looks at me, transfixed. And then I see it, the revelation of the next level below, going down deep inside him, soul-deep . . . and bringing it forth at last.

His undisguised dark *desire*.

Furthermore, if I were to look closer, there might even be *something more*.

But for now, it is quite enough.

For the first time, I am perfectly certain of it—merely from the look in his eyes.

Aeson Kassiopei wants me, desperately.

And knowing it, I become invincible.

Suddenly I am strong, fierce, free, in wild rebellion against the former limits of my own self.

The glorious, dark-haired young woman with the cherry-blood-and-crimson mouth blazing on the screens around the room, stretching her arms and throwing her head back while the grand sound pours from her, to fill every crevice of every object and every person in this chamber—she is *myself*.

She always has been.

But all these years she was hiding.

And now she is out, at last—no matter how briefly, for tonight.

I end on a triumphant high note that blasts away the last shadow of doubt, and the orchestra concludes the framing sound.

The crowd screams wildly, even before the music is over.

On a weird impulse, I grab the carnation flower that's tucked in my hair.

I try to locate Aeson Kassiopei with my gaze. But in that same instant I see him, he turns his back to me, moving almost violently, and starts walking away through the crowd, followed by Oalla and Keruvat.

I pause. . . . And I toss the flower out into the crowd, smiling widely at them—and in my mind, still at *him*, wherever he is, somewhere out there.

And even if he's not, it doesn't matter.

I started out singing for him, but I finished, singing for myself.

I climb down from the stage, and Xelio is right here, waiting for me. He is staring at me with absolute wonder.

"You're unbelievable!" he exclaims, while his eyes reflect

emotion and a deepening complexity. "Gwen Lark, tonight you've managed to surprise me for the second time!" He shakes his head, as though to clear away the stunned emotion.

"You liked it?" I exclaim with a brazen smile. At this moment I'm riding a wild high, and nothing can bring me down.

"Are you kidding?" He shakes his head again, while a slow amazed smile comes to him. "I've never heard you sing properly, not like this. But you just blew me away there! What was that glorious song? This style, it is your Earth opera? I must learn more!"

"Come, I need a drink," I say flippantly, throwing glances around us—at the teens in the vicinity who are still staring at me and clapping as I move past them. "And I'll tell you all about it."

We make our way to the perimeter toward the stations.

Toward Aeson and Oalla, I note with satisfaction.

Xel throws the CP and Oalla a daring grin and winks at me. "Wait here, *im nefira*, while I get your drink!" he intones loudly while nodding to the other Pilots. And off he goes in the crowd.

I stop before Aeson Kassiopei and Oalla Keigeri, as they stand off to the side, talking quietly. I'm still breathing much too quickly, my pulse is racing, and my eyes are sparkling with excitement.

Oalla glances at me and her one brow goes up, but she is smiling. "Wow!" she says to me. "Just, wow!"

And then I see Aeson. His face is averted slightly, and his arms are folded at his chest, while he seems to be examining something a few feet away.

Suddenly he turns to me. And—he is *cold* as ice. His expression is devastating. Oh, the frown, the barely leashed anger and accusation in his eyes!

He stands like a demon before me.

I am stunned.

All my joyous confidence and euphoria evaporates in the blink of an eye.

"*Lark.* We need to talk immediately. *Come!*" he says in a killing voice, and motions to me as he starts walking.

"Okay...." I glance briefly at Oalla and follow him as we move off a few steps away. Here he stops and turns to me.

"What you did out there—that was extremely

inappropriate," he says in a hard voice filled with derision. "You used the *desire power voice* in public."

My lips part. "I did what?"

But he does not relent.

"The *desire voice* is only to be used in private, and only with individuals with whom you have an intimate relationship," he continues, his gaze boring down at me. "Do you understand what you've done? You've just shamed the crew, all these people, my entire ship—"

"Wait, Kass—what are you talking about?" Oalla interrupts him suddenly. She obviously followed us, and is now looking from Aeson to me with a slight frown. "But—she didn't!"

Aeson Kassiopei suddenly grows very quiet and turns to look at her. "What?"

"I mean, she *didn't* use a power voice," Oalla repeats, craning her neck at him curiously. "Admittedly, it was a very lovely and strong voice, and Gwen sang that classical piece beautifully, but it was just a normal unenhanced singing voice."

"But—" he says, pausing. And suddenly his face flushes wildly. It's a deep scalding *red*, such a strong flood of color that it's noticeable even despite the brilliant red illumination in the room.

"I—" he says in a strange, quiet voice, and shakes his head. "I—I must go, excuse me. . . ."

And without looking at me, or Oalla, he turns around and swiftly walks past us, and continues toward the exit doors of the Resonance Chamber.

Oalla and I remain, staring at each other.

I am still reeling. "Okay. . . . What? What did I do? What happened?" I say breathlessly, while a bitter lump pushes at the back of my throat, so that I'm ready to cry.

Oalla pauses thoughtfully before answering me. She shakes her head slightly, bites her lips and says, "Don't worry about it. You did nothing wrong. It's all *him*. I'm sorry to say this—and *please* don't quote me—but sometimes your commanding officer is a real idiot."

My mouth parts at her reply.

Oalla throws a brief troubled glance in the direction that Kassiopei left. She then returns her attention to me. "In case I didn't make it clear, Gwen, you did a *wonderful* job singing. Really, really well done, I'm impressed. Now, why don't you go ahead and enjoy the rest of the dance. I am going to go after him and make sure everything is under control. If Keruvat comes looking for me, tell him I've left."

And with a friendly nod, Oalla Keigeri walks away quickly.

I remain standing alone in the crowd.

My mind—I think I've misplaced it somewhere.

Okay, what just happened?

Xelio comes back with my drink just as the last mournful strains of "Bohemian Rhapsody" by Queen dissipate into silence, and the four teenagers who've just performed the ancient classic do a wild, head-banging bow to the suddenly roaring dance crowd.

"Thanks," I say, taking the drink, while Xelio glances back at the stadium screens shaking his head with amusement.

"Your Earth music," he says. "It is so diverse and astounding."

"I'm not sure why everyone seems to be singing these really ancient songs tonight," I mutter with a smile. "Maybe because we're all a little homesick, and the old stuff has deeper roots."

"Where's everyone?" Xel says. "Did the CP take off already? Not surprising."

"Oh yes, he did," I say casually. "Oalla left too."

Xel laughs. "Their loss. Meanwhile, the dancing is about to resume. Ready for more zero gravity?"

I nod pleasantly as I stand sipping my drink, looking at him, listening to him absentmindedly, while my thoughts and my focus have been derailed completely. Right this moment I'm still trying very hard to understand *what* it is that just happened a few minutes ago, and whether it's a good or bad thing.

I decide eventually that it's a little of both.

First, the *good*:

I now know to a great degree of certainty that my commanding officer, Command Pilot Aeson Kassiopei definitely has *feelings* for me. Not sure how much of it has been achieved by my own provocative performance this evening, and how much has already existed beforehand, but the primary objective of this evening has been achieved—*I know*.

And now the *bad*:

The tragic aspect of knowing, is that now there's nothing much to be done about it.

That's it.

Nothing has changed, except maybe the fact that I've deeply embarrassed him on a personal level. But that's a sacrifice I was willing to take in order to learn the truth, going into this thing with all my passion and yes, my gorgeous war paint on.

I guess I've won the battle.

But the war is still going to overwhelm me in the end.

So let me just enjoy the rest of this Red Dance with a handsome, attentive, red-hot partner.

Because tomorrow—and in the days and weeks ahead—I must still face *him* every day, the Imperial Crown Prince of Atlantis. And he must face *me*.

Right now, I must confess, I have no idea how we're going to manage. However, I'm guessing sadly, it will be all things as usual.

Chapter 39

The very next day at the CCO confirms my expectations.
 I arrive just before 8:00 AM with a hammering heartbeat and a queasy feeling in my gut, and the two aides are not in yet.

A few minutes later, Kassiopei walks in.

My pulse goes wild.... Nervous cramps start tearing at me.

I'm not sure if he expected me to be there alone so early, or if he simply took a chance. But he takes one step, then sees me and goes very still. For just a fraction of that first instant, his face reveals the remnant of an intensely vulnerable, almost *frightened* expression. And then a wall slams down, and he becomes blank, unreadable—the usual.

"You . . ." he says quietly.

All the colorful events of last night flash before me in the blink of an eye.

"Command Pilot. . . ." I bravely look him in the eyes.

"I—" He starts to speak, and then suddenly I see his face begin to flame with the same furious blush I'd seen yesterday.

He shakes his head, as if he could shake it all away. And then he turns his face from me and simply goes to sit down at his desk, without another word.

I suppose there will be no apology forthcoming either—an apology for needlessly reprimanding me.

Something insane makes me get up from my seat and approach his desk. I stand before him and he glances my way, without meeting my eyes.

"I hope you're not upset about last night," I say softly.

"There is nothing to be upset about," he replies in a steady voice, looking at his computer screen.

"But you seemed to be—"

"I overreacted."

"I'm sorry if my song was too much."

In that moment he looks up at me with his lapis blue eyes. Oh, the look in those eyes!

"Everyone seemed to enjoy it." And he glances away again.

I bite my lip. "But not you?"

Suddenly he looks at me again, fiercely. "Lark, what do you *want* from me?"

In that moment, I don't know what to do with myself. My turn to blush like crazy—and I do. "Nothing," I mutter, as my pulse continues to beat wildly.

And then I return to my seat. All the while he watches me move, with a searing gaze that wants to swallow me whole.

I feel its impact along the surface of my skin, as my fine hairs stand up on end, and electric waves engulf me. . . .

Eventually he looks away.

And we get to work.

After that single outburst, the Command Pilot treats me with icy, aloof politeness and does not acknowledge anything that happened at the Red Dance.

At some point later, when I am able to think rationally again and analyze things, I wonder if Oalla ever caught up to him last night—and if so, if they had some kind of "talk."

I've lost count of the number of times over all these months, that I've wondered how much of a friendship there is between them. Seems to me like all the four Pilots on ICS-2 are the CP's "buddies" in one way or another. I suppose I will learn more eventually, as time goes by.

Meanwhile, not only does Aeson *not* acknowledge his feelings for me, or anything else that happened (and neither does he offer that apology for reprimanding me for something I didn't do) but he doesn't seem to show any reaction or concern over the fact that I had a fantastic date with Pilot Xelio Vekahat.

About that date—after the CP and Oalla left the Red Dance, Xel and I danced almost every dance and stayed till closing. Xelio, being in charge of things, had to stick around to make sure his crew wrapped things up properly. But right after midnight, he walked me back to my cabin, and just before I went inside, he stopped me.

"Gwen Lark," he said, leaning closely over me. "I thank you for a perfect night."

I expected a cheek-peck kiss maybe, or even a sweet kiss on the mouth. But Xelio took my hand, turned it over, wrist side up, pulled up my sleeve slightly and brought the hand up to his lips. He then kissed the inside of my wrist and his mouth lingered intensely . . . and oh wow, it sent a million electric currents throughout me.

"In Atlantis, this is how we acknowledge a special time together," he told me, after letting my hand go reluctantly—and I was equally reluctant to be released.

"A wrist kiss?" I said with a playful smile.

"A *pulse* kiss." Xelio's virile, dark-eyed gaze caressed me. "I hope it's only the very first one."

And then with a wicked smile he was gone.

I returned to my cabin, my mind overflowing, and my senses heightened to a fever pitch.

Then, it being after midnight, it was time for Cinderella to turn back into a Gwen.

So, that was the Red Dance, and its fallout. And now, business continues as usual at the CCO, and I expect nothing.

Yes, I still hurt, and every time I see Aeson Kassiopei, my heart is pulled apart with a lonely, hollow need for him. But I'm a big girl—I can live with it.

I continue with work and classes. One interesting side effect—Anu, at least, gives me a tiny bit more respect now that he's seen me all dressed up and with Xelio.

I also continue to train at the gym with Xelio on a regular basis, and now there's an extra layer of pleasantly exciting physical tension between us. . . . Plus it appears Xel is very good company in general, charming and funny, in some ways reminiscent of Logan when Logan and I were at our best—a sparkling couple together. Xel and I are not exactly dating, but we see enough of each other that it's safe to say we're some kind of friends.

Talking about Logan—I belatedly recall now that Logan

did see me at the Red Dance. In fact, I remember his intense multiple stares throughout the evening, even while he was with that blonde. But I was so focused, so occupied with Aeson and Xelio and everything else, that Logan's attention became a secondary thing.

Wow, funny how some things change. . . . Logan used to be the one person who anchored me, and whom I thought I needed desperately. And now, it still hurts, there are still complicated unresolved feelings, but there is no longer the urgency to be with him.

What's happened to me?

Meanwhile, the first month of Red ends, and with it, end our restrictions about flying in the Quantum Stream.

We're off the flight simulators once again, and real shuttle Pilot Training for Cadets resumes outside, all the way up to our arrival on Atlantis.

My new Pilot Partner Chiyoko Sato and I settle in, and find that we are both tolerably decent partners, and our joint flying gradually improves. Chiyoko might not be perfect, but compared to working with Hugo, she's a blessed angel.

It turns out, neither one of us is particularly good at being specifically either the Pilot or Co-Pilot, or at least not in any pronounced way. We switch constantly, and we do okay in either role. But it is frustrating sometimes that we are still not doing as well as some other people, by this point in our training.

Whenever we go out outside to take our limited turns with the shuttles (we all get only 5 runs a month per Cadet Pilot Pair), we end up scoring 3s and sometimes 4s on our performance. I don't remember getting even a single 5, which makes me wonder—how will I ever perform well enough to be a viable contender for the Games of the Atlantis Grail in Aeson Kassiopei's eyes?

Meanwhile Instructor Okoi watches all of us like a hawk, and we are continually reminded that the Final QS Race will be a grueling test of all our abilities.

Two more Red months pass, and during the third Red month, which coincides with February back on Earth, my brother Gordie has his birthday.

Wow, Gordie turns fifteen this year. And naturally he absolutely forgets the day it happens—February 7—because it's what he always does, and so does Gracie, because the only birthday Gracie ever remembers is her own—and for once so do I, which makes me an awful sister. So I end up trying to make it up to Gordie the following week, but it doesn't work out, I can't leave my ship that week, he can't leave his, so I give up and just leave him numerous video messages with air kisses. Yes, I suck.

And then we enter Yellow, the Atlantean season equivalent of Autumn.

The first month of Yellow—and the tenth month of us being on the journey—signals that we're in the final quarter of our journey. The fact that the Fleet is *decelerating* significantly is now visible, judging by the quality of the Quantum Stream around us—it is a finer, more translucent thing, and the view of the true interstellar space outside begins to intrude on the quality of the gray.

By the second month of Yellow, our month eleven in space, we begin to see actual stars again. For so long, they were only flickering shadows barely emerging out of the homogeneous grey darkness during the previous three months. . . . And now at last they are showing up as points of true light with extended tails.

What a weird wonder it is to know now we're in such a distant and impossible location in the universe, so far away from our original home, Earth.

We are now closer to Atlantis.

And our Final Test, the second Quantum Stream Race, is only days away.

With just three days to go until the QS Race, everyone's doing practice shuttle runs, both outside and on the flight simulator consoles. The classroom deck is always busy and there's a signup list to use the consoles even during after hours.

Chiyoko Sato and I manage to land a free half-hour time slot on the list, and so we meet up after dinner to use the flight simulator consoles one last time.

It's around 6:30 PM and the room is packed with Cadets running shuttle scenarios. There are several people milling around waiting for their turn on the consoles.

Chiyoko is already here, saving our spot. She looks up at me tiredly, with her usual startled expression.

"Hey," I say with a smile. "Let's do it!"

And we power up the simulator and begin a run.

"You be the Pilot first," she tells me.

I nod, and key myself to the Red and Green, Thrust and Brake, while Chiyoko takes the Yellow and Blue, Navigation and Adjustment.

Out of the corner of my eye, I see Logan and Oliver come in and take a console desk nearby. Logan gives me a brief look then turns away.

Immediately my heart skips a beat, and I hear the pulse in my temples pick up pace. *Yeah, Logan still has an effect on me. . . .*

So I force myself to ignore him and focus on the task at hand.

Chiyoko and I fly the virtual shuttle cleanly, and I engage the Red thrust to increase speed. Chiyoko handles the Blue Adjustment Grid, keeping us elegantly on course. "Time to slow down soon," she warns me in her mellow quiet voice.

I flip over to Green and engage the Brake. Our shuttle starts to slow down in a gradual deceleration as we enter the scenario's shuttle bay.

We finish and check our time. The Run Clock shows we took 17:04 minutes compared to the 15 minute Average.

"Damn," I mutter tiredly. "Is there anything we can do?"

This is pretty much the same time we keep getting on every run, and have been getting for the last several weeks. Our improvement is minimal, pitiful, and sometimes it can be counted in seconds.

Chiyoko looks at me and sighs. "I don't know," she says.

We look at each other and think. Unfortunately as we do so, we are also wasting our precious time slot. As of this moment, we only have time for another practice run, and that's it for our turn.

"Okay," I muse out loud. "What can we do to shave more seconds off? I tend to brake as soon as you tell me, right?"

"Yes," she says. "You do it very quickly, but not better than me. I think I brake a little faster."

"What about accelerate? Which one of us is better at it?" I rub my forehead.

Chiyoko pauses. "Uhm. I think you are. I tend to hesitate a little."

I sigh. "Okay, so which will gain us more of an overall advantage? To have a Pilot who accelerates faster but brakes so-so, or to have a Pilot who brakes faster?"

"I don't know." Chiyoko shrugs. "Maybe the Pilot should be the one who accelerates better, to account for speed."

"This is very frustrating," I mutter. "I wish we could just break up the roles and have each person do half of the Pilot's tasks and half of the Co-Pilot's. That way both of us get to cover whatever we're best at. . . ."

And then a crazy idea hits me. "Hey," I say. "What if we tried it?"

"Tried what?" She looks at me in confusion.

"Splitting the Pilot and Co-Pilot down the middle?"

"Huh?"

I point to the consoles. "Normally we key either Red-Green or Blue-Yellow. What if I took Thrust and you took Brake? And you took Adjustment and I took Navigation? So I key myself Red-Yellow, while you key as Green-Blue!"

Chiyoko starts to frown. "How is that possible?"

"Well, why not? A single advanced Pilot can fly solo while handling all four functions. No one *says* a Pilot has to do Thrust and Brake."

"But—" Chiyoko continues frowning. "That's not what we are being taught."

"Look," I exclaim with excitement, "nowhere does it say that's a hard rule. I mean, I think this particular role split is just a convenience."

Chiyoko bites her lip. "Okay. . . ."

"So let's just give this thing a try, for the heck of it," I say with rising excitement. "We have nothing to lose, right? Let's just try!"

"Okay. . . ."

And we do.

We re-key ourselves across functions, and start the shuttle

run. It's a little weird at first, for one person to just be responsible for going fast, and the other for slowing down. . . . But in minutes we realize we are doing very well with this new division of labor. I go really fast on Red, and Chiyoko takes over when needed to quickly slow us down with Green during turns and maneuvers.

We complete a clean run, almost effortless, and when we check our time, the Clock says we finished at 14:39 minutes!

"Oh, wow!" I exclaim. "That's our fastest time ever! And, we've *finally* beat the Average!"

Chiyoko stares in absolute amazement. "I have never gone so fast. . . ."

"I know! So let's make this split permanent!"

Her mouth falls open. "Will they allow us?"

"How are they going to know?" I grin. "Besides, it's not in any rulebook. No one says we are *not* allowed to do it. It might not be Fleet standard, but I don't think it's illegal."

Chiyoko puts her hand over her mouth and smiles.

I don't think I've ever seen this girl smile, *ever*.

"Instructor Okoi is going to kill us . . ." she whispers.

I laugh. "I'm willing to take that risk, if it means improving our chances in the Race!"

After just a tiny little pause, Chiyoko nods. "Me too!"

Chapter 40

The day before the Second Quantum Stream Race is filled with Pilot Training review sessions. I am allowed to miss most of my work duties at the CCO in order to attend the sessions.

First thing in the morning, we rush to see our Pilot Pair Standings that have been posted on smart boards in the corridor between the Cadet and Command Decks.

Chiyoko and I check our Pilot Pair numbers and we have a reasonable #314 score, which puts us somewhere in the healthy middle of our ship's Cadet Pairs. Our shuttle assignment for tomorrow is shuttle #47 in Shuttle Bay Four, and we are Pilot Pair two out of six in the relay lineup.

I note to myself that Logan Sangre and Oliver Parker are still at #3, with Alla Vetrova and Conrad Hart at #1 and Erin and Roy Tsai at #2. Meanwhile, Blayne and Leon manage to snag a very nice #173.

Oh, and Hugo Moreno? He and his "new and improved" partner Marc Goldstein got a #463, which makes me want to cackle with glee! Yeah, Chiyoko and I beat them by over a 100 points!

Now I eagerly look forward to calling up Gracie and Laronda later tonight to see how their numbers are.

But first, we have a Safety and Review session at 10:00 AM and a mandatory shuttle inspection at 1:00 PM.

When we get to Safety and Review, the classroom deck is filled with anxious teens.

Instructor Mithrat Okoi comes in, we salute, and he begins without any other preamble.

"This is your last class before the Final Test tomorrow," he tells us in a grim loud voice. "First thing you need to know is the type of race course you will be following. Instead of flying in a *straight line* around the Fleet as you had to do for the first QS Race, you will have to fly in a zigzag or *sine wave pattern* around each ship in the middle column of the formation. In other words, you will 'weave around' each ship in middle column #2 as you move forward, alternating going left then right in each horizontal channel between ships until you reach ICS-1 at the head of the fleet. Then you return the same way."

Immediately the classroom fills with nervous mutterings.

"Silence!" the Instructor says. "What this means for you is that you will have to treat each ark-ship in the middle column as an obstacle that you must carefully bypass without causing harm to yourself or the ship, or anyone else in your way. So—the primary test criteria you are getting evaluated on is *not* speed but *accuracy*. You need to go reasonably fast—it is a given. But—what's more important is for you to go with great care, for yourself and others."

Mithrat Okoi pauses, looking at us gravely, as though trying to impress the seriousness of it into our heads. "Now, there is a particular danger of collisions in this course. You will be using several vertical levels in order to avoid making collisions with oncoming ships that will be traveling in the opposite direction."

He calls up a Fleet formation diagram on the smart board behind him.

"When you are in the race channel going in the direction of the Quantum Stream, or *streaming* toward the head of the fleet which is ICS-1, you will use the upper levels, keeping your shuttles *above* the ark-ships. On your return, when you are *ripping* against the Stream you will use lower levels, flying *beneath* the ark-ships. The Quantum Stream Boundary extends a kilometer above and below the formation, so even here you will need to be very careful not to Breach upward or downward."

In that moment, various Cadets around the room throw meaningful stares at Hugo Moreno who's sitting a few rows away with his new partner Marc Goldstein—both of them looking overconfident and cocky—and then at me.

Oh, great . . . I think, remembering the terrifying experience I went through with Hugo the last time.

Meanwhile, Chiyoko throws me a nervous glance also.

"Because of the added difficulty, your Average time for this course is set at 20 minutes," Instructor Okoi continues. "Use all your acquired flight skills to keep an even, balanced flight. Do not rush beyond your abilities, and be careful. Note that you will once more be evaluated on both your individual shuttle run and the cumulative score of the other Cadet Pilot Pairs who use your specific shuttle—so, be courteous of others."

Instructor Mithrat Okoi talks for another half hour, giving us various course specifics, and repeats the QS Boundary Breach warnings many times over, with hard glances in the direction of Hugo Moreno and myself.

Yeah, we're never going to live that down.

At last the session is over and we are excused, until 1:00 PM when we have to do our shuttle hands-on inspections.

After lunch, Chiyoko and I get to the shuttle bay with the others and do our inspections in absolutely harmonious cooperation mode.

At one point as we're crawling around the ship, checking wall panels, she glances at me and says, "Gwen, do you really think we'll be okay if we fly tomorrow in the split roles?"

I bite my lip and sigh. "Well," I say with a tired smile. "I don't see if we have anything to lose. So, let's just go for it."

She nods at me. "Okay. Was just checking. Last minute jitters, I guess."

"No problem, I get it," I tell her. "I'm worried too, but I think it's the best thing we can do for us."

She allows her slightly frightened fleeting smile to show. "At least if we Breach," she says, "I know we can come back safely. You did it once, so you can do it again."

I bite my lip guiltily. Suddenly the burden of responsibility seems almost too heavy. If only she knew at what cost I got back into the Quantum Stream the last time. . . .

"I hope so," I mutter. "But we're *not* going to Breach. Instead we're going to do our best to win this dratted thing."

That evening I have my voice training session with Kassiopei. When I enter the CCO, he is just finishing up a call. Once done, he turns to me, blank-faced as always, and then looks away again, seeming to be preoccupied with his display screens.

"Command Pilot," I say, watching him with the usual elevated heartbeat. "I know you're considered to be the best Pilot in the Fleet, and it's your specialty. Is there any advice you can give me for tomorrow's Race?"

He glances at me. "I can," he says coldly. "But you will not listen to me, as usual."

I can't help it. *I smile.*

It's just a tiny little smile, but it makes my lips curve upward and probably gives me dimples or something, and I watch his face react to it. . . . His gaze softens, goes slack momentarily, almost in amazement, and he stares at me—at my mouth—with his oh-so-blue eyes.

The next moment he blinks, and all the traces of softness are gone.

"All right. Here's my advice." He leans forward, putting his hands flat against the desk, watching me, his neck craned slightly sideways. "You need to go *slowly*. You need to be as precise as possible during each turn—find a rhythm and stick to it. Without the rhythm you will not achieve balance. Since the race course is a regular wave pattern, you must visually find the center-point axis of each turn and *memorize* it. Then use it to create a repeating pattern in your mind."

"Okay," I say. "Thank you, that's really helpful."

He nods. "This is basic advice. More importantly, my advice for you is to *be careful*."

"I will."

"No, I mean it, Lark." He pauses, and his gaze overwhelms me with intensity. "Be careful . . . *please*."

I take a deep breath, hearing the sound of my pulse, the blood coursing wildly in my veins. "Do you really care if something happens to me, or is it only my Logos voice?"

"What do you think?" he says softly.

And then the mask slams down. He looks away, and we begin the voice lesson.

Today is the day of the Second Quantum Stream Race—a day that will determine the future of all the Cadets in the Fleet, and possibly myself, and by extension, my entire family.

I've had a nearly sleepless night, which does not bode well, but my stress levels more than make up for low energy.

I hurry through breakfast, forcefully cramming food while sitting with Chiyoko and Blayne and his Pilot partner Leon, since we all decided to meet up in the Cadet Deck Four Meal Hall before heading for the shuttle bays.

"Good luck, guys," I say to Blayne and Leon, as they are about to head for Shuttle Bay Three.

"You too, Lark. And this time, no Breaching, okay? Don't make us have to put you two on a quantum doggie leash or something." Blayne nods to me and Chiyoko with a sarcastic one-handed Atlantean salute, as he transfers himself from the bench over to the hoverboard, and angles it nearly upright.

Meanwhile Leon stands waiting for him with a mellow friendly expression on his dark face.

"Thanks," I mutter.

Chiyoko just nods to them silently.

Then Chiyoko and I rush to our own Shuttle Bay Four.

When we get there, just on time, there are already crowds forming.

We find shuttle #47, get in our relay line, and wait for the Race to begin.

"How do you feel?" I ask Chiyoko.

She pauses momentarily glancing around at the other Cadets dressed sharply and lined up around us. "Pretty good," she says, pursing her lips. She's about to say something else but then. . . .

"Attention, Cadets!" Instructor Okoi's thundering voice comes from the walls of the shuttle bay, and immediately everyone falls in line and there is perfect silence.

"Welcome to the Second Quantum Stream Race! This is your final test! Pilot Pairs, line up!"

And then he directs the first pair to start. "The Final QS Race begins on my mark! First pair—you have control of the shuttle. Go!"

Chiyoko and I stand tensely as the first pair in our lineup sprints for the shuttle, and the same thing happens in all the other lines around the platforms.

We're second in line, so we're next.

In moments, the shuttles all around the bay come alive, and launch, ten seconds apart into the tunnel.

We hold our breaths, imagining the crazy scene happening out there. In about twenty minutes, they'll be back and then it's our turn.

I glance sideways and notice that Chiyoko starts to hyperventilate.

Oh, crap. . . .

"Hey," I whisper. "We'll do great!"

In answer she only looks at me, nods, and continues breathing quickly, while her round face is paler than normal, and sweat breaks out on her forehead.

That's when I grab Chiyoko's clammy cold hand and squeeze it. "You and I are going to be amazing!" I tell her, over and over, for the next few minutes, as we continue to hold hands. Pretty soon, I think my hand is trembling too, but if I squeeze it hard enough neither one of us will know. . . .

Soon the launch channel fills up with wind as the shuttles start coming back.

And here comes our shuttle #47.

Oh crap, oh crap. . . .

The first Pilot Pair gets out, grim-faced, and relinquishes control to us.

"Let's go, girl!" I exclaim breathlessly, as Chiyoko and I race to climb the shuttle ladder.

"Which seat? Which seat?" Chiyoko momentarily panics.

"I'll take the Pilot chair!" I say quickly, and sit down.

She sits down next to me in the Co-Pilot one. We both buckle in, while she calls up the secondary console from the wall, and I key myself to the Pilot console.

Then we both swipe the console undersides to power on, and the window shields come down.

I don't waste a second and sing the ignition sequence while holding down the large four-color button. Immediately Chiyoko echoes me, activating her own console.

"Ready?" I say with a slightly crazed grin, while the shuttle hums to life all around us, and the golden threads of light race along the hull walls.

"Yes!" she says, glancing briefly at the fiery-red *QSBEP-1 Emergency Instructions* on the panel before her—while I stubbornly ignore mine.

Instead I stare at the Race Clock that reads 00:00.

"Ten second warning.... Shuttle #47, prepare to enter the launch channel."

"Here we go!" I exclaim, and I flip to Red Grid, while Chiyoko goes to Blue. Her hands are slightly unsteady, but I think her breathing is back under control.

". . . You may enter the launch channel."

I sing the sequence, swipe on Red, and we coast carefully into the launch channel. I can almost feel the wind gusts churning the air around the shuttle, a slight rocking motion. . . .

"Shuttle #47, you may launch now!"

I take a shuddering breath and swipe to engage the Thrust.

And, we're off.

Once we're outside, I waste no time getting us into the vertical stack of ten shuttles that wait at the side of the ICS-2 hull.

Meanwhile, even higher above us we see an endless cavalcade of speeding shuttles moving in sine-wave curves just at the periphery of the top of the ark-ship hull shape. That's the upper level lane.

The exact same thing is happening directly below us, at the bottom of the ark-ship, where shuttles are passing in zig-zags in the opposite direction, *ripping* against the Stream.

"Pilots, prepare to enter the race! Ten second warning...."

Chiyoko is poised on Blue, while I flip to Yellow Grid, set our Destination, and then wait tense and ready on Red.

". . . two . . . one. . . . Start!"

The Race Clock goes from 00:00 to rapidly moving milliseconds.

I sing and swipe the Thrust.

We separate from the stack, together with the others, and rise into the upper level racing lane, merging carefully between traffic.

And then we begin the zig-zagging wave motion, flying

directly above, and along the curvature of the next ark-ship's right side, turning left into the 5-kilometer gap between the ships in column #2, then doing the same thing along the left curvature of the next ship, then turning right into the next 5-kilometer gap....

It's truly hypnotic.

Command Pilot Kassiopei was right. There's a certain rhythm to it, and it would almost be easy, if not for the fact that we are surrounded by so many other ships on all sides, making the same curving arc maneuvers.

"How are we doing?" I mutter, swiping the curves on Red Grid.

"Okay," Chiyoko mumbles in reply, as she micro-corrects my motion on Blue.

I glance up and our clock says 02:35.

We keep weaving around the ark-ships in column #2, moving at a steady speed.

Breathe, in and out. . . . Breathe. . . .

There is something soothing about the motion, if you don't try to think too hard about what's happening.

With my peripheral vision I watch the rapid-fire pattern of Start/Finish Line holo-projections speeding by on both sides of us, as we move in and out of the left, then the right channels between formations.

Seconds tick away, as we weave around hundreds of ships, dizzying our vision. . . . We pass slower shuttles, while faster ones pass us. I have no idea how our speed is compared to the others.

"How much longer till the flagship and the top of the column?" I mutter, when the clock reads 06:34 minutes.

As if to answer me, the automated traffic controller says:

"Shuttle #47, prepare to turn ahead. . . . Fleet termination, ten second warning."

"Okay, Braking now!" Chiyoko exclaims hastily.

I relinquish the Red, and she takes over on Green, slowing us down gradually, and circle swiping in a nice clean arc, as we enter the 5-kilometer boundary between the second ark-ship and ICS-1.

We come around in a perfect circle, and then descend

below the ship to enter the bottom-level lane for the return leg of the Race. Other shuttles swoop down all around us, doing the same maneuver.

So far, so good, smooth sailing. . . .

We start *ripping* toward the back of the Fleet, once again weaving around the middle column #2, except now we're below the underbellies of the great ark-ships.

"Time looks good!" Chiyoko says, in a voice that's almost surprised.

I glance up and the Clock reads 09:26. Not bad at all. . . .

I keep circle-swiping on Red, weaving us in and out.

Hundreds of ships. . . .

The pattern starts to blur in my mind, and it's also become easy now.

I breathe evenly, and slowly, gradually increase our speed.

"What are you doing?" Chiyoko notices our increasing velocity.

"Don't worry," I mutter, focusing in utmost concentration on maintaining the Zen state.

"Are you sure?" Her voice sounds high-pitched and nervous, while her micro-corrections on the Blue Grid speed up to match mine on Red.

"Yup," I say. "Doing okay there, not too fast for you?"

"No, I'm okay, actually," she responds.

And we keep moving at the increased speed.

At some point we weave back around ICS-2, our own home ship, but we're not done yet—in this type of race course we have to keep going, because it's not considered a finish until we make a complete circle around the entire Fleet, so now we have to reach the anchor ship, ICS-4.

"Doing okay, Chiyoko?" I mutter, never taking my eyes from the gestalt of movement and flow in the window ahead.

"Yes," she replies, concentrating on her own Blue Grid.

I check the time, and wow, Clock says 11:42. We're making very decent time!

Meanwhile, the shuttle traffic around us is picking up now, as though everyone has figured out their rhythm, and is now trying to beat the clock.

Just a few minutes more, and we hear:

"Shuttle #47, prepare to turn ahead. . . . Fleet termination, ten second warning."

Okay, so we're just about to reach the back end of the Fleet and ICS-4.

"I'm on it!" Chiyoko takes over and goes Green to Brake.

I watch her turn us around in another wonderfully smooth perfect circle around the penultimate ark-ship, in that 5-kilometer gap between it and ICS-4.

It occurs to me momentarily, *this is the exact same spot where Hugo and I lost control during the first QS Race. . . .* The place where we were driven off course by those other out-of-control shuttles and where we spun out, then started to drift like crazy until we Breached. . . .

No, don't think.

Instead I take deep breaths and watch us do a perfectly controlled, beautiful maneuver, thanks to Chiyoko.

However, the two shuttles directly in front of us are not so lucky.

"Oh, crap, *no!*" I exclaim, as I watch in horror the sudden out-of-control wobble and then wild slide of one shuttle about a hundred feet ahead of us as it starts to turn, but instead goes spinning. . . .

Not again!

But it does not endanger us.

Instead it spins and flies directly at the same formation ark-ship that we are presently circumventing. And now it's on a direct collision course with the giant hull wall of violet plasma. . . .

Chiyoko and I both scream, and she Brakes forcefully to get us away from the out-of-control spinning *second* shuttle—which barely manages to regain its turning axis and then keeps going into the proper turn, and rises up to merge with the upper level traffic racing lane heading the same way as the Stream.

Meanwhile the first shuttle hurtles head-on into the ark-ship . . . and we stare as it slams at the plasma force field. . . .

And *disappears*.

"Oh my God . . ." Chiyoko whispers in horror.

We continue coasting carefully and slowly as we wait a few seconds . . . for what? For a silent space explosion, maybe?

Anything?

Instead, there is no trace of the shuttle.

There is *nothing*.

It's as if, the moment it made contact with the plasma energy shield it ceased to exist.

"Wow," I whisper. "Was it vaporized? I don't see any debris. . . ."

Chiyoko shakes her head. "I don't know. . . ."

"Okay, we should probably keep going then," I mutter. "We only lost about twenty seconds on the Clock."

And so we pick up speed and start rising in order to merge back onto the home stretch of the race course.

In that moment, just as we're almost at the upper level, I glance at the lower section of the viewport window and see a strange sight.

The shuttle that had disappeared about thirty seconds ago, suddenly *emerges* from the *inside* of the ark-ship . . . about three hundred feet away from its original disappearance spot.

At the same time, the *location* where it reappears seems to flicker peculiarly. The plasma crackles. . . . And then just for a brief crazy moment, the *entire outline* of the great ark-ship shimmers and flickers also.

For a moment it looks unreal, flat, two-dimensional.

And the shuttle that came out is perfectly *unharmed* and now makes its way back on course.

"Look!" I exclaim. "Did you see that? Okay, that's just impossible!"

"What?" Chiyoko glances up nervously, but she missed it, and she does not recognize the shuttle.

"That—that's the same shuttle—" I stammer. "It's back! It returned! But—that makes no sense."

"Huh?" Chiyoko mumbles.

Unless. . . .

And then the truly crazy thought comes to me.

The ark-ship—it is not real. It's a hologram.

Stunned, I almost forget to do my part on the Red Grid propulsion.

"Sorry, I don't understand," Chiyoko mutters. "Okay, can you please hurry up, Gwen? We need to merge."

"Right, never mind," I say, while my mind is reeling and I try to get a grip.

That ark-ship flickered like a standard hologram undergoing a brief static charge. I am completely sure of it. It explains why there was no collision, no debris, no destroyed shuttle.

But—what the hell does that mean?

What's a hologram of an entire ark-ship doing in the Fleet formation?

And then an even scarier thought comes to me: what if it's not the only one? What if the entire Fleet formation is full of ships that are holograms?

Holy crap! No, that can't be, that's just crazy. . . .

My mind begins to panic, but I don't allow myself the luxury. Instead, I slam down a steel wall of focus and concentrate on the weaving pattern before me.

A few minutes later, we reach the ICS-2 Finish Line.

As we pass the wide holo-strip of golden light projected from our home ship across the flight lane, our Race Clock freezes at 16:48. That's a great time.

Chiyoko exclaims in wonder. I force myself to smile back at her.

But instead of celebrating, it's with a heavy heart that I let Chiyoko take over on the Green Brake. And we enter the launch tunnel and return to ICS-2 Shuttle Bay Four.

Tonight I am going to see Command Pilot Aeson Kassiopei.

And he'd better have some answers for me.

Chapter 41

But first, we get out of our shuttles, give up control to the next Pilot Pair in the relay and stand aside nervously, watching the rest of the Quantum Stream Race along with the crowds in the shuttle bay.

The Race is over about an hour and a half later, as the last of the Pilot Pairs return in the shuttles.

Our Final Scores are tabulated instantly, and we all crowd to the smart boards to see our Cadet Standings. For a while I allow myself to forget the hologram ark-ship situation and just bump shoulders with everyone else as Chiyoko and I push our way forward to see our numbers.

The smart boards refresh, and here come our numbers for ICS-2 in one column, and our overall Fleet Scores in the other.... It's also interesting to see that the four Quadrant general rankings have changed slightly, so that Blue and Red are neck-to-neck, followed by Yellow and then Green. Go, Yellow—my Quadrant's moving up!

Everyone mutters, exclaims, holds their breath.

We watch as Alla Vetrova and Conrad Hart are the reigning champions, with a #1 standing for the ship, and a 100% perfect Fleet Score. Which means they could be in the top 200 across the Fleet overall—though, with top Cadets from 2,000 ark-ships vying for only 200 spots, there are no guarantees.

But if some of those 2,000 ships are only holograms, the crazy persistent thought plagues me, *then maybe their odds are way better....*

Okay, I really, really need some answers, and fast, before I go insane.

I watch the scroll and see that in spot #2 for ICS-2 is Logan

Sangre and Oliver Parker, with a 99% Fleet Score.

Wow. . . . Logan is really pushing his way up the ranks, I think.

Meanwhile, the Tsai siblings, Erin and Roy, have been knocked down to #3, with a 98% Fleet Score, followed by Leopold Deller and DeeDee Kim at #4 and a 97% Fleet Score.

And then, as Chiyoko and I stare in amazement, we see our names listed.

We're at #5 for ICS-2.

And, we have a 96% Fleet Score.

No effing way!

Chiyoko makes a stifled scream and puts her hands over her mouth, and starts crying. I scream also, and then hug her. . . . She hugs me back, and we sort of dance around and scream, holding each other, and getting out of the way of others.

"Oh my God! Oh my God!" she mutters and I mutter. I think we're both hyperventilating at this point.

"I don't know how, but we did it, Gwen! Thank you for being such a good partner!" Chiyoko says, smiling and sniffling at the same time, and constantly wiping her reddened face and the running tears.

"I can't believe it either! And no, thank *you!* You were awesome!"

Well, this definitely changes things for both of us—being in the top five for our ship. Chiyoko is going to have nice Fleet placement opportunities available. And me? My chances are so much better now—when at the end of next month we finally arrive in Atlantis and the CP has to make his decision about allowing me to compete in the Games of the Atlantis Grail.

Eventually we look up at the smart boards again and start to watch for other people we know and their numbers to scroll by. Looks like, after the initial rush to learn their own, everyone is doing it too.

Well, I don't have to wait long for Blayne Dubois and Leon Madongo—there they are at #18 and their Fleet Score is 93%! Way to go, Blayne and Leon!

Out of curiosity I stick around and wait to see Hugo Moreno's score. It's way down in the lower middle of the scroll, at #419, and the Fleet Score is a dismal 61%. I wonder if Marc

Goldstein now regrets becoming his Pilot partner. . . . Hey, not my problem.

The rest of the day goes by quickly. I get back to my cabin and call up Gracie and Laronda to make sure they both did okay, and apparently all is well.

Gracie and her partner got an excellent #35 for their ship standing, and a 90% Fleet Score, while Laronda has landed #104 for her ship and an 87% Fleet Score, which is not bad at all. With these numbers, both of them have a solid future in the Fleet.

Well, now the not-so-good part.

While most of the Cadets are celebrating or just recovering from the grueling event of this morning, I brood for the whole day, waiting for an opportunity to speak with Kassiopei. It's QS Race Day, so there are no duties scheduled for me at the CCO. However I do have the voice training at 8:00 PM.

And it can't come soon enough.

I walk into the CCO five minutes early.

Tonight my heart is racing for two different reasons. One, I get to see *him*, as always. Two, I get to ask him the scary questions, with possibly even scarier answers.

Aeson Kassiopei is standing near his desk, adjusting one of the mech arms for the display monitors.

The moment he sees me, he stops doing whatever he's doing and turns to me.

"Congratulations," he says in an unreadable voice. "You did very well on the Quantum Stream Race today. Better than expected."

"Thank you," I say with unusual composure, while my breath comes evenly as I attempt to control it. "I tried to follow your advice, and I think it helped."

"Following my advice? You surprise me yet again."

I nod, still breathing regularly and don't respond to his mild taunt.

He must be extremely well attuned to my nuances, because he raises one brow and looks at me in expectation. "You don't appear as pleased as you should be. Why is that, Lark? Tell me what is the matter."

My lips part. . . . How did he know?

"Command Pilot," I say, while a cold terror immediately begins to build up in my gut. "I'm very happy with my results. But—something happened today during the Race."

He continues looking at me, closely, with his unblinking masked expression.

And then I tell him the whole thing. "That shuttle emerged back out from the ark-ship, unharmed," I conclude, "while there was a strange visual effect—a ripple of sorts. Which is something that happens with *holograms*."

At the word "holograms" I notice him grow very still, more so than he already is. Okay, this does not bode well. . . . So, I persist.

"Was that ark-ship a hologram? And if so, are there others like it in the Fleet? Please, Command Pilot, I need to know! I must know what's going on!"

There is a long pause.

And then he exhales a held breath, and sits down at his desk. He points to one of the other empty chairs, and I sit down across from him in my usual spot.

"Please . . ." I say. "Please tell me, what is really going on?"

He frowns, watching me. "Sometimes, you're too perceptive for your own good. It is unfortunate that you had to discover the nature of that ship. Yes, it *is* a hologram."

"My God. . . ." I start to tremble.

"Don't be alarmed. There are *no* others like it in the Fleet. No other holograms. It is the only one."

"But why? How did it get there?"

He exhales another held breath. "I *put* it there."

"What?"

"I had to fill in the vacant space in the formation in order to maintain security, among other things. The actual ship has stayed behind, remaining in Earth's orbit."

"Oh!" I feel so many burning questions well up inside me.

He notices my anxiety. "These are all matters that don't concern you directly, so I wouldn't worry about it."

"Not worry?" I exclaim. Immediately I feel a stab of anger, and it gives me a boost of crazy energy. "Are you serious? How does it not concern me? What is that ship doing back on Earth?"

He starts to frown lightly. "Calm down."

"Don't tell me to calm down! This is my home! My family is there, I want to know—no, I *demand* to know what is going on!"

Command Pilot Kassiopei leans in closer to me, resting his hands on his desk. His composed expression hardens. "Right now, you are treading on dangerous ground, Lark. You are not to speak this way to me—*ever*. Remember yourself."

I let out my breath. I meet the look of his beautiful, terrifying eyes.

"Forgive me, Command Pilot," I say, in a careful voice like ice. "I have *overstepped* my bounds." And I continue to look at him fiercely, negating my compliant words.

For a few seconds, we are in a duel of gazes. And then, surprisingly, he relents first, by looking away.

"There's not much that can be disclosed to unauthorized personnel such as yourself," he says in an almost resigned voice. "However, I will tell you some of it—because I trust you sufficiently, as my Aide, and as a *human being*—someone who is intelligent enough to understand the complexity of the situation."

I blink and continue to watch him with absolute intensity. In that unexpected moment, I suddenly see the vulnerability in him, in the way his walls of composure break down momentarily, as he speaks to me on this very peculiar, human level of *equals*. And for some reason, it breaks my heart.

And then he begins to talk, looking off into space, and not meeting my gaze directly. Maybe it's easier for him to speak that way. . . . I know it's easier for *me*.

"The ship will remain in orbit around Earth all the way up to the arrival of the asteroid. It remains there for a number of reasons. Yes, obviously, it's a last resort, in case there's a sudden last-minute solution to the tragic situation. It also remains in order to establish a *communication link* with the Fleet in the Quantum Stream—otherwise we would not be able to receive news of Earth and transmit back to them."

He pauses, glancing at me briefly. "Your Earth United Nations governments and Earth Union have apparently relied on the fact that we are leaving ships in orbit—they expected several, not just one. My Father, the Imperator, has made them promises he never planned to fulfill. He is at least partially responsible for creating and escalating the tragic situation with Earth Union. He can never meet their demands, and they have an incomplete, false understanding of the situation."

I listen, while a frown gathers on my forehead from the tension. "And what *is* the situation?" I say softly.

Still looking away from me, Aeson Kassiopei shakes his head. And he does not reply.

In that moment I remember something else I've been meaning to ask. "Command Pilot," I say. "Thank you for explaining about the ark-ship. And . . . I'm sorry if this is again me stepping out of line, but there is something that has been bothering me ever since the hostage incident with Terra Patria. One of their demands—"

He looks at me, hard. "What?"

I swallow. . . . "A demand they made was for you to fly an empty ark-ship and crash it into the asteroid and cause a multi-megaton explosion that would destroy it. I was wondering, wouldn't it make actual sense to sacrifice an Atlantean ship—or even two or more ships, to make a really big impact explosion—if it meant that all of Earth could be saved? I know it's probably ridiculous, and there are some other considerations I'm not aware of, but—"

"It will not do any good." His answer comes softly.

"But why?"

"They will only send *another* one. . . ."

"What do you mean?" I frown. "They who? What? I don't understand. . . ."

But Aeson is looking at me with eyes filled with sorrow. "*They*—" he repeats softly—"will only send another *asteroid*."

My mouth falls open.

Oh . . . my . . . God.

I am stunned.

Truly, I have no words right now.

Who are "they?"

But Command Pilot Kassiopei preempts my further questions. "Enough," he says harshly, closing up again. "I have told you far more than I should, and at some point you will learn more—I *promise* you. But—not now, not today."

"But—" I stammer. "Who are they? Who are you talking about? Please! Is it the Imperator, your Father? The Atlantis Central Agency? *Who?*"

"No," he says, shaking his head. "*Not* my Father, and not the ACA. Furthermore, you must *not* speak to *anyone* about what I've told you. And now, this conversation is *over*."

As he reaches for the sound damper box containing the usual pieces of orichalcum for my voice lesson, I find that I'm shaking.

Later that night, and the following morning, I find that I am still stunned and mulling over the impossible implications of what I've learned from Kassiopei.

What is going on with that asteroid?

One thing is certain, *this changes everything*.

Instead of celebrating my great Pilot scores, or rehashing my carefully-laid plans for the future, about entering the Games of the Atlantis Grail in order to save my parents, or even wondering how my siblings and I will proceed once we get to Atlantis—instead of all that, I'm now obsessing over the true nature of the asteroid threat.

But I have no means of finding out anything more than I already know. My one source—the Command Pilot—is not giving me any more answers.

And so, over the next few days, and the remaining weeks, I force myself to put this on the back burner, and simply let the events play out.

Because either I do that, or I go insane with worry and soul-sickness. . . .

And right now, I need to conserve all the strength that I have for what's coming ahead.

Chapter 42

We've now entered the third month of Yellow season, which is the twelfth and final month of our journey to Atlantis.

The rate of our deceleration is making itself felt, because now when we visit the observation decks of our ark-ships, we can see real interstellar space and cosmic grandeur through the softly translucent curtain of the Quantum Stream.

The Stream itself has become rarified, fine and almost non-existent, its nature a wispy fabric.... Right now the Fleet is passing through a thick galactic cluster, a sea of infinite stars churning in a spiral that resembles a conch shell of pearl and rose, with a rich strange physical texture that looks like something you might see under a microscope.

It's absolutely stunning....

Supposedly, things on a grand macro scale often look the same as things on a tiny micro scale.... Galaxies resemble amoebas. It's only the in-between stuff that looks different to us, *homo sapiens*, the human race. Possibly because that intermediate scale is what we actually inhabit, and what makes sense to us. The super-big and the super-small are all *unreal*. Our world is somewhere in the middle.

In the third week of the third month of Yellow, with only one week before arrival on Atlantis, we have one final ship-board celebration to look forward to.

It's the Yellow Zero-G Dance.

And my Quadrant is hosting it.

Two days before the Yellow Dance, with everyone in the Fleet making fun plans, I talk to Gracie to ask her if she wants to be my guest once again, and visit ICS-2.

But my sister tells me that she has been invited by Blayne, and is coming to our ship already. "Oh, really?" I say with a little smile. "When was this planned?"

Gracie looks closely into the screen and I see a slight blush gather on her cheeks. "Oh, it's no big deal," she mutters. "Blayne and I were just talking recently, and he mentioned that he'll be around on ICS-2 the night of the Dance, so I said, why don't we hang out."

"Ah," I say. "So you invited *yourself* over, Gee Four. Nicely played!"

"I did not!" Gracie flares with embarrassment. "I mean, we were just talking, that's all, and since he's not busy that night—"

"Right," I say as my smile turns into a grin.

"Stop that!" Gracie is really blushing now.

"Okay, okay!" I put one hand up and bite my lips. "Just have a good time, and be sure not to drive the boy crazy too much, okay? I'll see you the day after tomorrow!"

So that's settled.

Then, I figure, I can invite Laronda. I call her up, and the girl sounds all excited and immediately says yes. So, now, I finally get to see her after all these months, at last!

"Oooh, what are you going to wear?" Laronda asks me, craning her neck. "Something stunning and outrageous like you did the last time for the Red Dance? Because I'm so mad I didn't get the chance to see your red-hot Carmen dress!"

"Oh . . ." I say. "Well, it's still here in my closet storage bin, so you can see it if you like when you get here. I was thinking about just returning it and having them recycle it. . . ."

"*What?*" Laronda exclaims. "No, no way! That's sacrilege! How can you even think of getting rid of a fabulous dress like that?"

I shrug. "It's not like I'll be likely to wear it again."

But Laronda shakes her head at me and wags her finger. "You never know, girlfriend. You never know. I mean, I'm still kind of wondering how come you're inviting *me* instead of that hottie Xelio as your date for this dance? Seriously, why not him again?"

I take a deep breath. "I dunno. He is smoking hot,

definitely, and there *is* an attraction. But . . . I just, well. . . ."

"What? *What?*"

"I—can't," I say. "It doesn't feel right. I don't really want to lead him on and—"

"And what?" Laronda raises both her brows. "Okay, is it because of the other guy? You know, *him?* Your commanding officer and Imperial Princely Hotness?"

"Yeah, well, kind of. . . ." I almost cringe as I say it.

Laronda looks at me sideways. "Oh, lord, you're in so much trouble, girl. You're still completely into him, aren't you?"

I nod sadly.

"Okay, never mind," she says with an energetic nod. "When I get there we'll talk about it. Meanwhile, let's decide what we're wearing!"

An hour later, after scouring the design database, Laronda and I have our outfits planned.

The theme of the Yellow Dance is sunshine—as in, harvest sun, and warm golden sunlight of early autumn. We send our selections and our body measurement templates off to the 3D printer here at ICS-2, to be ready for pickup tomorrow after 3:15 PM from the Manufacturing Deck.

"I'll pick up both of our outfits, and you can get dressed in my cabin when you get here," I tell Laronda.

"Perfect! Now, what are we doing about makeup?" Laronda muses. "I don't have that much here at all, just some crummy old lipstick from the last time I went to the Walden Galleria in Buffalo, New York, and also some nail polish and that's about it. Hey, maybe you can ask your Consul Denu again if he can hook us up with some of his amazing stuff?"

Yes, Laronda has heard all about my Red Dance Cinderella dress-up adventure, and I think she now wants in on that action.

"Hmm, I don't know," I say. "I'll ask, but not sure what the Consul will say."

"Hopefully he'll say 'yes' and send his personal assistant Kem to do our hair and makeup! Though, I tell you, that boy can do my face, but there's no way in hell he's touching this sistah's hair! Girl, I don't trust alien hair care products—"

I giggle, and then we blab some more, until Laronda's

barracks curfew kicks in. Afterwards, I send a polite email to Consul Denu, attaching the outfit template files for his reference.

The next day, I arrive at the CCO before 8:00 AM and Gennio and Anu are there early.

"With the CP's permission, we're helping Pilot Oalla Keigeri with the Zero-G Dance setup tomorrow," Gennio tells me. "Vazara and I will be doing the sound station tech once again."

"Oh, that's great!" I say cheerfully. "Will she be the Music Mage again?"

"Oh yes, she's the most popular one, and is certainly the best," Gennio says. "Pilot Keigeri requested her specifically."

Anu meanwhile gives me a sneaky sideways look. "So, Gwen, are you going with Xelio again?"

I glance at him and raise one eyebrow. "No, I'm not, and it's not really any of your business."

"Oh, yeah?" Anu makes his usual rude horsey laugh. "Hey, did Xelio drop you or something? How come? You broke up? He got sick of you, Earth girl?"

And Anu follows up by making awful kissy sucking noises against his arm.

In that awkward moment, *again*, Command Pilot Kassiopei has apparently walked in the door and now stands behind us. Did he hear Anu's loud stupidity *yet again*, just as it happened before the previous dance?

I have the feeling he did.

Oh, dear lord....

But this time Aeson Kassiopei says nothing. He does not acknowledge if he heard us, and simply makes his way to his desk. At one point he throws one cool fleeting glance at me, and quickly turns away.

I feel the usual flush in my cheeks and keep my eyes averted, and get back to my work. And later that morning, I obtain his permission to have Laronda Aimes visit this ship for the Yellow Dance, in addition to my sister.

"Since you're part of the Yellow Quadrant, you are excused from your duties tomorrow, and have my permission to assist with the setup and other aspects of the Yellow Dance,"

Kassiopei tells me.

"Thank you, Command Pilot," I say, then gather courage to ask: "I suppose you will not attend the Dance?"

He looks into my eyes with his composed, veiled gaze. "Very briefly," he says.

And that's that.

The morning of the Yellow Zero-G Dance has the usual buzz of excitement. Everyone around the Fleet is looking at this as the final opportunity to relax and have carefree fun one last time before the scary unknown of the following week—our arrival in Atlantis.

Maybe that's why there's so much energy in the air.

I go to Shuttle Bay Two to meet Laronda's shuttle. It arrives just on time, at 8:00 AM, and moments later the ladder comes down and out comes the familiar slim brown-skinned girl with the sassy relaxed bob hairdo, wearing her ordinary grey uniform and a big grin.

"Gwen!"

"Laronda!"

We both scream a little, and hug. Laronda looks like she's bulked up just a little, since the last time I saw her in person, which was months ago. Her skinny arms have more muscle definition, and she looks confident as always.

"Okay, let's go see if Gracie is here yet, and then we can get some late breakfast!"

Laronda and I chatter and laugh non-stop as we head for a different shuttle bay on the other side of the ship, where Gracie's supposed to be coming in.

"I'm sure Blayne will be there to get her," I say, as we pass through various ship decks and corridors. "But I just want to make sure she's okay too."

"Hey, you don't need to explain to me." Laronda punches me on the arm. "Let's go get your little troublemaker. I haven't seen her for nearly a year!"

"She's not so little anymore." I smile, biting my lip. "Thirteen and growing faster than I can deal with. . . ."

We get to Shuttle Bay One just to see Blayne and Gracie heading toward us and the exit. Blayne is hovering nearly upright on his board, and laughing easily at something Gracie just said. He appears bemused and very relaxed as he looks at her, and I notice his hair is out of his eyes, as he must have sleeked it back, revealing his blue eyes and his very nice looking face and forehead. He's not wearing his white Cadet dress uniform yet—I suppose he'll change later.

Gracie meanwhile is already in her dressy whites, wearing the Cadet uniform sharply. She also has very subtle, very grown up makeup on, and she is looking at Blayne constantly.

It occurs to me, Laronda and I could've just borrowed Gracie's cosmetics for this Dance. But then we wouldn't have the amazing Atlantean Face Paints and Kem's services.

Because, yeah—did I mention Consul Denu said yes, and he's sending Kem over again tonight? He is!

In moments they see us and there are more squeals and hugs, as Gracie and I, and then Gracie and Laronda, squeeze each other. And then Blayne gets a big hug from Laronda too, which makes him a little awkward, but he gets over it in moments.

We all head to breakfast together, and the day is looking good so far.

Later, around 11:00 AM, I get away from everyone briefly to go check up on the situation in the Resonance Chamber to see if I'm needed. Gennio is there, and I help out for about an hour with acoustic wall panel tests.

Then I come back and spend the rest of the afternoon with my friends and my sister.

"How is Gordie doing? I know he stubbornly refused to go to the Zero-G Dance here on ICS-2," I ask at some point, and Gracie just smiles.

"Oh, Gee Three's totally fine. He just prefers to go to the Dance on our own ship. I think he has a crush on a girl there!"

My mouth falls open. "Our Gee Three likes a girl? Noooo! Tell me more about this miracle!"

Gracie shrugs. "It's no big deal, really. She's just someone who works with him in Hydroponics, and I don't think he asked her out or anything. He just likes her from afar, you know. Like, from around trees. His notebook is filled with sketches of her and plants—that's the only reason I know."

I smile. "Aha! Well, that explains his insistence on staying on his own ship all the time. Poor Gee Three, the boy is growing up!"

Gracie rolls her eyes.

Laronda looks at both of us with a bemused little smile.

It occurs to me, *Laronda misses her own little brother Jamil, her own family.* . . .

And I force myself to remember that in many ways, having two of my siblings here in the Fleet, I am very lucky.

After dinner, it's time to get ready for the Yellow Dance, which begins at 7:00 PM.

Blayne briefly escapes our overpowering girl cooties and returns to his own barracks to get changed.

Meanwhile my tiny cabin turns into an overcrowded zoo, as Laronda, Gracie and I become disgustingly girly. Laronda and I take turns to use my shower, while Gracie remains in her Cadet parade uniform and fusses with her hair and makeup from her own cosmetics bag.

Laronda's and my outfits are still in their plastic packaging, lying on my bunk next to Gracie's makeup.

As soon as we are out of the shower and our hair is sufficiently dry, we start putting our dresses on.

Oh, wow. . . . They are both simply stunning.

Laronda puts on a slinky evening dress of flowing metallic gold, with a fitted sleeveless top that shows off her lovely neck and has a V-line plunging collar and slim waist, and below, a flaring princess skirt made of some kind of ethereal fabric in several pyramid layers. The fabric billows like a cloud around her feet, all the way down to her ankles, and her shoes are slim gold pumps with three-inch stiletto heels.

"Oh my lord, you are gorgeous!" I exclaim. "And the shoes! Can you actually walk on those heels?"

Laronda sticks out one foot before the other, and does an easy pirouette. "Two years of ballet lessons!" she mutters with a wink.

"Oh, wow! I didn't know you studied ballet!" I say, extremely impressed.

"Oh, yeah," Laronda says. "Was taking ballet for a while until Auntie Janice got her work hours cut, and couldn't afford to pay for more lessons."

And then I take out my own dress and put it on.

This time around, my dress is completely different from the seductive blood-red dress I wore to the Red Dance. Basically, I've given up on seduction, and embraced my simple side.

It is long and flowing, translucent pale gold. . . . It has a gently plunging round neckline and short sleeves, and a skirt that transitions from loosely-conforming at the waist to full at the bottom. The effect is very gradual and ethereal, a little like Laronda's skirt, except my entire dress is like that. And it's not puffy but gently cascading down. If I turn, it billows like a golden bell around me, but not just the skirt—the whole thing.

This dress makes me look innocent and dreamy, as if I'm some kind of airy nymph at a harvest festival. All I need is flowers in my hair and I could be running through fields of wheat.

And my shoes—they are simple golden pumps with tiny one-inch heels. No fear of tripping here.

"Wow, girl, you look dreamy and beautiful!" Laronda stands back to look me up and down with approval. "Doesn't she, Gracie?"

Gracie nods, and her mouth is partly open, as she admires both me and Laronda in our golden finery. "You guys look so good!" she mumbles. "I almost wish I got dressed up instead of this Cadet uniform."

In that moment we get the knock at the door—it must be Kem.

Kem comes in, carrying his usual bags and boxes. Introductions are made all around. And then he gets to work.

"Not the hair!" Laronda makes hectic gestures to him, and Kem nods gently and takes out the Face Paints instead. Fifteen minutes later, Laronda looks sophisticated and stunning, with golden highlights along her cheekbones and her eyelids, striking black eyeliner, and amazing liquid gold lipstick that makes her sexy full lips glitter like the essence of sunlight.

And then it's my turn.

"Hair, yes, please," I say with a shy smile. And then I

explain to him that I want something simple, and I want my hair down.

Kem nods again, with a little smile, and performs his magic on me.

First he brushes out my hair in layers, so that it attains unusual fullness and cascades in dark waves. Then he takes a fine golden net of exquisite fine chain garlands, and casts it over my hair, threading each strand with individual locks of mine, emphasizing the waves. And then he puts tiny white, gold, and clear snap-on beads along many of the strands. When he is done, my hair is a glorious carpet of harvest flowers.

Next, comes my makeup.

"Not too dramatic, please," I tell him.

And he understands, perfectly.

First, he enhances my skin with the same translucent foundation powder that gives me a soft rosy and porcelain glow. And then he applies golden and violet shadow over my eyelids, sculpting them. The sharp violet-black eyeliner and mascara come next, giving me just a little drama, but not as much as for the Red Dance.

Finally, a tiny amount of blush at the cheekbones, and the lipstick, a soft pale mauve that makes my lips delicate and ethereal, like rose petals.

"Consul Denu thought you might like a little borrowed jewelry once again," Kem says to me and Laronda both. He reaches into his bag and takes out a heavy gold collar for Laronda, made of gold filigree interspersed with colorful stones in shades of amber, lemon, citrus and apricot. There is something very Ancient Egyptian about it, and Laronda parts her lips in stunned amazement as the dramatic collar goes around her neck. There are also matching earrings, great garlands of gold and stones that sweep down Laronda's elegant neck and emphasize the beauty of her dark skin.

My jewelry is much more simple. Kem gives me a delicate choker necklace of amber and citrine stones, and matching drop earrings with tiny fringe gold chains cascading down to brush just below my ear.

"The sun will be hidden inside you, but this way you will still shine," he says, as he puts the finishing touches by tossing a tiny amount of golden dust along the edges of my hair.

He offers it generously to Laronda, and seeing how good it looks on my hair, the girl says, "Oh, all right! Sprinkle me too!"

And Kem does, until Laronda's short relaxed bob glitters like it's covered with faerie dust.

"What about Gracie?" I say. "Gee Four, want some gold hair sparklies?"

Gracie thinks for a second and then grins widely. "Okay!"

And in moments Kem gives her tidy updo hair a scintillating sparkle.

"Okay, all done!" he says with satisfaction.

We thank him and moments later, head for the Dance.

There is something magical about arriving at each Zero-G Dance. There's always the high energy, the crowd in the hallway, and this time is no different. The hub corridor around the Resonance Chamber is packed with teens dressed in golden outfits and white Cadet uniforms.

Even as we approach, a soft yellow-gold glow stains the entire corridor with warmth, and we can hear the rapid pounding beat of the dance track, a current popular chart-topping hit (or at least it *was* current, just as we Qualified and left Earth) by the international sensation boy band Ave Murakko, ironically called "Asteroid Burning Love."

"Scorch me, burn me, asteroid love!" Gracie sings with a giggle.

"Scorch me, burn me, crazy space m-a-a-a-n!" Laronda sings the next line.

"Okay," I say with a groan. "These have got to be some of the stupidest lyrics ever."

"Hey! I like this song!" Gracie whines, but she is laughing, and starting to dance in place.

"What's worse, it's really in bad taste, all things considered." I sigh.

"Yeah, well," Laronda says. "Tell it to all the brain-dead people who submitted this song for the Dance playlist. Must've been a bunch of votes for it, if it got chosen."

We reach the doors of the Resonance Chamber and enter. . . .

A golden universe.

The grand spherical chamber is burning like the inside of the sun—the Earth Sol. We're inside its golden belly, and the light is blazing almost white along the lower portions near the widest circumference level to where the dance floor has been raised. And then it gradually tapers off to yellow gold and fades into soft amber on the dome ceiling. . . .

Everywhere along the ceiling, small orbs and spheres hang, like golden light-filled champagne bubbles, or bunches of grapes, to suggest more suns, or ripe fruits.

The dance floor itself is like a pool of honey the size of a stadium. The illusion of liquid is so strong because a strange haze stands, rising about five inches off the floor so that people's feet literally seem to disappear—they dissolve in the smooth glow, as though sinking in the honey lake.

"Holy lord, wow!" Laronda says. "Unbelievable!"

"Oh, wow!" Gracie mutters. I notice she is already looking around the packed room for any sign of Blayne.

Meanwhile, the main floor is overflowing with dancers as usual. The perimeter walkway stations are busy serving refreshments, and I look for the glassed-off cube to indicate the sound tech station.

"Over there!" Laronda points. "Let's first grab the locator pins. We're gonna need them in this human zoo."

We head for the station that's handing out the couple locator pins, which are golden yellow this time. I grab my set and pin one on my dress and the other I give to Laronda who sticks it on hers.

"Gracie!" I say. "Give me one of your pins too! You can use Blayne's pair when you find him."

"Okay," she mutters, and surrenders one of her pins to me. I stick it next to Laronda's other one on my chest.

"Looks like I have an extra set," Laronda says, looking at the shining golden drops of light in her palm.

"Save it for the cute hottie you'll meet later," I say, wiggling my eyebrows at her.

"Good deal!" Laronda nods and sticks the spare pin pair on her sleeve.

I start to look around to see if there's anyone I know, but in that moment the great chamber grows silent, as the music fades.

A white spotlight falls on a platform floating ten feet above floor level, on which a golden goddess stands.

Oalla Keigeri is about to open the Yellow Dance.

Chapter 43

Tonight, Oalla Keigeri wears a floor-length sheath dress of liquid metallic gold that hugs her form. There's a single long slit on the side, through which one of her shapely legs is showing, up to the thigh, and her platform shoes studded with tiny glowing lights sport five-inch heels.

Her hair is gathered in a stunning perfect updo with a braided knot on top, and several long locks descend to swing down her back. They are intertwined with golden metal chain garlands that cascade from her earrings. One amber faceted jewel descends from her forehead to lie between her brows like a sparkling third eye.

Oalla raises her arms and the spotlight brightens. At the same time her bright voice rings out and echoes from the walls of the chamber.

"Attention, Cadets, Civilians and Crew! Yellow welcomes you!"

The dance crowd responds with a roar.

"Today, in this warm Season of Yellow, may you find joy and inspiration in the sunshine smiles all around you!"

Another wild roar comes from the dance floor.

"And now," Oalla exclaims, clapping her hands over her head in slow rhythm, "you all know the magic warning! So, what . . . is . . . it?"

"Gravity . . . changing . . . now!" the stadium screams like thunder.

"Then, no more waiting! You must Dance! *Orahemai!*"

In that moment, the opening power chords of a hot dance song explode from the sound system, and the crowd goes wild.

"Let's all dance now!" Gracie exclaims, pulling both of us

by the arms.

"Okay, just a moment while I check in with the guys," I say.

Swaying in time with the song, we all move around the perimeter walkway toward the sound station. Here I see Gennio, Anu, Vazara and several more Atlanteans, behind glass, dancing in place as they work the sound station consoles.

I wave and Gennio waves back, while Vazara smiles dreamily and then waves with both hands, doing an actual wave motion with her body. Tonight Vaz is wearing a little pale yellow dress sprinkled with glitter-beads and sparkling in the light. Her hair has yellow flowers and tiny golden spheres threaded throughout.

"Swimming through the air!" Vaz says to us, gyrating slowly and still moving her hands, while the guys look on.

I giggle. Then, since they already know Gracie, I introduce Laronda.

Anu steps up and makes an exaggerated salute, then slaps his forehead. "Oh, no, it's three Earth girls dancing!"

"Oh, no, it's Anu!" I exclaim.

Laronda does an exaggerated double take that mimics Anu's ridiculous lunge.

"Oh, wait," she says. "Is this the same crazy Anu you've been telling me about, Gwen?"

"Yup," I say, pointing to Anu's head. "There's only one, and it's him—all the crazy gathered in one place."

"Whoa!" Anu makes a loud snort, then glances from me to Laronda. "So you talk about me, Earth girl? Hey, you—other Earth girl—what did this one tell you?"

"Other Earth girl?" Laronda echoes him. "Seriously? I am *Laronda*. Repeat that and memorize it, troll boy!"

Anu's jaw drops open and then he laughs rudely, staring at Laronda with a grin.

But we're interrupted just in time by Vazara, speaking very slowly in her sultry voice:

"Gravity changing now. . . ."

Immediately the vertigo comes, and with it, the initial queasy sensation of falling. . . .

Everyone screams at the first gravity manipulation of the

evening.

"Okay, I'm going to find Blayne!" Gracie exclaims with urgency, and suddenly she is gone, rushing toward the perimeter seating area, in search of him.

Laronda and I start moving after her, semi-floating in the light gravity, while a slower song plays.

I can no longer make out Gracie among the crowd, but I see a familiar large girl standing a few feet away near the wall.

It's my Pilot partner, Chiyoko Sato. I notice, this time she hasn't bothered with a formal dress but instead wears her white Cadet uniform. She is holding a drink, sipping it through the straw, and watching the dancers.

"Chiyoko!" I exclaim, waving at her enthusiastically. In that moment I get a flashback to the very first Blue Dance when Command Pilot Kassiopei danced with her elegantly in the air, while Logan and I were breaking up. . . .

Don't think. . . .

Chiyoko notices me and her face comes alive.

I pull Laronda over and introduce them.

"This is my Pilot Partner, Chiyoko." I smile. "And this is my friend Laronda from Qualification."

And then I glance at the busy dance floor behind us. "Hey," I say. "Let's all dance together! We don't need partners! It's girls' night out! Let's go!"

Chiyoko gets a slightly surprised look on her face, while Laronda just nods confidently, then makes a loud woot noise and raises her hands over her head. "Yeah, bayyybeee, yeah! Girls, let's go boogie!"

And I grab Chiyoko and Laronda both, and together we hit the dance floor.

We dance hard for almost an hour, while the Music Mage switches the gravity at least three times. There's something absolutely amazing about holding hands with two other friends while you float weightless near the champagne bubble ceiling—and we do it repeatedly. We also do the low gravity high-jumping and tumbling, and then regular gravity dancing in a big group. By now, all our foreheads are glittering with a fine sheen of sweat from the workout.

"Drink! Hot! Hot! Must drink!" Laronda mutters, fanning herself with her palm, so Chiyoko, Laronda, and I head back to the stations and get tall glasses. We grab some seats along the wall and take a break while a really hard and fast track plays.

As I rest, and people-watch, I am constantly vigilant of a certain Command Pilot in the crowd. I see him at last—he walks in a small group with Oalla and Keruvat, as they make their way along the walkway.

Immediately my heartbeat speeds up again, and I stare. Frankly, I'm surprised he is still here—or is it that he's just arrived?

No matter.

I can't be sure if he's seen me yet. But Laronda sitting next to me definitely sees him.

She elbows me. "Gwen? Look! That's *him*, your gorgeous CP!" she whispers in my ear.

"Yeah," I whisper back.

"Ooooh! I think he's coming this way!"

"No, he's not," I mutter, as I feel my cheeks flushing instantly, on cue, damn it. . . .

"Yes, he is!"

Oh, crap, just hush, hush, Laronda. . . .

But she's right.

Aeson Kassiopei, sharp and handsome in his formal white Fleet uniform, sees me from a good distance across the walkway, and our gazes lock.

He grows very still.

My breath catches in my throat.

And then I see him turn briefly and say something to the other Pilots with him. In the next heartbeat, he separates from them, and starts walking through the crowd, directly toward us.

Toward *me*.

Laronda instantly gets up and gives me a meaningful look. "Chiyoko," she says to the other girl. "Come with me, I want to get another drink and see what the guys at the sound station are doing. Let's go, girl! Gwen, you sit—we'll be right back!"

And Laronda drags Chiyoko away, throwing me another meaningful glance.

Wow, Laronda!

I remain alone, sitting at the wall.

In moments, Aeson Kassiopei stands before me. His expression is carefully veiled, but his gaze takes me in with intensity—all of me, golden dress, glittering hair, subtle makeup. I think he must like what he sees because a faint trace of color appears on his cheeks.

"Lark . . ." he says. His voice is steady, composed.

"Command Pilot. . . ." My voice is as neutral as I can make it.

And suddenly, without asking, he sits down in the closest empty seat next to me.

There is a weird moment as my eyes widen, while I stare straight ahead of me.

And then, with my peripheral vision, I see his face is turned and he is watching me closely . . . and saying nothing.

"I'm surprised you're still here at the Dance," I say, because I have to say something. "I thought you hated these things."

"For the most part, yes, I prefer to leave as quickly as possible." He continues looking at me as he speaks, so that now I feel I must turn also and face him.

"I suppose you have to dance so much at Court," I mutter.

"Yes . . . too much."

There is an awkward pause.

"So," he says, looking slightly away and down, as though examining the floor. "How does it feel? A week remains. A week of *freedom*, and then we arrive in Atlantis."

"I don't know." I watch his fringe of dark eyelashes as they come down to shield his eyes. "Not sure what to think, actually. My fate, all of our fates as Earth refugees—they are the great unknown. At least you can return to your home and normal life."

"Ah. My *normal* life. . . ." He looks up again and his lapis blue eyes are suddenly vulnerable, tragic. "My normal life indeed awaits."

"I understand." I nod. "You must have so many unimaginable duties, so much additional responsibility . . . being who you are."

"And who am I?" he says, as his eyes bore into mine, his

gaze overwhelming me with its force, so that I have to blink.

"You are—the Imperial Crown Prince," I say.

"Yes," he says. "It is who I *am*. I may play at everything else—soldier, commander, pilot. But the one thing that I cannot escape is the fate of Imperial Kassiopei." And he grows silent with a bitter smirk. I have never seen him so strangely open, as he is in these bizarre moments.

"Gravity changing now!"

The playful disembodied voice of the Music Mage comes from the air around us. And immediately the beat of the music slows down while a physical sense of falling intrudes on our strange conversation.

I watch the strands of Aeson Kassiopei's pale metallic gold hair begin to float lightly at his slightest movement, his very breath. . . .

My own hair rises also as I turn my head, swept up by the low gravity.

"But there must be so many wonderful aspects about being who you are," I say softly after that small pause. "So much good that you can do for all your people with the power at your disposal. . . ."

"Oh, yes. Always so optimistic, Lark." He looks at me sideways with a sarcastic disdainful smile. "First and foremost, I can do what all Kassiopei do, and that is, perpetuate the bloodline. All that precious Imperial genetic material must not go to waste."

I frown slightly, with the tense effort of maintaining the impossible talk. "Is it true," I say, "that you have to get married soon?"

He blinks, looks down at his hands, flexes his long elegant fingers. "Yes." And then he turns to me, again watching me sideways, while individual strands of his golden hair float like cobwebs over his shoulder. "I will announce my beautiful Bride as soon as we arrive in Atlantis. What do you think about that, Lark?"

"I—" my breath stumbles, while my heart lurches painfully in my chest. "I wish you all happiness and all the best. Congratulations. . . . You must love each other very much. . . ."

"Oh, yes," he replies, with a strange expression. "Lady

Tirinea Fuorai and I . . . we are—" His words trail away.

"I think I saw you speaking to her once," I interject softly, awkwardly. "She seems very beautiful, amazing."

He smiles suddenly, a faint ghost smile. "Oh, she *is*." He speaks each word with a measured, barely-leashed force, all the while looking at me with a strange hard gaze. "And I can't wait to see her, as soon as we get back. . . . Even now, I want to hold her with my hands . . . feel her mouth against my teeth, and press her against the wall—"

My heart is beating so violently that I feel I'm about to have a heart attack. At the same time a bitter horrible lump is starting to build in my throat, and it's about to burst. . . .

I am about to burst, and become a horrible pitiful thing of tears.

I continue to look at him, because it is all I can do. And I think he sees that actual change in me, the inevitability of what is happening inside me. . . .

And he stops.

"No," he says suddenly, and his voice goes dark. "I *don't* want any of it. I *don't* want *her*—not with all her beauty and riches and genetic nobility and empty false smiles. But—I *must*. I must take her as my Consort, my Bride, and eventually my Wife, and I must *breed* her relentlessly until she produces fat litters of healthy children with perfect DNA for my Father to take comfort and pride in, to know that the divine Kassiopei bloodline continues well into the next generation. . . ."

He cuts off the avalanche of words, and stands up suddenly, and his hair billows around him in an angry golden halo.

He stands before me, Phoebos Apollo. . . .

I watch him with parted lips, stunned by what he just said, while vertigo comes to overtake me as I look up, seeing his face swim above me. . . .

"Gravity changing now. . . ."

This time the words of the Music Mage slither through the air as the music slows down completely, and the low gravity starts fading into perfect weightlessness.

"Enough bitter nonsense spoken for tonight," he says in that moment, looking down at me, with a strange mix of pain and fierce intensity. "My apologies for spoiling your mood, Lark.

Have a good night."

And then he turns his back on me and starts to walk away.

But then he stops.

He turns around.

And like the force of the tide, inevitable, Aeson Kassiopei comes back, looking at me with an impossible to describe expression in his eyes.

"Oh, what's the use . . ." he mutters softly, to *himself*, making a helpless gesture with his hand.

He stops again before me, and this time reaches out with his hand, palm up. "Come, Lark," he says. "Dance with me—for the *first* and *last* time."

I glance down at his outstretched hand, and then I look up into his eyes.

I stand up, while the winds seem to gather and stir around me, and the haunting song that plays from the walls of the spherical chamber is "Caribbean Blue" by the classic artist Enya.

And I take his hand, feeling with a shock, for the first time, the warm hard grasp of his fingers closing around mine, as he leads me onto the dance floor and into the aerial realm of awe. . . .

Aeson holds me by the hand—a gentle tug is all that's required to launch us upwards over the honey lake of light below, while the floor sinks deeper down and falls away completely.

And then he pulls me closer, and suddenly I feel his other hand, strong and warm, come around my waist . . . and the mere touch sends shivers of electric charges throughout me, like concentric waves made by a stone cast into a lake.

His hands . . . touching me.

We start circling gently to the ethereal rhythm of the waltz, and he pulls me in closer and closer with each turn, so that now his golden hair is mingling with my dark locks, and his face is inches away from mine, as he stares directly into my eyes with his clear blue ones. We are enclosed in a cocoon of floating strands and melody, and I feel his breath wash softly over my lips until I tremble with sweet honey agony that I don't even understand. . . .

I am *nothing*, a weightless thing of air and breath, and all he has to do is pull me in closer yet, to close the distance of just another microscopic space between us that's separating us, and I will *dissolve* into him. . . . Because right now, while it still exists, that tiny distance is the equivalent of infinity.

My hand that's held tightly in his is now *on fire* with the overwhelming flood of sensation and warmth coursing between us. And my other hand rests on his shoulder, trembling fingers tangled in his soft golden strands of hair. . . .

Oh, pull me in, my thoughts race in a fever, even as we soar toward the ceiling, where the honey flow of light has turned to rich deep amber—ripe, sweet light.

Closer, closer, please. . . .

I watch his face, mesmerized. It has grown soft and slack with a gentle *intimate* expression that's intended only for *me*.

"Lark . . ." he whispers, his breath washing against my lips, just as we rise close enough to touch the ceiling with its orbs of champagne bubbles and vines of cascading grapes.

And still holding my waist tightly, he lets go of my hand and suddenly brushes his fingertips against the side of my cheek, making me tremble, while sweet fever rises, in dissonant tendrils of chills and heat, buzzing inside me.

I see him in that moment of strange fragmented time . . . a sweet golden-haired boy with wise old eyes, a young man with a burning gaze of a child, a cold prince of blue ice and immeasurable distance, a selfless silent hero with a black band worn only by the ancient dead. . . . He is all of them and more, because he looks at me now, indomitable like a mountain and yet so *lost*—looks *inside* me, and through me, and somehow he *knows* me in that instant, more than I know myself.

"This cannot end," he whispers, following the trail of his fingers with his breath, as he speaks close into my ear, words like drops of rain, softly falling.

His eyes . . . they are perfectly *desperate* and perfectly clear.

In that moment at last I *know* him also.

My lungs expand raggedly with each inhalation. I shudder as I see the dying light in him, and I want to weep suddenly.

"Please . . ." I say. And I don't even know what I'm asking.

Please don't let go....

In response, his hand tightens around my waist. Our mingling breath and the air between us, it is now my entire world.

"Lark..." he repeats again, and he is drowning. "I—"

"Gravity changing now!"

I've never hated a phrase so much as I hate this simple one now, because it cuts him off, and indicates the end.

The end of the song.

The end of the haunting music.

The end of our beginning and any possibilities.

At once gravity starts to bloom, and with a shudder we both grasp each other's hands and begin the soft descent, at the same time as the floor starts rising up gently toward us.

All the meanwhile as we slow down our circling, he continues to watch me, with a raw, intimate, hopeless gaze.

At last we stand on the dance floor. Breathing, breathing....

He still holds one of my hands, as he leads me back to the perimeter walkway.

Here he stops and looks at me again.

"Thank you for the dance, Lark," he says.

"Thank you..." I echo him softly. My voice has lost all its resonance and is leached of energy. I feel his *loss* already, the fading of the touch and the growing distance.

But then he says something that makes me pause and freeze in place.

"Whatever has happened between you and Sangre," he says, "I hope it did not hurt you deeply. I am very sorry about it. You deserve to be happy. Whatever has happened, it is none of my business—"

"*You* happened," I say suddenly, finding my voice.

He grows still. And his eyes are wide-open, startled, vulnerable things.

"*You* happened between us," I repeat. "Logan and I broke up because of *you*."

His lips part. He blinks.

I'm not sure if it is astonishment or some other *insight*.

And then he only shakes his head, and nods to me. The next

instant, without saying another word, he turns away and begins walking swiftly through the crowd.

I remain standing, lost without him, while tears well up, blinding me, until everything in the world blurs. . . .

Chapter 44

I'm not sure what I am doing, still standing motionless and blurry-eyed, when Laronda and Chiyoko come upon me.

"Gwen!" Laronda says, immediately noticing my state. "Hey, girl, are you all right? What happened?" And she puts her hand gently on my shoulder, leaning in close to my ear.

I pull in a deep shuddering breath, and smile forcibly while carefully wiping parts of my face with my fingertips, so as not to smear the fabulous makeup that is now soaking up my tears.

"Oh, I'm, fine!" I lie blatantly, mostly for Chiyoko's sake, since I'm certain Laronda has a very good idea of what's really going on. "Sorry, I was just having a crazy moment there—heard a song that reminded me of Earth and home, and you know how it is—instant tear gusher!" And I snort and shake my head.

Laronda nods wisely, continuing to hold her hand on my shoulder, and then rubs it gently in circles. "Oh yeah, I know what you mean—happens to me all the time. I hear songs, snatches of dialogue that Cadets quote from holo-movies, even tiny little stupid things set me off. So, yeah, no problem. Take your time, girl. . . ."

"Thanks." I smile, then grin widely. "Okay, enough of me being a mush-ball. . . ."

"Yeah, well, you know, we were just hanging out with your Atlantean buddies Gennio and Vazara," Laronda says, picking up the conversation with great skill. "And also with that awful little prick Anu—my gawd! He's like—what is *wrong* with him?"

Chiyoko snorts and shakes her head. "Oh, yes. This Anu guy is really crazy!"

I shake my head and laugh with them, regaining my breath, forcing myself to be in the here and now, to push away all traces of what had happened between me and Kassiopei. With superhuman effort, I contain all thoughts of *him* deep inside, to be processed *later*.

"Anu is an acquired taste," I say lightly.

Laronda widens her eyes and rolls them. "Sweet lord, yes! Roadkill with horseradish! Seriously, why does your Command Pilot tolerate him?"

My Command Pilot. . . .

No, don't think.

"Well," I muse. "To be honest, I think on some level Anu is very smart and skilled at his job, believe it or not. But also, secretly, I think Anu kind of entertains him."

"He's a koo-koo clown, that's for sure," Laronda mutters. "That boy is *messed up!*"

"Okay, enough about Anu," I exclaim, as an out-of-control churning wave of emotion passes through me, and I must do something, anything to put it down. "Let's dance, guys! I think that's my song they're playing!"

And off we go, back onto the dance floor.

We dance for close to two hours, taking minor breaks. At some point during a zero gravity dance, Gracie and Blayne join us, and we all spin around the great honey-colored dome ceiling, holding hands, touching fingertips, and reaching to feel the glowing orbs attached to the panels, just because we *can*. What a strange glorious sensation, to fly through the air with friends!

"Gravity changing now!" the Music Mage whispers mischievously, and as gravity returns, we descend.

Blayne gets back on the hoverboard and Gracie fusses around him to make sure he is settled properly, while he glances at her with one raised brow. "Seriously, Lark Two, you may chill, I got this," he says at last, but his mouth quivers with amusement.

"*Im nefira . . .* Gwen!"

I turn around and there's Xelio. He is dressed in his sharp white Fleet uniform, and his long midnight hair is loose tonight, gorgeously unrestrained. Looks like he's just arrived late.

Better late than never. . . .

"So, did you save me a dance, golden goddess?" he says, stepping closer and giving me a long appreciative perusal.

I smile, while an energizing pleasant charge of energy comes to me—something I always feel around Xelio. "Of course, Xel!" I respond, with an almost flirty tone in my voice—and why the hell not? I no longer have anything to lose.

But. . . . Just for a moment, the deeply suppressed wave of despair comes overflowing upward inside me. However, I control it. . . .

And I smile at Xelio Vekahat and take his hand, allowing him to lead me in the swaying rhythm and beat of the music pulsing around us.

I leave the Yellow Dance close to midnight, with Laronda and Gracie following me to my cabin to get their things before boarding the shuttles for their own ark-ships.

Chiyoko says bye to us and heads to her own Cadet Barracks in the Green Quadrant.

As I hug Gracie, Laronda gives me a meaningful glance and promises to call me so that we can talk about things later. I nod at her, barely having the energy to maintain my happy front for Gracie's sake.

I need to be alone right now.

They leave, and I sit down on my bunk. I sit without moving for long minutes, and eventually the cabin lights go out, because the sensors no longer detect living motion.

They are correct.

I am dead inside. And the tears streaming down my face, they are just running water. . . .

But it gets worse.

Because I remember suddenly that today, based on the Earth calendar, is my birthday.

I just turned eighteen.

And no one, including myself, knew or cared about it.

The next morning, after a mostly sleepless night—made worse by the fact that I was plagued by thoughts of coming of age and everything that goes with it—I resolve to hold myself together for the remaining days on this journey to Atlantis.

I go in to work at the CCO at 8:00 AM, steeling myself for that initial moment of seeing Aeson Kassiopei after what had happened last night.

But he comes in wearing his own full suit of emotional armor—composed, cool, remote. He barely acknowledges me with an icy glance that is unreadable, and then works at his desk for half an hour, ignoring me and the other two aides. Eventually he gets up and leaves to do ship inspections, and is gone for the rest of the day.

Around dinner, I get a brief one-sentence email from Kassiopei that my voice lesson for that night is cancelled. Not a word of explanation or apology.

But somehow, it acts as the closest thing to what I might hope to have from him as a living human reaction—he can't deal with me right now, I get it.

I can't deal with him either.

And so I spend another numb evening alone in my cabin—thinking, planning I don't know what for myself and my siblings here in the Fleet and my family back on Earth—our vaporous future, maybe?—and constantly imagining what would happen only a few days from now when we land on the surface of the planet Atlantis.

In the morning, just before shipboard dawn, around 5:41 AM, I am awakened from a feverish shallow sleep by the voice of the computer.

"Ten second warning. . . . Interstellar space ends. . . . Now entering Helios solar system heliosphere. . . ."

I bolt awake and sit up, almost hitting my head against the bulkhead.

Oh, wow! I think. *We are now in the solar system of Helios, also known as Hel, the sun of Atlantis!*

Which means that approximately five days remain until we reach the orbit of our new home planet.

It's pretty much impossible to go back to sleep after that, and so I'm up early, feverishly recalling what I've been told about the structure of Hel's system.

In a nutshell, Helios is a radiant white star, about 10%

larger and 25% brighter than Earth's Sol, and it's orbited by five rocky planets including Atlantis (unlike Sol which has four—Mercury, Venus, Earth, Mars), and two gas giants (again, unlike Sol which has four—Jupiter, Saturn, Uranus, Neptune).

Hel's rocky planets in order of proximity to it are: Rah, Septu, Tammuz, Ishtar, Atlantis. And then come the two gas giants, Olympos and Atlas.

At the rate of our deceleration approach, we will likely be in the vicinity of Atlas's orbital region some time tomorrow.

On that same first day of our entry into Hel's solar system, the Fleet goes on general alert and all the ark-ships begin implementing the early stages of the arrival procedures.

Today is our last day of classes, after which we are going to be having interviews with our commanding officers and receiving our various placement instructions.

All class sessions are brief, and are mostly summaries and final thoughts given us by our Instructors. In Pilot Training, Chiyoko and I listen nervously as Instructor Mithrat Okoi tells us that all Cadets will receive specific Fleet assignment options during their career interview.

"I will be putting in my personal recommendations in your files which will then be reviewed by your commanding officers," Instructor Okoi says, pacing the classroom. "My recommendations carry fifty percent weight, and the rest will be up to your commanding officers. If you have any questions, you may see me after class today, or any time up to your interviews which happen starting tomorrow. Good luck, Cadets! You have come a long way since our first class many months ago. Many of you will make excellent, first rate Pilots, officers and crew. And now, dismissed!"

We salute and exit, as the Instructor watches us with his grim, serious gaze. For some reason he looks *affected*—if only for a brief fleeting moment. Indeed, it seems to me that Mithrat Okoi feels far more than he ever lets on. And right now, his gaze is telling us goodbye.

My Language class is next. Instructor Chior Kla speaks to us in pure *Atlanteo*, and surprisingly, after all these months of conversational practice, I and the rest of the class actually understand most of what she is saying. It's a strange feeling to hear the lilting beautiful language and feel the meaning coalesce at last.

"May you find and attain all your fondest wishes and dreams when you arrive on your new home, *Atlantida*," Instructor Kla says in her beautiful, emotionally charged voice. "You might be afraid and worried now, but you will be pleasantly surprised by what you'll find. Now that you are speaking our language, you will understand our thought processes so much better, and it will help you adjust. Think of it as another useful tool. Use the language well!"

And later on, in Culture class, we get a very similar sentiment from Instructor Nilara Gradat. "I have no doubt, you will fall in love, and so will the people of Atlantis when they meet all of you," she says to us, in parting. "It has been an unforgettable experience for me personally to have taken this journey with you, to Earth and back. Please, do not hesitate to keep in touch with me after we land. I will leave my personal contact instructions for you. In my regular life I teach at the Lyceum School in the coastal city Thetis Nereo, so if you are ever in the area, please come see me!"

Meanwhile, in Technology and Systems class, once again held in the garden paradise that is Hydroponics, Klavit Xotoi, our Tech instructor, gives us an inspirational rundown of career options for technically inclined Civilians. "You can apply for entry level jobs in most of our industries, as soon as we land," he says. "Or you can enroll in more advanced courses to get better positions. My recommendation is to take that entry level work and at the same time attend extra training courses in your off hours, especially if you decide to stay and make your home in the capital, Poseidon, or the provinces. You have many options, and as Earth refugees who have proven your various talents and skills simply by Qualifying for Atlantis, you will be in demand. Good luck, everyone!"

By the end of the afternoon, I have the final Combat Training class with Oalla Keigeri. "We will go through the Twelve Forms only one time, since it is our last class," she tells us seriously.

And we do.

By now, we are quite proficient in Er-Du, and we look good doing it—double rows of Cadets sharply lined up, moving in tandem and showing fierce elegance.

I admit, I feel a twinge of pride that I'm one of the better students here. Especially since my one-on-one personal training with Xelio for the last several months, I've been showing marked improvement, and now I'm possibly in the top five percent of the class in Sparring and Forms, and possibly in the top twenty percent in Yellow Quadrant Weapons. I am also glad that Oalla notices and approves. I haven't had a demerit in her class for *anything*, in ages. . . .

When we finish the final Form and grow still, Oalla paces before us in silence. "You have done well, Cadets!" she says at last, in a hard ringing voice. "I am honored to have every one of you serve on my ship, if it comes to it, and to fight alongside me if necessary. My final evaluations of your performance will be logged and analyzed during your interviews tomorrow. And now, Salute, Cadets! Show me your pride with the Form Salute of *Atlantida!*"

We salute and are dismissed. Oalla stands silently watching us file out of the classroom. She wears a hard, controlled expression on her face, but just as in the case of Instructor Mithrat Okoi, I realize she is holding back emotion.

And on that note, my classes are done.

I haven't had a Court Protocol Class with Consul Denu, but he informs me we will likely be continuing the lessons for quite some time, even *after* we land on Atlantis, and that's why there is no need for a class during this busy week. "I will see you shortly, my dear," he tells me graciously in passing as I come by his residence. "Right now, you and I and everyone on board will be busy with the arrival preparations. But fear not, you will have the fair opportunity to see me before we land."

That evening there is only one thing left—my voice lesson with Kassiopei.

However, once again I receive a curt lesson cancellation email: *"No voice lesson tonight. I will see you tomorrow at this time for your final evaluation interview. —A. K."*

And as soon as I see it, I am thrown into a cold terror. . . .

This is it. The thing I've been waiting for, and working for, all year, to see if he will judge me qualified and improved enough in all my general abilities, and permit me to enter the Games of the Atlantis Grail. . . .

And then another frightening and long-suppressed memory comes to me—the mysterious detail he mentioned in our conversation after the Final Quantum Stream Race, regarding the true nature of the asteroid. "They will only send another," he had said back then. For that reason, now all my best laid plans may not even matter in the greater scheme of things.

But then, I remind myself, I still don't know *anything*, and I can only go by what I know. My best bet to save my family is still to pursue the Citizenship and the Games of the Atlantis Grail.

And so I resolve to stand firm when I talk to the CP tomorrow.

Right now, my family is all I have left—the last ray of hope left to me, in the general sea of despair in which I've been living for these past several days since we danced the dance that broke my heart.

Chapter 45

The next day I spend waiting with trepidation for my evening interview with Kassiopei. When I go in to the CCO in the morning, the CP is not there, and according to Anu, he's dealing with Storage deck procedures, as the crew is getting ready to begin the long and careful process of unloading everything as soon as we achieve Atlantis orbit in about three days from now.

"They have to plan very extensively how to unload," Gennio adds. "The process is not just a reversal of the loading procedure. They also have to account for *where* the things will end up and in what order."

"What do you mean?" I say.

"Well, some of the things will be delivered on different continents. Also, some things will have to wait until the more favorable weather conditions are on the surface. . . . For example, different parts of the seed bank that contains all the specimens of the plant life and animal species on Earth, will be delivered to different landing sites for proper storage."

"I see."

He nods. "And the great works of Art from Earth will be divided between various museums in different cities. I believe the Imperial Poseidon Museum will take in most of your Leonardo da Vinci, Michelangelo, and Rembrandt into their permanent collection. On the other hand, the Sekar Mehet Museum will take Sandro Botticelli, Vincent van Gogh, the Terracotta Army sculptures of Qin Shi Huang, the complete Parthenon building that will be eventually reassembled on site—"

"Wow!" I exclaim.

"—and the whole Great Pyramid of Giza, which of course

took up the storage capacity of an entire ark-ship, just to house its components—"

"Wow!"

Gennio smiles. "Oh, yes, don't worry, we saved nearly everything."

For some reason it occurs to me to ask: "What about the two paintings from the Huntington in California? 'Pinkie' and 'Blue Boy?'"

"I can look it up right now." Gennio keys in something on his console and nods. "Yes, here they are, works by Thomas Lawrence and Thomas Gainsborough. They're currently on Ark-Ship 845, Storage Deck section 57."

I put my hand up to my mouth, as a welling of tears nearly overpowers me.

Gennio looks at me kindly, and then adds, "It will make you happy to know that we have safely in storage the entire contents of the Huntington Library and Art Gallery. Though, I am sorry we could not take the Botanical Gardens."

I break down and bawl.

The day drags on, and then it's 8:00 PM and time for my evaluation interview.

I arrive at the CCO with my heart pounding in my chest, and a cold sweat is breaking out even before I enter the office.

Aeson Kassiopei is at his desk, with two monitor screens active, but he appears distracted. He sees me and immediately his expression hardens and becomes inscrutable.

"Come in, Lark," he says coldly. "Take a seat."

I silently approach and take my usual chair before his desk. My palms are sweating, my forehead is damp, and I feel like I'm about to faint with terror.

Aeson glances at me once, then makes a point of looking at something on one of his screens.

"I have here," he says, "your official record. It now includes the notes and recommendations from all your Instructors."

"Okay," I mutter.

He turns and looks directly at me, for a long silent moment. I meet his gaze and it's like staring at the sun. I cannot endure it.

"Would you like to know what your Instructors think?" he asks, and it seems his voice is taunting me.

"Yes. . . ."

"Very well. Overall, your scores are very good across the board. Your Pilot Training Instructor Mithrat Okoi tells me that judging by your drastic rate of improvement combined with your demonstrated abilities, you would make a fine Cadet. He also recommends for you to formally apply to Fleet School and he'll give you a personal recommendation to advance you to second year level accelerated instruction. He gives you a 4 out of 5 possible score."

"Oh, wow," I say, trying not to look into his eyes for too long because I just *can't*. "Is that good?"

"A four is very good. Instructor Okoi is a harsh judge and does not give fives at all, with a few rare exceptions. I know, because he was my instructor too, when I was a Cadet in Fleet School."

"Oh, really?" And immediately I wonder what score Kassiopei himself received as a young Cadet. "So, who were the exceptions, if I may ask?"

For one moment Aeson seems uncomfortable. And then he says, "One of the exceptions was someone you know—Xelio Vekahat. Okoi gave Xel a five for excellence."

I feel a tiny smile gathering on my lips at the thought of Xelio. "I can certainly believe that," I say. "Makes all kinds of sense."

Aeson Kassiopei watches my fleeting smile and my reaction, and he blinks. "Speaking of Xelio Vekahat—he is not your formal Instructor, but I'm aware that he's been helping you train and work out on a regular basis."

"Oh, yes." I nod. "Xelio has helped me improve my Er-Du Forms tremendously, and he's been training me with weapons too."

"Good," Aeson says, glancing away from me and back at the display screen. I notice his voice has become hard, resonant. "Because I have here some informal recommendations from Xelio, and he tells me he thinks *you are spectacular, superlative, and are ready for any challenge you might take on*—his words, not mine."

My face erupts with a sudden blush. "Wow... I had no idea he thinks so highly of me."

Command Pilot Kassiopei watches me with a strange expression. "Surprising that you might not *know* what Xel thinks of you," he says suddenly.

He is jealous!

"Well, no," I backtrack, as my face blushes a deeper red. "I know that Xel seems to enjoy my company, I just had no idea he thought so highly of my fighting abilities. I find it super encouraging actually!"

"Fine—moving on." Aeson simply nods, and continues as though this is of little consequence. "Your Culture Instructor Nilara Gradat tells me you stand out because you ask so many good questions, and recommends you for any field you might choose, but particularly in communications. She does not give out formal grades, but gives you the equivalent of a 5 out of 5. So does your Language Instructor Chior Kla, who thinks your linguistic abilities are superior, and you have become very proficient in *Atlanteo*—"

"Oh, no," I say, somewhat flustered. "I hardly think I can speak it at all. In fact I don't think I'm ready to even ask for directions on the street—"

He raises one brow. "Regardless, you get 5 out of 5 from Instructor Kla."

I bite my lip and listen.

"Next, I have your Combat Instructor Oalla Keigeri. Oalla thinks you have improved tremendously and come a long way. She gives you a 4 out of 5 and thinks you can be a Cadet easily. However she makes a note here that she believes you will likely not become a Cadet because your interests are too varied—and yes, she knows all about your so-called greater aspirations—so she withholds her recommendation until you make up your mind and make the required effort to choose the Fleet over other career options."

He glances at me, to gauge my reaction, but I remain silent.

"Finally," he says, "I have here the glowing recommendation from Consul Denu, who does not give a grade but thinks you have the intelligence, flexibility, and cleverness to do very well as a public servant. Coming from Consul Denu, this is high praise indeed."

"Oh," I say. "Please relay my deepest thanks to the Consul."

"Relay them yourself," he says with a shadow of a smile.

I nod. "I will."

There is a pause. Aeson swings both display screens out of the way and faces me, with his hands palms down on the desk surface. "Now," he says. "My own evaluation."

My heartbeat lurches wildly. I clench my hands underneath the desk.

"Lark." His voice is composed and neutral. "It is an undisputed fact that you are bright, intelligent, and extraordinarily talented. Your achievements with the Logos voice are so far beyond the norm that I will not bother to give you a grade—not because I am unwilling, but because I'm simply incapable of evaluating you properly at such a high level. What you did with the Quantum Stream alone puts your abilities in a separate category. So, more of your voice training will be continued on Atlantis, but with dedicated specialist experts other than myself."

"You will no longer train me?" I say, forgetting to be nervous and suddenly feeling a terror of a different sort.

"No." He briefly glances down at his hands, taps his fingers against the desk lightly. "In fact, I will no longer see you on a regular basis."

"Oh. . . ." The sinking feeling washes over me, a dark wave of despair.

He looks up at me. "Officially, you are still a part of my staff, an Aide to the CCO, at least until designated otherwise by the Imperator. However, I don't expect you'll be in that position for long. As soon as we land, you will be introduced to your voice related duties, in addition to any career choice you might make. And yes, at some point you will be admitted before my Father at the Imperial Court—to that end you will continue to study with Consul Denu, to perfect your facility with Imperial Court Protocol. But for the moment, you have a choice before you."

He pauses, resuming the movement of his fingers along the surface of the desk. "So, what will it be, Lark? Cadet or

Civilian?"

I furrow my brow and face him. And I begin to speak in a careful measured voice, because what I'm saying *now* is about to determine *everything*. "Command Pilot Kassiopei, I choose neither. I still choose to become a Citizen. You said, back at the beginning of this journey, that at the end of the year you will evaluate my abilities, and as you can see I have come a long way. So, with your kind permission, I am going to enter the Games of the Atlantis Grail as I've always planned."

A long terrifying moment of silence, during which he looks at me, cold as ice.

"No," he says. "You will *not*. Gwen Lark, after reviewing your abilities and your personal record, I officially forbid you. And my decision is *final*. So I ask you again—Cadet or Civilian?"

Like a sudden twister falling out of the sky, fury rises inside me. I am so angry that I feel my head spin with vertigo. I open my mouth and take a deep breath, just to hold down the wild madness inside me. And then I lean forward, hands still clenched under my desk, now becoming white-knuckled fists.

"Command Pilot," I say, enunciating every word with barely controlled violence. "I have worked a whole *year*. . . . I did *everything* that was asked of me, and I have fought for this opportunity with every breath in my body. . . . So the *least* you can do is tell me *why*—why you cut off the last bit of hope left to me, why you make this *stone-cold* decision, knowing that it means *everything*?"

"I don't *have* to explain anything to you, Lark," he replies, leaning forward also, and staring at me with terrifying eyes.

"Well, then," I say with a sneer, "I suppose I don't have to explain anything to *you* either, when I *spit* on your 'decision' and simply do what I planned to do all along!"

I start to rise out of my seat. I am so mindlessly angry now, I cannot breathe. . . . And in that crazy moment I don't *care* if I die—I don't care what he does to me, how he punishes me, what he says. . . .

"Stop!" His power voice cuts through the blinding fury roiling in my mind. And although it does not affect me on any level, it breaks through the hurricane inside me enough to give

me a moment of clarity.

"Sit down," he says with force. "I understand the emotional state you're in right now, and it has blinded you to reason. For that, I will cut you some slack. But if you continue—if you do *anything* that goes against my decision, I will have you restrained and incarcerated as soon as we land on Atlantis. Do you understand? You will *not* disobey me!"

Like hell I won't....

I return to my seat and tremble, while fury continues to ride me, in waves of darkness. *Command Pilot Kassiopei, you have no idea.... You just wait and see ...* I think, starting to seethe, almost gleefully, on the inside. *You wait and see....*

I do not *accept this ... I do not....*

He watches me—watches me shaking. Does he suspect what's going on inside me? Apparently it does not matter. Because he remains unresponsive, like stone ... waiting.

And then my elemental fury runs its course.

Just like that.

Grim *reality* sets in.

And with it, something else, something *worse* happens to me, at this sight of him, stone-cold, silent, waiting for me to get a grip....

My throat, oh God, no!

Suddenly the painful lump is rising, gagging me, and with it, all the pent up pressure of tears, the result of anger, hopelessness, perfect despair. Everything has come together in a perfect storm—the absolute loss of *him* (not that there ever was any hope in that department, who am I fooling), the no longer deniable loss of *control* over my ability to help my family back on Earth, the fact that even if I *could*, it would probably make little difference, since the asteroid event is an unresolved mystery far more complex than we were given to believe....

All I can do now is become a Cadet or Civilian and do the best I can with my paltry life to make sure my sister Gracie and brother Gordie achieve their personal goals and have the best life possible on their new world.

Because that's all I have now—my two siblings.

And as far as my personal life, I have *nothing*.

Yes, I am being dramatic, I know. I will probably get a

decent job in Atlantis, and I might live a reasonably fulfilling life, and even find someone I can care about.

But it would be a different Gwen Lark, a dead and dull and mediocre one who does all these things instead of doing *all she could*.

Because right now, I am at a loss. I've lost the fight, lost *everything*—even more than he suspects—and all I can do now is hold back those tears.

Meanwhile, my beloved, perfectly cruel commanding officer continues watching me. And after a few seconds of silence and me struggling not to cry, he says: "The default choice is Civilian. If you do not make your decision by the time we land, I am recording you officially as a Civilian. Think well about what you are going to do with your life."

I nod silently, and I still make no sound. Because if I so much as open my mouth or modulate my breath, the dam of tears will burst. . . .

"Fine," he says softly at last. "We are done with the interview. You may go."

I stand up, feeling my head reeling with vertigo. And I leave the CCO.

That night, I call up Gracie and then try my brother Gordie, just to make sure they are both well. They are now my life, and I am their surrogate mother.

Gracie sounds fine, and she tells me her career interview went very well. "Can you believe it, Gee Two, I might get a Fleet assignment in the capital city itself, Poseidon, which is supposed to be highly desirable!" Gracie tells me, grinning into the screen. "Blayne thinks we'll probably get to find out very soon. After we land, we're supposed to report directly to the nearest Fleet Cadet Headquarters—"

I smile and nod and listen to her talk.

And then I chat with Gordie, who tells me he'll be likely staying in Poseidon too, depending on whether he likes it when he gets there. I have a feeling much of his "decision" depends upon a certain girl and her decisions—but I don't press poor Gordie on it, letting him have his dignity for now.

Then, I decide to talk to Laronda. I call her and she picks up immediately, with her noisy Barracks in the background.

We talk. First I ask her about her plans, which are reasonably solid—settle in, probably in Poseidon, get a good post with the Fleet, where, not entirely sure yet, et cetera.

And then I tell her nearly everything about what's happening with me. I tell her what happened at the Yellow Dance, and then what happened at my interview.

I tell her I will likely not see Kassiopei at all after we arrive.

Laronda listens to me gently, patiently, as my gusher tears begin to come again. And eventually I shudder with weeping, until I can cry no more.

Laronda puts her fingers up to her lips, and then presses them against the display screen, willing her kiss to transfer to me.

Afterwards, long after I disconnect our call, I sit in the cabin in silence.

At some point near midnight, the voice of the ship's computer intrudes upon my abysmal emptiness.

"Now entering Atlas orbital aphelion. . . ."

And then, about a minute later:

"Now leaving Atlas orbital perihelion. . . ."

But I ignore it, and instead pull down my sheet and blanket and get into bed.

As the Fleet continues to move closer and closer to Atlantis with every second, I sink into a dreamless abyss of sleep.

Chapter 46

The next morning, just three days before our arrival on Atlantis, I endure breakfast without any appetite, and then drag myself over to the CCO at 8:00 AM. I see that neither the CP, nor Gennio are here yet, while Anu looks very agitated.

"The Imperator just called!" he tells me with utmost dramatic importance. "He wants to speak with the Imperial Crown Prince immediately!"

"What's wrong?" I say with alarm.

"I have no idea! But I think I need to get the CP, right *now*."

Fortunately Aeson Kassiopei arrives within the next minute, and Anu starts talking in rapid *Atlanteo* to him, and all I can catch is that it's urgent and the Imperator seems more intense than usual.

"All right, I will call him," Aeson says, glancing from Anu to me. "Now, both of you—out in the hall."

And he points to the door.

We hurry outside, where we spend the next fifteen minutes milling around the corridor, hanging out with the guards, until Gennio gets there, and Anu informs him with pomp about the Imperator's call.

Eventually we are allowed to return inside the office.

When we walk in, the Command Pilot appears grim and upset. He paces, then stands near the desk, and does not speak immediately, and I can see his chest rise and fall with each breath. And then he looks directly at me.

"Lark," he says with dark intensity. "And both of you too—Vei, Rukkat. Major change of plans. We don't get a leisurely arrival. Instead, as soon as we arrive in orbit, we—the four of us plus Consul Denu and a few other officers—are all going to take a shuttle directly to the Imperial Palace in Poseidon. The Imperator has informed me that he will be holding Court on the same evening as our arrival, and I *have* to be there. Also, Lark, *you* have to be there too—apparently my Father has been informed in detail about you, Lark—about your voice, and quite a few other things. And he expects you to be brought before him immediately."

"Oh, wow . . . ." I say.

"Her voice?" Anu says, staring at me. "What's with her voice?"

"Nothing," I say.

"Later," Aeson says, with a dismissive motion of his hand to Anu.

At this point I am forced to remember that neither Anu nor Gennio know about my voice and its abilities.

"So . . . what does this mean?" I say, watching Aeson's grave expression. "What do I need to do?"

"You need to be ready to leave with us as soon as we arrive," he replies sharply, breathing hard—so much so that my eyes widen. Why is he so unsettled? "Have your personal belongings ready to go on a moment's notice."

My pulse starts racing with stress. "Okay. . . . What about my sister and brother?"

He shakes his head. "They will be brought down to join you later. Inform them that you are leaving early, ahead of the rest of the Fleet, and they are to wait until further instructions. That is all."

"But—" I begin.

"That is *all*," he repeats in a hard voice that borders on a power voice.

Wow. . . . I have never seen Kassiopei so agitated. Not even during our most emotional confrontations.

"Yes, Command Pilot," Gennio and Anu both hurry to say.

And then for the rest of the day the CP makes calls, speaking in a commanding voice to various personnel, then leaves the office for various meetings and inspections.

Gennio, Anu, and I have the presence of mind to take care and not to get in his way.

That evening I spend in my cabin talking to Gracie and Gordie, explaining the situation and my sudden new orders.

"OMG, you get to see the Imperial Palace on your first day!" Gracie exclaims.

"Not only the Palace, but the Imperator himself!" I remind her.

"Crap! What will you wear to Court, Gee Two?"

"I have no idea." I sigh tiredly. "And for now I'm not going to worry about it."

And then I look at Gracie. "You stay put, sis. Everything is going to be okay, you'll see. This is just a weird quick introduction to Atlantis, I realize. But, it will be okay."

"I know. . . ." She nods. But she does not look calm at all.

As for Gordie, he is not near his video screen as usual, so I leave him a detailed message explaining the situation of my early departure.

And then I get to bed early, because honestly, I can't take the stress and uncertainty any more, and the sooner it all happens, the better.

The next day—two days before our arrival in Atlantis—is mostly inconsequential. I have no classes, my work duties are light, and I can barely focus on anything. Kassiopei is mostly absent from the CCO, and about the only interesting thing that happens is around late afternoon. That's when the ship's computer announces that we are passing the orbital range of Olympos, the second of the gas giants.

Which means that, next up, is Atlantis itself. . . .

I spend a lot of that day on the ICS-2 Observation Deck, together with so many other Earth refugees. We stand and stare at Hel, a large radiant white star that is much brighter than Earth's Sol, and which now prominently resides in the viewport windows outside.

Atlantis is the fifth planet from Hel, and its orbit is at a greater distance than Earth is from the Sun, with a longer year. Because of Hel's size and brightness, the extra distance is actually a good thing—it allows the conditions that make it hospitable for life and similar to Earth.

"Please take care not to look at it directly for too long," we are warned by Atlanteans. "Even with the safety shields enabled, because of its particular brightness, vision damage can occur."

"What happens when we are on Atlantis?" someone asks. "What if we stare at Hel from the surface?"

"Not recommended," the Atlantean crew member replies. "Besides, you will all be issued strong sunglasses which you will be required to wear every time you go outside during daylight hours, for at least the first year of your arrival, until your eyes get better acclimated to the bright daylight glare."

"Well, drat, how bad is it?"

"Not too bad. But, it is a healthy precaution. And you will eventually get sufficiently acclimated. However, what will take a bit longer to get used to, is the somewhat heavier gravity."

And then we are all forced to remember the information from our Culture classes, about how initially we will feel somewhat more noticeably tired after ordinary physical exertion than we would on Earth with lighter gravity.

That should not be fun at all.

Maybe that's why Atlanteans are such big fans of zero gravity dancing, I think ruefully.

At last, it's the day before our arrival on Atlantis.
First thing in the morning we get Commander Manakteon Resoi's announcement transmitted to all the ark-ships in the Fleet. Basically he tells us that we arrive in orbit around Atlantis tomorrow morning, at 7:24 AM, Earth Universal Time Coordinated, which will be the last time we will be using Earth's time clock.

After we make orbit, the Fleet will begin unloading cargo for the first three Atlantean days. Only then will the Earth refugees start being ferried down to the surface to various designated locations and different continents. More will be explained to us at that point.

Of course, none of that applies to me or the other CCO Aides.

"Your schedule is as following," the CP tells us. "We arrive in Atlantis orbit at 7:24 AM. You are permitted to watch our historical approach from the Observation Deck, together with everyone else in the Fleet. However, immediately afterwards, you are expected to be in Shuttle Bay One at 8:00 AM sharp, ready to go, with all your personal luggage. That's when we board transport shuttles, and we depart to the surface, immediately. Understood?"

"Yes," I say, and Gennio and Anu echo me.

"Good, and don't be late under any circumstances." Kassiopei's expression is grim and forceful.

We nod again.

Later that afternoon I grab dinner with Chiyoko and Blayne at the Green Quadrant Cadet Meal Hall Three, basically to say goodbye—at least for now.

"I don't know where I will end up," Chiyoko tells me thoughtfully. "It might be interesting to start with Poseidon, their capital, and then, it depends on what post I get in the Fleet."

"Same here," Blayne says, picking up his glass of *lvikao*. "Most Cadets here on ICS-2 talk about Poseidon as their destination. I don't know, sounds good to me. Especially considering we've no frigging idea what anything's really like down there. The CP told me during the eval interview that he wants me to be stationed close to the Cadet Fleet School, so that I can continue with the LM Forms demos there. So, what about you, Lark?"

I tell them that I actually have to go down to the surface early, but withhold some of the details.

"Basically, I'm part of the CCO staff, so all of us Aides have to accompany the Imperial Crown Prince to the reception or whatever Imperial Court function it is."

Blayne whistles. "Wow, fancy."

Chiyoko raises her brows in interest.

"Hmm, does that mean that Lark Two is leaving with you early also?" Blayne asks, all innocent-like.

I hold back a smile. "Actually Gracie is staying put for now. I believe she'll be coming down to the surface at the same time as all the rest of you guys—about three days later."

We chat and eat for a while longer, and then say our goodbyes, because, hey, you never know if I'll have the chance to see them again before I depart.

As I head back to my cabin in the Yellow Quadrant,

moving roundabout past the Command Deck hub area in Blue, I run into Logan Sangre in the corridor.

Logan is walking alone in his usual determined stride. The moment he sees me, he pauses, startled, and then looks at me. His gaze goes cold and intense, and for just one moment I see a flicker of pain that quickly disappears behind a well practiced mask.

My heart twinges painfully at the sight of him ... there's that instant of familiarity, of all kinds of mixed memories being dredged up.

No, don't. ...

Our gazes lock, for a moment.

He nods curtly, but says nothing.

And then he resumes walking.

I stare in his wake briefly, then also continue on my way.

The morning of our arrival on Atlantis, the daylight alarms go on an hour early. I wake up to the gentle rising illumination and squint at the clock on the wall, and it's 6:00 AM.

Good, I think. It gives us more time to get ready.

I get into the shower, get dressed, and then start quickly putting away all my belongings into the two duffel bags. By 6:45 AM I'm ready to go, and my packed bags sit side-by-side on top of the blanket covering my neatly made bunk.

A strange pang of wistfulness comes to me when I look around at this tiny ship cabin that has served as my home for the last year. ... Feels like it's my last transition link between Earth and Atlantis.

Because, whatever happens, tonight I will definitely be sleeping somewhere down on the planet surface, on Atlantis. ...

Wow.

As I'm getting a quick breakfast at the Officers Meal Hall, the familiar ship's computer voice sounds from the walls:

"*Attention all personnel. ... Thirty minute warning. ... Arrival in Atlantis orbit. ... Thirty minute warning. ...*"

I finish eating, gulp down the last of my drink and head out of the meal hall to the ICS-2 Observation Deck.

It's time to watch the approach!

Chapter 47

It's not surprising that the Imperial Command Ship Two Observation Deck is packed with people all around the perimeter of the ship, so that it's standing room only, *everywhere*.

Against the black velvet of space, thickly scattered with distant stars, Hel shines large and bright in the windows, incandescent white, and about the size of a golf ball.

We are told that since Hel's solar system is in a general cosmic region that's densely populated with stars—basically somewhere halfway to the "urban" center of this galaxy, compared to Earth's solar system which is out in the periphery, out in the distant "suburbs," being on one of the out-flung spiral arms of the Milky Way Galaxy—because of it, the night sky of Atlantis will always seem a little thicker with stars.

"When will Atlantis appear in the window?" teens ask constantly, as waves of excited mutterings travel around the deck.

"Soon!" one Atlantean officer says with a smile. "Well, actually, it's already there. It's been visible to the naked eye for at least five days now—but only if you knew where to look. Just start watching for a large green-blue dot!"

We all go nuts, staring at the windows in exited agitation.

"There!" Someone points it out at last. The reason it's been hard to see is because Atlantis appears directly in-line, on approach with Hel, whose bright coronal glare prevents visibility.

But now, that we are so close, we see it briefly in transit across the face of Hel, a dark silhouette that gains in size, right before our eyes. And then, as we approach closer, it moves in perspective so that Hel is now right next to it, and we begin to see its natural albedo.

Atlantis!

It's a green-blue marble, and in a few minutes, a green-blue golf ball.

"Attention all personnel. . . . Fifteen minute warning. . . . Arrival in Atlantis orbit in fifteen minutes. . . ."

Everyone on the observation deck cheers.

Atlantis continues to grow in size, so that now we can make out distant blots and atmospheric features in aqua green shadow-colors.

In another few more minutes, it is the size of an orange, and then a balloon.

"Look! A moon!" someone exclaims. And indeed, we see it, a small violet-grey planetary disk orbiting at a significant distance around Atlantis.

"And there's another!" a girl exclaims. "And a third!"

The second and third moon of Atlantis appear one after the other, both slightly closer to it—a blue-gray tiny ball and a silver one.

"Attention all personnel. . . . Ten minute warning. . . . Arrival in Atlantis orbit in ten minutes. . . ."

We stare with held breath as Atlantis—a gorgeous blue-green-aqua planet of white clouds and navy-dark regions to indicate oceans—swells in the windows before us, its surface features finally taking shape, while the three moons now recede off the windows due to the loss of perspective.

"Oh my God . . ." a boy says in awe. "We're really here, aren't we?"

"*¡Claro que sí!*" a girl responds.

"Five minute warning. . . . Arrival in Atlantis orbit in five minutes. . . ."

I stand, motionless and frozen, willing with all my heart to be next to my sister and brother right now, wherever they are, probably on their own ark-ship observation decks, and to hold their hands and hold them to me as we arrive, together.

Atlantis, an immense glowing sphere, stands before us now, turning slowly, filling most of the window. The atmosphere lends a soft border of light, like a nimbus, and right below, we see continents, covered with green forests and great snow-capped mountain ranges. . . . Regions of whiteness that are likely polar ice caps appear in one area. . . . Clouds float softly, and there are no turbulent weather patterns, at least none we can see from here.

"One minute warning. . . . Arrival in Atlantis orbit in fifty seconds. . . ."

"Hey," someone says. "How's the weather down there? What is it, spring, now? You know, Green season?"

A few feet away from me an Atlantean crew member laughs. "This is a big planet," he says. "Just like Earth, the weather is different depending on the continent and hemisphere. Now, in Poseidon, capital city of Imperial *Atlantida*, specifically, it is Green season, and sometime late morning. Probably a pleasant 15 degrees Celsius."

"Ten second warning. . . . Arrival in Atlantis orbit in ten seconds. . . ."

"Holy crap, here we go!" Many teens start clapping, and woots and cheers begin cycling around the observation deck in waves.

Wow, I think, while nervous energy fills me with a buzz of excitement. It almost feels like a New Year's Eve countdown.

"Seven. . . . Six. . . . Five. . . ."

All of Atlantis now fills the window; there is no more space visible, only landmass and oceans. . . . A sudden welling of tears makes my eyes burn, as I see disks of violet plasma that are other ark-ships, slowly break formation and float like balloons all around us.

"Four. . . . Three. . . . Two. . . ."

My breath stills.

"Now establishing stationary orbit over Atlantis," says the ship's computer.

The entire observation deck erupts in shouts and applause. Teens of all Earth nationalities jump around and hug each other.

We have arrived!

And we can barely hear, over the din of human noise, the sudden *silence* that comes from the cessation of sound and vibration in the ship's outer hull. We'd gotten so used to that eternal sound that, now that it's no longer here, it's an amazing, almost frightening dead quiet.

The great ark-ship around us is suddenly silent as a dream.

But I cannot savor the moment too long.

Because, it is now time for me to go.

I quickly elbow my way through the celebrating crowds on the observation deck and run back to Command Deck Four, toward my own cabin. Here, I open the door for the last time, grab my bags, and head right back out to Shuttle Bay One where our transport awaits.

When I get to the shuttle bay, it is ten minutes before 8:00 AM, and both Gennio and Anu are already there, standing at the wall near the entrance with their personal bags and several crates of CCO computer equipment. Just as I approach them, we all see Consul Suval Denu in his grand gold wig and a flowing crimson robe, walking gracefully, followed by Kem, holding a mountain of very familiar boxes, and two Atlantean crew members carrying the Consul's infamous trunk.

The guards at the dispatch desk near the entrance point us to a large transport shuttle hovering on the platform nearby—not a personal flyer but the kind that we got to ride during the Semi-Finals and Finals during Qualification. I think of it as the shuttle version of a bus, and it can carry about a hundred people.

"So, this is our ride?" I ask Gennio.

"Yes," he says. "We're just waiting for the CP and his security team."

"Oh, really?" I ask. "So he'll have guards with him?"

Gennio nods.

"The Imperial Crown Prince is required to have a security detail," Anu adds.

A couple of minutes later, I see Command Pilot Kassiopei walking toward us. He is dressed in his everyday grey uniform—not sure why I notice this, maybe because I expected him to be dressed differently at this point. Right behind him I see six Atlantean guards with holstered weapons, lined up in two rows of three, flanking him from the back.

Aeson Kassiopei swiftly nears us and barely motions with the palm of his hand to all of us. "Let's go," he says in a hard voice, and keeps moving. He barely even glances at me.

Immediately we follow. I offer to help Gennio and Anu with the CCO crates, but they tell me there's no need, those will be loaded separately after we board.

We approach the transport shuttle and climb up the ladder. The interior looks familiar.

"Sit down anywhere and buckle up," the CP tells us, and he proceeds directly to the back where the Pilot's area is located.

After stowing my bags in the side panel storage compartments at the entrance, as directed by the guards, I grab one of the first row seats next to the two Aides.

Consul Denu takes a seat next to us, followed by Kem. The guards position themselves in various seats around the transport.

"Will the CP be Piloting this transport?" I ask.

"Of course," Anu says in a superior tone. "When you have the best Pilot in the Fleet, is that even a question?"

I shrug. We all engage the harnesses and make ourselves comfortable.

And then, moments later we hear Kassiopei's low voice over the amplifier. "We are departing now. Be prepared."

And in the next moment the shuttle's hull comes alive with vibration, while the hair-fine lines of golden light start racing around the etchings in the panels.

There are no observation windows here, so I have no idea what's going on outside. I can only feel the motion as we must be moving off the platform, and then, a smooth minor lurch, as we blast through the launch channel and outside. . . .

And then, we plummet. . . .

I feel the sickening lurch of transitioning gravity, and am temporarily reminded of the Zero-G Dances. At least it's something to think about as we fall, fall, fall, through the layers of atmosphere of Atlantis.

About ten minutes later the falling sensation stabilizes, while a slightly peculiar new feeling of *weight* settles in. And we come to a hover stop.

Anu makes a satisfied noise.

"And, here we are, Gwen." Gennio says mildly, looking at me. And then he smiles. "Welcome to Atlantis, your new home!"

"Thanks," I mutter. *This is just so weird.*

Moments later the hum in the walls ends and the hull lights disappear. Aeson Kassiopei comes out from the Pilot control section in the back and he looks at us with a sweeping glance. "We're here," he says. "Let's go."

Again, his glance at me is very brief. No other reaction or acknowledgement. I feel an instant pang of disappointment in my heart, as though I've been expecting something from him, maybe something a little more profound? Why was it Gennio and not *he*, who welcomed me?

I know these thoughts are crazy-irrational and bitter, so I try to put them down.

In that moment however, Kassiopei turns to Consul Denu, and momentarily glances at me. "Take her with you to the Palace Blue Wing residential quarters," he says. "Have her put in a guest room near you. Then, make sure you have her ready by six o'clock, properly attired for Court. Make all necessary arrangements in my name."

The Consul stands up and then bows elegantly before Kassiopei, speaking in a smooth pleasing voice. "Of course, my Imperial Lord, it shall all be done as you require. One small question—what should her attire reflect? Does my Imperial Lord need her to be dressed as High Court, Middle Court or Low Court?"

Okay, I have only a vague idea of what this all means, from my Court Protocol lessons with the Consul. . . . But I watch with growing trepidation as Aeson glances at me again with a look that's almost disdainful. "Low Court, of course," he says icily. "I need her to look sufficient to be presented before my Father, but nothing more. She will be standing with the Low Court during the presentation. I expect you to remain at her side for this particular event, Consul. Make sure she does nothing out of line. Is that clear? There must be nothing out of order. I do not want any problems, not tonight."

"As my Imperial Lord wishes, all will be done to your satisfaction." Consul Denu smiles and bows elegantly once again. And then he glances at me and nods graciously.

Okay. . . . There's nothing worse than being spoken about in third person when you are standing right there. I take a step forward and address Kassiopei, looking directly at him.

"Command Pilot, what's this exactly? How am I being dressed, and what should I be doing?"

But Aeson glances at me coldly and his lapis blue eyes meet my gaze with what again seems to be disdain. "Gwen Lark, you are never to speak to me again without permission. We are on Atlantis now, and I am no longer your commanding officer but the Imperial Prince of Kassiopei. As of this moment you must follow proper Imperial Protocol. Do not address me unless permitted to do so, do not question me or initiate a conversation unless I ask you. You may not approach me again. Stand back, and follow the Consul. You are dismissed!"

And with these terrible words that strike me like knife blows, he turns his back on me and goes to the hatch opening of the transport shuttle.

Moments later the hatch opens, and there's a blast of warmth, clear pure wonderful air, and blinding white sunlight. Two of the guards exit first, followed by Aeson Kassiopei, and then the rest of the security detail.

I remain standing, thunderstruck, heartbroken yet *again*.

"Here you go, Gwen," Gennio says softly, handing me a pair of large wrap-around black sunglasses. "You must wear these before you go outside. Keep them with you from now on."

"Yes, yes, good that you remembered, she will definitely need these," Consul Denu says in that moment. "Now, come along, my dear, and you too, Kem."

I nod and take the protective sunglasses from Gennio. I put them on, and pick up my two duffel bags.

It's a good thing my eyes are now heavily obscured—both from the bright light of Hel, and from their curious, or sympathetic, or pitying eyes.

Because, as I take my first step outside and down the ladder, and then put my right foot down on the ground of the planet Atlantis, *my new permanent home*, my vision is blurred and I am openly crying.

Chapter 48

Slightly warm, fresh, oxygen-rich Atlantean air surrounds me as I look outside and walk down the ladder. Even through the super-dark sunglasses, I can see that the sky is so bright that it looks white, with a hint of blue. There are no clouds, and Hel sits up near zenith, so I immediately squint and look away.

Our transport shuttle appears to have landed in the middle of a small airfield. It almost looks like a large and empty Earth parking lot, except it's paved with some other material, slightly reddish-mauve, a little like river clay, a little like European cobblestones. I am momentarily reminded of the iconic image of the Red Square in Moscow, Russia, that I've seen on TV—a similar expanse in tones of brick and mauve.

Except, on a far smaller scale.

Because only about three hundred feet ahead I see grand buildings inside a sprawling complex of what looks like a formally structured, landscaped park or garden, with amazing greenery and trees.

In contrast to this small landing field, the buildings are huge—and I don't mean merely tall skyscrapers in the style of New York or Chicago—but unbelievable wide-sprawling massive structures that resemble temples or palaces, reminiscent in style to the Karnak Temple in Egypt, but *bigger*. And, unlike the ancient and dilapidated Karnak with its crumbling stone, this is all *new* looking and very sharp and modern.

And oh my lord, the gold trim! *Gold*, gold is everywhere! The distant facades glisten yellow-white in the sun, and the fine ornamentation is stunning, with varicolored stone, in ebony black, river clay red, all shades of brick, rose, and cream.... Unbelievable!

If I didn't have my sunglasses on, I don't think I could look at it, it's that overwhelming.

As I stop and stare around me in perfect amazement, with my mouth open, I notice in the distance the retreating figures of Aeson Kassiopei and his guards, as they walk swiftly into the park area along a path and soon disappear out of sight as they enter the nearest building. I also notice all kinds of other people moving around the park grounds, dressed in distinctive clothing that looks far more colorful and flowing than what I'm used to seeing back in the United States. The closest to it on Earth would probably be the Middle Eastern or Far Eastern fashions.

"Hey, keep going, Earth girl!" I hear the brash voice of Anu behind me, as apparently I've frozen in place right before the ladder and now I'm blocking everyone's way.

"Sorry! It's just so amazing!" I mutter, and take a few steps away, letting Anu pass, followed by Gennio.

About that *gravity*—okay, now that I've taken a few steps on the surface of Atlantis, I can definitely feel it. . . .

Or at least, I can feel *something* being off. My limbs, my body, everything feels a little heavy, a little not quite right. Just lifting my hand up feels a little weird. I have no way to even describe it—maybe it's like the feeling you get after a long excruciating workout and all your limbs are "weak" and feel like noodles.

And my duffel bags! Oh wow, they are suddenly *heavy!* Like an extra five pounds each!

Gennio turns back and glances at me. "Are you okay, Gwen?"

"I don't know," I say, trying to smile. "My bags suddenly got very heavy!"

"Oh yes, the stronger gravity—sorry about that," Gennio says."Do you need some help carrying them?"

I look at him, overloaded with his own baggage and decide that he's got enough to carry on his own. "Thanks, but I think I'll manage," I say.

And then I begin walking. . . .

After a few steps I realize I've no idea where to go, so I glance back at the shuttle and see that Consul Denu is the last person out, walking carefully down the ladder, and Kem is with him, carrying many, many things. . . . I recall that I'm supposed to be going somewhere with the Consul, so I wait as they draw near.

"Come along with me, my dear," the Consul tells me mildly as he starts walking toward the buildings. "How do you like it so far? This is the Imperial Palace complex in Poseidon. We've landed in the private airfield."

"It's stunning," I say, following with some effort due to my heavy bags.

"Not too far now," the Consul tells me, noticing my plight, but he does not make any offer to help. I realize it is beneath him, or at least beneath the persona he is playing so carefully.

We walk through the landscaped area with a vast overwhelming array of green flowering plants, shrubs, and trees which I barely notice because of my growing discomfort with the bags that now feel like evil anvils. . . . And we go inside the first structure.

A grand hall interior with tall ceilings and what seems to be marble everywhere, greets us. Several people in light-colored uniforms, with golden metallic hair, kohl-lined eyes, and typical bronzed or river-red skin—who remind me of fancy hotel employees or servants—approach the Consul and he talks to them in Atlantean. I can recognize enough of the language now to know that he tells them to take my bags. Immediately, a porter comes up to me with a polite smile and takes my horrible bags, giving my arms instant relief.

Now that my hands are free, and we're indoors, I can take off my sunglasses—and I do. At that point I notice quite a few curious glances in my direction from the Palace personnel. It occurs to me, *they have probably never seen an Earth person before.* . . . And now I'm the alien, so no wonder they stare at me, despite their impeccable service training.

We start walking deep into the grand hall lobby to an area near the back that branches off into smaller corridors with lower ceilings.

Here we get into the Atlantean version of elevators. Except these are faster moving and more smooth, with ornate paneling.

"Fifth floor is our destination, Gwen," the Consul tells me.

"Then, on to the Blue Wing, where we'll be staying for now."

I nod, and follow him and Kem tiredly, dragging my limbs with difficulty. We emerge from the elevator into another long hallway trimmed in glorious red wood and more gold, and fascinating wall paneling that looks like embroidered silk squares under glass encrusted with expensive stained glass and stone mosaics. Wow. . . . If I weren't so tired, I'd take a closer look.

At some point in the maze of corridors, we stop before a specific door, and the porter opens it.

"This is your guest room, my dear," Consul Denu tells me, and we go inside.

The room is an airy bedroom suite decorated in an exotic and somehow old-world fashion. I have no other way to describe the rich deep rust and earthy colors of the fabric hangings, the heavy brocade-like curtains over the large windows, and the grand rectangle bed in the middle, vaguely comparable to a king-sized bed on Earth, the kind you might find in fine estates in United Industan or Europe. The bed is strewn with pillows and fine fabrics, and is upraised on a dais.

Several floor-length mirrors stand around the walls, and ultra-modern digital paintings of various stunning natural landscapes hang next to ancient-looking stylized tapestries. There are stands with vases filled with fresh pale flowers that look like acacia blooms, and bowls of exotic fruit resembling mangoes and pears and prickly cactus. A pillow-covered settee reposes along another wall, and several comfortable chairs are placed around the perimeter. There's even a small dining table and what looks like a writing desk and chair ensemble in another nook.

I notice there is a bathroom off to the side around the corner, and it's equally grand, with a sunken tub that looks big enough to be a small pool. . . .

Okay, I feel like I've stepped into a Presidential suite.

"This is all for me?" I say. "No, that's just crazy. It's too much! My God!"

But the elegant porter puts my bags down discreetly on a nearby stand. And the Consul dismisses him with a wave. "This is nothing, dear girl," he tells me. "By Imperial Palace standards you have been given a poor closet."

I put my hand to my mouth.

The Consul turns to me, with a very sympathetic look. "Now, this is what you need to do for the rest of the afternoon. In a few minutes you will have some refreshments brought up to you, so you need to have a nice solid meal—think of it as a brunch."

"Okay, thank you," I say. "I am not really hungry yet. . . ."

"No matter. You *will* try to eat. And then you will go directly to bed and sleep for at least three hours. If you cannot sleep, simply lie down and rest your body, to get yourself accustomed to the gravity—this is very important."

I nod.

"And don't worry about the time, or setting alarms," he continues. "If you do fall asleep, someone will come to wake you up gently. Next, you will be assisted with some spa treatments, and then you will be helped to dress. Finally, at five o'clock, I will arrive, with Kem, to do your final Court Face Art, and make sure you are ready to be presented before the Imperator. We will be done by five-forty-five, at which point we will proceed to the Imperial Reception. Court begins at six."

"Okay," I say. "As far as getting ready, I don't really need any spa treatments, and I think I can manage dressing on my own—"

But Consul Denu raises his hand up to stop me. "Not another word. This is all part of the procedure, and is required by Protocol. So please, dear girl, don't argue, and remember what I told you about *subtle acquiescence*. I know you are tired and overwhelmed, and you have had a *painful* emotional experience in more ways than one today. But, this is what must be done. We must follow the command given us by the Imperial Prince in regard to you."

I smile tiredly and nod. "Yes, I understand. . . ."

And on that note the Consul leaves me in my grandiose guest quarters.

As promised, refreshments arrive soon, carried on multiple trays by not one but three palace servants. They set the trays on the table and place tall carafes of drinks nearby. I thank them in Atlantean, then sit down and try to eat and drink.

Then I drag myself over to the huge pillow-covered bed and collapse directly on top of the silken coverlet. I lie, breathing heavily, feeling the added weight of every limb like it's not my own. . . . And then, tears come.

I cry silently, shaking, curled in a fetal position.

And then apparently I fall asleep.

I am awakened out of a deep slumber by a gentle touch on my shoulder. As I stare groggily, a sweet-faced Atlantean girl dressed in the Palace uniform leans over me. As I look around, my head still thick with the sleep and strange gravity, I notice that while I was asleep someone must've come in to clear away the trays, and now, a beautiful violet-colored outfit ensemble lies ready for me on top of the settee, underneath a clear protective cover.

"My Lady, I am Miwat," says the Atlantean girl in English. "I am going to help you wash and dress."

"Oh," I mumble, getting up. "Thank you." And then I add, "But I am not a Lady, so you can just call me Gwen."

"Forgive me, Gwen," Miwat says with a flustered look. "I am instructed to call any female guest in these quarters at least a Lady, but I will do as you request, of course."

"Oh, no problem!" Now I feel bad about even bringing this up.

I stand, feeling an initial head rush, but after having slept for a few hours, I do feel somewhat better, and my body is already adjusting to the slight additional weight.

And so we start getting ready.

While I take off my plain Fleet uniform and underclothes and shyly rush into the grand shower stall, with my arms and hands crossed over my chest, I notice that Miwat and two other servants I haven't previously noticed are moving around the suite laying out items of clothing and accessories from the outfit package. Meanwhile a fourth servant is doing something to the sunken pool—I have no idea what, but the water is running there, and a smell of flowers comes wafting to me in the shower.

As I am shampooing my hair with what I *think* is shampoo from one of the aromatic vials up on a ledge nearby, I see Miwat peer inside the shower enclosure.

I make a little squeal and try to cover myself.

"Oh, I am sorry, Gwen, but you will need to come out and use the bath instead," she says, completely ignoring the fact that I am buck naked, as if it's the most normal thing in the world. Oh wow, do Atlanteans have different standards of privacy? I suppose I will find out.

"But I am almost done," I say nervously. "And I'm not really comfortable walking around naked."

"My apologies," Miwat says with a small nod and no other reaction. "We will turn around and you can enter the bath, please."

Oh, this is just nuts....

I let them step away and watch as four girls turn their backs on me after Miwat explains my probably weird request to them.

Dripping wet, with Atlantean shampoo still in my hair, I streak across the bathroom and wade into the deep sunken bath which, thank goodness, is now filled with some kind of bath treatment that makes the water butter-creamy and opaque. I sit down and make sure the pleasantly hot water comes up to my neck.

"Okay to turn around," I say, feeling like an idiot.

But they don't seem to mind. Miwat and the girls immediately come around me and start working my hair with some kind of other gooey cream stuff, and massaging my shoulders and scrubbing my back, and just basically being extremely personally intrusive.

Ugh, if this is what spa treatments are like, how can people stand it? I think.

"Isn't this nice and pleasing? Please try to relax, Gwen," Miwat tells me constantly, and apparently to no avail. At this point I'm too polite to say anything, but I am as stiff and tense as a board. And no, all this fancy massage stuff is *not* relaxing.

About an hour later, I have been depilated, shaved, scrubbed, soaked, moisturized, and otherwise cosmetically tortured. But hey, my skin feels very, very smooth and clean!

Once out of the bath, I am covered in fluffy towels and then left to cool down for a few minutes while the girls do my nails, applying a glossy polish in pure liquid gold.

Oh, dear lord in heaven, I have gold fingernails and toenails....

After it dries, they return and start dressing me.

They allow me to at least put on the flimsy underwear by myself while they again stand with their backs to me. But then, as soon as I've pulled on the weirdly cut panties and whatever equivalent the Atlanteans have for a bra, they surround me and start putting on the layers. First, a slip-like long narrow tunic sheath of silky soft white fabric that goes to my knees. Then, a floor-length dark fitted violet dress of some kind of stiff, expensive and heavy material, with a high collar and no sleeves. Next, they put on a flimsy translucent gauze-like lavender overdress that floats over the darker base dress like a cloud. My hands and arms remain bare.

Next, come the sandal shoes. They are also violet, a cross between open sandals and boots, with several ribbon laces that wind around my ankle and are secured with a golden button above my heel. At least I can be thankful these are flats and there are no awful heels to contend with....

I stand, letting them do this to me. My mind is in a strange passive daze, a mixture of depression, shock, resignation, and alien wonder.

Just as they begin to brush out my long, almost dry hair, there is a loud knock on the door, and Consul Denu comes in, followed by Kem burdened with cosmetics boxes.

The Consul gives me a careful look-over and then nods in satisfaction. "You look well, my dear, precisely as intended," he says. "And now, we will complete the look to make you fit the intended station."

In other words, I recall, *Low Court*.

I am told to sit down, and the Consul sits before me, watching me carefully, while Kem lays out his cosmetics.

"We will keep your hair down, but gather it behind you loosely in a demure wide tail, with a barrette brooch." Consul Denu points with one polished finger to a box of accessories, and Kem knows immediately which to select.

Kem gathers my hair behind me, smoothing every unfettered strand into a perfectly controlled, deceptively loose wide tail. He clips it with the barrette, low at the back of my neck, leaving the nape covered.

Next, Consul Denu selects the colors of the Face Paints. Kem applies each layer as directed. I am given a very natural skin look, with faint traces of color, a delicate rose gloss over my lips, faint lavender and gold eyelid color, and in contrast very dark violet eyeliner and mascara that does give sudden drama to my eyes.

As final touches, Kem puts on two wide gold bracelets, one on each of my wrists, and hangs a pair of heavy gold pendant earrings with a tassel fringe of delicate chains through my earlobes. The earrings have great violet semi-precious jewels in the center to match my dress.

I stand up, and am told to look in the mirror.

Wow, I look ethereal, delicate, and stunning. If *this* look is Low Court, I'm afraid to think what High Court involves.

"Wow, thank you so much, Consul Denu—and Kem!" I say. "Yet again you work miracles and make me look amazing!"

"You are a fair canvas to work with, my dear," the Consul graciously replies. "Now, we have only ten minutes to arrive, and we are late already. Let us hurry now, to Court! The Imperator must not be kept waiting!"

Chapter 49

We arrive, through a confusing labyrinth of fine Palace corridors and levels, in the ante-chamber before a grand doorway that leads into the Imperial Throne Hall called the *Pharikoneon*—the ancient grand chamber dedicated to the highest Imperial ceremony.

As we walk, Consul Denu informs me as quickly as possible about the various specific details of this particular Court assembly. I try to absorb as much as I can, even though my mind is overwhelmed and I am sinking deeper and deeper into some kind of inexplicable numb state of terror and soul-sickness.

Crowds of splendidly dressed Atlanteans are gathering at the entrance, while the Imperial guards holding upright floor-length gold staffs stand in a line before us, preventing admittance until the proper time.

The formal outfits are amazing. . . . I see the difference now, between me in my delicate Low Court garb, my simple flow of hair and the austere fall of my dress, and the ladies in intricate headdresses, with upswept sculpted hair, dramatic makeup, sparkling webs and garlands of jewelry and dresses of so many layers that they are like sculptures in themselves. Yes, this is definitely High Court.

And the men are predominantly capped with grand golden wigs, also wearing amazing layers of makeup, perfectly fitted jackets and pants or floor-length robes and capes. To my untrained eye, the fine distinctions between Middle Court and High Court blur . . . but I suppose I can ask Consul Denu about it at some later date.

I also notice that here in this crowd of various degrees of nobility, there is a mixture of all ages, and not merely teens, as

I'm used to seeing in the Fleet. I see many older Atlanteans for the first time—gilded matrons with wrinkled faces, and old men with neatly trimmed beards. Most people have the usual metallic hair dye, but there are a few standouts with natural hair color in the crowd—black, dark brown, auburn, red. I am momentarily reminded of raven-haired Xelio Vekahat. . . . Yes, he's not alone in rejecting the metallic gold hair fashion.

"Notice, among the highest nobility of *Atlantida*, men and women wearing the long gold and white robes and the gold filigree skull caps," the Consul points out to me. "These are the members of the Poseidon Imperial Executive Council, the other branch of government, who serve to offset and balance the power of the Imperator."

"Okay . . ." I glance at the impossible crowds around us in this ante-chamber and note the white-robed individuals.

"Now, as soon as the Pharikoneon Gates open, the High Court is admitted first. Then, the Middle Court, and finally, the Low Court. You and I, my dear, will stand with the latter, but we will enter as close as possible to the front of our section, so that we end up in the first row, either on the left or the right of the throne. The trick to it is to stand precisely here—" And the Consul carefully takes me by the elbow and maneuvers me through the crowd to a certain spot near the walls and the edge of the marble colonnade.

"As soon as the doors open, walk quickly at my side, and do not slow your pace down under any circumstances."

"Okay," I say. "What exactly does it mean we will stand with the Low Court? Where exactly is that?"

The Consul smiles. "A fine question. It will be answered as soon as you see what is inside the chamber. The floor is colored in three sections, on both sides of the red path to the throne. Closest to the throne, the floor tiles are pale stone, almost white. That is the High Court. Only the highest nobility is permitted to stand there. Then you will see a section of stone floor in red—a divider—followed by an area in golden cream yellow—that is the Middle Court. Next, another divider in red, and at last, the section in rust orange, toward the back of the chamber. It is the Low Court, and it is where we will be."

I nod. "I see."

"Once the Court is assembled and the Imperator opens the Imperial Court Session, the red path to the throne and the red sections on the floor may not be tread upon by anyone who is not of Imperial blood, unless the Imperator or another member of the Imperial Family grants you permission.... What this means is, you must stand on the floor in your designated section, and you may not step on any red tile!"

"Wow.... Okay. Sounds scary and complicated."

Consul Denu squeezes my arm reassuringly. "Simply stay by my side, and you will be fine."

In a few minutes, a series of tones echo throughout the ante-chamber, followed by what sounds like deep bass, horns, and oboe. They form a grand C Major chord....

At the same time the guards at the doors stand aside and the Pharikoneon Gates open inward, revealing a brightly lit immense hall filled with soft golden glow. They announce admittance in loud Atlantean, and in that moment the crowd starts moving.

Consul Denu keeps a firm hold on my arm as we wait while the upper nobility enters. At last, when the ante-chamber has sufficiently thinned out, the Consul pulls me along and we walk rapidly past the guards into the Pharikoneon.

Oh, wow....

The sheer *immensity* and scale of the chamber takes my breath away.

It is like being inside a temple. Massive column supports of mauve stone circle the perimeter, and overhead looms a distant shadowed ceiling, formed like an inverted stair pyramid.

The distant wall directly ahead is pure gold. Against it, a sunburst relief of stunning intricacy frames the Imperial Throne of *Atlantida*.

The throne is a huge, tall-backed golden chair, placed upraised on a dais of five steps. To the right of it is a lesser gold chair, and to the left, another, both intended for other members of the Imperial Family. Next, come backless gold benches on both sides, for yet other relatives or those who are favored by the Imperator. The entire section is called the Imperial Seats.

At the moment the Throne and the Imperial Seats are unoccupied.

However, it is a different matter with the rest of the hall.

As we walk in, I understand now what the Consul was talking about. People fill the hall in six designated sections, three on each side of the central red tiled path. The main floor is red polished marble, off limits to all of us, and the paler colors are for the Court to occupy.

"Quickly now...." Consul Denu directs me to the left of the central red path walkway, and takes me into the Low Court orange floor section, so that we stand precisely at the orange corner. We are basically at the very edge where the red tile divider begins between Low and Middle Court and the Imperial path in the center.

Consul Denu takes the corner position, and I stand right next to him. Immediately other people take the spots around us. A young Atlantean woman in a long green dress stands next to me, a courtier in a grand gold wig similar to the Consul's stands behind me, and so on, until there is no room to turn....

I understand now why the Consul made sure we are in the front row, it is definitely more comfortable here. Of course, that we are in plain view of everyone present is not so comfortable, if you want to be inconspicuous.

"My dear, here is what you must do," Consul Denu says softly in my ear. "Stand quietly in place, until and only *if* the Imperator decides to notice you. This *may* or may *not* happen today. If you are lucky, it will be a very brief experience. Now—" And he points to the wide red path before us. "Once the Imperator calls you forward, you will step upon the red floor and you will walk in a quick but even pace toward the Throne. Do not ascend the dais at all, simply curtsey right before the first stair, in the middle. Remain with your head bowed until instructed otherwise. You may look up at the Imperator only if he is speaking to you. Then, once your audience is done, you curtsey again, then return the same way you came and take your place next to me. You may only turn your back on the Imperator during this brief time as you are walking away...."

Okay, now I'm officially terrified.

"Will the Imperator speak in English or Atlantean? What if I don't understand?"

The Consul thinks for a moment. "I believe you will be addressed in English, since the Imperator is aware of your situation. But if by any chance it happens to be in Atlantean, you are permitted to explain your difficulty. But—fear not, it will not come to it." And he squeezes my hand gently.

We stand a few minutes more as the rest of the Low Court fills the room. Then, grand tones once more sound, to indicate the arrival of the Imperator.

I hold my breath. . . .

The Imperator of Atlantis does not come up the red path as I imagined he would. Instead, a hidden doorway appears in the golden wall near the Throne, and he comes forth like a god from the darkness and steps directly onto the dais. . . .

Romhutat Kassiopei, the Archaeon Imperator of *Atlantida*, is a tall middle-aged man—as far as I can tell by the ageless features of his handsome stone face, at this distance. He wears a stunning floor-length robe of dark scarlet, and over it layers of gold cloth cascading from his shoulders glide along the floor behind him.

On the Imperator's chest a wide heavy collar lies, gold encrusted with jewels. His hair is natural Kassiopei, long and pale gold, and he wears the Imperial Crown of *Atlantida*—it resembles the Ancient Egyptian headdress known as the Khepresh, or the war crown, but it's made of scarlet cloth with a wide band of gold circling his head.

From the center of the forehead, a golden serpent rises. This is the Uraeus, the symbol of absolute Imperial power. This is the part of the crown that designates the Imperator.

The Imperator stands briefly before the Throne, looking at all of us. And then he sits down in the middle chair, straight-backed and motionless.

He is terrifying.

This is Aeson's Father, I have to remind myself. There is a vague resemblance in the features, yes, but more in the bearing and lines of jaw. I suppose the greatest resemblance would be in Aeson's mother who is purported to be the most beautiful woman of her generation.

Will the Archaeona Imperatris be here tonight?

For that matter, I wonder with a twinge of stress, *where is Aeson?*

Meanwhile, the hall remains in perfect silence as we wait for the Imperator to speak.

At last, he opens his mouth and his deep resonant voice strikes us with force. "My Court Opens," the Imperator says in Atlantean, and I understand this much with my rudimentary *Atlanteo* skills.

In the next instant, profound musical tones sound once again, and the entire Assembly, High, Middle, and Low Court, bows their heads before the Imperial Throne. Consul Denu squeezes my hand lightly and I lower my head with everyone else.

"You may Look upon Me," the Imperator says.

We all raise our heads once more.

And as I look up, in that surreal instant, my gaze falls upon the front row of the High Court and suddenly in a weird second of coincidence, I see a young woman there, dressed in stunning gold, who is, I'm perfectly certain, none other than Lady Tirinea Fuorai.

Oh, wow. . . .

Lady Tiri is tall and gorgeous, and even more amazing in real life than I expected—so perfect that my eyes hurt looking at her. And she stands next to several other similarly stunning girls, one more beautiful than the other. Though, I must say, she stands out slightly with her confident bearing and superior air.

While I stare at Lady Tiri, almost forgetting everything else, the Imperator speaks again. "I will now Receive You. First, the Imperial Crown Prince of Kassiopei may approach the Throne."

My heart immediately skips a beat painfully, and my eyes widen as I search the room for any sign of *him*. The rest of the Court seems to respond similarly as the Atlantean nobility stares. . . .

And then I see him.

Aeson Kassiopei strides upon the red path, walking from the back of the chamber toward the Throne.

Oh. My. God.

Aeson wears a formal jacket of deep blue, so dark it is nearly black, and similar trousers. His feet are encased in soft black leather dress shoes studded with gold. Gold wrist bands hold his sleeves in place, and a fine gold trim circles the fabric of his collar in an exquisite web rendered in lines of intricate symmetry.

His hair is long and loose, down his back. It is brushed to a gloss, and lies neatly back from his forehead to frame his stunning cold face.

Aeson wears no additional makeup, but he does not have to.

He is luminous and unreal.

The Crown Prince walks up to the dais, his footfalls against the stone floor causing echoes to rise in the hall. There he stops and inclines his head briefly.

Without changing his stone expression, the Imperator nods at him. "Welcome, My Son. I congratulate you on successfully accomplishing the important task given you, and returning the children of Earth here in safety. You may speak of your successful journey in detail."

At least, it's the general gist of what he's saying, because, again, my Atlantean language skills are barely adequate. Thank goodness Consul Denu taught me some basic common Court phrases and ceremonial language. This is all very traditional, highly stylized and formal stuff. One might hope the Imperator does not talk this way all the time. . . .

"My Father, Your Imperial Fleet and I are glad to be home," Aeson replies. His familiar low voice rings forcefully throughout the hall and sends strange pleasant chills down my back. Oh, it is so good to hear his voice in this surreal alien place!

"I have much to tell, and the achievements of this endeavor are historic in their ramifications, both for Earth and Atlantis," Aeson continues. And then he pauses slightly. "But before I go on, I would like to make an Imperial Formal Announcement before this Court. I believe this is an Announcement you have been waiting for me to make for quite some time. . . ."

There is another pause.

And then, for the first time, the Imperator smiles. I can see the shadow smile all the way from where I'm standing. And then he inclines his head, graciously. "My Son, I am glad to hear you have come to this decision at last. Yes, make your Announcement now, and we will Witness."

Aeson inclines his head once more, and then turns around to look at the Court with a sweeping glance that reveals a flash of energy overriding his carefully composed expression.

"My Father, as you have guessed, after much careful thought and consideration, I will now announce My Imperial Consort and Bride."

Oh God, no!

Sudden dark despair washes over me.

Meanwhile, excited soft whispers fill the great expanse of the chamber. And the High Court sections in particular react. . . . I can see Lady Tiri, and the other girls of noble families in that damned front row, all stand up straight. Lady Tiri looks at Aeson with a triumphant smile.

I am without breath now, faint and collapsing inside, as though all life has been leached out of me. . . . If I weren't standing in such a tight crowd, I think my feet would buckle from under me. Consul Denu must sense my sudden agitation because again he squeezes my hand and holds it tight.

In that moment, Aeson turns from the Throne and starts moving along the red path. Slowly he paces, glancing in both directions, to the right and left of the path, as though making careful considerations among those present.

In just a few steps, he is now by the High Court section, where Lady Tiri stands, turned toward him. Aeson pauses before her, looks at her and smiles also.

It's a smile I can see from all the way across the room, and it destroys me completely.

I am numb, barely breathing. . . .

The Assembly is filled with whispers, the High Court especially.

The Imperator watches with a satisfied smile.

Aeson looks at Lady Tiri.

And then he *resumes* walking.

I feel my heart pound in my chest as I watch Lady Tiri's expression go from confident triumph to slow fading confusion. She frowns and stares in Aeson's wake, as he continues to pace slowly down the red path, glancing leisurely on both sides of him.

He passes the Middle Court section and keeps walking.

There are more whispers everywhere. . . .

And then Aeson Kassiopei comes before Consul Denu, standing at the corner of the Low Court section. He glances at the Consul and then his composed gaze falls upon *me*.

I catch my breath, and my face must reflect a million things in that moment.

Suddenly Aeson's eyes come wide open and they are *wild*.

He takes an aggressive step forward and he reaches out for me and *grabs* my hand.

I almost stumble at the shock of contact, but there's no time, because suddenly I am being pulled forward and *dragged* along, as Aeson Kassiopei has me in a painful iron vise that compresses my fingers. . . . And all I can do is half-stumble, half-run after him as he rapidly walks back up the red path toward the Throne, taking me with him, while my mind is in shock.

A few steps from the dais, we stop. I see flashes of stunned faces on both sides of the aisle, and most of all, I see the Imperator suddenly frozen in his golden chair, his expression turned to stone, a frown gathering.

The Imperator is looking at *me*.

But before anyone can speak, I hear the loud ringing voice of Aeson Kassiopei at my side, and he is using a *power voice* of command.

"I have chosen my Bride and Imperial Consort and her name is Gwenevere Lark of Earth!" he exclaims, at the same time as he raises our clasped hands up for everyone to see—in the process pulling my arm up painfully, because he is so much taller than me, and I don't think he's fully aware of what he's doing right now—or for that matter, I don't think he is in his right *mind*. . . .

Or maybe it's *me*—I am not in my right mind, and I am about to fall. . . . Or I *would* if he wasn't clutching my hand and forcefully keeping me upright right now.

And then Aeson turns to me and faces me, and he still holds me tightly but no longer enough to crush my fingers.

"Gwen Lark," he says in Atlantean, and then repeats everything in English for my sake, all the while staring into my eyes with his lapis lazuli own—wild, completely raving mad with unspeakable emotion and violent intensity. "I take *you* as my Imperial Consort. . . . I claim you as my Bride. . . . I open you and seal you as my Wife! Let it be Known and Witnessed as my Immovable Will before the Imperial Court of Kassiopei!"

"What?" I gasp. And my voice sounds tiny and faint in the stunned silence of the great chamber.

But Aeson releases my fingers and now takes my upper arm, pressing my flesh forcefully as he draws me to him, so that now I stand directly before him, chest-to-chest, looking up into his eyes with absolute shock and disbelief.

"Gwen. . . ." he says, starting to lean in closer.

At first I think he is about to whisper something in my ear. But then he keeps going and turns his head slightly so that I feel the wash of his hot breath on my cheek. . . .

And suddenly, there is no more space between us, or between our breath.

Aeson Kassiopei kisses me, *hard*.

He opens my mouth with his and enters me, and it is like a live circuit closing, life force connecting with another source of life force, coming together as one, flowing between us in a stream and then a circulating ocean.

In that moment of shock I feel a stab of explosive indescribable *desire* pass through me. It *hurts* and burns and tears into me, rendering me into nothing . . . and it expands and fills me, like an empty vessel, so that I come *awake* at last.

This is what desire feels like. . . .

There had been no kisses before this one. That gentle, sweet flowing honey, the sensual lassitude I've felt with Logan, even the breathless euphoria—all of that was but a poor faded ghost, a shadow of the real thing that is happening to me *right now*, as suddenly I burn.

When he releases my mouth at last, and stands back from me, I gasp, pulling in air for the first time, and meet the intimate gaze of his eyes.

"The Sacred Opening of the Mouth has Sealed us, Gwen Lark, as it is written in the Book of Life and the Book of the Dead," Aeson says softly, yet his voice carries with power across the multitude of the great chamber. "My lips have kissed no other, and from this day forward I will kiss no other but you, my earthly Bride."

And then Aeson Kassiopei, the Imperial Crown Prince of *Atlantida*, takes me by the hand again and turns us both to face the wrath of his Father, the Imperator.

In that perfect moment, nothing can *compete* with us or conspire against us—neither Imperial wrath nor all the forces of the universe united against us—in that moment, we are one spirit.

And it soars and sings like a lark.

The End of COMPETE: The Atlantis Grail, Book Two

The story continues in . . .

WIN: The Atlantis Grail, Book Three

About the Author

Vera Nazarian is a two-time Nebula Award® Finalist and a member of Science Fiction and Fantasy Writers of America. She immigrated to the USA from the former USSR as a kid, sold her first story at 17, and has been published in numerous anthologies and magazines, honorably mentioned in Year's Best volumes, and translated into eight languages.

Vera made her novelist debut with the critically acclaimed *Dreams of the Compass Rose*, followed by *Lords of Rainbow*. Her novella *The Clock King and the Queen of the Hourglass* made the 2005 Locus Recommended Reading List. Her debut collection *Salt of the Air* contains the 2007 Nebula Award-nominated "The Story of Love." Recent work includes the 2008 Nebula Finalist novella *The Duke in His Castle,* science fiction collection *After the Sundial* (2010), *The Perpetual Calendar of Inspiration* (2010), three Jane Austen parodies, *Mansfield Park and Mummies* (2009), *Northanger Abbey and Angels and Dragons* (2010), and *Pride and Platypus: Mr. Darcy's Dreadful Secret* (2012), all part of her *Supernatural Jane Austen Series*, a parody of self-help and supernatural relationships advice, *Vampires are from Venus, Werewolves are from Mars: A Comprehensive Guide to Attracting Supernatural Love* (2012), *Cobweb Bride Trilogy* (2013), and *Qualify: The Atlantis Grail, Book One* (2014).

After many years in Los Angeles, Vera now lives in a small town in Vermont. She uses her Armenian sense of humor and her Russian sense of suffering to bake conflicted pirozhki and make art.

In addition to being a writer, philosopher, and award-winning artist, she is also the publisher of Norilana Books.

Official website:
www.veranazarian.com

Acknowledgements

There are so many of you whose unwavering, loving support helped me bring this book to life. My gratitude is boundless, and I thank you with all my heart (and in alphabetical order, cause in any other way lies madness)!

To my absolutely brilliant first readers, advisors, topic experts and friends, Jeanne Miller, Jeremy Frank, Katherine Akulicz, Susan Franzblau, and Susan Macdonald.

To the lovely and wonderful group of Vermont writers and friends, Ellen Jareckie, Lina Gimble, and Valerie Gillen.

To everyone on Facebook, for sticking with me and giving me sanity when the going got tough, inspiration, fact-checking research assistance and other support as needed!

To my awesome and fabulous Wattpad friends and fans who kept reading each chapter and making me smile, laugh, and otherwise delight in your hilarious, stunning, amazing, and insightful responses to the story! Thank you immensely, my dear friends!

If I've forgotten or missed anyone, the fault is mine; please know that I love and appreciate you all.

Finally, I would like to thank all of you dear reader friends, who decided to take my hand and step into my world of the Atlantis Grail.

My deepest thanks to all for your support!

Lightning Source UK Ltd.
Milton Keynes UK
UKHW040651080920
369553UK00003B/374